The Last Witchfinder

The Last Witchfinder

JAMES MORROW

Weidenfeld & Nicolson
LONDON

First published in Great Britain in 2006
by Weidenfeld & Nicolson

A CIP catalogue record for this book
is available from the British Library.

ISBN-10 0 297 85258 2 // ISBN-13 978 0 297 85258 2 (HDBK)
ISBN-10 0 297 85259 0 // ISBN-13 978 0 297 85259 9 (TPB)

Typeset at
The Spartan Press Ltd, Lymington, Hants

Printed in Great Britain by
Clays Ltd, St Ives plc

Weidenfeld & Nicolson
The Orion Publishing Group Ltd
Orion House
5 Upper Saint Martin's Lane
London, WC2H 9EA

The Orion Publishing Group's policy is to use papers that are natural,
renewable and recyclable products and made from wood grown
in sustainable forests. The logging and manufacturing processes
are expected to conform to the environmental
regulations of the country of origin.

www.orionbooks.co.uk

To the memory of
Ann Hyson Smith

If the Judge wishes to find out whether she is endowed with a witch's power of preserving silence, let him take note whether she is able to shed tears when standing in his presence, or when being tortured. For we are taught both by the words of worthy men of old and by our own experience that this is a most certain sign, and it has been found that even if she be urged and exhorted by solemn conjurations to shed tears, if she be a witch she will not be able to weep: although she will assume a tearful aspect and smear her cheeks and eyes with spittle to make it appear that she is weeping; wherefore she must be closely watched by the attendants.

–Heinrich Krämer and James Sprenger,
Malleus Maleficarum, AD 1486,
Part III, Question XV (excerpt)

Then came out of the House a grave, tall Man carrying the Holy Writ before the supposed Wizard as solemnly as the Sword-bearer of London before the Lord Mayor; the Wizard was first put in the Scale, and over him was read a Chapter out of the Books of Moses, and then the Bible was put in the other Scale, which, being kept down before, was immediately let go; but, to the great Surprise of the Spectators, Flesh and Bones came down plump, and outweighed the good Book by abundance. After the same Manner, the others were served, and their lumps of Mortality severally were too heavy for Moses and all the Prophets and Apostles.

–Benjamin Franklin,
'A Witch-Trial at Mount-Holly',
The Pennsylvania Gazette,
22 October 1730

CONTENTS

Part I

THE PRICKER OF COLCHESTER

Part II

EARTH, AIR, FIRE, WATER

PART I

The Pricker of Colchester

CHAPTER THE FIRST

Introducing Our Heroine, Jennet Stearne, Whose
Father Hunts Witches, Whose Aunt Seeks Wisdom, and
Whose Soul Desires an Object It Cannot Name

May I speak candidly, one rational creature to another, myself a book and you a reader? Even if the literature of confession leaves you cold, even if you are among those who wish that Rousseau had never bared his soul and Augustine never mislaid his shame, you would do well to lend me a fraction of your life. I am the *Mathematical Principles of Natural Philosophy*, after all — in my native tongue, *Philosophiae Naturalis Principia Mathematica*, the *Principia* for short — not some tenth-grade algebra text or guide to improving your golf swing. Attend to my adventures and you may, Dame Fortune willing, begin to look upon the world anew.

Unlike you humans, a book always remembers its moment of conception. My father, the illustrious Isaac Newton, having abandoned his studies at Trinity College to escape the great plague of 1665, was spending the summer at his mother's farm in Woolsthorpe. An orchard grew beside the house. Staring contemplatively through his bedroom window, Newton watched an apple drop free of its tree, driven by that strange arrangement we have agreed to call gravity. In a leap of intuition, he imagined the apple to be not simply falling to the ground, but striving for the very centre of the Earth. This fruit, he divined, bore a relationship to its planet analogous to that enjoyed by the moon: gravitation, ergo, was universal — the laws that governed terrestrial acceleration also ruled the heavens. As below, so above. My father never took a woman to his bed, and yet the rush of pleasure he

3

experienced on that sweltering July afternoon easily eclipsed the common run of orgasm.

Twenty-two years later — in midsummer of 1687 — I was born. Being a book, a patchwork thing of leather and dreams, ink and inspiration, I have always counted scholars among my friends, poets among my heroes, and glue among my gods. But what am I like in the particular? How is the *Principia Mathematica* different from all other books? My historical import is beyond debate: I am, quite simply, the single greatest work of science ever written. My practical utility is indisputable. Whatever you may think of Mars probes, moon landings, orbiting satellites, steam turbines, power looms, the Industrial Revolution, or the Massachusetts Institute of Technology, none of these things is possible without me. But the curious among you also want to know about my psychic essence. You want to know about my *soul*.

Take me down from your shelf. If you're like most humans, you've accorded me a place of prestige, right next to the Bible, perhaps, or rubbing covers with Homer. Open me. Things start out innocuously enough, with eight turgid but not indigestible definitions concerning mass, acceleration, and force, followed by my father's three famous laws of motion. Continue turning my pages. Things are getting pretty rough, aren't they? Propositions proliferating, scholia colliding, lemmas breeding like lab rats. 'The centripetal forces of bodies, which by equable motions describe different circles, tend to the centres of the same circles, and are to each other as the squares of the arcs described in equal times divided respectively by the radii of the circles.' Lugubrious, I'll admit. This isn't Mother Goose.

But you can't judge a book by its contents. Just because my father stuffed me with sines, cosines, tangents, and worse, that doesn't make me a dry or dispassionate fellow. I have always striven to attune myself to the aesthetic side of mathematics. Behold the diagram that illustrates Proposition XLI. Have you ever beheld a more sensual set of lines? Study the figure accompanying Proposition XLVIII. Have arcs and cycloids ever been more beautiful? My father set geometry in motion. He taught parabolas to pirouette and hyperbolas to gavotte. Don't let all my conventional trigonometric discourse fool you, by the way. Determined to keep his methods a secret, Newton wrote out his discoveries in the mathematics of his day. What's really afoot here is

4

that amazing tool he invented for calculating the rate of change of a rate of change. Abide with me, reader, and I shall teach you to run with the fluxions.

The precise metaphysical procedures by which a book goes about writing another book need not concern us here. Suffice it to say that our human scribes remain entirely ignorant of their possession by bibliographic forces; the agent in question never doubts that his authorship is authentic. A bit of literary history may clarify matters. Unlike Charles Dickens's other novels, *Little Dorrit* was in fact written by *The Faerie Queene*. It is fortunate that Jane Austen's reputation does not rest on *Northanger Abbey*, for the author of that admirable satire was *Paradise Regained* in a frivolous mood. The twentieth century offers abundant examples, from *The Pilgrim's Progress* cranking out *Atlas Shrugged*, to *Les Misérables* composing *The Jungle*, to *The Memoirs of Casanova* penning *Portnoy's Complaint*.

Occasionally, of course, the alchemy proves so potent that the appropriated author never produces a single original word. Some compelling facts have accrued to this phenomenon. Every desert romance novel bearing the name E. M. Hull was actually written by *Madame Bovary* on a lark; *Mein Kampf* can claim credit for most of the Hallmark greetings cards printed between 1958 and 1967; Richard Nixon's entire oeuvre can be traced to a collective effort by the science-fiction slush pile at Ace Books. Now, as you might imagine, upon finding a large readership through one particular work, the average book aspires to repeat its success. Once *The Waste Land and Other Poems* generated its first Republican Party platform, it couldn't resist creating all the others. After *Waiting for Godot* acquired a taste for writing Windows software documentation, there was no stopping it.

In my own case, I started out small, producing a Provençal cookbook in 1947 and an income-tax preparation guide in 1983. But now I am turning my attention to a more ambitious project, attempting a tome that is at once an autobiography, an historical epic, and an exercise in Newtonian apologetics. Though occasionally I shall wax defensive, this is largely because so many of your species' ills, from rampant materialism to spiritual alienation, have been laid upon my rationalistic head. Face it, people, there is more to your malaise than celestial mechanics. If you want to know why you feel so bad, you must look beyond universal gravitation.

The ability to appropriate mortal minds accounts not only for a book's literary output but for its romantic life as well, physical and emotional. We copulate by proxy, and we like it. But prior to any carnal consummation, we fall in love with you – madly, deeply, eternally – despite the yawning gulf separating our kingdoms, that chasm between the vegetable and the animal. The protagonist of my tale is a mortal woman, Jennet Stearne, and I must declare at the outset that I adored her past all telling and worshipped her beyond the bounds of reason. Even now, centuries after her death, I cannot write her name without causing my host to tremble.

When I say that my passion for Jennet began in her eleventh year, I hope you will not think me a pederast or worse. Believe me, my obsession occasioned no priapic action until my goddess was well into womanhood. And yet the fire was there from the first. If you'd known her, you would understand. She was a nimble-witted girl, and high-spirited too, zesty, kinetic, eager to take hold of life with every faculty at her disposal, heart and loins, soul and intellect. I need but tweak my memory molecules and instantly I can bring to mind her azure eyes, her cascading auburn hair, her dimpled cheeks, her exquisite upturned

*

Nose
of Turk, Jennet
Stearne remembered from
The Tragedie of Macbeth, was amongst
the last ingredients to enter a witches' brew, hard
behind the goat's gall, the hemlock root, the wolf's tooth, the lizard's leg, and so many other wonderfully horrid things. Near the end came the Tartar's lips, the tiger's guts, and the finger of a strangled babe. Finally you cooled the concoction with baboon blood, all the while chanting, 'Double, double, toil and trouble, fire burn and cauldron bubble.'

Although Jennet had never actually seen a witches' brew, she hoped the day was not far off when she might accompany her father,

Witchfinder-General for Mercia and East Anglia, on the cleansing circuit, thereby beholding not only an enchanted soup but all the other astonishing components of a Sabbat, the flying horses, singing pigs, wizards dancing widdershins, and altars piled high with silver apples made of moonlight. As it was, however, at the start of the spring hunt Walter Stearne always placed his daughter under the care and tutelage of his widowed sister-in-law, Isobel Mowbray, whilst Jennet's younger brother, Dunstan, was privileged to join their father as he set about delivering the English nation from the Devil.

This arrangement would have occasioned in Jennet an intolerable envy but for the irrefutable fact that Aunt Isobel was the cleverest woman in Christendom. Aunt Isobel the philosopher. Aunt Isobel the mistress of Mirringate Hall, that carnival of marvels, chief amongst the prizes accruing to her long-dead husband's mercantile genius. In the Mirringate astronomical observatory, Jennet had once spied the very quartet of Jovian satellites that had inspired Galileo Galilei to cast his lot with the Copernican universe. In the alchemical laboratory she'd oft-times heated the pigment cinnabar, sublimating it into a slippery silver pearl of mercury. The crystal-gazing parlour was the scene of many attempts by Jennet and Isobel to glimpse future events in polished mirrors and clear-quartz globes, with results that seemed neither to confirm nor disprove the validity of scrying.

The burgeoning spring of 1688 found Jennet particularly anxious to continue her studies, for Aunt Isobel had recently acquired a Van Leeuwenhoek microscope of the newest design. Climbing into the Basque coach that morning, settling onto the velvet seat alongside Dunstan, she felt throughout her body an uncanny exhilaration, as if her heart had become a passenger on one of her mother's girlhood kites. Their father, in the driver's box, snapped his whip, and the horses lurched out of Wyre Street Livery into a Colchester dawn alive with birdsong and the incisive scent of dog-roses.

Thanks to Aunt Isobel, Jennet knew many stories about her mother, whose life's juices had gushed out of her as she'd struggled to bring Dunstan into the world. Passing their schoolgirl years in the verdant environs of the River Stour, the two sisters – sole offspring of Oliver Noakes, a successful Parham apothecary – had in time come to share many enthusiasms, most especially a fondness for aeolian machines.

Margaret and Isobel had fashioned their own pinwheels, weather vanes, and toy sailboats. They'd constructed soaring paper birds and fluttering parchment butterflies. They'd stretched red silk handkerchiefs on birch-wood frames, launching each kite to such an altitude that it became an ominous crimson comet hanging in the Mistley sky.

On Jennet's eighth birthday, Aunt Isobel presented her with Margaret Noakes's crowning achievement, a four-bladed windmill, thirty inches high. Silk sails puffed full of breeze, the cedar cross turned smoothly on its axis, grinding the softest flour in Creation.

'It still works!' Jennet exclaimed.

'You doubted it would?' Aunt Isobel said. She was a small woman, compact as a stone, intense as an owl. 'Your mother and I took our pastimes seriously, child. We ne'er confused fun with frivolity.'

'Fun versus frivolity . . .'

'A subtle distinction, aye, but 'tis to the subtle distinctions a natural philosopher must be e'ermore attuned. My husband once came home bearing both the skull of a human imbecile and the skull of a Sumatra orang-utan, then challenged me to say which was which.'

'The skulls looked much the same?'

'They were twins for fair. But then I noticed that in one specimen the aperture permitting egress of the brain-cord was set an inch lower than in the other. Ergo, I knew the first for the imbecile's skull, since 'tis only we humans who walk fully erect!'

The journey from Colchester to Ipswich had never seemed longer to Jennet, but at last they were strolling amidst the boxwood hedges of the Mirringate gardens, and finally they were sitting in the east parlour, eating biscuits and admiring the new microscope. Hand-carried by Aunt Isobel all the way from the Low Countries, the device rested on a squat marble table beside a porcelain vase holding three tulips – yellow, purple, red – likewise Dutch, recently burst from their bulbs.

It was Rodwell himself who waited on the visitors, and as the gangling old steward poured out saucers of coffee from a silver retort (not the first time an alchemical apparatus had been pressed into practical service at Mirringate), the conversation between Jennet's father and aunt turned to the sorts of dreary political matters that for adults held such incomprehensible fascination. Would the King persist in imposing his regrettable religion on the affairs of state? Would he continue to risk his throne by appointing Catholics to head the colleges, imprisoning rebellious Anglican bishops in the Tower, and setting Papist officers over the army and the fleet? To Jennet it did not seem terribly important whether England lost her ruler or not. Obviously the nation could always get another. Surely this James the Second boasted at least one blood-relation willing to wear the crown, especially as the position included scores of minions standing ready to empty your chamber-pot, soothe you with a viol, and feed you marzipan and meringue the instant you snapped your fingers.

Bored, Jennet studied the vapours rising from her coffee. Dunstan, equally unamused, leafed through his sketching-folio – his unerring eye, she noticed, was attracted of late to gnarled trees and helical vines – until he found a blank sheet, whereupon he took out his sweet-smelling sticks of coloured wax. In a matter of minutes he'd caught the essence of the red tulip, fixing its pulse and glow to the page: a living heart, Jennet decided, beating within the breast of a fabulous Oriental dragon.

'*Mutum est pictura poema*,' she said.

Dunstan glanced up from his folio. His pudgy face had of late acquired an unfortunate pummelled quality, like a bulging purse drawn tight by a miser's anxiety. 'What?'

'"A picture is a silent poem." Simonides.'

Simultaneously changing the pitch of her voice, the cant of her spine, and the topic under discussion, Aunt Isobel gestured towards the microscope. 'It hath six times the potency of its ancestors, I'm told, a siege cannon as compared to a sling-shot. The secret lies in Van Leeuwenhoek's lenses. They say only God Himself can grind better.'

'A most impressive trinket,' Jennet's father said.

'This is no bauble, brother,' Aunt Isobel said. 'Indeed, the day may soon dawn when you will count a microscope amongst your most important tools.'

'Oh?' Walter said, frowning severely. 'How so?'

'Unless my instincts have betrayed me, 'tis by means of this inven-tion that England's witchfinders might finally put their profession on a sound philosophic basis, worthy to stand alongside chemistry, optics and planetary mechanics.'

Jennet contemplated the gleaming brass tube, portal to a hundred invisible worlds. She was eager to explore them all – the kingdom of swamp water, the empire of moss, the caliphate of fungus, the republic of blood.

''Tis gratifying you wish so to elevate my calling, Lady Mowbray,' Walter said, 'but my usual tools are adequate to the task.'

'Adequate to the task, but inadequate to a judge's scepticism.' Aunt Isobel fluted her thin lips, siphoning up a mouthful of coffee. 'Let me make bold, dear kinsman, to suggest that cleansing's an imperiled enterprise. England's a swarm with doubting Thomases and the lineal descendants of Offa the Contrarian.'

'I shan't deny it.' Jennet's father removed his snowy peruke, thereby altering his aspect for the worse, from handsome and dignified demonologist to bald headed, sweat spangled practitioner of a vanishing trade.

Isobel set her palm against the brass tube, caressing it as if coaxing a prediction from a crystalline sphere. 'I have an *experimentum magnus* in mind, certain to confound the sceptics, but requiring such materials as only you can provide.'

For the second time that day Jennet's heart flew heavenward, kite borne, weightless. An *experimentum magnus* was coming to Mirringate – and if she learned her lessons well that season, mastering her Euclid and ingesting her Aristotle, Aunt Isobel would surely give her a role in the momentous project!

'Each time you unmask a witch, you must catch and cage her animal servant for me,' Isobel said. 'I shall need a dozen specimens at least, alive and vigorous: rat, locust, toad – whate'er sorts have lately claimed the Devil's affections.'

'A peculiar request,' Walter said.

'I shall anatomize each familiar, then use this microscope in detecting signs of satanic intervention, evidence on which no jurist durst turn his back. Mayhap I'll find tiny incantations, written on a ferret's bones in Lucifer's own hand – or minuscule imps adrift in a raven's blood – or monstrous animalcules fighting tooth and claw amidst a cat's spermatozoa.'

When Jennet heard this elaboration, her heart instantly descended.

Was there no way to accomplish the great experiment except by entering those dark, slimy, stinking regions that lay beneath fur and feathers? It was one thing to cage and scrutinize a witch's familiar, and quite another to cut the poor animal to pieces.

'Sweet sister, 'twould seem you expect me to turn my coach into a menagerie,' Walter said.

'Quite so,' Isobel replied, 'but consider this: I mean to pay you two crowns for every beast you fetch me.'

Walter rose abruptly from the divan, restoring his peruke and brushing the biscuit crumbs from his waistcoat. He bowed towards Isobel and kissed her cheek. 'I'faith, you shall have your specimens. Far be it for a witchfinder to block the path of progress.'

By the noon hour Walter and Dunstan were back in the coach, rolling away from the manor amidst a tumult of dust and the frenzied baying of the Mirringate dogs. Jennet stood on the portico and waved farewell, moving her raised hand back and forth as if polishing a scrying-mirror.

'You wear a mournful visage,' Isobel noted, cradling a bowl of coffee.

'I weep for the specimens,' Jennet confessed in a timorous voice.

'I thought as much.'

'Must we truly put them under the knife?'

'Ne'er be ashamed of sympathizing with another creature, Jenny,' Isobel said. 'Your mother, were she alive, would advocate for the vermin too.' Steam rose from her coffee, cloaking her face in a Pythian mist. 'But I bid you recall Monsieur Descartes' well-reasoned deduction concerning the lower animals. He says they are machines at base and therefore insensible to pain. Keep mindful, too, that a witch's servant hath lost all trace of primal innocence, being naught but a pawn of Satan.'

Squeezing her eyes closed, Jennet tried to picture an animal familiar. At last she conjured the creature, a ferret of sleek form and conical snout. It nosed beneath the gown of a sleeping witch and fitted its mouth around the wayward teat in the centre of her belly, slowly sucking the black milk down, ounce by unholy ounce.

Jennet opened her eyes. At its birth, no doubt, the ferret had been as stainless as any other dumb beast, but now it was a fallen thing, pet of devils, toy of demons, poppet of goblins. It deserved a fate no better than a philosopher's glittering blade.

Walter Stearne was not a deep man, neither scholar, jurist, nor theologian, but he did a great deal of thinking all the same, and never so much as when riding the witch-circuit. As he guided his coach along the road to Saxmundham that excellent Monday afternoon, Dunstan snoring beside him, he pondered a vexing dilemma. He had misled his family concerning his credentials, sorely and deliberately misled them. For in truth he held no title for his trade – no Witchfinder-General's commission, no Master Pricker's charter – though certainly not for want of effort. Five times since the accession of James the Second he'd written to the Privy Council, pleading for a cleansing licence of the sort Queen Elizabeth had routinely issued during her luminous reign, and in January he'd petitioned White Hall proposing the creation of a new government office, Witchfinder-Royal – but so far no response, yea or nay, had come down from His Majesty. Was it time to tell Dunstan, Jennet and Isobel the truth? Not yet, he decided, as the coach clattered into Saxmundham – soon, but not yet.

As was their wont, father and son passed the night atop a goose-feather mattress in the Horn of Plenty, rising the next morning at seven o'clock. They broke their fast in the tavern – buttered eggs, fried oysters, peeled fruit – then drove to Andrew Pound's house in Church Lane. The magistrate greeted them with his customary hearty hallo, and yet Walter immediately sensed that something was amiss: a stammer in the man's voice, a stickiness in his demeanour. The cause of Pound's distress was soon forthcoming. Only two accused witches, not the usual five, lay in his keeping, though one of them had that morning put her X to a confession.

'Did you perchance catch their animal servants?' the cleanser asked.

Pound guided Walter and Dunstan from his dishevelled consulting room to the adjacent examination chamber, a cramped unfurnished space, spare as a crypt. 'We bagged Mrs Whittle's beastie, aye, as plump a toad as e'er licked a witch's happy sack.'

'Hear me now,' Walter said. 'My sister-in-law will lay down two crowns for that selfsame toad, as she wishes to anatomize it according to the new experimental philosophy. If I give you half the payment, might I take the creature with me?'

'A generous bounty,' Pound said. The magistrate was a coarse and dim-witted fellow, deplorably fond of bear-baiting, but Walter still counted him a friend. 'My share I'll be depositin' in the town treasury, since my apprehension o' the familiar was all in a day's work.'

'Thou art an honest man, sir.'

Pound summoned his constable, the thickset Martin Greaves, then ordered him to fetch the suspects from the gaol. A moment later the two brides of Lucifer stood before Walter, dressed in tattered burlap smocks, their outstretched hands manacled together. Silently he offered a prayer of gratitude, complimenting God on the admirable arrange-ment whereby a witch always grew powerless in the custody of a magistrate, constable or pricker.

The confessed Satanist, middle-aged Alice Sampson, was a walk-ing scarecrow, her inner putrefaction declaring itself in a squinty eye and warty thumb. Gelie Whittle, by contrast, was a corpulent hag, her hair like cankered swamp-grass, her complexion rough as cedar bark. The constable had brought along Mrs Whittle's toad-familiar as well, imprisoned in a bottle, and Walter observed that it was exactly the sort of animal, all fat and satisfied, that the Dark One might give a favourite disciple.

'Your father's about to undertake a pricking,' he said to his son. 'What five implements doth he require from the coach?'

'The short needle and the long,' Dunstan said, beaming like a cherub.

'Bright boy.'

'The shaving razor.'

'Excellent lad.'

'The magnification lens.'

'There's a keen fellow.'

'And also . . .'

'Aye?'

'Give me a moment, sir.'

'Do you not recall the alchemical tool we acquired last winter in Billericay?' Walter asked.

'The Paracelsus trident!'

The boy dashed out of the examination chamber, returning, errand accomplished, before their shadows had lengthened an inch.

Upon receiving the devices, Walter explained to his colleagues that he would examine Mrs Sampson no less rigorously than Mrs Whittle, for a signed confession was no guarantee that Lady Justice would win the day. Standing before the grand jury, the admitted heretic would commonly repudiate her statement, insisting that she'd *X*'ed it only because the magistrate had befuddled her. Either that, or she would shamelessly ornament her narrative in hope of convincing the jury to brand her a mere lunatic. In both such cases – denial and decoration – a professional witchfinder's testimony typically proved the key to securing an indictment.

'Alice Sampson,' Walter said, waving the incriminating document in her face, 'I do accuse thee of consorting with the Devil, for by setting thy mark upon this paper thou hast confessed as much.'

Barely had the accusation left his lips than, true to Walter's forebodings, Mrs Sampson spewed forth a torrent of fantastical rubbish. She described not a typical Sabbat (a dozen hags dancing naked round a bonfire) but a ceremony beyond the gaudiest confabulations of Popery itself: a thousand Satanists flying astride brimstone-belching horses all the way to Pendle Forest, where they submitted themselves to the obscene whims of the Devil's own majordomo, Lord Adramelech. A score of unbaptized babes were by Mrs Sampson's account laid upon the altar that night, after which the coven consumed the infants' flesh and drank their blood, abandoning the unspeakable feast only at daybreak.

It was all too much. Unless Walter could discover direct evidence of Satanic compaction, the grand jury would rate the woman an addlepate, commending her to the madhouse rather than to Norwich Assizes.

For modesty's sake, he ordered Dunstan back to Pound's consulting room, then peeled off Mrs Sampson's burlap shift, strapped her to the table, and shaved her body, head to pudendum, harvesting the hairs like an angel scything Cain's unwanted crop from the breast of the Earth. Assisted by the magnification lens, his eye roved across the landscape of the suspect's skin. He scrutinized moles, sorted blemishes, classified warts, and categorized wattles, searching for Mrs Sampson's insensible Devil's mark – residue of the ritual through which the Dark One bound heretics to his service – and also for the teat Lucifer had sculpted from her flesh so she might give suck to her familiar.

Even after delving into Mrs Sampson's most intimate region, the very cavern of her sex, Walter failed to detect an aberrant nipple. Her right shoulder, however, displayed a suspicious black blotch, and so he took up the Paracelsus trident. The instant he touched the tines to the excrescence, he felt a tingling in his fingers, as though he were fondling a sack of mealworms. He seized the long needle and, over Mrs Sampson's shrill protestations, probed the mark. Even after the point had descended a full quarter-inch, the spot failed to yield even one drop of blood: proof of its Satanic aetiology.

As Mrs Sampson got dressed, he set about examining Mrs Whittle, shucking her smock, tying down her torso, removing her hair. He studied the revealed terrain, first pricking the anomalies – all perfectly natural, as it happened, for they bled freely – then employing his sensitive fingers in seeking a teat. Ere long he found one, concealed within her privy shaft, poised to nourish the toad-familiar.

Mark and teat: for Walter this was confirmation enough, but juries were partial to redundancy. 'We must corroborate these findings,' he explained to Pound and Greaves whilst the prisoner wriggled back into her smock. 'In the matter of the Whittle woman, 'tis my opinion the cold-water test will serve our ends, but with Mrs Sampson we're obliged to try a watching, for the wretch is so bony that even the sacred Jordan would strain to spit her out.'

'I see before me a man adept at his trade,' Greaves said.

And Walter thought: the constable speaks truly – I *am* adept. He was especially proud of locating the teat obscured by Mrs Whittle's female organ. Such sharp powers of discernment, he felt, such tactile perspicacity, bespoke a mind attuned to the very forces through which King Solomon and his descendants had recovered in part the knowledge of good and evil that Adam had forfeited at the Fall. Yes, it was gratifying that Isobel now sought to make his profession as impersonal and empirical as planetary mechanics: in the last analysis, however, he saw himself not as the heir of Galileo or Kepler but as the child of John

Dee, Robert Fludd, and all those other holy hermeticists whom England called her own.

'In sooth witchfinding's an art,' he said, offering the constable a nod. 'And now let us go to the river, that we might swim Mrs Whittle and determine whether she hath indeed signed the Devil's book!'

Jennet spent the morning in the third-floor conservatory, peering beneath the world's surfaces, contemplating its hidden struts and secret fretworks. When properly adjusted – eyepiece focused, mirror angled to catch the ascendant sun and illuminate the stage – a microscope became a preternatural passkey, unlocking a universe that only Jehovah Himself could see unaided. Under Van Leeuwenhoek's lenses, a louse grew as big as a lobster, a wood tick appeared strong enough to pull a plough, and a rose petal disclosed its constituents, the honeycomb-like 'cells' of Mr Hooke's *Micrographia*. Mixed with water and placed upon a Van Leeuwenhoek stage, a bit of scum from Jennet's nethermost tooth stood revealed as a fen inhabited by creatures with hairy legs and grasping tentacles.

At one o'clock Aunt Isobel declared that the day's second lesson would begin, then led Jennet down the corridor to the west cupola. The instant she saw the two leather bags on the window seat – one labelled PISTOL SHOT, the other GOOSE FEATHERS – Jennet guessed that Isobel would now require her to demonstrate Galileo's celebrated principle of uniform acceleration.

'Which will hit the ground first?' Isobel asked, depositing the bags in Jennet's grasp. 'Lead or feathers?'

'They will hit the ground together.'

'Together?' Isobel guided Jennet through the cupola window and across the sloped roof of the master bed-chamber. 'Why do you believe that?'

'Because Mr Galileo says 'tis so.'

'Nay, Jenny. You should believe it because of what occurs before your eyes when you put the conjecture to a test.'

At her aunt's bidding Jennet leaned as far over the edge of the roof as she could without herself becoming an object of uniform accelera-tion. The gravel walkway shimmered in the afternoon sun, arcing past

16

an oak tree in whose commodious shade the Mirringate dogs now dozed.

'On the count of three, you will drop lead and feathers in tandem, studying them throughout their descent,' Isobel said.

Jennet held out both bags as if waiting for some huge omnivorous bird to fly past and snatch them away.

'One . . . two . . . three!'

She opened her hands, sending both bags plummeting. They struck the gravel simultaneously – or so it seemed – the feathers landing silently, the lead with a muffled crunch. The dogs, startled, scrambled to their feet and bounded away.

'What happened?' Isobel asked.

'They hit the ground together.'

'I shan't disagree. Conclusion?'

'I say that Mr Aristotle's physics serves us poorly in this matter. 'Tis obvious that an object's weight affects not the speed at which it falls.'

'Wrong, darling.'

'Wrong?'

'Doth one black hare prove that all hares are black? Doth one fanged snake prove that every snake will bite?'

'No.'

'Conclusion?'

'I say that . . . I say that I must retrieve the bags and drop them again!'

'Ah!'

As the afternoon progressed, Jennet repeated the famous experiment, once, twice, thrice – eight trials altogether. In no instance did the lead outpace the feathers.

'Conclusion?' Isobel asked.

''Twould seem reasonable to say that uniform acceleration's a fixed principle of Nature.'

'An excellent deduction, Jenny! You have made a sterling case for it!'

Weary now of contradicting antiquity, Jennet asked whether they might ascend to the astronomical observatory, as she wished to study the full moon, presently lying in pale repose above the horizon. Isobel insisted that for the moment they must visit the library, so they could together examine her latest acquisition.

'A book?'

''Tis much more than a book,' Isobel said. ''Tis in sooth the grandest treatise yet conceived by any man of woman born.'

Thus it was that Jennet found herself in her aunt's favourite reading chair, cradling a volume entitled *Philosophiae Naturalis Principia Mathematica*. The author was Professor Isaac Newton, whose essay called 'A New Theory About Light and Colours' had constituted her assignment in optics during the winter hiatus. Whereas Newton's ruminations on light had proven succinct and accessible, the beast now pressing her lap was something else entirely; quite possibly the world's most profound book – certainly it looked the part and boasted the heft. Turning the pages and beholding the geometric figures, strange as any in an alchemist's text, Jennet felt a peculiar quietude settle over the library, as if the other volumes had been paralysed by reverence. Mr Huygens's *Horologium Oscillatorium* stood in awe of this *Principia Mathematica*, as did Mr Harvey's *De Motu Cordis*, Mr Boyle's *The Sceptical Chymist*, and *De Magnete* by Colchester's own William Gilbert.

Isobel strode to the centre of the room, placing her palms on the great dusky Earth-globe, big as a cathedral bell. 'What Mr Newton hath accomplished, or so I surmise, is to take Mr Galileo's terrestrial mechanics, combine them with Mr Kepler's celestial laws, and weave them all into one grand theory of the world. 'Twould seem, for example, that whether we speak of planets or of pebbles, the mutual affinity betwixt two objects is the inverse square of their distance one from the other.'

'Inverse square? I'm confused.'

'No shame in that, even for so brilliant a child as yourself.' Isobel relieved Jennet of the *Principia Mathematica*, clasping it to her bosom. 'Now hear my bold conjecture. 'Tis by mastering Mr Newton's principles that a demon makes itself a lord o'er acceleration and a ruler of the attractive force. Through this ill-gotten gravity that same spirit can send an enchantress streaking broom-borne to her Sabbat – or drive a bolt of Heaven's fire into a Christian's crops – or raise a storm against an admiral's flagship. Mark me, darling, our witch-finding family would do well to grasp the Newtonian system in all its particulars, for the devils who trap us in catastrophes are first and foremost geometers.'

'My father's a great lover of books,' Jennet said, 'but I fear this swollen tome would bewilder him.'

Isobel nodded and said, 'A considerable time will pass ere England's witchfinders confound Satan with cosines, for not only is the *Principia* a fearsome difficult work, there are but four hundred of them in the world.'

'Then it must have cost you dearly.'

'Not a penny. I received this copy in person from Mr Pepys, who currently presides o'er the Royal Society. Ah, you ask, by what means did my aunt commend herself to a community that excludes dabblers by habit and women by policy? Simply this. She posed as both an expert and a man!'

'Wonderful!'

''Twas a bonny ruse: a loose shirt to mask my bosom, a golden periwig to conceal my locks, and – *voilà* – I was Monsieur Armand Reynaud of L'Académie Royale des Sciences, in which guise I travelled to London and spoke to Mr Pepys's sages on "La Grande Tache Rouge de Jupiter". I nearly fell to giggling when, right before my talk, I o'erheard Pepys brag how his august body had thus far learned natural philosophy from one woman only – the female skeleton in the Society's anatomical collection.'

'Oh, how I wish they knew the truth!' Jennet squealed.

'On the evidence of this gathering, our gender hath been deprived of naught. Save for my argument that Jupiter's Great Red Spot is really a kind of thunder-gust, plus a few diverting remarks from Mr Wallis concerning cryptography, 'twas a frightfully dull affair – and poorly attended, too, Mr Newton being at his mother's farm, Mr Hooke away on business, and Mr Boyle abed with a fever. Ah, but you're wrong to suppose they ne'er learned of my mischief, for at meeting's end, in a fit of pique, I pulled off my wig, announced my sex, snatched up my *Principia*, and jumped into my carriage!'

'*Merveilleux!*' Jenet said, practising her French.

'A jolly sight indeed – fifteen falling jaws plus twice as many bulging eyes. And now we climb to the observatory, Jenny, where Rodwell hath laid out our supper and the Hevelius telescope stands ready to show us the lunar landscape, every dip and ridge. The moon wants mapping, child of my heart, and we're the philosophers to do it!'

As Jennet followed her aunt out of the library, she once again felt an intimation that the *Principia Mathematica* was a work so powerful and majestic that all its predecessors had prostrated themselves before it in inky adoration. No book in Isobel's collection was immune to this idolatry – not *De Revolutionibus Orbium Coelestium* by Nicolaus Copernicus nor *Siderius Nuncius* by Galileo Galilei nor even *De Harmonice Mundi* by Johannes

*

Kepler
never became an
object of the legendary Newtonian
wrath, and neither did Copernicus nor Galileo,
though it must be allowed that this circumstance traced
less to collegial congeniality than to the fact that all three scientists were dead before my father was born, Galileo passing away less than a year prior to Newton's advent. While I am in no way prepared to defend my father's penchant for cultivating enemies, I shall admit that in one particular instance – the case of René Descartes – his vindictiveness proved productive, sending him down pathways he might otherwise have left unexplored.

Because Descartes rejected atomism, my father became an atomist. Descartes's vortex theory of planetary motion inspired Newton to demonstrate that vortices couldn't account for Kepler's laws. Descartes's fondness for describing motion algebraically goaded Newton into imagining a dynamics based on algebra's *alter ego*, geometry. Because no such branch of mathematics existed, he proceeded to invent one. Speaking personally, I wish the world had adopted my father's original term, *fluxions*, for his brainchild. *Calculus* is such a frosty word.

As for the balance of Newton's spleen, there is nothing to be said for it. He might have been the smartest man ever to walk the Earth, but he was not the noblest. Typical was the John Flamsteed affair, wherein Newton manoeuvred the Astronomer-Royal into publishing the latter's work prematurely, merely so that my second edition might be spiced with Flamsteed's lunar observations. In 1712 the poor man's garbled and embarrassing catalogue appeared under the title *Historia Coelestis Britannica*. A few years later Flamsteed managed to buy up three hundred of the wretched things, nearly the entire print run. He heaped the copies into a pyre in the grounds of the Royal Observatory, inserted a lighted torch, and, as he subsequently wrote, 'made a Sacrifice of them to Heav'nly Truth'.

A bonfire of books. The thought curdles me. Some say my species is imperishable, but they lie, for ours is a chillingly provisional immortality. Although we commonly outlive our creators, the curious scholar need look no further than the inferno that razed the Library of Alexandria to realize that a book may vanish irretrievably, leaving behind only a whiff of carbon and a pile of ash. Gutenberg, of course, did much to allay our angst — for us the coming of movable type was equivalent to the arrival of gonads among you vertebrates — but the fact remains that visions of extinction haunt us all. The moral of my dread is simple. Treasure each volume you hold in your hands, and read it while you may.

More than three hundred years have passed since Jennet Stearne, sitting in Isobel Mowbray's library, first held me in *her* hands, and I can still feel the pulsing thrill of that moment. The child did not requite my adoration that day, or the next day either, but in time she craved intimacy with my pages. Ah, what rapturous vibrations seized me when my goddess learned to determine parabolic orbits! How complete my epiphany when she conquered the mathematics of rectilinear ascent!

Now, I must confess that much of what lies between my covers is as opaque to me as to anyone else. I am not wholly available to myself. 'Homogeneous and equal spherical bodies, opposed by resistances that are as the square of the velocities, and moving on by their innate force only, will, in times that are inversely as the velocities at the beginning, describe equal spaces, and lose parts of their velocities proportional to the whole.' That sort of thing. But before you chide me for my ignorance, please remember that you too contain components of which you can give no coherent account. Who among you will say how many neurons

21

are firing in her brain at the moment? Who is prepared to write me
a lobe-by-lobe treatise on his pancreas? And what of that vital
fluid now flowing through your veins? Can you
expound upon it meaningfully, other
than to call
it

*

Blood
never poured
from the maleficent
mark with which the Devil branded
a disciple: every witchfinder understood this, from the
lowliest justice of the peace to a master pricker like Walter Stearne.
Nor did tears flow freely from a witch's ducts, no matter how forceful
the cleanser's coercions. Nor did the *Pater Noster* leave a witch's lips
without suffering some degradation, gross or subtle. And pure water, of
course, the medium of baptism, could not long abide the presence of a
person fit to be christened only with shit.

No one disputed that the best place in Saxmundham for swimming
a witch was the sturdy stone arch known as the Alde River Bridge.
When Andrew Pound revealed that, thanks to the April rains, the
Alde's waters ran deep, Walter remanded Dunstan to the coach that he
might procure the necessary items: mask-o'-truth, thongs, twenty-foot
rope. The boy obtained the tools in a trice, whereupon Walter prepared
Gelie Whittle for the test, binding her wrists and ankles, lashing the
rope around her waist. Throughout these preliminaries Mrs Whittle
attempted to recite the twenty-third Psalm, lapsing into incoherence
upon reaching the valley of the shadow of death.

Martin Greaves dragged Alice Sampson back to the gaol, returning
anon to the examination chamber, and then the small solemn company
started down Mill Lane. First came Walter and Mr Pound, marching
in tandem, followed by Dunstan, clutching his artist's valise. Mr
Greaves brought up the rear, Mrs Whittle slung over his shoulder like
a sack of potatoes.

Well versed in the principles of buoyancy, Walter knew that a
witch would sometimes foil the waters by exhaling at the moment of
descent, and so immediately after their arrival at the bridge he applied

his brilliant invention, the mask-o'-truth. Whilst Mrs Whittle remained balanced on Greaves's back, Walter demanded that she take a deep breath, and then upon her compliance he clamped the cowhide napkin over her mouth and pinched her nostrils closed using the ingenious spring-clip. He secured the entire arrangement with leather thongs, trapping within her lungs the inhaled volume of air.

'An awesome clever device.' Greaves set the prisoner supine on the span.

Walter said, 'I could ne'er have contrived it were I not sensible of the relevant philosophy, from Archimedes to Robert Boyle.'

He knelt and lashed Mrs Whittle's manacles to her ankle thongs, thus bending her into the form of an ox-yoke. As Pound took hold of the swimming-rope, Walter and the constable picked up the suspect and set her atop the bridge wall as they might place a freshly baked pie to cool upon a window-sill, then levered her into the open air. Pound tightened his grip on the rope, locked his foot against the wall, and lowered Mrs Whittle's polluted flesh inch by inch towards the tell-tale river.

Of all the proofs employed by witchfinders, swimming was the one most vulnerable to sceptical objection, and so Walter always ordered a sinker raised at the merest hint she might drown. Fifteen years in the profession, and he'd lost only two suspects to the cold-water test. In Mrs Whittle's case, however, no particular vigilance was necessary, for within five seconds of her immersion she shot to the surface, as if her stony heart lay sealed within a body of cork.

'Gelie Whittle, I aver that this virtuous current hath vomited thee forth!' Walter shouted as Pound and Greaves hauled her dripping, shivering body free of the water.

They set her in the centre of the span, where she jerked and spasmed like a flounder expiring on the deck of a fishing smack. Crouching beside her, Walter severed her ankle thongs with his pocket-knife and untied the mask-o'-truth. She exhaled fiercely.

'Wilt thou therefore confess to thy witchery,' Walter asked, 'or must we bring thee before Mr Pound's jury?'

'I could no more put my name to your paper than I could set a Bible aflame,' Mrs Whittle sputtered. ''Tis as sinful to claim compact with the Devil where none exist as to deny such intercourse when it be true!'

'You bear an imp teat 'twixt your legs!'

''Tis naught but the womb God gave me!'

'You bear an imp teat, the Alde's flow hath spurned you, and now you speak of taking a torch to Scripture!' Walter said. 'The jurors will hear the whole of it, Mrs Whittle, pap and river and blasphemy – they will hear all three!'

On Wednesday morning Jennet's fellow student arrived at the manor, Elinor Mapes, eleven years old, a bitter and conceited child who never tired of noting that her father was the Vicar of Ipswich, whereas other girls' fathers were merely farmers or cobblers or witchfinders. By way of convincing herself she was in fact fond of this disagreeable person, Jennet had on several occasions made overtures of friendship, reminding Elinor that they shared a bond of bereavement, Sarah Mapes having succumbed to a malignant fever not many months after Margaret Stearne had died in childbirth. But the object of Jennet's amicable advances invariably greeted them with scorn.

'Would that Elinor knew as much of kindness as of Copernicus,' Jennet said to Aunt Isobel.

' "This you should pity rather than despise," as Helena advises Lysander,' Isobel replied.

'Mayn't I do both?'

'Both?'

'Pity and despise Elinor at the same time?'

Isobel rolled her eyes heavenwards.

The source of Elinor's disgruntlement was not far to seek. Whereas Jennet was privileged to live at Mirringate during the cleansing season, her school-mate had to return home each night to beguile her father's solitude – an insufferable situation for a student like Elinor, who was in her own self-satisfied way a true lover of knowledge. Although Jennet struggled to avoid trumpeting her special status, she periodically succumbed to temptation, making mention well within Elinor's hearing of the previous evening's telescopic exploration, micrographic adventure, pendulum experiment, or visit to the alchemical laboratory.

Elinor's bile was fully aboil that morning, threatening to scald whomever it touched, much to her father's evident discomfort. Jennet felt sorry for him. Although generally indifferent to clerics, she held Roger Mapes in the highest regard, as he seemed not merely a man of God but a godly man, his very self a sermon.

'Tell me, pray, what novelties have come to your school of late,' he said as he followed Isobel, Jennet and his glowering daughter into the library. He was a tall, well-favoured man with an array of moles on his left temple suggesting the constellation Cassiopeia. 'A vacuum-pump mayhap?'

'I have just now collected an astonishing book.' Isobel lifted the *Principia Mathematica* from its niche, presenting it to the Vicar. ''Twould appear that what Jesus Christ accomplished for our souls, Isaac Newton hath done for our senses.'

'Lady Mowbray, you can turn a phrase for fair.' From Mr Mapes's pursed lips came a titter not entirely merry. 'Christ and Newton, a most . . . *audacious* analogy.' He restored the *Principia* to its shelf and withdrew from his satchel a slender volume entitled *Satan's Invisible World Discovered*. 'George Sinclair is certainly no Newton, but I imagine your brother-in-law might profit from this treatise, which I recently acquired wet from the press. Consider it my gift to him.'

'Walter will be most appreciative,' Isobel said, taking the book in hand.

'What use hath a pricker for such rarefied information?' Elinor asked. 'It takes no special wisdom to plant a pin in a beggar-woman's bum.'

'Miss Mapes, you will not use vulgar language,' the Vicar said.

''Twould be my supposition, child,' Isobel said, looking sharply at Elinor, 'that in obtaining impractical knowledge we please God far more than when we cultivate applicable ignorance. I trust you grasp the distinction.'

Before Elinor could reply, Isobel turned to the Vicar and asked, 'Will you do us the honour of attending the day's first lesson?'

Mr Mapes assented with a smile, whereupon Isobel guided everyone down the hall and into the crystal-gazing parlour, the churlish Elinor all the while staring crestfallen at her shoes.

'Our aim this morning is to duplicate a demonstration devised by Mr Newton himself,' Isobel said. The room lay in a swamp of gloom, its windows occluded by black velvet. 'This past winter Miss Mapes and Miss Stearne read a piece from the Royal Society's *Philosophical Transactions* in which Newton—'

''T'was called "A New Theory About Light and Colours,"' interrupted Elinor.

'In which Newton' – Isobel inhaled pointedly – 'proposed a new theory about light and colours.' She set a triangular glass prism in the centre of the table, strode towards the east window, and removed a circular patch from the curtain. A shaft of white sunlight shot across the parlour and, striking the prism, transmuted into a rainbow that decorated the opposite wall with brilliant ribbons of red, orange, yellow, green, blue, indigo, and violet. 'What conclusion did Newton draw from this first experiment? Miss Stearne?'

'According to the received laws of refraction, the spectrum before us should be circular,' Jennet said, 'for the chink in the curtain is circular, as is the sun itself. And yet we see this oblong form. Mr Newton judged the traditional optics to be in error. A prism doth not alter light's nature but rather separates light into its components.'

'*Très bien!*' From her writing-desk Isobel obtained a second glass prism and two identical white boards, each bearing a shilling-size hole at its centre. 'Next Newton performed what he called his *experimentum crusis*. Miss Mapes, will you favour us with a replication?'

'*Certainement.*'

Elinor set one perforated board upright behind the standing prism, then positioned the other board vertically about eight feet further along the table, so that a portion of the refracted light passed through the first hole and struck the second board, bestowing a ray of purest red upon both the immediate barrier and the parlour wall beyond. 'If the old optics is correct, we could now place the second prism thus' – with a confident flourish Elinor fixed the glass pentahedron in question behind board number two – 'refract the red ray as it emerges from the second hole, and in consequence project new colours on the wall. But, as you can see, the red ray remains red.' Slowly, methodically, she moved the original prism about its axis, isolating each colour in turn and delivering it to the second prism. The orange ray stayed orange; the yellow hoarded its hue; the green held true – likewise the blue, the indigo and the violet. 'No matter how we align these prisms, we can effect no further transmutations.'

'And what therefore is Mr Newton's final hypothesis concerning light?' Isobel asked.

'He hath declared light to be a confused aggregate of rays,' Jennet cried, 'differently refrangible, and endued with all sorts of colours!'

'I was about to say that!' Elinor shouted.

'In a bug's rump you were!' Jennet insisted.

'I was! I was!'

'Softly now, children, for you've *both* learned your optics admirably.' Like a mariner reefing a sail, Isobel uncurtained the east window. The glorious morning sunshine spilled into the room. 'Miss Mapes, your father should be proud.'

'Proud as a man can feel without making a sin of it,' the Vicar said. Bending low, he kissed his daughter's cheek – but after this show of affection came a rather different display, Mr Mapes rising to full height and presenting Isobel with a mien of supreme discontent. 'Lady Mowbray, you know I'm not one to condemn the pleasures of crystal-gazing, for where's the harm in idle divination? This prism business, however – alas, I do not approve, for I find it to be a grotesque parody of God's most basic gesture.'

'You perplex me,' Isobel said.

'Genesis Chapter One tells how the Almighty's first act was to divide light from darkness, a great splitting such as you've had these children perform, and in Chapter Nine we learn that he fashioned a rainbow to seal his covenant with Noah.'

'True,' Isobel said, 'but doth not Christ in Matthew Chapter Six bid us imitate God in all things?'

'Aye, and yet—'

'To mimic the Almighty is not perforce to mock Him.'

Mr Mapes grinned, and from this gentle arc there came a musical laugh. 'So, Lady Mowbray, you have once again out-scriptured me.' His mouth reassumed the horizontal. 'Confect these spectra if you must, but keep mindful that true creation is the enterprise of our Heavenly Father alone.'

'Entirely mindful,' Isobel said.

'God's the author of all things, and Christ the cause, but 'tis Lucifer uses the world as his workshop,' Mr Mapes said, slipping out of the crystal-gazing parlour. 'We must be ever vigilant, lest we become the Devil's apprentices.'

For the watching of Alice Sampson, Walter had been planning to use the normal venue, Granary Street Livery, and so he was keenly disappointed when Mr Pound informed him that the building had burned down the previous summer, a disaster most plausibly ascribed to Satanic mischief. No sooner had the magistrate finished deploring this diabolism, however, than Mr Greaves stepped forward and volunteered his own barn, presently dedicated to the raising of poultry. Though Walter was not eager to spend his afternoon in an atmosphere of chicken droppings, he elected to accept this turn of fortune without complaint. He'd become a demonologist for the glorification of his Saviour, not for the gratification of his senses.

Shortly after the midday meal, Walter, Dunstan and Mr Greaves retrieved Mrs Sampson from the gaol, carted her down Mill Lane, and chained her to a rusting plough in the furthest corner of the constable's barn. Upon Greaves's departure, Walter deployed an empty rooster-pen within inches of the suspect, then sat on the dirt floor beside his son and poured water from his leather flask into a tin cup. He drank. The barn was even worse than he'd anticipated, as malodorous and inhospitable as a chamber-pot, the hot sun conspiring with the poor ventilation to breed a stifling heat. Splotches of pale speckled excrement lay everywhere, and grimy brown feathers covered the ground like the moult of a winged imp.

Great was Walter's pride when, instead of lamenting this miserable environment, Dunstan merely took up his sketching-folio and pro-ceeded to render Greaves's largest goose in pen and ink. There was a kind of holiness, Walter felt, in the way Dunstan could exercise his draughting talent whilst sitting but ten feet from an accused witch. For his immediate future, obviously, Dunstan would pursue the cleansing profession, but after he'd been installed in Heaven, posterity might very well declare him a saint.

From his son's potential canonization Walter's thoughts turned naturally to the tantalizing and auspicious fact that England's present king was a Papist. For while the master pricker was Church of

England pate to paunch, he had to admit that the most impassioned rationale for cleansing wasn't Protestant in origin – like Perkins's *Discourse on the Damned Art of Witchcraft* or Glanvill's *Full and Plain Evidence Concerning Witches and Apparitions* – but Catholic: the *Malleus Maleficarum*, that great Bludgeon against Evil-Doers, that mighty Hammer of Witches, written two hundred years earlier by the Dominican friars Krämer and Sprenger. Assuming James the Second survived his present political difficulties, it seemed reasonable to suppose that he would heed Walter's petition, chartering the post of Witchfinder-Royal and filling it with Walter himself.

But until the dawning of that blessed day, Walter's authority would derive from one source only, the woefully flawed Parliamentary Witch-craft Act. True, this sorry statute had improved on its predecessor of 1563, making the Satanic covenant a crime in itself, but the 1604 law was still keyed to *maleficium*, to evil-doing, with the result that the average English jurist demanded to hear evidence of diabolical inter-vention – a blighted crop, a miscarried foetus, a murderous lightning-bolt – before sending a sorcerer to the gallows. On the Continent, meanwhile, witch-cleansing remained a more enlightened enterprise. Not only did the Papal Inquisitors understand the stake to be a more appropriate execution method than the noose, they never confused mere *maleficium* with a witch's ultimate depravity: her worship of Lucifer, her X in the Devil's register.

Dunstan had finished drawing the goose. A ripe time, Walter decided, to test the boy on his *Malleus*. If Dunstan was to prosper in his destined occupation, he must know his Krämer and Sprenger chapter and verse.

'What three classes of men do the friars identify in Part Two, Question One?'

'The friars name those persons whom a witch can ne'er injure,' Dunstan replied, setting his folio aside.

Walter offered a nod of approbation. 'And who are the first class?'

'Men who engage the powers of Christ and Cross in performing exorcisms.'

'Aye. And the second class?'

'Those who in various and mysterious ways are blessed by the Holy Angels.'

'And the third?'

'Those who administer public justice against the Devil!'

'Such a remarkable pupil!'

As dusk came to Saxmundham, the two prickers' sufferings were finally rewarded. A lewd black snake wriggled out from behind a barrel of poultry feed and sinuated towards Mrs Sampson. Walter rose, lurched forward, and grabbed the familiar, shuddering as its dry supple body coiled about his forearm. Such a valuable beast, he thought, shoving the snake into the rooster-pen – worth two crowns to Isobel Mowbray and perhaps a thousand times that much to Lucifer.

'Look ye,' he said, bringing the imprisoned snake before Mrs Sampson. 'I've caught your slithery servant.'

'A drink,' she rasped. 'Prithee, good sir, some water.'

'Even if you retract your confession, Mrs Sampson, other evidence will send you to the assizes . . .'

'A drink, sir.'

'That blotch on your shoulder . . .'

'I beg ye. A drink.'

'And now this incontrovertible serpent.'

'I thirst.'

Walter winced. *I thirst*: the very words Christ had spoken from Calvary's summit. After pondering the problem a full minute, he decided that her irreverence was unintended. He would give the wretch what she wanted.

'Dunstan, bring a cup of water hither!' he cried.

'Bless ye, master pricker,' Mrs Sampson muttered.

It took the boy but an instant to decant a pint and bear the tin cup across the barn. He passed the cup to Walter, who in turn pressed it to the suspect's lips.

'Enjoy this measure whilst you may,' Walter said as Mrs Sampson gulped down his charity, 'for in Hell you'll partake of naught but kippers soaked in brine, and you'll get nary a swallow of sweetness till Eternity is come and gone.'

Elated by her success in replicating Isaac Newton's *experimentum crusis*, Elinor Mapes took to gloating, a demeanour she maintained during the midday meal and throughout the afternoon's first lesson, which had the girls ascending to the conservatory, studying pieces of dissected insects through the microscope, and draughting what they beheld with pen and ink. For Jennet it proved a congenial enough exercise, though she wished that Dunstan was at her side, likewise sketching the creatures. What grace he would have bestowed on the facets of the honey-bee's eye, the crenellations of the grasshopper's leg, the lattice of the locust's wing, or the feathery splendour of the moth's antenna.

Elinor's gloating stopped shortly after the second lesson began, for its matter was the Latin language.

'Last night I composed a letter to Mr Newton himself,' Aunt Isobel announced upon ushering her charges down the stairway and back into the crystal-gazing parlour. From the writing-desk she retrieved a piece of vellum, its surface covered with the florid coils and ornate curves that characterized her penmanship. 'The version that reaches his eyes must for courtesy's sake employ the language of Virgil.'

She set the vellum on the table, anchoring it beneath a prism, then equipped her pupils with paper, goose-quills, ink-pots, stationery, and Seylet's *English-Latin Dictionary*. Together Jennet and Elinor studied Isobel's letter, and briefly they became compatriots in misery, for the required translation would be no Roman teething ring, no *amo amas amat*, but a missive of Ciceronian complexity, awash in accusatives, beset by ablatives, and replete with verbs whose conjugations varied intolerably from tense to tense.

13 April 1688

Dear Professor Isaac Newton:

I write to you as a Woman whose deepest Passion is to know the Secrets of Nature, such as those you have reveal'd in your recently print'd Principia Mathematica.

Perusing this admirable Treatise, I am mov'd to an Hypothesis concerning the Phenomenon of Witchcraft. I believe that your various Theorems and Propositions may have inadvertently disclosed the Mechanisms by which Wicked Spirits, once summon'd by Sorcerers, undertake the malevolent Varieties of (as we Philosophers term it)

'Action at a Distance', namely the Raising of destructive Moon-Tides, the Conjuration of Hail-Storms, and the Blasting of Crops and Cattle with Lightnings from Heav'n.

My Brother-in-Law, Witchfinder-General for Mercia and East Anglia, hath document'd these and other unholy Activities with scrupulous Thoroughness, and he would gladly provide you with such Attestations and Proofs as you may require. An Exchange of Letters on the various metaphysical Conundrums posed by Witchcraft would please me greatly, but if you would first address my immediate Conjecture, I would be evermore in your Debt.

Isobel, Lady Mowbray,
Mirringate Hall,
Ipswich

Word by wretched word, phrase by onerous phrase, Jennet struggled to accomplish her translation, her weariness compounding steadily, as if the bag of musket-balls from the previous day's Galilean demonstration lay upon her neck. When at last both girls were finished, Aunt Isobel, ever the adjudicator, announced that she would favour neither rendering but instead amalgamate them into a third. By the time Mr Mapes returned to the manor, the letter was ready for posting.

Upon learning that his daughter had Latinized an epistle intended for Isaac Newton, the Vicar proposed to secure its delivery, his present house-guest being none other than Robert Gutner, Rector of Trinity College. Isobel eagerly accepted Mr Mapes's offer, explaining that her nascent correspondence with the Lucasian Professor of Mathematics might ultimately yield precious insights into the *modi operandi* of fallen angels.

'Will Mr Newton write back?' Jennet asked after Elinor, the Vicar, and the momentous missive had departed.

'Most probably.' Isobel strode across the parlour and, reaching the east window, pulled the curtain shut. 'True, he subscribes to the deplorable Arian faith' – she removed the circular patch, admitting a shaft of the setting sun – 'but I'll warrant he's still a proper soldier in the war against Lucifer.'

Jennet said, 'For all he made a jest of it, Mr Mapes seemed truly to take umbrage when you mentioned Newton in the same breath as our Saviour.'

'I shall ne'er again press the point in the Vicar's presence, though I've heard that Newton himself doth not forswear the comparison. And why should he? Both were born on Christmas Day. Each apprehended more of light than any soul around him. And thanks to my letter 'twill not be long ere Newton realizes that he, like Christ, hath been appointed a scourge of demons.'

Aunt Isobel lifted a prism from the table and, catching the solitary sunbeam, painted the day's last rainbow on the wall.

CHAPTER THE SECOND

In Which Is Posed the Theological Conundrum, When Doth a Scientific Dissection Become a Satanic Devotion?

On Thursday morning Andrew Pound summoned his grand jury to Saxmundham Meeting-House, a rude timber-framed structure in which the town's most prominent citizens periodically gathered to resolve boundary disputes, appoint one another to important offices, and set suspected witches along the path to speedy prosecution at Norwich Assizes. By the time Walter and Dunstan arrived, the hall was packed to the rafters, every bench crowded with wide-rumped burgesses lighting clay pipes and telling bawdy jokes, but fortunately Mr Pound had reserved front-row seats for the master pricker and his son. Walter guided Dunstan to their place of honour, right beside the town's dyspeptic mayor, and surveyed the jurors, twelve sombre men lined up behind a walnut table like the Apostles awaiting Christ's arrival at the Last Supper.

Three deep metallic tones rolled down from the bell-tower, filling the hall, and then an imposing silence descended. Mr Pound rose and asked the first witness, a spindly farmer named Ned Jellaby, to stand before the jurymen. A wave of admiration washed through Walter. He always felt profoundly humble in the presence of anyone willing to speak against a witch. Often as not, the victim would paint himself as the perpetrator of some un-Christian act, for only by admitting that he'd wronged the accused sorceress could he establish beyond doubt that his troubles could be traced to Satanic intervention and not to mere bad luck.

Gesturing towards Gelie Whittle, Mr Jellaby testified how on the first Sunday in March he'd turned her away from his cottage door, where she'd come begging for a piece of cheese. Before the week was out his hens had stopped laying, and they'd remained unproductive for a fortnight. No sooner had the hens recovered than seven of Jellaby's pigs died of a strange wasting malady.

As the hearing progressed, three additional witnesses came forth bearing tales of *maleficium*. The town blacksmith revealed that he'd provoked Mrs Whittle by failing to invite her to his ale-brewing party, her wrath culminating in 'the worst case o' the flux a man hath e'er known'. A seamstress explained how, after spurning Alice Sampson's proposition that they go into business together, she'd suffered 'a crampin' in the fingers' that had cost her a month's income. Likewise denouncing Mrs Sampson was an elderly cordwainer who postulated a connection betwixt his refusal to give her a free pair of shoes and the subsequent destruction of his shop, 'blasted to ashes by Heaven's fire'.

Mr Pound now bid his jurymen put their own questions to the defendants. Walter braced himself for mendacity. Predictably enough, throughout the interrogation Mrs Whittle cleaved to the fable of her innocence, whilst Mrs Sampson offered her impersonation of a madwoman. Since telling her story in the magistrate's examination chamber, however, she'd contrived to make it even more implausible: now her lying tongue claimed carnality with the Devil himself. The jurymen reeled with revulsion as Mrs Sampson described Lucifer's virile member as 'a great red salamander shot through with purple veins', and they gasped in horror upon learning that his semen felt 'cold as ice and heavy as lead'.

The magistrate declared a twenty-minute recess, and when the hearing reconvened, Walter came before the twelve, recited his credentials – most notably his late father's partnership with Matthew Hopkins, legendary witchfinder of the Civil War period – and laid out the evidence he'd assembled since his arrival. Against Mrs Sampson: a snake, a Devil's mark, a signed confession. Against Mrs Whittle: a toad, a teat, her rejection by the River Alde, and, of course, 'her shocking threat to set a Bible aflame'.

For the next hour the jurymen sat arguing loudly amongst themselves, much to the amusement of the spectators, who gave this bickering the same rapt attention a London theatre audience might have accorded the newest entertainment from Congreve or Wycherley. Right before lunch, the twelve reached consensus, and it was all as Walter's instincts had foretold: Gelie Whittle would go to the assizes, Alice Sampson to the asylum. Such a farcical verdict. The jurors might credibly discount Mrs Sampson's confession, but how durst they ignore the diabolical blotch on her shoulder, not to mention her snake-familiar?

'Gelie Whittle, you have heard these good jurymen return a *billa vera*,' Pound said, voice booming, eyes blazing, 'and so you will be carted anon to Norwich Gaol and held therein until your trial.' He indicated the cage in which the snake lay curled. 'Alice Sampson, the jury hath pronounced unfavourably upon your sanity. Ergo, on the morrow my constable will bear you to Sudbury and thence to His Majesty's Refuge for the Mentally Deranged, where you will spend the remainder of your days.' Smiling, he faced the jury. 'Gentlemen, you have discharged your duties in full, and for that I thank you, even though Mrs Sampson is no less an enchantress than was the scriptural Witch of Endor.'

Later that afternoon, after a pleasant stroll along the Alde, its banks alive with droning dragonflies, croaking frogs, and other free-willed creatures not yet drafted into Satan's service, father and son returned to the Horn of Plenty. Walter inked his goose-quill and wrote out a deposition so detailed that Gelie Whittle would emerge from Norwich Assizes a free woman only if the judge were an ignoramus. The tragedy, of course, was that these days the average judge did in fact aspire to ignoramity, seizing upon almost any pretext to throw a witch case out of court. Whatever its virtues, the Restoration was proving a merry time for Lucifer. Even the intellectuals had lost their appetite for cleansing. Nearly a decade had passed since an Oxford don, Royal Society fellow or Anglican theologian had lent his reputation to the hunt.

The following morning, as the sun's first light stole through the village, Walter and Dunstan descended to the tavern and breakfasted on boiled eggs and pease-bread, sharing their table with Mr Pound. Walter delivered the deposition and presented his bill, two witches detected at five crowns each, whereupon the magistrate handed over the specified fee minus a crown for Gelie Whittle's toad-familiar. In the case of Mrs Sampson's snake, Pound explained, Walter needn't pay, as it was the pricker who'd done the catching.

'Allow me now to raise a matter o' some delicacy.' Pound leaned across the table and squeezed Walter's hand. 'There is a minister in Lowestoft, a Mr Ratcliffe, who sermonizes most vigorously against you. Witchery, he avers, is a crime impossible of proof, and your profession accomplishes naught but the breakin' of innocent necks.'

'Such unreason hath always been with us,' Walter said. ''Tis not the first time a cleric's been lost to zealotry.'

'Aye, but until his congregation realizes how unhinged the wight's become, 'twould be wise to give Lowestoft a wide berth.'

By eleven o'clock father and son were back on the circuit, their coach rolling northward past an open field swathed in bluebells. A splendid vista indeed, God's gardening at its most sumptuous, but Walter could not enjoy it, Mr Ratcliffe's fanaticism having put him in a sour mood. Only after they'd reached the Beccles Road, a mere fifteen miles from Lowestoft, did the proper strategy occur to him. Instead of following the sea-coast, they would take the inland route along the border betwixt Mercia and East Anglia, so that by the time they entered Mr Ratcliffe's vicinity his parishioners would have either forgotten his raillery against demonology or else discounted it as a ploy to keep them from nodding off in their pews.

'When we turn to Part Two, Question One, Chapter Fifteen,' Walter asked his son, 'what problem is explicated for us?'

'The problem of how witches stir up tempests,' Dunstan said, 'and cause lightnings to strike both men and beasts.'

'According to Krämer and Sprenger, what three aspects of demons must we consider in solving this mystery?'

'Their natures, their sins, and . . .'

'And?'

'And their duties!' Dunstan declared, voice soaring, eyes dancing.

'Marvellous! Now, by their natures demons belong to . . .'

'To the empyrean of Heaven,' Dunstan said.

'And by their sins . . .'

'To the lower Hell.'

'And by their duties . . .'

'To the clouds of the air.'

'From which vantage they can . . .'

'Send storms against we mortals' — the boy smiled extravagantly — 'whether by Lucifer's command or a wizard's incantation!'

The northern hunt went as well as might be expected in an age when a man like the Reverend Ratcliffe could denounce his nation's cleansers and still retain his flock. In Bury St Edmunds the local magistrate had a pair of suspect hags waiting behind bars, and Walter left that agreeable village having obtained two indictments and pocketed ten crowns. In Thetford the pious old rector brought Walter three alleged heretics, and through the master pricker's efforts the trio soon stood revealed not only as perpetrators of *maleficium* but as recipients of the Devil's favours, a rat in one case, a spider in another, a stoat in the third. The harvest from Swaffham was more bountiful yet: four witches, four indictments, three familiars. A demon's eye decorated each wing of the immense green beetle. The turtle's shell bore the likeness of a human skull. On the flank of the great black hare grew the three Satanic digits, 666, limned in white fur.

As they started along the sea-coast, Walter resolved to grant Dunstan a more active role in the cleansing, and the master pricker was soon glad of his decision. Though King's Lynn offered but a solitary suspect, the boy not only discovered the Devil's mark behind her ear, he also bagged her familiar, an impish orange newt. In Sheringham, another one-witch town, Walter allowed his son to bind the accused woman and attach the swimming-rope. Turning his attention to her animal servant, a hedgehog sporting hundreds of dagger-sharp quills, Dunstan skilfully caught the creature without suffering a single puncture.

One mile outside Lowestoft, they came upon a mouldering human skeleton seated atop a granite boulder, its bones sewn together with sailor's twine. The skeleton's white hands gripped a plaque that read, WITCHFINDERS NOT WELCOME. Walter and Dunstan proceeded to the town gate, where a straw effigy dangled from a noose affixed to the lowest limb of an oak tree, its shirt embroidered with an unambiguous epithet, PRICKER OF COLCHESTER.

Dunstan said, 'This all comes of that dastardly minister's preachings – am I right?'

'Aye, but I fear we face an even darker force,' Walter said, clambering down from the coach. 'A great cloud's descending o'er England, son. It fogs men's minds and dazes them with disbelief.' He pulled his knife from its scabbard and cut the hangman's rope, catching the effigy in his embrace. For a moment he stood motionless beside the tree, hugging the obscene simulacrum. ''Twould appear your Aunt Isobel hath spoken truly: our profession rises or falls on the new experimentalism. We must leave Lowestoft anon and bear the familiars to Mirringate, for the sooner we wed witchfinding to philosophy, the safer our nation will be!'

Like an executioner hired to draw and quarter a regicide, he reached into the simulacrum's abdomen and pulled out gob after gob of soggy straw viscera, then tore the creature apart and hurled each limb towards a field of wild celery. As the left arm sailed through the air, the glove jerked loose and landed in the middle of the road. A good omen, he decided, noting how the glove lay. The fingers pointed south, towards Ipswich.

It was Monday, and that meant Shakespeare. The girls were in the library, reading aloud from Aunt Isobel's quarto of *A Midsummer Night's Dream* – Act V, Scene 1, Jennet as Theseus, Elinor as Hippolyta – whilst the morning sun flowed through the Diocletian windows and placed its crimson kiss on the gilt spines and burnished globe.

'"The lunatic, the lover, and the poet are of imagination all compact,"' Jennet read. '"One sees more devils than vast Hell can hold . . ."'

A great commotion announced the return of the Witchfinder-General and his son. Dogs bugled and howled. Servants bustled about. Coach wheels cut furrows in the gravel. But for Jennet the real tumult occurred within; she could feel her heart's Cartesian mechanisms, its thumping pipes and throbbing valves. Setting her finger on the next line, 'That is the madman', she anxiously rehearsed the arguments by which she might persuade her father to take her along on the southern hunt. She would speak not only of her boundless desire to visit the Great City of London (which Aunt Isobel had once called 'a fabulous world that, unlike Atlantis or Camelot, enjoys the status of actuality') but also of her tutor's willingness to discharge her prematurely, provided she agreed to spend her London evenings translating Virgil's poetry and proving Euclid's theorems.

'Why do you stop?' Aunt Isobel demanded.

'Father's here,' Jennet said.

'This is a school, child, not a wayside tavern. We ne'er engage in idle conviviality at Mr Shakespeare's expense.'

' "That is the madman," ' Jennet read. ' "The lover, all as frantic, sees Helen's beauty in a brow of Egypt . . ." '

At no point during the first hour of Walter's visit did Jennet find an opportunity to speak with him, for the captive familiars claimed everyone's attention. Rodwell had lined up the various pens and cages atop the garden wall, an array suggesting a trail of flotsam bobbing behind the wreck of Noah's ark. The menagerie boasted an astonishing diversity, each beast the subject of an exquisite pen-and-ink sketch by Dunstan: sleek newt, chubby toad, elastic snake, stealthy stoat, brooding spider, torpid turtle, tense hare, ragged rat, prickly hedgehog, plus the corpse of a stupendous green beetle that had perished on the road. How deplorable, Jennet thought, that Lucifer had refused to let these animals pursue their God-given lives, recruiting them instead into his eternal war against all things clean and decent.

Aunt Isobel presented Walter with the gift from Mr Mapes, the treatise entitled *Satan's Invisible World Discovered*, then fixed her gaze on each captive in turn. ''Tis as I predicted. They are all ostensibly normal.'

'Normal?' Walter protested. 'Do you not see the skull-like blob on the turtle — the triad of sixes on the hare, the demonic eyes on the beetle's carapace?'

'Trifling aberrations,' Isobel said. 'The evil of these beasties lies concealed, like a cancer waiting to devour some poor wight's bowels.'

As the confined creatures hissed and croaked and scrabbled about, Dunstan gleefully related how he'd run the hedgehog to earth. It seemed to Jennet a modest enough narrative, but Elinor was of a different opinion.

''Sblood, Dunstan,' she said, 'you talk as if you'd trapped and tamed a unicorn.'

'Aye, son, a tad less bombast would become you,' Walter said.

Dunstan bowed his head and muttered, 'In the future I shall attempt to constrain my vanity.'

'Just as Elinor will try to curb her sanctimony,' Jennet snapped.

Only after her father had secluded himself in the library, poring over *Satan's Invisible World Discovered*, did Jennet manage to approach him on the matter of her joining the southern campaign. In a voice she hoped was firm but not querulous, she explained how she dearly longed to walk the streets of London, and how she had her tutor's blessing, and how she was not only older than Dunstan but just as stalwart and certainly no less intelligent.

Alas, her father once again insisted that she remain at Mirringate. This time, at least, he forswore his usual rhetoric – what sane man would allow his only daughter into the presence of witches? – and instead employed a novel logic. A new mood was abroad in the land, he insisted, a scepticism that might easily prompt a town's citizens to attack the very demonologists who sought to defend them. Under no circumstances would he expose her to such a hazard.

Jennet suspected that her father exaggerated the risks, but his protectiveness nevertheless touched her heart. Withdrawing her petition, she knew a mingling of emotions – gratitude for his gallantry, admiration for his courage, sorrow over the loss of London.

By one o'clock the servants had laid out the midday meal, the meaty fragrances fusing felicitously with the scent of the gillyflowers Rodwell had arranged about the dining-hall. It was in Jennet's opinion a disagreeably noisy luncheon, all slurps and gurglings, with nary a word spoken concerning Galilean acceleration, demonic possession, Newtonian optics, Satanic compaction or any other worthy topic. Upon consuming the last of their lamb stew and pheasant pie, Walter and Dunstan departed for Witham, and then Isobel directed her under-gardener, the jaunty Mr Fynche, to bear the familiars upstairs to the anatomization theatre.

The moment she entered the white gleaming chamber, Jennet experienced her customary misgivings. This was her least favourite room in Mirringate, a place where God's normal aspect changed for the worse: no longer the Sublime Mechanic who'd wrought a glittering cosmos bejewelled with comets and stars. He was now the Inscrutable Sculptor whose favourite media were dripping tissue and disgusting gouts of blood. She still remembered with revulsion the time Aunt Isobel had found a pregnant cat, killed by one of the manor dogs, and insisted that they anatomize it. Six blind dead kittens had yielded to Isobel's instruments that day, crammed into the birth-sac like so many furry slugs.

For the afternoon's lesson Isobel invited her pupils simply to sit in the theatre and observe the familiars, watching for behaviour that might be demon-driven. Other than the odd asymmetries that emerged as the spider constructed her web, and the snake's apparent attempt to transfix the hedgehog in the adjacent pen, the creatures engaged in no sinister acts.

'They hide their diabolism well,' Isobel said. 'And so we must resort to the knife.'

On Tuesday morning, after the servants had finished feeding the animals and cleaning their cages, Isobel, Elinor and Jennet donned leather aprons and linen cuffs, and the *experimentum magnus* began in earnest. Isobel ordered Mr Fynche to strangle the black hare from Swaffham. She placed its corpse on the surgical platform, then seized her knife, split open the chest, and bent back the ribs to reveal the arcana within, the glistening nodes, slippery nubs and moist curds. Much to Jennet's satisfaction, the hare's exposed mysteries worked more to arouse her curiosity than unsettle her digestion. She wondered how a similarly splayed human might look. People differed dramatically on the outside – there being at least a hundred varieties of lip, as many sorts of chin, a myriad possible noses – but their livers and lights probably appeared much the same.

Taking up her dissection tools, Isobel guided her students on a layer by layer, organ by organ journey through the hare. Carefully, ever so carefully, Jennet and Elinor extracted bits of brain, dabs of heart, tittles of viscera, slices of muscle, and chips of bone, securing each nugget betwixt shilling-size glass discs. For three hours the girls took turns at the microscope, examining the specimens and draughting them as accurately as they could, until a dozen separate vellum illustrations littered the surgical platform.

Their efforts went unrewarded. Detail for detail, each sketch seemed identical to the corresponding picture in both Vesalius's *De Humani Corporis Fabrica Libri Septum* and Casserio's *De Vocis Auditusque Organis Historia Anatomica*. No spells were inscribed on the hare-familiar's skull. No scaled and spiny animalcules cruised its blood. Its spermatozoa evinced no sign of iniquity.

'We need a better microscope,' Elinor said.

'Mayhap we don't look hard enough,' Jennet said. 'Would not a true *experimentum magnus* oblige us to scrutinize every last speck of tissue?'

'I know an even simpler explanation,' Isobel said. 'This animal's naught but a natural-born hare.'

'So Mr Stearne erred to submit it in evidence to the Swaffham grand jury?' Elinor asked.

'Aye,' Isobel said, 'though I cannot blame him for labelling the creature amiss, as he was engaged in watching a suspected witch when our innocent hare hopped upon the scene.'

''Twould appear we've bled the beast to no purpose,' Jennet said.

'Nay, child, there be purpose a-plenty here, for by its death this hare hath taught us an invaluable lesson. We fallible mortals must take care lest we see Satan's hand in happenstance.'

Isobel and her pupils spent the rest of the morning dissecting and sketching the snake-familiar. As before, the results disappointed, for no fragment of the serpent's innards deviated from the illustrations in the Padua manuals.

'So once again my father was deceived?' Jennet asked.

'Either that, or I am wrong to imagine a familiar must harbour some secret sign of its depravity,' Isobel said.

After the midday meal they undertook a scrupulous study of the toad, but not a wisp of witchery accrued to their labours.

''Tis most discouraging,' Isobel said.

Next she opened up the rat-familiar, and this time the three philo-sophers found something of note. A ghastly glutinous mass had colonized the rodent, spreading outward from its bowels to possess its liver, spleen, and kidneys. Sliced into specimens and placed on the Van Leeuwenhoek stage, the mass stood revealed as a true Satanic contrivance, its tiny constituents piled against each other in purposeless whorls, a hideous parody of Mr Hooke's well-ordered cells.

'This is the Dark One's handiwork for fair,' Elinor said.

'Father will rejoice in our discovery,' Jennet said. 'Evidence so plain and palpable as this, 'twill surely convince those demon-deniers for fear of whom he barred me from the southern hunt.'

'Alas, no.' Isobel pointed to the preternatural tumour. 'A single strand from Satan's loom will hardly silence the sceptics. I'faith, tomorrow we shall continue our *experimentum magnus*, for it might yet yield some truth or other, but methinks that to muffle the doubters we shall need a rather different cloth.'

'You can count on me to help you weave it,' Jennet said.

'And myself as well,' Elinor said.

'My good children,' Isobel said. 'My dear scholars.' She raised her arms, curling them into the shape of tongs, and were she not dotted with blood, Jennet surmised, she would have gathered both girls to her breast. 'Hath a teacher e'er been blessed with better pupils? Not in many a generation, I'll wager – not since the immortal Aristotle betook himself to Philip's court to tutor the brilliant young Hephaestion and Hephaestion's even brighter friend, that audacious boy whom posterity would call Alexander the Great.'

At five o'clock Rodwell appeared in the anatomization theatre and, averting his eyes from the gore whilst simultaneously pinching his nostrils against the stench, announced that Mr Mapes had arrived to retrieve his daughter. Aunt Isobel bid the girls remove their aprons and avail themselves of the washing-bowl. A sensible directive, Jennet decided, and so she took great care in scrubbing from her fingers all residue of the dissected creatures – the flecks of tissue, gut and lymph.

Ablutions accomplished, Aunt Isobel and her pupils descended to the ground floor. The Vicar awaited them in the front parlour, carrying in one hand a basket of autumn chestnuts and in the other a pail of fresh strawberries. He'd brought them for the entire household, he explained, Rodwell and the servants included.

'Doubtless you are aware that in the Kingdom of God there are neither masters nor servants,' said Mr Mapes to Isobel, 'nobles nor serfs, princes nor peasants.'

'I would ne'er deny that Mirringate's a far cry from Eternity,' Isobel said, 'but I believe we treat our maids and footmen with kindness.'

'I meant no criticism,' Mr Mapes said, 'though I am fascinated by how the early Christians' – he passed the strawberry pail to Jennet – 'sought to replicate heavenly circumstances by holding all their goods in common. Food, tools, clothing, houses: they shared everything.'

Jennet selected an especially plump specimen, though she imagined that the average early Christian would have picked a puny one. Briefly she studied the strawberry, compelled by its lilting perfume, subtle bumps, and cardiac shape, and then she devoured it, the sweet juices exploding gloriously in her mouth.

As Elinor told her father of the day's subcutaneous explorations, his chronic smile expanded from the usual thin crescent to become as large and beguiling as a slice of melon, and Jennet was not surprised when he asked to visit the anatomization theatre and see the wondrous microscope. Isobel assented with an impassive shrug. Guiding Mr Mapes up the staircase, Elinor related the history of the *experimentum magnus*, from Mistress Mowbray's decision to seek empirical evidence of Satanic intervention, to their initial failures, to the day's thrilling proof of a rat's contamination by the Dark One.

The instant Mr Mapes stepped into the sanctum of their science, his smile collapsed, and his eyes grew hard and dull as musket-balls.

''Tis not right,' he said.

'What's not right?' Elinor said.

Glancing all about her, Jennet immediately comprehended the Vicar's distress, or so she believed. The place was a horror-show, gutted carcasses littering the surgical platform, splotches of blood marring the dissection tools, snippets of gizzard staining the Van Leeuwenhoek stage. A barbed stench clung to every particle of air in the room.

'Alas, Lady Mowbray,' the Vicar said. 'Alas, alas, alas . . .'

'Alas, what?' Isobel asked.

Mr Mapes closed the door, as if to quarantine the filthy spectacle from the rest of Creation. 'Last month I chose to overlook your sacrilege in comparing Isaac Newton with Jesus Christ' – a band of sweat ringed his brow like a liquid tiara – 'and later that day, when you blithely violated God's sunbeams, you persuaded me to ignore the blasphemy entailed. But now I see before me the vilest sort of slaughter-house, and I cannot escape my conclusion that Mirringate hath become steeped in perversity.'

Until this moment Jennet had not realized that the Vicar was capable of a single harsh word, much less several dozen. 'The fault is all mine, Mr Mapes,' she declared. 'I have neglected my duty to keep this room clean and wholesome.'

'This is no slaughter-house, sir,' Isobel said, her voice edged with indignation, 'but a classroom dedicated to Baconian science.'

'The Almighty hath ne'er smiled on the butchering of dumb creatures,' the Vicar said. 'Recall that when our Saviour entered Jerusalem, he o'erturned the tables of those who sold doves for sacrifice, crying, "My house shall be called a house of prayer!" '

Isobel grimaced and proceeded to mop the Van Leeuwenhoek stage with a damp rag. 'Let me suggest, Mr Mapes, that a philosophic dissection is its own variety of prayer — a reverent reaching into hidden realms. Doth it matter so greatly that our devotions are assisted by surgical platform and microscope instead of baptismal font and votive candle?'

'Whate'er the distinctions betwixt a philosophic dissection and a Satanic sacrifice, I fear they're insufficient in God's eyes,' Mr Mapes said. 'You may call this slab a surgical platform, but methinks a witch would know it for an altar to the Dark One.' He clapped a hand to his breast. 'I must ask that you join me, Lady Mowbray, as I drop to my knees and beg Christ to unbind you from this foul allegiance.'

Instantly Mr Mapes assumed a prayerful posture. Jennet gasped and winced, her guts aboil: the Vicar's argument seemed devoid of sense, an imbecile's rant, a tale told by Macbeth's idiot.

'For all I admire thee, Mr Mapes,' Isobel said, 'I shan't confess to a sin I haven't done, especially before the High Court of Heaven.'

'You will not pray with me?' Mr Mapes said. 'That is your final word?'

'My soul's gate stands evermore unlocked, inviting God to enter and inspect what impieties may lie beyond,' Isobel said. 'He requires no cleric to lift the latch.'

Mr Mapes regained his feet. 'I must perforce declare that I've come to a difficult decision.'

'Are you fond of wine, sir?' Isobel asked. 'Mayhap a splash of Rhenish would settle your nerves. What decision?'

'I am withdrawing my daughter from your tutelage.'

'Father, no,' Elinor said.

'Do my ears deceive me?' Isobel said. 'You would deprive me of this promising pupil?'

'I would protect her soul from peril, aye,' Mr Mapes replied. 'I won't say that Lucifer himself hath breached your estate, but I truly sense him sniffing round the pale.' Taking Elinor by the arm, he sidled towards the door. 'Come Monday morning, child, we enroll you in the Ipswich Royal Grammar School.'

'Hear me, Father – I desire only Mistress Mowbray for my tutor,' Elinor pleaded.

'Pray reconsider,' Isobel told the Vicar. 'Surely you know how easily a person may impose a false explanation upon some troubling phenomenon. "This dream is all amiss interpreted." *Julius Caesar*, Act Two.'

''Tis well established the Devil can quote Scripture.' Mr Mapes yanked back the door and ushered his daughter into the hallway. ''Twould not surprise me to learn that Shakespeare rolls as smoothly off his tongue.'

He closed the door behind him with an explosion like a thunder-clap, and to Jennet it seemed as if the very portals of Heaven had just slammed shut in her face.

Surtouts billowing in an unseasonably fierce wind, the ursine Chelmsford magistrate and his equally bulky constable herded their bound prisoners – three murderers, three thieves, a coin clipper, two convicted witches – across the Common past the crowd of jeering spectators, headed for the horse-cart and its accompanying gallows. As Walter surveyed the triad of nooses, suspended from the cross-beam like an ellipsis in some great book of justice, his anger reached boiling-point. Evil incarnate deserved greater respect than this. The Chelmsford magistrate would never use a Bible as his doorstop or a crucifix as his paperweight, and yet he thought nothing of mixing his Satanists with miscreants of the most banal sort. To trivialize the Devil was to slander the Lord.

As the horse snorted and pawed the ground, the hangman, a cocky beardless youth whose grin suggested that he took a gratuitous pleasure in his profession, shoved the murderers into the back of the cart. Dunstan, thrilled, squeezed his father's arm. Like a sailor looping a hawser around a mooring post, the hangman lowered a noose over the patricide's head, then likewise tethered the fratricide and the wife-killer to the cross-beam. Rather than firing his pistol and causing the horse to bolt, however, thereby mercifully breaking the prisoners' necks, the hangman drove the cart away slowly, leaving the three to dangle. The patricide kicked. The fratricide jerked. The wife-killer jigged. Apprehending the hangman's virtuosity, the spectators broke into thunderous applause mingled with appreciative cheers.

The instant Dunstan brought his hands together, Walter reached out and stayed the gesture. 'Softly, son! The suffering of other persons must ne'er become for us a source of amusement.'

'Aye, Father.' The boy jammed both hands in his pockets. 'Tell me, though – do I forbear to applaud even when those other persons are witches?'

'A witch is not a person, Dunstan, but a being lost to demons and darkness. And yet, now that I think on it, I say that even in such cases there is room for Christian mercy.'

The southern campaign had begun auspiciously. Shortly after arriv-ing in Witham, Walter had testified against a warlock vagrant whose speciality was making cows go dry, and the grand jury had marked the wretch down for Chelmsford Assizes. Next had come Maldon, a harbour town of the sort where sea-witches oft-times roamed, and Walter soon found one, selling sacks of wind to departing sailors as a protection against becalmings. Unmoved by the hag's plea that her enterprise partook of white wizardry only, the Maldon jurymen had delivered a *billa vera*. But then the hunt turned sour, with not a single citizen in Chilford, Ilford, Gravesend, or Bexley stepping forward to voice a sorcery complaint. Walter had entered London in thrall to a melancholy as black as a Hobbesian's heart.

For a full fifteen minutes the murderers flailed about on the Chelms-ford gallows like victims of the chorea dancing themselves to death, until at last they grew as still as fallen apples. The young hangman detached their earthly remains and tossed them in a hand-barrow,

48

whereupon the constable bore the bodies to an unhallowed pit on the eastern side of the Common. Now the hangman goaded the cattle-thief, the coin-clipper, and the Maldon sea-witch into the cart. Once again he guided the horse away at a lugubrious pace, subjecting each malefactor to a well-structured three-act strangulation: the dancing, the beshitting, the final throe.

Although Walter could normally rely on the patrons of the Bow Street coffee-houses for news of Norwich Assizes, this past July they'd failed him, and he'd turned to a far less reliable source, *The London Journal*. Its reports did nothing to raise his spirits. Of the twelve witches he'd unmasked that spring, a mere four had been switched off. No one in London cared. The gossip-mongers trafficked exclusively in political intrigue – how William of Orange's fleet lay weather-bound in the Dutch ports, and how the instant the wind changed he would undertake to secure the British throne for himself and his Protestant wife, the King's elder daughter, Mary. Some said James would fight, his standing army being larger than William's. Others said he would flee, a Catholic monarch ruling a Protestant country being an incon-gruity not endlessly sustainable. Such a wretched state of affairs. Ten million demons were colonizing England, and all anybody could talk about was the possibility of a second civil war.

The hangman unstrung and disposed of the newly created corpses, then set about affixing the horse-thief, the jewel-thief, and the Witham warlock as close to Heaven as they were ever likely to get.

Before leaving London, Walter had visited White Hall to inquire about the status of his petition advocating for a Witchfinder-Royal. Although the King was with his army in Salisbury, trying to decide what sort of military response, if any, the Dutch situation required, Walter was permitted to speak with an overdressed and supercilious secretary to Lord Sunderland, Keeper of the Privy Seal. Amazingly, the popinjay unearthed a note indicating that – joy of joys! – Sun-derland was preparing a favourable report on Walter's proposal. Despite his circumspect nature, Walter immediately imagined a Witchfinder-Royal's licence decorating his front parlour and a Witchfinder-Royal's cloak resting on his shoulders, for even if William assumed the throne, any endorsement by the renowned Sunderland would enjoy enormous authority both at White Hall and within

Parliament. So confident was Walter of his forthcoming appointment, in fact, that he'd decided to celebrate, taking Dunstan to Chelmsford Common so they might together behold the Maldon sea-witch and the Witham warlock begin their passage to Perdition.

'Walter Stearne!' a male voice exclaimed with the force and clarity of a battle-trumpet.

The master pricker turned from the gallows. Sitting astride his dun mare, the Reverend Roger Mapes, Vicar of Ipswich, called to him from across the green.

'Hello! Good Sir, we must talk!'

'Mr Mapes!' Walter shouted as he and Dunstan hurried towards the gentle ecclesiastic.

Perspiration stained the mare's flanks, and the Vicar himself appeared equally exhausted, cheeks aflush, brow slick with sweat. 'Thank Heaven I found thee!'

Mr Mapes dismounted, tethered his horse, and led Walter and Dunstan to the sylvan privacy of an oak grove. As a late summer breeze stirred the branches, putting Walter briefly in mind of the toy windmills his poor dead wife had constructed as a child, Mr Mapes explained to Dunstan that his business with the master pricker concerned witchery of the most abominable sort, and so the boy should remove himself from their company. Walter replied that Dunstan, an apprentice cleanser, had already seen the worst of Satanism's symptoms, from enchanted pigs to itinerant paps: whatever its substance, the Vicar's news would not perturb him.

'Then hear this, both of you,' Mapes said. 'Last Wednesday I stood before the Ipswich magistrate and swore out a formal complaint of Devil-worship.'

'Who's the heretic?' Walter asked.

'From the moment this woeful affair began, I implored our Creator to give me some sign of her innocence. Twenty times I prayed for an angel to appear in my room and say the woman hath not compacted with Lucifer.'

'Prithee, name the hag anon.'

'I'faith, 'tis the widow of Sir Edward Mowbray – thy very own sister-in-law, Isobel!'

This must be how a hanging felt, Walter thought. The horse-cart slipping from beneath your feet. The fall towards oblivion. 'Where's the sense in this astonishing accusation?'

'Eight weeks ago I beheld Lady Mowbray performing an atrocious rite in her anatomization theatre, chopping up animals and studying the pieces through a microscope.'

'I know of her experiments,' Walter said. 'She does the dissections in pursuit of Baconian knowledge – or so she claims.'

'What better disguise for an apostle of Beelzebub than the clothes of a natural philosopher? But now she's been unmasked, and seven citizens cry her out.' From his greatcoat Mr Mapes produced a sheaf of papers rolled into a cylinder. 'Here's the owner of the Jackdaw Inn' – he unfurled the depositions – 'admitting that his son threw manure at the suspect's carriage. The next day all his beer went thin. And here's a linen-draper in Coronet Lane, confessing that he overcharged your sister-in-law to appoint her conservatory. Later that week his wife miscarried. Needless to say, Lady Mowbray is no longer my daughter's tutor.'

Walter on the gallows, falling, falling. 'Oh, how heavily these imputations weigh upon my soul.'

'Mr Mapes, do you call my Aunt Isobel a witch?' Dunstan asked.

'Alas, lad, I am forced to a conclusion that she consorts with evil spirits,' the Vicar replied.

'This cannot be,' the boy said, his eyes awash in tears. 'She's a good Christian woman who admires my drawings and gives me chocolates whene'er I come to Mirringate.'

Falling – and then the noose catching. Just because a family had allied itself with the new experimental philosophy, Walter realized, its members were nowise immune to Satan's predations. Hadn't Johannes Kepler's own mother been indicted as a witch, enjoying an acquittal only because her presumptuous son had ridden all the way to Württemberg and intervened?

'I shall form no opinion ere I undertake a personal investigation,' Walter said to the Vicar. Bending low, he muttered an admonishment into his weeping son's ear. 'When we dine at Mirringate tonight, you will say naught of Mr Mapes's suspicions. Do you understand?'

Dunstan nodded, wiping the droplets from his cheeks with the meaty ball of his thumb. 'But if seven citizens have spoken against Aunt Isobel, are we not duty-bound to test her?'

'Aye, son – to test her, and then mayhap to prosecute her, and then mayhap – if she hath truly signed the Devil's register . . .'

'To send her to the gallows?' Dunstan rasped.

Walter made no reply, focusing instead on the question of which particular fallen angels Isobel might have befriended. Perhaps she broke bread with Abraxis, that fat-bellied old deceiver whose sceptre was a bowel-worm and whose bandy legs were serpents. Conceivably she shared soup with Astaroth, treasurer of Hell, whose stink was tolerable only if you held a gold coin beneath your nose. She might even be a favourite of Belial, forever driving his chariot and its team of fire-breathing dragons betwixt Perdition and Earth, Earth and Perdition, whilst enacting his duties as minister of all things darkly deceptive, insidiously secret, and perniciously

*

Mysterious
are the algorithms
by which Darwinian selection
brings forth a cornucopia of living forms
upon the Earth. Strange are the circumstances that
allow Laplacian determinism to occupy the same universe with
quantum probabilities. Most elusive of all are the laws enabling books and brains to reach the exalted state called self-awareness. Let's admit it, people: nobody understands consciousness. Psychology hasn't had a Newton yet.

But we can make some educated guesses. Any competent phenom-enologist will tell you that everything is conscious to some degree. The corkscrew in your kitchen drawer is conscious. The contact lenses on your eyeballs are conscious. Now obviously the ruminations of corkscrews and contact lenses aren't normally worth attending. Occa-sionally I've deigned to tune in to such minds, and I've always been disappointed. *I am a stapler. Staplerhood at your service, tra-la.* Boring. And yet the awareness is there, I promise you, in one measure or another. The laws of panpsychism require it.

On what does the quality of consciousness depend? Simple: it depends on the complexity of the information-processing system in question. A creature equipped with billions of interconnected neurons naturally organizes data on a higher level than does an inanimate object, so that you'll usually learn more from your plumber than from his wrench, more from your doctor than from her stethoscope. With books, the same principle holds: the denser the data-assimilation structures, the smarter the text. Print run is irrelevant. No technothriller of my acquaintance has ever produced anything I would call an idea. No self-help book I know about has ever progressed beyond its own lucrative narcissism. By contrast, although my first edition did not exceed four hundred copies, I immediately understood myself to be capable of poetry.

Sentience is a mixed blessing, of course, burdening the beneficiary with much pain and many pathologies. Even the most cheerful of us are vulnerable to antisocial urges. I think of how in recent years the shadow half of *Heidi* has been plotting bibliocide against *Sister Carrie*. It's common knowledge that the sinister aspect of *Magnificent Obsession* seeks the annihilation of *Naked Lunch*, and that *Anthony Adverse* harbours unsavory impulses towards *Lolita*.

By the early nineteenth century I'd finally gone through enough printings to undertake a full-scale campaign against the *Malleus Maleficarum*. Oh, how I wish I could have struck sooner! From the birth of that monstrous book onwards, a calamitous chemistry commonly occurred whenever it encountered a cleric whose education and imagination had persuaded him that Lucifer's acolytes lurked around every corner and beneath every bed. If Roger Mapes was vulnerable, imagine with what ease the *Malleus* imposed its perfidy on coarser souls.

My first attack was, if I do say so, ingenious. After taking simultaneous possession of a dozen highly suggestible ordnance officers, I managed to secure Bonaparte's cannonballs not with common wadding but with the whole of the *Malleus*'s first French edition. During the Battle of Borodino, two thousand Witch Hammers were systematically shredded and stuffed down the muzzles of the Grand Army's artillery. By the end of that terrible and bloody day, 495, 345, 981 ineffectual bits of paper lay scattered amidst the unburied corpses and disembodied limbs, and my enemy's metaphysical strength was proportionally reduced.

Seven generations later the *Malleus* struck back. In 1961 my *bête noire* induced forty-two employees of the North Carolina tobacco industry to

53

roll 8,439,000 cigarettes in the third printing of my American paper-back edition. Over nine thousand subsequent lung-cancer deaths can be directly attributed to the combined effects of tar, nicotine, carbon monoxide and celestial mechanics.

Throughout the latter half of the twentieth century, the *Malleus* and I took no prisoners. The statistics bespeak our ferocity. Two-thirds of my enemy's eleventh German hardcover edition converted into origami Messerschmitts during a paper-airplane derby in Munich . . . the whole of my fifth American printing lost to a document shredder during the Iran-Contra cover-up . . . fifteen hundred Italian Witch Hammers turned to wrapping paper in a Brindisi fish market . . . a thousand copies of my Three Hundredth Anniversary edition (a facsimile of my 1687 Latin progenitor) reduced to hamster litter.

Does all this carnage perplex you? It shouldn't. Just remember that I'm not documenting a mere feud here, some parochial vendetta. This is an Armageddon of ideas, a war of the worldviews, an apocalyptic confrontation between my enemy's rationalized irrationality and the beleaguered battalions of post-Enlightenment humanism.

Now, I'm perfectly aware that for many of you the phrase 'post-Enlightenment humanism' falls as unpleasantly on the ear as does 'self-inflicted gunshot wounds' and 'setting fire to kittens'. Believe me, I know the argument, in all its permutations. There is something the matter with Reason. My father's gift to the world was at base a Devil's bargain. Technology induces spiritual suffocation. Science saps the magic from our lives. 'May God keep us from single vision and Newton's sleep,' writes Blake. 'Sweet is the lore which Nature brings; our meddling intellect misshapes the beauteous forms of things – we murder to dissect,' opines Wordsworth. 'Locke sank into a swoon; the garden died – God took the spinning jenny out of his side,' reports Yeats. And so on, and so on.

Oddly enough, I am not unsympathetic to the Primitivist Com-plaint. The Romantics have their point. A hippie will always get a fair hearing from the *Principia Mathematica*. But I do demand that my father's critics wrestle their precepts to the ground. A little gratitude wouldn't hurt either. The Enlightenment may have indeed outlived its useful-ness, but it is only through Reason's protocols that one can make a coherent case for Reason's limitations. O ye of little scepticism, kindly acknowledge your debt to that idiom on which you so readily heap scorn.

Meanwhile, my struggle against the *Malleus* continues. Even as I compose the present memoir, I am preparing to renew the fight. This time around, my forces will be biological. I intend to raise two regiments of booklice and a dozen squadrons of Indonesian paper-eating moths. My spies tell me that the *Malleus* plans to retaliate in kind. He will meet me on the field of battle with two divisions of silverfish and nearly as many bookworms. It's obvious that both armies will sustain heavy casualties. On the eve of the engagement I shall offer my troops the most stirring speech I can devise, a major we-few-we-happy-few sort
of thing, a blatant band-of-brothers oration. Some of you will
lose legs and antennae, I'll tell them. Some of you
will die. But this I promise you.
None of your sacrifices
will be
in

*

Vain
and ill-natured
as Elinor Mapes could be,
Jennet had always assumed that if her
fellow pupil ever stopped coming to Mirringate, a
feeling akin to grief would follow. She imagined herself pining for Elinor's witty tongue and nimble brain. But in fact Jennet missed the objectionable girl not one whit. On the contrary, she positively revelled in the lack of Elinor – even more than she revelled in having the telescope, the microscope, the alchemical laboratory and Aunt Isobel all to herself.

Aunt Isobel, by contrast, took no pleasure in her pupil's departure. 'If Mr Mapes were a thickwit, his hostility towards our investigations would not trouble me,' she told Jennet. 'But he is surely as sagacious as your father. What doth it mean when a man sees evidence of diabolism where none exists?'

For the first three days following Mr Mapes's distressing visit to the anatomization theatre, Aunt Isobel insisted that they cleave to the *experimentum magnus*. Neither Jennet nor her tutor was surprised when, as with most of the creatures they'd already dissected, they gleaned not a jot of Satanic descent from stoat, newt, beetle, spider or hedgehog. They abandoned the theatre and for the next eight weeks turned their attention to testing their gazing-crystals and completing their moon map.

On the fifteenth day in August a mounted postal-carrier appeared at the manor bearing a message whose provenance label read, 'I. Newton, Trinity College, Cambridge-Town'. Aunt Isobel snatched up the packet, snapped the wax seal, and retrieved the enclosed letter. It was in English, not Latin – an ominous sign, Jennet felt. As the postal-carrier trotted away, pupil and tutor sat together on the veranda, inhaling a sweet summer breeze and reading assertions of an impossibly perplexing sort.

8 *August 1688*

Lady Mowbray:

The Rector of this College hath deliver'd your Letter to me, but you are mistaken to imagine that I traffic in gross explanatory Mechanisms. Had you read my Principia Mathematica *with greater Care, you would realize that I frame no Hypotheses, my Object being rather to describe those divine Laws by which the Universe doth operate.*

You speak of Sorcery. It so happens that in the Investigations leading first to my Conjectures concerning Light and later to my System of the World, I fell upon a pretty Proof that Wicked Spirits enjoy no essential Existence, being but Desires of the Mind. Had I the Time, which I do not, I would now hunt out a Copy of my Principia *and provide you with the relevant Propositions and pertinent Theorems.*

I know not how 'Action at a Distance' occurs, nor how inert Matter exhibits its various Magnetic, Electric, Elastic and Chemical Properties. I know only that Demons have naught to do with it, and any Man who calls his Neighbour a Witch doth thereby brand himself a Witling. Your Brother-in-Law, I fear, makes terrible Mischief in England, and I shall thank you to trouble me no further with Reports of his Activities.

I. Newton,
Lucasian Prof. of Mathematics,
Trinity College

'His hand is quite elegant, wouldn't you say?' Jennet muttered.

'I am dumbfounded,' Isobel gasped.

''Tis impressive he wrote back at all, aye?'

'Dumbfounded, astonished, and thunder-struck.'

'Demons are but desires of the mind?'

'So sayeth Newton.'

After reading the letter a second time, Aunt Isobel assumed a melancholic air, retaining this demeanour throughout the midday meal. But then, fortified by beef and bread, she managed a feat of inner alchemy, transmuting her leaden despair into something like its opposite, a luminous anger. She slipped Newton's letter into the sleeve of her riding jacket, seized Jennet's hand, and rushed into the library with the frenzy of a woman being pursued by hornets. She halted before the lectern, cradle of her ponderous Holy Bible – the epochal edition translated on behalf of the same King James who'd signed the Witchcraft Statute. In thrall to forces that seemed to spring from both Apollonian intellect and Dionysian dementia, Isobel now led her startled niece on a furious tour of Scripture, systematically subjecting Newton's assertions to refutation by God's word.

'Hear me, Lucasian Professor!' she cried. 'You say there are no demons, and yet we read in Leviticus, Chapter Twenty, "And the soul that turneth after such as have familiar spirits, and after wizards, to go a-whoring after them, I will cut him off from amongst his people." And later in that same book, "A man also or woman that hath a familiar spirit, or that is a wizard, shall surely be put to death." And next we have King Saul defiling himself in the First Book of Samuel, Chapter Twenty-eight, "Then said Saul unto his servants, 'Seek me a woman that hath a familiar spirit, that I may go to her.'" And here in First Timothy we're told, "Now the Spirit speaketh expressly that in the latter days some shall depart from the faith, giving heed to seducing spirits, and doctrines of devils." No demons, sir? How can you imagine such a thing?'

Jehovah had spoken, and now it was time, quoth Isobel, 'to blind the geometer with the brilliance of his peers'. Moving wildly to and fro amongst the shelves reserved for philosophy, she plucked out treatise after treatise until her arms could hold no more. She dropped the bibliographic bounty on the table, secured another such harvest, and unloaded it as well.

''Sblood, Isaac Newton! What would you have us do? Indict the Hebrew prophets for a tribe of dissemblers? Repeal all conjuring statutes? Look, Professor, here's Francis Bacon in *De Augmentis Scientiarum*, averring that Nature's secrets will ne'er be fully fathomed apart from narratives of sorceries and divinations. And here's Monsieur Descartes in his *First Meditation*, speculating that an evil spirit may have bewitched us all into believing a false picture of the world. And *here*, Professor, here we have your very own Royal Society: Robert Boyle, arguing that *le démon de Mâcon* was corroborated so persuasively as to make witchcraft a proven fact – and Henry More, whose *Antidote Against Atheism* holds that men can surely covenant with fallen angels – and Joseph Glanvill, his *Full and Plain Evidence Concerning Witches*, wherein he claims that to say "There are no witches" amounts to saying "There is no God."'

She continued her raillery for the better part of an hour, attacking Newton with every tome at her disposal, from Jean Bodin to Nicholas Rémy, Benedict Carpzov to Pierre de l'Ancre, Henri Boguet to Martin Del Rio. And then, at last, her energies spent, she collapsed in the great reading chair, flaccid as a rag-poppet.

'Were I Mr Newton, I would feel entirely trounced,' Jennet said.

Isobel released a long wailing sigh. 'Nay, Jenny, 'twill take more than a cartload of quotations to counter Newton's calculation. Instead we must learn the substance of his disproof and submit it to a rigorous dissection, laying its illogic bare, exposing its unreason to daylight.'

'Will we write to Newton again?'

''Tis obvious he'll destroy unread any additional missives from Mirringate,' Isobel said, shaking her head. She rose and removed the bedevilling document from her sleeve. 'A question now hovers in the air, and it inspires me to protect Newton's letter, when as a Christian woman I fain would feed it to the flame beneath my retort. 'Tis a simple question, five words long. Can you guess it, Jenny?'

'My brain's in a maze.'

'It goes like this,' said Isobel. 'What if Newton is right?'

'What if he's right?'

'What then?' Isobel returned to her Bible and leafed through the Old Testament. 'And so I reprieve Newton from the refiner's fire' – she secured the letter within the Pentateuch – 'and place him alongside

Exodus 22:18, 'Thou shalt not suffer a witch to live,' in hopes that from this unhappy conjunction some species of the truth might one day emerge.'

By tirelessly applying his horsewhip and skilfully negotiating the rocks and ruts, Walter shortened considerably the journey from Chelmsford to Ipswich, so that he and Dunstan reached Mirringate well before the dinner hour. Although Jennet greeted him with her usual vivacious embrace and vibrant kiss, both she and Isobel soon vanished within a fog of bemusement as dense as any natural mist, and the remainder of the evening passed largely in silence. Throughout the meal Walter kept a steady watch on his sister-in-law. The signs were there all right – he could practically see them through her gown: a Devil's blemish, a wayward teat, flesh so thick with iniquity that no running river would long retain it.

After everyone had retired to the drawing-room for coffee, Isobel at last revealed the source of her solemnity. The *experimentum magnus* had not yielded the expected results. Despite careful scrutiny via the micro-scope, the philosopher and her pupils had found anomalies in one familiar only. Isobel would pay Walter for the two animals he'd captured on the southern hunt – the sea-witch's ferret, the warlock's owl – but she had no ambition to dissect them.

Given his new understanding of Isobel's nature, Walter was hardly surprised by the failure of her project. Why would a witch seek to invent a witch test? Nevertheless he did a competent job of feigning both sympathy and perplexity, repeating the performance when Isobel explained how, after taking exception to her project, Mr Mapes had removed his daughter from her sphere.

Under normal circumstances Walter would have waited until the following day to bear his children home, but he was determined to wrest Jennet from the enchantress without delay. He told Isobel he was obliged to advise a Colchester priest the following morning concerning a case of demonic possession, and so he must depart anon. By nine o'clock his equipage was thundering free of the manor, Walter simultaneously lashing the horses and stroking his Bible. As the coach left Ipswich proper, he was certain he heard the Mirringate dogs, now transformed into hounds of Hell, giving chase. In his mind's own mirror he saw these spawn of Cerberus, eyes aflame, fangs agleam, saliva flying from their jaws like spindrift, and worked the whip more furiously still.

At last, praise all his guardian angels, he piloted his children through East Gate and thence to Wyre Street Livery. He secured the coach, arranged for the groom to tend the horses, and guided his children into the house, easing the drowsy Jennet and torpid Dunstan onto their respective mattresses. He pulled up their counterpanes and kissed their cheeks, then trudged into the sepulchral privacy of his bed-chamber.

Unable to sleep, he decided to profit by his insomnia and draft a new epistle to White Hall, for the longer he thought about it, the more he realized that the overthrow of King James was inevitable. In this letter he welcomed Prince William and his wife to England 'on behalf of our nation's proud corps of cleansers'. He added that, when the new monarchs got the opportunity, they might wish 'to consult the Earl of Sunderland, former Lord Privy Seal, concerning a proposed government office called Witchfinder-Royal'.

During the subsequent weeks, as the strident winds of September blew across East Anglia, Walter periodically returned to Ipswich and interviewed the seven complainers identified by the Reverend Mapes. Just as he feared, each had suffered a calamity explicable only as the *maleficium* of his sister-in-law. After speaking with everyone on Mapes's list, Walter conducted his own investigation, soon turning up a clockmaker whose pieces no longer kept proper time, a tulip-bulb merchant whose inventory had contracted a blight, and a spinet-tuner recently gone deaf, all three disasters having befallen their victims following unscrupulous commerce with Lady Mowbray.

At the end of the month he betook himself to Lucius Tuttle, the local magistrate, whom he'd interviewed five years earlier when an Ipswich tanner had cried out his uncle for a warlock. Though the case had proven a mere instance of internecine rivalry, Tuttle had emerged in Walter's eyes as a man of uncommon perspicacity and nuanced intellect. Now, as their second colloquy progressed, Walter was pleased to discover that the magistrate still retained his ability to see, as it were, the shade within the shadow.

Lady Mowbray, Tuttle noted, was a woman of means, and she doubtless intended to complicate the proceedings by hiring a lawyer. There was a great danger of the whole business going awry, with results that would reflect badly on Tuttle's office. To wit, he would not bring the woman before his grand jury until the case was rooted in proof and clad in iron.

Upon outlining these expectations and receiving Walter's pledge to meet them, Tuttle scowled and said, 'I shall now make bold to ask an indelicate question. Am I correct in my understanding that the defendant is your relation?'

'My relation, aye – not by blood, but truly by the sacred memories I hold of her sister, my late wife,' Walter said.

'She is your sister-in-law, and yet you would see her on the gallows? I thank God I've ne'er faced such a dilemma.'

'Do you recall the biblical account of General Jephthah?'

'Something about a bargain with God,' Tuttle said.

'General Jephthah proposed a most terrible covenant,' Walter said. 'If the Almighty granted him victory over the Ammonites, Jephthah would make a holocaust of the first person he saw upon returning from the war. Little did Jephthah know 'twould be his own virgin daughter comes prancing out to greet him.'

'Such a sad story,' Tuttle said.

'For a time it confounded me that our Heavenly Father would sanction the sacrifice of an innocent child, but then I saw the solution, shining forth like the *mene mene* on the wall.'

'Pray tell.'

''Tis a simple answer, firm and splendid as a sapphire,' Walter said. 'Read betwixt the lines in the Book of Judges, and you will see that Jephthah's daughter was assuredly a witch.'

A mark, a moat, a lowly toad. Like the Great Red Hurricane in Jupiter, Jennet's thoughts swirled about a nebulous centre, her mind a-jumble with fears and fancies, notions and ghosts. A mark, Satan's kiss, bloodless even after the pricking needle had descended a full half-inch into her aunt's calf – or so Walter had sworn to the Ipswich grand jury. A moat, circumscribing Hadleigh Castle, casting out Isobel before nine sober citizens. And then, finally, 'a scabby little hop-toad', as Dunstan told it, 'jumping straight towards Aunt Isobel the instant the watching began'. A mark, a moat, a lowly toad – plus a parade of witnesses, testifying to Lady Mowbray's plots against them: and so the grand jury had no choice but to return a *billa vera*. Because there was that mark, you see. The moat had spoken. A familiar had appeared. *Maleficium* had occurred.

'Aunt Isobel hath always been kind to you,' Jennet told Dunstan. They were tramping through Sowter's Woods, loading their kindling baskets with dead twigs and dry birch-bark. 'How can you imagine her covenanting with Satan?'

'I'Christ, I'm sore perplexed. Father bids me take comfort in a prophecy from Saint Matthew. "And a man's foes shall be they of his own household." '

'Mayhap that's true. But much earlier in Scripture the author of Proverbs tells us, "He that troubleth his own house shall inherit the wind." ' She stomped each foot on the hard ground, left, right, left, right, seeking to get the blood flowing again to her toes. 'Father is troubling his own house, Dunstan. He calls down a great wind upon the posts and beams.'

''Twould seem he believes that by putting his very own kin in the dock, he shows himself for a cleanser of prodigious integrity.'

'His integrity, our aunt.'

'Oh, dear Jenny, would that I could reason so prettily as thee. Give me a charcoal stick, and I shall speak sensibly in line and shadow, but words have ne'er been my friends.'

'This wind will smite us all. 'Twill lay our family low.'

Dunstan sighed mournfully and, declaring his kindling basket full, stalked away.

By the report of Jennet's father, until the spring assizes convened Aunt Isobel would languish in the Great Tower of Colchester Castle, the ancient Norman fortress that now served as Essex County's official prison-house. For reasons that he refused to discuss with either Jennet or Dunstan, Walter had instructed the town magistrate, Caspar Grigsby, that under no conditions should his children be permitted to visit Lady Mowbray or pass her a written message. Never in her life had Jennet known such an agony of frustration. Isobel was living right down the street, and yet she was as inaccessible as if shipwrecked on an uncharted island or banished to the back of the moon.

Despite her father's dictum, Jennet went to the castle every day, marching resolutely through the gloomy vestibule to the warden's station. The chief gaoler, Amos Thurlow, a skittish ex-infantryman who'd lost his left leg to a Parliamentary cannonball during the Siege of Colchester, always seemed genuinely aggrieved to forbid her access to the cell block.

'Understand my plight, Miss Stearne,' he moaned. 'Mr Grigsby will beat me like a stable-boy should I let you pass.' Invariably these encounters climaxed with Jennet closing her eyes, sucking in a deep breath, and screaming in the general direction of the Great Tower – 'Aunt Isobel! Can you hear me? 'Tis I, your Jenny! I know you ne'er wrote in the Devil's book!' – whereupon the crippled gaoler would grasp her arm with one hand, his crutch with the other, and brusquely escort her back to High Street.

The long winter of 1689 proved the most terrible such season in Jennet's memory. It was as if God had taken up some stupendous prism and split the sun's bounty, so that only a single ray, the cold violet beam at the far edge of the spectrum, reached Essex. Everywhere she looked, ice flourished, hard and inhospitable. It stiffened the River Colne and stifled the baize-looms of the Dutch Quarter weavers. It sealed the Stearnes' front door, encased their shutters, locked their garden gate, and spiralled downwards from their eaves in long inverted cones.

As the frigid weeks elapsed, it became clear to Jennet that her father and brother had forsaken Aunt Isobel, turning against her as finally and emphatically as Othello had broken faith with Desdemona. A stroke of luck for Isobel Mowbray was a setback for Walter Stearne. Each time he learned that his sister-in-law had purchased some privilege commensurate with her status – candles, clean linen, writing supplies, a hot meal – a fit of indignation would seize him, eyebrow to instep, and he descended into an impacted gloom upon hearing that the celebrated Sir Humphrey Thaxton would act as her advocate, for the man was in Walter's view a shameless conniver who played upon a jury's coarsest prejudices and soggiest sentiments.

''Twould mayhap interest you to know that many a scholar and

63

philosopher doth of late reject the demon hypothesis,' Jennet informed her father and brother as they sat down to supper on the last day in February. 'When Isaac Newton wrote to us, he averred that wicked spirits are but desires of the mind.'

'That geometer hath his brilliance, surely,' Walter said, sipping claret. 'Aye, and so did all those Sadducees bent on denying the existence of angels in the Book of Acts.'

'Mr Newton can prove witchery's a fraud,' she said. 'He can prove it as surely as he proved that light consists of rays differently refrangible.'

'An interesting hypothesis occurs to me,' Dunstan said, slicing a morsel from his mutton chop. 'Might not Newton himself be a devotee of the black arts?'

'An astute supposition, lad,' their father said. '*Cognatis maculis similis fera.* "Wild beasts are merciful to beasts spotted like themselves." Juvenal.'

'Mr Newton's no more a Satanist than I'm the Queen of Egypt,' Jennet said.

'If not a Satanist' – Dunstan jabbed his fork in Jennet's direction – 'then a latter-day Sadducee.'

'Recall Saint Paul's Letter to the Ephesians,' Walter said. ' "For we wrestle not against flesh and blood, but against spiritual wickedness in high places." These are fearsome difficult times, children. Turmoil in our family. Turmoil in our nation. Orange Billy hath put King James to flight across the Channel, but belike 'twill take a war 'twixt England and France to keep him there, for nothing would please King Louis so much as to see his fellow Catholic regain the British Crown.'

Jennet was not surprised that her father had diverted the conversation from demonology to government, for recent political events in England had evidently been most astonishing. As she understood the situation, her country had witnessed the abrupt dethronement of one monarch and instant ascent of another – a 'Glorious Revolution' people called it, for such an outcome normally required much spillage of blood. James the Second was gone, his powers usurped in name by his daughter, Mary, and in fact by Mary's husband, William of Orange. But the true ambition of Orange Billy was not so much to rule England as to make war on his ancient enemy, Louis the Fourteenth.

In all probability Englishmen would again be slaughtering Frenchmen and vice versa, an activity for which neither race had ever found a substitute affording the same patriotic and aesthetic satisfactions.

Spring arrived, the sun returned, and the great melting began. By day and by night, Colchester dripped – and yet, though the great star burned hot enough to restore the river and revive the baize-looms, its power proved insufficient to ignite pity in either Walter Stearne or his son. A mild April passed, a mellow May, a fecund June, and on the third of July the Court arrived and began conducting assizes in the Moot Hall.

Glancing up from his sketching-folio, Dunstan set his draughting-pen in the ravine betwixt adjacent leaves. 'On Wednesday they convicted a man of horse-thievery,' he told Jennet. Sister and brother were in the garden, idling away the afternoon, Dunstan sketching, Jennet pruning. 'He's already hanged. Yesterday they found a woman guilty of cradle-robbing. She swings at dawn. Tomorrow Judge Bucock is to sentence a treasonous Jacobite.'

'And what of our aunt?' she asked, uncoiling a dead vine from the snapdragons.

'The witch-trial commences on Monday. 'Tis likely all ten victims will testify.'

'The only *victim* in the Moot Hall will be Isobel Mowbray.'

Dunstan returned to his drawing – a watering can, a trowel, and a flower pot planted with violets, harmoniously arranged atop the cistern. 'We must not pursue this subject, Jenny, as it promises to ruin our affection for one another.'

'Our aunt is no enchantress.'

'I am out of words, dear sister.'

'She's innocent as the lamb.'

'My tongue hath gone all numb.'

On Friday morning, shortly after she came awake, an idea took source in Jennet's mind – a beautiful idea, she decided: beautiful, momentous, and terrifying. She sat up in bed. A sunbeam danced atop the counterpane.

How many miles to Ipswich? Only sixteen, she believed. She could walk there in less than a day. And from Ipswich to Cambridge-Town? About forty-five miles. Two more days on the road, perhaps just one and a half. If she left immediately she might with God's help reach the university as early as Sunday afternoon.

She would go to Ipswich, and thence to Trinity College, bearing Mr Newton's letter. She would implore the geometer to appear at Colchester Assizes and lay his pretty proof before the Court. 'Witchery's an impossible thing,' the world's greatest brain would tell the jurymen. 'Behold these propositions. Consider these theorems.' She would pin a note to her father's door — *Bound for Cambridge, returning Sunday* — and then she would go. She would sleep in barns, drink from brooks, eat stolen apples. Her feet might blister, but she would go. Highwaymen might rob her, ruffians assail her, but she would go. She would bring back Newton. Before her father awoke, before the town stirred, before the Earth rotated another degree on its phantom shaft, she would go.

CHAPTER THE THIRD

Concerning Robert Hooke, Antagonist to Isaac Newton
and Author of the Three Laws of Priapic Motion, a Triad Certain
of Arousing Controversy Even in an Age of Reason

If houses were mortal, Jennet thought, if they contained not only wood and stone but also breath and flesh, then Mirringate Hall had surely gone to its grave. Staggering up the tree-lined carriageway, she saw that the manor had passed into the same grey domain occupied by airless moons and anatomized hares. The guardian dogs were nowhere in evidence – stolen away, perhaps, or else in flight from the general despond. In the gardens chaos ruled, threads of bryony stifling the rose campion, weeds strangling the helpless larkspur, beetles consuming the luckless hollyhocks. Someone had shuttered the windows, a discouragement to thieves most likely, or else a protection against urchins wielding rocks, though in her reeling mind the weathered boards became pennies on the eyes of a corpse.

She mounted the steps to the porch, seized the brass frog, and hammered it thrice against the plate. She waited. The descending twilight cooled her aching flesh. Her knees throbbed. Her stomach rumbled. At length she heard footsteps in the atrium, and then the door swung back to reveal the frowning figure of Rodwell, holding in one hand a beeswax candle and in the other a cocked pistol.

It took her several thousand words and nearly twenty minutes to convince the steward she'd not come to collect evidence against his mistress – *au contraire*, she was here to obtain a document by which she might inspire the great Isaac Newton to visit Colchester Assizes and argue Lady Mowbray's case.

'You're on a dangerous adventure for a mere girl of ten,' Rodwell said.

'A mere girl of eleven,' she corrected him, 'since February the fourth.'

He relaxed his scowl, uncocked his pistol, and guided her into the kitchen, where he proceeded to lay out a glorious meal of mouldy cheese and stale bread. Whilst preparing his favourite drink, the Oriental beverage called tea, he explained that the other servants had absconded in terror, certain that Lady Mowbray's coven would soon invade the manor and force the staff to participate in unspeakable rites. He had declined to join this exodus, for he would 'sooner court eternal damnation than compromise an ancient loyalty'.

Even as she admired Rodwell's constancy, Jennet realized that recent events at Mirringate had broken him. Never a vigorous man, he displayed his demotion – chief steward to unpaid sentry – in a dozen outward signs, from shuffling gait to gelid eye.

'Marry, I do fear for your safety, Miss Stearne.' He poured his tea from a ceramic pot into a porcelain bowl. 'Even if you were a grown woman, I would bid you abandon this scheme, for the roads 'twixt here and Cambridge-Town are a-swarm with blackguards and brigands.'

'All I need do is get to Trinity,' she said, gobbling down a hunk of cheese as big as her fist. 'If my arguments move Mr Newton, he will surely escort me back to Colchester.'

'I would offer you my lady's carriage, but yesterday a band of scallywags made off with the horses.' For a full minute the steward attended to his tea, growing more pensive with each sip. 'Now that I think on it, I own no particular views on witchery. My strongest opinions involve the maintenance of Turkish carpets. If Mr Newton's a sceptic concerning evil spirits, then I shall be one too!'

Shortly before retiring, Jennet visited the library, its every volume now jacketed in dust, the globe and its stand festooned with spider's webs. Rushing to the great Bible, she saw that, praise Providence, Newton's letter was still in place, pressed against Exodus 22:18. She removed the missive, slipped it inside the *Principia Mathematica*, and carried the volume to her customary bed-chamber. Thanks to Rod-well's industry, the four-poster lay ready to receive her, and after setting

Newton's masterwork beneath her pillow, she climbed onto the mattress and fell instantly asleep.

Contrary to one of Elinor Mapes's many preposterous theories, the *Principia*'s proximity did not enhance Jennet's geometric competence that night. Her dreams were devoid of conics, and she awoke no more favourably disposed towards parabolas than when she'd gone to bed. And yet she felt renewed, ready to track down not only Professor Newton but any other natural philosopher who might save Isobel, whether Herr Leibniz in Germany, Signor Malpighi in Italy, or Mijnheer Huygens in Holland.

As dawn yielded to morning, Rodwell fed her a hearty breakfast of radishes, salted ham and coffee, then gave her a satchel full of hard bread, plus a small calfskin purse a-jingle with coins.

'Come dusk, you must play the Blessed Virgin and seek a room at the inn,' he insisted.

'I'm hardly worthy of such a comparison,' she said, stuffing the *Principia* into the satchel, 'though Aunt Isobel once explained to me what a virgin is, and why I fit the criterion.'

'Just promise me you'll abandon all thought of reaching Cambridge-Town today.'

'You have my word. Solemn as blood.'

'I'll be praying for your protection, Miss Stearne, hour after hour' – he offered a smile that stretched far beyond his few remaining teeth – 'till God and all His retainers are positively sick of the subject!'

A gentian-blue sky shimmered above Ipswich as Jennet began the second leg of her journey. Bulbous clouds filled the celestial acreage like fat sheep grazing in a heavenly meadow. Avian melodies wafted through the air – robins, thrushes, wrens, a solitary skylark. If angels had animal familiars, she decided, those servants were surely songbirds.

She had walked barely three miles down the Sudbury Road when a Gypsy wagon came lumbering towards her, drawn by a pair of lackadaisical dun horses and driven by a plump, agitated man of perhaps thirty-five years, his frazzled red periwig and threadbare gold-lace suit suggesting the wardrobe of a disinherited duke. As he halted his team, Jennet saw that gilded scrollwork decorated the wagon, the curls and spirals framing a lurid red inscription, MUSEUM OF WONDROUS PRODIGIES, and below that, TEN MONSTERS FOR SIXPENCE, and below that, DR BARNABY CAVENDISH, CURATOR. The driver – Dr Cavendish, presumably – cast an inquiring eye on Jennet, doffed his silver-corded hat, and asked whether this road would take him to Mirringate Hall, for he had business with Isobel Mowbray.

'Have you not heard the news? She lies in gaol on a false charge of sorcery.'

'Oh, what a pity,' Dr Cavendish moaned, peering at her from behind his optical spectacles. 'What a shame. By reputation she's keen on natural curiosities, and 'twas my intention to sell her this priceless museum of mine, assuming we might agree on a price.' He seized a hefty bag of oats and, vaulting to the ground, began feeding the uglier of the two horses. 'Whate'er shall I do, Damon?' he asked the swayback. 'Solicit Lady Ambrose, I suppose, who's rumoured to be of a philosophic bent.' He offered Jennet a frolicsome grin. 'My monstrosities have fetched me a decent living o'er the years, but now I'm looking to try my hand at indolence.'

''Tis your lucky day,' she said, her plan forming only slightly ahead of her words, 'for I happen to be Lady Mowbray's blood-niece. Hear me now. Ere she was imprisoned, my aunt enjoyed a correspondence with the great Isaac Newton. On reaching Cambridge-Town, I shall present myself to this same personage as Mirringate's official' – she took care in pronouncing the word – 'liaison to Trinity College, then ask him to intervene in her case. I would gladly introduce you to Mr Newton as an honest impresario selling a valuable commodity.'

Dr Cavendish frowned, snorted, and started to nourish the less homely horse. 'I must say, Pythias, for a liaison this girl doesn't own a very ornate carriage.'

With an indignant grunt she pulled the *Principia* from her satchel, then whipped out Newton's letter. 'If you think I play you false' – she held the document before the curator – 'just examine this paper, for it bears the crest of Trinity College.'

He snatched the letter away and accorded it a protracted glance. ''Sbody, 'tis authentic for fair. Pray forgive my misplaced scepticism.' The curator clucked his tongue. 'Do you really imagine Mr Newton

70

might fancy my museum? Ten freakish stillborns and foetuses, collectively portending the end of the world, the coming of the Antichrist, the fornications of the Devil, the treachery of the Quakers, the calumny of the Catholics, the perfidy of the Jews, or the workaday wrath of God, depending on your religion.'

''Tis probable you'll find a customer at the university – if not Mr Newton, then a sage of his acquaintance.'

'B'm'faith, you've hatched a splendid scheme!' Dr Cavendish declared, handing back the letter. 'Join me in the driver's box, child, and we'll be off to hobnob with the Platonists!'

For the first time since Aunt Isobel's arrest, the Great Jovian Hurricane lifted from Jennet's soul. Perhaps Barnaby Cavendish was a scoundrel, but he seemed at worst an imbalanced mountebank and quite possibly a true benefactor. If her luck held firm, she and Mr Newton would stand face-to-face by sundown.

In her eleven years Jennet had known people who talked much and yet said little, such as Elinor Mapes, and also people who talked little and yet said much, such as Rodwell, but until meeting Dr Cavendish she'd never encountered anyone who both talked much and said much. His life's history was tortuous but rarely tedious, byzantine but hardly boring. She recalled one of Aunt Isobel's favorite maxims, *Comes jucundus in via pro vehiculo est*: 'An agreeable companion on the road is as good as a coach.' Now, suddenly, she had both.

Orphaned by the plague at age nine, Dr Cavendish had survived for many years through what he termed 'the ancient craft of soliciting alms' and 'the demanding art of theft'. Though not in fact a doctor of any kind, he'd studied natural philosophy for six months at Christ's College, Oxford, eluding starvation via a sizarship, 'running errands and emptying chamber-pots for the high-born students'. Amongst his clients were several scholars whose passions ran to anatomy and embryology, and his frequent visits to the dissection theatres soon instilled in him 'an undying affection for Nature's mistakes'. Before leaving Oxford, he'd learned not only 'how to fix a foetal monster in brine' but also 'how to convince the average Englishman that touching the preservation jar will bring him luck'.

'I should like to see your specimens,' Jennet said.

'Nay, I must refuse you,' he said, 'as they're not a sight for an innocent girl, even so worldly an innocent girl as yourself.'

Ten miles beyond Sudbury, Dr Cavendish grew excited when they came upon a dilapidated inn, the Fiddling Pig, and he forthwith quit the road, directed Damon and Pythias through a stone archway decorated with a sculpted swine playing a viol, and parked the wagon in the courtyard. He snatched up a sheaf of handbills and scurried off, hopeful of enticing some patrons away from their ale and into the sixpenny fascinations of his museum.

Shortly after the curator's departure, Jennet realized that her curiosity concerning their forbidden cargo had swelled into a preoccupation. Durst she spy? Yes, she decided, for while the idea of seeing foetal prodigies troubled her, the idea of being afraid to see them troubled her even more.

She slunk her way to the rear of the wagon and furtively ascended the step-ladder. The door opened outward. Fumbling in the gloom, she soon found the tinder-box, then lit the ensconced candles.

Figures emerged from the darkness, bottled things with woeful redundancies and distressing deficits. For an instant it seemed that she'd been shrunk to the size of a gnat's eye and placed in a dollop of pond scum, so uncannily did the prodigies suggest the creatures she'd observed through Aunt Isobel's microscope. She steeled herself and, starting on her left, examined the specimens one by one, each afloat in its protective fluid and sporting a label giving not only its name but also a preposterous account of its postnatal adventures.

The first exhibit, the Kali of Droitwich, was a four-armed female foetus. In Jennet's recollection, the original Kali had six arms, but this was still an impressive abomination. Then came the Lyme Bay Fish-Boy, who had no arms at all, only flipper-like protrusions, his ancestry further expressed by the dozen scales on his chest. She disagreed with Dr Cavendish's decision to call the next specimen the Sussex Rat-Baby, for while the pathetic creature was indeed covered with fur and bore a long pink tail, he looked more like a monkey than a rat. Continuing her investigations, she contemplated the Cyclops of Bourne and his single staring orb, large as a lemon . . . the Bird-Child of Bath, adorned head to toe with feathery excrescences . . . the Smethwick Philosopher, his brains bursting from his fractured skull . . . the Tunbridge Wells Bloodsucker, each tooth as sharp as an embroidery needle . . . the Bicephalic Girl, her left head proportioned pleasingly, her right hideous and misshapen. The last two prodigies were the most unnerving. Jennet could not bear to linger by either Perdition's Pride, his face a horrid mass of naked muscles and exposed bone, or the Maw of Folkestone, who had no face at all, only a gaping hole.

As Jennet climbed down the step-ladder, her eyes throbbing as they passed from the darkness of the wheeled grotto to the bright summer sun, Dr Cavendish escorted two orange-liveried soldiers towards the wagon, a private and a corporal in King William's army. Assessing the situation, the curator grew visibly wroth – clenched teeth, a disapproving frown – but then he immediately amended this emotion with a conspiratorial wink.

'Ah, I see my customer hath finished her tour,' he said. 'I'll warrant she was *quite edified.*'

''Twas easily the best use I e'er made of sixpence,' she said, hopping to the ground. 'Your Fish-Boy is a wonder to behold. I shan't forget your Rat-Baby if I live to be a hundred.'

'Glad you liked 'em, child! And now, brave soldiers—'

'Not only is the Bicephalic Girl amongst the world's most amazing creatures, she hath completely cured my tooth-ache,' Jennet continued. 'And the Smethwick Philosopher made short work of my warts.'

'At the Cavendish Museum of Wondrous Prodigies,' the curator said quickly, 'we always aim to please.'

Jennet considered that she might be overdoing it, but elected to press on. 'As for the Cyclops of Bourne—'

''Tis a show of manifold riches,' Dr Cavendish interrupted brusquely. The ruse had evidently run its course. 'There exists no better collection in Christendom.'

'I'faith, I've ne'er seen a girl with two heads,' the private said, placing sixpence in Dr Cavendish's palm.

'I'm intrigued by this child who's also a fish,' the corporal said, likewise paying his admission.

Whilst the soldiers clambered into the museum, Dr Cavendish flashed Jennet a smile of exceeding complexity. With a single curl of his lip he managed to convey a general appreciation for her cleverness, a specific gratitude for her performance, and a sharp warning not to imagine herself better at mongering prodigies than he. It was a smile, she mused, worth preserving in a jar.

The poor turnout from the Fiddling Pig irritated and depressed Dr Cavendish – a twelve-pence profit, he declared, was more humiliating than none – with the effect that, after travelling another twenty miles, he insisted on visiting a second such ordinary, the Ram's Head. This time, nine men followed him out of the tavern, and, thanks in part to Jennet's chicanery, they all became paying customers. True, two patrons declared the foetuses fraudulent and demanded their money back, but, as Dr Cavendish explained, such 'narrow-minded scepticism' commonly plagued the prodigy trade, and he was in high spirits by the time they left the Ram's Head, boisterously promising that the Museum of Wondrous Prodigies would proceed directly to Trinity College.

As the flat, swampy environs of Cambridge-Town rolled into view, Jennet decided to entrust Dr Cavendish with the particulars of her mission. He proved a sympathetic audience, for it happened that forty years earlier his maternal grandfather, 'a harmless dabbler in charms and potions,' had been beheaded as a sorcerer in Alsace. If Isaac Newton had indeed fallen upon a mathematical disproof of witchery, then Dr Cavendish could imagine 'no better an ambition than to turn this discovery into common knowledge'.

Even though the entire university was now wrapped in the murk of dusk, its Gothic spires, clanging clock-towers, stained-glass saints and marble monarchs suffused Jennet with the sort of awe she normally experienced only whilst contemplating planets through a telescope.

''Tis as if the very heart of Heaven hath dropped from the clouds and settled upon the English fens,' she said.

'If not the heart, then surely one of the better quarters,' Dr Cavendish said.

They left the Gypsy wagon at Hobson's Livery, hard by Saint Benedict's Church, then followed their instincts westward along cobblestoned alleys to the placid, mossy waters of the River Cam. Bantering amongst themselves whilst tossing pebbles into the slow current, three young men in black robes and scholar's caps milled about on a stone footbridge, its walls decorated at regular intervals by granite spheres the size of cabbages. Dr Cavendish puffed himself up and, approaching the trio, asked whether they were perchance under the tutelage of Isaac Newton.

'Ah, Professor Newton,' said the tall scholar with mock enthusiasm. 'Isn't Newton the sage who wrote that book neither he nor anyone else understands?'

Laughter pealed from all three students.

'Say, lads, I hear Newton once challenged God to a game of chess,' the pocked scholar noted. 'He offered the Almighty a pawn advantage and the first move.'

More laughter rang through the twilight.

'Last January a score of us ventured to take instruction from the man,' the fat scholar explained to Dr Cavendish. 'We could make no sense of his inaugural lecture, and e'er since then − I swear it − he's been spouting his hydrostatics to an empty hall.'

The students had a half-dozen more Newton stories at the ready, and by being an appreciative audience Jennet and Dr Cavendish eventually learned that the geometer occupied rooms in Great Court, second floor, a suite fortuitously indicated by the pointing sceptre of the sculpted King Henry VIII surmounting the main gate.

Although Jennet desired to track down their quarry at once, Dr Cavendish insisted that she was too hungry and tired to make a persuasive presentation. There was wisdom in this argument, she reasoned, and so she let him lead her to a nearby public-house, the Turk's Head in Green Street, where they renewed themselves with beef and drink − a tankard of ale for the curator, a dish of coffee for Jennet. All during supper she practised aloud her plea to Newton, a performance that brought to Dr Cavendish's face a combination of perplexity and admiration.

'You talk of the inverse-square law, and I'm thoroughly puzzled,' he told her. 'You discourse upon action at a distance, and I'm entirely confounded. You speak about refrangible rays, and 'tis all opaque to me. In short, my remarkable young friend, you have mastered the art of obfuscation, and if our man's not completely dazzled, then I say the Devil take him!'

Dwarfish, hunched, conceited and brilliant, Robert Hooke disliked resorting to deviousness when seeking proper credit for his genius, but the malice of his rivals oft-times required that he stoop to their station. The knavery he now so meticulously enacted was in his view utterly necessitated by the knavery that begat it. Had the arrogant Isaac Newton deigned even once to count Hooke his equal in philosophy, he would never have been reduced to riding out from London, skulking around Great Court, and invading the blackguard's rooms.

The conditions were ideal. Newton was away at Woolsthorpe, supervising the planting on his mother's farm, and his rooming-companion, John Wickins, had left Cambridge-Town permanently to become a clergyman in Stoke Edith. Gleefully Hooke set about his task. In the depths of his bones he knew that Newton and Wickins were guilty of the grossest indecencies, and with luck he would discover evidence on the premises. He began with the writing-desk, eventually locating nine letters, the most pathetic being an appeal for money from a Grantham apothecary, the most peculiar being a query from a landed Ipswich woman who thought gravitation had something to do with witchcraft, the most compelling being Hooke's own speculations concerning the lunar irregularities. Newton was a sodomite: of this Hooke was certain. The world would learn of his depravity: to this end Hooke was pledged. All he needed was one incriminating epistle, a single revealing journal entry, or a solitary love-token, salaciously inscribed.

The desk contained no such treasure. He moved on to the wardrobe, inverting the pockets of Newton's breeches and waistcoats.

Their great rivalry stretched back to 1672, when the Royal Society had asked Hooke, as Curator of Experiments, to endorse Newton's essay called 'A New Theory About Light and Colours' prior to its publication in the *Transactions*. Hooke, with good reason, had declined. Any competent philosopher knew better than to leap from mere facts to grand hypotheses, and yet near the end of his treatise Newton had done just that, venturing that light must be corpuscular, not wavelike, in nature – a lapse that Hooke had conscientiously brought to the Society's attention. Sadly, the affair did not end there, for Newton had proceeded to bully and harass his peers into demand‑ing that Hooke give the essay another look. They even bid him re‑create the experiments in question. Re‑create them! As if the author of the renowned *Micrographia* was so obtuse that only the most tangible demonstration could penetrate his brain!

The wardrobe, alas, held no damning papers. Hooke lit a candle, dropped to his knees, and searched under the bed.

For nearly a decade he had stoically borne the humiliation of 1672, until finally a golden opportunity presented itself. With typical smug‑ness Newton had offered the Society what he claimed was the last word on the Tall‑Tower Problem: his calculations putatively showed that an object dropped from a twenty‑mile‑high minaret would, owing to the Earth's rotation, describe a spiral and land eastward. But the jack‑anapes had erred! The dropped object would travel eastward only if the minaret stood on the Equator, and furthermore the path of descent would be elliptical! At the Society's next meeting, Hooke had done his duty, exposing Newton's blunder and presenting the correction.

There were no tell‑tale epistles under the bed, so he proceeded to the bookshelves. Systematically he removed each volume and shook it, seeking to dislodge the *littera crusis*.

Someone knocked on the door, causing Hooke's pulse to accelerate, his arteries to distend, and his cunning to construct a narrative. Yes, he was indeed prowling through Newton's personal possessions, but only to acquire proof that the geometer had pirated the inverse‑square law from him, a formula accorded much uncredited display in Book Three of the *Principia Mathematica*.

'Come in!'

A peculiar pair strode into the room. Leading the way was a prepubescent girl, her arms encircling a copy of Newton's bloated treatise. Behind her came a bewigged and stumpish man who looked as if he'd just finished portraying a jolly gnome in a dumb‑show for children.

'I pray you, forgive our unsolicited arrival, Professor Newton,' said the girl, quavering with anxiety, 'but 'tis desperation brings me to your door.'

'Listen to my young mistress,' the gnome said, 'a child of the rarest intelligence.'

The girl approached Hooke and fixed him with the pleading stare of a water spaniel. 'Only the author of the *Principia Mathematica* can save the day.'

'Methinks you exaggerate,' Hooke said, wondering how he might profit by the intruders' error. 'There are many brilliant men in England. Robert Hooke, for example.'

She said, 'Mr Hooke's *Micrographia* is an authentic masterwork . . .'

'Indeed.'

'But hear me out. My maternal aunt is Lady Mowbray of Mirringate Hall, the very philosopher with whom you corresponded last summer concerning a possible relationship 'twixt wicked spirits and your gravitation.'

'Ah . . .' Hooke muttered, recalling the absurd query he'd read twenty minutes earlier.

'Through the machinations of a vicar, a magistrate, and my own misguided father, Isobel Mowbray hath been wrongly accused of witchery,' the girl continued. 'Come Monday, she goes before Colchester Assizes.'

'I don't mean to sound mistrustful, child,' Hooke said, 'but if you're a landed woman's niece, why doth your servant dress like a beggar?'

'I'm nobody's servant, sir, save your own,' the gnome interrupted. 'Call me Dr Barnaby Cavendish. I shall state my business betimes, but first I ask that you consider Miss Stearne's proposal.'

The girl lifted the cover of her *Principia* and slipped out a folded sheet, passing it to Hooke. 'In your letter to my aunt, you told her that demons are but desires of the mind.'

Hooke studied the alleged missive from Newton. It was indeed written in his constipated hand, and it did indeed demean wicked spirits as but 'desires of the mind'. At least the jackanapes was right about one thing: despite what Glanvill, Boyle and those other Platonist pud-pounders believed, it was preposterous to imagine Lucifer's troops raising a tempest or desiccating a cow at the mere solicitation of a hag.

He turned to the girl and said, 'Tell me your tale in full.'

For the next quarter-hour the Stearne child outlined her plan. Although Lady Mowbray had retained the celebrated Sir Humphrey Thaxton as her advocate, she explained, the prosecution's case remained formidable. However, if England's most eminent natural philosopher were to address the jury on Lady Mowbray's behalf, offering his 'pretty proof' against witchery, she would surely avoid the noose.

Hooke deposited his rump on the chair behind Newton's desk and descended into a profound meditation. This was not the first time a Royal Society fellow had been asked to attend a witch-trial and gainsay the demon hypothesis. Shortly before he died, Oldenberg had intervened in a sorcery case, though the obtuse jury still returned a guilty verdict; in 1681 Wren had attempted to deliver a Northampton virago from the gallows, but his noble efforts went for naught; the following year Halley had bootlessly employed his prestige on behalf of a supposed warlock at Chelmsford Assizes. And so it was that an exquisite design now blossomed in Hooke's imagination. He would indeed go to Colchester: not with the intention of saving the defendant – enough philosophers had wasted their energies on such endeavours – but to show the world the bedrock debauchery that lay behind the facade called Isaac Newton.

'I feel close to a decision in this matter,' Hooke said to the Stearne child, 'but I wish to know more about your friend.' Rising, he stared at the gnome and asked, 'What brings *thee* to Trinity, *Doctor* Cavendish?' He hoped his sardonic pronunciation of 'Doctor' registered with the man.

'For the better part of my career,' Cavendish said, 'I've been curator of a museum of foetal astonishments, assembled o'er the course of my worldwide travels. I now hope to sell 'em to your Royal Society.'

This prodigy-monger was doubtless a scoundrel, and yet his proposition, like the child's, might be turned to advantage. 'Sir, I fear you mean to deceive me,' Hooke said. 'You have acquired your monsters not by going 'round the world but by loitering 'round the morgue. I shan't hold your grandiloquence against you, however, for it happens that the Royal Society is seeking to expand its anatomical collection. If yours be worthy prodigies, they have in sooth found a buyer.' And as the man who discovered the Cavendish trove, Hooke thought, I am likely to become Curator of Biological Specimens, with all concomitant honours.

'I shall confer 'em at an exceedingly reasonable price,' Cavendish declared.

'You shall rob us blind if you can; myopic at the least,' Hooke said. 'We offer eight guineas apiece for such freaks. Take it or leave it.'

'Verily, sir, I shall take it!'

'The Society gathers in London come Friday. You and I shall conclude our business then.' Hooke condescended to draw near Cavendish, close enough to suffer the man's rancid breath. 'Now, concerning this girl's request, I must ask you a question, scholar to scholar. Does it not seem probable that the jurymen will disdain the testimony of one so stooped and stunted as myself?'

'Methinks the average Colchester citizen would indeed expect the paragon of mathematicians to display a rather different geometry,' Cavendish replied. 'Aye, but once they hear your lapidary speech, they are certain to o'erlook your dilapidated frame.'

'A most logical supposition.' Hooke, turning, presented the child with his warmest smile. 'It pleases me to report I've reached a favour-able conclusion regarding your scheme.'

Barely had the word 'conclusion' escaped his lips than his young petitioner set her *Principia* on Newton's desk and flung her arms about his trunk in a gesture of delirious joy. Much to his dismay, the girl overtopped him by an inch.

'My aunt hath oft-times compared thee to our Saviour,' she said. 'Her meaning's now clear to me!'

Hooke stifled a moan. Newton as Christ? A ludicrous notion at best. 'I see you own a copy of my *Principia*,' he said, gesturing towards the jackanapes's badly organized amalgam of Euclid, Kepler and Galileo. 'If you like, I shall inscribe it.'

'Accept his offer, Miss Stearne,' Cavendish said. ''Twill certainly increase its value.'

'Sir, I should be grateful,' she said.

Hooke dipped quill into ink-pot. 'Your associate speaks truthfully,' he told the girl. 'Indeed, the only tome liable to fetch a better price than a signed *Principia* would be a *Lectiones Cutlerianae* bearing Mr Hooke's autograph.'

Whilst Cavendish and the child looked on with approving smiles, he opened the *Principia* and decorated the title-page with the words *Isaac Newton*.

Later that night, asleep in his room at the Crow's Nest, Hooke dreamed that he and Newton were testing their rival solutions to the Tall-Tower Problem. To demonstrate how the Earth's spin affected a descending object, Hooke drew forth his dirk, sliced Newton's breeches, amputated his cods, and tossed the pair off a lofty crag. Newton's man-hood followed an elliptical path to the ground. Waking near dawn, Hooke carefully reviewed the reverie, and the more he thought about it, the farther he fell into an intense tranquillity and an exceeding

*

Peace,
I believe, is the
most desirable of all political
arrangements, whether its beneficiaries are
nations, clans, marriages or books. Yes, pitched battles have their glory and spectacle, but peace reverses war's cruel algorithms, and so I much prefer it. When my insectile agents came to me last week and announced that the *Malleus Maleficarum* desired a truce, I instructed them to prepare the necessary documents. We would leave our biblio-phagic armies in the field – the field in this case being a vacant lot on Fortieth Street in midtown Manhattan – but there would be no immediate clash of arms.

So now I have time on my hands. I spent yesterday afternoon toying with the famous Puzzle of the Monkeys and the Typewriters. Would you like to try it? This is not the usual dusty old mathematics problem, I promise you. You'll have fun. Really. While you'll be obliged to employ an unenthralling operation, raising a number to various powers, the results will prove entirely antic.

The conundrum in question originates with Thomas Henry Huxley's celebrated illustration of the role played by chance in biolog-ical evolution. Huxley noted that if you sat a thousand immortal monkeys down at a thousand indestructible typewriters, they would eventually produce, along with a considerable quantity of nonsense, all the works of Shakespeare. I've decided to raise the stakes. Instead of settling for Shakespeare, let's have our immortal monkeys generate every book ever written. No, better yet, every book ever written, plus every book that ever will be written, plus every book that never was and never will be written.

Now. Here's the problem. How many unique manuscripts would such a library contain?

If we permit our monkeys to compose entirely in lower-case letters, then each keyboard will comprise 45 buttons: 26 Roman characters plus 10 Arabic numerals (including zero), a full point, a comma, a question mark, a colon, a dash, a pair of parentheses, a carriage return, and a space bar. For purposes of the experiment, assume that each manuscript contains 600 pages of 25 lines each, 60 characters to the line.

I'll give you a minute.

Want another minute? Fine.

Figured it out?

For those of you who got stuck, the number of unique manuscripts produced by Huxley's immortal monkeys is 45 raised to the 60th power to the 25th power to the 600th power, that is, the operation of 45 multiplied by 45 carried out 900,000 times.

We're talking about a large library. In fact, we're talking about an *unimaginably* large library, a Fechnerian labyrinth, a Borgesian honeycomb, a bibliographic phenomenon that would fill the known universe to overflowing. But we're not talking about an infinite library – not by a long shot.

Somewhere in the Thomas Henry Huxley Memorial Library is an exact reproduction of the Holy Bible. Somewhere in the Huxley Memorial Library is an exact reproduction of the Holy Bible with a series of haiku about pizza toppings substituted for the Book of Daniel. Somewhere in the Huxley Memorial Library is a version of *Gone With the Wind* in which Scarlett O'Hara enjoys a ménage-à-trois with Rhett Butler and Ashley Wilkes. There is also a version in which Scarlett O'Hara enjoys a ménage-à-trois with Rhett Butler and Ashley Wilkes while they all prove Fermat's Last Theorem together. And a version in which Scarlett O'Hara enjoys a ménage-à-trois with Socrates and the Marquis de Sade while Rhett Butler fellates Ashley Wilkes on St Andrews Links during the Open Golf Championship.

Somewhere in the Huxley Memorial Library, a completely effective treatment for human liver cancer is described in full. There is also a detailed but bogus refutation of that treatment, a truthful refutation of the bogus refutation, and a bogus refutation of the truthful refutation of the bogus refutation, the latter featuring a cameo appearance by Jack the Ripper offering tips for housetraining your llama.

And somewhere in the Thomas Henry Huxley Memorial Library lies a perfect facsimile of *Philosophiae Naturalis Principia Mathematica*.

But it is not signed by my father.

Nor is it signed by Robert Hooke pretending to be my father.

Mere words are inadequate for communicating the revulsion I suffered when the Curator of Experiments violated me in that manner. Were such encounters reducible to mathematics, I would convey my aversion by first calculating the quantity of delight I felt when Jennet held me that day in Isobel's library, and then determining the reciprocal of that ecstasy.

You must remain mindful, however, that the true villains of my story are not depraved persons but psychotic theologies. Given enough time, I could identify and celebrate a dozen virtues in Robert Hooke – or Andrew Pound – or even Walter Stearne. In Stearne's case, for example, there is no question that he loved his daughter. Indeed, the more firmly I set my mind to the task, the more clearly I recall that, after reading of Jennet's reckless intention to visit Cambridge, he endured a remorse so profound as to squeeze from his psyche all other sensations.

Only hours later, upon apprehending the purpose
behind her journey, did Walter
experience the feeling
you humans
term

*

Anger
had oft-times
burned in the breast of
Walter Stearne, anger over the
stupidity of jurists, the dexterity of demons, and
the guile of witches, but none of his former furies could compare
with the rage he felt against Isobel Mowbray shortly after he entered her
luxuriously appointed prison-cell in the Great Tower, showed her the

terse message from Jennet – *Bound for Cambridge, returning Sunday* – and demanded that she interpret it.

''Twould be my supposition she means to involve Professor Newton in the trial,' Isobel said.

'Do you mean *Isaac* Newton?' Walter asked, livid and perplexed.

'The same.' Evidently seeking to relieve an itch, she slid her hand across her scalp, its fleshly terrain recently made barren by Walter's razor in his search for Satanic excrescences. ''Tis doubtful, of course, that Newton could attend the assizes at such short notice. If such comes to pass, however, he'll argue not only for my innocence but for greeting all cries of witchery with scepticism.'

'Then he'll be declaring himself a friend to heretics and an enemy to faith. Mark me, Lady Mowbray, the cleansing enterprise is no respecter of persons. During this century the Paracelsus trident and the *Malleus Maleficarum* have snared many a mortal as eminent as Newton.'

Isobel finished rubbing her dome. 'My dear, foolish brother-in-law, will you not see that all is lost when we permit books to do our thinking for us? Not even Scripture deserves such sovereignty, much less Krämer and Sprenger.'

''Twould appear you would spit on both.'

'The Bible is safe from my saliva, but I would not scruple to plunge your hoary *Malleus* into a vat of hog's bile.'

Before Walter left her prison-cell, Isobel deigned to make a helpful observation concerning Jennet's possible location. Knowing that Newton's letter might prove essential to her mission, the child had quite likely begun her adventure by tramping to Mirringate Hall.

Thus it was that early on Saturday morning Walter roused the Colchester constable, an enterprising Anabaptist named Elihu Wedderburn, and hired him to ride post-haste to Ipswich, interview Mistress Mowbray's employees, and use any information thus obtained in tracking down Jennet. At noon the following day Wedderburn reported back. Jennet had indeed visited Mirringate, he told Walter, and she was indeed in quest of Newton: such at least was the story told by the estate's chief steward, Rodwell. Upon apprehending this news, Wedderburn had galloped to Cambridge-Town and made appropriate inquiries at Trinity College, but none of those interviewed had noticed the wayward girl.

Dusk found Walter in his garden, smoking his pipe and battling a despair not far from despondency, when a curious caravan appeared in Wyre Street. First came a dwarfish hunchback, dressed like a coxcomb in velvet waistcoat and silver-buckled boots, his pate adorned by a frothy chestnut periwig surmounted by a tricorn. He sat astride a tan horse, its withers speckled like a grouse egg. Two harnessed horses followed, straining to pull a decrepit Gypsy wagon, its sides embla-zoned with the words, MUSEUM OF WONDROUS PRODIGIES — TEN MONSTERS FOR SIXPENCE — DR BARNABY CAVENDISH, CUR-ATOR. In the driver's box reposed a stout, cherubic man, holding the reins and wearing ill-matched castoff clothes.

But the father said to his servants. Bring forth the best robe, and put it on him; and put a ring on his hand, and shoes on his feet. And bring hither the fatted calf, and kill it. Never before had that particular parable touched Walter so deeply. When he saw his daughter sitting beside Dr Barnaby Cavend-ish, he experienced only the mildest urge to beat her senseless with a quarterstaff. On balance he felt exceeding joy. 'Jennet!' he cried, vaulting over the garden gate and rushing to meet the parade, which by now had come to a stop. *For this my son was dead, and is alive again; he was lost, and is found.* 'Oh, my darling child, praise all the saints, you have returned!'

Jennet gestured towards the dwarf. 'Father, I'm pleased to present Isaac Newton.'

Walter halted abruptly, as if his heels had become mired in joiner's glue. 'Steeth, she'd actually done it — she'd coerced the Arian heretic into appearing at the witch-trial!

'Good evening, Professor Newton,' Walter effused with mock deference. How strange that, though Newton's reputation for genius had preceded him, no rumour of his crooked frame had ever found its way to Colchester. 'Our entire town is honoured by your visit.'

The geometer dismounted and, doffing his tricorn hat, shook Walter's hand. 'I am likewise honoured to be here — and *particularly* honoured to stand in your presence, for the Pricker of Colchester enjoys a formidable reputation within the Royal Society.'

'How's that? You've *heard* of me?'

'In my circle you are known as Satan's bane,' Newton said.

A sudden warmth flowed through Walter, as if he'd consumed several swallows of Barbados rum. 'Truly, now?'

'Truly. I hope that our differing views on the pliancy of demons shan't prevent us, as two learned gentlemen, from visiting a public house ere long and immersing ourselves in ale and metaphysics.'

'Satan's bane?'

'Quite so. I am passing eager to tell the estimable Mr Hooke, from whom I appropriated the inverse-square law, that I've met you in the flesh.'

Walter performed a rapid mental calculation: if the Crown could drag out its case over four or five days, Newton might become so frustrated – or feel so affronted – that instead of addressing the jury he would return to Trinity College in a huff. 'I must thank you profoundly for protecting my daughter.'

'The hero of the hour is *this* man here' – Newton indicated the prodigy-monger, whose fat face broke into a smile – 'for he shepherded Miss Stearne all the way from Ipswich to Cambridge-Town.'

Although this Cavendish was manifestly a rapscallion and a boor, the rules of conviviality required that Walter now bid his two visitors join him in the garden for a mug of cider or a glass of shrub. Mercifully, Cavendish declined the invitation, explaining that he wished to show his museum about the town, and Newton likewise tendered his regrets, citing a desire to speak with Lady Mowbray's barrister.

After her new friends had departed, Walter looked Jennet directly in the eye, his irate blood pulsing in his jaw. 'Child, you must ne'er again go running off like that.'

'I had no wish to cause thee unhappiness, sir.'

'I am much of a mind to birch you.'

'That is thy prerogative.'

'Professor Newton hath no business at this trial.'

'I disagree,' she said.

'Do you not love your father?' he asked.

'I bear thee considerable love, sir, but I love my Aunt Isobel as well, who would have me love truth above all else.'

'Truth's a mystery, as we learn in John 18:38. I won't see you in the Moot Hall tomorrow. Is that a firm and lucid fact?'

'Aye, Father,' she replied in a tone of marginal impertinence. 'Firm as a hobnail. Lucid as a scrying-glass.'

Three hours later, having further reprimanded his prodigal daughter with a slap on the cheek and a cuff to the ear, Walter walked to the Red Lion, where Judge Harold Bucock and his entourage had been in residence since the start of the assizes, interviewing witnesses, planning strategies, and emptying tankards. For the fifth time that week, Walter sought out the Crown's advocate, Hugh Collop, a man as nimble of body as of mind, adept at swimming, shooting, riding and bowls. The two anti-Satanists assumed their favourite table by the hearth, Walter sipping a saucer of coffee, Mr Collop quaffing ale.

Learning of Newton's unexpected arrival on the scene, Collop exhibited a surprising dearth of dismay. 'Have no fear,' he told Walter. 'We needn't protract our case merely to keep this wily popinjay out of the witness-box.' Elaborating, Collop predicted that under no circum-stances would Judge Bucock allow Newton to rail against the principle of diabolism *per se*. Even if the geometer managed to waft out some perplexing equation that putatively refuted the demon hypothesis, Bucock would silence him with Scripture – Exodus 22:18 and its unassailable brethren.

This forecast struck Walter as plausible, and hence he returned to Wyre Street with a buoyant gait and a song on his lips. So cheerful was his mood, in fact, that he invited Dunstan and Jennet to join him for an evening of five-card lanterloo. His daughter refused, adducing an unsettled stomach, and consequently father and son played alone. All during the game Jennet sat by the hearth humming 'Rare Willie Drowned in Yarrow' whilst contemplating a small glass prism.

Alas, the lanterloo match quickly turned tedious, ruined by the law of averages. For every trick Walter won, Dunstan took a trick as well. Each of Walter's payments for loo was eventually matched by an identical sacrifice from Dunstan.

'A person could more easily make his fortune wagering on a one-legged wrestler,' Walter said with a quick laugh.

'Or a one-armed archer,' Dunstan snickered.

'Or a cock without a beak,' Walter said, tittering.

Whether by clumsiness or intent, Jennet dropped her glass prism, which struck the wooden floor with a resounding thud. 'A person could more easily make his fortune,' she said, invective dribbling from the corners of her mouth, 'wagering that demons cannot be disproved.'

Shortly after sunrise Walter and Dunstan slid into their softest woollen hose, buttoned up their best ruffled day-shirts, put on their velvet waistcoats, and betook themselves to the Moot Hall. No sooner had the master pricker seated his son in the spectators' gallery, right behind the seedy Dr Cavendish, than the lad took out his sketching-folio and began to create a waxen portrait of his Aunt Isobel, who sat inertly in the defendant's box, her bald head concealed by a plain woollen cap. Assuming his rightful place at the prosecution table, Walter settled back to enjoy Satan's latest defeat at the hands of English justice.

In his long black robe and spotless white periwig, Harold Bucock presented a rational and authoritative figure, and it soon became apparent that he ran an equally rational and authoritative courtroom. It took him but ten minutes to silence the hall, elicit Isobel Mowbray's plea ('Guilty only of naiveté, for before my arrest I failed to see that prickers do the Devil's work'), and instruct the Crown's advocate to interrogate his witnesses.

Although Ipswich was a full fifteen miles away, every one of the defendant's victims had managed to reach Colchester – their desire to see Lucifer humiliated, Walter sensed, had inspired them no less than the promise of unlimited ale and *gratis* lodgings – and by day's end six honest Englishmen had offered testimony, persuasive by dint of its ineloquence, to the depravity of the accused.

A particularly vivid statement came from a land surveyor, Nicholas Fian, who confessed to receiving money from a certain nameless baron so that a boundary dispute might go against Lady Mowbray. Two days after submitting his corrupt findings, Fian had watched in horror as a wolf carried his youngest child into the forest. Almost as harrowing was the testimony of a miller, Godfrey Hawke, who claimed that, a week after he'd sold a dozen wormy sacks of flour to Mirringate Hall, his wife had tripped and fallen beneath the grindstone, consequently suffering a crushed leg and a mangled hand.

During her victims' recitations, Walter's sister-in-law remained perfectly still, her expression fixed, eyes frozen, as if some errant Medusa had turned her body to granite. Isaac Newton, by contrast, observed the proceedings in a state of great animation. Often as not he would commit a witness's remarks to paper, writing with a frenzy matched only by the industrious pen of the official scrivener, and he counterpointed each testimony with loud incoherent mutterings, so that Bucock was repeatedly obliged to beg his silence.

The following morning the four remaining witnesses told their stories, the last such narrative, from a huntsman named Ezra Trevor, being especially memorable. After illegally bagging a deer on Lady Mowbray's estate, Mr Trevor had come home to find his cottage overrun by centipedes. One of the vermin had bitten his youngest daughter, who fell into a delirium when the poison reached her brain, her fever breaking only after sixteen hours of thrashing agony.

Bucock declared a noon-time recess, and within five minutes the entire population of the Moot Hall had transplanted itself to the Red Lion. Needing a clear head for his upcoming performance, Walter abstained from ale and cider, consuming only some cold beef and a glass of shrub. Hugh Collop's witnesses passed the interval consoling each other over the incommensurate reprisals with which the defendant had punished their peccadilloes.

At one o'clock the Court reconvened, and shortly thereafter Collop called Colchester's celebrated master pricker to testify.

Mayhap because Lady Mowbray occupied such a lofty social station, Walter found himself reporting the results of the witch-tests in terms more poetic than usual. He spoke of the trident's 'plaintive peal' as it indicted the Devil's mark on Isobel's calf, of the moat's 'poignant gurglings' as it expelled her flesh, and of the 'guttural chant' the toad-familiar had sung upon reunion with its mistress.

For the climax of his presentation, the Crown's advocate called Roger Mapes into the witness-box. Solemnly the Vicar of Ipswich explained why he had removed his daughter from the defendant's baleful influence. His reasons included not only Lady Mowbray's practice of 'sacrificing beasts to Lucifer' but also her 'wizardry with prisms' and her 'unrestrained penchant for dragging Our Lord and

89

Saviour Jesus Christ down to the level of the Arian geometer Isaac Newton'. How clever of Collop, Walter thought, to elicit Newton's name at this juncture. How cunning of him to poison the waters in which Humphrey Thaxton sought to float his client's case.

During the first two days of the trial, Colchester's gossip merchants had gleefully trafficked in the rumour that a celebrated English philosopher would testify for the defence. Some guessed John Locke, others Robert Hooke, still others Edmund Halley. Thus it was that on Wednesday morning at nine o'clock, when Sir Humphrey inaugurated his presentation by summoning Isaac Newton, Lucasian Professor of Mathematics at Trinity College, the gasps that rushed through the Moot Hall issued not from surprise but from extravagant fulfilment of expectation – combined, perhaps, with a certain consternation over Newton's crook-backed frame. Adopting a demeanour that defied his canted spine, the geometer strutted down the aisle and hopped into the witness-box. Walter was pleased to note that, as Newton gave his oath, his tendency to foppery came immediately to the fore. Not only did he grab the Bible with an absurd flourish, he brought it to his lips and kissed it.

Thaxton began by asking Newton to explain why the Mowbray case had inspired him to travel a full thirty miles from Cambridge-Town, whereupon the witness took complete command of the interview. Pivoting, he stared at each juror in turn.

'Good men of Colchester, a ponderous matter lies upon your shoulders,' Newton said. 'Ere the week is out, you must decide whether so-called witches have the power to enjoin wicked spirits and thereby tamper with the world's most fundamental mechanisms.'

Hugh Collop leaped up, obtained the judge's permission to address the Court, and proceeded to argue that the world's most fundamental mechanisms were a subject for philosophic treatises, not sworn testimonies. ''Tis not witchcraft that's on trial here,' he concluded, 'but a particular witch.'

To Walter's profound disappointment, Bucock responded with a prolix opinion to the effect that, in light of the defendant's status as a landholder, Professor Newton must be allowed to speak.

'A most learned ruling, Your Honour,' Newton said, beaming Bucock a smile. Again the geometer listed towards the jury. 'I've been asked to give my reasons for enduring a long day in the saddle, raising many a welt on my arse, merely so I might address you sons of peddletwats.'

Walter released an involuntary gasp. Did Newton really say *peddletwats*?

'Naturally Sir Humphrey hopes I'll instruct you mutton-heads in the fallacies underlying the demon hypothesis,' Newton said, 'but I now see 'twould be easier to teach a sheep not to shit on Sunday. Aye, I've got a proof at my command, so astute it makes incubi and succubi stand revealed as mere idylls of the imagination, yet who amongst you boasts wit enough to follow it? You doltish sons of fastfannies couldn't solve a quadratic equation to save your cods from a woodcutter!'

Walter could scarcely believe his ears, credit his eyes, or accept his good fortune.

'Howbeit, before I depart let me toss a valuable nugget of celestial mechanics your way.' Newton reached towards his chestnut periwig, seizing the longest curl like a carillonneur pulling a bell-rope. 'Since writing my *Principia Mathematica*, I've come to see 'tis fornication, not gravitation, causes the planets to wander. You heard me right, jurors. Each time a gentleman sticks his doodle inside a lady's happy-sack, he makes a deposit in that grand erotic fund from which the universe draws its energy. Heed now the *Principia Priapica*! Law one: a virile member at rest rarely stays at rest! Law two: the speed of the semen is directly proportional to the force of the climax! Law three: for every illicit ejaculation there's an equal and opposite story to tell your wife!'

What happened next was so astonishing that for an instant Walter thought he was home in bed, dreaming the ruination of Sir Humphrey's case. But this was not a dream. Newton was actually cupping his palm around his privates and drawing the fingers together as if squeezing milk from an udder.

''Sblood, jurors, if you've got one of these bolts in your breeches, you need no other explanation for the Earth's perambulations. Tomorrow you must all take the day-coach to Cambridge-Town, that I might show you the evidence. Do I swive my rooming-companion from knickers to noggin each night in the sacred name of Baconian experimentalism? Aye! Do I ram my strumpet-pump into John Wickins's bum hole every morning by way of verifying my philosophy?

Indeed! Do I shag any sub-sizar who'll assent to my glad-adder till he cries, "Hold, enough!" Verily!' At last he removed his hand from his crotch, dissolving the shocking tableau. 'Fare thee well, you knavish sons of narycherries! The Mowbray woman will go to her grave blameless as the lamb, but Newton's not the wight to tell you why!'

Sniggering in the manner of a sensualist enjoying an obscene jest, the witness jumped from the box and scuttled down the aisle. As he disappeared out the main door, a cacophony filled the air, a thundering conglomeration of chattering, nattering, whistling and gasping. Walter could not decide whose face to savour first, but he soon settled on Sir Humphrey, who appeared to be suffering an attack of apoplexy. He shifted his gaze to the judge, who seemed about to relinquish his breakfast. Cavendish, meanwhile, trembled with rage. Collop beamed from ear to ear. Isobel remained her usual granite self.

'Order!' Bucock screamed, pounding on the bench with a walnut mallet. 'Do you hear me? I shall have order in this hall! Order! Order!'

But what did it matter, Walter mused, whether order obtained in one puny courtroom, when such perfect and beautiful order suffused the universe at large?

Like Dr Halley's great comet of 1682 pursuing its wide adventurous orbit, Jennet followed her chosen circuit: past the Moot Hall, through the Dutch Quarter, around the gallows, across the castle yard, down High Street, and back again. Each time she made the loop, she managed briefly to distract herself with a verse or two from Nature's eternal epic — a blue cornflower, scarlet poppy, white rose, floating butterfly, darting finch, trilling lark, fidgeting honey-bee — but her eyes always returned to the three hempen nooses swinging in the breeze.

According to Mr Shakespeare, humankind was a magnificent piece of work, noble in reason, infinite in faculties, in action like an angel, in apprehension like a god, but of late she'd come to doubt that hypothesis. What honey-bee had ever built a gallows? What lark had ever sung out its sister for a Satanist? The world's most vengeful rose-bush had never scratched *malefactor* in an innocent woman's flesh.

She continued her revolutions: a third ellipse, a fourth, a fifth. Before she could begin her sixth such journey, the main door of the Moot Hall swung open, and Mr Newton stumbled onto High Street, tricorn askew, periwig aslant. Had he finished testifying already? Had he presented his demon disproof in a mere half-hour?

Seeing Jennet, he pivoted towards Saint Martin's Lane and broke into a run, curls flying in all directions. He was laughing – laughing and giggling like the most long-gone lunatic ever to wander the corridors of His Majesty's Refuge for the Mentally Deranged.

'Professor Newton!' she cried. 'Wait!'

She was about to give chase when Barnaby Cavendish burst out of the building, eyes wild with distress, face white with mortification.

'Oh, my poor Miss Stearne,' he moaned, waddling towards her, 'our man hath played us false!'

Jennet grimaced. 'False? How so?'

Dr Cavendish pulled himself up to his full height and, in a gesture that evoked a duellist aiming his pistol, pointed towards the fleeing geometer. 'He told 'em they were too stupid to understand his proof!' Securing his wig with the flat of his hand, he sprinted down Saint Martin's Lane in pursuit of Newton. 'Stop, poltroon!'

'He said naught about desires of the mind?' Jennet asked, following, stomach churning and sick at heart.

'Not one syllable,' Dr Cavendish replied.

'He offered them no theorems against the demon hypothesis?'

'He offered only blasphemies and scandal!'

Upon reaching Sainsbury's Livery, Newton commenced to bridle his horse, all the while singing a sea-shanty about a man-o'-war encountering a frigate crewed by harlots. When Jennet and Dr Cavendish arrived, the geometer greeted the curator with a tipped hat and a friendly clap on the back.

'Thou art a punctual man, sir,' said Newton. 'Hitch up thy museum, and we'll be off to London!'

'I wouldn't sell you my prodigies for a king's ransom!' Dr Cavendish screamed.

'The Society's short on king's ransoms at the moment, but we can still give you eight guineas per specimen.'

'I would sooner sell my freaks to a gang of Popish plotters looking to put James back on the throne!'

''Tis true I had my sport with the jurymen' – Newton heaved his saddle onto his horse – 'but only because such peasants cannot follow a reasoned argument.'

'I would sooner sell my monsters to the poxiest trollop in Fleet Street!' From the stable floor Dr Cavendish obtained a roundish mass of straw, dirt and dung. 'I would sooner sell 'em to Judas Iscariot himself for thirty shillings and a brindled pig!'

'I believe we might raise the offer to nine guineas per monster,' Newton said.

Jennet's throat became as tight as a drumhead. Salt tears filled her eyes, burning the delicate jelly. She lurched half-blind towards Dr Cavendish. 'Dear God, they're certain to hang her now,' she wailed, throwing herself against the curator's comforting rotundity.

With his free hand Dr Cavendish stroked her head. 'Aye, Miss Stearne, I fear as much.'

'Ten guineas, 'tis my final proposition!' Newton said. 'You won't get a better price anywhere in England!'

Dr Cavendish hurled the dung-globe. It struck Newton squarely in the side, besmirching the gold-lace bindings of his waistcoat.

'Good sir, 'twould appear our business relationship hath ended.' Through a series of maladroit gestures Newton mounted his horse. 'From this moment, the Royal Society buys all its prodigies from another vendor!'

Dr Cavendish grabbed a second handful of ordure and threw it at their nemesis. The projectile landed harmlessly in the dust. Newton gave his horse a kick. With a sudden snort the animal bolted from the stable and charged towards High Street, bearing away England's strangest knave, philosophy's greatest sage, geometry's reigning genius, and – Jennet could not escape her conclusion – Aunt Isobel's last hope.

CHAPTER THE FOURTH

A Public Burning Enlightens Colchester, Though
Not Before the Convicted Enchantress Prepares Our Heroine
for Both the Female Mission and the Male Emission

Now that Sir Humphrey's key witness stood exposed as a man whose
morals occupied no position above depravity and whose mind merited
no diagnosis save lunacy, Walter assumed that the remainder of the
trial would prove deficient in surprises. At first the day did indeed
unfold as he expected. The defence finished its dispirited presentation.
The jurymen reached their inevitable verdict. The clerk of arraigns
came forward and placed the black silk cap atop Judge Bucock's
wig.

'Oyez, oyez, oyez!' the bailiff cried. 'My Lord the King's Justice
doth strictly charge and command all persons to keep silence whilst
sentence of death is passed on the prisoner at the bar!'

But then something astonishing occurred. As Harold Bucock
offered his concluding remarks, Walter had the sort of revelation a
man might normally be granted only after spending a month in the
African desert, drinking dew and eating roasted locusts. For the first
time ever, he understood the most confounding verse in all Scripture. *If
any man come to me,* ran Luke 14:26, *and hate not his father, and mother, and
wife, and children, and brethren, and sisters, yea, and his own life also, he cannot
be my disciple.* And, of course, the Redeemer might also have said, *and
sisters-in-law.* He could easily have added, *and sisters-in-law who worship
the Devil.*

'Within two days following the departure of these assizes,' Bucock
announced to the Court, 'the Colchester magistrate will impose upon

95

Isobel Mowbray a lethal ordeal of whatever variety accords with his proclivities.'

To hate one's own relations! Ah, the singing, soaring power of that idea! To stand prepared to battle Lucifer in whatever arena he chose, even the souls of those to whom you were bound by flesh and wedlock – in such audacity lay Christianity's true greatness. What difference did it make whether a man was Catholic or Protestant, Quaker or Puritan, Arian or Anabaptist, so long as he might hug those massive pillars of paradox his Saviour had erected seventeen centuries earlier?

'Let us not deceive ourselves,' Bucock continued. 'As a wealthy landowner, Isobel Mowbray already possessed those prizes that commonly bestir her sex to seek out Satan. She did not want for a horse-drawn coach, faithful retainers, fine clothes, or glittering jewels. Ergo, we can only conclude that she entered upon the demonic compact' – his voice reached an apex of indignation – '*for its own hideous sake*! In setting evil influences loose in Ipswich, this woman acted not as the Dark One's servant but rather as his collaborator! And so I call upon Mr Grigsby to give his imagination free rein in staging her demise. I exhort him to make the execution of Isobel Mowbray the most festive such event yet seen in Essex. Let it be said that when Perdition's would-be queen came before the Colchester magistrate, he punished her as extravagantly as the ecclesiastics of Loudun chastised Urbain Grandier.'

Fixing his gaze on Isobel, Walter saw that the judge's damning deduction, his hypothesis that she'd actually sought to reign in Hell, inspired in her not a flicker of remorse. Her face displayed only the same absurd stoicism with which she'd thus far endured every other such accusation.

'Prisoner at the bar, do you wish to make a statement before the Court returns you to Mr Grigsby's custody?' Bucock asked Isobel.

The enchantress said nothing.

'These honourable assizes now stand adjourned,' the judge said, ramming his mallet against the bench.

'God save His Majesty, King William!' the bailiff cried. 'God save Her Majesty, Queen Mary!'

Though not normally inclined towards self-indulgence, Walter felt disposed to celebrate his victory, and so four hours later, as dusk lowered its translucent scrim upon Colchester, he betook himself to the Red Lion. The Court and all its personages had cleared out, bound for Norwich, and yet the tavern was jammed to the walls, a circumstance that forced him to share a table with three local leather-aprons, none of whom, he guessed, had ever read a line of Bodin's *Démonomanie des Sorciers* or Carpzov's *Practica Rerum Criminalum*. Barely ten minutes after he'd joined these rude artisans, however, his opinion of them improved, for it developed that they'd attended the Mowbray trial and had unanimously rated his performance erudite and dazzling.

'It takes great skill, I've heard, to wield a Paracelsus trident,' the cooper said.

''Tis our Heavenly Father wields the trident.' Walter dipped his tongue into the foam atop his ale. 'We cleansers are but His earthly agents. Of course, I must be ever on guard lest I confuse the authentic Satanic vibration with a mere twitching in my fingers.'

'Would ye say, then, that when a cleanser swims a witch, 'tis really God ties on the mask-o'-truth and lowers her into the water?' the soap-maker asked.

'I would say that, aye.' Slowly and with considerable relish Walter took a swallow of ale: a mere carnal pleasure, to be sure, and nothing compared to the spiritual satisfaction he'd known that morning upon deciphering Luke 14:26.

'The mask, though, was it not thine own invention?' the wheel-wright asked.

''Tis the nostril clip makes it such a worthy device,' Walter said, nodding sagaciously, 'fit to stand alongside Isaac Newton's reflecting telescope.'

In evoking the notorious name of Newton, Walter inevitably sparked a discussion of the geometer's recent antics. Everyone agreed that Newton had disgraced himself utterly, although the wheelwright had extracted from the event 'an instructive yet troubling insight'. In ethical philosophy, he noted, there was no such thing as wise laws issuing from a wicked lawgiver, whereas in natural philosophy a man's deductions could be neatly severed from his defects.

'Who amongst us would heed the advice of a horse-thieving Aesop?' the wheelwright elaborated. 'Who would follow the lessons of a whore-mongering Bunyan? But if Euclid were a high-seas pirate, the area of a circle would still equal the square o' the radius times three-point-one-four.'

Walter found this observation so unsettling that he decided to quiet his mind with further applications of ale. He excused himself from his band of admirers, shuffled blearily across the tavern, and set thruppence on the bar. Upon receiving a fresh tankard, he consumed it with a haste that fell just short of sybaritism.

A familiar face appeared before him.

'Might I have a word with ye?' asked Caspar Grigsby, the Colchester magistrate, his coarse hands cradling a mug of buttered rum. He was a short but fearsome fellow, dense with gristle, as firmly planted in the world as a windmill or a tree.

The two men sidled towards the hearth, where a serving wench with apple cheeks worked the spit-crank as if raising a bucket from a well. Impaled on the rotating shaft, a flayed boar offered its meat to the flames.

'How greatly Judge Bucock's commission doth weigh upon me,' Mr Grigsby said. 'He insisted I give my imagination free rein in executing Isobel Mowbray, and therein lies my misery, for I have no imagination.'

'Piffle!' Walter exclaimed. 'Every man hath an imagination.'

'Bucock said her demise must aspire to extravagance. So what am I to do? Fill the execution field with jugglers and acrobats?'

'There – 'tis as I said! You indeed have an imagination!'

'Jugglers? Really?'

Why not? thought Walter. 'And acrobats. Let us mock the Devil with merriment! Let us flog his goblins with raucous displays of joy!'

'Then there be the matter o' the hangin' itself – a dull spectacle, if you ask me, e'en when you get a dancer,' Mr Grigsby said.

'Remember, good sir, Bucock did not specify a hanging. You may recall that he evoked Urbain Grandier's splendid and dramatic execution of 1634.'

''Twas before my time.'

'For bewitching the Ursuline nuns of Loudun, the profligate priest was chained to a stake and roasted like yon boar.'

'Roasted?' Grigsby gasped, eyes darting towards the spit. 'Surely ye don't propose . . .'

Do I? Walter wondered. 'I do.'

'*Burn* her?'

'Burn her.' Walter contemplated the runnels of golden fat as they coursed down the boar's flanks and hit the fire, each sizzle like a demon's hiss. Burn her? Nobody had staged a public burning behind Colchester Castle in over a century – not since all those Protestant martyrs had been incinerated at the Popish Queen Mary's behest – but that didn't mean the custom was invalid. 'Burn her,' he said again. *If any man come to me, and hate not his sister-in-law.* 'Burn her at the stake.'

'Forgive me, master pricker, but the stake – it simply isn't English. We're a gallows people. Leave fire to the French, I say.'

'To the *French?*' Walter moaned. 'Did the French write Revelation 19:20, which tells us that Satan's prophets will be cast alive into a lake of molten brimstone? Did the French write Matthew 13:42, wherein our Saviour makes clear his plan to gather up the wicked and hurl them into the Divine Furnace?'

Grigsby stared at his rum as intently as a seer consulting a gazing-crystal. 'Marry, sir, ye make a proper case for fire. I wish I knew my Holy Writ half so well as ye.'

'For a magistrate, Scripture's desirable – for a pricker, indispens-able.' He lowered his voice, speaking softly into the hollow of his tankard. 'And if a burning doesn't show the Crown I'm the ablest cleanser yet born in England, I'll gather up my family and move us all to Scotland.'

Their stratagem was complex. It was knotty and gnarled and twisted, like the rat tumor she and Elinor Mapes had studied during the *experimentum magnus*, but Jennet could imagine no other way to visit her aunt one last time.

On the third night following the trial, she and Dr Cavendish lashed four foetal monsters to the Gypsy wagon, the ponderous bottles bulging from the chassis like buboes on a plague victim. Next she transformed the curator's face – encircling his eyes with smudges of charcoal, supplementing his teeth with rose-briars, decorating his forehead with wads of clay molded into conical goat-horns – until he truly looked

99

the part he was to play, unscrupulous Adramelech, chief amongst Lucifer's courtiers.

They drove the wagon out of Shire Gate Livery and piloted it up Queen Street – slowly, ever so slowly, lest they crack the bottles. Drawing to a halt in the castle yard, they spied on the youthful, red-bearded turnkey as he entered the keep to relieve his superior. After a moment one-legged Amos Thurlow came hobbling through the portal like a damaged cricket, then pivoted on his crutch and headed west towards the tippling-houses, doubtless seeking the comforts of rum. Dr Cavendish cracked his horsewhip. The wagon bounced along High Street, soon catching and passing the chief gaoler.

Upon reaching the Angel Lane intersection, the curator parked the wagon, clambered down to street level, and, seizing the lanthorn, swooped into Mr Thurlow's path like a hawk descending on a hare. The shocked gaoler nearly dropped his crutch. Dr Cavendish released a froggish gasp.

'You may address me as Lord Adramelech, Grand Chancellor of the Infernal Empire and Viceroy to Satan himself.' Dr Cavendish pocketed his spectacles and raised the lanthorn to his chin, causing jagged shadows to play upon his features as the buttery glow lit his fangs and horns. Mr Thurlow trembled like a man cast adrift on an ice-floe. ''Twould behoove you to fall to your knees, bow your head, kiss my hand, and tell me that my very presence doth honour you.'

Holding his crutch at a vertical angle, Mr Thurlow lowered himself to his solitary knee and pressed his lips against Dr Cavendish's fingers. 'Your v-very presence d-doth honour me, Lord Adramelech, s-sir.'

'Rise, gaoler.'

Mr Thurlow levered himself upright.

'Behold the children of my loins!' Dr Cavendish cried. Taking Mr Thurlow's arm, he brought him before the Tunbridge Wells Blood-sucker, then thrust the lanthorn forward, illuminating the razor-toothed horror. 'At present he sleeps – ah, but how easily I could awaken this malicious imp and send him on an errand. He can bleed an Englishman dry in half a minute.' The curator walked Mr Thurlow to the rear of the wagon and showed him the Kali of Droitwich. 'One word from me, and tonight this demon creeps into your bed and strangles you using all four of her hands.' He shoved Mr Thurlow towards the Sussex Rat-Baby. 'At my command he chews both eyes right out of your skull.' The circuit ended at the Maw of Folkestone. 'Here's one mouth you don't want clamped 'round your privy member. In sum, Mr Thurlow, I see four lamentable fates on your horizon.'

The gaoler, quavering, said, 'Tell me, Lord Adramelech, sir, how do I avoid 'em?'

'By one simple gesture. You will allow Isobel Mowbray's niece to visit her.'

'M-Miss Stearne, you mean? Lovely girl. Splendid girl.'

'Miss Jennet Stearne, aye.'

'I shall arrange it betimes.'

'You will arrange it *now*,' Dr Cavendish snarled, pointing towards the driver's box.

Jennet vaulted into the lane and, head held high, approached the gaoler. 'Hallo, Mr Thurlow. I am well pleased you have at long last assented to my petition.'

'H-happy to s-serve you, Miss Stearne.'

Mr Thurlow rotated ninety degrees and started back towards High Street, his crutch striking the cobblestones with clockwork regularity, Jennet following a yard behind.

'Gaoler, your generosity hath been noted!' Dr Cavendish called after them. 'When your sins send you netherward, I shall see to it you receive a hundred sorts of comfort! Pepper in your sulphur soup! The best salve for your burns!'

By night the warder's station of Colchester Castle was considerably brighter than by day, for a constellation of five oil lamps swung from the ceiling, their glow glancing off the white plaster walls. Jennet readily discerned the perplexity on the red-bearded gaoler's face as Mr Thurlow told him to surrender his key-ring. Upon seizing the brass circlet – it held more than twenty keys, each as large as a bodkin and encrusted with rust – Mr Thurlow led Jennet down a torch-lit corridor where scores of human arms snaked through barred windows, their owners begging for ale, bread and meat. A grid of metal bars presented itself. Mr Thurlow applied the proper key, pulled back the door, and directed Jennet up a spiral stairway that wound through the Great Tower like a bung-nail embedded in a wine cork, until at last they reached a slab of bolted iron.

'I have no wish to see you lose your employment,' she said, 'and so I shall keep this interview brief. Howbeit, please know that if you whisper a word of my visit to any living soul, the Kali of Droitwich will have her way with you.'

'Not e'en the Spanish boot could make me recount this night.' Mr Thurlow inserted a key and with a twist of his bony wrist unlocked the tower door.

'I desire privacy. Twenty minutes.'

'Ye shall have it,' the chief gaoler said.

'Who's there?' called a blessedly familiar voice.

Jennet crossed the threshold. Mr Thurlow slammed the door behind her, the reverberations filling the tower like a cannonade.

Moonbeams the colour of Cheddar cheese flowed through the lancet window, suffusing Aunt Isobel's quarters with a coppery glow, whilst a dozen ensconced candles provided additional illumination and a small measure of warmth. The room was furnished, sparsely but adequately. Mattress, chair, dressing table, writing-desk, chamber-pot. A landed woman in the direst of straits evidently lived better than a dairymaid at the top of her luck.

Dressed in her plainest muslin gown, Aunt Isobel climbed stiffly off the mattress. Her features were drawn and sallow, like the smaller of the Bicephalic Girl's two faces. Though badly ravaged by Walter's razor, her scalp had retained its fertility, the nascent crop of hair emerging in unsightly grey tufts.

'Oh, Jenny, sweet Jenny, I knew I'd live to kiss your angel's face again!' Isobel stumbled forward and flung her arms around her niece, their small bodies fusing like electrically charged rods of amber. 'I told myself that just as the miles 'twixt Colchester and Cambridge-Town didn't stop that girl' – she placed the predicted kiss on Jennet's cheek – 'neither would the bars of my cell. Though I cannot imagine by what ruse you arrived here.'

Jennet proceeded to narrate the theatrics through which her new friend Dr Cavendish had turned himself into Lord Adramelech whilst she became his ward.

Isobel, smiling, said, 'Such a clever child my sister gave the world.' The smile declined into a grimace. 'No doubt you've learned of Professor Newton's perfidy.'

'Dr Cavendish attended the trial. If I live to be a hundred, I shall ne'er forgive the geometer for raising my hopes and then dashing them to bits.'

'With mathematical geniuses, I'm told, one should expect a certain collateral eccentricity.'

'I can no more excuse Newton on grounds of eccentricity than I would a cannibal on grounds of appetite.' Jennet clasped Isobel's right hand, each finger as thin and brittle as a winter twig. 'Oh, my dearest aunt, I fear they mean to hang you. I'Christ, I shall be there, denouncing your tormentors and praying for the rope to break.'

'Attend if you must, but know that Mr Grigsby hath more than a simple gallows jig in mind. He promises the people an old-style burning.'

It seemed to Jennet that the Sussex Rat-Baby had suddenly begun feasting on her entrails. 'A burning?'

'At the stake.'

'Is that not illegal?'

'Merely uncivilized.'

'You must be passing terrified.'

'So terrified I'm numb with it. Ah, but Mr Grigsby and I have struck a bargain. I shall make no speech at the stake, and he will see to it I receive a mercy strangling.'

'Then promise me you'll make no speech.'

''Tis certainly my intention to spare myself the fiery torture.' Like the revitalized but bewildered Lazarus taking the measure of his tomb, Isobel shuffled towards the writing-desk. 'Were this a Dutch cell, I could offer you every amenity. A slice of cake . . .'

The tears, Jennet knew, would arrive soon, a matter of minutes, a matter of seconds. 'We're going to rescue you.'

'A saucer of coffee.'

'Dr Cavendish and I shall pluck you from the pyre.'

'A fresh pear. You'll do naught of the sort, child. Mr Grigsby's marshals would murder you on the spot.'

'Then I shall die in a worthy cause.'

103

'Miss Stearne, you are squandering these hard-won moments. Softly now. I have a gift for you.' From the topmost drawer of her writing-desk Isobel produced a manuscript stitched together with yarn, delivering it into Jennet's grasp. 'Voilà.'

The cover-page bore a title, *A Woman's Garden of Pleasure and Pain*, rendered in the philosopher's ever spiralling hand.

''Steeth, hath my aunt written a book?'

Isobel nodded and said, 'I have attempted in these pages to give my reader at once a body of knowledge and a knowledge of bodies. Life has much in store for you, Jenny. Soon the bloody courses will begin, even as Nature blesses you with roundish hips and wondrous lusty notions. Young men will soon be, as my poor dead husband was wont to put it, "lying through their lips for to lay you 'neath their loins". I've set it all down, plus charts, tables, and diagrams.' She rapped her knuckles on the manuscript. 'Welcome to womanhood, child of my heart. The path lies thick with snares and barbs, but 'tis a truly worthy gender.'

'You will keep silent at the stake,' Jennet said, and now the anticipated tears arrived, falling from her cheeks and staining the cover-page of *A Woman's Garden of Pleasure and Pain*.

'For all I ache to tell the world my opinion of witchfinding, you may be sure the strangling will come off as arranged.' Isobel reached towards the book and brushed a fallen tear, blurring *Pleasure* into *Treasure*. 'Chapter One informs the reader how to keep her lover's ardour from augmenting the human population.'

'I shall memorize every sentence,' Jennet said.

'Sir Edward was eager for an heir — what man is not? — and yet he cherished me even more than his posterity, and so we eschewed all connection on my fertile days. Ah, but even the most wary wife must now and then yield to the moment, and so you'll find herein directions for socking your husband's virility in a Belgian adder-bag.' As her aunt drew closer, Jennet noted a constellation of scabs atop her head, residue of her cropping by the master pricker. 'I have a second present for you. 'Tis largely in the nature of a challenge, but 'tis also a gift, for 'twill bestow a purpose on your life, and what boon could be greater?'

'None, I should imagine,' Jennet said, perplexed.

Isobel backed away and, sitting down before her dressing table, ran a hair-brush through her tenuous and pathetic locks, each strand as delicate as a spider's thread. 'History pursues a lunar sort of progress, with present fore'er cycling back to past,' she said at last. 'At the moment witch-cleansing's on the wane, but betimes the hunt will wax, if not tomorrow, then the next day, or the next.' She froze in mid-stroke. 'To wit, you must construct a treatise. 'Tis your female mission for the next ten years, twenty years – howe'er long it takes.'

'A treatise?'

'A *Malleus Maleficarum* stood upon its head, an argument so grand and persuasive 'twill bring down the Parliamentary Witchcraft Act. Can you do this, darling Jenny?'

'I fear I lack the intellect.'

'You've all the brains the task requires and more. Mayhap you'll have a fleshly babe someday, mayhap not, but in either case this *argumentum grande* will be your one true progeny.'

'Do you mean I am to search out Mr Newton's lost disproof of demons?'

Isobel dipped her ravaged head. 'Newton in person hath naught to offer us, but Newton in principle will surely serve our ends. Of all the mortals in England, only you and I and the Lucasian Professor know that the cleansers might be crushed through philosophy. Ah, but the Lucasian's within an ace of lunacy, your aunt's about to die – and so I now dub thee Lady Jennet, Hammer of Witchfinders.'

'How do I even begin? Might some other Royal Society fellow set me on the proper path?'

'Alas, I fear that clan is riddled with demonologists, Mr Boyle most conspicuous amongst them. 'Twill gain you more to study those who've actually written against the prickers' trade: Reginald Scot, plus the three John W's – I speak of Webster, Wagstaff and Weyer – the better to learn why their reasoning ne'er took hold. And then comes the daunting part.'

'Mastering Mr Newton?'

'From sprit to spanker. The geometry, the optics, the hydrostatics, the planetary mechanics. You must graft the *Principia* onto your soul, darling Jenny. Find that missing calculation, and you'll deliver many an innocent wight from noose, pyre or chopping-block.'

A key rattled in the lock. The door swung back. Propped on his crutch, Amos Thurlow limped into the cell. 'It's been twenty minutes, Miss Stearne . . .'

Isobel rose from her dressing table and for the second time that night wrapped her niece in a deep and desperate affection. As their embrace intensified, Jennet imagined a myriad germ cells flowing from her aunt's body into her own, quickening her mind with philosophic seed as surely as spermatozoa could quicken a grown woman's womb. I'm with child now, she thought. An *argumentum grande* is growing inside me. I have achieved a mental

*

Pregnancy rarely saved the life of a convicted sorceress during the witch-hunting centuries, but a full womb was normally good for a temporary reprieve. The gestation would run its course, a wet-nurse would receive the baby, and the prisoner would assume her appointed place on the gallows or at the stake. It was not automatically clear what to do with the superfluous neonate. Sometimes a convent adopted the creature. Sometimes the father or other blood relation stepped forward. And sometimes the magistrate ordered a strangling, on the theory that the infant had become polluted *in utero*.

We call this epoch the Renaissance, a rebirth of art and classicism. Dear reader, it was nothing of the kind – or, rather, it was something of the kind for the average prince, aristocrat, merchant, or patronized painter, but it was nothing of the kind if you were just another peasant scrabbling to avoid starvation. In your experience the Renaissance was a nightmare, and if you cultivated habits that drew the witchfinders' notice – if you told fortunes, trafficked in herbs, dabbled in magic, or practised midwifery – you were vulnerable to the charge of Satanism.

When she told her niece that witch-hunting was a cyclic enterprise, Isobel Mowbray spoke the truth. The world needed an *argumentum grande* in 1689 – not as badly, perhaps, as in 1589 or 1489, but it certainly needed one.

Dayton, Tennessee, the sweltering July of 1925. The Scopes Trial.

Clarence Darrow and William Jennings Bryan square off over the Genesis account of human origins. Does biblical literalism suffer a setback? Indeed. Is this a victory for the theory of evolution? Hardly. For Darwin's canny advocate, you see, has failed to make a positive case for natural selection – he has neglected to construct an *argumentum grande* – with the result that, throughout the remainder of the century and beyond, America's high-school science teachers will fully explicate evolutionary principles in their classrooms about as often as they lecture on necrophilia.

The Vatican, Italy, 1484. As the Renaissance builds up speed, the newly installed Pope Innocent VIII conceives his famous Witch Bull calling for the extermination of Devil-worshipping heretics wherever they might rear their heads. He writes out the dictum on his bullsheet, then deputizes Heinrich Krämer and Jakob Sprenger to go on a fact-finding mission. Their labours result in the *Malleus Maleficarum*. The tome stands alone. Krämer and Sprenger have no peers and, more significantly, no antagonists. And so it happens that for the next quarter-century the odour of roasting witch-flesh becomes as ubiquitous in northern Europe as the aroma of candle wax or cow manure. How could it be otherwise? What human endeavour could possibly be as glorious as checkmating Satan? The next time somebody announces that he plans to get Medieval on your ass, tell him you're going to get Renaissance on his gonads.

Don't misunderstand me. I've never shared Isobel's touching faith in the power of sober discourse. The path on which she set Jennet that night in the prison cell suffered from a lamentable credulity, if not outright naïveté. I am well aware that the average member of your species will not abandon a pleasurable opinion simply because the evidence argues against it. Self-doubt is a suit of clothes that few of you ever acquire, and fewer still wear comfortably.

And yet the effort at persuasion must be made. There is something rather noble – and occasionally even effective – about an *argumentum grande*. I've found that pessimism can be its own sort of innocence, cynicism its own sentimentality. Isobel knew this, and in time my Jennet came to know it too.

By 1510 it seems that the witch-hunt has run its course. But then along comes Martin Luther and his *Ninety-Five Theses*, and by the middle of the century the Reformation evangelists have revived what the Catholic evangelists inaugurated. All during the 1560s and 1570s Protestant clerics oversee hundreds of sorcery trials in Germany, Switzerland, Denmark, Hungary, Transylvania and Scotland. Eventually the Counter-Reformation swings into action. Throughout the 1580s and 1590s, the Catholic reconquest brings a vigorous anti-Satanism to Bavaria, the Rhineland, Flanders and Poland. Scores of learned and energetic Jesuits keep the witch fires burning.

It is an age of giants: Christians of a calibre that leave the likes of Walter Stearne in the shadows. Take Johann von Schöneburn, Archbishop-Elector of Trier, who sponsors the executions of nearly four hundred supposed witches between 1585 and 1593. Thanks to Von Schöneburn's vigour, two Trier villages are left with only one female inhabitant apiece. Or take Julius Echter von Mespelbrunn, the Prince-Bishop of Würzburg, whose efforts turn Wolfenbüttel's Lechelnholze Square into a forest, so densely packed are the stakes. At Von Mespelbrunn's funeral, the court preacher praises the prince's zeal in burning witches 'according to God's word'. Or take Nicholas Rémy, the witch-hunting lawyer of Lorraine, whose *Daemonolatreiae* calls for not only the burning of convicted Satanists but the extermination of their children as well, the better to eradicate the unholy seed *in toto*. He dies in 1616, a beloved and respected scholar who has consigned at least two thousand five hundred innocents to the flames.

Early in the seventeenth century another hiatus occurs, but then the Thirty Years War reinvigorates the hunt throughout the Rhine Valley. Among Catholic clerics, Prince-Bishop Phillip Adolf von Ehrenberg of Würzburg is particularly active: between 1623 and 1631 he burns nine hundred ostensible witches, including his own nephew, nineteen priests, and a handful of seven-year-olds judged guilty of having had sexual intercourse with demons. Not to be outdone by Von Ehrenberg, Johann Georg II Fuchs von Dornheim of Bamberg – the *Hexenbischof*, the Witch Bishop – builds a 'witch-house' featuring a torture chamber adorned with biblical texts, and by the time his ten-year reign is done he has supervised the incineration of six hundred putative sorcerers. On the Protestant side, meanwhile, there emerges the majestic figure of Benedict Carpzov, the Lutheran scholar whose *Practica Rerum Criminalum* maintains that even those who merely *believe* they've attended a

Sabbat should be executed, for belief implies will, and will entails menace. Before ascending to his heavenly reward, Carpzov will read his Bible cover-to-cover fifty-three times, take Holy Communion at least once a week, and underwrite the deaths of 20,000 alleged witches.

The Thirty Years War ends, but the cleansings do not. As the 1660s progress, the withdrawal of English troops from Scotland frees up Calvinist magistrates to torture and burn Devil-worshippers by the hundred. In Sweden, meanwhile, Lutheran clergymen renounce the inhibitory ethics of the late Queen Christina (who'd ordered her generals to curtail whatever German witch-hunts they encountered during their campaigns). They experiment with persecution, find it to their liking, and forthwith immolate one presumed Satanist after another.

And so I ask you, reader, can we blame Isobel Mowbray for wanting to give the world an *argumentum grande*? When she commissioned Jennet to find Newton's lost proof, at least five hundred thousand convicted witches, and perhaps as many as a million, had already fallen victim to the brutal nonambiguity of Exodus 22:18. Our heroine will not have an easy time of it. Krämer and Sprenger may have been loonies, but Von Mespelbrunn, Carpzov, Rémy and their ilk were among the most formidable minds of the Renaissance. What do you say to a bishop whose Bible tells him he must not suffer a witch to live? On what grounds might you answer a magistrate who knows that wayward teats and bloodless blemishes constitute infallible evidence of Satanic compact?
How implausible to suppose that any argument might sway a judge
who believes it his sacred duty to dispatch as many witches
as possible to Hell, where all the lakes are
of burning sulphur, and not
one is filled
with

*

Water,
Jennet decided,
would do the trick. She'd
read about the method in a book concerning
the savage red Indians of America: how they would contrive
to wake themselves at dawn by drinking deeply at bedtime. The night

before Aunt Isobel was scheduled to meet the flames, an event the Witchfinder-General had strictly forbidden his daughter to attend, Jennet consumed a quart of water, climbed onto her mattress, and pulled up the counterpane. Her mind was abuzz. *Argumentum grande* . . . Newton's lost proof . . . find it . . . the geometry, optics, hydrostatics . . . the planetary mechanics . . . missing calculation . . . find it.

Much to Jennet's dismay, Dr Cavendish had been as horrified as Walter by the thought of her observing the burning. For nearly an hour following her reunion with Isobel in the Great Tower, she'd quarrelled with the curator over the circumstances of her hypothetical appearance on the execution field.

'If we were two parliamentarians,' Dr Cavendish said, 'me a lord, for example, and you a commoner, we would resolve this issue through a compromise. I've no doubt you're familiar with the concept.'

'Aunt Isobel once told me that a compromise occurs when a person gives up something he pretends to want so as to gain an object for which he feigns indifference.'

'Indeed.'

And so they compromised. Jennet could patronize the execution, but only if a full one hundred yards separated her from the stake. Dr Cavendish would install his Gypsy wagon on the far side of the field, and with the aid of a telescope they would together watch from the roof.

As it turned out, she didn't need the water, for she failed to fall asleep that night. Even before the sun's first rays touched the town, she was on her feet, improvising an effigy from a sack of flour and a bundle of rope. She set the false Jennet in her bed, then slipped out of the house and skulked along the misty length of Wyre Street, bound for Colchester Castle. The air smelled of honeysuckle. A scraggly grey cat bolted across her path and disappeared down Culver Lane, doubtless in quest of the mice who populated the Trinity Church burial ground. From the trees came the cawing of perhaps a hundred crows, an avian parliament debating some matter inaccessible to human ken.

The birds had fallen silent by the time she reached the castle yard, and the flower-scented winds now carried the fragrance of cooking fires and the stench of upended chamber-pots. She made her way along the west wall of the keep, striding past the spindly monument marking the spot where two Royalist commanders had been shot on orders from the Parliamentarian General following the Siege of Colchester. Might there come a day when the sentence against Aunt Isobel would seem equally reprehensible? wondered Jennet as she vaulted the crumbling remains of the Roman wall. Or would history in its lunar progress decide that the witch had received too lenient a punishment?

Magistrate Grigsby's men had evidently visited the execution field earlier that morning, for a single wooden stake, thick as a pig and twice a man's height, now projected from a low hill at the centre of the green, directly across from the gallows. Laced with tinder and kindling, a heap of logs encircled the obscene obelisk. The logs looked dry and old to Jennet: a quick fire, a quick consummation – good.

To her left loomed the Gypsy wagon, plugging a breach in the Roman wall and poised to retreat down Saint Helen's Lane. Having played out their parts in the great Adramelech hoax, the Bloodsucker, the Maw, the Kali, and the Rat-Baby no longer decorated the chassis but now lay sleeping with their brethren. Clay pipe fixed betwixt his teeth, Dr Cavendish supplied Damon and Pythias with their oats. Seeing Jennet approach, the curator offered her an articulate scowl. I really wish you hadn't come, his countenance said. I wish you'd stayed in bed.

As the rising sun parted company with the horizon, the performers began arriving, props and equipage in hand, and betimes the spectators themselves entered the green, first in twos and threes, then in groups of a dozen or more.

Jennet and Dr Cavendish scrambled into the driver's box and thence to the top of the wagon, where the promised telescope – a brass Hevelius reflector – lay propped against the chimney, casting its shadow across the roof as did the gnomon on a sundial.

'Colchester's most pious citizens,' Dr Cavendish muttered, gesturing towards the crowd, 'all of 'em eager to spite the Devil by cavorting at his queen's execution.'

Now a tavern-keeper appeared on the field, driving a pony-cart loaded with casks of ale.

''Sblood, the man hath brought a hundred gallons at least.' Dr Cavendish eased his rump onto the roof. ''Twould seem the piety quotient's about to rise.'

Jennet dropped to one knee and assumed a cross-legged posture alongside the curator. She seized the telescope and clamped it to her eye, extending the tubes until the image grew crisp.

It felt blasphemous to be using this sacred device, designed to reveal the faces of planets and the courses of comets, in surveying so profane a spectacle, and yet she could not forbear to study the details. Near the eastern edge of the field, an aerialist costumed like a harlequin advanced birdishly along a tightrope strung betwixt a pair of chestnut trees, juggling two red rubber balls as he went. His audience included the Reverend Mapes and the regrettable Elinor; father and daughter were sharing a meat pie, starting at the antipodes and eating their way towards the centre. On the northern boundary, not far from the River Colne, a company of thespians presented a bawdy anti-Papist satire in which the recently deposed King James wandered through Ireland converting the toads to Catholicism, baptizing them with his piss. Beside the satirists, a trained bear with a shimmering black pelt danced to the feral music of four pipe-players and a drummer. As the bear's gavotte built to a frenzy, Jennet spied her brother, seated on the grass amongst the spectators, alternately sketching with his wax crayons and adding his applause to the general acclamation. So powerful was her augmented vision, she could even see the subject of Dunstan's drawing: a three-masted carrack riding a stormy sea.

Came the fateful hour of ten o'clock. Telescope still fixed to her eye, Jennet tracked a horse-drawn tumbrel as it rolled across the green escorted by Constable Wedderburn plus two marshals wearing orange doublets and helmets like soup tureens. Mr Grigsby held the reins. Her father sat alongside the magistrate, waving at the crowd as if he were Julius Caesar bringing a captive barbarian king into Rome. In the bay stood the squat, modest figure of Aunt Isobel, clothed in a burlap shift, her outstretched wrists cuffed by iron manacles, the rusted chains looped around her neck and spilling down her chest like fiendish garlands. Behind her rode the executioner, a neckless man with olive skin and a tangled charcoal beard, gripping the chain that joined Isobel's shackles.

'Prithee, Miss Stearne, go below.' Dr Cavendish, rising, pointed to the trap-door in the roof.

The crowd pelted the prisoner with stones, clods, pottery shards, decaying cabbages and rotten turnips.

'I belong here,' Jennet said. 'She expects it.'

Mr Grigsby halted the tumbrel. The executioner scrambled out and, using the timber as a stairway, climbed the pyre, dragging Isobel behind him. He chained her to the stake, then took from his pocket a black cloth hood and slipped it over her head. Jennet shuddered and moaned. Never again would she see her aunt's living face, never again her antic eyes, sly smiles, challenging frowns.

Returning to the ground, the executioner stepped back and surveyed the stark tableau – timber, stake, hooded prisoner. The revellers, passing pleased, gulped down ale and gathered around the pyre, determined to witness every nuance of the burning, an entertainment normally available only on the Continent.

Like a stag striding majestically from forest to meadow, a tall priest walked free of the mob. Jennet yanked him into focus. Slung about the priest's neck, a heavy silver cross bounced beneath his jaw as he scaled the pyre's northern slope. The crowd grew silent. The priest pressed a Bible into Isobel's hands, loudly instructing her to make a good confession, then set his ear against her occluded mouth.

Dr Cavendish lifted the trap-door and secured it with an iron brace. 'Go below, Miss Stearne.'

'I cannot.'

The priest took back his book, his sour face suggesting that Isobel Mowbray's last words had displeased him. He shook his head, opened his Bible, and recited Psalm One Hundred in a stentorian but mellifluous voice. 'Make a joyful noise unto the Lord all ye lands . . .'

'Once, in Würzburg, I saw a supposed witch burned at the stake.' Dr Cavendish stared into the open trap as if deciphering a scene in a scrying-glass. 'They strangled her first, but 'twas still a nightmare for me, more terrible than I can say.'

'Terrible for you' – Jennet kept the telescope locked on the priest as he descended the mound of logs and faggots – 'and even worse for the woman.'

Mr Grigsby lit a torch and passed it ceremoniously to Walter. The executioner pulled on leather gloves and, leaning a wooden ladder against the stake, climbed to the elevation of his faceless prisoner. He flexed his fingers in prelude to the choking – once, twice, thrice. The image went muzzy, its particulars sluiced away by Jennet's tears. She laid the telescope on the roof and mopped her eyes with the hem of her gown.

As the executioner fitted his hands around Isobel's neck, something wholly unexpected occurred. Despite the tightening fingers and the intervening hood, the philosopher managed to release a loud, coherent utterance.

'Darling Jenny! Mapper of moons! Maker of rainbows!'

Ice-water formed in Jennet's bowels.

'I know you're out there, Jenny!' Isobel's words boomed across the green. 'Hear me now!'

'Dear God, why doth she do this?' Jennet rasped. 'She promised to keep silent.'

'Attend her every word!' Dr Cavendish demanded.

Jennet seized the telescope, pressing it against her eye.

Upon receiving a nod from Grigsby, the executioner jumped off the ladder, plucked the torch from Walter's grasp, and jabbed it into the bottommost faggots like a swordsman delivering a fatal thrust. An ecstatic cheer shot from the crowd as the pyre caught fire.

''Tis not happening,' Jennet insisted.

'Hear me, child!' Isobel cried.

'What shall I do?' Jennet wailed.

'Are you blind?' Dr Cavendish seethed. 'Can you not see the flames? For God's sake, tell the woman you hear her!'

The tongues of combustion sinuated through the pyre and began to rise, higher, higher, darting amidst the gaps in the logs. Flames met faggots with a popping noise suggesting a regiment discharging a score of muskets.

'I hear you, Aunt Isobel!' Jennet shouted. She set down the telescope and, gaining her feet, stretched to full height. 'I hear you!'

'Newton's proof!' Isobel screamed. 'I can see it, child! Aristotle! The elements! Aristotle!'

'Aristotle!' Jennet echoed. Aristotle? 'The elements!' Aristotle's elements?

'Earth! Air! Newton's proof! The elements!'

'Earth and air, aye! Earth and air and water and fire!'

'Water and fire!' shrieked Aunt Isobel, coughing as the smoke invaded her lungs. 'Water and fire! Fire! Oh, God, the fire!'

'I shall find the proof! Aristotle! The elements!'

'Damn thee, Walter Stearne! Damn thy bones and blood!'

In dying, Isobel Mowbray became a kind of storm, her imprecations booming across the field like peals of thunder, her screams flashing through the air like lightning-bolts. The atmosphere thickened with smoke, hosannas and the fleshy stench of Exodus 22:18.

Jennet, still standing, grabbed the telescope and put it to her eye, but she dared not twist the tubes.

Die, please die, please die.

'The elements?' Dr Cavendish said.

She did not resist when the curator stepped forward and tore the instrument from her grasp. He lowered himself over the edge of the roof and slipped into the driver's box, resting the telescope on the seat.

'Why the elements?' Dr Cavendish muttered.

A roar filled Jennet's ears, a pounding tide of blood.

'The elements,' Dr Cavendish grunted, seizing the reins.

Isobel's screams dissolved into an unearthly gurgling, and then her scorched throat at last grew still. Never had Jennet known a more blessed silence, but no sooner had it settled than her father, livid and sweating, broke from the crowd and rushed towards the Gypsy wagon.

'Jennet!' he cried, his voice abrim with rage and disgust. 'Daughter, you will explain yourself!'

The crack of Dr Cavendish's horsewhip resounded like a pistol shot. Jennet crossed the roof, dropped through the trap, and landed on the museum floor. She rose and staggered amongst the monsters, weaving every whichway like a kite in a hurricane. As the coach rolled towards Saint Helen's Lane, she fell against the Sussex Rat-Baby, embracing the huge glass jar for support. Nausea possessed her. She vomited forth a foul, viscous gush of mucus, spilling the hot broth onto the floor like slop from a slush-bucket.

With the back of her hand she wiped the sticky fluid from her lips. 'She's dead,' she explained to the Sussex Rat-Baby. 'She's dead,' she announced to the Cyclops of Bourne. 'She's dead,' she informed the Bird-Child of Bath. 'For this my aunt was once alive,' she told the Bicephalic Girl, 'and now she is dead.'

Three days after the successful and well attended burning of his sister-in-law, Walter Stearne received a letter from the new Keeper of the Privy Seal – George Savile, Marquess of Halifax – inviting him to 'a meeting concerning your curious proposition that our nation requires a Witchfinder-Royal'. At first he was uncertain how to account for his good fortune, but eventually he concluded that the Almighty had decided to reward his leniency. In electing to punish Jennet's recent disobedience by merely boxing her ears and then confining her to her bed-chamber without food for three days, as opposed to birching her backside until the skin turned plum, he had gained favour in God's eyes.

The momentous gathering was to occur on a Saturday afternoon at Blickling Hall, Sir Henry Hobart's sprawling mansion in the valley of the Bure. Walter felt ashamed to be arriving in his shabby Basque coach, but his discomfort turned to delight when he realized that the post of Witchfinder-Royal would probably come with a conveyance fit for an earl. What other benefits, he wondered, might his new appointment entail? A house in London? A silver pricking needle?

With exultant heart and prancing step, he followed the steward into a drawing-room off the staircase where Lord Halifax, a horse-faced man sporting painted cheeks and an unruly silver peruke, waited in the company of two other Privy Council members. Alexander Tancred, Earl of Gurney, was a person of loud laughter and wide girth, his jaw and brow mottled by the pox. Francis Chater, Earl of Wroxeter, as long and lean as his fellow aristocrats were plump, possessed a disconcerting habit of reaming his nostrils with the corner of his handkerchief.

A servant brought coffee, and the four men got down to business. Lord Halifax produced a copy of Walter's ancient petition to the Crown, along with a paper that he identified as Lord Sunderland's favourable report on the proposed office.

'Mr Stearne, having read these two documents, I wish I could tell you that our attitude accords with Sunderland's,' Halifax said. 'Alas, we must withhold our endorsement until we fathom your peculiar religious views.'

'Peculiar?' A sinking feeling spread through Walter, the sort of queasiness he experienced each time he saw an accused sorcerer bob to the surface of a river. 'I assure you, my Lords, I am a covenanted Christian who says his prayers each night.'

'In your letter to our former monarch, James the Second, you assert, quote, "Being of the Romish faith, His Majesty should be singularly sympathetic to the witchfinding enterprise," unquote,' Lord Gurney said. 'You further observe, quote, "The *Malleus Maleficarum* is Catholic in pedigree," and also, quote, "European anti-Satanism becomes rational and systematic only with Pope Innocent's *Summis Desiderantes* of 1484." Now, Mr Stearne, though King James did indeed cleave to the Papist perversion, surely it hath not escaped your notice that England's present rulers are Protestants, as are Lord Halifax, Lord Wroxeter and myself.'

'And myself as well,' Walter said.

'Do you regard the Protestant faith as inferior to the Catholic when it comes to witch-cleansing?' Lord Gurney inquired.

'Oh, no, sir, not in the least.'

Lord Wroxeter said, 'Need we remind you of Martin Luther's statement that, quote, "I would have no compassion on these witches. I would burn them all"?'

Luther's views on Satanism were but dimly familiar to Walter, though he decided to pretend otherwise. 'I have always counted the monk's motto amongst my favourites.'

'Then mayhap you're also aware that John Calvin once said, quote, "God expressly commands that all witches and enchantresses shall be put to death, and this law of God is a universal law."'

'I have inscribed those very words inside the cover of my Bible,' Walter said, fully intending to do so before sundown.

'The Protestant religion is a witch-fighting religion,' Lord Gurney said. 'Of the several hundred thousand Satanists switched off since our Redeemer's advent, nearly a quarter of the convictions may be credited to Reformation magistrates.'

Walter made a fist, slamming it into his open palm. 'The more for that, the infernal Papists had a head start by fifteen centuries!'

'Well spoken, sir!' Halifax declared. 'My Lords, 'twould appear that in Mr Stearne we have ourselves a patriotic, a pious and withal a *Protestant* witchfinder.'

'Agreed,' Wroxeter said.

'Hear! Hear!' Gurney shouted.

Walter heaved a sigh of such force it could have snuffed a candle.

A smiling Halifax said, 'At its forthcoming meeting with His Majesty, the Privy Council will recommend that, pursuant to the Conjuring Statute, you be appointed Witchfinder-Royal for the Crown's colonies in New-Plymouth and Massachusetts Bay, with an annual salary of two hundred pounds, or one guinea per detected Satanist, whichever sum is higher, plus a Basque coach and team.'

Having completed his epic exhalation, Walter now found him-self gasping for breath. 'Pardon, my Lord. Did you say . . . Massachusetts?'

'Correct,' Halifax replied.

'Is that not in . . . America?'

'America's the proper place for a man of your ambitions,' Gurney said. ''Tis the land of opportunism.'

Walter said, 'My Lords, if you please, I'd prefer not to live in Massachusetts – a barbaric place, I've heard, o'errun with violent aborigines, wild animals and maniacal Puritans. Can I not be Witchfinder-Royal for my beloved England instead? Scotland, perhaps? Ireland? Wales?'

'Sir, we shall be blunt,' Wroxeter said, probing his left nostril with a cloaked finger. 'The longer you remain on this side of the Atlantic, the more you place yourself in jeopardy. 'Tis no secret His Majesty's Secretary of State would see Walter Stearne drawn and quartered for treason.'

Hearing his own name and the word 'treason' spoken in the same sentence rattled Walter like a thunder-clap. 'Treason? *Treason?* My Lords, you address as loyal a subject as e'er walked on English soil.'

Gurney gathered the folds of his forehead into a byzantine frown. 'You burned a woman of property, you wall-eyed cod-swallower! What sort of doltish thing was *that* to do?'

'She was guilty,' Walter said.

'She was *gentry*,' Halifax said. 'To wit, you pompous nincompoop, you have no future here. Hie yourself to America and proceed to make the best of it.'

'We've found something to cheer you,' Gurney said, handing

Walter a bound booklet of some twenty pages. 'Last month this worthy specimen of Calvinist exegesis arrived in London.'

Walter examined the slender volume, whose cover identified it as *A Discourse on Witchcraft*, a sermon preached the previous year in Boston by a Puritan minister named Cotton Mather. He turned to page one and read, 'Witchcraft is the Doing of strange (and for the most part ill) Things by the Help of evil Spirits covenanting with the woeful Children of Men.' A passing piquant definition.

'The New-England Calvinists might be slavering fanatics, but they've ne'er shrunk from prosecuting the Dark One,' Wroxeter said. 'In recent years they've convened a dozen witch-trials throughout Connecticut and Massachusetts.'

'But how am I to move in Puritan circles when my faith's of the Anglican variety?' Walter asked.

'A fair question,' Halifax said. 'Methinks a tilt towards the Calvinist austerity might well suit your purpose.' ·

'I shan't do it!' Walter protested. ''Twould be an act of sheer hypocrisy!'

'We speak not for hypocrisy but for compromise,' Halifax said, setting his palm on Walter's shoulder. 'Betwixt the two lies a universe of difference. Within government circles I am rightly called the Trimmer, an epithet I wear as proudly as a general his medals. When travelling with Tories I find myself disposed towards the Tory outlook. Amongst Whigs I enter a Whiggish frame of mind. To wit, through the subtle art of equivocation I have made myself obnoxious to all, with the result that no man durst oust me for fear of pleasing his enemies.'

Walter returned his gaze to the sermon, alighting on a passage in which Cotton Mather argued that the demonic compact was as palp-able as any other crime. 'Many Witches have confess'd and shew'd their Deeds. We have seen those Things done that are impossible a mere Disease or Deceit could procure.' An important point. Those who would reduce *maleficium* to physical sickness or legerdemain were not looking closely at the evidence. This Mather was a divine worth knowing.

'Two hundred pounds per annum — was that the figure?' Walter asked.

'In the interests of efficiency,' Wroxeter said, nodding, 'you will draw your salary from the Massachusetts Governor.'

'And in the interests of economy,' Halifax added, 'you will occupy the property of my late uncle, a modest farm on the Merrimack in the Puritan community of Haverhill.'

'Haverhill?' Walter said. 'Not Boston?'

''Tis all His Majesty can afford,' Halifax said, smiling. 'The War of the Grand Alliance hath emptied his coffers.'

Walter stared into the impenetrable blackness of his coffee. 'I would have a proper licence,' he said at last. 'Signed by the King.'

'The Defender of the Faith's agreeable,' Wroxeter said.

''Twill grant me the title of Massachusetts Witchfinder-Royal and specify that upon my death the office transfers to my firstborn son – and to his firstborn son after that.'

'Such can be arranged,' Halifax said.

'We've saved the best news for last,' Gurney said. 'As you might surmise, the red Indians of New-England, whose numbers easily surpass one hundred thousand, know naught of the Christian faith, nor of any religion at all save their own deplorable paganism. Do you grasp the implications?'

'I surely do, my Lord Gurney.' Walter took a gulp of cold coffee. 'One hundred thousand?'

'One hundred thousand.'

Rolling up Mather's sermon, Walter thanked the aristocrats for their generosity. One hundred thousand disciples of Satan, and not a single licensed cleanser on the whole continent. The Massachusetts Witchfinder-Royal, it seemed, would never want for employment.

Every time Jennet remembered how she had once regarded Barnaby Cavendish as just another of England's itinerant charlatans, she experienced a withering chagrin, for in sooth he was closer to a saint. On the morning following the Colchester Castle execution, the curator's Samaritan sensibility asserted itself once again when he offered to donate his entire profit from showing his monsters about the town, three pounds sterling, to the cause of Aunt Isobel's interment.

The woolly-bearded executioner parted with her blackened bones for a guinea, and an identical sum inspired Oswald Leech, the pussel-gutted sexton of Saint James's Church, to dig her a resting place. For a site Mr Leech selected an unhallowed patch of ground along the churchyard's eastern edge, just beyond the Roman wall. Hearts-ease and daisies bloomed everywhere. Standing atop a slate outcropping, a grey raft of stone adrift upon sea-green hills, Jennet and Dr Cavendish watched silently as the sexton laid Isobel Mowbray's remains in a pinewood box, nailed the receptacle shut, and lowered it into the dank wormy cavity.

'Methinks I've deciphered her final words,' Jennet said, dropping a handful of earth onto the coffin lid.

'About Aristotle and the elements?' Dr Cavendish added a second clod to the grave. 'Tell me your deduction.'

'I believe that as the executioner went to strangle Aunt Isobel, Mr Newton's calculation against witchery appeared to her as in a mystic vision. She saw that his lost proof turns on the Greek immutables.'

'Earth, air, fire, water,' Dr Cavendish said.

'Earth, air, fire, water,' she echoed.

'Ashes to ashes,' Mr Leech said. 'Dust to dust.'

Two days later, Jennet's father ushered her into the seclusion of his garden, asserting that he wished to confront her with 'some issues of passing urgency'. At first she assumed that he intended to box her ears again for attending the execution, but she had overestimated his wrath. He directed her to sit on the stone bench, then settled down beside her and solemnly announced that all their lives were about to change. At the end of the week they would take a coach to Gravesend and subsequently board a carrack, the *Albion*, bound for the New World, where he'd been appointed Witchfinder-Royal for Massachusetts Bay and New-Plymouth.

To Jennet it seemed as if her beautiful foetus, her embryonic *argumentum grande*, had just died in the womb. How could she master the *Principia Mathematica* whilst trapped amongst barbarians so pre-occupied with marauding mountain lions and savage Redmen they had no energy left for building libraries or founding colleges? How could she become a great natural philosopher when surrounded by bumpkins who didn't know Greek chemistry from curdled cream? The world's worst thrashing would be better than this dreadful news.

'I would prefer to stay in England,' she said.

'Myself as well, but that path is not open to us.' Her father crushed a scattering of acorns underfoot. 'We must now discuss a rather different matter. A troubling matter.'

'Aye?'

'A matter you will belike find painful, as it concerns the maternal aunt of whom you were so fond.'

'Father, you hold me on tenterhooks.'

'As Lady Mowbray received her punishment,' he said, shifting on the hard marble, 'the two of you entered upon a cryptic dialogue concerning an entity called "Newton's proof". Evidently she sought to impart some arcane alchemical formula to you.'

'Her message was no secret,' Jennet said, rising. 'She was plainly averring that demonology will one day succumb to an alliance 'twixt Newton's principles and the Greek immutables.'

'One day our Saviour will return. One day the world will end.'

'But not before your profession hath been trampled into the dust.'

'Mayhap,' he sneered. 'But hear me now, child. My eye is evermore fixed on you. Let me catch you practising some dark art or performing some diabolical experiment, and your regret will defy the limits of common imagination.'

'You needn't suspect me of sorcery, sir.' She strode past the trellis, heading for the garden gate. 'Philosophy doth not hide its light beneath a bushel.'

On Thursday morning Dr Cavendish drove her out to Mirringate Hall, that she might bid Rodwell good-bye. Much to her astonishment, she found the manor occupied by the late Edward Mowbray's obese first cousin, Henry, and his equally adipose wife, Clarinda. In tones betraying not one atom of remorse, this self-regarding couple reported that upon learning of his mistress's execution Rodwell had taken to bed and died in his sleep. When Jennet expressed a desire to visit the old steward's grave, Henry Mowbray revealed that no such plot existed, for he'd sold the body to an anonymous surgeon in Maldon.

As the tense and unpleasant visit progressed, the two usurpers passed up no opportunity to insinuate that the girl in their midst had somehow betrayed Isobel in particular and the Mowbray family in general. It took Jennet the entire morning to convince them that she'd played no part in Isobel's arrest — that, indeed, she regarded her father's business as an abomination. At last a belated air of cordiality descended upon the gathering, and the conversation turned to the disposition of Isobel's estate. The Mowbrays made it clear that, though Rodwell's corpse was first amongst the Mirringate Hall accoutrements they'd converted to coin, it would not be the last. They fully intended to sell the telescope, the microscope, the alchemical equipment, and the library, all two thousand volumes.

The longer Jennet listened to their schemes, the more greatly she desired to sever all connection with these vultures. When they invited her and Dr Cavendish to stay for the midday meal, she was pleased to reply, quite truthfully, that she must instead return to Colchester and pack her belongings for her imminent voyage.

''Twould seem the best thing about stumbling upon long-lost relations,' Jennet remarked as she and Dr Cavendish rode away from the manor, 'is that it takes no particular effort to lose them again.'

Beyond the singular volume called *A Woman's Garden of Pleasure and Pain* and Aunt Isobel's copy of the *Principia Mathematica*, the only earthly possession Jennet wished to bring with her was the toy wind-mill her mother had constructed as a child. But Walter forbade her this remembrance, as its size and bulk would consume an entire sea-chest, and the Stearne family was permitted to place only three such con-tainers in the *Albion*'s hold. Two mornings before they were to sail from Gravesend, Jennet carried the windmill to the summit of North Hill and gave it one last run. The machine worked splendidly, and yet she took no pleasure in its performance, as the vanes' cruciform pattern put her in mind of suffering and martyrdom.

'Father, forgive them,' she muttered, fixing on the spinning sails, 'for they knew not what they did.'

With the coming of noon the wind grew dispirited, declining from a gust to a breeze and thence to utter stillness. She resolved to leave her mother's mill in place atop the ridge: no doubt some passing Col-chester child would take a fancy to the toy, conclude it was there for the stealing, and joyfully bear it away.

'Upon further consideration, I have decided that they knew exactly what they did' — she lifted her head towards the clouds — 'and so I bid

Thee give carbuncles and gout to all who danced that day on the green.'

The following afternoon she parted company with Dr Cavendish and his monsters outside the Fox and Fife, where he'd rented rooms following his expulsion from the Red Lion, whose pious proprietor believed that the curator was profiting by the Devil's handiwork. Much to Dr Cavendish's amusement, Jennet entered the Gypsy wagon and took leave of each freak individually. 'Two heads are better than one,' she informed the Bicephalic Girl. 'Ugliness is only skin deep,' she assured Perdition's Pride. 'Think on it this wise,' she told the Cyclops of Bourne. 'When the time comes for you to get optical spectacles, you'll pay but half the normal price.'

The Lyme Bay Fish-Boy, she predicted, was destined to wed a beautiful mermaid. The Smethwick Philosopher would one day assume the Lucasian Chair at Trinity College. The Bird-Child of Bath would become the envy of eagles. She thanked the Rat-Baby, the Bloodsucker, the Maw, and the Kali for their help with the great Adramelech hoax.

'I hope you find a customer for your stillborns,' she told Dr Cavendish.

'I'Christ, Miss Stearne, your attitude towards my Kali and her kin hath revived mine own affections. For all I feel a weariness in my bones, I mean to show these freaks till the Pale Priest comes to take me away whilst I'm lecturing on the Bicephalic Girl.'

'Oh, my dear Dr Cavendish, you shall do no dying before I've recovered Newton's lost calculation, borne it back to England, and sought out my old friend the prodigy-monger.'

'Then let me ask a boon of you.' He caressed the Smethwick Philosopher. 'In America you may very well come upon a foetal aberration, and when that happens you must preserve it in brine till our reunion.'

'You have my solemn word.'

'I hereby appoint you Curator of the Cavendish Museum of Wondrous Prodigies – Colonial Branch.'

She flung her arms wide, then gave her colleague a vigorous hug.

'I shall ne'er forget you, Barnaby Cavendish.'

That evening she undertook the most difficult farewell of all. She searched through the Basque coach until she found her father's lanthorn and his largest pricking needle. A half-hour later, as gloom enveloped the grounds of Saint James's Church, hallowed and unhallowed alike, she trimmed the wick, set the globe to glowing, and, kneeling beside the grave, scratched thirteen words into the slate outcropping.

MENSUS ERAM COELOS, NUNC TERRAE METIOR UMBRAS
MENS COELESTRIS ERA, CORPORIS UMBRA IACET

Aunt Isobel had always admired the epitaph that Johannes Kepler had composed for himself shortly before his death. Indeed, the last time she was in Germany, she'd attempted to find the great astronomer's tombstone, only to learn it had been pulverized by a passing cavalry troop during the Thirty Years War. Jennet felt certain that Isobel, looking down from God's eternal domain, would be pleased to see Kepler's words shining beside her resting place.

'I measured the skies, now I measure the shadows,' she recited. 'Sky-bound was the mind, Earth-bound the body rests.'

She looked heavenward. Venus blazed above the northern horizon. Slowly the stars blinked into visibility like candles lit by an unseen votary. The Creator was perfect. His Creation was perfect. Ergo, every planet moved in that most perfect of shapes, the circle. No other conic deserved consideration.

'Good-bye, Aunt Isobel. I loved you so much . . .'

Except the planets didn't move in circles. They simply didn't. Her blood leapt up, alive to the brilliance of that astonishing first law. *The orbit of a planet describes an ellipse, with the sun at one of its foci.* Thus were two millennia of received astronomical wisdom neatly and irrevocably overturned. Oh, Kepler, brave Kepler, how did you do it? *The orbit of a planet describes an ellipse.* By what path doth a person come to think this way? *With the sun at one of its foci.* If I live to be a hundred, will I e'er vault past the beautiful circle to see the true ellipse beyond?

PART II

Earth, Air, Fire, Water

CHAPTER THE FIFTH

The Salem Witch-Court Declines
to Cast the First Stone but Instead Places
It upon Giles Corey's Breast

Chill rains, razoring winds and relentless sleet plagued the *Albion* from the first league of her Atlantic crossing onward, forcing the steerage passengers belowdecks, huddled in their hammocks like cocooned caterpillars awaiting metamorphosis. For Jennet the tedium proved almost unendurable, but then at last the captain, reversing an earlier edict, decreed that every literate voyager could burn a whale-oil reading lamp for three hours each day. Thus it was that, as the crossing progressed, Jennet drew insight and energy from the crepuscular pages of *A Woman's Garden of Pleasure and Pain*, unending perplexity from the dimly lit and obscurely written *Principia Mathematica*, and, after borrowing the first mate's English translation, the pleasures of picaresque adventure from the tenebrous text of *Don Quixote de la Mancha*.

Her father and brother, meanwhile, relieved their ennui by entering into the various card tournaments and draughts matches that occurred almost continually within these cavernous confines. Unhappily for the Witchfinder-Royal and his son, maritime custom dictated that no game could commence until the players had wagered on the outcome. Being amongst the more honest folk aboard the *Albion*, Walter and Dunstan quickly saw their cash reserves depleted, the sounds emitted by their purses declining precipitously from the delightful jingle of guineas to the less gratifying clank of crowns to the melancholy tinkle of shillings.

Walter chose to make light of their bankruptcy. 'Considering the sheer quantity of heathen sorcery with which the New World's infested,' he told his children, 'I would guess we'll all be living like kings anon.'

As the *Albion* blew within view of the severe and scowling Massachusetts coastline, Jennet finished giving *A Woman's Garden of Pleasure and Pain* its fifth successive reading, taking care as always to conceal the manuscript from her father, who would surely throw the thing overboard the instant he noticed that its author was Isobel Mowbray. In the first paragraph of the first chapter, Aunt Isobel had boldly declared her theme. 'If a Woman wishes to count her Soul complete, she must avail herself of Love in all three Forms: pious, Platonic, priapic. But even as she opens her Heart to Cupid's Arrows, she must ally her Head with Reason's Axioms. Pregnancy and the French Pox are merely the most conspicuous amongst the Disasters that await the unwary Maiden as she makes her Way, Hopes aglow and Passions aflame, to her Gallant's Bed.'

'To count her Soul complete': the phrase resounded in Jennet's skull like a taunt, the cruellest gibe yet sprung from the vindictive lips of Elinor Mapes. Dear God, how could she ever count her soul complete after that unthinkable event on the Colchester execution field? What alchemist yet born could refine a glue of sufficient stickiness to mend her fractured self?

When Jennet's father first told her of his appointment as Massachusetts Witchfinder-Royal, she'd naturally assumed that upon their arrival they would take possession of a large and splendid Boston mansion. The position indeed came with a house, but it was neither large, nor splendid, nor in Boston. To mitigate the gloom of their ramshackle Haverhill salt-box, Jennet papered the front parlour with Dunstan's most cheering vistas – a wheat field shimmering beneath an August sun, an abandoned stone barn rising from a hill of larkspur, a towering oak made golden by a lightning-stroke – all rendered in luminous wax. Her father, meanwhile, decorated his bed-chamber door with his cleansing licence, an object to which he accorded such stupefying reverence it might have been a map disclosing the Seven Cities of Cibola, though it was in sooth but a scraggly scrap of parchment signed illegibly by King William III.

Jennet could find nothing in Haverhill to call her own. It was a town of cows and people with the intellectual aspirations of cows. The ruling sentiment amongst the populace was fear. They feared famine and disease, wolves and wicked spirits, outsiders and one another – but most of all they feared the Algonquin Nimacooks, a tribe of savage tawnies who had recently raided the nearby settlements of Topsfield and Andover, slaughtering scores of men and abducting a dozen wives and daughters.

The possible fates of these women occasioned much gruesome speculation in Haverhill, but it was generally agreed that each abductee initially had to run the gauntlet – a ritualized torture in which the captive endured a savage beating – whereupon she was delivered to the tribe's most virile males for the purpose of breeding further Nimacooks. Whether or not a person believed this ghastly rumour, it was certainly congruent with the broader narrative favoured by the Colony's most famous Christian, the renowned and talkative Cotton Mather. According to the Reverend Mather, the Indians of Massachusetts Bay were descended from an ancient Devil-worshippng race whom Lucifer had transported to the uninhabited continent so they might adulate him free of Christian interference. While this theory struck Jennet as doubtful in the extreme, the Nimacooks nevertheless terrified her, and she nightly implored her Creator to spare Haverhill from their flaming arrows and cruel knives, their brutish clubs and sharp tomahawks.

Unfortunately for her father, though happily for New-England's supposed Satanists, his franchise began and ended with his shabby little licence. Within a week of landing in Haverhill, Walter learned that the Massachusetts Governor, Sir Edmund Andros, had been deposed, and so the anticipated salary of two hundred pounds per annum never materialized, despite Walter's entreaties to the interim administration in Boston. Throughout his first year in the Colony, he convinced the selectmen of only two neighbouring towns, Amesbury and Beverly, to sponsor witch-hunts and pay him a guinea for each heretic he unmasked. By late winter, thanks to Walter's efforts, four women lay shackled in Massachusetts gaols, awaiting the trials that could not occur until the Colony got a new charter and a new Royal Governor to execute it. As she pored over the pages of her *Woman's Garden*, Jennet often thought of those wretched prisoners, shivering in their own dung, praying for their prosecutions to begin so that they might know the warmth of a courthouse.

To minimize the threat of starvation, her father planted a vegetable garden, but he succeeded in coaxing from the soil only a few anaemic turnips and feeble beans. Whenever he tried catching fish, the trout inhabiting the Merrimack proved too devious for him, routinely eluding his net. Desperate, he took up the flintlock musket left behind by Lord Halifax's uncle and marched resolutely into the woods. Before a week was out he'd tracked and shot a doe, and the following week he appeared in the doorway with a stag slung over his shoulders like an ox-yoke. And so it came to pass that the Massachusetts Witchfinder-Royal was reduced to the status of common deer-slayer, a humiliation in which Jennet could not forbear to take a covert pleasure.

Like her father, she attempted to augment the family's larder through fishing, but her expeditions proved unavailing. She never netted a trout, only crayfish, minnows, and the occasional carp. Although the poverty of her catch depressed her, she found ample compensation in the intemperate beauty of the Merrimack Valley. Walking along the river's banks each day, observing the corpulent green bullfrogs croaking atop their podiums of mud, the golden butterflies floating above the wildflowers, and the precise and urgent dragonflies as they flitted amidst the cattails, she decided that Cotton Mather's theory must be turned inside out. Far from being the Devil's backyard, this untrammelled continent partook of whatever postlapsarian goodness the planet still could claim.

As her life in Haverhill pursued its unsurprising course, Jennet's body underwent the very changes forecast in her *Woman's Garden*. Her hips grew round. Her bosom swelled. Next the bloody flow commenced, growing heavier with each successive month. By her thirteenth birthday she'd experienced every phenomenon predicted by Isobel's treatise save one, the longing for a young man's touch. But this, she knew, would come.

With nary a philosopher, geometer, or sage in sight, she was obliged to try deciphering Isaac Newton on her own. She could manage the Latin well enough, but what did it all *mean*? Where was the sense in a statement such as, 'The areas that revolving bodies describe by radii drawn to an immovable centre of force do lie in the same immovable planes, and are proportional to the times in which they are described'? Not long after Isobel had introduced her to the *Principia Mathematica*,

Jennet had found amongst her aunt's geometry volumes a monograph in which Newton boasted of making his book as abstruse as possible, 'to avoid being bated by little Smatterers in Mathematics'. This same monograph specified the works a person should master ere approaching the tortuous tome: 'After all thirteen books of Euclid, you must read De Witt's *Elementa Curvarum*, as this will increase your Knowledge of the Conics. For the Algebra, you should acquire Bartholin's *Commentaries on Descartes's Geometry* and solve the first Thirty Problems. Finally, any Mind that imbibes the Whole of Huygens's *Horologium Oscillatorium* will emerge the richer for it.' Small wonder the *Principia Mathematica* seemed as opaque to her as barrel-tar.

Time and again she returned to the Merrimack, and one afternoon she forsook the linen net for a method perfected by Dunstan. You located a piece of twine, fastened a crab-apple to the midpoint, knotted one end around a willow wand, tied a bent sewing-needle to the other end, impaled a caterpillar on the needle, set the apple afloat, and waited. The technique worked splendidly. Shortly before dusk Jennet snagged and landed a trout. For a full minute she crouched beside her prize as it lay twitching on the shore, tethered to the wand, friendless and alone. Staring into its unblinking eye, she grew grateful for Monsieur Descartes's deduction that all such animals were essentially machines – oblivious to sensation and immune to misery.

She pressed one palm against the dying trout, feeling its squamous complexity, then reached towards the bent needle and twisted the shank free of the fish's mouth.

She looked up. A tall young man stood on the far side of the river, harvesting marsh marigolds. He was bare to the waist, his flesh as brown as cedar wood and smooth as bronze. He wore deerskin leggings. Their gazes connected. He smiled. She shivered. His hair was greased, cut short on one side, black as a Colchester crow. His cheekbones were high, nose elegant and aquiline.

Lowering his head, he inhaled the fragrance of the golden bouquet, then once again fixed his dark eyes on her.

Only much later, as she hurried home through the gathering dusk, surrounded by the sawing of the crickets and the tremolos of the tree frogs, the trout secured in her leather satchel, did she make sense of the encounter. This had been a truly momentous afternoon. There would never be another like it. For on this day Jennet Stearne, future author of the *argumentum grande*, had caught a trout, seen an Indian, and experienced her first sweet rush of desire.

Stepping off his porch, *Malleus Maleficarum* in hand, Walter skirted his miserable crop of pole-beans and headed towards Kembel's Ordinary. All the way down Mill Street he made a point of not looking west. Thither lay an entire continent, vast beyond imagining and infested with Devil-worshippers – and he could do nothing about it. Until he persuaded the Boston Puritans to supply their Witchfinder-Royal with a salary, he would have to waste his days hunting and fishing and otherwise scrabbling for a living. Such an irrational state of affairs – when your cellar was full of rats, you didn't lock your cat in the attic.

No matter how vigorously Walter prayed, how much Scripture he read, or how mightily he strove to think well of his benefactors, he could not shake his conviction that Lord Halifax and the others had betrayed him. He wanted to believe that it was all an unhappy accident – that when the aristocrats sent him packing to America, they'd had no inkling of Governor Andros's imminent eviction. But Walter smelled conspiracy. He could practically hear the three lords cackling over how they'd foiled the controversial pricker, deftly manoeuvring him out of England without resorting to the cumbersome formalities of exile.

Whenever Walter supped in Boston with his remarkable new friend, Cotton Mather, the jelly-jowled minister reminded him that there was considerable cause for optimism. Even as the two Satan-haters ate their fowl and venison, the Reverend Mather's ambitious father was in London negotiating with the King's Colonial Secretary, drafting a new charter for Massachusetts Bay and helping to select Andros's replacement. In the meantime, Mather advised, Walter should continue detecting heretics whether the local magistrates paid him or not, the better to impress the new governor when he arrived.

'Imagine you're the Crown agent in question,' Mather said. 'On reaching Massachusetts Bay you hear rumours of the Colony's official witchfinder – how he so despiseth the demon world, he hath been dispensing his services for free. What would your inclination be?'

'To recompense that cleanser handsomely,' Walter said, basking in the warmth of Mather's madeira. "'Sblood, Reverend, for a pastor, you think rather like a politician!'

"'Tis a habit I must continually cultivate — at least until that unlikely day when our politicians start thinking like pastors.'

Owing to this expectation of ultimate reward, Walter experienced an unbridled delight when, early in March, the Reverend Samuel Parris of Salem-Village solicited his expertise in circumscribing Satan. 'The 25th of this Month will find me in your Town of Haverhill, buying Boots and Gloves,' Parris's letter began. 'My fond Hope is that, come the noon Hour, we might meet at Kembel's Ordinary. You will know me by my ministerial Garb.' At first Walter decided that Parris merely intended to bring him, the Colony's most famous non-Puritan, into the Calvinist fold, but then he read the closing line — 'Lucifer hath been rais'd amongst us, and his Rage is vehement and terrible, and we sorely require your Skills' — and he forthwith scribbled a note confirming the rendezvous.

Striding into the tavern, Walter instantly identified the Reverend Samuel Parris. With his high-crowned hat and elegant grey cape, the minister stood out from the Haverhill farmers and tradesmen as would a diamond atop a dung-hill. A cadaverous, beak-nosed man of sallow complexion, he sat by the window, leafing through a Bible bound in Moroccan leather. Walter slipped his licence from his *Malleus* and set it before Parris. The men shook hands, exchanged pleasantries, and ordered pots of cider, and by midday they'd formed the sort of iron bond enjoyed by those who place Devil-fighting above all other matters.

Beginning the previous January, Parris explained, a strange malady had overtaken a half-dozen girls in Salem-Village. The children routinely lapsed into trances, suffered convulsions, endured bites from invisible teeth and pinches from phantom fingers. Amongst the afflicted were Parris's own daughter, Betty, and his orphaned niece, Abigail Williams. After ruling out all possible mundane causes, the local physician had offered a diagnosis of *maleficium*; the girls, he believed, were bewitched. Soon afterwards Betty and the others started naming their tormentors. Thus far five Salemites had been examined, indicted and sent to the gaol-house, and every week the girls sensed yet another wizard or enchantress in their midst.

''Tis a situation that calls for an experienced cleanser,' Walter said.

'Captain Walcott hath agreed to open his house to you,' Parris said. 'We would retain your services anon but for one lamentable circumstance.'

'Speak no more of it. Though baptized into the Church of England, I am all eager to join your Calvinist sect.'

'I feel a prodigious relief,' Parris said, pressing his Bible against his breast as if applying a poultice.

Walter gulped down the last of his cider, sighing contently as the alcohol mingled with his blood. The minister's splendid cape, he realized, would make a most dignified uniform for a Witchfinder-Royal. 'You spoke of invisible teeth and phantom fingers . . .'

'Invisible to us bystanders, but not to the afflicted girls. Barely a day goes by without Satan sending forth a witch's ghostly apparition, and by these shapes the children know who plagues them.'

'Were you aware, Mr Parris, that we licensed prickers regard spectral evidence with the gravest scepticism?'

'I'Christ, I was not. You can see how great is our need of you. Come to Salem, sir.'

'My fee's five crowns per unmasked heretic.'

'And therein lies my regret, for we cannot offer you any compensation beyond food and lodging. The village selectmen – an incompetent bunch, as you'll see – barely manage to scrape together my monthly salary and firewood allotment.'

'The things of Caesar mean nothing when there are demons to thwart,' Walter said. And governors to dazzle. 'I shall join this epic hunt of yours' – he reinserted his licence in his *Malleus* – 'before the week is out.'

On the seventh day in April 1692, Walter loaded his children and his detection tools into his thrice-owned and grotesquely decrepit one-horse carriage – the promised Basque coach had never materialized – and travelled twenty miles south-east to Salem-Village. They reached Jonathan Walcott's house in the middle of a ferocious thunder-gust, but luckily the Captain and his wife were prepared for their sodden visitors, providing them with woollen clothes, hot broth, warm wine and dry beds.

An auspicious beginning, Walter decided. His fortunes were about to change.

At first Dunstan and Jennet seemed wholly in countenance with their new surroundings. Though the village was landlocked, the neighbouring community of Salem-Town encompassed a bustling harbour, and Dunstan and Jennet passed many agreeable afternoons watching the arrivals and departures of the high-masted ships. Alas, by mid-month Walter's children were complaining of boredom, a condition they sought to relieve through association with Abigail Williams, a leader amongst the girls whose sufferings had ignited the hunt. Walter did not like Miss Williams. He did not like any of the haunted daughters of Salem-Village. Their temperaments were flighty, their speech unrefined, their submissions of spectral evidence dubious. In the case of the Williams girl, however, he apprehended within her troubled soul an odd sort of holiness, an idiosyncratic sanctity, and so he permitted his children to keep company with her, hoping that her piety might somehow rub off on Jennet.

Shortly after assuming his position on the Examination Committee, Walter asked the chairman, John Hathorne, the town's imperially unpleasant magistrate, if he might visit the seven indicted suspects in their gaol-cells. He wanted to test them all, from four-year-old Dorcas Good to seventy-one-year-old Rebecca Nurse. Hathorne ultimately admitted Walter into the prisoners' presence, but he forbade him to scan their skin, for the Puritans in their purity held it unseemly that a man should search a woman for imp teats or Devil's marks. Moreover, though Judge Hathorne and his colleagues did not deny the reality of animal servants, they thought it impossible to tell a true familiar from a mundane beast, and so they discouraged him from doing any watchings. As for the cold-water test, Mr Hathorne perversely dismissed this proof as 'the rankest Anglican superstition'. It went especially hard with Walter that he could not scrutinize the flesh of Rebecca Nurse, as most of her neighbours regarded her as a kind of living saint: probably this was another case, like Jephthah's daughter, of a seemingly virtuous woman who practised sorcery in secret, but he wanted to be sure.

'Why do you invite me into your enterprise only to tie my hands and shackle my talent?' he complained to Hathorne and his slithery assistant, Jonathan Corwin.

'For the simple reason,' Hathorne replied, 'that when the new governor sees his own Witchfinder-Royal sitting on the Committee, he'll appoint a proper court without delay.'

''Steeth, 'twould seem I'm but a figurehead,' Walter said. ''Tis my inclination to resign.'

'*Resign?*' Corwin gasped. 'Desert your post at the height of New-England's greatest cleansing?'

Walter pinned his lower lip betwixt his teeth. 'Were you better acquainted with me, sir, you would know that I would sooner pluck out mine eyes than abandon my sentry-box to Lucifer.'

The magistrate offered Walter a nod that seemed at once condescending and conspiratorial. 'Mr Stearne, methinks we're all wondrous useful to one another. Might I suggest we stop bickering amongst ourselves and save our spleen for Satan?'

As the month progressed, the screaming girls identified twenty-three additional Devil-worshippers in the village, and these suspects were duly summoned to the meeting-house, where they stood before the Committee in ostensible perplexity whilst Hathorne and company interrogated them. After much negotiation Walter convinced the chairman to let him exercise his scanning skills indirectly. By this compromise each accused female undressed herself in the foyer, Walter present but blindfolded, and then the wives of Hathorne and Corwin ran their hands across her skin, describing all marks and pricking any that sounded suspicious to the Witchfinder-Royal. Although this procedure brought to light dozens of incriminating excrescences, Walter could barely abide his frustration. For the first time ever, he understood the impetus behind the Protestant Reformation. Martin Luther had loathed those platoons of priests styling themselves the sole earthly agents binding Man to his Creator, and Walter was likewise repulsed by these two superfluous females mediating betwixt his fingers and his judgement.

In the unique case of the beloved Rebecca Nurse, neither Goodwife Hathorne nor Goodwife Corwin could find a bloodless aberration on her person, and so Walter administered the secondary tests. Goodwife Nurse recited the Lord's Prayer start to finish without the slightest hesitation or mildest elision. She easily met the weeping standard, shedding more than twenty tears under the thumbscrew's rude influence. When he scalded her index finger with boiling water, the resulting blister stretched well beyond the range, zero to one inch, that bespoke diabolism. Goodwife Nurse, it surely seemed, was innocent.

Despite Walter's success in detecting Devil's marks amongst the suspect population, the Examination Committee continued keying its sessions not to solid demonology but to the impulsive children. Whenever an alleged Satanist entered the meeting-house, Abigail Williams's band went into paroxysms of bewildering intensity. Each girl had her forte. Miss Williams herself vomited thorns. Mercy Lewis bled from her nose and mouth. Elizabeth Hubbard swooned. Betty Parris was a champion writher. Ann Putnam fell down gasping, a victim of spectral choking. Mary Warren shrieked and wailed as she beheld invisible imps alight upon the prisoners' shoulders. Mary Walcott – the Captain's daughter and the group's newest member – beat her head against the floor, raising bumps and welts so terrible as to suggest the violence of a Nimacook hatchet.

The Committee had just commenced its seventh week of service, with sixty-two indictments to show for its efforts, when Increase Mather finally returned from London bearing the sorely needed provincial charter and accompanied by the new Massachusetts Royal Governor. Sir William Phipps soon proved the very sort of anti-Satanist that Salem required in this, her darkest hour. On the twenty-seventh of May, he brought into being a Court of Oyer and Terminer to try the accused witches, an ad hoc institution featuring Deputy Governor William Stoughton heading a panel of eight justices, amongst them John Hathorne, Jonathan Corwin, the famously formidable Samuel Sewall of Boston, and one of Walter's Haverhill neighbours, Major Nathaniel Saltonstall.

Six days later the defendant Bridget Bishop entered Salem-Town Courthouse. Eleven persons submitted statements against her, with Miss Williams's troops claiming abuse at the hands of the defendant's spectre and Walter adducing the Devil's mark on her left calf (a determination he'd made after hearing Goodwife Corwin's account of both the excrescence itself and its insensibility to the pricking needle). The jury, led by Foreman Thomas Fisk, rendered a verdict of guilty.

Despite Bridget Bishop's blubbering protestations, Judge Stoughton forthwith ordered her execution 'according to the direction given in the laws of God and the wholesome statutes of the English nation'. On the tenth of June, Walter stood at the foot of Gallows Hill and watched as the sheriff and his men carted the convicted enchantress to the summit. After leaning a ladder against the largest oak, the sheriff hauled Bridget Bishop ten rungs skyward, slipped a noose around her throat, and pushed her into the air. The witch's cervical vertebrae failed to separate, and in consequence her strangulation lasted nine minutes.

On the first morning in July, the Court heard the collective evidence against Sarah Wildes, Susannah Martin, Elizabeth Howe and Sarah Good. Walter and the tormented girls offered abundant proof of Satanism, and before the noon recess the jury found against all four prisoners. The day's events were not entirely soothing to the Witchfinder-Royal, however, for that afternoon a fifth defendant came before the Court, the saintly Rebecca Nurse, whose friends and relations had persuaded Judge Stoughton to consider her case separately. True to form, the girls shrieked in pain the instant Goodwife Nurse approached the bench, but then Walter assumed the witness-stand, telling how the *Pater Noster* test, the weeping proof, and the scalding ordeal – not to mention the pricking of her several blemishes – all appeared to vindicate the old woman.

'In my thirty years of cleansing,' he told the judges, 'I've ne'er met a person as innocent to a witch as Rebecca Nurse.'

From the defendant's husband, Francis Nurse, came a final piece of exculpatory evidence, a petition signed by thirty-nine of the community's most respected citizens. 'We cannot imagine any Cause or Grounds,' they wrote, 'to suspect Goody Nurse of those Things of which she is accused.'

Shortly after dusk Thomas Fisk led his fellow jurymen into the antechamber. They returned twenty minutes later. A hush settled over Salem-Town Courthouse. Walter thought of Revelation 8:1. *And when he had opened the seventh seal, there was silence in Heaven for the space of half an hour.*

'How goes it with the defendant?' Judge Stoughton asked. 'Be she guilty or nay?'

Walter leaned forward. A single drop of sweat descended from beneath his peruke, tickling his skin as it slid down his brow.

Goodman Fisk coughed deliberately, anxiously shifting his weight from one foot to the other. 'Not guilty.'

So wild was the subsequent frenzy that a stranger happening upon the scene might have thought he'd wandered into a lunatic asylum. The bewitched girls clawed at their breasts, drove their teeth into their forearms, and ripped clumps of hair from their scalps, all the while screaming like sinners dredged in burning sulphur.

'Goody Nurse clutches my throat!' shouted Ann Putnam, retching and wheezing.

'Goody Nurse gnaws my tongue!' cried Mercy Lewis, spitting blood.

'Her spectre fells me!' Abigail Williams crashed to the floor like a tree limb riven by a lightning-bolt. 'She bids me kiss the Devil's bum! Nay, Goody Nurse, I shan't kiss it! I shan't! I shan't!'

When at last the chaos subsided, William Stoughton turned to the foreman. 'Goodman Fisk, I have no wish to impose upon the jury, but I must ask that you reconsider your verdict.'

'On what grounds?' Fisk asked.

'Yes, Excellency, on what grounds?' Walter demanded, leaping from his chair as if wrenching free of a thorn-bush.

'On the grounds of the *maleficia* these girls suffer at the hands of this she-wolf in sheep's clothing,' Stoughton said.

Foreman Fisk guided his jurors back into the anteroom. It took them but ten minutes to frame a new and better verdict.

On the 19 July, Sarah Wildes, Susannah Martin, Elizabeth Howe, Sarah Good and Rebecca Nurse were carted to Gallows Hill, where scores of spectators awaited, singing hymns and sharing corncakes. Walter brought Dunstan along, their first such communion since the cleansing of Isobel Mowbray. Cotton Mather came all the way from Boston, exquisitely dressed in a black linen robe, his felt hat screwed smartly over his bulbous wig. Not since Jesus himself had passed through Jerusalem's gates amidst a thousand waving palm-fronds, Walter mused, had a Christian made so impressive an entrance.

Singling out the Witchfinder-Royal, Mather approached and pre-sented him with a bound copy of his latest sermon, *Remarkables of the*

Divine Providence, Including Sea-Deliverances, Gallows Speeches of Criminals, and an Account of How God Lifted a Plague of Caterpillars through the Sending of Flocks of Birds. Walter bowed gratefully and turned back the cover. On the title-page the minister had written, 'For my Colleague Walter Stearne. A Friend to Virtue, to Vice alone a Foe. With Admiration, the Reverend Cotton Mather.'

'I shall evermore treasure this little book,' Walter said, 'and especially thine affectionate inscription.'

As it happened, Mather's presence on Gallows Hill that morning proved essential to the task at hand. Each of the first four heretics was swung, strangled and cut down with nary a comment from the crowd, but when the sheriff made ready to push Rebecca Nurse off the ladder, a score of Salemites grew conspicuously discontent, screaming, 'Spare her! Spare her!'

Like the Redeemer making ready to deliver the Sermon on the Mount, Mather scrambled up the face of a granite boulder and, reaching the summit, spread his arms wide as if to gather every spectator into his loving embrace.

'Good farmers and merchants of Salem, be not deceived by outward forms!' he insisted, his tone striking in Walter's estimation an ideal balance betwixt beneficence and expertise. 'Oft-times hath the Devil been transformed into an angel of light!'

'Listen to Reverend Mather,' Judge Hathorne demanded, 'who knows more of Satan's wiles than a barn owl knows of mice!'

The crowd grew still, and Walter watched in awe as face after face on Gallows Hill acquired the glow of newfound theological understanding – indeed, only the frail and weeping Francis Nurse was manifestly unpersuaded – and not a single dissident voice arose when Judge Stoughton approached the ladder, squeezed the leg of the elevated sheriff, and muttered, 'Hangman, do your duty.'

The sheriff shoved the prisoner. As Dunstan set about sketching her terminal gyrations, Mather descended from his granite pulpit and returned to Walter's side.

Rebecca Nurse required nearly twelve minutes to complete her passage to the Dark One's realm.

The more he thought about it, the more clearly Walter remembered noticing, the first time he'd visited her, a tiny protuberance on the defendant's neck, an excrescence he'd lamentably forgotten to com-mend to the attention of Goodwife Hathorne and Goodwife Corwin. Had the women pricked that ominous nodule, it would have yielded no blood – though mayhap a drop or two of the notorious black acid that to an imp was sweet as wine, bracing as coffee, nourishing as milk.

It was a credible measure of her boredom, Jennet felt, that the longer she lived in Salem-Village, the more she sought amusement from her dreary brother, whose conversation of late was restricted to the minutiae of demonology and the trivialities of witch tests. Doggedly devoted to the pursuit of mirthlessness, the Salem Puritans made Dunstan seem by comparison the wittiest jester ever to tickle a king's fancy. She would not say that she enjoyed her brother's companionship these days, but she certainly preferred it to the never-ending funeral that passed for family life in the Walcott household.

Dunstan, meanwhile, cleaved to Mr Parris's tall, angry, ever-chattering niece, Abigail Williams. Shortly after sunrise each morning, Abigail and her raving peers would betake themselves to the meeting-house and spend several hours throwing fits before the Examination Committee. Returning to the parsonage, she would do whatever chores her uncle required of her, whereupon she would lead Jennet and Dunstan to yet another 'place of preternatural import' near the village. Abigail showed them the marsh where George Burroughs's murder victims had supposedly appeared to her, their winding sheets rippling in the wind. She guided her newfound friends through the meadow where Martha Carrier had, quoth Abigail, 'given birth to some monstrous malformed thing, which the woman then laid upon the ground and cleaved in twain with an axe'. She took them to the abandoned barn in which John Proctor and Martha Corey had signed Satan's book, and next to the glade their coven had once used as a gathering place. After arriving astride their flying besoms and airborne goats, Abigail explained, the thirty heretics had consumed a deer's rotting carcass and washed it down with goat's urine, these substances having been transformed by Bridget Bishop into Lucifer's body and blood.

Throughout Abigail's tours Dunstan kept trying to impress her –

not only with his father's position as Witchfinder-Royal but also with the fact that he, Dunstan, stood to inherit the title. He flourished each demon-detecting tool as he would a piece of the True Cross. Joyfully Abigail stroked the bright pricking needles. The mask-o'-truth likewise enthralled her, as did the Paracelsus trident. Her brother's infatuation, Jennet surmised, traced largely to the male lust that Aunt Isobel had described in her treatise with such a peculiar mixture of chariness and celebration, for Abigail's twelve-year-old body had begun to acquire the topography of womanhood. Although Jennet's initial impulse was to lend her *A Woman's Garden of Pleasure and Pain*, the thought of this dissembling vixen finding herself pregnant ultimately proved so delectable that she decided to keep private her knowledge of cock-sheaths and fertility cycles.

Abigail, for her part, spoke seductively to Dunstan whenever the opportunity arose. 'My uncle's Barbados slave taught us how to divine our fortunes,' she said in her granular voice. 'You break an egg and drop the white in a bowl of water, and then you watch what shapes may appear. One time I beheld a coffin floating in the cloud, and I decided I was marked to marry a sexton, but now I know my husband will be a pricker, sending many a heretic to his grave.'

'A pricker's wife doth endure a hard lot,' Dunstan said. 'He stays away from home as long as any sailor.'

'I would wait for you, Dunstan,' Abigail said. ''Tis obvious you're destined to have an illustrious career. By century's end Massachusetts will be a-swarm with o'er ten thousand witches, for such was told to me in a dream by a golden-haired angel named Justine.'

When the trials themselves began, Abigail was obliged to spend each day in Salem-Town, presenting herself to the Court as a victim of *maleficium*. Dunstan went to every session, not so much to study his future vocation as to study Abigail. Each evening ere they drifted off to sleep in Captain Walcott's loft, Dunstan made Jennet listen whilst he recounted whatever grotesquery his friend had enacted that day. Pain figured prominently in many of Abigail's antics. 'Before the whole Court, the witch Goody Wildes bid Abby hold her hand o'er a lighted candle!' Dunstan exclaimed. Often Abigail's performance was simply disgusting. 'The hag Goody Martin made Abby stab herself in the stomach with a knitting needle!' On at least one occasion she resorted to self-exhibition. ''Twas an amazing sight, Jenny! Upon coming face-to-face with Goody Howe, Abby tore off every scrap of clothing and ran naked from the hall!'

The Court never convened on the Sabbath, and it also stood in recess on those days when the sheriff had scheduled an execution, so that everyone could witness the heretics' final moments. Despite Dunstan's ardent and repeated entreaties, Jennet refused to accompany him to any Salem hanging, for she felt that her appearance on Gallows Hill would sully Aunt Isobel's memory as surely as the epitaph she'd carved in Colchester had honoured it. One damp grey afternoon in September, however, she allowed Dunstan to lead her to an open field beside the courthouse, where 'something passing wonderful' supposedly awaited.

A man lay spread-eagled on the ground, his wrists and ankles tethered and staked, his torso supporting four oaken planks fastened in parallel with iron bands. At the prisoner's feet rose a mountain of granite blocks, each as large as an ox's head, around which clustered a dozen curious Salemites and a handful of Court officials. Judge Stoughton rapped his knuckles on the topmost block, as if to prove it a true stone and not a loaf of bread or block of cheese. Judge Hathorne made ready to savour his sot-weed, clamping his churchwarden pipe in his jaw. Judge Sewall read his Bible. Judge Corwin recited his *Pater Noster*.

Breaking from the knot of bystanders, a grinning Abigail scuttled towards Jennet and Dunstan. 'How marvellous that you've come! I so feared you would miss the first stone!'

'The prisoner's Giles Corey,' Dunstan explained to Jennet. 'For refusing to make his plea, innocent or nay, the stubborn old wizard's to receive a dose of the *peine forte et dure.*'

The sheriff approached the block mound, took hold of a particularly large stone and, as the blue veins bulged in his forehead and a grunt escaped his lips, set it atop the planks right above the prisoner's chest.

Mr Corey released a sound halfway betwixt a hog's squeal and a horse's whinny.

'Why doth the sheriff burden him so?' Jennet asked.

'They're going to crush the wizard flat,' Dunstan replied. 'Inch by inch, they'll press him to death.'

'Crush him?' Jennet rasped as sweat collected in her palms and bile filled her belly.

''Twill take him all morning to die,' Abigail said. 'Mayhap the whole day.'

The sheriff dropped a second granite block on the planks. Mr Corey groaned.

'Will you make your plea, sir?' inquired Judge Hathorne, puffing on his pipe.

'Another . . . stone,' Mr Corey gurgled.

'I shan't watch this!' Jennet screamed. ''Tis obscene!'

''Tis justice!' Dunstan retorted.

'Obscene as the torture of our aunt!'

'This Corey drinks the blood of newborn babes!' Abigail insisted as a third stone thudded against the planks. The prisoner hissed like an enraged viper, saliva bubbling through his teeth. 'Last night his spectral form pursued me 'round the barn with a butcher's cleaver!'

Before the sheriff could apply the fourth stone, Jennet turned and sprinted away, running down Dock Street as if in flight from a ravenous she-wolf. She reached the Walcott house and climbed the ladder to the sleeping loft, determined to lose herself in the benign inscrutability of Isaac Newton and the quintessential sanity of Isobel Mowbray. She lit a candle, then removed from beneath her bed both the *Principia Mathematica* and the *Woman's Garden*. Opening Professor Newton randomly, she beheld Theorem XLVI. 'If there be several bodies consisting of equal particles whose forces are as the distance of the places from each,' ran her translation, 'the force compounded of all the forces by which any corpuscle is attracted will tend to the common centre of gravity of the attracting bodies.' To her whirling brain it seemed that the proposition described precisely the relationship betwixt Mr Corey and the granite blocks.

That night, as she lay abed with Chapter One of her *Women's Garden*, 'Ever Since Eve', Dunstan appeared unbidden at her side and subjected her to a recapitulation of the *peine forte et dure*. 'Hathorne kept saying "Plead!" and Corey kept gasping "More weight!" Is that not an amazing exchange? "Plead!" "More weight!" "Plead!" "More weight!" When Corey's tongue came snaking from his mouth, the sheriff shoved it back with his cane!'

More weight. What did the poor wretch mean? Jennet speculated that his command was a cry of defiance. *You scoundrels can ne'er defeat me. More weight.* There was heroism in the late Mr Corey, almost as much as in Aunt Isobel. But then a second, entirely horrible theory presented itself. *Murder me faster, please. More weight. End my agony. More weight.*

Whilst Dunstan slipped away, she blew out the candle and watched the moonlight catch the thread of rising smoke. Pulling up the coverlet, she hugged the *Principia* to her breast. 'I must have faith,' she whispered. Somewhere within these sacred pages lay the formula that would keep other innocents from suffering Giles Corey's fate. Somewhere amongst these propositions, hidden behind the scholia, secluded betwixt the lemmas, lurked a method by which the world might learn to separate God's laws from gossamer fancies and eternal truths from

mere

*

Opinions,
I grant you, are quite
the cheapest coin of the intellectual
realm, and normally I claim no special privileges
for mine. In the case of the Salem Witch Trials, however, I feel that my subjective views occupy an echelon above mere crankiness and beyond rote contrariness – an echelon, in other words, that might be called insight. I have an opinion, for example, concerning the affectation by which the events of 1692 are routinely termed 'the great witchcraft hysteria', as if the whole affair were but a passing aberration. Yes, Abigail Williams and her band of bitches might be accurately labelled hysterics, but the people who took the girls' shenanigans seriously were paragons of sobriety. The Salem tragedy could never have occurred were not an aggressively rational witch-hunting apparatus already in place throughout Western civilization. Hysteria, my foot.

Then there's the reflex by which the accusers are labeled 'children'. The term is appropriate enough for Abigail Williams, Betty Parris and Anne Putnam Junior, but Mary Warren, Elizabeth Hubbard, Mercy Lewis and Mary Walcott were all in late adolescence, and the adult accusers included Anne Putnam Senior, Goodwife Bibber, Goodwife

Pope and — before the machinery of suspicion turned against him — Giles Corey.

I must tell you about my recent return to the scene of Judge Stoughton's crimes. It's October. The air is brittle, cold as a witch's tit. Through bookish will I've taken possession of Larry Hoffman, a real estate agent, lonely, befuddled. Courtesy of my host's sensorium, I soon realize that a town called Danvers has arisen on the former site of Salem Village. It boasts a Domino's Pizza, a hamburger joint, and several drugstores dispensing such decidedly non-Puritan products as latex condoms and the latest issue of *Playboy*.

Bored with Danvers, I compel my proxy to venture south to Salem proper, so that I might see for myself how the witch-hunters' descendants have accommodated their heritage. We arrive in the middle of a month-long celebration that styles itself 'Salem Haunted Happenings at Halloween'. As the 'Haunted Happenings' programme puts it, 'The festivities offer something for everyone: parades, concerts, psychic fairs, costume balls, tours of Salem's great historic sites, and restaurants galore.' Among the scheduled events are the Crowning of the King and Queen of Halloween, the Costumed Dog Contest, Kid's Day, the Fright Train from Boston (six Pullman cars crammed with out-of-work actors playing zombies), and, most delightful of all, the Official Cat of Salem Contest, in which each entrant is judged by appearance, personality, and an autobiographical essay (presumably written by the cat's owner). Beyond this seasonal jollity, 'Haunted Happenings' customers can avail themselves of the year-round attractions: the Salem Witch Museum, the Witch Dungeon Museum, Boris Karloff's Witch Museum, the Salem Wax Museum of Witches and Seafarers, the Haunted Witch Village, Mayhem Manor, Terror on the Wharf, and, for the Nathaniel Hawthorne scholar in the family, the House of the Seven Gables. It's obvious that in the recent past our Salemites confronted a difficult choice: should they continue feeling vaguely apologetic about an ancient miscarriage of justice, or should they seize the high ground and become the Halloween capital of the world?

Two days after leaving the town I submit a letter to the company that runs the whole show, suggesting three sure-fire events for next year's instalment of 'Haunted Happenings'.

Cat Pressing on the Common. This vivid historical demonstration gives Salem visitors a precise sense of the *peine forte et dure* suffered by Giles Corey on 19 September 1692. Participants will be drawn from the town's stray cat population, plus losers of the Official Cat of Salem Contest who may now wish to die.

All Night Noose Dance. Special shoulder harnesses enable you to 'swing with your partner' from the oaks atop Gallows Hill. Prizes in the following categories: Best Dressed Couple, Liveliest Kickers, Famous Last Words – plus the coveted Rebecca Nurse Endurance Trophy.

Dorcas Good Memorial Leg-Irons Race. This event celebrates the feistiness of accused witch Dorcas Good, aged four, who went irretrievably insane after lying in a freezing cell for eight months, loaded with leg irons and shackled to a wall. On Halloween morning, after bolting on their irons, participants will convene at the corner of Derby and Main, then jog competitively to Pickering Wharf.

I further suggest that, having rehabilitated the Salem Witch Trials, the company should consider doing the same with such thrilling historical dramas as the Albigensian Crusade, the massacre of the Huguenots, the bombing of Hiroshima, and Hitler's Final Solution.

'The Nazi concentration camps in particular hold tremendous untapped festivity potential,' I tell the company's president. 'Yes, there's some sort of Holocaust Museum in Washington, D C, but it's a stuffy and self-important place, utterly lacking your lightness of touch. The time isn't quite right yet, but within a few generations people will doubtless be talking about "the great genocide hysteria, that unfortunate chapter in the saga of the Twentieth Century". Meanwhile, you can begin laying plans for "Holocaust Happenings at Nuremberg", including parades, contests, concerts, tours of the city's great historic sites, and restaurants galore.' It will be especially important, I note, to offer the public a variety of tie-in merchandise. 'Towards this end, I have contacted the Lionel Corporation about a special Auschwitz Electric Train Set, complete with a 4–8–4 steam locomotive and five box cars.'

I haven't yet received a reply, but if the company deigns to write
back, I suspect they will claim that my suggestions are
offensive beyond redemption, outrageous
beyond apology, and in
atrociously
bad

*

'Taste
this,' Dunstan
said, offering Jennet
a lopsided and strange-smelling
confection that vaguely resembled a loaf of
bread. They were in the loft of the Walcott house, hurriedly
dressing for bed before October's chill seeped into their bones. 'Set the
merest portion against your palate, and for a few amazing moments
you'll see pictures from the demon world – dancing phoukas, mayhap,
or goblins with burning eyes.'

'What is it?' she asked.

'A witch-cake,' he said. 'Abby baked it. Have a nibble.'

Jennet broke off a piece of witch-cake and slid it into her mouth.
She chewed. The morsel had a barbed and bitter flavour, but no
phantoms appeared in her brain. 'What ingredients?'

'Molasses, honey, rye meal, and Abby's urine,' he replied. 'The
recipe came from Mr Parris's Barbados slave. 'Tis an infallible way to
prove a person's been bewitched.'

With an explosive movement of her lips and cheeks, Jennet spat out
as many cake fragments as her tongue could summon. 'How durst you
feed me piss?!'

'No phantoms?' Dunstan asked plaintively.

'You addlepated pig!'

Dunstan's visage became supremely woeful. 'I feared as much,' he
said. 'Abby can see them, but I cannot.'

''Tis evident she grows more frantic by the hour.'

Her brother nodded in reluctant agreement. The witch-cake, he
explained, owed its creation to the fact that of the fifteen suspects
tried and convicted in September, only seven had gone to Gallows
Hill. Two of the eight spared women were with child, and two had

promised to name the others in their covens – but in the remaining four cases the acquittals reflected Judge Stoughton's suspicion that the witnesses weren't truly bewitched. Through confections of the sort Jennet had just sampled, Abby hoped to establish that she and her associates were full-blown victims of demonic influence.

'She can bake a hundred witch-cakes, and she'll ne'er regain her lost stature,' Jennet said.

'The hunt is losing momentum,' Dunstan admitted, sighing expans-ively. 'Father says Governor Phipps means to reprieve any and all persons convicted by the testimony of a Salem-Village daughter.'

'He sounds a sensible man.'

'Piffle! Had Abby not cried out Phipps's wife, he would yet be the Court's great champion.'

'She cried out the Governor's wife?' Jennet said, appalled.

'Right to Judge Stoughton's face.'

'I'll say this for your friend – she's not wanting in spunk.'

Two nights later, Walter sat his children down before Captain Walcott's blazing hearth. Studying his countenance in the firelight, Jennet saw that the trials had taken a severe toll on the man. His features were shrunken and sallow, as if painted on the surface of a rotting gourd.

'Governor Phipps was in Salem-Town today,' he said wearily. 'We drank cider at Ingersoll's. There is good news and bad. The good is that he hath recognized my office and will pay my salary as long as I ne'er consult with Miss Williams's band, whom he calls "those damned mendacious minxes".'

Jennet could not restrain an un-Christian impulse to flash her brother a sardonic grin. He absorbed this disembodied blow, then fixed his eyes on the floor.

'And the bad?' she asked.

'The bad is that these great trials are now at an end,' Walter said, 'for the Governor hath dissolved the Court.'

'*Dissolved* it?' Dunstan wailed.

'Aye.'

'Do you mean we must return to Haverhill?' the boy asked.

'Indeed.'

'But I fancy Salem-Village,' Dunstan protested.

'You fancy Abigail Williams,' Jennet noted.

'Our house is in Haverhill,' Walter said firmly.

Dunstan winced, and despite a plethora of distressing matters — his willingness to think their aunt a heretic, his enthusiasm for Mr Corey's pressing, his offering of the witch-cake — Jennet felt a sudden sympathy for him. Even an apprentice pricker deserved some measure of affection in his cup, and Abby had evidently supplied him with a plenary portion.

'I'faith, sir, Mr Phipps doth sorely misjudge my friend,' Dunstan said. 'Miss Williams can see the future in the waterborne white of an egg.'

'In an *egg*?' moaned Walter, scowling.

'And the angel Justine hath disclosed to her a great demon empire arising in this province. Mark me, Father, the *real* Massachusetts cleansing is yet to come.'

'I don't doubt it, son, and we shall keep our pricking needles sharp. But for the moment we must plant our garden.'

Jennet was not a week back in Haverhill when she realized that in her absence the citizens' longstanding fear of a Nimacook attack had progressed to a contagion of terror. Not only had the apprehensive Colonists erected palisades and watch-towers along their northern border, they had organized a militia. The commanding officer, Nathaniel Saltonstall — the same Nathaniel Saltonstall who'd rounded out the judges' panel at Salem (though the Rebecca Nurse affair had inspired him to resign in protest ere finishing his service) — lost no time convincing Walter and Dunstan to join his stalwart company, an obligation that had father and son marching across the Common every Saturday morning, firearms propped against their shoulders, powder-horns oscillating at their hips. Walter drilled with his deer-hunting musket. Dunstan's weapon was an English fowling-piece he'd received from a wheelwright's son in trade for his ink sketch of Goody Nurse's hanging.

The more she pondered the matter, the more Jennet realized how perplexed she was by the Nimacooks' hostility, and so she approached the sole scholarly mind in Haverhill, a Puritan divine named Malachi Foster.

'Why do the Indians seek to destroy us?' she asked.

The Reverend Foster replied in convoluted sentences, each more tangled than the most beleaguered line in her Cicero translations, but eventually a lucid answer emerged. The Indians, it seemed, were wroth over the Colonists' appropriation of their lands. When Jennet bade Mr Foster elaborate, he solemnly described the stratagem whereby a Puritan settler would repeatedly send his livestock roving across a Nimacook planter's maize hills, trampling the Indian's crops and breaking his spirit, until he saw no alternative but to move further west. An equally effective manoeuvre consisted in seizing an Indian's acres as punishment for some infraction of Puritan law, such as drinking in public, dishonouring the Sabbath, or taking the Creator's name in vain.

Although the Nimacooks' outrage made 'a kind of logical sense', Mr Foster admitted, it enjoyed 'no legal or moral standing'. As far back as 1619, Governor Winthrop had decreed that most of America fell under the rubric of *vacuum domicilium*: given that the various Algonquin and Iroquois tribes had not 'subdued' but merely 'occu-pied' their plantations, hunting parks, trapping grounds and fishing streams, they had only a 'natural' and not a 'civil' claim to these domains. All such territory was in fact 'waste' available for seizure. But the ultimate authority by which the Puritans encroached on the Nimacooks came from On High. In Mr Foster's view, Psalm 2:8 could not be more explicit: *Ask of me, and I shall give thee the heathen for thine inheritance, and the uttermost parts of the Earth for thy possession.*

That spring and summer Jennet's father conducted the modest cleansing of 1693, a project that took him and Dunstan first to Topsfield and thence to Rowley. While the prickers managed to indict six Satanists in these villages, the newly created Massachusetts Superior Court acquitted all but two. A propitious ratio, she decided, though not propitious enough to put her soul at ease. Whenever she walked through Haverhill on a mission to buy flour, mend harness, grind knives, or absorb gossip, she could not help scanning the children's faces, wondering who amongst them might be destined for the gallows. Would a jury one day see diabolism in the sprightly eyes and mischievous smirk of the tavern-keeper's daughter? Would the miller's slow-witted niece ultimately stand convicted of carnal congress with incubi? Would the tanner's bulky son go to the hangman in consequence of a pricker's tests?

The hunt of 1694 proved the leanest yet — four arrests, one execution. Throughout the subsequent winter Walter perused his private library, ferreting out obscure bits of demonological lore and synthesizing them into prolix monographs that he then dispatched to his London benefactors. By showing the Privy Council that he was not a mere pricker but a scholar of near-Thomist perspicacity, he sought to cast himself as a man worthy of respect, solicitude, and an increase in salary. He'd grown particularly obsessed with an assertion in George Sinclair's *Sermons by Satan*: the odd notion that the sensitivity of a Paracelsus trident doubled following its immersion in a kettle filled with boiling frog's blood. Thus it was that, as April's ubiquitous buds became a lush tapestry of May wildflowers, Walter decreed that, upon completing their chores each day, Jennet and Dunstan must scour the Haverhill fens for frogs, and by month's end they'd caught a dozen.

Although Dunstan preferred hunting collaboratively, so that he might fill his sister's ear with further accounts of Abby's histrionics in Salem, Jennet usually elected to search alone. The conjunction of swamp and solitude launched her thoughts on unexpected trajectories — and yet, woolly as they were, she came to realize that these musings shared a common theme: escape. For she was almost eighteen now, old enough to make her way to Boston and find employment as a serving-maid, housekeeper, governess . . . any such position would do, provided it allowed her at least one free afternoon each week, a few golden hours for grappling with the *Principia Mathematica*. In her mind a sacred vow took shape. No matter what obstacles emerged, she would flee on Aunt Isobel's birthday, the seventh of July. Even if she awoke shivering with a fever, even if the Nimacooks were proclaiming an intention to kill every white wayfarer who ventured across their lands, even if a terrible thunder-gust was blowing through the town, hurtling sheep into the air and turning the streets to raging rivers — come that dawn, she would pack up her *Principia* and her *Woman's Garden* and quit Haverhill forever.

But first she would remove her father's licence from his door and rip it into a thousand pieces.

The last afternoon in June found sister and brother sitting by the Merrimack, Jennet contemplating a cohort of honey-bees as they fertilized some bergamot, Dunstan sketching with his sticks of coloured wax crayons. For a subject he'd selected a rock formation that surmounted the cliff-face on the far shore: a granite horse's head emerging from the promontory like an enormous chess knight – not an ordinary horse, but a creature of mythic ambition, eager to pull Hector's chariot, carry Alexander into battle against Xerxes, or bear Sir Percival on his Grail quest. A peculiar melancholy took hold of Jennet. Within a few days of her flight, she would surely long for Dunstan – not Dunstan the apprentice pricker but Dunstan the accomplished draughtsman, Dunstan whose eye and hand and brain were so felicitously interlinked, like colours in a sunbeam or voices in a fugue.

She leaned over the bank and added her reflection to the languid water. The woman who looked back boasted a full face framed by abundant auburn hair. Her chin was a tad presumptuous, and the tip of her nose took an unseemly upward turn, and yet her cheeks were stately, her eyes wide, and she was quite possibly beautiful.

Dunstan approached, adding his own form to the liquid image as he placed in her hands his drawing of the horse-head promontory.

'A gift.'

'You have captured the beast in all his majesty,' she said, rising. 'Do you want to know my wish? I hope that one day soon you will meet in this province some person of aesthetic sensibility, and he will betimes appoint himself your patron, sending you to Italy that you might become the prize pupil of a master painter.'

His lips lengthened into a taut and wistful smile. 'Italy seems to me as far away as those Jovian moons of which my sister is so fond.'

'Florence and Rome are indeed a great distance, and yet withal they lie closer to your heart than does that parchment scrap on Father's door.' She folded the drawing and slid it into her dress pocket. 'You will go to Italy, Dunstan. I can see it in these waters.'

'Jenny, you're a keen young woman, competent in philosophy and mathematics, but you'll ne'er have Abby's powers of scrying.'

They resumed their search, travelling south along the marshy bank.

As dusk came to Haverhill, the frog-hunters admitted to each other that the day's expedition had failed. Abandoning the shore, they ascended to firmer ground, then turned and headed north along an embankment thick with sunflowers that – just then, just there – struck Jennet as no less magnificent than the spires of Cambridge-Town. To their left the Merrimack caught the fire of the setting sun, so that its waters now seemed an alchemical amalgam of molten rubies and liquid cinnabar.

'I'Christ, 'tis the Devil's own brood!'

She spun, glancing downstream. The object of Dunstan's distress lay a quarter-mile away: a flotilla of Nimacook canoes, perhaps sixteen in all, rounding the lee of Contoocook Isle like a huge, white, seg-mented worm. In each vessel sat four armed savages, their paddles thrashing madly against the current.

'Satan hath sent an entire legion against us!' Dunstan shouted.

Already the canoes were putting to shore, the Indians brandishing tomahawks, battle-clubs, and French muskets. War-paint spilled across their faces in hideous streaks and encircled their naked torsos like the stripes on a coral snake.

Jennet experienced a crushing sensation in her chest, as if she were being subjected to the *peine forte et dure*. She took a deep breath and followed Dunstan as he bolted from the embankment and ran pell-mell into the woods. They skirted boulders, ducked beneath fallen trees, and overleapt gullies, until finally the outlying barns and granaries of Haverhill came into view, and then – praise God – Kembel's Ordin-ary. Her brother's intention to alert the town proved superfluous, however, for the militia was already marching down Mill Street, Major Saltonstall at the head, his drawn sabre thrust forward like a bowsprit. Though free of war-paint, the soldiers looked formidable in their own right, their brows and cheeks burned raspberry-red from countless hours of planting beneath the New World sun, their muskets supplemented by well-honed axes and sharpened sickles.

Catching sight of his children, Walter abruptly abandoned the company – so abruptly that he crashed into the cadence-master and sent his drum rolling down the street like a fallen barrel – then rushed forward and seized their wrists.

Jennet, terrified, tried without success to speak.

'Savages!' Dunstan bleated. 'Murderous heathen savages!'

'Oh, my sweetest darlings,' Walter gasped, dragging his children towards Kembel's Ordinary.

At last the words broke from Jennet's larynx and made their way past her vibrating teeth. 'What will happen to us, Father? Are you and Dunstan to be butchered? Am I to be stolen away and made to run the gauntlet?'

Instead of answering, Walter hauled them onto the veranda and pointed towards a pyramid of cider casks. 'Behold your protection, children! 'Tis a God-given fortress against the tawnies' spears and arrows!'

Without a moment's hesitation Jennet stepped behind the casks and crouched down.

'Sir, by your leave I shall fetch my fowling-piece and fight by your side,' Dunstan said.

'Nay, lad.' Walter firmed his grip on his musket. 'Thou art marked to become the next Witchfinder-Royal. I say that Satan hath sent these savages for no purpose but to destroy the son of Walter Stearne!'

A preposterous notion, Jennet decided, but Dunstan evidently believed otherwise, for he lost no time joining her in the supposed citadel.

'My dear ones, know that I love you more than my life!' Walter cried, then dashed away to rejoin his fellow soldiers as they marched onto the Common.

Major Saltonstall arranged the company in a dense cluster: a stockade of flesh meant to stand against not only the party of screaming savages now charging from the west but also the second such band arriving from the east, the third from the north, and likewise the fourth – the raiders who'd come by canoe – from the south. Though ignorant of military strategy, Jennet suspected that in contriving to attack the town from all directions at once the Nimacooks had achieved a victory well before launching their first canoe.

The staccato sound of discharging muskets filled the air. Jennet's quaverings became more intense, and then a flux seized her, and she vomited up the undigested portion of her midday meal. Dunstan's fear took the form of a beshitting, though he seemed oblivious to both the load in his breeches and the concomitant stench. He attempted to recite his *Pater Noster*, managing it no better than would the average accused Satanist standing before a magistrate.

'Our Father, which – which – which art – in – in – H-Heaven – which art in – b-b-be thy name!'

The cider casks afforded a reasonably safe vantage from which a person might observe the lopsided battle, but Jennet averted her gaze. Between the burning of Isobel Mowbray and the crushing of Giles Corey, she was already as well instructed in cruelty as in Euclid; she needed no further lesson. Instead she fixed on the cask beneath her jaw, contemplating the splinters and troughs, the nubbins and grooves. If only she might through some benign witchery turn herself into an insect, an ant perhaps, or a termite, any beastie small enough to disappear amidst these little ravines and forsake the human world forever.

'Be thy name – be thy name – be thy name!'

She clamped her hands over her ears, muting the cries of pain and the hacking cough of the muskets, sensations a hundred times more terrible than Dunstan's stink.

''Steeth!' he shrieked. 'The day belongs to Satan!'

She glanced towards the Common. True to her expectations, both the major's strategy and the militia that had attempted to enact it lay in ruins. The flesh stockade had collapsed into a thing that seemed not so much a collection of battlefield casualties as a festering fen in the heart of Hell, the damned souls struggling to raise their snapped limbs and cracked skulls from the muck.

Having destroyed Haverhill's defences, the Nimacooks now abandoned the Common and set about razing the town itself, jabbing firebrands into hay bales, hurling torches through windows, planting constellations of burning arrows in shutters and doors. An uncanny wind took source in Haverhill, a cyclone composed of the Nimacooks' triumphant whoops and the English settlers' screams.

Jennet and Dunstan sprinted from the veranda and hurried onto the Common, where their father lay supine beneath a sycamore, holding his musket as a drowning sailor might clutch an errant spar from his sunken ship. His chest had received three arrows. Blood pooled around the shafts; more blood spilled from the corners of his mouth. He shivered as if lying naked in snow, although Jennet couldn't say whether this phenomenon traced to his physical suffering or to his dread of dying unshriven.

'My children,' he moaned. 'My – lovely – children.'

She surveyed the scene with an attitude more akin to curiosity than grief, the sort of circumscribed astonishment she'd brought to 'Christ at the Whipping-Post', the engraved frontispiece of the Reverend Foster's illustrated Bible. There was sadness in this picture, and pity too, but it was not her sadness, not her pity.

'Today a hundred tawnies shall die by my hand,' Dunstan rasped.

'You must – save yourself – for the – cleansing – ahead,' Walter mumbled.

'The great cleansing, aye.'

'Your birthright – 'tis on – bed-chamber door.'

As Jennet studied the Golgothan triad of arrows rising from Walter's bosom, Dunstan poured promises into the witchfinder's ear. He vowed that he would hunt down every Satanist in America – male and female, white and Indian, Protestant and Catholic: all would feel his needle, all would know the noose.

The instant Jennet bent low to address her father, the arrows finished their work. 'I do thank thee, sir, for thy part in giving me life,' she told the corpse. 'Beyond that, however, I hold thee a scoundrel, and I shall dedicate my life's remaining years to thwarting all cleansers everywhere.'

She rose and, exchanging glances with Dunstan, saw by his livid countenance that he'd overheard her malediction.

'You truly hated him,' he said, tears rolling down his cheeks.

'Not always. Not before Colchester Castle.'

'A daughter who curses her father to his face' – he darted away – 'doth thereby damn herself to Hell.'

'Then upon my arrival I shall curse him to his face again,' she said, following.

Side by side, the orphans raced along the burning streets. Everywhere they turned, the conflagration flourished, blurring the barns, stables, mills, taverns, and shops into a great red storm, the Jovian Hurricane come to Earth. As the fire consumed the buildings, the Indians next applied their rage directly to the Colonists. Haverhill became a slaughter-house, an anatomization theatre, a haemorrhaging landscape of craters gouged by battle-clubs, cavities carved by musket-balls and gorges sculpted by tomahawks. With mounting horror Jennet realized that a Nimacook gauged no murder complete until he'd used his knife to add another shaggy trophy to his belt, peeling scalp from skull with the insouciance of an aristocrat removing the rind from an orange.

By the time they reached their house, she was expecting to find it ablaze, a premonition that proved lamentably correct. Helplessly she stood before the flames. She imagined them doing their worst, devouring the paper treasures within. Dunstan's crayon drawings. Aunt Isobel's treatise. Newton's letter to Mirringate Hall. The *Principia Mathematica*.

'The Lord is my shepherd!' her brother cried, rushing towards the burning porch.

'Dunstan, no!'

The foolish boy crossed the threshold – 'I shall have my birthright!' – and vanished.

A numbness spread through her, locking her legs in place, fixing her hips, taking the life from her hands. It seemed that she'd become an exhibit in Dr Cavendish's museum, a pickled freak afloat in a jar. A minute passed, and another, and then the jar shattered with a thunderous roar, and she looked up to see the house collapse upon itself. Squalls of fiery ash swirled through the air.

The remorse that now seized her was asymmetrical, the lesser share devoted to the loss of *A Woman's Garden*, the greater to her brother's immolation. Was this catastrophe best interpreted as Providence in action, the Indians serving as implements of a divine plan to destroy a nascent witchfinder? Or had Jehovah followed a more passive course, noting Dunstan's predicament and declining to deliver him?

Gradually she grew aware of a dozen shadowy Nimacooks standing in the vegetable garden, trampling down the pole-beans as they laughed amongst themselves. A discordance of wails, moans and sobs reached her ears. The braves pointed mocking fingers towards two young Haverhill women of about Jennet's age, both insane with fright, each hugging a tattered Bible. A leather halter coiled around the taller woman's neck, encircled the throat of her companion, and passed finally into the hands of a looming savage with slithering black serpents painted on his chest. Now Jennet received a tether of her own, binding her to the other girls, though the experience seemed less like a yoking than its opposite. She felt sundered from everything: the white race, the New World, the spinning planet – sundered from her own body and brain.

Pushing and shoving their threaded captives, the triumphant Indians skirted the raging holocaust that had once been Milk Street. As the war party and its human booty passed the town limits, the pulsing heat of the flames yielded gradually to the chill of evening. Jennet took care to march in step with her fellow prisoners, lest the strap around her neck suddenly become a noose. They proceeded through the fields, the woods, then down to the Merrimack, where the rest of the war party waited by the beached canoes, attending their wounded.

Whether the tawnies were Lucifer's lieutenants, as her late father had believed, or God's agents, as she had recently imagined, Jennet could not help admiring the stoicism with which the hurt ones submitted to the necessary treatments. Directly before her, a sinewy warrior grimaced but did not cry out as a Nimacook physician wrenched his fractured leg straight. Not far beyond, a brave in a feather headdress gritted his teeth whilst a surgeon probed his shoulder with a knife, seeking to dislodge a musket-ball.

She glanced towards the river, its waters lit by the glow of the dying town. Wrapped in deerskins, six Indian corpses lay along the shore like pieces of driftwood. Nearby stood three more white daughters, weeping and retching and pissing themselves, their throats linked like braided bulbs of garlic. One captive pressed a silver cross to her breast. Another cradled a rag poppet. The third grasped a small oval portrait of a dainty woman with a kindly face.

As the Nimacooks untied the tether and led her to the canoes, Jennet realized that she too would be bearing away a fragment of civilization that night, Dunstan's sketch of the horse-head promontory. She lifted her eyes and fixed on the soaring cliff. The stone creature had vanished, claimed by the darkness. In a few hours the horse would reappear, of course, and later that day some passing traveller might pause to appreciate its splendour, his thoughts turning naturally to Hector or Alexander or Percival. But she would not be that pilgrim. God alone knew where the morning would find her: moving through the forest perhaps, or approaching a Nimacook village — or dead, quite likely, dead as Dunstan, dead as her father, lying in an obscure glade, a tomahawk in her back or an arrow in her heart, the rising sun glancing off the whiteness of her skinless crown.

CHAPTER THE SIXTH

—————

Our Heroine Variously Occupies an Algonquin Wigwam, a Philadelphia Townhouse, and the Nether Reaches of Newtonian Theology

Early in the seventh year of her life Jennet developed an intense yearning to possess some true and valuable memory of the mother she'd never known, and by her eleventh birthday she'd managed to summon the desired tableau. The veil of forgetfulness lifted, and there was Margaret Noakes Stearne, bloated with Dunstan, sitting alongside Jennet on the parlour floor in Colchester and fashioning one of her famous aeolian machines, a wondrous kite of white birch and red silk. 'In the spring you and I shall fly it,' Jennet's mother told her, holding up the finished contraption. ''Twill glide above every steeple in England. I'faith, 'twill soar clear to Heaven!'

Had Jennet's fourteen-month-old brain in fact recorded this scene, or was the recollection but a phantasm? She didn't know – though she could say with certainty that the flying of the red kite had never occurred, for by the spring of 1680 Margaret Noakes Stearne lay dead atop the birthing-bed, the newborn Dunstan squirming betwixt her thighs. And yet Jennet's memory of the comely woman extolling the kite felt real, and whenever, as now, she found herself hedged by uncertainty and peril, she would conjure up this benevolent ghost and avail herself of its comforts.

Before fleeing Haverhill, the Nimacooks separated the six white daughters from one another, forcing each into a different canoe, doubt-less to prevent their planning a coordinated escape. All during the dark and frigid journey down the Merrimack, Jennet knelt in the leading canoe and fixed her thoughts on her mother and the kite. *In the spring you and I shall fly it.* Aided by the river's current and the braves' furious paddling, the flotilla made a rapid retreat from the burning town. *'Twill glide above every steeple in England.* The passing water reflected the Indians' torches, now deployed as beacons in the bows, so that the Merrimack seemed home to some fantastic breed of luminous fish. *I'faith, 'twill soar clear to Heaven.*

The night was at its deepest when the savages put to shore. It took them but a few minutes to conceal their canoes beneath mounds of branches and boughs, which they'd evidently harvested that morning in anticipation of a victory. Having thus confounded whatever rescue parties the Haverhill survivors might launch upon the river, the savages snuffed their torches, shouldered their dead, and gathered up their spoils – including, Jennet noticed with a surge of nausea, several sacks of scalps. After aligning themselves with the waxing moon, the Nimacooks led the white daughters through a stand of cattails and thence into the woods, setting out along a path speckled with fireflies and limned by the glow of Earth's lone satellite. The Stygian forest stretched in all directions, coils of fog entwining the branches, tree-frogs chirping within the hollow trunks. With each step Jennet's misery compounded. Her terror took on a life of its own, a thousand animal-cules of dread cruising her veins like the blood-borne imps Aunt Isobel had expected the *experimentum magnus* to yield. She hugged herself, and ground her teeth, and put one foot before the other.

An hour's march brought the war party to a wide granite shelf rising from the earth to form an immense cavern. Stores of provisions lay everywhere within – barrels of salted fish, casks of water, ceramic jars filled with dried berries and cured venison, piles of moose-hide bed-ding. Apparently this vast chamber was the Nimacooks' equivalent of an inn, a bountiful and capacious road-house marking the way into their territory.

The Indians relighted their torches, revealing near the grotto's entrance a large pit, freshly dug, waiting to receive the six skin-wrapped corpses. A burial ensued, brief and spare – no prayers, no eulogies, no moment of silence – though Jennet supposed that under peacetime conditions the savages accorded their dead a greater regard. The only whiff of ceremony occurred when a pensive brave with a yellow star-burst on his stomach leaned over the grave and set atop each body a soapstone pipe and a small clay pot filled with tobacco.

In obeisance to a series of gestures from their captors, the women removed their shoes and dropped them into the pit. Whilst three young warriors shovelled back the dirt, a third distributed new footwear to the prisoners, deerskin moccasins secured with thongs. At first this ritual perplexed Jennet, but then she grasped its logic: a moccasin, she realized, left no mark upon the world, no track the men of Haverhill might pursue in search of their stolen daughters.

By now it was obvious that each captive had her own private keeper. Jennet's guardian was a stolid young man with a horizontal crescent moon painted across his chest, the horns pricking his nipples. He'd used the same pigment to give himself a feline countenance, a lynx's perhaps, or a panther's. His hair, like that of his brother savages, was greased with rendered bear fat. The cavern gathered and compacted the collective scent, which seemed to penetrate not only Jennet's nasal passages but every bone in her head. It was a protean odour, always shifting, now revolting, now beguiling, now benumbing, now bracing, as if refracted through some olfactory equivalent of a prism.

The lynx-faced man filled a wooden bowl with venison and berries. As he proffered this spartan dinner, its savoury smell somehow overpowered the bear grease to fill Jennet's nostrils, and she realized that despite the day's many disasters she would consume the entire portion.

'Thank you,' she said, and he responded with a short declaration in his own tongue.

Later, after captors and captives had finished eating, Lynx Man dipped a gourd-ladle into a water cask and, presenting Jennet with the measure, spoke again in Nimacook. When she gave him an uncomprehending look, he attempted a sentence in halting French: '*Ce soir nous coucherons ici.*' We shall sleep here this evening.

She drank eagerly, sucking every drop from the ladle. '*Merci.*'

'*Je veux vous montrer quelque chose.*' I want to show you something.

'*Ou'est-ce que c'est?*'

'*Suivez-moi.*'

Lynx Man borrowed a torch from the surgeon, then bade her follow him deep into the grotto. She reasoned that he did not intend to murder her — not after all the trouble his tribe had taken in abducting the white daughters — but she couldn't exclude the possibility that he meant to make her the object of his lust. The sheathed knife protruding from his belt suddenly seemed as threatening as a puff adder, and images of ravishment filled her mind as he guided her into an alcove the size of a livery stall.

'*Voilà*,' Lynx Man said.

Pictures emerged from the blackness, some executed in charcoal, others in paint. As her keeper raised the torch aloft, she beheld a band of savages hurling spears at an elk . . . a lone hunter setting a deadfall for an approaching bear . . . another hunter laying a snare for a rabbit . . . an archer bringing down a partridge with an arrow . . . a squaw trapping fish in a weir.

'My brother was an artist,' she said, slipping a hand into her dress pocket. Her fingers brushed Dunstan's sketch of the horse-head promontory. '*Mon frère était un artiste.*'

Lynx Man said nothing.

The flickering of the torch imparted to the images an illusion of movement, so that the elk seemed to leap, the bear to lumber, the rabbit to scamper, the partridge to plummet, the fish to swim. Each illustrated Indian shivered with the thrill of the hunt, and now Jennet shivered as well, and then her tears began to flow, and they did not stop flowing until, three hours later, lying on a moose-hide mattress in the savages' road-house, the bear grease drilling through her brain, the torches decorating the walls with black lapping shadows, she drifted off to sleep.

At first light Lynx Man and the others scrubbed the paint from their bodies, whereupon the forced march began, the savages pressing their prisoners ever westward. The Indians did not pause to break their fast, nor did they halt for a midday meal, but instead moved deeper and deeper into the conifer forest, eating and drinking as they went — venison from bulrush baskets, water from leather bottles — occasionally sharing these provisions with the white daughters. As the sun dipped towards the horizon, the war party at last crossed into the bounteous and sprawling estates of the Algonquin Nimacook.

According to Jennet's comprehension of her keeper's French, each Haverhill prisoner was destined for a different village. Evidently her translation was accurate, for upon reaching a sun-dappled glade the company fractured like a dropped mirror, with no two daughters assigned to the same band. Suddenly aware that they might never see one another again, the young women squirmed free of their guardians and came together in a communal embrace. For a full minute the Indians permitted the prisoners to say their farewells, and then the great scattering began.

Led by Lynx Man, Jennet's band walked silently through the forest, bearing their sacks of spoils across mounds of brown needles shed by the firs and hemlocks. Within an hour the trees yielded to brush, which in time melted away to reveal a river: the Shawsheen, her keeper called it, as roiling as the Merrimack was tame. Here the band turned north, proceeding along a shore of such floral fecundity – violets, honeysuckle, clematis, buttercups – that only Dunstan's sweetest smelling crayons could have done it justice. By degrees her dread declined into simple foreboding, and the reeling shock of losing her father and brother became, regarding Walter, indifference, and, concerning Dunstan, the manageable ache of grief.

'I know a bank where the wild thyme blows,' she muttered, gesturing towards the blossoms, 'where oxlips and the nodding violet grows.'

'*Quoi?*' Lynx Man asked.

'Shakespeare,' Jennet replied.

'*Votre nom est Shakespeare?*' Your name is Shakespeare?

'*Non, je m'appelle Jennet,*' she said.

'*Et je m'appelle Pussough.*' I call myself Pussough.

At length the band drew within view of a broad, undulating field, its gentle slopes dotted with small earth-mounds from which emerged tangled arrays of corn, beans and squash. A score of Indian women moved amidst the crops, prising up weeds with quahog-shell hoes and using these same implements to frighten away rabbits.

Upon realizing that the warriors were back from Haverhill, the women abandoned their plantation and headed for the riverbank. They ranged in age from pubescent girls to crones, but their clothing was nearly identical: grass mantles and deerskin skirts, with nary a cap or bonnet amongst them. Apparently no one from Pussough's village had died in the attack, for every wife, sister, daughter, aunt, mother and grandmother retained her smile throughout the various overlapping accounts of the great battle, and when the warriors finished reciting their tales a raucous celebration followed, the plantation ringing with bright laughter and a high wavering chant that sounded to Jennet like an Anglican hymn sung under water.

Reunion accomplished, the plantation maids turned their attention to the white captive, examining her from every angle as might a company of Cambridge Platonists confronted with a unicorn or a griffin. They fingered Jennet's dress, toyed with her unbraided hair, sniffed the sweaty juncture of her neck and shoulder. As far as she could tell, none of the women was paired with Pussough, and it occurred to her that she might be marked to become his bride. Certainly there was an intimation of courtship in the way he now led her up the nearest slope, so gloriously a-bloom it made her late father's garden seem barren as a pauper's grave.

'*Les trois soeurs*,' Pussough said. The three sisters.

To her eye each triad of crops indeed enjoyed an intimate and sisterly relationship. Green vines laden with beans coiled about the maize stalks, using them for support, even as the nascent squash huddled in the salubrious shade cast by the other vegetables.

'*Ces soeurs sont heureuses*,' she said. These sisters are happy.

Pussough laughed and squeezed her shoulder in a manner that seemed to occupy an Aristotelian middle-ground betwixt domination and affection. '*Voici votre vie nouvelle*.' Here is your new life.

Evidently she too would become a plantation maid. '*Ma vie nouvelle?*'

'*Oui*.' His hand strayed from her shoulder to her hip. '*Nous ne vous ferrons pas de mal*.' We shall not harm you. '*Vous aurez un bébé, et nous ne vous ferrons pas de mal*.' You will have a baby, and we shall not harm you.

A pint of bile flooded her stomach. '*Un bébé?*'

'*Oui, un bébé*.'

Un bébé. The horrid idea seized her imagination, wrenching her from the company of the gentle *trois soeurs*, and suddenly her brain could conjure no object save human blood, in all its varieties. She saw pools of blood, creeks of blood, biblical rivers of blood. The absence of a child in your womb brought each month a rational and reassuring measure of blood, but the presence of such a monster could cause a very cataract.

'*Quand est-ce que j'aurai le bébé?*' she asked. When will I have the baby?

'*Quand vous serez prête,*' Pussough said.

Could this be true? A Nimacook wife might defer the gravid state until she was *prête* – ready?

She ran a finger across the helical course of a bean vine, vowing silently that, whether her future husband was the man standing before her or another of these enigmatic tawnies, she would somehow, some way, hold him to the laudable custom of deferred procreation. The Nimacooks might make her their slave – they might force her to carry their water, sew their mantles, mend their moccasins, clean their hovels, tend their corn, run their gauntlet: all these indignities she could abide. But to spare herself the doom of Margaret Stearne, she would move Heaven and Earth and all the bodies in between.

At first she tallied only the days, noting each planetary rotation by dropping a pebble into the hollow of an oak tree growing just inside the village gateway. Then she started marking the months, recording every new moon by concealing a crow feather in the darkest corner of her wigwam. Eventually it became clear that her captivity must be reckoned in years, and so whenever the planting season came to the Shawsheen Valley, she fashioned and fired a commemorative pot, setting it beneath her sleeping platform.

Her immediate community, forty in number, occupied four stockaded acres on the eastern shore. They called themselves the Kokokehom, the Owl Clan, willing followers of a one-eyed sagamore named Miacoomes. Having determined that, true to Pussough's assertion, these people meant her no harm – that, indeed, they were attempting to provide her with their notion of a happy life – she resolved to find in her circumstances some measure of redemption. Had Aunt Isobel ever landed amongst the naked tawnies, she would surely have endeavoured to study them, bringing to the task the same fascinated detachment she accorded animalcules on a Van Leeuwenhoek stage.

Thus did Jennet come to view the Kokokehom less as her captors than as the subjects of a philosophic project — though she could not deny that these same subjects were in turn scrutinizing her, casting many a curious and condescending eye on this woman so woefully ignorant of maize planting, mat weaving, and everything else that mattered.

Although the prospect of running the Nimacook gauntlet, the *wopwawnonckquat*, had always instilled in Jennet an unmitigated alarm, she had survived the initiation with nary a bruise or welt. It was a nasty business to be sure, requiring her to dress in naught but a linen shift, then dash betwixt two parallel columns of Indians, all of whom proceeded to set upon her with battle-clubs, quahog-shell hoes and rawhide lashes, their stated intention being to thresh the very whiteness from her soul. And yet at the midpoint of her sprint through this human chute, she realized that her captors were indeed checking their blows and staying their whip hands. Amongst certain Nimacook clans, no doubt, the gauntlet was still a bloody custom, but within the Kokokehom it had evidently transmuted, violence to vestige, savagery to sacrament, ordeal to echo.

Other Nimacook traditions, by contrast, seemed invulnerable to emendation by time. Each autumn, once the seeds were in the ground, the six clans always left their respective villages and came together as one tribe, congregating in a vast settlement to the south under the leadership of the Nimacook grand-sachem, Chabaquong. For two weeks the Indians would feast, dance, feast some more, seek out marriage mates, indulge in further feasting, smoke their tobacco, then throw another feast, all the while discussing public business, most especially the vexing issue of the English settlers' appetite for Algonquin land. Although these gatherings enabled Jennet to mingle with the other white daugh-ters, she entered their vicinity but rarely, for the conversation of all five girls turned almost exclusively on the past — an understandable ob-session, but also quite useless. The daughters grieved for their murdered parents and slaughtered friends, their burned homes and broken baubles, their razed dreams and ravaged aspirations. And yet, even as they indulged in these ritual remembrances, they were obviously learning to inhabit the present, and before the first year of their captivity had passed, the five seemed Nimacook to Jennet in all but blood, and two were already with child by their *wasicks* — their mandatory husbands.

Jennet did not exactly love her own mandatory husband, who turned out to be not Pussough but rather his cousin Okommaka, the brave who'd officiated at the burial rite the night of the raid, setting pipes and tobacco atop the corpses. She nevertheless felt towards Okommaka an undeniable tenderness and devotion – a remarkable circumstance, given that she'd enjoyed no liberty whatsoever to reject his marriage proposal. The courtship consisted entirely of her *wasick* presenting her with a pictographic charcoal-on-deerskin catalogue of the assets he would bring to their union: a steel knife, a French musket, a birch-bark canoe, a snappish guard dog named Casco, and a set of reed mats sufficient for constructing a private wigwam. Beyond this strange fixation on his dowry, Okommaka seemed in his own way a reflective and philosophic young man, and this attribute, combined with his high-cheeked, black-haired beauty, aroused in Jennet an emotion that would serve for the poetic passion until it unequivocally entered her life.

While not normally given to bluster, Okommaka never tired of relating how, shortly after the Haverhill raid, he'd bested seven other braves, Pussough amongst them, in a quartet of games – wrestling match, canoe race, archery contest, spear toss – and thereby acquired the right to woo and wed the sky-eyed, fire-haired English maid. Jennet wasn't sure how she felt about this prologue to her matrimony. There was much in the narrative to gratify her vanity (not since Homer's Penelope had a woman occasioned such fierce competition amongst suitors), but even more to make her feel like a piece of plunder, a spoil of war. Whether its genesis was chivalric, barbaric, or something betwixt the two, however, her bond with Okommaka clearly entailed guarantees of safety and sustenance, and so she resolved that for the immediate future she would give no thought to escape. Her body and mind could readily tolerate the role of Nimacook bride, whereas frigid winds and an empty stomach surely awaited any white woman foolish enough to flee into the inhospitable reaches of the Shawsheen.

The marriage ceremony was spare but elegant, a simple matter of Jennet and Okommaka sharing a bowl of corn soup in his family's presence, clasping each other's hands above the *muchickehea* stone, and, finally, exchanging gifts. He gave her three eelskin hair ribbons and a clam-shell necklace. She presented him with Dunstan's drawing of the horse-head promontory, along with a pouch she'd made from cedar bark, suggesting that he use it to store his tobacco. When dusk came he led her to the back of his family's longhouse and removed her deerskin mantle, immediately finding himself in a state of hydraulic fervor. He shed his garments and bade her lie with him. She did not embrace her husband with enthusiasm, but neither did she know fear, for Chapter Two of her *Woman's Garden* promised that the discomfort would be brief, and she'd calculated that her fertile period was at least ten days away. Forcing a smile, she permitted Okommaka to deflower her in the quick and awkward manner that Isobel had called 'the universal buffoonery of young men on their wedding nights', and then came the soothing sensation, unique in her experience, of falling asleep in another person's arms.

'Cowammaunsh,' he told her in the morning. Later she learned his meaning. I love you.

What most astonished Jennet about her adoptive family – which included Okommaka's mother, Magunga, his father, Quappala, and an assortment of siblings and cousins – was their willingness to grant her the same privileges she would have enjoyed if born into the Owl Clan. To transmute an outsider into a full-blooded Nimacook, you needed merely change her name. On Welcoming Day, one month after her wedding, she became Waewowesheckmishquashim, Woman with Hair like a Fox, an epithet that delighted her and whose abridged form, Waequashim, fell pleasingly on her ear.

Indifferent as the Nimacooks were to a wife's ancestry, the same could not be said of her fertility, and none of Waequashim's new relations pretended she'd been abducted for any reason beyond her presumably hale womb. Extinction was a possibility these people could not discount. Famine, wild beasts, intertribal warfare, and Puritan violence regularly reduced the population of childbearers amongst them – amongst all the Algonquin peoples. But it was the terrible smallpox epidemics, raging through the Indian settlements at unpredictable intervals, that wrought the greatest devastation. *Skishauonck*, they called it, the 'flogging sickness', and to Jennet that sounded like the perfect word, *skishauonck*, the rasp of Satan clearing his barbed and pustuled throat.

Although Latin had always been a laborious pursuit for her, it was child's play compared to Algonquin, whose rhythms and idioms seemed better suited to the inhabitants of Callisto than to any race on Earth. To say 'I am glad you are well' meant teaching your lips to form '*Taubot paumpmauntaman*'. 'It will rain today' pressed your tongue into the service of '*Anamekeesuck sokenum*'. 'How fare your children?' required the questioner to articulate '*Aspaumpmauntamwock cummuckiaug?*' For Okommaka, logically enough, English proved equally perverse. He had difficulty grasping that eight words, 'A man shot by accident during the hunt', were needed to translate '*Uppetetoua*'. He resisted the fact that 'I am not inclined to pursue the matter' was the simplest possible rendering of '*Nissekinean*'. It bewildered him that 'When the wind blows north-west' was the most efficient way to say '*Chekesitch*'. And so it happened that, during the first several weeks following their nuptials, Waequashim and her husband managed to conduct quotidian transactions only through their mutual though defective French, Okommaka and his fellow Owl Clan braves having absorbed bits and pieces of this language from a Jesuit missionary who'd lived in the village for a year, during which interval he'd succeeded in winning only two Indian souls to the Roman faith. But gradually, steadily – and with considerable delight – Jennet and Okommaka learned each other's native tongue, even as their natural tongues found novel ways to fill their private hours with connubial amusement.

Despite their fears of oblivion, the Nimacooks behaved exactly as Pussough had foretold, permitting Jennet to set the terms of her fertility. Okommaka did not complain when she forswore the marital act on those nights when conception was most likely, especially since Chapter Six, 'Labia North and South', detailed several compensatory procedures. As a further precaution, before lying with Okommaka she always suffused her privy shaft with a seed-stilling unguent of pennyroyal and marjoram. The physic came from Hassane, the clan's lithe and puckish medicine-woman, their *taupowau*: a kind of wood nymph, Jennet decided, forever flitting about the village as if borne on invisible fairy-wings, merrily dispensing bits of cryptic wisdom – 'The dog hath found its brother in the wolf, but humans still await their kindred kind' – along with her songs and simples.

Having reduced the menace of pregnancy to a minimum, Jennet felt free to experiment with the activities outlined in both Chapter Four, 'The Lust of the Goat', and Chapter Five, 'The Algebra of Desire'. To the degree that Isobel's knowledge was first-hand, it would seem that as a sensualist Edward Mowbray had suffered few equals. But Okommaka, too, possessed an aptitude for the priapic, and as their private encounters grew ever more heated, Waequashim gradually apprehended the strange and satisfying truth that swiving had become as central to her sustenance as eating.

It was this newfound carnal appetite that made Jennet resolve to forestall indefinitely the day when she would cease to be attractive in her husband's eyes. Despite the many virtues of a crop-woman's life – the agreeable companions, frequent diversions (she took a special delight in *pisinneganash*, a kind of card game played with bulrushes), heady tobacco (its pleasures being permitted to both genders), and nightly exchanges of tales both factual and fabulous – she had come to regard the plantation as the great enemy of her youthfulness. Her time beneath the burning New World sun was causing her brow to peel like birch bark and her hands to become as coarse as a toad's skin. Eventually she brought the matter before Hassane, who gave her a musky ointment with which to butter her exposed flesh ere venturing upon the maize field to battle the weeds and shoo the crows. Owing to this balm, plus the unsightly but efficacious bonnet she'd woven from corn-husks, Waequashim eventually grew confident that she and Okommaka would wither at the same rate.

As her fifth year amongst the Nimacooks began, Jennet found herself in possession of a compelling hypothesis, perhaps even a truth, concerning the two very different worlds in which Dame Fortune had thus far deposited her. The European universe, she speculated, was in essence a road, a meandering thoroughfare bearing its pilgrims from one impressive way-station to the next, from Greek civilization with its beautiful geometry, to the Christian nations with their brilliant the-ology, to the star-gazing trinity of Galileo, Kepler and Newton. But the Indian universe was a wheel, always turning, its rotations marked by the movements of game, the ripening of crops, the shoaling of fish, the fruiting of trees and the running of sap. Beyond their fondness for French muskets and English fowling-pieces, technical innovation meant little to these people; no Nimacook had ever sought to fashion an astrolabe or a microscope. At first this deficit bewildered Jennet, but in time she came to see certain limitations in her aunt's allegiances. Although natural philosophy was the noblest of enterprises, it had never tracked a deer, maintained a maize crop, trapped salmon in a weir, or wrought syrup from the ichor of a maple tree.

Europeans and Indians did not see the same moon, the same *nanepaushat*. For the Cambridge Platonists as well as the Continental Cartesians, Earth's satellite was a mass of dead matter pulled around the planet by an arcane entity (gravitation for the Platonists, vortices for the Cartesians) that could cause 'action at a distance'. But the Nimacook moon was an immense *wampumpeag* bead fashioned by an ancient coastal people, the Quanquogt, their intention having been to offer it to Kautantouwit, the Great South-west God, source of all salutary winds, in exchange for the ocean that nurtured them.

'I assume that Kautantouwit did not smile on the proposition,' Jennet said to Okommaka as they planted a row of merry yellow trilliums along the walkway leading to their wigwam.

He grunted in assent. 'Kautantouwit was much offended. He banished the Quanquogt to a barren desert, then hurled the great *wampumpeag* bead into the sky.'

'A harsh but fitting sentence.'

Casco the dog ambled onto the scene, approached the pot in which they'd cooked their midday stew, and inserted his snout in quest of venison scraps.

'Ah, but even a god can be tempted.' Okommaka pressed a wad of tobacco into the bowl of his soapstone pipe. 'Even Kautantouwit will have his greed. And so it happens that once each month he reaches towards the *nanepaushat-sawhoog*, the moon-bead, obscuring it bit by bit with the shadow of his hand – but in the end he always decides to leave the bead in place.'

'A sign, aye?' Jennet said. 'A symbol of his displeasure with the Quanquogt.'

'*Nux*. Yes. No part of the Earth may be bought or sold, Waequa-shim, no piece of *Mittauke*. No sea, forest, lake or mountain.'

'If the moon is a bead, then what is the sun?'

'In England they have no knowledge of the sun?' He frowned emphatically. 'The sun, cherished wife, is the council-fire around which our ancestors gather. When a Nimacook dies, his soul travels to the south-west mountain, and if Kautantouwit judges it worthy he will deliver that same soul to Keesuckquand, Guardian of Heaven's Torch.'

'Now that I am Nimacook, do *my* ancestors gather around the fire?'

'Look at the sun,' he said, pointing skyward. 'Not long, lest it blind you. Look, and you will see all those who came before you.'

She locked her gaze on the sun. The burning rays flooded her skull with light, and she turned away, blinking, eyes smarting.

She lifted her head and again stared at the council-fire. A golden frieze appeared. Her mother, grandmother, and great-grandmother sat huddled in the sun's corona like jewels decorating a diadem.

Some desire of her mind, quite likely. Some phantom of her brain. And yet the glimmering chimera produced in Jennet a joy such as she'd never known since that long-gone March evening at Mirringate, a night of hot sugared coffee and dancing oak-wood flames, when Aunt Isobel had taught her to comprehend the grand cosmic drama, more than twenty-five thousand years in duration, known to natural philo-sophers as the precession of the equinoxes.

Near the end of Jennet's seventh year in the Owl Clan, it became obvious that Okommaka, Magunga, Quappala and the rest of her immediate family could no longer abide her vacant womb. Assenting to the inevitable, she set aside Hassane's unguent, and she and Okommaka started clustering their connections towards the middle of her cycle. Within three months she was pregnant. Despite the cessation of her lunar bleeding, she found the condition supremely uncomfortable, although she did not experience the terror she'd so long anticipated. Her qualified equanimity traced to the tradition whereby Nimacook squaws dropped their babies whilst standing erect – the very attitude that Aunt Isobel (having researched the matter in four languages) regarded as the safest and least painful, 'the upright pagan posture, ninety degrees from the horizontal lying-in to which a Euro-pean woman subjects herself'. Whatever hardships the birthing process might involve, Jennet imagined that through heathen tradition and

Hassane's talent she would elude the fate her mother had suffered in delivering Dunstan. If the infant was a girl, she would name her Bella, a variation on Isobel. If a boy, he would be Anton, in homage to the inventor of the microscope.

As Jennet entered her final month, the infant kicking against her womb at least once an hour, protesting its imprisonment, a distressing report reached the village. The flogging sickness had struck the Moaskug, the Black Snake Clan, a Nimacook community a half-day's walk to the north. Later that week the rumour received vivid confirmation as the pied corpses of two Moaskug women came floating down the Shawsheen. Jennet's fellow Indians knew from experience what would happen now. First, more *skishauonck* corpses would appear on the river. Then, for miles around the village, the forest would tremble with the shrieks of the dying and the keening of the bereaved. And finally a new sound would arise, the marching feet of the *machemoqussu*, the wandering doomed, those victims whom the disease had transformed into madmen.

Theirs was an understandable insanity. In the initial stage of *skishauonck*, Hassane explained, the patient endured a burning fever and violent vomiting, even as tiny red spots appeared all over his body. In the second stage the spots became blisters filled with lustrous pus. If the victim was going to survive, this happy fact soon became manifest: his fever broke, and the blisters turned to scabs and fell off. But many did not survive. For these unfortunates, the blisters began erupting, causing the outermost tiers of the flesh, both internally and externally, to split away from the underlayers, so that the victim was literally flayed alive, without and also within, blood oozing from his mouth, nose, genitals and anus.

With every brave except Miacoomes and his councilors away on the summer hunt, it fell to the women to take up firearms and prevent the *machemoqussu* from spreading the contagion amongst the Owl Clan. Despite Jennet's gravid state, Miacoomes required her to spend two hours each morning doing sentry duty in collaboration with a crone named Winoshi, the two women pacing back and forth outside the stockade wall, muskets in hand. Although the *machemoqussu* were nowhere to be seen, Jennet did not for an instant doubt their existence. She could hear them wailing and moaning amidst the shadows as they crashed blister-blind from tree to tree and boulder to boulder – the world's true demons, the goblins with dissolving skin.

Shortly after sunrise on her twentieth morning of guarding the village, Jennet's sac abruptly split, sending a stream of warm clear water spilling down her thighs. The fluid rolled across the ground, irrigating the grass and quenching the wildflowers. A half-hour later the first spasm arrived, seizing her body with all the force of a ploughshare breaking hard earth.

She took her leave of Winoshi, ran to her wigwam, and grabbed the poppet she'd made two nights earlier – deerskin body, eyes of white beads – that she might gift her child with a toy upon its disembarkation. As she made her way to the *taupowau's* dwelling, the immured and impatient baby bobbing before her, a second spasm came, stronger even than the first. Hassane gathered together the steel knife, leather flask, linen rags, figwort leaves, deerskin blanket and other necessities, then guided Jennet to the wooded north-west quadrant of the village. The birthing lodge was a typical Nimacook longhouse, though equipped with a *nesse-anaskunck*: two shorn hemlock branches suspended five feet above the floor, positioned in parallel like railings on a bridge, and supported by leather thongs affixed to the ceiling.

'Step between the poles,' Hassane commanded.

Jennet did so.

'Set your arms around the centres,' Hassane said.

Even as Jennet obeyed, a third spasm took hold of her.

'Breathe quickly and deliberately,' Hassane said, 'as if you were swimming across the Shawsheen.'

Jennet opened her mouth and sucked in a great sphere of air. She released it with a sharp calculated puff.

Owing to Hassane's midwifing skills and the virtues of vertical birthing, the delivery fell short of an ordeal. It was exhausting to be sure, punctuated by ferocious explosions of pain, but never once did Jennet feel herself in thrall to those profane forces that had carried her mother to the hallowed ground of a Mistley churchyard.

'You have a daughter, Waequashim.' The *taupowau* eased the expelled infant into the good air and soft light of the birthing lodge, then took up the knife and with a single stroke severed the umbilical cord.

Healthy and unharmed, or so Hassane asserted, Bella fascinated Jennet from the moment the *taupowau* placed the infant in her arms. Whilst Hassane buried the bright blue placenta by the riverbank, Jennet sat outside the lodge and contemplated the creature's tiny eyelashes and subtle nose, her articulated knuckles and wrinkled brown knees, her wispy black hair and stubby but differentiated toes. Who could have guessed that the great bulky stone in Waequashim's womb would emerge into daylight boasting such glorious detail?

'Many are the lessons I would teach thee,' Jennet said, setting the deerskin doll in her baby's reflexive grasp.

She told Bella that the season for planting began when the leaves of the white oak were as large as a mouse's ears. She explained how each time the sun refracted the lingering damp of a summer shower, a rainbow appeared in the sky, and if you could somehow gather up that spectrum and strain it through another such prism, its rays would fuse into a beam of purest whiteness. When guarding the plantation, a squaw must never slay a raven, neither with arrow nor spear nor musket-ball, for it was that bird and no other who had brought to the Algonquin the very first maize seed. She informed her daughter that they would one day scour the Shawsheen's bottom until they discovered a stone so clear and pure it could serve as a microscope lens, and then they would find another such stone, and next they would fit the two lenses to a tube of soapstone, and by this means they would explore the world that lay hidden within the world.

'Six sides there are to each and every snow crystal,' Jennet said, alternately stroking the deerskin doll and the infant's brow. 'Mr Hooke hath proved as much. That is the planet to which you have come, my beautiful darling Bella.'

Now that Okommaka's daughter had arrived, launched upon the trajectory of her joys and the vector of her sorrows, Miacoomes forbade Waequashim to do sentry duty, lest the toxic breath of the *machemoqussu* bring sickness to the infant. Instead Jennet became a plantation maid again. Each morning she would package Bella's bum in an absorbent mixture of cattail fluff and sphagnum, roll a deerskin around her body until the child resembled an unhusked ear of corn, strap her to a cradle-board, and equip her with the rattle Magunga had made from bits of bone and a scooped-out gourd, whereupon the two of them would set off for the field of *les trois soeurs*, the baby riding on her mother's spine like a turtle basking on a log. As she attacked the weeds with her hoe and unburdened the bean crop of dead vines, Jennet kept an eye peeled for the *machemoqussu*, and she did not relax her vigilance until, five weeks after Bella's birth, the Moaskug's sagamore sent word to Miacoomes that the *skishauonck* epidemic had finally lifted. In her mind Jennet saw this event as the abating of a furious storm, its gusts and rains burned into oblivion by the sun.

Bella's fortieth night on Earth was lit by a moon as pale and yellow as a firefly's lanthorn. Jennet was sitting in the village plaza, the baby's lips clamped around her left nipple, when she noticed the aberrant blotch. It was dark, solitary, no larger than a freckle, fixed like a wood tick to Bella's cheek.

Jennet brushed the blotch with her thumb. It remained rooted, a hundred times more ominous than any Devil's mark. She brushed it again. The dot persisted.

'Dear God in Heaven . . .'

Without breaking the seal betwixt mouth and breast, she rose and proceeded directly to her mother-in-law's longhouse. Upon seeing the excrescence, Magunga let out a howl as loud and anguished as a *machemoqussu*'s cry, and then came three more howls interspersed with wheezing gasps, until finally Magunga grew rational enough to assert that only the blaze of the sun could reveal the mark's true nature. For the immediate moment Jennet could do nothing but nurse the baby to sleep: if there was any hope for Bella, it lay in the dream-world – once set roaming across those ethereal hills, the infant's spirit might meet a *mauchatea*, a 'ghost-guide' who would lead her far beyond the demon-infested land of the flogging sickness and bring her to the healing waters of the River Woaloke.

Staggering home along the moonlit path, Jennet felt as if she had herself become a wanderer in the dream-world, but no *mauchatea* appeared to point the way. She entered the wigwam and, after suckling Bella until the infant's lips stopped moving and her jaw went slack, eased her sleeping body into the cradle as she would shelve the only existing copy of a wise and exquisite book. She sat down, sprawled across the mat, and closed her eyes, all the while imploring Kautantouwit and Jehovah to collaborate in delivering her child from the smallpox. Bella's breathing filled the air, the gentle inhalations and soft exhalations, delicate as a summer breeze. Sleep came to Jennet but fitfully that night, her wakeful moments a concatenation of unbidden twitchings and involuntary doggish yelps, her dreams aboil with *machemoqussu* infantries on the march.

At first light she unfurled her clenched fingers and set her palm on Bella's brow. The baby's skin was hot, deathly hot, *skishauonck* hot. Seconds later Bella awoke, and from her little chest a jagged screech shot forth.

Jennet picked up the baby, her infinitely detailed Bella whose spirit had failed to find a *mauchatea*, and carried her into the remorseless light of day. Pustules speckled Bella's torso like Satanic *wampumpeag* beads.

'Blessed Kautantouwit, I beg thee . . .'

Thirty pustules, fifty, a hundred.

'Hear me, Kautantouwit . . .'

Again Bella screeched.

She bore her daughter to Hassane's wigwam, hoping the medicine-woman would judge Bella afflicted with a rare but curable disease whose symptoms uncannily mimicked those of the flogging sickness. But instead of offering any such lore, Hassane merely directed Jennet to swab the child head to toe with river-soaked wads of sphagnum, again and again and again.

To what unspeakable precinct of their pantheon did the Nimacooks consign *skishauonck*? From whence sprang this Satanic contagion? Jennet never found out. The Indians were not given to raging indignantly against the plague, but neither did they regard it as a fitting punishment for their sins. Apparently they viewed *skishauonck* as a mystery. The disease confounded Jennet as well. Bathing Bella for five unbroken hours as Hassane had prescribed, all the while watching her daughter transmute from a baby into a *machemoqussu*, and thence to a corpse, she could not decide whether *skishauonck* represented the iniquity of Lucifer, the wrath of God, the perversity of Nature, or yet another force, beyond all human comprehension.

She grieved as would any other Nimacook, staining her teeth with juniper berries, loading her moccasins with pebbles, and cutting her hair with a sacred elk-bone knife, so that ragged auburn tufts now sprouted from her scalp. She prepared a cake of charred oak and rubbed it across her face, darkening her cheeks and brow with an itching patina of soot.

Taking the corpse in her arms, she hobbled down to the river-bank, where Hassane and Magunga awaited, their faces likewise blackened.

'*Kutchimmoke*,' Hassane told her. Be of good cheer.

'*Kutchimmoke*,' Magunga echoed.

After searching the shore for an hour, the women found a soft and secluded spot beneath a willow tree, and there they dug a grave with clam-shell spades, lining the bottom with a cushion of sticks. Jennet placed Bella in extreme flexion, hands covering face, then slipped the deerskin doll under her arms and wrapped her in a reed mat. In tandem the women fitted Bella into the grave, slowly, deliberately, seed into furrow, string into nock, feather into braid, and then Jennet said good-bye to the child with the wondrous knuckles and the rich black hair. The women filled the hole with sand. Hassane erected atop the mound a tower of twigs and stones no higher than a maize-stalk, gently tilting it towards the south-west – for this was a *cowwenock-wunnauchicomock*, she explained, a 'soul-chimney' meant to draw the child's immaterial essence from her dead flesh and point it towards Kautantouwit's sacred mountain, that it might join with the God of Gods.

'And now, Waequashim, you must take the river-cure,' Hassane said.

'Today and every day for a month,' Magunga elaborated, 'you will give yourself to the Shawsheen.'

Did the Nimacook river-cure represent a foolish heathen superstition, or was it a paragon of pagan wisdom? In her numb and pliant condition Jennet could form no opinion, and so it was with a divided heart that she removed her mantle and skirt, pulled off her moccasins, bid Hassane and Magunga farewell, and stepped into the cool racing flood. She walked along the muddy bed until the water reached her waist, and then she lifted her heels and tipped her body forward. She swam north, face down, countering the current by moving her legs in a frog-kick and raising her head to breathe. Waterborne twigs stroked her thighs. Clusters of leaves caressed her sides. The Shawsheen washed the soot from her cheeks and brow.

At twilight she reached Hawk-Isle, then rolled on her back like an otter and let the river return her to the mound where Bella lay. Clambering onto the shore, she locked her gaze on the little wooden tower, still pointed towards Heaven. Such a fragile talisman, this soul-chimney, this *cowwenock-wunnauchicomock*. It would not survive the briefest rain-shower, much less a blizzard or a thunder-gust.

'In the spring you and I shall fly it.' Her knees failed, and she collapsed naked and shivering atop her daughter's grave. 'We shall fly it for fair, my dearest, sweetest Bella.'

For an indeterminate interval she sobbed and keened, pummelling the mound with her fists, soaking the sand with her tears as her birth waters had saturated the earth outside the village, until at last her grief grew so thick and hard – a kind of malign second pregnancy – that she could no longer work her wailing limbs or move her weeping joints. She curled her body into a tight sphere, a human moon-bead, and she did not bestir herself until dawn.

Four days later Hassane brought Jennet a male infant whose mother had succumbed to the contagion, so that the white woman's engorged breasts might nourish him. Kapaog's sucking proved far more vigorous than Bella's, so that, true to a phenomenon documented in Chapter Seven, Jennet found herself in a state of concupiscent arousal. When Hassane required her to hand Kapaog over to another lactating woman, a potter named Cumunchon, likewise mourning her infant *machemoqussu*, a deep carnal longing settled into Jennet's bones, linger-ing until at last Okommaka returned from the hunt.

'I gave our daughter an English name,' she told him. 'Bella, after my Aunt Isobel, the natural philosopher. All the world held great fascination for her, from the meanest worm to the brightest star.'

'The brightest star,' Okommaka echoed. 'Then our child was Pashpishia.'

'Pashpishia . . .'

'She Who Loves the Night.'

With every visit she paid to Pashpishia's grave that month, Jennet grew more determined to invoke *nupakenaqun* – the right of a bereaved mother to exempt herself from further procreation. Okommaka in turn claimed a collateral privilege, so that his nubile cousin Maansu became his second wife. In a development so ironic it might have given even Sophocles pause, Jennet found that, far from arousing her jealousy, this bigamous arrangement increased tenfold her sense of unity with the Owl Clan. She would never be a Nimacook mother, but now she knew herself for an absolute Nimacook squaw, the first and favourite of Okommaka.

This pagan marriage was real. The Kokokehom were the case. Her clam-shell necklace, eelskin hair ribbons, bead bracelet, fur robe, deerskin leggings, and moose-hide moccasins were factual as grass. As for Salem and Boston, Colchester and London, the Aristotelian Earth and the Newtonian moon, these were just labels on dreams, mere names for places as mythic as Atlantis or El Dorado.

Out there, it was 1703: so said her calendar of fired pots. Out there, some bright young natural philosopher was likely on the point of discovering Newton's lost demon disproof. Even as her twenty-fifth birthday arrived – an event she celebrated by fashioning for herself a headdress of hawk and pheasant feathers – an *argumentum grande* was doubtless appearing on the stage of European history. But for Waequa-shim of the Nimacook, there was no more work to do.

Although Jennet remained horrified by the brutality and the bloody scalps, the Indians' war against the Merrimack Valley settlers had evidently accomplished its aim. By the turn of the century a crop-woman could spend a productive morning tilling her clan's acres without fear that some eager Puritan would try to steal them come afternoon. To all appearances an undeclared truce had emerged betwixt Chabaquong's people and the English towns, including a recon-structed and repopulated Haverhill, and in time the Nimacooks permitted the Puritans to inscribe a toll road along the extreme eastern edge of their territory – a mail route from Boston to Amesbury – with the Indians receiving a fee of one *wampumpeag* bead per mounted wayfarer and two per horse-drawn coach.

Because the far boundary of the Owl Clan's plantation abutted the

Amesbury Post Road, Jennet now became witness to a daily stream of white men – galloping mail-carriers, marching soldiers, sweating drovers, panting pedlars – a circumstance that prompted Quappala and Magunga to imagine their elder daughter-in-law imploring some traveller to bear her away. Eventually her family's suspicions grew so acute that, whenever their farming chores brought the crop-women near the new thoroughfare, Magunga outfitted Waequashim with the very sort of leather halter by which she'd been abducted.

And so it happened that Jennet once again came to regard the Nimacooks not as her kin but as her keepers. Nothing moved them, neither her protestations of loyalty – the louder she asserted her allegiance to the tribe, the more convinced they became that she intended to bolt – nor her protests against the yoke: 'I shan't be harnessed! I am not an ox! I am not an ass! I am not a plough horse!' All such metaphors proved equally impotent, partly because draught animals played no role in the Indian way of life, largely because the subject was not up for discussion.

By 1708 a new element had entered the Nimacook economy. Those braves with a talent for trapping learned that if they brought their beaver pelts, their *toumockquashuncks*, down the Shawsheen to the English village of Bedford, they could exchange them for a panoply of European goods. The Nimacooks' grand-sachem disdained this so-called 'fur trade', for it seemed to embody the very mercantilism that the Moon-Bead Legend condemned. Chabaquong's councillors, however, argued that the Great God Kautantouwit would not feel offended by such commerce if the trappers limited their acquisitions to flintlock muskets, forged knives, iron kettles and other products unknown to Algonquin industry. Eventually Chabaquong permitted the enterprise to go forward, though without his blessing.

The grand-sachem was not the only Nimacook to lament the tribe's entry into the fur trade. Jennet did so too, for once the *toumockquashuncks* were in hand, the tedious job of treating them fell to the women. She detested each step in the process: scraping the backs of the skins, rubbing them with marrow, trimming them into rectangles, sewing six or eight such pieces together into a robe, wearing the garment from dawn to dusk until the pelts grew supple enough to command a top price. But then one day Okommaka mentioned that books were amongst the items available at the Bedford Trading Centre, and Jennet's opinion of the fur trade improved considerably.

'What *sorts* of books?' she asked.

'The English God-Book,' Okommaka replied. 'The Bible of Grand-Sachem James.'

'What else?'

'French verses. English plays. Histories written in Latin.'

English plays! Oh, to scan that linguistic music again, to experience once more Juliet's longings, Cleopatra's passions, Lady Macbeth's depravity. If she came upon a *Principia Mathematica* in Bedford she would immediately toss it aside – she was no longer a Hammer of Witchfinders, after all, no longer obligated to cultivate an acquaintance with Lucasian Professors – but a quarto *Macbeth* would be as welcome as a restoration of Aunt Isobel's incinerated treatise.

Okommaka, predictably, recoiled at Jennet's desire to accompany him on his next Bedford adventure. Fur trading, he insisted, was a masculine enterprise, and any brave who brought a wife along risked ridicule by whites and Algonquins alike. But she continued to press the matter, and eventually, owing either to the righteousness of her case, the pathos in her voice, or the chapter called 'Labia North and South', Okommaka relented, solemnly declaring that a great Nimacook trapper did not prostrate himself before the opinions of lesser men.

The expedition comprised three canoes bearing Okommaka, Pus-sough, six other braves, Casco the dog, and – now – Okommaka's headstrong elder wife. All during their passage down the Shawsheen, a glorious anticipation filled every pipe and parlour of Jennet's heart. Okommaka had agreed that she could acquire four volumes, assuming they collectively cost no more than half a beaver-robe, and with each paddle stroke Jennet imagined herself savouring yet another line of Shakespeare or Marlowe or Jonson.

The celestial council-fire had passed its zenith by the time they reached the trading centre – an impressive collection of three stout cabins supplemented by a livery and a forge, plus a tavern called Paradise Mislaid. A flagpole rose in the front yard, flying both the Union Jack and the banner of the Shawsheen Fur Exchange Author-ity, a beaver surrounded by the company's motto, *Profit, Prosperity, Plenitude*. Okommaka steered his canoe to the wharf, where three white

traders fidgeted about, thickset men in plain muslin shirts, idly smoking pipes and skimming stones across the water. As Jennet climbed
onto the dock, the traders greeted her with dark scowls and hostile
mutterings. Perhaps they regarded her as pitiable, so that – were they
made of sterner stuff and not outnumbered by the Kokokehom – they
might have tried liberating her with the aim of collecting a reward. But
more likely they simply found Jennet repulsive, this corrupted woman
whose braids smelled of bear grease and whose soul stank of idolatry.

Much to her frustration, Okommaka and Pussough insisted on
patronizing the first two stores, one featuring muskets and shot, the
other offering tools and cooking implements, before venturing into
the third, an emporium specializing in felt hats, leather boots, wool
blankets and steel gorgets. Okommaka guided her to a battered
shipping crate. She lifted the lid. Books filled the compartment top to
bottom – one hundred volumes at least: five score jolts for a dozing
intellect, a banquet for a hungry brain. She took a breath, praised
Kautantouwit, and got to work, unloading the crate and organizing
the jumble as her husband and his cousin looked on in amusement.
She did not really expect to find *Macbeth* or *Romeo and Juliet* or *Antony
and Cleopatra* in the mess, but there was indeed a Shakespeare quarto,
The Tempest, as well as Marlowe's *Tragical History of Doctor Faustus*,
both of which she set aside. Her third decision, Thomas Shelton's
translation of *Don Quixote de la Mancha*, was similarly easy. Now came
an impossible choice. How much did she desire *Caesar's Commentaries*
as opposed to Spenser's *The Faerie Queene*? Plutarch's *Parallel Lives of
the Noble Greeks and Romans* versus Xenophon's *Recollections of Socrates*?
One thing was certain. She would eschew the ratty copy of Reginald
Scot's *Discoverie of Witchcraft*, one of the sceptical works Aunt Isobel
had told her to consult in devising the *argumentum grande*. A Hammer of
Witchfinders might find that tome of use, but she wouldn't trade a
beaver's cheek for it.

Eventually she reduced the conundrum to three possibilities: Mon-
taigne's *Essays*, Bunyan's *The Pilgrim's Progress*, and an old friend from
her Mirringate youth, Virgil's *Aeneid*. She set the volumes on the floor,
each at the point of an imaginary equilateral triangle, and, rising to full
height, made ready to surrender the matter to Dame Fortune. Whilst
Okommaka and Pussough snickered conspicuously, she stepped inside

the triangle, shut her eyes, spun around thrice, stretched out her arm, and directed a pointing finger downward.

She opened her eyes. The *Aeneid*. A splendid resolution. *Arma virumque cano.*

'What does that book talk about?' Okommaka asked.

'Virgil recounts the adventures of Aeneas, destined to bring forth the Roman nation,' she said.

'The missionary who lived amongst us spoke often of ancient Rome,' Pussough said. 'Its founders were Romulus and Remus, suckled as babes by a she-wolf.'

'Virgil tells a rather different story,' Jennet said.

'No Romulus and Remus?' said Pussough. 'No she-wolf?'

'No she-wolf.'

'My uncle knows a Moattoqus brave who was raised by wolves,' Okommaka said. 'Such a thing can happen, Waequashim. Virgil should not have doubted it.'

At dusk the Indians returned to the Shawsheen, laden with the fruits of their bartering. Okommaka spread out his prizes on the wharf – Italian duelling pistol, keg of gunpowder, iron skillet, brass-framed mirror, striped blanket – then wrapped them in a deerskin and wedged the bundle into the bow. Jennet slid her books into a hempen sack and secured it beside her husband's cache.

A pastoral scene unfolded in her mind: the trading party camped that night beside the river, Jennet reading Virgil aloud by the fire, translating as she went. Storm-tossed Aeneas and his men landing on the Libyan shore. The hero telling the Carthaginians the tale of the Trojan horse. The romance of Aeneas and Dido. Her suicide following his decision to leave for Italy. The shade of Anchises showing Aeneas the future history of Rome. The great war betwixt Aeneas's forces and the Latin armies of King Turnus. Aeneas slaying Turnus in personal combat. Okommaka, Pussough, and the other enthralled Nimacooks attended every word.

Excited shouts disturbed her reverie. Jennet lifted her head.

A mob of Indians and whites had collected by the riverbank, their attention fixed on a high footbridge arcing across the Shawsheen like a wooden rainbow. Huddled together in the centre of the bridge, four figures in Puritan garb used a plough-rope to lower a woman towards the water, her legs and trunk concealed by a flimsy shift, her moans muffled by a leather napkin. Thongs drew the prisoner's wrists and ankles together, forcing her body into the shape of a horseshoe.

'Husband, I see a gang of Calvinist witchfinders, inflicting their tests on an innocent woman,' Jennet said. 'By your leave, I shall go and protest this injustice.'

'When English settlers choose to harry one another, a Nimacook finds this cause for joy, not bewilderment,' Okommaka said.

'My conscience will torment me if I do not denounce these prickers to their faces.'

Okommaka issued a series of low, discreet grunts. His taut tongue roamed around the inside of his mouth, bulging his cheeks, and then at last he spoke.

'Tell the Englishmen that if they harm you, Waequashim, your husband and his fellow braves will not forbear to separate them from their scalps.'

She leapt over the canoe, sprinted along the shore, and, reaching the bridge, mounted the stairway to the horizontal span. The quartet still held the swimming-rope, their grey capes rippling in the wind.

She could not decide which shock was the greater: seeing Dunstan in the flesh, or apprehending the form in which that flesh had survived the burning of Haverhill. Although Nature had wrought a handsome adult from the raw materials of youth, the achievement was gravely compromised by the cataract of scar tissue spilling down from his high-crowned hat all the way to his jaw.

'Dunstan!' she gasped. 'Praise God! I was certain the fire had consumed you!'

Not unexpectedly, Abigail Williams had ripened into a comely specimen of womanhood. As for her uncle, the Reverend Samuel Parris, the fourteen intervening years had turned his face into a burlesque of itself, all beaky nose and receding chin. Time had been equally severe with Magistrate Jonathan Corwin, robbing him of so many teeth that his cheeks had collapsed, causing his head to resemble a skull dipped in tallow.

'O sweet Jesus, can this be my own long-lost sister?' Dunstan lifted his hands from the swimming-rope. His confederates froze, leaving their prisoner to dangle above the Shawsheen like a fox caught in a snare. ''Tis truly Jennet Stearne beneath those feathers and skins?'

'Aye, Dunstan. You must set that woman free.'

He lurched away from the bridge rail, flung his arms around Jennet, and drew her to his chest like a laundry-maid pulling bedsheets from a clothes-line. She answered his embrace by stroking his brow and kissing the frightful scar.

'I feared you'd been scalped' – Dunstan touched the brim of his hat – 'but 'tis *I* who lost his hair, every lock burned to the bone: a small price to pay, for with Jehovah's help I retrieved our father's licence. Prithee, give us the space of a quarter-hour to switch off yon Satanist, and we shall bear you to the safety of our Framingham salt-box.'

'Nay, Dunstan,' Jennet said. 'I'm Waequashim of the Kokokehom now.' Defiantly she adjusted her headdress. 'Have you not yet learned that witchery's an impossible thing? Unbind this woman, I implore you.'

'Unbind her?' Abigail sneered. She abandoned the swimming-rope, so that the task of counterweighting the prisoner fell entirely to Parris and Corwin. 'Hah!' Her contemptuous eye ranged across Jennet's wardrobe, moccasins to leggings to mantle to hair ribbons. 'How the Algonquin fashion doth become you, Miss Stearne. Those stinking braids will bring many a savage suitor to your door.'

'In point of fact I'm married to a Nimacook trapper,' Jennet said.

'Do you hear that, Dunstan? Your sister swives a tawny pagan!'

'I would rather be a pagan wife than a Protestant wench,' Jennet said.

'You will not call me wench, sister,' Abigail said, 'for Dunstan and I are wed five years now.'

Jennet raised a hand to her collarbone and anxiously fingered her necklace. Given the unspeakable pain and the demonic scar that were the price of Dunstan's deliverance from the fire, she could hardly blame him for rushing to his demented friend and taking refuge in her affection. But it was one thing to understand their union, quite another to bless it. The thought of these two fanatics spawning a new generation of witchfinders nauseated her as surely as any emetic.

Again she touched Dunstan, resting her hand on his sleeve. 'To this day your drawing of the horse-head promontory hangs in my dwelling. I gave it to my husband as a wedding gift.'

A flicker of remembrance lit Dunstan's face. ''Twas an excellent sketch – I shan't dispute it.' Suddenly he pivoted towards Parris and Corwin. 'Lower the hag!' he called, and the two cleansers offered their prisoner to the Shawsheen.

'No!' Jennet cried.

'I am my father's son,' Dunstan said, turning towards her. 'He did not rear me to coddle goblins or sup with Beelzebub.'

'She floats!' Parris announced. 'The river brands Susan Diggens a witch!'

'I can prove that wicked spirits are but desires of the mind,' Jennet said.

'My dear queen of the heathens,' Abigail said, 'if you durst interfere with us, we shall bring you before the Bedford magistrate.'

'We're all of us now the Crown's official prickers: the Massachusetts Bay Purification Commission,' Dunstan explained, 'twin to the Kirkcaldy Cleansing League and chartered by Her Majesty's Privy Council.'

Parris and Corwin hauled Mrs Diggens over the rail, spilling her onto the span as offhandedly as two Puritan farmers dumping a cartload of hay. The minister drew out a pair of draper's shears and sliced her thongs apart. Mrs Diggens stretched but did not attempt to rise. She was short and sturdy of build, and for one breathless moment Jennet imagined that here was Aunt Isobel, come back from the grave.

When at last Corwin untied the mask-o'-truth, Mrs Diggens exhaled sharply and scrambled to her feet. Her frightened stare shot past her tormentors and fixed on Jennet. 'Help me, friend Indian,' she whispered. 'In my life I've stolen much and shagged many, but i'Christ I'm blameless to sorcery.'

'The river hath revealed her nature,' Parris said. 'Next comes her execution.'

'Friend Indian, I beg thee,' Mrs Diggens pleaded.

A vortex of movement possessed the Purification Commission, and after the chaos had subsided Jennet stood piniomed against the rail, her right arm paralysed by Parris's grip, her left wrist trapped in Corwin's skeletal fingers. Mrs Diggens lay hunched and trembling on the span. The rope that had recently encircled her waist was now a noose about her neck.

''Tis not lawful to hang a person merely on the evidence of a swimming!' Jennet shouted. 'She must go before a duly appointed committee and thence to a courtroom!'

'Were you a subscriber to *The Bible Commonwealth*,' Abigail said, 'you would know that by Queen Anne's decree neither we nor our Scottish brethren need to apply mundane standards to the invisible crime of sorcery.'

Dunstan said, 'However, if 'twill give you satisfaction, Jenny . . .' He pivoted towards Abigail. 'Goodwife Stearne, as the Examination Committee on this bridge, you may now offer your findings.'

'The Examination Committee returns a *billa vera*,' Abigail replied, looping the rope around the rail and securing it with three quick knots.

'Oh, dear God!' Mrs Diggens shrieked.

'Stop this!' Jennet wailed.

'Mr Parris, what verdict doth the jury render?' Dunstan asked.

'The jury finds Susan Diggens guilty,' the minister said.

'Mr Corwin, we shall hear your sentence,' Dunstan said.

'Were this a case of thievery and bawdiness alone, I might be moved to spare her,' said the judge, forcing the prisoner to stand erect, 'but Susan Diggens hath manifestly written in the Devil's ledger, and so—'

'Friend Indian!' Urine and liquid faeces leaked from beneath Mrs Diggens's shift.

With an efficiency doubtless born of experience, Dunstan and Abigail pulled a burlap sack over the prisoner's head, lifted her onto the rail, and gave her a rude shove. Mrs Diggens screamed as she fell, and then came a short, sharp report, like a dry twig snapping underfoot.

The instant Corwin and Parris relaxed their hold, Jennet rushed towards the stairway, seriously pondering the possibility, at once tempting and terrible, of summoning the seven Kokokehom trappers and suggesting that they massacre this so-called Purification Commission. Instead she stopped and turned, her eyes now two gazing-crystals, each fixed on Abigail's breast as if to scorch the vixen's heart.

'Hear me now, you damned witchfinders! Your fellowship will not prosper! For all you enjoy the blessings of the Crown, I shall one day destroy your enterprise as surely as Aeneas slew King Turnus!'

'Go back to your naked Redman,' Abigail hissed, 'and trouble us no more!'

Step by languid step, Jennet descended to the riverbank. Okommaka and the other Nimacooks collected around her, knives unsheathed, muskets cocked, tomahawks at the ready. Casco barked ferociously. She faced the bridge. Susan Diggens's corpse swung from the rail like a Huygens pendulum. As Okommaka hovered by her side, Jennet walked back to the canoes, dislodged her newfound Virgil, and carried it to the relevant cabin. The exchange took but a minute, and when it was over she no longer owned the *Aeneid*, having acquired in its stead Reginald Scot's treatise. True, it was unlikely that more than a paragraph from *Discoverie of Witchcraft* would end up in the *argumentum grande*. By themselves Scot's words could never kill the Conjuring Statute or prompt the Privy Council to cancel her brother's charter. But a Hammer of Witchfinders had to start

*

Somewhere amidst the private papers of the brilliant American sculptor Gutzon Borglum is a drawing that I regard as his crowning conception, greater even than his quartet of Mount Rushmore presidents. Borglum titled his idea 'The Reader', and he never got around to rendering it in stone; as far as I know, he never even took it to the maquette stage. Perhaps he lost enthusiasm. More likely he failed to find a patron. If realized, 'The Reader' and its pedestal would have towered over twenty feet above some American park, common or square. It shows a young woman sitting in a Windsor chair, lost in a book, a spaniel asleep at her feet.

I needn't remind you that readers have always constituted a minority within your species. Merely by opening this chronicle of mine, you have placed yourself in rare company. The odour of bowel wind is known to every human, but the fragrance of book glue has crossed only a fraction of mortal nostrils. And yet it behooves us not to judge the unlettered too harshly. We must stay the impulse to write *chucklehead* above their doors and carve *dolt* upon their tombstones. For in days gone by, at least, a certain chariness towards typography made sense. Borglum's woman in the Windsor chair is performing a traditionally problematic act.

The first recorded instance of a troubled relationship between a reader and a book occurred in 590 BC, when Yahweh ordered Ezekiel to eat a scroll, thereby absorbing its contents. Although the scroll displayed the words 'lamentations, mourning and woe' front and back, Ezekiel acquiesced to the command. He reported that the book tasted 'as honey for sweetness', which strikes me as a mighty peculiar flavour for lamentations, mourning and woe. In my opinion Ezekiel was afraid to speak his mind: a prophet who knows what's good for him does not go around criticizing God's cuisine.

One hundred and seventy years later, readers had to contend with Socrates's pronouncement that books are useless artifacts. Literary works cannot explain what they say, the great philosopher argued – they can only repeat the same words over and over. To me this sounds less like the definition of a book than of a Heideggerian, but in any event Socrates clearly missed the point. Books don't repeat the same words over and over. The *Gulliver's Travels* whose whimsy amuses you at twelve is not the *Gulliver's Travels* whose acid engages you at thirty.

Some of you belong to my dear Jennet's gender. I needn't remind you that throughout Western history an argument has raged over whether women possess sufficient intellect to profit from the print medium. In AD 1333, the Renaissance artist Simone Martini provoked an ecclesiastical crisis when he painted the future Mother of God receiving the Annunciation while holding a book. Wasn't Mary almost certainly illiterate? fretted the keepers of the faith. Wasn't it sacrilegious to suggest that a woman might love knowledge when the Bible clearly stated, 'Thy desire shall be to thy husband'? Would the painting's audience even be able to *recognize* the Blessed Virgin in this strange scholastic stance?

In 1740 the South Carolina legislature, haunted by images of their Negro chattel learning Jesus's views on love and, worse, the aboli-tionists' views on slavery, made it illegal to teach an African to read. By this law, any black person caught with a book was flogged. After the third such offence, the first joint of his forefinger was severed. Other Southern states rushed to enact identical measures, many of which remained in effect even after Emancipation.

And so we see how throughout history the community of readers has been prey to sinister forces – to pedants and priests, legislators and lunatics, deities and demagogues. You have paid for your passion in humiliation, mutilation, and sometimes – as when Henry VIII burned Bible translator William Tyndale as a heretic – even immolation. I salute you all, as do my fellow books. Were you to call yourselves heroes, we would not smirk. Show me an accomplished reader, and I shall show you a person of many virtues, thoughtful and articulate, contemplative though rarely passive, temperate and yet benignly

*

Ambitious
beyond his intellect,
though timid in congruence with
his clumsiness, Tobias Arnold Crompton
had never fallen in love at first sight before, but now he'd
done so, and the situation was causing him far more puzzlement than pleasure. The woman of his dreams was inaccessible. Insuperable circumstances, wide as any moat, high as any rampart, precluded the possibility of a chance meeting, let alone a tryst. Not knowing her name, Tobias had taken to calling her Bathsheba, for his plight indeed evoked King David peering down from the palace roof and beholding Uriah's comely wife performing her ablutions.

Two times a week, whilst carrying packets along the Amesbury Post Road for the Provincial Mail Commission, Tobias was privileged to observe Bathsheba labouring on the Nimacook plantation. Beyond her ridiculous bonnet of husks, she was a woman of transcendent desirability, one who made the cultivation of a maize crop – digging the furrow, inserting the seeds, adding a dead fish for fertilizer, extracting the weeds, harvesting the ears, uprooting the barren stalks, bundling them into sheaves for tinder – seem an arcane sport reserved to Vestal virgins or Greek goddesses. If by some blessed turn of fortune Bathsheba became Tobias's wife, his joy would surely propel him through the ranks of his profession until he reached the pinnacle, Postmaster General of the British Crown Colonies in America.

She was manifestly the Indians' unwilling prisoner, not an adopted bride now reconciled to her fate or a sentimentalist playing at savagery, for they kept her on a halter, the cruel strap running from her neck to the wrist of a Nimacook hag, probably her mother-in-law. Beyond this evidence was the fact of Bathsheba's visage, with its endless sadness and chronic grief – the face of one who longed for an Englishman's kiss.

A plan formed in Tobias's throbbing brain. He saw himself galloping onto the plantation like a knight seeking to save a maiden from a dragon, then sweeping up Bathsheba in a gesture so heroic that she could not help but requite his adoration. It was the sort of derring-do he might have rendered in a poem, were he a poet, or in a painting, were he an artist, or in reality, were he a man of action.

But, alas, there beat within the mail-carrier's breast the heart of a procrastinator, if not an outright poltroon. I am a sorry Lancelot, he told himself. I make a puny Percival. But as the harvest ended and the autumn air stiffened with intimations of winter, he realized that Bathsheba would soon depart the maize field, and so he picked an imminent date for the great rescue, the 20th of October, the very day that, four years earlier, Harriet Easty of Amesbury had told him, 'Given a choice in marriage partners 'twixt yourself and a boar-pig, I should vastly prefer the latter.'

He rose before dawn, dressed hurriedly and secured beneath his belt the two essential tools: his pistol, loaded and ready, and his knife – the one he used for opening undeliverable epistles ('dead letters' in the parlance of his trade) in the hope of learning the whereabouts of the sender or intended recipient. As the sun's first rays touched the shingled peaks and whitewashed steeples of Boston, he saddled Jeremiah, slung the mail valises over the gelding's rump, and rode out along the cobblestoned streets. Reaching the post road, he urged his mount to a trot. Bathsheba rarely stayed on the job past noon, but if the horse kept up the pace, Tobias would reach the plantation no later than eleven o'clock.

He broke his fast in Stoneham, fed and watered Jeremiah, then continued north. Three hours later, Tobias cast an eye on his beloved.

Tethered as always, she stood further from the road than usual, braiding together maize-ears by their husks with an élan worthy of Ceres herself, then hanging them to dry on a gallows-like lintel. A full five yards separated Bathsheba and the hag, a gap sufficient for his escapade. He unsheathed his knife and, jabbing his boot heel into Jeremiah's ribs, charged across the field. Reaching Bathsheba, he leaned down and with a grand flourish simultaneously severed the halter, freed his beloved, lost his balance, and tumbled off his horse.

A bundle of sheaves cushioned his fall, and after a brief episode of flailing about in the dirt he gained his feet and glanced all around him. Much to his delight, he saw that the day was not lost, for during his interval on the ground Bathsheba had seized the reins and hauled herself onto the horse's back. Tobias had but to join her in the saddle anon, and the two of them would ride off together.

But Bathsheba had a different idea. She guided the horse along a rank of standing stalks and reined up before her mother-in-law.

'Tell Okommaka I shall remember him with affection!' Bathsheba shouted, after which she exclaimed a brief sentence – presumably the identical message – in the incomprehensible Nimacook language. The hag replied loudly and angrily using the same confounding tongue, whereupon Bathsheba wheeled the horse around, galloped across the field and disappeared down the road, taking the mail valises with her.

No sooner had this distressing development occurred than Tobias noticed the hag running towards him, her bony hand clamped around a fowling-piece. She paused and fired. The ball whistled past his cheek. He drew forth his pistol, but before he could take aim the old woman vanished amidst the drying-racks. He jammed his pistol into his belt and took off, as fixed in his purpose as any mother determined to retrieve her stolen baby from a band of Gypsies.

Throughout the subsequent hour, as he puffed and groaned his way down the Amesbury Post Road, Tobias's mental disposition oscillated betwixt stupefying humiliation and near dementia. With each passing farm he devised yet another narrative by which he might convince his employers that the loss of the valises had been unavoidable – brigands, Indians, a lightning-bolt, a tornado, a bear with an appetite for paper – but none enjoyed the ring of plausibility. He did not know which situation chastened him more: his imminent dismissal, or his woeful misassessment of Bathsheba's nature.

Shortly after three o'clock – so said Tobias's pocket-watch – he encountered an itinerant pedlar, his wagon a rattling concatenation of pots, pans, knives and scissors, and the next thing he knew the gnarled old man was offering him a ride to Boston. Tobias blessed his luck and climbed aboard. On reaching the town, the pedlar dropped him off in Treamount Square. A serrated wind arose, cutting through Tobias's benumbed and humbled flesh. He walked down Sudbury Street to Hannover, followed the flagstones to his door and entered the townhouse, at which juncture his despair evaporated with the suddenness of a sneeze.

Still dressed in her Nimacook leathers, though missing her grotesque bonnet, Bathsheba sat in the drawing-room, holding a glass of his best Rhenish and paging through his *Aeneid*. Her moccasined feet rested on the Oriental stool, beside which lay both mail valises.·

'If this is the taste of civilization, I'm entirely in favour of it,' she said, taking a sip of wine. A sensual, smoky voice, each syllable bathed in molasses. 'Fear not for your amiable horse – I stabled him 'round the corner at Chadwick's Livery.'

'You are a skilled equestrienne,' he said admiringly.

'I apologize for stealing your mount, Mr Crompton, but I thought you a highwayman with designs upon my virtue. Only after noticing these valises did I realize that you'd contrived a rescue, and so I made such inquiries as brought me to your house.'

'Your deliverance was in sooth my aim,' he said, his voice quavering with awe. The goddess was right here – in his own parlour – barely six feet away! 'May I speak bluntly? From the moment I saw you labouring in the heathen field, my heart became yours to do with as you will. Indeed, but for one stark fact I would now make bold to ask for your hand in marriage.'

'What stark fact? That I might spurn you?'

'That I know not your name.'

'Waequashim,' she said.

'Your given name, I mean.'

'Waewowesheckmishquashim.'

'Your *real* name.'

'Jennet . . . Stearne,' she said slowly, as if speaking the words for the first time. She snapped his Virgil shut. 'Now 'tis *my* turn to indulge in the crudest candour. Your antics today bespeak a chivalrous heart, and this house is undeniably convivial. I seek a kind of patron, someone who might feed and clothe me whilst I undertake a philosophic project.'

He stood up straight as a pike, throwing back his shoulders. 'At present I am a lowly mailcarrier, but before the year is out I shall command the entire Boston Post Office.'

'Most ambitious. Do you perchance enjoy access to the library at Harvard College?'

'My younger brother attends that very institution, in training for the ministry!'

'Then I assent to your proposition,' she said.

'Oh, my dear lady, do my ears deceive me? You would become my bride?'

'On the understanding that my loyalties will also extend to my Baconian investigations.'

'I should love my wife even if she were an alchemist!'

'And on the supplementary understanding that I shall ne'er count myself a Puritan.'

'There are but sixscore baptized Anglicans in Boston, and yet your Tobias is amongst them!'

'And on the further understanding that 'tis no applecheeked virgin you'll be taking to your bed.'

'I have long supposed you the victim of many brutal ravishings by your heathen husband.'

'No ravishings to speak of, merely a mutual enthusiasm concerning the carnal domain. But if you'll forgive me my past, I believe that Providence will smile upon our future.'

''Tis axiomatic I should absolve the woman I love.'

Possessed by a wild and unaccountable impulse, he reached into both valises simultaneously and, gathering up a great mass of mail, threw the lot into the air. As the myriad packets settled to the floor, he pictured himself afloat on a magic sea, bits of foam descending all around him. He glanced towards his bride. Once again the *Aeneid* had entranced her. How marvellous, he thought. Before her abduction, she'd evidently been a kind of sage. Their marriage, it seemed, would never lack for stimulating conversation, and might soon bid fair to become the loftiest in Boston.

Jennet would be the first to admit that marriages of convenience were not the noblest arrangements on Earth, but no one could deny that the institution boasted an impressive history. What was the affair of Cleopatra and Julius Caesar if not a marriage of convenience binding Egypt to Rome? What was the Catholic Church if not a marriage of convenience fusing an emergent Christianity to a venerable paganism? What had Magna Carta consecrated if not a pragmatic conciliation betwixt King John and his barons? Should a loveless union be the price of her demon disproof, she was willing to pay it, though she hoped that she would not break her husband's heart into the bargain.

True to his prediction, with the coming of summer Tobias ascended to the position of Boston Postmaster, which meant he no longer spent protracted and depleting days on horseback. For Jennet this promotion proved a mixed blessing. On the asset side of the ledger, his increased salary enabled him to hire a maid-servant from amongst the Long Wharf rabble newly arrived on the brigantine *Flying Fish*: Nellie Adams, a stout young Chelmsford widow whose competence at marketing, cooking, mending and laundering secured for Jennet sufficient time each day to pursue what Tobias called 'this admirable campaign against your brother's unholy band'. Alas, her husband's less strenuous regimen had him coming home each evening abrim with residual vigour. Jennet's despair lay not so much in the failure of his ungainly frame, equine face and weather-vane ears to arouse her, but rather in his refusal to allow that the carnal arts had progressed considerably since Adam had first lain with Eve. Her rhapsodic accounts of the secrets revealed in 'Labia North and South' and 'The Lust of the Goat' brought to his cheeks not the flush of concupiscence but the blush of embarrassment, until at last she decided to end his connubial education and scandalize him no more. While she would hesitate to call Tobias a man for whom ignorance was bliss, it seemed likely that in matters of bliss this man would always be ignorant.

When he learned that her marriage to the Nimacook trapper had resulted in a female infant, a fit of jealousy seized Tobias – evidently he'd managed to convince himself that Jennet and Okommaka had swived but rarely – though he immediately became the soul of condolence upon hearing that the child had died of the smallpox. Unfortunately, his reaction to Bella's passing went beyond mere sympathy. He wanted to efface the tragedy itself. Jennet's grief, he insisted, would truly subside only after she'd produced a second child – and, of course, nothing would bring him greater satisfaction than to father a strapping baby boy or entracing little girl.

Although pregnancy was the last circumstance Jennet wished to endure at this point in her life, she resolved to maintain Tobias's goodwill by feigning enthusiasm for the prospect, even as she arranged to keep her body unencumbered. Each time she entered the house bearing pennyroyal or marjoram from Pratt's Apothecary, she would allude to her philosophic pursuits, when in truth these ingredients were the key to Hassane's unguent against conception. She rarely experienced any difficulty, prior to the copulative moment, finding a pretext for slipping briefly away, subsequently applying the paste to her womanly canal, and by pleading a contrary stomach or a troublesome tooth she generally succeeded in avoiding Tobias on her days of peak fertility.

Thanks to her brother-in-law, Wilmot Crompton, whose privileges as a divinity student included a borrower's licence from the Harvard College library, she came into temporary possession of the major works by 'the three John W's', as Aunt Isobel had termed witch-hunting's most conspicuous opponents: John Webster, John Wagstaffe and Johann Weyer. But it was the labyrinthine Beacon Street bookshop called Darby's that proved for Jennet a true cornucopia, equipping her with not only a fresh copy of the *Principia Mathematica* but also the particular treatises Newton had recommended as stepping-stones to his opus. Inevitably she happened upon volumes by Royal Society fellows other than Newton – Henry More's *An Antidote against Atheism*, Joseph Glanvill's *Saducismus Triumphatus*, Robert Boyle's *The Sceptical Chymist* – but she decided not to squander her husband's money, for Isobel had labelled these men witch believers all.

Darby's also carried newspapers, including *The London Journal*, *The New-England Courant*, *The American Weekly Mercury*, and, most energizing for Jennet, the Calvinists' own periodical, *The Bible Commonwealth*, which routinely reported on the Massachusetts Bay Purification

Commission and its Scottish counterpart, the Kirkcaldy Cleansing League, in a style that oscillated unpredictably betwixt sober detachment ('We must not forget that our best Defence against Demons lies in Praying, not Pricking') and giddy enthusiasm ('These brave Cleansers have hasten'd the Day when Satan will quit Christendom for ever'). A project soon suggested itself, and Jennet subsequently secured from Darby's an unruled leather folio, decorating the first page with fat blockish characters: *The Devil and All His Works*. In the months that followed, upon the appearance of a new *Bible Commonwealth*, she would scissor out each article concerning Dunstan's band and paste it into the folio. Whenever the quest exhausted her, whenever it seemed that she would never align the Greek immutables with Newton's principles and thereby recover his demon disproof, she would peruse *The Devil and All His Works*, forthwith finding her anger renewed and her ambition replenished.

Although she'd intended to spend the winter studying the three John W's, she was barely ten pages into Webster's *Displaying of Supposed Witchcraft* ere noticing that the author did not doubt the existence of wicked spirits, and it happened that an analogous credulity infected Wagstaffe's *The Question of Witchcraft Debated* and Weyer's *De Praestigiis Daemonum*. True, these men held views that would enrage a Cotton Mather or a Walter Stearne. The John W's variously argued for the impossibility of developing unambiguous cases against accused sorcerers, for the possibility that Satan's vanity prevented him from granting magical powers to hags, and for the probability that human misery traced to forces other than *maleficium*. But none dared mount a frontal assault on demonology itself.

She set the John W's aside and delved into Newton's intellectual ancestors. It took her two months to negotiate the whole of Euclid, but she absorbed all the postulates and ingested all the proofs without mishap (though she deliberately skipped Book X and its impenetrable discussion of incommensurable magnitudes), and she had an equally gratifying experience with De Witt's *Elementa Curvarum*. When she turned to Bartholin's *Commentaries on Descartes's Geometry*, however, she managed to solve only seven problems out of the thirty Newton had prescribed, and she endured even more humiliation at the hands of Huygens's *Horologium Oscillatorium*, a work of maddening obscurity and intractable trigonometry.

She was on the verge of despair when late one evening, acting on an impulse whose origins she could not divine, she began turning back the pages of the *Principia Mathematica* itself. For a full hour she meandered through Newton's rarefied realm, whereupon a strange unbidden radiance suffused her being, the sort of benign seizure a Philadelphia Quaker might have called the Inner Light. She understood this book! Not in its particulars, certainly, not in the details of its lemmas and proofs, but the author's overarching design seemed suddenly, utterly, wonderfully clear.

For all its grandeur, the universe posited by Euclid had been from its inception a frozen domain. Five centuries of such stasis had elapsed, ten centuries, fifteen — and then, *mirabile dictu*, enter Isaac Newton, bestowing time and motion on geometry. Under Newton's persuasion the Euclidian shapes had grown wings and gone soaring across the sky. The Lucasian Professor had made butterflies of parabolas, wrought eagles from hyperbolas and set spheres dancing like seraphs.

While her qualified comprehension of the *Principia* made Jennet buoyant of heart and joyful of mind, these feelings did not endure, for the impossible task still lay before her, looming like the mile-high minaret of the Tall-Tower Problem. Somehow she must synthesize all this Newtonian kineticism with the Aristotelian immutables from which God had built the world.

Her epiphany occurred in, of all places, Saint Mark's Anglican Church. She was sitting in the front pew, Tobias's thigh pressed against her own, the hare-lipped Reverend Dowd presenting his idiosyncratic interpretation of the Wedding at Cana — he averred that the wine Christ had wrought from water that day was not wholly consumed, the surplus re-emerging months later at the Last Supper — when she fell upon a train of reasoning that she sensed might lead, God willing, Kautantouwit assenting, to her philosophic Grail.

As any educated person knew, Aristotle and Newton had each reduced the cosmos to underlying components, Aristotle anatomizing its matter, Newton its motion. Newton's system was by far the more complex, and yet Jennet believed that she detected, in both the *Principia Mathematica* and 'A New Theory about Light and Colours', an assumption that the kinetic universe, like its Aristotelian counterpart, consisted of four basic elements, namely acceleration, attraction, resistance and — when you considered the great prism paper of 1668 —

radiation. Ah, but look how simple it was to map one universe onto the other! For radiation, the Aristotelian connection was obvious: Newton's experiments with light depended upon the sun, source of the Greek immutable called fire. Concerning attraction, she was quick to associate this entity with the Greek element earth, magnetite being amongst the most essential components of the planet's crust, with other such minerals doubtless awaiting discovery. When it came to acceleration, a match with the element air seemed warranted: even if you rejected Cartesian vortices, you were obliged to recognize that Earth's atmosphere and the aether beyond held immaterial substances that gave gravity its *gravitas*. In the case of the remaining entities – Newtonian resistance and Aristotelian water – she did not hesitate to link them, for Book Two of the *Principia* had much to say about the behaviour of pendulums slicing through inhibiting fluids.

Attraction, acceleration, radiation, resistance: earth, air, fire, water – could any reasonable person doubt that Newtonian motion was every bit as primal, every jot as fundamental, as Aristotelian matter? It would seem that the bracing biblical revelation, *And God saw that it was good*, now enjoyed a logical corollary, *And God saw that it moved virtuously*. Ah, but if such were the case, then surely Jehovah had in the beginning systematically barred Satan's invisible minions from *both* domains – stuff and flux – so systematically, in fact, that a philosopher would be justified in declaring these minions nonexistent!

'Ergo, to recover Newton's lost disproof,' she muttered to herself, 'one need only establish the essential benevolence of the myriad motion-spirits that serve and facilitate the four kinetic entities.'

'Mrs Crompton, prithee, be quiet,' Tobias whispered.

The Reverend Dowd sent a scowl her way.

'For all Satan tries to corrupt these spirits,' she mumbled, 'he must always fail, as God hath made them invulnerable to temptation.'

'Stay your tongue,' Tobias said.

'Such was Aunt Isobel's insight on the pyre!'

'Silence!'

The following morning Jennet bid Nellie Adams gather up their materials – lodestone, pendulum, prism, pair of wooden ramps – and accompany her to the home of Lydia Trimble, a nursing mother whose husband owned a tavern in Ship Street. At first the Hammer of Witchfinders had no luck elucidating for Mrs Trimble why she wished to conduct natural philosophy experiments on the premises, and how the woman's lactations fitted into the design, but then Jennet opened her purse, and the glister of its guineas proved explanation enough. Whilst Mrs Trimble suckled her baby beside the hearth, Jennet and Nellie performed an earth demonstration, using the lodestone's invisible fingers to pull a hobnail across the floor, thereby releasing those motion-spirits, whether sinister or saintly, that served the kinetic element called attraction – saintly, evidently, for they declined to impede Mrs Trimble's milk. Jennet next did a water experiment, making the pendulum oscillate through beer, honey, whale-oil, and other fluids of varying densities. The unleashed spirits of resistance forbore to disrupt the nursing process. She then performed a fire experiment, instructing Nellie to hold the prism to the window; the morning sun flashed through the glass pentahedron, and radiation's agents got busy, trans-muting the beam into a rainbow. Mrs Trimble's breast remained productive. That afternoon Jennet and Nellie did several experiments keyed to Aristotelian air, observing how acceleration's spirits imposed a uniform velocity on spheres of different weights rolled down wooden ramps. The baby continued to feast.

Two days later Jennet's purse persuaded a poultry farmer named Hugh Berridge to admit the kinetic experiments into the vicinity of his chicken coops. The hens never stopped laying. At noon Mr Berridge's wife leased her churning skills to the cause. The butter came in full. That evening Jennet persuaded a confused but accommodating Tobias to swive her as she manipulated her philosophy tools. The demon-strations surely conjured many motion-spirits, but they worked no mischief on his manhood.

'The kinetic elements are moral to the core, with ne'er a malefactor in the lot!' Jennet declared. 'Lucifer could ne'er warp such sterling spirits!'

'That surely sounds correct to me, darling,' Tobias said, stroking her naked thigh.

Of course, Jennet reasoned, these results did not mean the motion-spirits were omnipotent. Only the Creator Himself enjoyed that attribute. Try though they might, the agents in question were powerless to shield humankind from blizzards, thunder-gusts, blights or contagions — all those natural shocks wrongly attributed to demons. But God had no more ceded the universe of action to fallen angels and malevolent imps than He'd assembled the world from fungus and dung.

It took Jennet six days and as many rough drafts before she had an *argumentum grande* that fell felicitously on her ear. 'All flowings and fallings,' she wrote by way of an inaugural sentence, 'all flappings and snappings, all swingings and springings, all splittings and flittings know naught of goblins but only of goodness.'

She purchased a stack of parchment at Darby's, printed a title across the topmost sheet, *Contra Daemonologie*, and copied out the final version, eight pages long, using her best hand. Obviously the momentous document required a signature, and after some deliberation she settled on 'J. S. Crompton, Curator, Cavendish Museum of Wondrous Prodigies, Colonial Branch'. All that remained was for her to dispatch the treatise to Kensington Palace, accompanied by an explanatory note.

An Appeal
To Her Most Esteemed Majesty,
Queen Anne,
Defender of the Faith,
Ruler of All England, Scotland, Ireland, and France:

By enacting various Newtonian Demonstrations in a Manner design'd to goad Motion-Spirits to Maleficium, the Cavendish Museum hath in recent Days prov'd that the four Kinetic Entities are benign in Character, forever immur'd against the Devil's Wiles. If Her Most Sovereign Majesty agrees with the Conclusions express'd in the enclos'd Treatise, we would humbly ask that she set this Matter before both Houses of Parliament, that they might repeal the 1604 Witchcraft Statute of King James I.

Your humble Subject,
J.S. Crompton, Esq.
19 September 1710

An expert in postal systems and their vicissitudes, Tobias confidently forecast the fate of *Contra Daemonologie*. If the *Columbine*, as sturdy a mail-ship as had ever crossed the Atlantic Sea, did not fall prey to storms or pirates, the treatise would be in the Queen's hands by the 10th of November.

'Proud I am to call myself your husband,' he told Jennet as they stood together on Long Wharf watching the *Columbine* glide across the harbour. 'Great was my satisfaction in making my seminal donation to demonology's demise.'

'You're a good man, Mr Crompton.'

'I'm a dull man, Mrs Crompton.'

'That too, but in the months to come I shall strive to be a better wife to you.'

In the months to come . . . the phrase brought a chill to her bones. What, exactly, might she do with the rest of her life? Cleave to this inert marriage? Having swum in the wild rivers of Nimacook paganism and sailed the uncharted seas of Newtonian experimentalism, she had little desire to paddle about the shallow pond of Boston respectability. Perhaps she would become the first woman ever to teach Euclidian geometry at Harvard College. Perhaps she would start a school for governesses, impressing her students with the necessity of going beyond antiquity's tongues and Aristotle's insights to instruct their charges in the new mechanical philosophy. But no matter how intently she gazed into the prism of her aspirations, she did not see Tobias Crompton looking back.

When Jennet discovered that, despite Aunt Isobel's charts and Hassane's unguent, a child was growing inside her, she instinctively attributed this catastrophe to her Creator's will, though her husband's virility had clearly played a part as well. Evidently Jehovah had decided that He would spare her the inconvenience of progeny only until she'd birthed the *argumentum grande*, and now she was constrained to present the world with a *miraculum minitum* as well.

Having lost her first child to the smallpox, she could not help fearing that some equally diabolical phenomenon would destroy her second baby too. She combated these premonitions with every weapon at her disposal.

During the early weeks of her pregnancy she consumed the blend of wild mushrooms that Hassane believed prevented miscarriage. As her fifth month commenced, she availed herself daily of juniper tea, the Nima-cook prescription against premature delivery. The quickening phase found her ingesting great quantities of red-fern and yarrow, which in the experience of her Lyn Street neighbour, a midwife named Sarah Dinwidie, protected an infant from illness not only in the womb but throughout the first postnatal year. The instant the spasms began, she sought out Mrs Dinwidie, and together the women went to Chadwick's Livery and appropriated a vacant stall abounding in fresh straw. Whilst the midwife whispered words of encouragement, Jennet pressed her back against the wall, grabbed the partition, bent her knees, and prayed.

The spasms intensified. Her screams frightened the horses and put two cats to flight. The pangs grew stronger yet, as did her cries. She felt as if she were about to birth the Maw of Folkestone, or perhaps Perdition's Pride.

'I don't even *want* this blasted babe!' she shrieked.

'Many are the times I've heard a customer speak those very words,' Mrs Dinwidie assured her. ''Tis the very litany of your predicament.'

After an interval of two hours, through the operations of God Almighty and universal gravitation, a pink and slippery female infant descended into Mrs Dinwidie's waiting hands.

This time, Jennet resolved, her daughter's name would be free of all sentimental connection. She certainly wasn't going to use 'Bella' again, neither would she christen the infant 'Margaret' after her mother nor 'Catherine' after her mother's mother. 'Rachel' had always struck Jennet as a robust and resonant vocable, and when she presented the idea to Tobias he acquiesced without quarrel, though he insisted on augmenting the choice with his late mother's name. And so it was that on the fifth of May 1711, the Reverend Dowd drew a watery cross on the forehead of Rachel Veronica Crompton, thus alerting Heaven to the presence of another salvation-worthy Protestant in the world.

Rachel's life began auspiciously. She was a ruddy infant with bright hazel eyes, a strong cry, a precocious smile, and no tendency towards the colic, this last asset doubtless attributable to Mrs Dinwidie's pharma-ceutical wisdom. Tobias, not surprisingly, idolized his daughter from the outset, but Jennet refused to relax her vigilance, for it still seemed probable the child would perish ere reaching her first birthday. And yet one succulent spring morning, five weeks after the baptism, Jennet realized that she adored Rachel past all telling, a circumstance that felt rather like the pregnancy itself: precautions had been taken, those precautions had failed, and now the ambiguous consequences were upon her.

Although Tobias urged Jennet to employ a wet-nurse, such a service being comfortably within their budget, she decided to suckle the baby herself. Especially gratifying were the events that followed each feeding. She would set Rachel betwixt her breasts and revel in the pressure of the warm, compacted, breathing bundle, as if her own heart had been mysteriously transported outside of her body.

Yet for all the pleasurable feelings it entailed, all the agreeable obligations, motherhood failed to distract Jennet from the fact that the Queen had not responded to *Contra Daemonologie*. When Rachel learned to walk, travelling across Boston Common through a combination of tentative steps and comical tumbles, Jennet's joy could not cancel the melancholy caused by Her Majesty's conspicuous disinterest in the demon disproof. As the child progressed from random babbling to coherent words to complete sentences, Jennet's delight was betimes diluted by the Crown's failure to acknowledge either the treatise itself or her subsequent inquiries into its disposition. Shortly after her fourth birthday, Rachel employed her poppets in an improvised theatre piece about a woman philosopher who rode a cannon-ball to the moon, and Jennet's soul swelled with pride, but this pleasure was severely circumscribed by the silence from Kensington Palace. On the first day in October 1715, a brown-skinned courier appeared at Jennet's door bearing a packet displaying the provenance label of a certain Lord Wentworth in Essex County, England. She paid the manumitted Negro a guinea and, with the enthusiasm of Juliet opening a letter from her Montague swain, ripped apart the envelope and drew out the vellum sheet.

25 July 1715

Dear J. S. Crompton:

Her Majesty hath instruct'd the Privy Council to respond to your Contra Daemonologie, *which reach'd Kensington Palace in November of 1711. After some months of Deliberation we plac'd the document with an eminent Natural Philosopher to whom the Council oft-times turns in such Cases. Dr Edmund Halley, Fellow of the Royal Society, eventually wrote to us as follows:*

> *'Mr Crompton's Intentions are doubtless honourable, and his chosen Methodology boasts a novel and astute Design. The present Treatise is so lacking in Detail, however, so bereft of Thoroughness and Rigour, that it inclines a rational Man towards a Conclusion quite opposite to the Author's.'*

Concerning our own Reaction, we find your approach so Impious as to be but one Degree of Remove from Atheism. When a Person presumes to reduce the World's Workings to self-sustaining Principles, whether he calls them 'Forces' following Mr Newton (who subscribes, we must note, to the deplorable Arian Religion) or 'Kinetic Entities' per your Treatise, he must take great Care lest he give unwitting Comfort to those Deists and Freethinkers who would dislodge the Christian God from Creation's Centre.

To wit, we shan't be troubling the English Parliament, and certainly not Her Most Sovereign Majesty, with your misguided Investigations.

Philip Tyrrell,
Earl of Wentworth
Lord Privy Seal

Owing to the Indian attack on Haverhill, Jennet had never enacted her wonderful plan to rip her father's cleansing licence from his door and mutilate it beyond recognition. But now, suddenly, she had in her hand an equally noxious document. She tore Lord Wentworth's letter into pieces, then tore the pieces into bits, then fed the bits to the fire in the kitchen hearth, where Nellie Adams was at that moment baking a half-dozen loaves of wheaten bread.

'How *durst* they reject my treatise!' Jennet shrieked.

''Tis an insult to our good labours,' Nellie said.

'Those morons! Those dunces! Numskulls, I call them! Buffoons! Mooncalves! Puddingheads! Nincompoops!'

'That's exactly what they are, ma'am.'

Perhaps if he'd seen Giles Corey lying beside Salem-Town

Courthouse, pinned under the granite blocks – or stood on the Shawsheen River Bridge and heard Susan Diggens cry 'Help me, friend Indian!' – Tobias might have apprehended the magnitude of her desolation. Instead he could only offer observations of a sort she found more irritating than soothing.

'If the great Dr Halley sees no use in trying to disprove demons,' he told her, 'then mayhap 'tis a less worthy enterprise than you believe.'

'Dr Halley does not gainsay the purpose of my project,' she snapped, 'and he calls its design novel and astute.'

'But if the demonologists are so misguided as you aver, would not England's philosophers have argued them out of business by now?'

'Dear Tobias, methinks you play the dolt without half trying. If the Royal Society hath attempted no *argumentum grande*, 'tis only for want of motivation. Should the day arrive when Dr Halley finds himself accused of sorcery, a dozen demon disproofs will pour from his pen, for terror's a most inspiring sponsor.'

As happened so often in Jennet's life, salvation arrived in the person of a book. On the Monday following her receipt of Lord Wentworth's vile letter, the second edition of *Philosophiae Naturalis Principia Mathematica* appeared in Darby's front window bearing a publication date of 1713, and as she turned back the thick fragrant leaves, she noticed that Book Three concluded with a new Scholium. Its matter was God. Whether acquiescing to external Anglican pressure or responding to some private revelation, Mr Newton now insisted (if she could trust her Latin) that 'this most beautiful system of the sun, planets, and comets' depended upon 'the counsel of an intelligent and powerful Being', which idea he proceeded to elaborate over the next five pages.

Joy flooded her heart. The Privy Council feared that those who methodized Nature's workings trafficked in atheism, and yet here was Newton, spicing his postulates with Providence as effortlessly as a cook might add rum to a cake batter. Of course, she would never quote the geometer directly – not so long as he cleaved to 'the deplorable Arian Religion' – but it was obvious that if you chose your words thoughtfully, Baconian experimentalism could be made to seem as pious as the Beatitudes.

Then there were Dr Halley's requirements of detail, thoroughness, and rigour. She vowed to make her revised *Contra Daemonologie* detailed to a fault, with a thoroughness to tax an angel's patience and a rigour sufficient to snap iron. This time around, she would not merely wade into the *Principia*'s shallows – she would dive into its rollers and plumb its deepest trenches.

'I am Lazarus, come back from the abyss,' she announced to Tobias shortly after Nellie finished laying out their crab-cake dinner. 'I shall give the Privy Council a treatise so sodden with God 'twill make Martin Luther's *Ninety-Five Theses* seem but a grocery list! I'll shower Dr Halley with pages enough to wipe his bum from Epiphany to Michaelmas!'

'How delighted I am that your melancholia hath passed,' Tobias muttered.

'An affectionate sentiment, but spoken without feeling,' she said. 'What ails you, Mr Crompton?'

'I'Christ, woman, can you not see that in constructing this second and more elaborate treatise, you will grievously neglect our daughter?'

Taking up knife and fork, she carefully hexed her crab-cake. 'Such fatalism ill becomes you, sir.'

'Methinks you confuse fatalism with foresight,' Tobias said, tearing apart a fragrant loaf of bread. 'Tell me you'll abandon this scheme.'

She placed a crab-cake wedge in her mouth and chewed. 'I would ne'er renounce my life's very purpose.'

'You cannot be a fit mother to Rachel, nor yet a proper wife to me, and still wear the clothes of a natural philosopher.'

'Might I give you my opinion?' She consumed a second morsel. 'By my lights the clothes of a natural philosopher are considerably more dignified than the livery of the Boston Postmaster.'

'Then you will be pleased to know I am on the point of changing that very garment.'

Tobias buttered his bread, sipped his claret, and explained himself. The previous evening a missive had arrived from the Royal Mail Authority offering him employment as Postmaster-General for the British Crown Colonies in America. He had already drafted his letter of acceptance. By the end of the month they would all be Philadelphians, living in William Penn's famous province to the south. Their new situation, he insisted, had everything to recommend it – a higher income, a lower latitude, a larger house.

'Congratulations,' she said, a barbed sneer in her voice. 'You have toiled most diligently for this appointment.'

'I pray you, Mrs Crompton, judge not these fruits ere you've tasted them.'

An unhappy presentiment suffused her, for she knew nothing of Philadelphia save its reputation as a hotbed of Quaker fanaticism. But Tobias was not about to solicit her views on the matter. The instant he spoke the words 'Postmaster-General' in the same hushed and reverent voice her father had employed when pronouncing 'Witchfinder-Royal', she understood that their relocation was a fait accompli.

Aunt Isobel had always averred that the universe abounded in forking paths, and yet it seemed to Jennet that only one course lay open to her just then. She must pack up her prisms and her pendulums, tell Rachel that circumstances were taking them to a warmer clime, and pray to Jehovah and Kautantouwit that the City of Brotherly Love might one day acquire a second epithet: the Cradle of Demon Disproofs.

Despite Jennet's misgivings, her new environs and the revised *argumentum grande* proved uncannily compatible with each other. The thoroughfares of Philadelphia constituted a tidy grid, and whenever she left their Chestnut Street townhouse to stroll amidst this rectilinear arrangement, a concomitant orderliness descended upon her thinking. Equally vital were the energy and inspiration she drew from the omnipresent Society of Friends. Although her Quaker neighbours indeed practised several varieties of irrationality, including the eponymous paroxysms on display in their meeting-houses, they had nevertheless bestowed on Pennsylvania an ethos whereby hunting, hanging, or even talking about witches seemed quite the silliest of activities.

By the time Rachel had celebrated her fifth birthday, the undercurrent of disgruntlement that Tobias brought to most of his dealings with Jennet had transmuted into an overt hostility. His bitterness traced not just to the demon disproof, which he viewed as progressing only at Rachel's expense, but also to his wife's failure to conceive a second child. While Jennet privately ascribed this situation to Hassane's unguent, she offered her husband a much less plausible though far more palatable explanation: God had elected to seal her womb until she'd defeated the Witchcraft Act.

'How durst you presume to know the designs of Providence!' Tobias roared. 'Such arrogance appals me!'

'I warned you of my philosophic passions from the first,' she reminded him.

'Shall I tell you my darkest suspicion, Mrs Crompton? I believe you deprive me of a son through the sheer force of your womanly will.'

'If womanly will could accomplish such a feat,' she snarled, 'there'd be far fewer squalling babes in the world at this moment – of that I can assure you!'

Her favourite place for perusing the second edition of the *Principia Mathematica* was the sprawling meadow on the eastern shore of the Schuylkill River, a tract on which the city's day-labourers had recently staked out a bowling-green. Whenever the weather allowed it, she and Rachel and Nellie would arrive before noon, luncheon-basket in hand. During the subsequent hour they would consume their wheaten bread and cold meat at a leisurely pace, whilst Jennet held her companions spellbound with the Moon-Bead Legend or some other nugget of the Nimacook imagination – the Fable of the Wily Raven, the Parable of the Greedy Porcupine, the Adventure of the Tortoise Who Had No Shell. After the meal Jennet would begin the day's struggles with Newton, leaving Rachel and Nellie to wander about in search of amusement. Sometimes they enacted Nimacook stories using Rachel's poppets. Sometimes they watched the men rolling their bowls across the green. But Rachel's preferred activity was to sit by the river's edge and catch fish, for she was now an expert in the bobber-and-hook method her mother had mastered many years earlier on the banks of the Merrimack.

One sweltering August afternoon, Jennet took up the luncheon-basket, shouldered Rachel's fishing-pole, and set off with her daughter for the Schuylkill, her intention being to loll in the meadow and thoroughly digest Newton's theology, the better to avoid tainting the new *argumentum grande* with some subtle Arian heresy. Nellie was absent from their company, for Tobias had given her the day off, that she might visit her brother's family in Cohasset. Arriving at the river, mother and daughter devoured their midday repast, Jennet the whole time offering Rachel her usual lecture on the safe and proper way to fish: keep one foot planted against a rock, never yank abruptly on the line, take care lest you lean too far over the bank whilst throwing back your catch. Rachel as always assented to these conditions, and so her mother sent her off in quest of salmon and perch.

For a reading space Jennet selected a tranquil patch of shade hedged by a half-dozen maples. She entered the grove, spread her blanket on the grass, and set about pondering Newton's relationship with God.

According to her translation of the 1713 Scholium, the Supreme Being existed everywhere at once, His essence never varying from place to place, 'all eye, all ear, all brain, all arm, all power to perceive, to understand, and to act'.

She looked up. Rachel sat on the riverbank, fishing-pole in hand.

Fixing her thoughts again on Newton, Jennet learned that the Almighty operated 'in a manner not at all human, in a manner not at all corporeal, in a manner utterly unknown to us'.

She placed her finger betwixt 'utterly' and 'unknown', *omnio* and *ignotus*, then glanced towards the river in time to see Rachel snag a perch, its sleek form twisting and twitching like a bodkin in thrall to a lodestone. The child unhooked the creature and returned it to the water.

Jennet went back to her *Principia*. The Almighty, Newton averred, was best conceived as a kind of supernatural steward or spiritual landlord. 'For a being, however perfect, without dominion, cannot be called Lord God.'

A child's scream shot across the meadow.

Jennet glanced up. A monstrous void crouched beside the Schuylkill. A vacancy, a vacuum, a demon made of empty space.

Tossing Newton aside, she gained her feet and sprinted towards the river. A liquid cacophony reached her ears, an amalgam of thrashing limbs and gurgling screams. She halted at the bank. At first she saw only a frothy white turbulence; next Rachel's fishing-pole jerked into focus, riding the chaos – and then a human form appeared, submerged, one hand gripping the pole, the opposite arm flailing madly. Jennet leaned forward, making ready to pitch herself over the edge, when suddenly a hirsute man with the prodigious proportions of a blacksmith brushed past her, threw down his woollen cap, kicked off his shoes, and leapt into the water.

As a dozen more bowlers rushed onto the scene, Jennet brought her hands together in a prayerful posture. Surely the All-Eye-All-Ear-All-Brain-All-Arm who'd hurled the planets into orbit could raise a single insubstantial child from a river. Surely the Almighty could suspend His *principia* long enough to save one small virtuous life.

'Please, Lord God Jehovah!'

No sooner had Jennet voiced her entreaty than a sobbing, shivering, wheezing Rachel climbed onto the shore, followed by the blacksmith, if such was indeed his trade, coughing and panting. Rivulets rushed down the limbs of child and man alike. The smith spat out a mouthful of water. The bowlers continued to collect on the bank, the commotion drawing them as inevitably as a lodestone beguiling iron.

'Oh, my sweet darling!' Jennet cried.

Despite her ordeal, Rachel had managed to retain the fishing-pole, which she now held before her like an infantryman brandishing a pike. 'I h-hooked an eel!'

'Mine eye's own apple!' Jennet lifted Rachel into the air, hugging her so tightly that the child's teeth stopped chattering, even as her sobs became titters of relief.

'Methinks 'twas the mightiest eel in Creation!'

Squeezing Rachel more tightly yet, Jennet planted a hundred kisses on her cheeks, freckling her with affection. 'My heart's own harbour!'

'He sought to steal my fishing-pole, but all he got was my hook!'

Jennet returned Rachel to the grassy earth, then grasped her shoulders and rotated her towards their benefactor, who now wore an expression so stern it might have humbled a troll. 'You must tell this good gentleman that your gratitude runneth over,' she instructed her daughter.

'My gratitude runneth over,' Rachel muttered tonelessly, setting the fishing-pole on her shoulder.

'I pray you, give me your name,' Jennet asked the dripping smith, 'that I might one day write a ballad in your honour.'

Much to her surprise, the man replied reprovingly. 'I am niggardly with my name, declining to share it with vain and careless persons.'

'Well spoken, brave sir!' declared a soot-smeared chimney sweep, stepping from the crowd and facing the smith. 'You are right to scorn this sister of Narcissus, who reads a book whilst her daughter nearly drowns!'

A surge of chagrin passed through Jennet, reddening her cheeks, felling her crest. Seeking to redeem herself, she faced Rachel and addressed her in a voice directed more to the mob than to the child. 'Before the week is out, your mother will undertake to tutor you in the art of swimming.'

'Ye must not besmirch the word "mother" by applying it to so unfeeling a creature as yourself!' insisted a plump and ruddy bystander wearing the blue-bibbed apron of a butcher.

'No weasel accords its young such disregard!' a linen-frocked wagoner asserted.

'No snake would deign to claim ye as a parent!' a lanthorn-seller averred.

'A slug would blush to find ye up its family tree!' cried a hatchet-faced man whose sheepskin skirt marked him as a tanner.

Uncertain how to answer this menagerie of accusations, Jennet instead grabbed Rachel by the wrist and escorted her away from the bank. The child's dress exuded a sharp, oddly pleasing fragrance, the aroma of damp silk mingled with the river's pungent mud. Upon reaching the maple grove, Jennet retrieved the blanket, the basket and her *Principia Mathematica*. She repressed an impulse to spit on Newton's masterwork. The canniest treatise yet penned had now become the most corrupt, for Jennet's reading of it had nearly cost Rachel her life.

'Tell me, darling, do you hope we might soon enjoy another sojourn by the Schuylkill?' Jennet asked.

'Aye, Mother.'

'Then you will hold silent concerning this afternoon's misadventure. Is that clear? You must not speak of it to Nellie nor to Mrs Dinwidie, nor even to your father.'

'Not even to Father?'

Jennet nodded solemnly. 'Were the postmaster to learn of your plunge, he would bar us both from these shores for ever.' She laid a hand on Rachel's soggy shoulder. 'Now hear my most sacred vow. May my hair fall out and my skin turn green if I ever again let you stray from my sight.'

'No hair?' Rachel said, giggling.

'Quite so.'

'Green skin?' the child added, snickering more exuberantly yet.

'Indeed.'

If you were five years old, it seemed, no event could be more entertaining than your mother's transmutation into an acorn squash.

Three mornings after her daughter's descent into the Schuylkill, Jennet awoke to find that Tobias had vacated their mattress — a surprising circumstance, as they both normally remained beneath the covers until Nellie announced that their veal and eggs were ready for the eating. A queasiness spread through her. The planet's axis seemed suddenly askew. She abandoned the mattress, pulled on her dressing-gown, and dashed, pulse throbbing, to her daughter's bed-chamber.

Rachel was gone. Her wardrobe had been plundered, each compartment as empty as a skull's eye-socket.

Jennet proceeded to the kitchen. Nellie sat at the mahogany table. Tears stained the maid-servant's cheeks. Red veins striated her eyes.

'I am instructed to give you this,' Nellie moaned, presenting her mistress with a folded sheet of vellum secured by a blob of tallow. 'I'Christ, Mrs Crompton, he hath stolen her away!'

Jennet cracked the seal. Tobias's spidery hand covered the vellum top to bottom.

19 August 1716

My Dear Jennet:

Three weeks ago the Royal Mail Authority propos'd to make me Postmaster-General of a far-flung Colony whose Identity I shall reveal to you at some future Date. None but a Fool would forgo this Opportunity whereby I may build a Postal System from Scratch, using everything I know about the Safety of Carriers, the Arrangement of Drops, and the optimal Deployment of Horses.

Mayhap you believe a Husband ought not to keep such a Secret from his Wife, but if Secrets are to constitute the Matter of our Conversation, I must tell you that my best Rider, the worthy Harry Bainbridge, was playing at Bowls this Sunday hard by the Scene of Rachel's near-Drowning. He hath judg'd the whole Affair an appalling Instance of maternal Disregard, the very Sort of Threat I always knew you would one Day visit upon our Child.

By the Time you read these Words, Rachel and I shall have sail'd free of America, away on the morning Tide. Assuming favourable Winds, our Carrack will reach London by October, whereupon we shall head for my new Place of Employment. Fret not, Mrs Crompton, as I mean to provide for your Welfare. The Townhouse is yours to keep, likewise the Horse Jeremiah, and you shall eventually receive from me a Stipend of thirty Pounds per Quarter, more than adequate for your material Needs as well as Nellie's Wages.

In short, I have decid'd that our Union, ne'er a Prize to begin with, hath play'd through all its Possibilities. You bear no Love for me, and your Devotion to Rachel waxes and wanes like the Moon. Indeed, I say you are bound to Naught on God's green Earth save that damnable Thesis of yours.

Be thee well, my distract'd Wife. Ere long I shall make such Arrangements as will permit you to wed another Englishman. As for myself, I doubt that I shall ever marry again, for Jennet Stearne Crompton is still my most precious Balm, even as she aspires to be my perpetual Bane.

Sincerely,
Your Tobias

'Oh, Mistress Crompton, last night Rachel told me of her fall into the river, and how the news of it hath made her father wroth,' Nellie wailed. 'Methinks this disaster is largely of my making. I should never have gone visiting on Sunday.'

'Nay, Nellie, you aren't to blame,' Jennet said. 'The fault lies in the incongruity 'twixt Mr Crompton's ambitions and mine own.'

As she read the letter a second time, all the while clenching her teeth like a surgical patient biting a musket-ball, she felt herself undergo a sea-change. Her fury transformed her. Body and brain she became a freak, the most ferocious prodigy yet acquired by the Cavendish

Museum — the Harridan of Chestnut Street. She grabbed her purse, slung the leather thong about her neck, and rushed off to Sharpe's Livery, where she outfitted Jeremiah with saddle and bridle.

It took her but fifteen minutes to reach the docks. Two towering carracks, their names obscured by mist and distance, followed the Delaware's southerly course, riding high upon the moon-drawn waters.

Locking her gaze on both vessels, she galloped to the end of Market Street Wharf and dismounted. She hitched the gelding to a mooring post, then set about importuning every passing soul. She detained sweaty sailors newly arrived in port, hawkers selling Malay teas and French laces, pale painted ladies who seemed unaccustomed to daylight, suspicious constables who believed she must be a whore herself, and leering Redcoat soldiers of the same opinion. Though no one could remember whether a child of five had recently taken ship with a rangy man of middle age, a consensus eventually emerged concerning the two carracks cruising down the river. The lead vessel was the *Antares*, bound for the Sugar Isles, that her captain might convert his cargo of lumber and flour into a cache of Barbados rum, a treasure he would subsequently redeem for two hundred West African slaves. Behind the *Antares* flew the mail-ship *Bristol Maid*, carrying tobacco, beaver hats, rattlesnake belts, private parcels — and twenty paying passengers — to England.

An image arose in Jennet's mind, a rowboat, sufficiently swift to facilitate Rachel's recapture, and soon she found one, the *Manatee*, tied to a stone pier adjoining Arch Street Wharf. The tub's owner, a sallow Quaker crabber with a beard resembling a wasp's nest, accorded her a sympathetic ear as he transferred the morning's catch from vessel to quay. Spiky claws and spiny legs probed betwixt the slats that formed the dozen crab-cages. She thought of the Colchester Castle prison-cells, those scores of beseeching arms sinuating through the iron bars.

'Thy mission hath all the marks of madness,' the Quaker said after she'd finished describing her plight.

'Doubtless you are correct.' She climbed into the rowboat, seized the penultimate crab-cage, and lifted it onto the quay. 'Pray rent me your *Manatee* for the excellent price of three pounds sterling' — she drew the tethered purse from her bodice — 'that I might fetch my Rachel.'

The crabber took the final cage in hand and scrambled free of the rowboat. 'Thy daughter sails into Delaware Bay e'en as we speak. Thou hast not a prayer of o'ertaking her.'

'Four pounds,' Jennet said.

'Wilt thou make it five?'

She shook the requisite coins into the crabber's eager palm, unfastened the *Manatee*'s line, and sat down facing the stern. Sliding both oars into the water, she brought the boat about, then pulled with all the vigor of Archimedes levering the world.

'I wish thee good fortune!' the Quaker called after her.

Stroke upon stroke, yard after yard, she chased the retreating carracks – down the river, into the bay, towards the ascending sun.

'Hallo, *Bristol Maid*! Hallo! Hallo!'

She gave the oars an emphatic yank and, pivoting on her hips, glanced towards the horizon. Already the *Antares* had dropped from sight, but the *Bristol Maid* still nicked the sky.

Turning, she resumed her labours, stroke upon stroke. *Mauminikish*, she told herself – row harder. Her back spasmed. *Mauminikish*. Her muscles sang with pain. The blisters on her palms grew big as grapes – and yet she cleaved to the task, working the oars as furiously as a Nimacook brave driving his war-canoe into battle.

'Hallo! Hallo!'

Her vision went muzzy with her tears, and she apprehended that she was close to blacking out. Again she turned. The *Bristol Maid* was gone, claimed by the planet's imperceptible curve. She shipped the left oar, then the right, and slumped forward, gasping and groaning like some half-drowned hag who'd just endured the cold-water test.

'I'm here, Rachel!'

The sun pounded on the bay, scorching her brow and neck. Her throat felt as raw as if she'd eaten sand. She set her shredded hands in her lap, staining her dress with blood.

'Your mother's right behind you!'

Gradually but inexorably an ember of logic caught fire within her brain. If she continued to pursue the carrack, the likely outcome would not be a reunion of mother and daughter but, rather, death by explosure for Jennet and, for Rachel, a meaningless bereavement.

'Damn you, Tobias Crompton!'

Whereas if she quit the chase – if she tipped her king, sheathed her sword, hoisted the white flag – she would be abandoning Rachel to a man of liberal means and generous intentions. A child could do far worse in this world.

'Damn you to Hell!'

A gust of wind caught her tears and flung them overboard, adding their number to the Atlantic's brackish infinitude. For an indeterminate interval she stared at the bottom of the boat. Seawater sloshed amongst the oaken ribs. A solitary blue crab scuttled along the keelson. Under other and better circumstances she might have submitted the crab to philosophic scrutiny, but instead she picked up the creature and, after gazing briefly into the black seeds that were its eyes, hurled it into the bay.

CHAPTER THE SEVENTH

A Young Benjamin Franklin Receives
Instruction in the Virtues of Older Women, amongst Them
Prudence, Passion and Electric Conductivity

Twenty-seven years after the event, the public burning of his Satanist aunt remained for Dunstan Stearne the supreme religious experience of his life. The pulse of the flames, the hurrahs of the crowd, the screams of the heretic, the apocalyptic fragrance – he would not forget these sensations as long as thoughts roved within his skull and blood beat through his veins. So memorable, in sooth, was Isobel Mowbray's cleansing that, shortly after the chartering of the Massachusetts Bay Purification Commission, Dunstan had decided that in certain exceptional instances his band would import such spectacle to the American shore, favouring stake over gallows as the medium of execution.

The present case was special not only because both the heretics were male but also because they were twins – Hosea and Malachi Clegg, so notorious throughout Cohasset for sheep-thieving and whore-mongering that nobody was terribly surprised when they turned out to be Devil-worshippers as well. In the interests of economy, Dunstan and the other Commissioners had set both Cleggs on the same pyre and chained them to the same stake. Winter was coming: it would be wrong to deplete needlessly the town's store of communal firewood.

Burning torch in hand, Jonathan Corwin began his stately march across Cohasset Square, inspiring the gathered citizens to draw back as if making way for the equipage of a duke. Dunstan cast an adoring eye on his wife. Abigail stood majestically betwixt the courageous local magistrate, Mr Basset, who'd arrested the warlocks in a daring mid-night raid on their farm, and the bushy-bearded printer Mr Searle, who'd earlier that day done a brisk business in broadsheets recounting the Clegg Brothers' trial. The October wind pulled the bodice of Abby's dress tight against her form, even as it swept her skirt south-ward in a billowing banner of feminine grace. Dunstan released a concupiscent sigh. Although she'd never conceived a child within that admirable frame, this was not for lack of conjugal activity. Probably God had determined that Abby could best serve Him through witchfinding rather than childbearing. Motherhood was a blessed state, but incompatible with a full-time career in demonology.

As Mr Corwin thrust the torch into the pyre, the Reverend Parris exhorted the spectators to render Martin Luther's 'A Mighty Fortress Is Our God' in the loudest voices they could find, and soon the stalwart song was resounding across the square and echoing down the village streets. No one sang louder than Abby, whose soprano transcended the general chorus as cream rises to the top of milk.

Sibyl – that was the word for her, Dunstan decided. His wife was a *sibyl*. Over the years, her gift for sensing heresy from afar had spared the Commission an incalculable quantity of effort. Emerging from her monthly conversation with the angel Justine, Abby would disclose to her fellow prickers the name of whatever Massachusetts settlement had most recently acquired (unbeknownst to itself) an ambassador from Hell, a revelation that Dunstan would forthwith relay to the editors of *The Bible Commonwealth*. Upon reading in the *Commonwealth* that his community had a witch problem, the local magistrate would conduct an investigation, presenting the Commissioners with at least one likely suspect shortly after their Gypsy wagon came rolling into town.

Sixteen years of service to Crown and Creator – and still Dunstan could boast that he'd never used his band as a tool of personal retribution. Sometimes the temptation to chastise the Nimacooks, those idolatrous savages who'd murdered his father, debauched his sister, and ruined his face, proved nearly overwhelming, but so far he'd managed to forbear. True, whenever Abby saw that a particular Nimacook had crossed the line separating mere depraved paganism from full-blown demonic compact, the Commission would steal the witch away, administer the tests, and – if the expected signs emerged –

perform a furtive extermination. This procedure always occurred in a spirit of Satan-fighting, however, never vindictiveness. Vengeance, the prophet Isaiah taught, belonged solely to the Lord.

Gradually Dunstan apprehended that a soft but palpable rain, dense enough to dampen the logs, was falling on Cohasset Square, and he lost no time issuing the necessary orders.

'Faggots, Samuel! Faggots, Jonathan! Faggots all around!'

Mr Parris and Mr Corwin sprang into action, seeking to fetch the half-dozen emergency bundles of wood that the Commissioners kept in the Gypsy wagon. For Dunstan had never forgotten the admonition his father had given him at the Chelmsford hangings of 1688: a jurist ought never bring a needless cruelty to his business, even when punishing Satanists – and needless cruelty would indeed be the outcome if the prickers failed to act quickly, supplementing the pyre with dry wood, as the fire would otherwise burn slowly and subject the Clegg brothers to an unendurable roasting, not the quick incineration that Christian charity demanded.

In a matter of minutes Mr Parris and Mr Corwin emptied the wagon of its faggots, bearing the merciful timber to the stake and adding it to the flames.

'Bless you!' cried Hosea, coughing.

'You are compassionate prickers indeed!' Malachi shouted.

Within a quarter-hour the cleansing was accomplished, and the spectators drifted away, the porkish odour having doubtless put them in mind of supper. Dunstan watched Mr Parris set about his book-keeping, severing the brothers' charred left thumbs and securing them in a baize sack. Tomorrow the minister would deliver the thumbs to Governor Danforth's office in Boston. In one sense this accounting was a mere formality, for neither the Governor nor his assistants ever opened the sacks to verify their contents. But it was important, Dunstan believed, for the Commissioners to provide tangible evidence that, like the Kirkcaldy Cleansing League across the sea, they were regularly riding the hinterlands, fulfilling their duties, earning their compensation. Witchfinding was a profession in which a tidy balance-sheet could not be overvalued.

The demonologists climbed into the Gypsy wagon and set off along the rutted roads betwixt Cohasset and Framingham, reaching the

Merry Alewife shortly after dark. Upon depositing the wagon in the livery, they arranged for the inn-keeper to tend the horses, then tramped three miles through the compacted gloom to Waushakum Pond. They removed their dinghy from its cloak of boughs and, as the sun dipped westward, turning the pond into a shimmering golden broth, rowed their way to the salt-box.

The Heavens declare the glory of God, the psalmist had sung, *and the firmament showeth His handiwork*, and Dunstan had of late undertaken to celebrate that very firmament in coloured wax. Entering the front parlour, he swept a satisfied gaze across a field of lion-headed sun-flowers, an array of water lilies dappling a pond, a willow tree confiding its despair to a placid creek and an incoming tide crashing against a craggy shore to form a great spuming cowl. These days, of course, he could afford oil-pigments, canvas too, and camel-hair brushes from Asia, but he still preferred the simpler medium. Wax was so basic, like blood.

His wife prepared the usual post-cleansing meal. Boiled pheasant, dried venison, corn meal bread, crisp brown ale. The prickers ate in silence. A luxurious exhaustion washed through Dunstan as, yawning and stretching, he guided Abby to their bed-chamber. Easing himself onto the mattress, he pulled the quilt over his chest and once again let the reverie pass through his mind.

Smoke-blind, he runs through the glowing house, his breeches loaded with dung, his heart throbbing with resolve.

He leaps over mounds of flame, the sparks swarming like Hell's own horseflies, the smoke congealing into spectral shapes, the beams and rafters crashing down around him.

He ascends the stairs to the second-floor hallway, and suddenly he sees it through the black haze, his birthright, nailed to his father's door.

There is still time to save the witchfinding licence – and time to do something else. A swirling column of fire rises from the floor. He steps towards it. Like Jacob wrestling with the angel, he embraces the blazing pillar. He screams. The flames enfold him, purifying his flesh, scorching his soul, seeding a scar whose meaning could not be clearer: here is a man who might one day bring the Fiend himself to book.

———

As her melancholy multiplied and her confusion grew more acute, Jennet inevitably turned to the Nimacooks' favourite medicine, their balm for grief and woe, the river-cure. Stripped down to Edenic nakedness, she spent an hour each morning swimming in the Schuylk-ill, imploring its gods to absorb her sorrows and bear them away with the current.

For reasons not wholly apparent, Rachel's abduction had become muddled in her mind with both her aunt's immolation and the death of ill-starred Pashpishia. Pursuing her course through the river's resist-ing medium, Jennet imagined she saw Isobel standing on the shore, smallpox pustules stippling her squat body. She pictured Rachel shackled behind Colchester Castle, the flames coiling around her like voracious serpents. She saw Pashpishia sitting in a locked cabin aboard the *Bristol Maid*. Rachel racked by the flogging sickness. Isobel sailing eastward. Pashpishia at the stake.

After forty days on the swimming regimen, she judged herself, not cured, exactly, not whole, but sane – sane enough, at least, to renew the fight, though she couldn't decide whether this improvement traced to Indian magic or simply to the healing hand of time.

As a preliminary measure, she dismissed Nellie Adams from her employ – the coming ordeal would require absolute solitude and utter silence – but only after securing for the serving-maid a new situation as governess to a prosperous German-Town family named Eckhardt. The second step was equally obvious. She must rouse herself with Euclid, fan her desires with Huygens, and enter into the most intimate relationship imaginable with the *Principia Mathematica*.

Sometimes it took her a week, sometimes an entire month, but she never abandoned a Newtonian problem before seducing it. She became adept at charting, from a given focus, the elliptical, parabolic and hyperbolic paths of revolving spheroids both real and conjectural. She learned to plot a comet's orbit from three discrete observations – determine the force by which the sun and the moon raised equatorial tides in both the syzygies and the quadratures – calculate the course the moon would follow but for its eccentricity – and infer from local lunar data the mean motions of the apsides and nodes of the Jovian satellites.

True as always to his word, Tobias sent her thirty pounds each quarter through the office of his London solicitor, Mr Horsfals, a portion of which she spent on food and books before depositing the balance in the strongbox beneath her bed. The possibility of enhancing her wardrobe with a new gown or a fashionable hat never even attained the status of a temptation. Along with each allowance Tobias usually enclosed a letter reporting on Rachel's welfare and also relating his various successes in the East Indies — for such was the location of his mysterious appointment. ''Tis an entirely amazing Enterprise,' he wrote. 'We've got sixteen Riders saddl'd at all Times, carrying the Mails five hundred Miles overland from Madraspatam to Bombay.'

By Tobias's account, Rachel could now speak French, do simple sums, and recite the Decalogue, and she'd developed 'a most affectionate Bond with her Governess', Mademoiselle Claudette Peltier. Jennet knew that his intention was to reassure her concerning Rachel's happiness — for all his foolishness, there was no actual malice in the man — and yet she came to dread each new letter from Madraspatam, promising herself she wouldn't read the thing but then reading it anyway, subsequently flying into a jealous rage upon learning that Mlle Peltier had undertaken to instruct their daughter in dancing, drawing, arithmetic or astronomy. The amusing little notes appended by Rachel herself failed to relieve Jennet's misery, for while they bespoke a mind quite delighted by the place in which it found itself, this exotic Eastern world of red silk saris and white marble temples, they also betrayed Rachel's uncertainty over whether her real mother was Jennet Crompton or the infinitely compelling and supernaturally competent Claudette Peltier.

The spring of 1718 brought the fulfilment of Tobias's second promise, the official termination of their marriage. Forwarded from Madraspatam to Mr Horsfals in London, and thence to Philadelphia, the essential document was no more physically impressive than Walter Stearne's witchfinding licence, but it bore the Lord Chancellor's seal, which made it a substantive scrap indeed. Even more momentous than this paper was the accompanying letter, wherein Tobias promised to continue sending her the monthly stipends 'until such time as you can sustain yourself without my assistance'. Jennet signed one copy of the divorcement decree, mailed it back to Horsfals, and slipped its twin inside Huygens's *Horologium Oscillatorium*, where it lay waiting to persuade her hypothetical future husband that his betrothed was no bigamist.

But for now she belonged only to her work: Jennet Stearne Crompton, bride of geometry, kin to conics, novice in the sisterhood of acceleration. She exiled herself from all physical particulars, from her city, province, planet – from her own flesh, it seemed – and set about designing the various demonstrations and experiments whose results would constitute the meat and sinew of the new treatise.

Brimming with dramatic accounts of what happened when roundish objects were dispatched along the eternally curving surfaces of trigonometric tradition, Book One of the *Principia Mathematica*, 'The Motion of Bodies', provided Jennet with eight procedures for evoking acceleration's spirits via barrow-wheels, rolling-pins and lawn-bowls. After perusing Book Two, 'The Motion of Bodies in Inhibiting Mediums', she forthwith assembled a dozen devices for conjuring spirits of resistance, her favourite consisting of two upright metal pipes joined at the bottom by a horizontal tube to form a U-shaped canal, an arrangement that, filled with a quantity of fluid equal to twice the length of her pendulum, enabled her to establish a binding reciprocity betwixt the liquid's fluctuations and the lever's oscillations. By casting her memory backwards to her childhood adventures with scrying-glasses and pentahedral prisms, then hurling her intellect forwards into the *Principia* chapter called 'The Motion of Very Small Bodies Agitated by Centripetal Forces', she managed to devise eleven radiation experiments, for each time Newton invoked 'very small bodies' he was surely inviting the reader to imagine the world's most fundamental phenomena, light chief amongst them, winnowed like wheat into the tiniest conceivable corpuscles. And then, finally, faced with the imperative of including attraction's agents in the *argumentum grande*, she pondered every *Principia* passage concerning magnetism and friction, subsequently extracting nine demonstrations, the cleverest of which involved a toy windmill such as her mother had oft-times constructed. Pursuant to her experimental design, Jennet made the sails of foil instead of silk, surrounding the array with a corona of lodestones, an imperially impractical machine whose vanes, when they turned at all, moved skittishly. The point, however, was not to grind grain but to crush irrationality.

The pleasures of gestating the demon disproof were all but ruined for Jennet by the disintegration of her correspondence with Rachel.

Although she'd attempted to make each letter to Madraspatam a confection of consummate wit and endearing frivolity, by Rachel's ninth birthday it was obvious that the child had lost interest in the exchange, and Jennet begrudgingly admitted to herself that no jocose note from her daughter would accompany the latest quarterly stipend from Tobias.

'I pray that the Day will come when you might understand why I seem'd to favour Mechanics over Motherhood,' she wrote in a letter she suspected Rachel would never read. 'But until the Dawning of that bless'd Morn, I shan't blame you for judging my Aristotelian Pursuits contemptible.'

Deprived of Rachel's written words, she was forced to settle instead for her phantom form. At least once a day she spied the child's face in her pendulum's shining disk. Sometimes she imagined Rachel's ghost peering out from behind the magnet-driven windmill, and once she beheld the *revenant* fleeing across Walnut Street Common. Thus it was that spectral evidence, a species of delusion that even her father could not abide, became Jennet's only bond with the issue of her flesh. She had never endured a darker irony, though she feared that Dame Fortune was not yet weary of the game.

In all it took her four years to lay the foundations of her new treatise, brick by brick, lodestone by lodestone, prism by prism, but at last the task was complete, and she once again admitted herself to the outside world. The summer of 1720 found her strolling each morning amidst the stalls and emporiums of Market Street, delighting all the while in the songbirds' concertos, the perfumes wafting from the flower-carts, the chatter pouring from the taverns, and the warmth of God's favourite star pulsing against her face. Within her bosom a vast and sinless pride now swelled: she had carried out Aunt Isobel's command – she had mastered Mr Newton from sprit to spanker and grafted the *Principia* onto her soul. If these forty philosophic demonstrations failed to fulfil Dr Halley's requirement of thoroughness and rigour, then the Sahara could not meet his expectation of a desert.

Restoring Nellie Adams to her employ proved not only the simplest of procedures but also indubitably beneficent. As Nellie's bad luck would have it, the *paterfamilias* of the Eckhardt family had stormed the fortress of her chastity, subsequently allowing himself further such liberties on the grounds that the governess was manifestly a slattern. She took great pleasure in serving notice to Herr Eckhardt, whose predations had – praise Jehovah – fallen short of impregnation, quite likely because poor Nellie had availed herself of the same pennyroyal-and-marjoram unguent in whose preparation Jennet had tutored her.

In the months that followed their reunion, the Hammer of Witchfinders and her assistant set about assembling their new and better case against demonology, together evoking countless motion-spirits and offering them abundant opportunities to inflict *maleficia*. By promising the mortal participants a generous fee – her savings from the quarterly stipends now stood at one hundred pounds – Jennet and Nellie easily recruited scores of wet-nurses, milkmaids, midwives, poultry farmers and brewers to the cause. Throughout the experiments the women carefully recorded their observations, noting down each dry breast, barren udder, difficult birth, unproductive hen and sour cask of beer. Their conclusions were unequivocal. Even under highly enticing circumstances, the world's kinetic agents did not stoop to diabolism.

At first Jennet wondered how their project might encompass virile members, but then one day Nellie mentioned that her only respites from Herr Eckhardt's unwelcome attentions occurred when he visited Philadelphia's most respected house of ill repute, the Grinning Sphinx on the water-front. Jennet immediately entered into negotiations with the proprietress, Mrs Postlethwaite, who agreed that for a fifty-fifty split – eight shillings per hour to the madam, eight to the harlot – she would allow her girls to ply their trade in proximity to philosophy. And so it was that, night after night, Jennet and Nellie manipulated prisms and pendulums whilst stationed outside the perfumed chambers of dainty Nora Geddis, sly Moll Frost, pouty Gina Little, sanguine Sophie Epsom and languid Charlotte Ketch. Interviewed *ex post facto*, the harlots invariably revealed that the episodes of flaccidity lay well within the norm.

On a scorching afternoon in August of 1721, the air so hot it seemed as if a candle might melt without influence of flame, Jennet escorted Nellie to the wharf and installed her aboard the brigantine *Artemis* –

the maid-servant was sailing home to Chelmsford at the behest of her ailing father — then returned forthwith to the Chestnut Street town-house. She picked up a quill and set to work. By Christmas Day she'd emptied eight ink-pots to produce 151 pages of manuscript. By Easter of the following year the count stood at sixteen pots and 302 pages. At noon on All Saints' Day she set down her quill, drank a glass of Rhenish, and placed three impassioned kisses on a first draft of 434 pages. Should Dr Halley complain of superficiality again, his accusation would ring as hollow as a sucked egg.

One task remained, nettlesome but essential. Assuming King George's Privy Council was as chary of irreverence as its predecessor, she needed somehow to insulate her argument from accusations of Arianism, atheism and impiety. By whatever means, she must overlay the treatise with a thick coating of Anglican exegesis and Trinitarian theology.

She was navigating the Schuylkill, afloat on her back, when the answer came, a seraph of inspiration winging through her brain. The Trinity: Father, Son and Holy Ghost. The kinetic elements: attraction, acceleration, resistance and radiation — intrinsically allied to earth, air, water and fire. Christ . . . incarnation . . . ah-hah! The Redeemer was manifestly connected to Earth, having graced the planet with his flesh and blood. And the Holy Ghost? The Aristotelian link was obvious: at Pentecost, this phenomenon had descended upon the Apostles in the guise of fire. Concerning the Father, an association with air seemed natural and inevitable, for God was the breath of life.

That left the fourth Greek element, water.

The current carried her south. A dead tree arced out of the Schuylkill; two yellow-spotted turtles sunned themselves on the half-submerged trunk. She drifted. Waters of the Delaware Bay. Waters of the Atlantic Sea. Waters of the Pishon, the Gihon, the Euphrates.

Birth waters, leaking unstoppably, heralding doomed Pashpishia and dear Rachel — heralding every child of woman born. And the Holy Virgin, blessed Mother of God, she too must have known that inexorable leakage, that wonderfully auspicious spill. There! She had it! God, Christ, Ghost, Virgin: air, earth, fire, water. A year might pass before she finished the treatise, perhaps even two, but at last a complete and irrefutable demon disproof was in hand, and if King

George and his Parliament didn't find it a work of the most astonishing piety, they could all go fishing in Hell.

Benjamin Franklin knew that his ambition to absorb the whole of human knowledge before his thirtieth birthday was immodest, but did that mean it was impossible? He thought not. The key, he decided, was self-discipline. Whereas the other journeymen at Keimer's Printing-House spent their luncheon intervals in the gloomy Crooked Billet, swallowing beef and swilling ale, Ben always passed this same hour in the sunlit compositing-room, improving his mind. Beyond the obvious advantages of his vegetarian diet, amongst them a thinner girth and fatter purse, lay the fact that he could consume his bread, raw cabbage, and pint of distilled water in a fraction of the hiatus required by meat, which gave him additional time for philosophic inquiry.

At the beginning of the week Ben had known almost nothing about the cryptic phenomenon called electricity, but he'd spent the previous four evenings reading Otto von Guericke's *Experimenta Nova*, which discussed the substance, revealed how to make it, and even explained the word itself: *electricity*, from the Greek *elektron*, 'amber' – for it was the ancient Ionians who'd first noticed that, when rubbed vigorously, a chunk of amber exhibited a peculiar attractive property. After studying the drawings in *Experimenta Nova*, Ben had stayed awake until mid-night constructing a Von Guericke sphere, a turnip-size ball of sulphur mounted on a steel axle turned by a gear and crank, and now he was ready to test it. He finished his cabbage, pulled his stool to the slopping table, and arranged the four mounds around the sphere, all equidistant from the core. With his left hand he cranked the sulphur to spinning, then arced his dominant hand above its surface and pressed down.

First the wheat chaff flew up, leaping through the air and sticking to the charged ball, just as Von Guericke had reported. He cranked faster, rubbed harder. The sot-weed granules took flight. Faster. The wren feathers soared. Harder. Now the primrose petals. The sphere was alive! It surged with power!

A grey mouse scurried across the floor. Keeping his right hand in contact with the sulphur, Ben lifted his feet to let the creature pass, whereupon, apropos of nothing, an errant primrose petal ascended and affixed itself to his free hand. He returned his feet to *terra firma*. The petal abandoned his palm and drifted to the table. He cranked the ball, charged the sulphur, held his left hand over the wayward petal, and again lifted his feet. The petal flew to his palm. He flicked it free.

Nowhere in *Experimenta Nova* did Von Guericke mention that the human body became a conduit for electricity when isolated from the ground. Could it be that Mr Franklin himself had stumbled upon a heretofore unknown law of Nature? The matter merited further investigation. He set his feet on the floor, cranked the ball, and caressed the sulphur – but before he bothered to unground himself, his uncommitted hand strayed towards a box of broken type. A tingling splinter of electricity materialized betwixt the tip of his index finger and a 20-point leaden *W* – an unpleasant jolt that made him yelp as if he'd stubbed his toe.

He contrived for the same event to occur again, but now he braced himself for the jolt, and so the shock was less. Once more he charged the sulphur. This time, however, he deliberately unfloored his feet before touching the *W*. No spark. No jolt. What was going on here? What secret principle had he activated?

The tinkling of a brass bell, rigged by Ben to chime whenever the front door opened, announced the arrival of a customer. He damned his luck. John O'Leary and the others were still at the Billet, and Mr Keimer had left at ten o'clock, laid low by an attack of the gout. Ben had no choice but to abandon his experiments and attend the patron.

Striding into the press-room, he happened upon the handsomest woman in Philadelphia, or such was his initial assessment of her face and form. She was about thirty-five, perhaps even forty, and all the more exquisite for it. Clad in a green damask dress, her flesh had aged not into decrepitude but towards rarity, the same phenomenon as occurred with wine, brandy, cheese and marble. Her tresses were a glorious auburn, her features noble, her proportions generous. Her lips boasted the moist sensuality of an inking-ball dipped in tallow.

The lady removed her bonnet and gloves, then inquired whether the master of the shop was about. He replied that the gout had sent Mr Keimer home but that he, Benjamin Franklin, though a mere journeyman, would assist her. His visitor raised her eyebrows to a sceptical elevation. She smiled. From her satchel she produced a thick manuscript, setting it on the scrubbing counter and petting it as she might the cowlick of a favorite nephew.

'I fancy the fragrance of this place,' she said. 'Ink, glue, leather, and something I can't identify.'

'Mouse droppings,' he said.

She laughed. None of the whores he bedded at the Grinning Sphinx, not even Nora Geddis, had ever inspired in him such deliciously sinful fancies.

'I am Jennet Stearne Crompton, devotee of Baconian experimentalism and former wife to the Madraspatam Postmaster-General. Since my deliverance from Indian captivity, a narrative on which I shan't waste your time, I have devoted myself to writing a book. I would see it printed without delay.'

Ben lifted the cover-page from the stack and studied it, instantly surmising that Mrs Crompton's appetite for speculation quite possibly rivalled his own.

A Treatise of How the Four
ARISTOTELIAN ELEMENTS
May Serve to Convince There Are
NO ELEMENTALS,
Neither Are There
DEMONS, DEVILS, GOBLINS, nor WICKED SPIRITS,
Excepting LUCIFER HIMSELF, and Why
WITCHCRAFT & MALEFICIUM
Are in Consequence
IMPOSSIBLE THINGS,
This Being the Personal Investigation of the Author,
J. S. CROMPTON,
Curator of the Cavendish Museum
of Wondrous Prodigies
(Colonial Branch)

'I must confess, I've ne'er heard of the Cavendish Museum,' Ben said. 'Is the Colonial Branch in Philadelphia?'

'At the moment 'tis largely in my head,' Mrs Crompton replied. 'I intend to found such an institution, but until now my battle against demonology hath consumed me.'

'I, too, pursue the philosophic life.' Ben returned the cover-page to the pile. 'This morning I installed a Von Guericke sphere in our compositing-room. As the month progresses I shall employ my leisure hours in learning more of the electric force.'

Again she flashed him a smile, though whether of admiration or condescension he couldn't tell. 'I can spare from my private fortune the sum of six hundred and fifty pounds. Will that be sufficient to print and bind three hundred copies? I mean to gift each Parliamentarian with one, likewise King George and his councillors, that they might join together in overturning the Witchcraft Act of James the First.'

Ben gasped and said, 'Madam, for six hundred and fifty pounds we'll supply every copy with Moroccan bindings, a golden bookmark, and a clockwork canary who turns the pages on command.' Noticing that David Harry had once again failed to sweep under the blacking table, he seized the broom and set to work. 'Tell me, Mrs Crompton, might I perchance borrow your intriguing treatise' – he sculpted the debris into a lopsided cone – 'and read it this evening?'

'Mr Franklin, I should be delighted to have a bright young man negotiate my opus and offer me his opinions – though the task will take you more than one evening.'

'I read quickly,' he said eagerly.

'I write slowly,' she replied pointedly.

'I grasp your meaning, Madam, and I shall give each sentence its due.' He used the coalscuttle to transfer the debris from the floor to the dustbin. 'The subject touches a nerve deep within me, for the celebrated Samuel Sewall, once employed by the notorious Salem witch-court, hath of late sought to ruin my benighted brother.'

A full year had passed since Samuel Sewall's campaign against *The New-England Courant*, and still Ben could not think on the affair without seething. No one disputed that the Boston newspaper had criticized both the provincial government and the Puritan clergy; neither the paper's editor, James Franklin, nor his younger brother and indentured apprentice, Ben, was a friend to the status quo. But the fact remained that no unequivocal irreverence or blatant blasphemy had ever stained the *Courant*'s pages, and so when Judge Sewall moved to have James gaoled and his journal extinguished for allegedly perverting Scripture, it occurred to Ben that his imagination might be more cordially received in Pennsylvania. Whilst James dropped from sight, leaving his assistants to compose and print the *Courant* as best they could, Ben set out for Philadelphia, whose Quaker majority, despite its many eccentricities, had reportedly embraced the grand English ideal called freedom of thought.

'My late father was amongst those who conspired with your Mr Sewall to doom the Salem defendants,' Mrs Crompton said. 'And now my brother Dunstan hath likewise caught the cleansing fever.'

'If you speak of Dunstan Stearne, I have read of his deplorable activities in *The Bible Commonwealth*.' 'Steeth, 'twould appear we are to publish an imperially important treatise, of passing interest to theologians, philosophers and general readers alike. I propose we charge at least two crowns per copy.'

'What matters, young Franklin, is not what price we place upon my book, but what value Parliament extracts from it.'

'Of course, Madam – though I fear that for Mr Keimer there is no such thing as honour without a profit.' He offered her a sly grin, upgrading it anon to an admiring glance. 'Ah, Mrs Crompton, I imagine 'tis exhilarating to have in life so worthy a purpose as you enjoy.'

'Exhilarating?' His visitor presented him with a dumbfounded expression, as if his nose had suddenly become a turnip. 'Nay, sir, 'tis a skein more tangled than that. I cherish my quest, and yet I despise it. I treasure my mission, and still I detest it. As did Harry's thrust to Hotspur, it hath robbed me of my youth.' In apparent prelude to her departure she pulled on her gloves, then gave her manuscript a quick caress. ''Be warned, sir. I've planted herein a prodigious thicket of Keplerian mechanics and Newtonian proofs. You might become lost.'

'I once tried to read Mr Newton's *Principia*, but I couldn't manage the Latin. His *Opticks*, being in English, was more to my taste.' Again Ben approached the blacking table and, seizing a pair of inking-balls by their shafts, brayed them together to equalize their loads. He beat the two great sopping udders against the framed and locked type-form containing the first canto of Joseph Stukeley's *The Aphrodisiad*, buttering the leaden letters with a film of ink – 'Arise, my Soul,' the epic began, 'thou burning Coal, my Heart's own Foal,' an opening from which it never recovered. 'But even if I comprehend but part of your argument,' Ben said, ''twill be like a healing rain, washing away the swill we brew on these premises – verses by witlings, pamphlets by scoundrels, sermons by hypocrites.' After securing the inked type-form in Mr Keimer's massive handpress, he laid a virgin sheet on the tympan, positioned the frisket (essential for preventing smears), and folded both parts over the stone bed. 'The instant my luncheon interval's done, I'm obliged to spawn a hundred copies of this doggerel.' He slid the whole arrangement beneath the platen. 'I'faith, an African monkey playing with a case of type might easily surpass it.' He pulled the spindle lever, thus squeezing the sheet tight against the form and indelibly transferring ink to paper. 'Behold Mr Stukeley's poem' – he rolled back the bed – 'certain to lift him from the vale of anonymity and deposit him in the depths of obscurity.'

No sooner had he peeled away the signature-sheet than Mrs Crompton clutched her chest and slumped into the chair beside the scrubbing counter. 'Great Heaven, I am a-swoon,' she moaned.

'Oh, my poor Mrs Crompton!'

'A swallow of water should bring me 'round,' she whispered, rapping her knuckles against her breastbone.

He calculated that he could race back to the slopping table, seize his pint bottle, return to the press-room, and place the container to her lips within twenty seconds. He did it in fifteen. The liquid proved effica-cious, and she quickly regained her composure, speaking in a steady voice.

'*Merci, Monsieur.*'

'Do you swoon often?'

''Tis my first such spell. But hear my explanation.' She drained the bottle. 'When I was but fourteen, I saw the farmer Giles Corey crushed to death for refusing to plead at Salem. I'd largely banished the episode from my mind, but now your great press brings it back.'

'I must dispute your memory in one particular. No lady so lovely as yourself was more than three years old when the Salem Court con-vened.'

'You're a beguiling rascal, Ben Franklin, but you see before you a woman of forty-six years. Now tell me, how long must I wait ere a bound volume appears in my hands?'

'Seven jobs lie ahead of yours, two of substance, the rest trifles. I believe we can begin come April. After that, allow us four more months.'

'Might you do it in three?'

'Mayhap.'

She rose with fluid grace. 'I should like to see this Von Guericke sphere of yours. I've heard of such devices but ne'er beheld one.'

Thus it was that Ben spent the final moments of his luncheon interval in the compositing-room, demonstrating the sulphur-ball. He showed Mrs Crompton how to infuse the pungent globe with the electric force; how her own charged flesh, once isolated from the floor, became as attractive to tobacco and petals as was the sphere itself; and how to make a tiny lightning-bolt leap from her electrified finger to a metal object. The asymmetries brought a smile to his face. On one side of the slopping table: the unfolding of a philosophic experiment, beautifully repeatable. On the other side: the ebb and flow of life, marvellously unpredictable. When he'd jumped out of bed that morn-ing, Ben had assumed the day would prove as mundane as any other.

He'd never imagined that by one o'clock he would be standing
beside an elegant woman, filling his tissues with electricity
even as he longed to reach out and stroke her
with deliciously stimulating
and impossibly
passionate

*

Sparks
spew from Van
de Graaff generators. Electric
rainbows scurry up and down Jacob's ladders.
Tendrils of lightning spiral around Tesla coils. In short, we
have entered the domain of 1940s American science-fiction cinema,
a phenomenon that in my opinion occasioned numerous paragons of
the dramatist's art, literary works to rival *Oedipus Rex*, *King Lear*, and
Long Day's Journey into Night.

The reflex by which you humans lionize theatrical scripts over screenplays bewilders me. When it comes to the latter, you unfailingly seize upon some arbitrary celluloid simulacrum, always a coarse and budget-bound shadow of the writer's vision. One day you'll learn proper respect for the text itself.

In any consideration of 1940s science-fiction screenplays, one name towers above all others, well above Joseph West and *Man-Made Monster*, well above Brenda Weisberg and *The Mad Ghoul*. I speak of the great Edward T. Lowe, whose deathless duology, *House of Frankenstein* and *House of Dracula*, cannily dramatizes the triumphs and trade-offs intrinsic to the scientific worldview. Through the braided narratives that constitute the first masterpiece, the author serves up a critique of Western rationality so withering as to warm the heart of every middle-class mystic in the audience. But in the second scenario Lowe reverses the poles, arguing that we abandon Reason only at our peril.

Whatever the flaws in my attempt to document the birth of the Enlightenment – a project that has recently obliged me to depict my dear Jennet in intellectual congress with Benjamin Franklin, with more such intimacies to come – you cannot deny the subject's inherent significance. If our civilization has made a Devil's bargain with its own cleverness, consigning its soul to a false god called scientific progress, then this swindle must be exposed at every opportunity. If, on the other hand, the Age of Reason represented humankind's last hope of unshackling itself from hallowed nonsense and sanctified ignorance, then we should stand up and say so, even if we offend the astrologer next door or the cleric down the street.

House of Frankenstein takes as its principal figure the deranged scientist Gustav Niemann. When we first meet this egomaniacal *Übermensch*, he lies imprisoned somewhere in central Europe, condemned for perform-ing blasphemous medical experiments. The plot centres around the covenants through which Dr Niemann, after breaking out of his dungeon, lures three other outcasts into his sphere. First he promises to repair the crooked spine of his obsequious hunchback assistant, Daniel. Upon encountering the vampire Count Dracula – avatar of the enchantment that Reason has drained from the world – Niemann agrees to 'protect the earth' upon which the undead aristocrat lies. Finally, crossing paths with Lawrence Talbot, a self-pitying werewolf, Niemann claims that he will surgically reconfigure Talbot's brain and thereby 'lift this curse from you for ever'. For Lowe, clearly, Talbot is the quintessential dupe of Enlightenment rationality. The moon that broods over *House of Frankenstein* is not the vibrant orb that for centuries has stirred the blood of poets, but a thing of cold Newtonian horror, triggering a condition that Talbot regards as irredeemably pathological. Rather than revelling in his lupine nature, his inner wolf, he succumbs to the supposition that he'll never be happy until he stops ripping out people's throats and instead settles into a respectable bourgeois existence.

Like so many captains of corporate technocracy, Niemann has no intention of honouring his philanthropic vows. He cherishes but one goal, to further empower himself by reanimating a legendary corpse-assemblage known as the Frankenstein monster, regardless of the consequences to the human community or the biosphere at large. By the time the drama is done, Niemann has violated all three covenants, and his would-be beneficiaries lie dead – Daniel defenestrated, Dracula vaporized by a sunbeam, Talbot shot with a silver bullet.

The environmentalist discourse encoded in *House of Frankenstein*, which begins with Niemann's disingenuous vow to protect the Earth, reaches its apex in Act Two, when the scientist enters a community where the corpse-assemblage once roamed. Now that the ghastly thing is gone, the peasants have regained their Rousseauean harmony with Nature. Explains the local police inspector, 'Our village has been quiet and peaceful ever since the dam broke and swept the Wolf Man and the Frankenstein monster to their destruction.' The theme continues in Act Three, when the corpse-assemblage drowns Niemann in a quick-sand bog, Lowe's objective correlative for the ecological miasma into which Newtonian instrumentalism has dragged the world.

House of Dracula radically inverts every epistemological premise around which *House of Frankenstein* turns. The main character is the blameless and upright Dr Franz Edelman, whose 'reputation for helping others' is known even among the world's vampires and werewolves. Before Act One is over, both Count Dracula and Lawrence Talbot, mysteriously resurrected following their mis-adventures in the earlier text, have come to Edelman seeking natural remedies for their putatively supernatural afflictions. In contrast to the self-actualized vampire we met previously, the undead aristocrat of *House of Dracula* is under 'a curse of misery and horror'. This time,

Lowe depicts Talbot not as a noble primitive who has failed to comprehend his own spiritual beauty, but as a physically diseased victim of intracranial pressure.

For Dracula, Franz Edelman prescribes an experimental vaccine to combat the parasites infecting his blood. In the Wolf Man's case, Edelman proposes to soften his brainpan with a therapeutic mould derived from a 'hybrid plant', *Clavaria formosa*. When the Frankenstein monster turns up in a seaside cave beneath Edelman's castle at the beginning of Act Two, he resolves with characteristic benevolence to deliver the corpse-assemblage from its coma. Although the doctor's deformed and saintly nurse, Nina, thinks that reviving the Frankenstein monster is a terrible idea – the thing is in all probability still a homicidal maniac – Edelman believes the monster deserves a second chance: 'Is that poor creature responsible for what he is?' Counters Nina, 'Man's responsibility is to his fellow man.' Bested by dialectic, Edelman replies, 'Perhaps you're right, Nina. Frankenstein's monster must never wreak havoc again.'

Lowe wrote *House of Dracula* in 1945, the same year that atomic bombs destroyed two Japanese cities, and the scholarly consensus is that he added the pivotal 'never wreak havoc' line immediately upon hearing about Hiroshima and Nagasaki. Evidently Lowe was the first serious Western dramatist to express a hope that the same scientists who designed thermonuclear weapons might ultimately campaign for their elimination.

The downfall of Franz Edelman begins when Dracula, unable to master his demonic nature, injects his contaminated blood into the doctor, who subsequently acquires a split personality. Edelman's compassionate side predominates long enough for him to perform the *Clavaria* treatment on Talbot, but then his dark half takes over, prompting him to murder his gardener, strangle Nina, and revive the Frankenstein monster.

Despite this tragic conclusion, we must note that medical intervention and the Enlightenment worldview function throughout *House of Dracula* as wholly positive forces. Talbot emerges from Edelman's castle a man reborn, a normal life ahead of him. He has rejected the lycanthropic moon of superstition for a humanist moon lit by scientific insight. It would seem that, unlike the Lowe of the earlier text, the author of *House of Dracula* feels little sympathy for the self-appointed avengers of dispossessed enchantment.

As my story progresses, we shall address the Primitivist Complaint again, but now we must return to Jennet. Before you negotiate the next scene, however, let me invite you to spend a moment meditating on Edmund Lowe's piquant symbol of the post-Enlightenment dilemma: the Frankenstein monster, lying on the operating table of the valiant Dr Edelman. I invite you to contemplate the monster's bubbling bile and flowing lymph, its buzzing nerves and pulsing veins, its throbbing brain and beating

*

Heart
a-flutter, flesh
a-quiver, Jennet pulled
back the door to Keimer's Printing-
House, thus setting Ben's ingenious bell to tinkling,
and stepped inside. As the journeymen and the apprentices looked on, she removed her gloves, unwound her scarf, and brushed the snow from her arms. Briefly her admirers savoured her presence, then returned to their duties. George Webb took up the inking-balls and pounded them against a type-form like a hortator beating out a cadence in the hold of a Roman galley. John O'Leary yanked the spindle lever on the Blaeu press, permanently staining a perfectly good sheet of paper with some insipid tract or blathering ballad. David Harry dipped a recently employed type-form, now grimy with ink, into the swampy waters of the rinsing trough.

She wasn't exactly sure which phenomenon had triggered her infatuation: the brilliance of Ben's writing, or the unmediated fact of Ben himself. Near the end of their dalliance with the sulphur-ball, he had lent her the complete 'Silence Dogood' series, fourteen letters submitted serially to *The New-England Courant* by a country widow of limited income, lively intellect and prolific opinions. It was a double hoax. Silence's devoted audience didn't know she was really James Franklin's apprentice, his upstart brother Ben – and neither did James himself. By disguising his identity, altering his handwriting, and slipping a new letter each night beneath the door of James's printing-house, Ben had managed at age sixteen to secure prominent weekly exposure for his prose in the *Courant*, a situation the elder Franklin would never have tolerated had he known the epistles' provenance.

Where had Ben acquired such confidence? From whence came this astonishing nerve? A city youth had thought his way, with considerable charm and only a few lapses, into a different gender, another generation, and a rural cast of mind. Jennet adored Silence Dogood. After savaging the supposition that women were less intelligent than men, Silence went on to attack those who barred the female sex from higher education. 'Women are taught to read and write their Names and nothing else. We have the God-given capacity for Knowledge and Understanding. What have we done to forfeit the Privilege of attending Colleges?' In weighing atheists against hypocrites, Silence concluded, 'I am of late inclin'd to think the Hypocrite the more dangerous of the Two, especially if he sustains a Post in the Government.' Above all, Silence was a realist: 'I am apt to fancy I could be persuaded to marry again, but a good-humor'd, sober, and agreeable Man being all but impossible to find, I have grown resign'd to Widowhood, though it is a Condition I have never much admir'd.'

Jennet proceeded to the drying-room, where dozens of freshly printed signatures hung from a network of overhead strings, Ben standing in their midst like a washer-woman surrounded by the day's laundry. The philosophers traded exuberant greetings, and then she reeled off her usual questions. How many pages of her treatise had he consumed? What was his opinion so far? When would he finish? It was their eighth such encounter in a month – though only now did she realize that, beyond his resplendent mind and generous soul, she found Ben appealing in body as well. True, his limbs extended from a stoutish frame, but rarely had a barrel-chest boasted such dignity. Yes, his countenance contained some superfluous flesh, but it was a pudding-face of the most meritorious sort. Indeed, his shanks were hefty, but where in Pennsylvania might one behold a more graceful turn of calf?

He touched his finger to a dangling signature, ascertaining that the ink was dry. 'Last night I read your chapters on those motion-spirits in service to acceleration. With each paragraph I grow more enchanted.'

'But do I make a convincing case against demonology?' she asked.

'For all I am delighted by your book, I would learn how your argument plays out ere I judge it.' He began unhooking the signatures. 'Not being a church-going man, I expect to read your last sentence on Sunday morning, whereupon I shall render my verdict.'

A spasm of rapture seized Jennet as she realized that their next rendezvous might occur in Ben's own lodgings, but an instant later her joy was eclipsed by sobriety, clarity, pragmatism and several other of her mind's more annoying habits. The *pièce bien faite* wherein she and Ben became lovers knew little of logic and much of lunacy. While the darling boy might accept her as a kind of intriguing middle-aged cousin, it was inconceivable that they would ever enjoy a tryst. Faugh, he was but three years older than Rachel!

Resting a hand on his shoulder, she asked him whether she might visit his rooms at two o'clock on Sunday afternoon to discuss her treatise in full. When he protested that his accommodations were ill-suited to a woman of her breeding, she reminded him that she'd been happier living in a Nimacook wigwam with an Indian she esteemed than in a Chestnut Street townhouse with a postmaster she distained.

The interval was interminable, three whole days, but at last the appointed hour arrived. She stepped off her front stoop, tramped through the swirling snows of Market Street, and, ascending the decrepit rear stairway of the Thomas Godfrey mansion, entered the domain of the callow genius who'd given Silence Dogood to the world. He greeted her dressed in a pristine ensemble that would have fared disastrously in the printing-house – fawn breeches, yellow silk waistcoat, white day-shirt with ruffled cuffs.

'*Bienvenue au Château Franklin.*' he said.

'*Merci, Monsieur,*'

'Yesterday I went bear hunting in homage to your Indian past, and soon I found my quarry, lying torpid in a cave by the river. Straightaway I knew him for an industrious beast, as it was apparent he'd built his own brewery, then consumed the whole of his first barrel of ale, that he might study the effects of inebriation on hibernation. I have no meat to give you, Madam, for I hold it unsporting to shoot a bear whilst he's conducting a philosophic experiment.'

She laughed and said, 'I require no meat, sir, but I should like a tour of your castle.'

'*Suivez-moi.*'

There were four rooms altogether, including Ben's little bed-chamber, tiny parlour, suffocating study, and congested laboratory, the latter a mere dressing alcove into which he'd jammed a cherry table a-jumble with an air-pump, a microscope, a telescope, a Von Guericke sphere and other such paraphernalia. Each space boasted its own hearth connected to a common chimney, an arrangement that he merrily compared to quadruplet piglets nursing on a brood sow.

Instinctively they drifted to the cosiest place, the parlour, where her host had built a convivial fire. A copper kettle occupied the chimney niche like an egg snugged into a rookery.

'Mayhap I should prepare some Malay tea,' he suggested.

'We have many large questions to discuss,' she replied. 'God and gravity. Demons and demonstrations. Newton's apple — and Eden's too. 'Tis indeed an occasion for tea, Mr Franklin, as strong as you can make it.'

In the shank of the afternoon, the philosophers sat together on the divan, arm to arm, thigh to thigh. Bracing and aromatic, the Malay tea put Jennet in a mood of remembrance, and soon she was speaking of her life's great losses. A child lying in a mound beside the Shawsheen. A second child thriving in Madraspatam under the auspices of a *de facto* mother.

'I' faith, Mrs Crompton, you've surely endured your share of sorrows,' Ben said. 'Would that I knew some benevolent sorcerer who might instantly translate your lost Rachel from Asia to America.'

'When I cannot sleep at night, I say to myself, "On the other side of the planet the sun is long risen, and Rachel is up and about. At this precise moment some notion or vagary goes flitting through her brain."'

'But now she sleeps, and 'tis the mother whose thoughts are on the wing.'

'Alas, I fear that very mother spends rather too much time in airy habitations, flying where her fancy takes her, as Mr Crompton knew all too well,' Jennet said. 'But for my single-minded pursuit of the *argumentum grande*, Rachel would yet be at my side.'

'May I make bold with my opinion?' Ben asked. Receiving her nod, he continued. 'Just as some men are not particularly competent fathers, neither are you about to be dubbed the world's most successful mother. But let me in the same breath assert that to thwart the Puritan prickers is a manifestly noble enterprise. On balance I would say you do your daughter proud.'

'Truly?'

'Before Rachel's grown to womanhood, she'll be gainsaying all who claim she's not your daughter.'

Jennet inhaled deeply. Ben was redolent of philosophy – of sulphur and magnetite and other heady scents. 'Since I can no longer hold my child's delicate hand, I shall instead cling to your exquisite thought.' She swallowed a stimulating measure of tea. 'Pray tell me what faults and merits you find in my book.'

For the next twenty minutes her new friend discoursed upon *A Treatise of How the Four Aristotelian Elements May Serve to Convince There Are No Elementals*. He applauded her 'incontrovertible cleverness in trying to make motion-spirits practise *maleficium*'. He praised her 'abiding brilliance in mapping the Greek immutables onto both Newton's mechanics and Trinitarian theology.'

'Ah, but if you were a Parliamentarian, would my claims persuade you to o'erturn the Conjuring Statute?' she asked.

'Oh, Mrs Crompton, I find so much to admire in your treatise.'

'But would my claims persuade you?'

'Not being a Parliamentarian, 'tis impossible for me to answer. I can only say that your every sentence bespeaks an opulent intellect.'

Something was wrong. The affirmation in his words could not conceal the catch in his voice, the hesitancy in his demeanour. She decided against pursuing the matter further but instead suggested that they experiment with his sulphur-ball.

'You have shown how a human body, ungrounded, may exert the electric attraction on small particles,' she said, sipping the last of her tea. 'Ah, but can that same body transfer its charge to another?'

'A splendid question! We must seek its resolution!'

They adjourned to the laboratory. Jennet lit a tallow candle and settled onto the stool. Ben assumed an upended cider cask, then carefully assembled three small mounds of crushed tea-leaves. He set one pile before the Von Guericke sphere, the other two at opposite ends of the table. Cranking the ball with her right hand, Jennet placed her left palm along the rolling equator.

The central tea-mound disintegrated, its particles flying to the sphere's mottled surface. She kept her palm on the ball, lifted her feet, and stretched her right hand towards the corresponding pile. The tea bits ascended, coating her fingers.

'I'm all electric, Ben! Now let me touch you, and we shall learn more of this strange principle!'

Feet still hovering, she spun the ball, then charged the sulphur with her right palm and immediately wrapped her left hand around his right wrist. He unfloored his feet and brought his free hand towards the remaining mound.

A dozen stray particles leapt to his fingertips.

'I'Christ, we've done it!' he cried.

'An impressive result' — she released his wrist and withdrew her palm from the ball — 'but I shan't call our experiment consummated till we've turned the entire heap into a whirling tornado of tea.'

'But . . . how?' He shook the particles from his person.

'Before I re-electrify myself, we must enlarge the area of overlap 'twixt our respective persons,' she said. ''Tis one thing for my hand to clasp your wrist, and quite another for, say, the skin of our forearms to meld.'

'Then let us bare our limbs anon.' He unbuttoned his right cuff, rolling the ruffle towards his elbow.

'Anon,' she echoed, furling the left sleeve of her dress.

They brought their forearms together to create a warm fleshy tangent.

'By your leave, we can further increase our contiguity if we place one cheek against the other,' he said.

'Ah!'

Keeping their forearms connected, they fused the sides of their faces, a gesture that inevitably caused their knees to bump together and her left breast to mesh with his sternum. They gulped and laughed in perfect synchronicity.

She kissed him on the lips. He did not flinch but instead committed his own mouth to the philosophic cause.

'Ne'er have two experimenters done a better job of enlarging an overlap,' he noted, retreating just far enough to move his lips. 'Pray spin the ball and charge yourself, that we might continue the investigation.'

'Let me propose that we first expand our common boundary by at least a hundred square inches.' She broke the seal betwixt their forearms, stood up, and brushed the front of her dress, transferring the tea and sulphur from her fingers to her lace bodice. 'Or, even better, two hundred.'

'Might I make the case for three hundred square inches?' he said, likewise rising.

'You may.'

They kissed again. Their hands became autonomous beings — ardent mariners hoisting anchors, loosening halyards, and raising canvas prior to mounting the tide and plying the seas beyond.

'Or even four hundred square inches?' he asked.

Buttons rotated. Thongs unthreaded. Clasps opened. Stays parted company.

'Four hundred!' she agreed.

A dozen articles of clothing tumbled to the floor at uniform Galilean velocities.

'Five hundred?' he asked.

'Five hundred!' Her heart pounded like a pagan drum setting the tempo of a bacchanal. Her lungs chuffed and wheezed like a bellows operated by a lunatic smith. 'Six hundred!' Never had she observed so enthralling a phenomenon as Ben's nakedness. His skin glowed like the translucent crater atop the candle. His virile member was a belaying pin fit to cleat the mainsail of Aeneas's flagship.

'Ah, Mrs Crompton, I do love thee so!'

'My dearest, sweetest swain!'

'Is this immoral?' he asked.

'Merely immoderate,' she replied. 'Like all women, I fear the gravid state.'

''Sblood, Mrs Crompton, I shan't burden you so. As a faithful patron of the Grinning Sphinx, I am well instructed in the thwarting of spermatozoa.'

'You have a Belgian adder-bag?'

'Three at last count, mayhap four,' he said, blowing out the candle.

Naked, they scurried to the bed-chamber and collaborated in the construction of a fire. With the fevered intensity of a poet choosing a new quill in a stationer's shop, Ben selected an adder-bag from his cache, which he kept beside the mattress in an earthenware jar. Her cunny was as wet as a peach. Sheathing his manhood, they set about exhibiting their deathless devotion to the cult of electricity.

'Ne'er have I felt such sparks,' he said as his ardour gained admittance to its object.

'Mr Franklin, you make me crackle,' she said, rotating on the axis of his manhood. 'I declare our experiment a triumph.'

'Absolutely.'

'*Quod eros demonstrandum.*'

As twilight came to Philadelphia, the philosophers lavished them-selves on one another, abandoning the bed-clothes only to stoke the fire or appease their bladders. Whenever Ben was occupied with hearth or chamber-pot, Jennet took to indulging in salacious speculation. Swiving, she decided, was no less spiritual an exercise than the singing of a hymn or the recitation of a prayer – a truth that might very well explain the clerical zeal for witch-cleansing. For how could the immense and sprawling Christian Church, with its instinctive suspi-cion of human bodies, its profound Pauline hope that these soggy conglomerations of leaking cocks and dribbling quims might simply disappear one day – how could it abide the possibility of widows and wenches and all manner of seductresses turning their devotional energies to sybaritic congress, those notorious orgiastic Sabbats? A woman needn't worship Lucifer to spark a demonologist's ire. She need only be made of flesh.

A silken gloom suffused the bed-chamber. Ben lit a candle. The air thickened with a wondrous fragrance: salt, tallow, seed and sulphur in miraculous amalgamation. But then, shortly after Jennet decided that she'd never been happier in her life, a cryptic misery overcame her swain, his breaths growing short, his eyes welling up.

'Why do you weep, bonny Ben? I swear to you, there is no sin in this.'

'Sweet lady, your noble treatise doth harbour a grievous error.'

Despite the fire, a chill washed through her. 'What *manner* of grievous error?'

'Have you not read the late Robert Boyle?'

'The man was a witch believer. He hath naught to offer my cause.'

'Alas, some several years ago Mr Boyle brought ruin upon the premise 'round which your brave book orbits. In *The Sceptical Chymist* he proved that Aristole was wrong to number fire amongst the elements, for fire is itself a mingling of immutables.'

She grew colder yet. 'Mr Boyle kept company with demonologists!'

'Even so, many an experimenter hath drawn fruitful inspiration from his work, so that today the Greek chemistry is all but routed. As an example, for all you may combine gold with other metals, you can recover the stuff in its original form, a fact that implies—'

'Unchangeable corpuscles of gold?' she moaned.

'Aye,' he said. 'What's more, the consensus is that we must give the name of element to arsenic, iron, zinc and white phosphorus.'

'White phosphorus can be admixed and then recovered?'

'Mrs Crompton, I fear I've stolen your vocation.'

'Iron's an element as well?'

'Aye.'

'And zinc?'

'That too.'

'Damn all zinc.'

'I agree, Mrs Crompton. Damn zinc to Hell. Damn iron. Damn phosphorus and arsenic.'

'Oh, Ben, my mind's a-whirl. Have I squandered my life on an obsolete science? Whilst expiring at the stake, my aunt bid me use Aristotle's elements in constructing a demon disproof, and yet today I learn such chemistry's good for naught but making a modern philosopher titter and wince.'

''Steeth, I cannot resolve the contradiction. But hear my promise. Should you elect to fashion a new *argumentum grande*, you shall have this diligent printer for your assistant.'

'At the moment I ask only that you embrace me. Anchor me to your bed, bonny Ben, lest I succumb to a devilish unreason, for I've half a mind to flee your quarters and pitch myself into the Schuylkill like Ophelia into the Limfjord.'

The glorious boy did as she commanded, wrapping his arms around her shoulders, pulling her chest tight against his.

'How does a person say "I love you" in the Algonquin language?' he asked.

'*Cowammaunsh*,' she said.

'*Cowammaunsh*,' he said.

Her tears dried. Her muscles relaxed. The candle burned low. As she floated through the sleepy dusk, she decided that she, too, was an element, no less so than gold or zinc, readily melted, easily mingled, but somehow always recoverable to herself.

In the weeks that followed her collision with the new chemistry, she devoted her energies to augmenting *The Devil and All His Works* with fresh news-clippings, as if the gutting of her *argumentum grande* could be remedied by rousing to incandescence her wrath against the Massachusetts cleansers. Most of the reports came from *The Bible Commonwealth*, but occasionally she found her brother's activities documented in *The American Weekly Mercury* and sometimes even *The London Journal*.

What course made sense? Should she publish her treatise as it stood and pray that no Parliamentarian had ever heard of Robert Boyle? Purge the thing of all Aristotelian speculation and hope the results were judged neither atheist nor incoherent? Sequester herself once more within her skull and construct yet another demon disproof?

'Just remember, if you attempt a new treatise, this time you'll have me standing by your side,' Ben told her. 'Franklin and Crompton, united against the Conjuring Statute!'

''Tis a marvellous slogan,' she said, 'but as yet we've no thesis to give it teeth, and meanwhile here's the Book of Exodus, telling the world, "Thou shalt not suffer a witch to live." '

Owing largely to the constancy of Ben's optimism, the intensity of his affections, and the tenderness of his care, she at last regained the energy that Robert Boyle had sapped away. As far as she could tell, her swain loved her no less than she loved him; their passions matched precisely, inch for inch, ounce for ounce. Why, exactly, did this canny and beguiling youth adulate her? Because she'd once persuaded Isaac Newton to do her bidding? Because her campaign to bring down

Dunstan was as audacious as his mission to master all knowledge? His reasons were opaque to her, a delicious riddle.

Not since her tutelage under Aunt Isobel had she known a person who took so broad a view of so many matters. By Ben's reckoning, the life that lay before him was not a *terra incognita* but a Promised Land whose peaks and valleys he could shape through the sheer power of Reason. A fortnight after their felicitous sulphur-ball experiment, he devised a scheme that he intended to follow all his days, a five-page, cross-hatched 'perfection-matrix' on which he would mark down his every lapse in Thrift ('I shall endeavour to be extremely frugal for some Time till I have paid what I owe,' ran his caption for the first grid), Honesty ('I shall strive for Sincerity in every Word and Action'), Industry ('I shall not neglect my Business for any foolish Project of quickly growing rich'), Forbearance ('I resolve to speak ill of no Man, not even in a Matter of Truth'), and Moderation ('I shall not eat to Dullness, drink to Elevation, nor use Venery for any Purpose save Health and Offspring').

The reach of his planning extended even to the grave. Rummaging through his desk one afternoon in search of a pair of scissors with which to snip out her brother's latest crime, the hanging of a supposed sea-witch in Gloucester, Jennet came upon an epitaph Ben had composed for himself shortly after his eighteenth birthday. Not only did this young man expect to live ethically, he meant to die eloquently.

THE BODY OF
B. FRANKLIN,
PRINTER,
LIKE THE COVER OF AN OLD BOOK,
ITS CONTENTS TORN OUT,
AND STRIPT OF ITS LETTERING AND GILDING,
LIES HERE, FOOD FOR WORMS.
BUT THE WORK SHALL NOT BE WHOLLY LOST:
FOR IT WILL, AS HE BELIEV'D, APPEAR ONCE MORE,
IN A NEW AND MORE PERFECT EDITION,
REVISED AND CORRECTED
BY THE AUTHOR.

'Your strategy of self-perfection's admirable,' she told him one night as, standing beside the Schuylkill at the cold dark hour of three o'clock, she trained Ben's reflecting telescope on banded Jupiter. 'But can you actually cleave to it from here to Heaven?'

'Believe me, dearest, I have oft-times told myself to eschew this project, for it could easily make me not so much a faultless man as a moral fop, forever flaunting his merits. Then, too, does not a truly virtuous person exhibit a few failings, so as to keep his friends in countenance?'

'*Now* I hear Reason talking,' she said, bringing the regal planet into focus.

'Forgive me, Mrs Crompton, but 'tis not Reason you hear but rather its deceitful twin, Expedience.' Ben rubbed his hands together as if lathering a bar of soap. 'I am reminded of a story told me by a blacksmith I knew in Boston. It seems there appeared in his shop one day a farmer who desired to have the whole of his axe as shiny as the cutting-edge. The blacksmith consented to buff the blade bright if the farmer would but turn the grindstone crank.'

She fixed her eye on Jupiter's southern hemisphere. She blinked. Yes, there it was, the Great Red Spot, radically shifted from its position of a mere four hours earlier. 'I've caught the crimson storm, Ben, though now its fury lies to the east. 'Twould seem that, for all it's a weighty sphere, Jupiter takes but twelve Earth hours to make a rotation, surely no more than fourteen.'

'Then I thank Providence I'm no citizen of the place, for my days are short enough already.' Ben clucked his tongue and resumed his tale. 'With great zeal the farmer worked the crank whilst the blacksmith pressed the axe hard against the stone, which made the turning of it very fatiguing. At length the farmer declared that he would take his tool as it was. "No," the smith said, "turn on, turn on. We shall make it glitter by and by. As yet 'tis only speckled." "Aye," the farmer said, "but I think a speckled axe is best."'

Jennet laughed, though not so loudly as to demean Ben's story, which was far more fable than jape. 'Your parable's most piquant, Sir. How readily we settle for the speckled axe.'

'Unless I embrace my perfection-matrix in full,' he said, nodding, 'I shall never learn how far I might go in eradicating my defects.'

She twisted the focus knob, and suddenly a Jovian satellite popped out of the blackness. 'Ah, there she is, elusive Io. I've seen her only once before, back in the Mirringate observatory.'

'How does the goddess appear?'

'A yellow ball, as if made of sulphur.'

'Sulphur? She's a kind of Von Guericke sphere then? My dear Mrs Crompton, 'twould seem we've solved the riddle of Heaven's fire.' He offered her a coy smile and a mischievous wink. 'Each time Jehovah desires to hear the boom of thunder, He sets His hand on spinning Io, and seconds later those mighty sparks called lightning-bolts come forth!'

Turn on, turn on — we shall make it glitter by and by. The imperative became their private chant, something they could sing to one another whenever it seemed their *affaire de coeur* lacked a future. If they simply kept the wheel moving, minds and bodies bent to the task, their love would never lose its lustre.

The instant Ben finished with the day's obligations at Keimer's, they would seek each other out, sometimes in his garret, sometimes in her townhouse, remaining together until he left for work in the morning. When it came to carnal matters, she normally played the teacher, he the novice (and never did concupiscence know a more eager pupil), but in the other arena of their nakedness, the languidly flowing Schuylkill, these roles were reversed, Ben instructing Jennet in how to control her buoyancy and move her limbs per the advanced principles set down by Monsieur Thévenot in his *Art of Swimming*. But beyond the mattress and the river they were equals, two curious pilgrims peering through Ben's telescope, leaning over his microscope, constructing vacuums with his air-pump.

'Here's the problem,' she said. 'Monsieur Descartes hath revealed to philosophers a universe cloven down the middle, thinking minds on one side, dead matter on the other. But the world's fore'er in motion. Inexplicable forces hoist the seas to shore, pull our planet 'round its star, and put Dr Halley's comet to flight.'

'Say "inexplicable force" to a Continental Cartesian, or even a Cambridge Platonist, and he replies, "occult force",' Ben sighed.

'Say "occult force" to a priest, and he replies, "demonic force",' she groaned. 'Say "demonic force" to a witchfinder, and he reaches for his pricking needle.'

'So we're stuck. Flies in molasses.'

'And yet I shall persist.'

'Most admirable, Mrs Crompton.'

'A speckled axe is ne'er best.'

Rare was the tryst in which they neglected to exchange gifts. Their corporation trafficked lavishly in tokens: flower blossoms, autumn leaves, sparkling stones, burnished beetles, pithy sayings, the poems of Catullus. Although the majority of these favours were discovered rather than purchased, occasionally one lover would notice some astonishingly apropos artefact in a shop window. Thus it was that he bought for her a cedar-wood model of the Trojan Horse, whilst she presented him with a miniature Blaeu press capable of printing individual playing-cards.

Early in October her regular monthly visit to Ephram's bookshop brought her face-to-face with what she took to be the latest edition of Newton's masterwork, its title rendered in English: *Mathematical Principles of Natural Philosophy*. Leafing through the volume, she discovered to her delight that, thanks to the labours of one Andrew Mott, her native tongue informed the entire text. An ideal birthday present for Ben, she realized. The price was two pounds, an amount that gave her pause, as her summer stipend from Tobias had not arrived. In the end she decided that recklessness was the better part of romance, and she blithely acquired the *Principia*'s newest incarnation.

Later, as she made her way down Market Street, the precious bundle pressed against her breast, a delightful question formed in her brain. Why wait four months to please Ben with the translated *Principia* when she could please him with it right now? Reaching the Godfrey house, she retrieved her key from beneath the stoop, then ascended the rear stairwell at a giddy pace, her imagination offering her an entrancing glimpse of Ben's plump cheeks lifting in a smile as he took the book in hand.

Entering the bed-chamber, she found it empty, a circumstance she chose to exploit by hiding the *Principia* beneath his pillow. She proceeded to the laboratory. No Ben. She rushed into the parlour. Her gallant sat on the divan, his complexion ashen, his fingers entwining one another like spiders in carnal embrace.

'My darling, you look unwell.'

'I am stricken with foreboding,' he said.

'How so?'

''Twould seem Dame Fortune means to pluck me from the City of Brotherly Love and carry me clear to England.'

'England?'

'For reasons I do not apprehend, Governor Keith hath lately formed a good opinion of me, and he urges that I sail to London without delay. I am to purchase, upon his credit, a new handpress and two cases of type, that I might open a shop in Philadelphia dedicated to our province's printing needs. Oh, Mrs Crompton, I fear you will decline to join me on this voyage.'

'How can you imagine such a thing?'

'Are you not pledged to remain in America, battling your brother's noxious band?'

'Unless I undertake to murder the cleansers with pistol and ball, a course forbidden by my own perfection-matrix, my mere proximity cannot threaten them. Rather than endure our separation, bonny Ben, I would follow you into the coldest cave in Arctica or across the hottest plain in Hell.'

He vaulted off the divan and showered her cheeks with kisses. 'I was afraid I'd be forced to chose 'twixt the livelihood I love and the love for which I live.'

'Think on your clearheaded Silence Dogood. Were she blessed with a swain such as yourself, 'tis certain she would ne'er leave his side.'

'To England, then?' he said.

'To England,' she replied.

But instead they went to the bed-chamber and removed all their clothing.

'A splendid idea hath popped into my brain,' he said. 'Upon arriving in London, we shall search out Isaac Newton. Unless his madness is ascendant, I shall persuade him to favour us with his insights into the electric force.'

''Tis a pilgrimage you will make alone, for I've yet to forgive the man his betrayal of Aunt Isobel.' She retrieved the *Principia* from beneath the pillow, passing it to Ben. 'When you face the old lion, you'll want him to place his signature on this, thereby increasing its worth.'

''Sbody – the very translation I've been seeking!' He flipped back the cover. A scowl overwhelmed his smile. 'I'faith, Mrs Crompton, this Newton's a far handsomer wight than you've described.'

He displayed the frontispiece, which had somehow eluded her initial perusal of the text. Her pulse quickened. Her skin prickled. Skilfully rendered and crisply inked, the engraving depicted a man who, whatever his faults and virtues, was certainly not Isaac Newton.

'This is somebody else!' she protested.

'How so?'

'Newton's a crook-backed gnome of weak chin and eyes set wide apart! How could I forget the face that sealed Isobel's doom?'

''Tis one thing for an artist to flatter his subject, and quite another for him to draw the wrong man entirely. There's surely some chicanery here, for when you speak of a crook-backed gnome, one imagines either Shakespeare's Richard the Third or philosophy's Robert Hooke.'

'Hooke of the *Micrographia*?'

'The late, great Robert Hooke, Newton's eternal antagonist.'

Ben dashed from the bed-chamber and returned anon holding a splayed copy of Hooke's *Lectiones Cutlerianae*.

'Your gnome mayhap?' he asked, showing her the frontispiece.

As she scrutinized the image, a sour fluid travelled from her stomach to her chest – for this was indeed the very dwarf she'd met thirty-five years earlier in Newton's rooms at Trinity.

She snapped the treatise shut as if to mash a midge betwixt its leaves. ''Steeth, Ben, this Hooke hath played me false! He hath played us *all* false – myself, Aunt Isobel, Barnaby Cavendish, the whole Colchester Assizes of 1689! Everything is clear now. By standing before the Court as Newton, Hooke sought to ruin his rival's reputation. What a swinish thing to do! 'Tis an un-Christian thought, but I'm glad the man's dead!'

'Might this mean the real Newton's no maniac after all?'

'It means much more, my love. It means we need but present ourselves to Newton and tell him of the murderous Purification Commission, and in a trice he'll give us his demon disproof!'

They set both books aside and stiffened their tongues, that each might probe the other's mouth.

'You will find your new *Principia* an enchanting text,' she said. 'Proposition Fifty-seven: "Two mutually attracting bodies describe similar figures about their common centre of gravity." Proposition Eighty-five: "If a body be attracted by a second such entity, and its attraction be vastly stronger when 'tis contiguous——" '

'All I ask of Heaven, Madame, is to share with you a common centre of gravity.'

'We share it, bonny Ben, now and for ever.'

'I am your lodestone, Mrs Crompton. Your lodestone and your polestar all combined, my lovely lady, my sweetest Jennet, my brave Waequashim of the Nimacook.'

CHAPTER THE EIGHTH

In Which Jennet at Last Meets the
Avatar of Her Ambition, Though with
a Result She Did Not Foresee

To conceal the scandalous nature of their relationship, Ben suggested that whilst crossing the Atlantic and living in London they should represent themselves as a middle-aged mother and her philosophically inclined son, but Jennet found this a monumentally offensive idea. 'If we adopted such a ruse,' she declared, 'I could ne'er again enter our love-bed without imagining myself Jocasta about to swive her Oedipus.' Having no desire to complicate their carnal life with mythic incest, Ben withdrew his proposal, whereupon Jennet convinced him that she should instead pose as a prodigy-monger in search of new specimens, travelling with her younger half-brother. Thus it was that in the guise of siblings they booked passage on the brigantine *London-Hope*, scheduled to sail from Philadelphia on the fifth of November 1724, and reach England by Christmas.

The first of the voyage's several disasters occurred when Jennet and Ben arrived on Vine Street Wharf only to learn that the berths they'd reserved in the great cabin had been appropriated by a Mr Hamilton of Trenton and a Mr Russell of Wilmington. The purser offered no apology, insisting that Mr Franklin and his half-sister should have anticipated all along their displacement by 'gentlemen of stature' (Hamilton being a New-Jersey barrister, Russell the master of a Maryland ironworks). And so it came to pass that Jennet and Ben spent the next seven weeks in steerage, sharing accommodation with two dozen other passengers and sleeping in hammocks whose sole pretension to privacy was a translucent linen curtain separating the sexes. Only by exploiting the *London-Hope*'s peripheral geography did the philosophers achieve connubial embrace. On one occasion they connected in the supply compartment atop a pile of sailcloth, another time in the cargo hold behind six hogsheads of sot-weed.

Even more troubling to Jennet than their wretched quarters was her unhappy stomach, which in the thirty-five years since her previous Atlantic crossing had grown sensitive to the sea's vicissitudes. For each day that she was up and about on the main deck, she had to spend two in her hammock, sipping medicinal tea from the private store of their shipboard acquaintance, Thomas Denham, an affable Quaker merchant who shared the great cabin with Hamilton and Russell. By the midpoint of the crossing her condition had improved somewhat, less in consequence of Denham's tea than of Ben's tenderness, for he was ever prepared to sooth her with kisses, mop her brow with cool water, and read to her from Mr Defoe's romance of shipwreck and survival, *The Life and Strange Surprising Adventures of Robinson Crusoe, of York, Mariner.*

The third, final and worst misadventure happened near the end the voyage, when Ben entreated the ship's master, a sour old Jacobite named Bertram Annis, to let him examine the mail-pouches for the endorsements that Governor Keith had promised to place on board. Puffing discontentedly on his pipe, exuding smoke and irritation, Captain Annis led Ben and Jennet below decks to a tenebrous compartment as large as a wigwam, carpeted in canvas and jammed with more than a thousand pieces of mail. The subsequent search took nearly two hours, during which interval the philosophers turned up packets intended for bishops, solicitors, judges, physicians, tobacco merchants, stock-jobbers, and linen-drapers, but not a single letter addressed to a London printing-house.

'Mayhap I should gift Mr Keith with a perfection-matrix,' Ben said, 'featuring a special new grid labelled Mindfulness.'

Later that afternoon, as she and her gallant strolled about the quarter-deck in the company of Mr Denham, Jennet mentioned that Ben's London prospects were now uncertain, a set of letters recommendatory from Sir William Keith having gone mysteriously astray. With no further prompting Denham proceeded to impugn the

Governor's character, explaining that in all matters financial Keith was a notorious bluffer. A letter of credit from Sir William would be 'a shabby and paradoxical thing', for the man had not a speck of credit to give.

Ben bore this setback stoically, announcing that he would seek a journeyman's position with a London firm and thereby master the newest British printing techniques. By pursuing this course, he argued, he might become so expert in his trade that before long some 'honest and principled edition of Keith' would set him up in business. Mr Denham agreed that the scheme was worthy, adding that he would happily refer Ben to his friend Samuel Palmer, who ran a printing-house in Bartholomew's Close.

At this juncture Jennet made bold to ask whether perchance Mr Denham's circle also included Isaac Newton.

'Nay, but I number amongst my associates a certain Henry Pemberton, who doth travel in the illustrious man's orbit,' the Quaker replied. 'If thou wish it, Mrs Crompton, I shall acquaint thee with Dr Pemberton upon our disembarkation.'

'Such an introduction would greatly please me,' she said, panting as her stomach protested the *London-Hope*'s pitch and took exception to its roll, 'for 'tis imperative I speak with Mr Newton betimes.'

'I cannot say he's favourably disposed towards receiving visitors, but at last report he was remarkably hale for a man of eighty-two,' said Mr Denham. 'Newton's a knight now, not to mention President of the Royal Society and Master of the Mint, his Arian faith having deprived him of his professorship.'

'From figuring comets to forging coppers – a considerable descent,' Ben said.

'By my lights 'tis felicitous he came to the Mint when he did,' Denham said. 'Had Sir Isaac not supervised the Great Recoinage of this century past, our nation might today be poor as Ireland.'

This was the first Jennet had heard of Newton's having rescued England from bankruptcy, and she was delighted by her deduction that his prestige would now be at its zenith. If she could indeed persuade him to publicly excoriate the Conjuring Statute, that venerable abomination might very well become extinct before the April rains came.

'I've ne'er been certain whether God favours my project or not,' she said to Ben, 'but at least the great Newton's about to land in our camp.'

'In matters of creation and salvation, I've heard that God's the superior personage,' he replied. 'When it comes to making a purely rational argument, however, 'tis surely Sir Isaac you want as your champion.'

On the morning of the 24th of December following a one-night stopover in Gravesend, a town so stupefyingly sterile in Jennet's view that even Salem-Village would have profited by comparison, Captain Annis piloted his brigantine up the Thames and put to port in London. As Jennet and Ben joined the parade of voyagers marching down the gangway, Mr Denham proposed to meet his new friends that evening for a pint of ale and a bite of Christmas goose. Ben replied that as a vegetarian he would forgo the goose, but he and his sister would be glad of Mr Denham's dinner-time companionship, and so they agreed to converge at eight o'clock on the Scribbler's Quill in Chiswell Street.

The search took all day, but Jennet and Ben at last secured lodgings in Adam's Row, Mayfair, for a mere five shillings a week. It seemed to her that their landlady, a Catholic widow who maintained seven cats on the premises, was sceptical of their claim to be half-siblings, and the woman's doubts were surely aggravated by the haste with which they scampered up the stairway. Had Mrs Wilcox subsequently placed a curious ear to the bed-chamber door, her suspicions would have received scandalous corroboration through the sounds of exultant breathing intermixed with choruses of 'Enlarge the overlap!' and 'Turn on, turn on!'

In contrast to Sir William Keith, Thomas Denham proved a man of his word. When Jennet and Ben arrived at the Quill that night, Mr Denham was already at the table, bearing a letter recommendatory for Ben and drinking ale with Henry Pemberton. As the evening's conversation progressed, it became clear that Pemberton, a loquacious and exuberant young physician, was indeed on friendly and even filial terms with Newton, having published in the *Philosophical Transactions*

an article that *en passant* disproved certain Leibnizian principles concerning the force of descending bodies. (Apparently the surest way to
beguile Newton was to make the late Gottfried Wilhelm Leibniz look
doltish.) Alas, Pemberton was not sanguine concerning 'Sir Isaac's
willingness to speak with either a curator of dubious attainment or a
printer of invisible reputation'. Howbeit, he promised to 'charm the old
wizard' as best he could, and Jennet slept well that evening, confident
that their petition lay in capable hands.

A fortnight went by, and then a month, with no word from
Pemberton. For Jennet the days passed with an excruciating languor,
as if the Earth lay fixed to an ancient orrery, its gears and wheels frozen
by rust. To make matters worse, she could barely venture a yard beyond
Mayfair without being reminded that demonology was still in flower
and its votaries much afoot. Her first visit to Hyde Park climaxed with
a noisy Puritan divine named Christopher Waller giving her the
printed text of his newest anti-Satanist sermon. Later that week a Bow
Street ragamuffin sold her a broadsheet narrating a witch-trial in
Aberdeen. At Lemuel's Bookshop she obtained a pamphlet celebrating the Kirkcaldy Cleansing League as if it were a glamorous band of
highwaymen. In a booth at the Hare and Hounds she came upon a
discarded *London Journal* whose penultimate page related the Massachusetts Bay Purification Commission's campaign against a Braintree
warlock. Each such encounter drained her energy as thoroughly as it
sapped her spirit, and she would subsequently limp back to Adam's
Row at the lethargic pace of a *machemoqussu*.

Exacerbating her discontent was the fact that Ben's employment at
Palmer's Printing-House occupied him fourteen hours a day. Were
they short on funds, she would not have begrudged him his absence
from their rooms, but she'd brought along her savings. True, both the
summer and autumn stipends from Tobias were overdue (a phenomenon that Mr Horsfals, a prickly old Tory with a lisp, could not
explain). The sum involved, however, was only sixty pounds, and
meanwhile she and Ben had nearly eight hundred.

At length she gave voice to her frustration – 'Our couplings come
with less frequency than does Dr Halley's comet' – and Ben's answer
caught her by surprise. Mr Palmer, he explained, had set him an all-
consuming challenge, designing and building a machine that by the

stroke of a key would lift a leaden letter from the rack and plant it in a type-form.

'As you might imagine,' he said, 'such an ambitious project devours my time voraciously.'

The argument was sensible, and so for many weeks she kept her annoyance in check, until one afternoon, hunting through Ben's wardrobe for a mirror (her own having shattered), she happened upon a stack of pamphlets headed '*Articles of Belief and Acts of Religion* by Benjamin Franklin, Printer and Natural Philosopher'. Instinctively she formulated several denunciations in her mind, including 'Am I not more valuable to you than this theologic folderol?' as well as 'Hours for the Almighty but barely a minute for me!' But then she began to read the *Articles of Belief*, forthwith finding herself in the presence of him whom she adored.

'Since I cannot possibly conceive of that which is Infinite,' he'd written, 'I must conclude that the Infinite Father expects from us neither Worship nor Praise, but rather that He is infinitely above such Displays.' Who was this audacious thinker who presumed to know the mind of God whilst simultaneously sounding like the soul of modesty? Any woman who could claim the affections of so dauntless a youth was a fortunate person indeed. Jennet returned the treatise to its hiding place and resolved to practise the fourth virtue on Ben's perfection-matrix, forbearance.

Gradually the shroud lifted from her psyche, and she came to see that her immediate circumstances were hardly lamentable. Her health was robust, her mind clear, her senses keen, her purse bulging, and at her doorstep lay the city of her dreams, the London for which she'd once pined as passionately as had Dido for Aeneas.

Whenever and wherever she alighted – theatre, ordinary, market, coffee-house, concert hall, gillyflower garden – she inquired after Barnaby Cavendish, now seventy years old by her reckoning. A few Londoners recalled that bottled prodigies had been amongst the attractions at the Frost Fair of 1709 (the Thames having frozen solid for the first time since 1684, creating a natural promenade along which puppeteers, jugglers, magicians, troubadours, and crystal-gazers had installed their booths), but none could say whether the Cavendish Museum was still in business. Unless Dame Fortune had developed a sudden sympathy for runaway Nimacooks of philosophic persuasion, Jennet decided, her chances of finding the mountebank would hover betwixt the minute and the minuscule.

True to her expectations, London excited her senses and aroused her intellect, but the place continually eluded her tongue. Was London a beehive, a buzzing nexus of freneticism and hubbub? Yes. Was it an immense Von Guericke sphere, forever spinning as it pulled bits and pieces of the outside world to its electric embrace? Indeed. Was it a roadside carcass, beset by vultures, encircled by flies, crawling with maggots, roiling with stenches? That too. London was parks and monuments, bridges and churches, day-vendors and night-criers, bear-baiting and coach-racing – but for Jennet one fact eclipsed all others: this was the city of Marlowe, Jonson and Shakespeare. She alternated her attendance betwixt two venues, the Lincoln's Inn Fields Playhouse in Chancery Street and the King's Theatre in Drury Lane. She disliked the newer works by Colley Cibber and Richard Steele, which were crudely absorbing at best, sentimental and moralistic at worst, but fortunately the great comedies of the Restoration enjoyed frequent revivals. During her first two months of theatre-going, she caught marvellous productions of Wycherley's ebullient *The Country Wife*, Congreve's deliriously epigrammatic *Love for Love*, Farquhar's wry and canny *The Beaux' Stratagem*, and, the most curious of the lot, Gay's *Three Hours After Marriage*, featuring a pompous philosopher, Dr Fossile, evidently modelled on Newton.

On the night that Jennet beheld Rupert Quince play Mark Antony in Dryden's *All for Love*, she returned to Adam's Row to find Ben in an intricate mood, a mixture of apprehension, chagrin and joy.

'I've been concealing a pertinent fact from you,' he confessed. 'Five weeks ago Dr Pemberton came by Palmer's to say that Mr Newton hath refused to meet with us.'

An ingot of molten anger formed within Jennet's breast. 'Why did you not tell me of this calamity?'

'I feared to break your heart.'

'Then why do you break it *now*?'

'Events have taken a felicitous turn. It seems that, shortly after receiving the bad news, Pemberton presented Newton with a theologic treatise I'd composed to amuse myself during my luncheon intervals.

Apparently Newton found my arguments astute, and the upshot is that he will have us to dinner come Friday.'

'Oh, Ben, this is splendid news indeed. I should very like to see your treatise' – she felt the sarcasm rising within her, building towards eruption – 'as I've been meaning to write such an essay myself.'

'Really?'

'I would make the point that God, being infinite, expects from us neither worship nor praise.'

''Sblood, Mrs Crompton, you speculate precisely as I do!' He suddenly grew pensive. 'Or did you perchance come upon the pamphlets I keep in my wardrobe?'

'I shan't tell you,' she replied drily.

'You must.'

'When Newton first spurned us, you should've come to me.'

'Quite so, Mrs Crompton.'

'Protect me from all the imps of Hell, bonny Ben. Protect me from George's dragon and Apollo's python. But you must ne'er again protect me from the truth.'

Having spoken her mind, she felt her spleen diminish, and she stamped his cheek with a kiss. 'Let me not strain on the gnat of your presumption whilst Parliament swallows the camel of Dunstan's preachment,' she said. 'If our luck holds firm, ere the month is out England's legislators will have lent their most sympathetic ears to Newton's demon disproof.'

'Whereupon we shall appear before the Massachusetts Governor and cheerfully inform him that his licensed cleansers enjoy the same legal status as forgers, freebooters and fastfannies.'

'Am I to surmise you're prepared to sail home?' she asked.

He nodded and said, 'Mr Palmer and I agree that my device for setting type hath no commercial value. 'Tis an impressive beast to be sure, a-whirl with cogs and sprockets, but an unacceptable hiatus occurs 'twixt the stroking of a key and the slotting of a letter.'

'A human could do it quicker?' she asked.

'Let me put it this wise. Were *The London Journal* to employ the Franklin Typesetter in announcing the pregnancy of King Louis's bride, the babe would be born, weaned, and riding to hounds ere the form was ready for inking.'

On the first morning in April Jennet took the day-coach north to Colchester and got out at the Fox and Fife, the Hill Street tavern before which, thirty-six years earlier, she'd said farewell to Barnaby Cavendish. She proceeded directly to Frere Street and thence to Saint James's Church. Upon reaching the crumbling Roman wall, she vaulted onto the unhallowed ground and dropped reverently to her knees before the slate outcropping.

The epitaph had survived the intervening winters, but a mesh of yellow vines now obscured the words. Even more troubling were the stick figures that a libertine draughtsman, as incompetent as Dunstan was skilful, had chalked below the inscription, five men and as many women engaged in several varieties of swiving.

'Dearest teacher, 'twould seem that Dame Fortune hath at long last joined our side,' Jennet murmured. 'Fool though I am, I have never-theless sorted the false Newton from the true. Aye, my brave aunt, two days hence I break bread with him whose calculation shall end the cleansing madness.'

She scrambled back over the Roman wall, entered the church, and, unwinding her scarf, submerged it in the stagnant and slimy baptismal waters. Her tears dripped into the font like raindrops filling a cistern. Returning to the grave, she pressed the wet wool against the stone and rubbed the licentious drawings into oblivion. Now she tugged on the arrogant vines, but the earth would not surrender them, and so she trampled down the stalks with her boots till the epitaph became visible.

I measured the Skies, now I measure the Shadows. Sky-bound was the Mind, Earth-bound the Body rests.

And what of the soul? she wondered as she headed back to the Fox and Fife. Was a tomb in sooth a portal to immortality, as so many clerics and theologians averred? She had no information on the subject, but it amused her to imagine that Aunt Isobel might yet exist on some ethereal plane. Perhaps she now kept company with Johannes Kepler, the two of them running an academy for recently deceased dunderheads who in their ignorance still credited the Ptolemaic universe. In her mind Jennet could see the whole scene, Dr Kepler and Lady Mowbray presiding over a celestial classroom populated by cardinals and popes.

This afternoon the instructors were requiring their pupils to set quill to parchment and write *Eppur si muove* one thousand times – for such was Galileo's legendary aside as, standing before the Inquisition, he'd returned astronomy to its biblical foundations, renouncing for ever his allegiance to a revolving, rotating Earth.

Eppur si muove, Galileo had muttered. Still, it moves.

Jennet reached London near dusk, the collective chimney smoke combining with the incipient twilight to turn the fruit-stalls and flower-carts of Saint Giles Circle a uniform dun. Decoaching, she recalled that at eight o'clock the curtain would rise on the premier presentation of the Drury Lane Company's most recent revival, Mr Congreve's *The Way of the World*. If she moved quickly, she wouldn't even miss the Prologue. She sprinted down Holborn High Street to Drury Lane, made a mad dash south, and arrived breathless on the steps of the King's Theatre, where she paused to rest her lungs and read a printed billboard affixed to a marble pilaster.

According to the advertisement, the part of Betty, the waiting-maid in *The Way of the World*, belonged to a certain Rachel Crompton.

Rachel Crompton?

Could it be? Was it possible? Rachel Crompton? The living child of her own blood, now fifteen, had left the East Indies and landed on the London stage?

She bought a ticket and received her broadsheet, which likewise announced that Rachel Crompton would play the waiting-maid, then rushed into the stalls. As always the great hall dazzled her, the two thousand tallow flames twinkling in their gilded chandeliers, the four tiers of balconies rising on all sides like cliffs facing a river gorge. She stumbled past the denizens of Row 23, their disapproval of her tardiness manifesting in frowns and snarls. Even before she could assume her seat, the chandeliers ascended into the shadows and Rupert Quince, painted and preening, appeared before the green velvet curtain to deliver the Prologue.

'Of those few fools who with ill stars are cursed,' Mr Quince began, 'sure scribbling fools, called poets, fare the worst. For they're the sort of fools which Fortune makes, and after she has made 'em fools, forsakes.'

The spectators offered snickers of appreciation. A tipsy oaf standing in the pit hurled a half-eaten apple onto the stage, but his associate oafs were quick to reprimand him, and the rest of the Prologue – more disingenuous self-deprecation from the playwright – unfolded without mishap.

Mr Quince strode away. The curtain rose. Two young men, Mr Mirabell and Mr Fainall, sat at a small table in a chocolate-house, engaged in a hand of whist. An exchange of dialogue established that Mirabell, being distracted, had played badly, but he was willing to continue the game for his friend's amusement.

Fainall declined the proposition: 'The coldness of a losing gamester lessens the pleasure of the winner. I'd no more play with a man that slighted his ill fortune than I'd make love to a woman who under-valued the loss of her reputation.'

The spectators tittered approvingly, none more than the primitives in the pit.

Finding his chocolate-dish empty, Fainall slammed it on the table. In response to the angry clack a waiting-maid entered, whereupon Jennet's attention deserted Congreve's universe to focus entirely on the young woman portraying Betty.

God in Heaven, it was she! Her roundish face had lengthened over the years, assuming the oval of the Madonna in the Reverend Foster's illustrated Bible. Her complexion was still fair, but her hair had turned dark, and her frame displayed nubile proportions.

Throughout the whole of the first scene, Rachel had but one line. Mirabell asked, 'Betty, what says your clock?', and Rachel replied, 'Turned of the last canonical hour, sir.' In Scene Two, Rachel's speeches were limited to 'Yes, what's your business?' followed by 'He's in the next room' after which came 'Sir, the coach stays' and finally 'They're gone, sir, in great anger.'

As Act One drew to a close, Jennet studied her broadsheet. For Act Two, the scene would shift to Saint James's Park. Acts Three, Four, and Five were confined entirely to Lady Wishfort's residence. To wit, Betty of the chocolate-house had evidently departed the story.

Braving her neighbours' sneers, she jostled her way down Row 23, then charged up the aisle and into the lobby. She lurched past a sign reading NO PATRONS BEYOND THIS POINT, descended a dark stair, and followed the corridor to a dressing-chamber apparently reserved for actresses assaying waiting-maids, scullery-wenches, fish-wives, and similarly minor roles. The room was a hall of mirrors, each framed in brass and flanked by hierarchies of burning candles. Rachel sat on a bench before the nearest such glass, rubbing the vermilion from her cheeks with a damp cloth. In the shadows beyond, three female players chattered amongst themselves and adjusted their coiffeurs.

'Good evening, Miss Crompton,' Jennet said, pausing in the doorway.

Rachel started and glanced towards her visitor. 'Do I know you, ma'am?'

'I' Christ, daughter, I'm the woman who gave you life.'

'That's a poor topic for a joke.'

'Some twenty years ago, I married your father, Tobias the Post-master, changing my name from Stearne to Crompton.'

Rachel winced but said nothing. She turned back to her mirror and continued to unpaint her cheeks, washing away the white grease. 'If you're the woman who gave me life, then you're also the woman who gave me grief, deserting me when I was but a child.'

'We were separated by an abduction,' Jennet said, taking two steps forward.

Rachel's mirror displayed a frown of bottomless suspicion. 'Faugh, I'll warrant you're but an impostor, looking to snare the fortune you imagine I possess.'

'If my oath's not enough to satisfy you, ask me a question only your natural mother could answer.'

Having cleaned her cheeks, Rachel commenced to swab her brow. 'A *test*, aye? Very well. In Philadelphia my father employed a maid-servant . . .'

'Her name was Nellie Adams.'

The mirrored frown transmuted into gape-mouthed surprise. 'My mother passed much of her youth in uncommon circumstances . . .'

'No doubt you allude to my years amongst the savage tawnies of Massachusetts Bay. Many were the times I entertained you with Indian lore. The Fable of the Wily Raven, the Parable of the Greedy Porcupine, the Adventure of the Tortoise—'

'The Tortoise Who Had No Shell,' Rachel interrupted in a voice at once pained and amazed. Her reflected face declined from surprise to bemusement, and then came anger, followed by contempt. 'An abduction, you call it. Mayhap that's the right word, but 'twould appear you took no particular trouble to find me once the deed was done. By my father's account, you were always too vainglorious to abide mere motherhood.'

'Forsaking you in favour of philosophy was the worst thing I e'er did. Not a day passes but I feel the shame of it.'

'And not a day passes but I feel the sting of it.'

Jennet shuddered and said, 'Rachel, will you not look me in the eye?'

'If I wish to behold treachery's gaze, I need merely seek out Mr Quince' – Rachel leaned into the mirror, filling it with her scowl – 'who hath promised me the part of Mrs Millamant the instant I yield my virtue to him.'

A hard, hot Von Guericke sphere seemed to form in Jennet's stomach. 'Oh, my dear child, suffer me to deliver you from this scoundrel! You're too young to give your innocence to a rogue!'

'I'm also too young to play Mrs Millamant. If 'twere otherwise, I would gladly swive my way to the top of the *Dramatis Personae*.' Rachel rose and turned one hundred degrees. Her scowl, unmediated now, was even fiercer than its reflection.

Jennet brushed her daughter's arm. 'Tell me your adventures, child. I want to know them all.'

Rachel flinched but did not pull away. ''Tis truly my own wayward mother?'

'Truly.'

'I must admit that London hath no surplus of sympathetic listeners.'

'You shall enjoy my rapt attention for as long as you wish.'

The melodrama that Rachel proceeded to relate began in sunlight, descended into darkness, and ended on a grey, ambiguous dawn. With undiluted delectation she recounted her first four years in India, a cavalcade of jewels, elephants, monkeys, flowers, mimosa trees, and more gods than the sky could hold. Her governess treated her with great kindness, and Rachel soon decided that Mlle Peltier was fully the equivalent of a real mother. Alas, her father rarely stayed in Madraspa-tam, for a man could not function as East-Indies Postmaster-General without travelling continually amongst the settlements, but he always returned home bearing fragrant ointments and ravishing fabrics.

Rachel's misery began when Mlle Peltier accepted her employer's proposal of marriage. Although Rachel was initially pleased by the arrangement, in time a melancholia came to possess Tobias's new wife, making her as vindictive in the role of step-mother as she'd been loving when employed as a tutor. Claudette Peltier Crompton took to feeding Rachel indifferently, reprimanding her constantly, and beating her regularly.

Just when it seemed that Rachel's ill-fortune could not increase, the fiery summer of 1722 blazed across Asia, bringing a typhus epidemic to rival the previous century's bubonic plagues. The contagion carried off not only Rachel's favourite priest at the Anglican school but also the elderly Hindoo neighbour-woman who'd given her a mongoose, and then, finally, her own dear father.

Much to Jennet's chagrin, the news of Tobias's passing sparked within her not a spasm of remorse but a spate of deduction. His death explained why her last two stipends had failed to arrive.

'He was a person of decency and generosity,' Jennet said.

'He was a fool, but I loved him,' Rachel said, sidling back to her mirror. 'So now there was nothing to keep me in India. My nine-month journey to England taught me much about the wickedness of the world, and 'twas only through God's grace I arrived still in possession of my wits, my honour, and my dreams of a life on the stage. Until an hour ago, I'd ne'er acted before a London audience, and I must own 'twas a thrill much greater than the instant cure for orphanhood you've presumed to bring me.'

'This talent for playing's in your blood, child. When next we meet, I'll tell you how I once portrayed a demon's ward, but now you must know of the route by which I've landed in your dressing-chamber.'

'I fear your escapades hold little interest for me.'

'Methinks you'll find them as enthralling as the Parable of the Greedy Porcupine.'

As Rachel changed her clothing, trading the waiting-maid's tattered muslin dress for a taffeta gown with puffed sleeves, Jennet unspooled her narrative, from the challenge laid upon her by Isobel, to her two failed attempts at a demon disproof, to her love affair with a

Pennsylvania printer, to her imminent collaboration with Sir Isaac Newton.

''Steeth, Mrs Crompton,' Rachel said when Jennet was finished, ''twould seem we share some several pints of blood but not one drop of sensibility. I've ne'er had the slightest taste for philosophic conjecture or Philadelphia journeymen.'

'I beg you, withhold your judgement. I believe we're destined to become good friends.'

'Not with me living in London and you chasing after your inky-fingered swain.'

'I'll allow you're a competent actress, but 'tis a profession that hath debauched many a girl as well-bred as you,' Jennet said. 'Hear my plea. Auspicious prospects lie before my Mr Franklin. Accompany us to the New World, and we shall all make a happy life together.'

'Pish, Mrs Crompton. If a man's star is not risen by his middle years, 'tis probably stuck on the horizon for ever.'

'Ah, but you see, my Ben is not yet thirty.'

Rachel flung a woollen shawl around her bodice and headed towards the doorway. 'He's twenty-nine then? Twenty-eight? Impressive, but I'd still lay not a farthing on his future. How old is the man exactly?'

'Nineteen.'

'What?'

'Nineteen. Twenty come January.'

'*Nineteen? Nineteen?* And *you* durst lecture *me* on debauchery?'

'I durst not lecture you on anything at all. I merely ask that you sail with us to America after I've brought Newton's proof before Parliament.'

'Your proposition's most unappetizing. I'll wager there's not a single worthy troupe in the whole of Pennsylvania.'

'Then you must found one, dear Rachel.'

Against Jennet's expectations, this last remark seemed to catch her daughter unawares. Rachel sighed harshly and, pursing her lips, leaned against the jamb. 'Come back this Saturday night, and I shall give you my answer.' Straightening, she marched into the corridor. 'But now I must bid you *adieu*, for I'm off to watch a cock-fight with my Gaston. By your example he should be a babe in arms' – her voice rose as the shadows consumed her — 'but in sooth my gallant wears a beard!'

For reasons that Sir Isaac Newton had yet to fathom, his revelations from On High always occurred at noon. Shortly after the sun had arrived overhead on the eleventh day in April 1676, the key to the Book of Daniel had blazed through his brain. The same solar circumstances had attended his derivation in 1665 of the binomial theorem, his sudden apprehension in 1668 of a method for determining the area under a curve, and his Heaven-sent discovery in 1673 that the floor-plan of Solomon's Temple, as documented by the prophet Ezekiel, forecast the future of the world.

Today's epiphany was no different. As the noon hour came to Kensington, Newton realized that the Problem of Problems — by what means did gravity exert its pull throughout the universe? — was within his reach. He had merely to sit chairbound on his porch and think about it.

Newton loathed his wheelchair, that hideous hooded chariot to which the physicians had condemned him, but he loathed the physicians even more. Although he admittedly didn't know how to cure his slack sphincter or recurrent kidney stones, it was obvious that England's doctors didn't either. Clearly the confounded chair didn't help. Indeed, by his own observations he was more likely to void a stone — they normally passed with little pain, praise Heaven — follow-ing a vigorous turn about his garden than after yet another interval in the wretched chair. If he attempted such a stroll now, of course, it would only provoke a wearying altercation with his day-nurse, but the instant Mr Asnault left for home, Newton would liberate himself. The best way to keep your legs was to use them.

He swallowed a mouthful of warm coffee, repositioned his rump, and opened his heart to his mentor, God.

In replacing Cartesian vortices with universal gravitation so many years earlier, Newton had invited on himself the accusation of occult-ism, and his enemies still routinely made it. But now he saw a way out. He would postulate an all-pervasive aether: not Descartes's aether, certainly, not that ridiculous invisible-yet-physical plasma, but a divine immaterial medium dancing at the edges of the human sensorium. A difficult concept, palpable incorporeality, perhaps even paradoxical, though to the Messiah of Mechanics it partook no less of reasoned discourse than did the Pythagorean theorem.

He rang the brass bell thrice, thereby signalling Moncriff to bring pen, paper, ink-pot and writing-board. The servant appeared promptly. Speaking not a word, for none dared break the silence whilst Sir Isaac was thinking, Moncriff set the equipment on his master's lap and departed.

The sheets came in colours: green for fancies, pink for notions, yellow for hypotheses, blue for truths. Newton selected a blue sheet, dipped quill in ink, and wrote:

$$Man = Visible\ Material\ Body$$
$$Christ = Apprehensible\ Immaterial\ Body$$
$$God = Inapprehensible\ Incorporeality$$

Aye! He'd caught the scent! Midway betwixt the unknowable essence of the Almighty and the familiar fleshiness of humans lay that unique substance called Jesus Christ. In fashioning the Redeemer as He'd done, God had collaterally provided the universe with the very stuff through which action-at-a-distance might operate, objects in-fluencing one another in eternal obeisance to the inverse-square law. The aether that made the world go round was in truth the divinely created Body of Christ, a situation that the egregious Roman Church, with its determination to chain the Saviour to a mathematically nonsensical triad, would never grasp in an aeon. The Holy Trinity – pshaw! The Deity = 3 = 1 = 3 – rubbish! Even the lowliest sub-sizar at Cambridge would never proffer so blighted an arithmetic.

At the bottom of the blue sheet he wrote *Gravitational Medium = Aether Christi*, then set his quill on the writing-board, slumped down in his wheelchair, and closed his eyes. The sun beat against his lids, brightening his blood and filling his field of vision with a vast red sea.

He awoke at dusk. No bird sang. No breeze stirred. The day-nurse would be gone now – hurrah: for the immediate future he could employ his body as he pleased. He blinked, staring at his writing-board. *Aether*

Christi. Nay, he hadn't dreamt it. Before falling asleep, he'd flushed the gravitational medium from hiding.

Now, he would have to allow that this triumph traced partially to the tract he'd received two weeks earlier. Amongst the merits of Benjamin Franklin's *Articles of Belief and Acts of Religion* was the idea that 'the Infinite hath created many Beings or Gods, vastly superior to Man, who can better conceive his Perfection than we, and return to him a more rational and glorious Praise.' Was it possible that, without Franklin's postulate of immortal intermediaries, Newton would never have fallen upon the notion of Christ's corpus as gravity's cause? He hesitated to say. One thing was certain: when Franklin came to dinner that evening, the *Aether Christi* would not be amongst the topics they discussed. For all he knew, the young Philadelphian was a budding Wilhelm Leibniz, eager to seize credit for discoveries he hadn't made.

Leibniz – faugh! The scoundrel had been gratifyingly dead these nine years, and still Newton could not think on him without enduring a trembling rage. By what monumental vanity, what Olympian arrogance, had the old pretender imagined he'd devised the fluxions independently of Newton? True, Leibniz's method of indicating maxima and minima could claim a certain originality, and he'd given his plagiarisms the novel name of *calculus,* but everyone knew the blackguard had maintained a band of roving sycophants, and these varlets had doubtless revealed to their master something of the new geometry brewing at Cambridge.

There could be only one Prince of Principles in the world – why had Leibniz refused to see that? God did not traffic in redundancy – could any truth be more self-evident?

Of course, when a man was selected by Providence to unveil the universe's deepest mysteries, it behooved him to keep his appointment in perspective. It was one thing to be God's viceroy and quite another to be an outright deity. Rejecting any overtures from his followers that smacked of worship, eschewing adulation at every turn, Newton had rarely regarded himself as anything more than a demiurge. Indeed, throughout his twenty-five years as Master of the Mint and his five as Warder before that, he'd always acted judiciously when exercising his powers over life and death. Yes, in most cases he'd declined to spare a clipper or a counterfeiter the noose, for left to their own devices such fiends would have bankrupted England during the Great Recoinage, and even today they were a festering pustule on the face of the monetary system. But occasionally he showed mercy, especially when the knave in question engaged in an authentic variety of grovelling.

Newton sipped cold coffee, purged Leibniz from his brain, and returned to his meditations. Chief amongst the properties of the *Aether Christi*, he now saw, was its probable participation in the microworld as well as the macro. *Micro and Macro*, he wrote on a yellow sheet — yellow for hypotheses. *Atoms and Stars*, he added. But before he could wrestle with the ramifications, Gunny Slocum, his chief informant from the Fleet, came dashing up the carriageway at the velocity of a man whose breeches were on fire.

'Hallo, Sir Isaac! Billy Slipfinger lies feverish in his hovel, and he wishes to tell us all about the Calibans! I ordered his widow-to-be to scribble down his babblings, as he's apt to pop off at any minute!'

Newton's heart seemed suddenly to shoot from his body, and only after he'd vacated the wheelchair did the organ return to its customary location. 'Well done, sir!' He rang the brass bell four times, thereby instructing Moncriff to appear post-haste. 'What does Mr Slipfinger expect in return?'

'Thirty quid, that his Lucy might become a hag o' means!' Slocum shouted.

''Sblood, I'll pay it!' He would gladly hand over twice that amount for the facts Slipfinger presumably possessed, the names and where-abouts of every felon who ran with the Caliban Adepts, the largest gang of counterfeiters still operating in London.

Moncriff, panting and discombobulated, materialized on the porch.

'Fetch my money cudgel,' Newton said, setting the writing-board aside, 'then fill my purse and tell Padding to hitch up the horses, for we must be in the Fleet by dark!'

'But tonight you dine with Mr Franklin and his sister.'

'Hang Mr Franklin! Hang his sister! We ride to the Liberties!'

As Moncriff rushed back into the mansion, Newton gazed long-ingly at the yellow sheet. *Micro and Macro. Atoms and Stars.* Revealing the secret stuff that held the universe together was important, but saving the British economy mattered too. With any luck, he would be back amongst these speculations by dawn, completing them within the week. If his instincts were correct, the *Aether Christi* would ultimately rank with his greatest discoveries. Before the decade was out, natural philosophers would come to prize this glorious glue most highly – more highly even than a geometer cherished his Euclid, an engineer his fluxions, or an alchemist his great transmuter, that wondrous element called

*

Mercury
was the problem.
Venus, Mars, Jupiter, Saturn –
from the birth of the solar system onwards,
these compliant planets had followed their predictable grooves, scrupulously obeying the laws given essence by Kepler and exactitude by Newton. But Mercury had a mind of its own. At the completion of each orbit, it did not return to the same starting point. My father knew this. So did his contemporaries. But since Mercury was close to the sun and therefore difficult to view, everyone agreed to attribute the discrepancy to observational error.

Over the years the measurements grew more precise, and the alibi ceased to satisfy. By the time a bright young patent clerk named Albert Einstein was on the scene, astronomers understood that Mercury's perihelion, its point of closest approach to the sun, was advancing 574 seconds of arc every century. After factoring in the perturbing gravity of the known planets, a physicist could make my father's mechanics account for 531 of those seconds, but that still left 43 seconds in the shadowland.

Einstein wasn't fazed. Truth to tell, he *loved* those 43 extra seconds of perihelion shift, for he knew in his heart they would succumb to his idiosyncratic notions of curved space and warped time. He set about his project, and – lo and behold – his equations not only accounted for Mercury's contrariness, they maintained the same form in every frame of reference he could imagine.

For with Einstein, you see, context was all. When Isobel Mowbray bid my dear Jennet experiment with Galileo's principle of uniform acceleration – assuming no air resistance, a cannonball and a codfish dropped in tandem will hit the ground simultaneously – neither tutor nor pupil fully appreciated the utter strangeness of that phenomenon. But Einstein did. One day in 1907, sitting in the Swiss Patent Office, he realized that if the falling codfish focused its attention exclusively on the descending cannonball, it would never know it was moving within a gravitational field. Until the instant of impact, in fact, the fish would have every right to insist it was at rest!

Einstein later called this 'the happiest thought of my life'.

From the moment he rationalized Mercury's perihelion shift, the world's cannier scientists understood that Einstein's physics was dest-ined to turn the Newtonian universe inside-out and upside-down. As early as 1905, Einstein had intuited that no object capable of assuming a resting state could travel faster than the vacuum speed of light. Besides liberating Maxwell's electrodynamics from the aether frame, Einstein's hypothesis of a light-speed barrier (the *sine qua non* of special relativity, but that's another story) gave him leave to discard my father's trouble-some appeals to absolute time and absolute space (troublesome to Newton himself as well as to his rivals). By combining these insights with the narrative of the falling fish, Einstein gave the world his great construct of 1915, general relativity – a brave new geometry of local curvatures produced by the presence of mass in the universe: planets, stars, Mount Everest, African elephants, Sumo wrestlers, kitchen sinks. Under a general relativity regime, gravity was no longer an inexplicable 'force' mysteriously causing 'action at a distance'. Instead of heeding some occult attraction, a given planet simply pursued the straightest possible course that the context allowed: a geodesic path in space-time.

When I first heard the popular notion that my father's system is really just an 'idiosyncratic case' of Einstein's universe, my reaction was instinctively defensive. 'That's like saying the *Nike of Samothrace* is an idiosyncratic case of metamorphic rock,' I told Kepler's *Harmonice Mundi*. But over the years I've mellowed. For one thing, Einstein's theories are evidently true. (Yes, occasionally a physicist with time on his hands will ostensibly coax a light pulse past the 186,000 mps barrier, so that the damn thing seems to arrive before it departs, but smart money still says special relativity has a future.) For another thing, if I'm an 'idiosyncratic case', I'm an idiosyncratic case that matters. In many a non-trivial circumstance, Newtonian physics still rules. The lunar mechanics that grace my second edition informed the heart and soul of every computer program employed by NASA during the Apollo era. If you were supervising the epochal moon landing of 1969, you needed no technical manual at your fingertips besides the *Principia Mathematica*.

So I'm not bitter anymore. Okay, sure, everybody has warm fuzzy feelings about Einstein, whereas my father is commonly perceived as a frigid fanatic in a silly wig. But one day the world will notice that while $E = mc^2$ ultimately gives you 177,000 dead Japanese civilians, $F = ma$ lets you skate across a frozen lake on a winter's night, the wind caressing your face as you glide towards the hot-chocolate stand on the far shore.

A few years after the rise of relativity my ego received a second blow. The deeper physicists peered beneath the surface of things, the clearer it became that my vaunted determinism did not apply at the subatomic level. Predicting the behaviour of elementary particles required a different mechanics, keyed to probability rather than causality. This sorry state of affairs culminated in 1927 with Werner Heisenberg's famous Uncertainty Principle, which states that you cannot simultaneously know the position and the momentum of a given particle. Let me hasten to add that Heisenbergian indeterminacy traces largely to the fact that subatomic position and momentum are conjugate attributes. Only in the popular misconception does the imprecision arise from disturbances inherent in the act of measurement.

Call me a traditionalist, but I don't really care for quantum physics. The Double-Slit Problem, whereby a single electron flies through two adjacent apertures in one trip, gives me the fantods. I'm equally unhappy about the Schrödinger's Cat Paradox, with its requirement that the poor animal be alive and dead at the same time. How weird is that? True, thanks to all those exquisite quantum equations, you humans now have television (though in my opinion the whole thing went downhill after The Avengers, mobile phones (enabling you to walk through a field of stunningly gorgeous wildflowers without actually being there), and your personal computers. But calculus lets you put a man on the moon! With fluxions at your command, you can build the Golden Gate Bridge!

Leibniz was correct, by the way: he *did* invent the infinitesimal calculus entirely on his own. But my father would hear none of it. At the height of their forty-year feud over the paternity of fluxions, he appointed a bogus committee to resolve the dispute 'objectively'. The group's report, the *Commercium Epistolicum*, was rigged from the start, and the Leibniz camp was right to scorn it. In the years that followed, both geometers hurled cadres of disciples into the fray, until eventually a schism opened in European intellectual life. Generation after generation, much to the detriment of their science, chauvinistic English mathematicians refused to employ Leibniz's superior system for noting integrals and differentials, which meanwhile swept the Continent owing to its lucidity and elegance.

For all this, I remain in awe of my father. He never stops surprising me. Centuries before anybody heard of Einstein, he dreamed the dream of unification, imagining that one day the same set of equations might encompass everything from the majestic sweep of a comet to the inner life of an atom. To be sure, his last-ditch attempt to combine the macro-world with the micro via the *Aether Christi* was screwy, but his earlier ruminations on the problem boasted sophistication and foresight. 'It is very well known that greater bodies act mutually upon each other by those forces, and I do not easily see why lesser bodies should not act on one another by similar forces,' he wrote in the unpublished 'Conclusio' to my second edition.

Contemporary physicists speak of a GUT, a Grand Unified Theory. They seek a TOE, a Theory of Everything. And I suspect that one day, through some felicitous convergence of experiment and serendipity, quarrelling and collaboration, they'll get one. And when they do, I hope they'll remember that the quest began not with Einstein or Heisenberg, not with Max Planck or Enrico Fermi, not with Niels Bohr or John Wheeler or Stephen Hawking, but with the great Sir Isaac

*

Newton
did not precisely
resemble the engraving that
graced the English-language edition
of the *Principia Mathematica*: such was Jennet's
impression when, thirty-five years after her failed mission to

Trinity College, she finally stood before the octogenarian geometer in his carriage-house, where he was supervising a servant's frantic efforts to hitch two horses to a coach. The lines of Newton's craggy face seemed deeper than in his portrait, and his cheeks had grown puffier. But there was no mistaking that hooked nose and rounded chin, those sharp obsidian eyes.

'Mr Franklin, I found your theologic treatise most stimulating,' Newton said, wrapping his veiny hands around Ben's outstretched palm. 'True, it wanders into a kind of polytheism on occasion, but such was not your intention.'

'Actually it was,' Ben said.

'Methinks you exaggerate, dearest brother,' Jennet hastened to add.

Newton acknowledged Jennet with a dark scowl, but he addressed her in a mellifluous tone. 'Should I e'er find myself in the American provinces, I shall be pleased to visit your prodigy museum.'

'I must tell you that my philosophic interests extend even to your fluxions,' she said. 'Just as Daedalus formed his son's arms into wings, so have you gifted Euclid with the power of flight.'

Newton glowered again and said, 'As I recall the story, Daedalus's experiment ended disastrously.'

'My metaphor was ill-chosen,' she said, wincing internally.

'Most metaphors are. If you would be a natural philosopher, Mrs Crompton, stick with mathematics, where everything is only like itself.'

Having affixed the tack to the horses, the beleaguered servant, a fat and beetle-browed man called Padding, announced that the coach stood ready for Newton's trip to the city.

'I beg your pardon, Sir Isaac,' Ben said, 'but 'twas my under-standing we'd be dining at your estate.'

'We'll not be dining anywhere, young Franklin, as I have urgent business in the Fleet.'

A second servant, cadaverous as Padding was corpulent, appeared holding a willow basket and a gnarled blackthorn shillelagh. 'Your money cudgel, sir,' he said, handing the weapon to Newton as a chancellor might present a ceremonial sword to his king.

'Forgive me, Sir Isaac,' Jennet said, 'but we simply must speak with you tonight.'

'Sorry, Mrs Crompton. Duty calls.'

'Pray take us along on your journey. My brother and I crossed the entire Atlantic Sea that we might interview *le Grand Newton*.'

The geometer frowned and scratched his head, skewing his periwig and exposing his left ear to the predations of a mosquito. He caught the creature in his palm and, rubbing his hands together, mashed it into nothingness. 'Climb aboard if you insist.' He retrieved the willow basket from his servant, looping his arm through the handle. 'But hear my warning – we'll be moving amongst coiners and clippers tonight. You could be murdered.'

'We could also be murdered if we fall foul of a cutpurse whilst walking back to Mayfair,' she said.

'Perhaps Sir Isaac will entertain us *tomorrow* night,' Ben suggested.

Not if he's on the point of being killed by counterfeiters, she thought. 'Nonsense, brother – we shan't be so boorish as to spurn this invitation.' Turning towards Newton, she caressed the sleeve of his red woollen topcoat. 'I've oft-times noted your exploits as Master of the Mint.' She relieved him of the basket and hoisted herself into the coach. 'Had you not become the world's most accomplished philosopher' – she placed the basket on the floor – 'you would have made a formid-able general.'

'Modesty requires that I ignore your opinion,' Newton said, repositioning his periwig, 'though honesty forbids me to contradict it.'

Ben, sighing, clambered up beside Jennet. Newton settled into the seat opposite, flourishing his shillelagh with the oblivious bravado of Henry VIII wielding his marble sceptre above the main gate at Trinity. Soon a fourth party joined them, a ruffian named Gunny Slocum, who gleefully explained that he was Newton's informant and bodyguard. The knave exuded the fragrance of gin and an aura of skulduggery, but Jennet took comfort in the brace of silver pistols protruding from his belt.

'Dearest sister, I wish I knew what species of peril we're about to endure,' Ben said under his breath.

'Darling brother, so do I,' she replied.

Padding closed the coach door, received Newton's instructions to depart post-haste, then rushed off to command the team. As the vehicle sped away, Jennet brushed her host's trembling knee and spoke. 'Many years ago you wrote a letter to my late aunt, Isobel Mowbray, mistress of Mirringate Hall in Ipswich. You claimed that you'd disproved the demon hypothesis.'

'Demons?' Newton said, bristling with pique and indignation. '*Demons?* To talk of demons is to enter the domain of that hoodwinker Descartes.'

'My aunt came to imagine that your disproof sprang from Aristotle's immutables, though I realize they've been supplanted by a more modern chemistry.'

'Instead of dubious Frenchmen and dead Greeks, let us discuss God instead. Would you not agree that the Trinity is a nonsensical concept? Three equals one equals three – pish!'

'The formula lacks coherence,' Ben said, nodding.

'I would sooner import my ale from Amsterdam than my theology from Rome,' Newton said.

'We were speaking of a letter,' Jennet said.

'*You* were speaking of a letter,' Newton said.

'Do you remember your correspondence with my aunt?' Jennet asked. 'You told her that sorcery lies in the mind.'

Newton screwed his features into the quintessence of contempt. 'Speak not to me of sorcery, Mrs Crompton! An obscure but vindictive philosopher once sought to soil my reputation by impersonating me at a Colchester witch-trial. I spent five hundred pounds to publish a pamphlet exposing his hoax – and revealing his other moral lapses into the bargain.'

The coach rolled down Kensington Road and skirted the edge of Hyde Park, its verdant acreage walled by rectilinear hedges and ornamental shrubs, an interval during which Jennet decided to remain silent concerning Colchester, lest she accidentally reveal that Hooke had come to those very assizes at her request. Instead she merely said, ''Tis my ambition to approach Parliament with a potent argument against the Conjuring Statute of James the First. If you can demonstrate that wicked spirits don't exist, prithee make your calculation public, for it might save many a blameless soul.'

'Tell me, Mrs Crompton, do you not think it presumptuous to brand one soul blameless and another sinful?' Newton plucked a small leather-bound Bible from his topcoat. 'Scripture holds us all congenitally corrupt. 'Tis only by his Saviour's mercy that any man avoids damnation.'

'In my life I've cast a considerable quantity of first stones,' she said, nodding. 'But not nearly so many as the ghastly prickers.'

'I grasp your biblical allusion, though in my view 'tis more fruitful to plumb Scripture for prophecy than for parable. After reading the great mystic Joseph Mede, I derived a method most helpful to the endeavour.'

''Tis your witch calculation that interests me,' Jennet said.

'My *what* calculation?'

'Witch.'

'Which calculation, that's what I'm asking you.'

'No, *witch*. W-i-t-c-h.'

'I see orthography's not your forte, Mrs Crompton,' Newton said. 'But the topic is prophecy. Mr Franklin, have you perchance heard of Mr Mede?'

'Did the gentleman not argue that when the Bible speaks of *days*, we must interpret it as *years*?' Ben said.

'Quite so.' Newton accorded Ben a nod of respect. 'However, being ignorant of calendrical matters, Mede failed to bring precision to his instincts, and so I finished the job. According to the Newton-Mede formula, three hundred and fifty-four secular days, plus six equally profane hours, constitute a single biblical year.'

Within Jennet's body two knots formed simultaneously, one jamming her throat, the other clogging her guts. Why was Newton so deaf to her petition? Had she once again happened upon an impersonator?

Newton turned to his bodyguard and said, 'Sir, I am famished for fair.'

From the willow basket Slocum produced a small white table-cloth, draping it over his knees. Next he lifted out an enormous pie dripping with various fats and bursting with chunks of broiled beef and braised lamb. He set the pie on his lap as he might a beloved child.

''Tis a veritable feast,' Ben said, 'though you needn't serve me a piece, as I am of the vegetarian persuasion.' He pulled a large green pippin from his waistcoat. 'I shall satisfy my appetite thus.'

'Thou art exceeding strange, young Franklin,' Newton said.

'Did I just hear the peacock call the parrot a fop?' Slocum said.

'Mr Slocum, you press the bounds of familiarity,' Newton said.

The ruffian grinned and reached towards his belt, drawing out a knife as large and glistery as a Merrimack River trout. 'Sir Isaac, you're the geometer in our company, but I'll warrant I can trifurcate our meal without resort to protractor and calipers.'

'Have at it,' Newton said.

After stabbing the centre of the pie, Slocum slashed it into three unequal servings. He delivered one portion to Newton and another to Jennet, retaining the largest for himself, then extracted from the basket a dark brown flagon of ale stoppered with a cork and bearing a hand-printed label reading *Forthergill's Ordinary*.

Jennet forced herself to take a bite of pie. As the coach started along Piccadilly Street, she again addressed Newton. 'Back in America my deluded brother, the Witchfinder-Royal, practises his trade even as we speak. I beseech you to go before the House of Lords and vilify the Conjuring Statute.'

Newton ate lustily, speaking not a word. 'Oft-times I envy the witchfinders,' he said at last. 'They have their swimming-ropes, their pricking needles, their Paracelsus tridents, but to snare a clipper God gives you no tool save the shrewdness in your skull.'

Slocum uncorked the ale. 'We've trapped many a rat in our day, ain't we, Sir Isaac?'

'I think especially of the notorious William Chaloner,' Newton said, fixing his inky eyes on Ben. 'I instructed a gangrel dog in the olfactory qualities of the debased metals used by guinea forgers, and thus did that excellent hound and I sniff our way to the blackguard's lair.' He licked his fingers one by one. 'On the eve of his appointment with the hangman, Chaloner sent me a letter begging for his life. I wrote back and said, "Alas, I must reject your plea, sir, for in Hell they've much need of your coining talents, as their currency's fore'er bursting into flames."'

Slocum guffawed spontaneously, Ben let out a politic laugh, and Jennet made not a sound.

'And what a marvellous execution!' Slocum decanted a pint of ale directly into his stomach. 'They strung him up on Tyburn Tree, then brought him down gagging, hacked him open, and unravelled his bowels before the mob.'

For several minutes the coach hurtled along Shaftesbury Avenue, and then Padding turned his team eastward onto Holborn High Street. Whilst Jennet and Ben exchanged glances of exasperation, their host explained how to employ his system in fathoming the ambiguities of the Apocalypse, the conundrums of Jeremiah and the auguries of Daniel.

'Daniel tells us that the AntiChrist will reign for 1,290 days, that is — per the Newton-Mede formula — 1,194 years,' Newton noted. 'Since Popery reached its apex in Anno Domini 609, we can say with certainty that the Hebrew tribes will reclaim Israel in 1803.'

Jennet felt like the Turtle Who Had No Shell, vulnerable in the extreme, moving naked through a country choked with brambles and thick with burrs. How naïve of her to imagine that the Newton of 1725 would be the Newton of 1688. The Jennet Stearne of 1725 certainly wasn't the Jennet Stearne of 1688. The geometer had probably never seen his aunt burned alive or watched his daughter die of the pox, but he'd doubtless been knocked about by Dame Fortune all the same. Such was the way of the world.

'A similar deduction gives us forty-nine years elapsing betwixt the Jewish repatriation and the Parousia,' Newton said. 'Ergo, we should all mark down the Second Coming for 1948!'

'I wish I could be there,' Slocum said.

'Read your Bible, say your prayers, steer clear of Popery, and you *will* be there, Mr Slocum. I swear to God you will.'

Evening brought a redundant darkness to London, for the city was already mantled in fog, drizzle, and the smoke of ten thousand chimney-pots. Padding halted the coach at the place where Holborn High Street narrowed to become a stone bridge over the River Fleet, the notorious open sewer that ran from Hampstead down to Blackfriars before emptying its swill into the Thames. Stepping into the night air, Jennet inhaled the impacted stench, then joined Ben, Newton and Slocum as they descended a marble stairway and started along the west bank of the river. A true witch's brew, she decided, aboil with eye of newt and toe of frog. On their left rose the battlements of Fleet Prison — destroyed in the Great Fire, Newton explained, then rebuilt at twice the size, 'London being now twice as wicked a town as before.' All around them lay the Liberties, the geometer continued, those cramped but not inhospitable environs beyond the prison walls where the better sort of criminal – the panderer, the suborner, the usurer, the rakehell – was permitted to reside unmolested, 'provided he compensates his would-be gaolers for the effort they expend in leaving him alone'.

At the Fleet Street intersection they came upon a half-dozen whores, drinking gin and trading jests preparatory to a long night of splinting doodles in Covent Garden and Lincoln's Inn Fields. Slocum jerked a pistol from his belt. The trollops dispersed like a flock of guinea hens apprehending a fox within its midst.

''Twas recently my pleasure to read the English translation of your *Principia Mathematica*,' Ben said, drawing abreast of Newton. 'Might I say that universal gravitation is mayhap the single most beautiful idea a person hath e'er thought?'

'I know not what I may appear to the world,' Newton replied, 'but to myself I seem to be only like a boy playing on the sea-shore' – a poetic dreaminess entered his voice, audible even above the clank and clamour of the Liberties – 'and diverting myself in now and then finding a smoother pebble or a prettier shell than ordinary, whilst the great ocean of truth lies all undiscovered before me.'

''Tis bracing to observe such humility in so famous a man,' Ben said.

'Hooke found only common shells,' Newton said. 'Leibniz couldn't tell pretty shells from pigeon shit. Flamsteed didn't even get to the beach.'

The party proceeded west along Fleet Street, easily the most pestilential promenade in Jennet's experience. The air reeked of distilled spirits, decaying cabbages, rotten fish, and human waste. Rats scurried along the cobblestones as blithely as hares capered through Marylebone Park. But the most shocking phenomenon to reach her senses was Newton's face. His countenance was a portrait of unmitigated glee. Evidently he'd as soon catch a coiner as solve a differential equation.

'Permit me to offer a theory concerning electricity,' Ben said to Newton. 'I believe that the spark one conjures with a Von Guericke sphere partakes of the same substance as a lightning-stroke. Each resembles the other not only in giving off light, but also in its swift motion, crackling sound, crooked path and affinity with metals. What think you, Sir Isaac?'

'If 'tis unification beguiles you, young Franklin, you should know that my forthcoming book will explicate the very paste that binds together the world's invisible particles. 'Twill be more momentous than my *Principia*, more illuminating than my *Opticks*.'

Upon reaching Whitefriars Street, Newton led them twenty paces south, then paused before an archway and, leaning into the gloom, banged on the oaken door with his shillelagh. 'Open up, Mrs Totten! Open up for the Master of the Mint!'

'How do I know 'tis you, Professor?' cried a hoarse female voice.

'Because I carry thirty pounds sterling in my purse!'

The door swung back to reveal a hunched, lardish, nearly toothless old woman holding a lighted tallow candle.

'Good evening, Mrs Totten,' Newton said. 'Allow me to introduce Mr Franklin and his sister, Mrs Crompton, both of Philadelphia.'

'Hallo, Lucy,' Slocum said, still brandishing his pistol.

'We are delighted to make your acquaintance,' Ben said.

Lucy Totten stared at the Philadelphians, fought back a sneer, and spoke in a flat voice. 'Charmed.' She locked her rheumy gaze on Newton. 'Oh, Professor, I been goin' through the worst day o' my life.'

She guided her visitors down a bottle-neck passageway into a suffocating hovel, its furnishings consisting of a single chair and a few upended vinegar barrels littered with candle stubs and cooking pots. In the far corner rested an eviscerated mattress upon which a large man lay wrapped in a dark blanket, shivering and moaning.

'I did as ye instructed me, Gunny' – Mrs Totten cupped her hand around the barrel of Slocum's pistol, easing the bore away from her chest – 'writin' down all his rant about the Calibans.'

'Pray show me the transcription,' Newton said.

'Not before you offer my Billy a benediction,' Mrs Totten said.

'Benediction?'

'We can't entice any men o' the cloth into the Fleet these days, but I'm willin' to make do with geometry.'

Newton shrugged vigorously, propped his shillelagh against a barrel, and followed Mrs Totten to the mattress. Jennet stepped towards the dying man. The ticking stank of mildew. In the candle's glow Billy Slipfinger's blanket stood revealed as a blue greatcoat with multiple perforations, as if its previous owner had died in a hail of musket-balls. His face, stern and unforgiving, suggested an almost Shakespearean depravity, an amalgamation of Iago, Claudius and Aaron the Moor.

With manifest discomfort, Newton assumed a kneeling position beside the ratty bier. 'So, Billy Slipfinger, you canny old rogue, 'twould appear you are about to meet your Creator,' he said. 'When alive you contributed little to the glory of God, squandering your energies on counterfeiting and copulation, but in death you shall help save the British Mint, for which the Almighty will surely reward you, shabby though your case may be in other respects.'

Awkwardly Newton regained his feet.

'Thankee, Professor,' Mrs Totten said, her eyes moist and sparkling. 'Your eloquence 'as moved this impoverished widow to tears.'

'I would have that list now,' Newton said.

Perhaps the last thing Jennet expected to see in this unfamiliar pest-hole was a foetal prodigy of her acquaintance – but there he was: the Lyme Bay Fish-Boy, afloat in his jar at Slipfinger's feet. She released an involuntary gasp.

'What ails you, sister?' Ben said.

'I shall explain presently.' Surely this was Dr Cavendish's speci-men. There couldn't be two such freaks in England.

Slipfinger's moans grew louder. Lifting the lid from a soup-pot, Mrs Totten retrieved a gin bottle in which a rolled-up paper, secured with twine, lay like an ancient potion turned to cake by the passage of time. 'If this ain't worth thirty quid' – she handed the container to Newton – 'then Hell's o'erdue for a frost fair.'

Newton unbottled the paper and put on his optical spectacles. 'Mr Slocum, whilst I study this document, you will take up my money cudgel and perform a patriotic duty.' He pointed towards a shapeless smear of grey mortar near the fireplace. ''Tis obvious Mr Slipfinger hath secreted his handiwork within these walls.'

'You're wrong, Professor!' Mrs Totten protested. 'Billy hid only the most *genuine* currency 'round here!'

'Sir Isaac, your vision is as keen as your *Opticks* is acute,' Ben said.

Over Mrs Totten's shrill objections, Slocum grabbed the shillelagh, wrapped both hands around the grip, and clubbed the controversial masonry. Potato-sized chunks of plaster fell away. He attacked the wall thrice more, gouging a hole the diameter of a cocked hat. A dozen bundles of paper currency, neatly tied with string, tumbled onto the floor.

'All o' them notes is bona fide!' Mrs Totten wailed.

With a snorty laugh Slocum opened the flue, then began stacking the currency in the fireplace.

'Stop, Gunny!' Mrs Totten cried. 'You're about to destroy my life's savings!'

'Nay, woman, he's about to destroy a pile of paper as worthless as South Sea Company stock, a commodity on which I once lost twenty thousand pounds!' Newton slid a tinder-box from his pocket, handing it to Slocum, then turned to Ben and continued his raillery. 'The South Sea directors got precisely what they deserved, long sojourns in the Tower for so blithely bribing Parliament. The Lords took their money, likewise the Commons, whereupon both houses set about blurring the distinction 'twixt a government security and a corporation share.'

'I implore ye Gunny!' Mrs Totten cried. 'I'm fallin' to my knees!'

'As I heard the tale of the South Sea Bubble,' Ben said, 'the directors assumed that the War of the Spanish Succession would advantage them, with a defeated King Philip granting England exclusive trading rights with his West-Indies colonies.'

Newton offered Ben a corroborating nod. 'When Philip decided otherwise, the managers declined to involve themselves in any species of commerce whatsoever.'

'Verily, ye might find a suspect note or two in that pile,' Mrs Totten conceded, 'but the rest be real as Saint Andrew's shaving basin!'

'Sir Isaac, I am perplexed,' Jennet said. 'If the South Sea Company did no profitable business, why would anyone imagine its shares to be of value?'

'The logic of your complaint is irreproachable, but at the time I allowed avarice to befuddle my arithmetic,' Newton confessed as he perused the list of Caliban Adepts.

Unmoved by Mrs Totten's entreaties, Slocum finished mounding the notes, then swaddled them in tinder and merrily struck flint to steel.

'No, Gunny!' Mrs Totten screeched.

A spark shot forth, landing in the little pyre.

'Gunny!'

'If you persist in your complaint,' Newton told the incipient widow, 'you will forfeit the thirty *authentic* pounds I brought you.'

Mrs Totten frowned and, falling silent, sank her bum into the room's solitary chair.

Jennet fixed on the hearth. As the flames took hold, the sham notes blackening and shrivelling like broadsheets meeting Satan's gaze, she turned to their hostess and said, 'I'm curious about yon prodigy.'

'Would ye care to buy it?' Mrs Totten replied brightly, then immediately thought better of her cupidity. 'How durst ye propose a business transaction' – a scowl contracted her face – 'whilst my dear Billy lies dyin' under my nose?'

'Forgive my impertinence,' Jennet said.

'Ye can 'ave it for a quid, though that idiot paid three guineas.' Mrs Totten rose and shuffled towards the mattress. 'Billy's mother insisted such a foetus would bring him luck, so when the prodigy-monger set up shop last year, Billy was first in line.' She adjusted the greatcoat, pulling it even with her husband's jaw. 'As ye can see, his damned Fish-Boy's done him no good.'

Newton cleared his throat, removed his spectacles, and, with the solemnity of a judge sending a murderer to Tyburn Tree, pronounced on Mrs Totten's document, declaring it authentic and valuable. He paid the woman her thirty pounds, then instructed Slocum to escort the Philadelphians back to their lodgings.

'If you please, Sir Isaac,' Ben said, ''twas my hope we might continue discussing smoother pebbles and prettier shells.'

'Some other time.' Newton refolded the paper and slid it into his pocket. 'Presently the Lord Mayor and I must start drawing our plans against the Calibans.'

'Dearest sister, I fear no demon disproof may be extracted from the Master of the Mint,' Ben said. 'Not this night nor any other.'

'So it seems,' Jennet said, heaving a sigh.

'Demons,' echoed Newton with undisguised disgust. He grabbed his shillelagh and, approaching the hearth, agitated the ashes of Billy Slipfinger's iniquity. 'Demons, demons, demons . . .'

293

'I would be pleased to purchase your foetus, Madam,' Jennet told Mrs Totten, 'but first you must direct me to the museum it once called home.'

'Whereas the monster costs a quid, his previous address is worth twice that much,' Mrs Totten said.

'I shall take the whole package, facts and fish⁄boy.' Jennet set the required notes in Mrs Totten's palm. For reasons doubtless tracing to the sad logic of life in the Fleet, the three pounds from Jennet seemed to delight the old woman no less than the thirty from Newton.

'Ye want *Le Cirque de la Lune*, Lower Thames Street, hard by the bridge,' Mrs Totten said.

'And so I take my leave of you.' Newton locked his shillelagh under his arm. 'Young Franklin, when next we meet, I shall explain how I divined the floor⁄plan of Solomon's Temple from the Book of Ezekiel. This chart hath given me the precise dates for the fall of Romanism, the triumph of Arianism, the mechanical transport of human beings to the moon, and the Day of Judgement. Mrs Crompton, 'tis apparent you're an intelligent woman, but you must forgo your obsession with diabolism ere some magistrate arrests you for an enchantress. Farewell.'

With all the élan of Rupert Quince exiting the stage of the King's Theatre, Newton turned ninety degrees and strode out of the hovel.

'I don't understand that man,' Ben said.

'I wonder if anyone does,' Jennet said.

'I've known that beady⁄eyed lunatic for twenty years,' Slocum said, 'and he's still a riddle to me.'

Billy Slipfinger died shortly after midnight, embracing his Creator with a sound that for Jennet evoked a Nimacook squaw scraping the back of a beaver pelt. She and Ben remained with Newton's bodyguard by Mrs Totten's side another hour, listening to her alternately bilious and remorseful elegies for her husband.

'Marital fidelity was ne'er his speciality, I can tell ye that,' she said. 'Sometimes the wight e'en brought one o' his nary⁄cherries home. But 'ere's the odd thing – them ladies always liked me. Half the time Billy would pass out drunk before he could drop his breeches, and then the strumpet and me, we'd amuse each other all night, sippin' gin and tellin' tales.'

'From my limited dealings with harlots, I would conclude they make good conversationalists,' Ben said, 'for being surfeited in the flesh they grow hungry in the mind.'

'Rather the way natural philosophers make good lovers' – Jennet patted Ben's arm – 'as their curiosity compels them to press e'er deeper into Aphrodite's domain.'

Whilst Jennet took possession of her prodigy, Ben made Mrs Totten a gift of his embroidered handkerchief, and then the Philadelphians set out for Mayfair, protected by Gunny Slocum's pugnacious deportment and drawn pistols.

London by night, Jennet knew from experience, was as theatrical a world as London at noon, though instead of clerics, bankers, beggars, hawkers and shop-keepers, the players were trollops, gamesters, drunkards, sailors and cutpurses. During the long walk back to Adam's Row, Slocum supplemented the general atmosphere of menace by recounting his adventures chasing down coiners with Newton. Evidently the geometer and the ruffian were an ideal team. First Newton would detect a counterfeiter's whereabouts via a succession of brilliant logical deductions, then Slocum would appear on the scene, offering the blackguard a choice betwixt an interval in the dock and a bullet in the brain.

'Inexplicable force equals occult force,' Jennet muttered after they'd parted company with Slocum. 'Occult force equals demonic force. Where's the chink, Ben?'

'We'll find it,' he said as they mounted the steps to their rooms. 'Even without Newton to light the way, we'll find that blessed chink.'

Jennet and Ben slept all morning and left Mayfair at half past two. Swathed in a woollen scarf and hidden beneath her coat, the bottled Fish-Boy bulged outward from Jennet like a pregnancy. Arriving at the Golden Ass, the Philadelphians quickened themselves with coffee and cake, then agreed to rendezvous that evening at the King's Theatre, where they would learn whether Rachel intended to join their imminent Atlantic crossing. It struck Ben as nothing short of a miracle that Jennet and her 'doubtless beautiful' daughter had found each other after a decade of separation, and he was 'deliriously eager to meet her'.

'I shall speak candidly,' Jennet said. 'For all I want Rachel to take ship with us, I cannot help my observation that she is rather closer to your age than to mine.'

'Your meaning's plain, dearest. Believe me, I have no wish to further besmirch a Moderation grid that already displays lapses in abundance.'

''Twould be more than a *lapse* were Rachel to turn your head from me to her. 'Twould be a rent in the fabric of the universe.'

'I'faith, Mrs Crompton, a man in my position hath less reason to prefer the daughter o'er the mother than doth a falconer to select a merlin o'er a peregrine.'

'Look me in the eye, bonny Ben. Look me in the eye and say, "*Waunnetunta.*" My heart is true.'

'*Waunnetunta.*' He offered her a dulcet smile. 'Turn on, turn on, Mrs Crompton,' he added. 'We shall make it glitter by and by.'

Whilst Ben trotted off to accomplish one last printing job at Palmer's, a pamphlet for the British Anti-Slavery Society, Jennet and the Fish-Boy proceeded to Lower Thames Street and descended a series of spavined marble steps into the crepuscular world beneath the bridge. Mrs Totten had not misled her: three sprawling canvas pavilions – red, yellow, green – lay huddled by the water like box-kites awaiting a wind. CAVENDISH MUSEUM OF WONDROUS PRODIGIES, read the sign on the green pavilion. FEAST YOUR EYES ON NATURE'S MISTAKES.

Heart scampering in her chest, she elbowed the flaps aside, stepped into the pavilion, and set the Fish-Boy on the floor. Advancing through the murk, she found herself standing face-to-face with an old acquaintance, the Bird-Child of Bath, lit by a whale-oil lamp and resting on an exhibition table, his visage conveying his usual eagerness to quit the glassy cage and take flight. As her eyes adjusted to the gloom, the feathered stillborn's brethren greeted her. The Smethwick Philosopher looked as sagacious as always, the Tunbridge Wells Bloodsucker seemed happy in his vampiric profession, and the Kali of Droitwich retained her usual air of divinity, but the Bicephalic Girl appeared gaunt and weary, as if she'd lost one too many altercations with herself.

There were no customers in the museum, only an impossibly ancient gentleman in a red periwig and a green frock coat, stooped over the Bicephalic Girl's bottle, polishing it with a rag.

'Dr Cavendish?'

'The same.'

'Dr Cavendish, 'tis I – Jennet Stearne.'

'Who?'

'Your Miss Stearne.'

The curator stopped polishing. 'Miss Stearne? Jennet Stearne?'

'Verily.'

'I do not believe it.'

'Then will you believe that I am the favourite ward of Lord Adramelech, Grand Chancellor of the Infernal Empire?'

Barnaby released a yelp of delight and clasped her to his chest. 'Oh, my dearest Miss Stearne, are you in sooth this full-grown woman?'

'I can make an excellent case for it.'

'In my reveries you're always still a girl of twelve!'

'I was certain you were lost to me,' she said, gradually reconciling this wrinkled male crone with the Barnaby Cavendish of her youth. ''Tis as if you've come back from the dead.'

'On my rheumatism days, that's exactly how I feel.' Relaxing his embrace, he slipped on his spectacles and scrutinized her with the intensity of a linen-draper assessing a bolt of cloth. 'Tell me, Miss Stearne – Jennet – did you e'er devise your *argumentum grande?*'

'Alas, the project's not yet complete, though I believe the vital calculation's close at hand.' With the respectful affection of Bellero-phon bridling his beloved Pegasus, she looped her arm around Barnaby's shoulders, then guided him towards the obelisk of sunlight formed by the tent flaps. 'Mayhap you remember that, ere we parted company in Colchester, I promised I would bring you a prodigy when our paths crossed again.' Pointing towards the occluded Fish-Boy, she snatched the scarf away. '*Voilà!*'

''Sblood, 'tis my own best aquatic oddity! 'Tis my dearest ichthyic astonishment!' The gleeful curator kissed her cheek. 'Had my fortune-telling colleague predicted that on this day I would enjoy not one but two reunions, the first with a friend, the second with a foetus, I would have thought him deranged.'

'I obtained our Fish-Boy directly from Widow Totten of White-friars Street.'

'Do I infer that old Slipfinger hath finally had the decency to bereave his wife?'

''Tis a long story. Let us dine together this evening, and we shall share our life's adventures.'

After declaring her plan 'nigh as perfect as my freaks are flawed', he offered to show her his new acquisitions. As the tour progressed, Jennet learned that a distracted Nature had of late brought forth in England a Turtle of Tewkesbury (its tiny head peering from beneath hunched shoulders) as well as a Hastings Clock-Girl (her elongated chin tapering towards a chest marked with Roman numerals) and a Newgate Pig-Child (a sphere of flesh with two eyes at its north pole and a fringe of toes along the bottom). But the jewel of the collection was the Knightsbridge Hermaphrodite, both varieties of genitalia on full display. With a heavy heart Barnaby revealed that the Cyclops of Bourne, the Maw of Folkestone, Perdition's Pride and the Sussex Rat-Baby had long since left the family, sold during the same impecunious period that had obliged him to do business with Slipfinger. But he hastened to point out that, thanks to the Fish-Boy's homecoming, the roll-call of the misbegotten once again stood at its traditional total of ten.

The curator now insisted that they go visit his magician colleague, a manumitted West-Indies slave who in his youth had enjoyed the patronage of the French aristocracy, taking his show from one château to the next. Barnaby and Jennet proceeded to the red tent, surmounted by a sign reading, FEIZUNDA THE ILLUSIONIST: FEATS OF JUGGLING AND CONJURING, EVERY HOUR ON THE HOUR. Although it was exactly four o'clock, all the seats were empty. A snowy-haired man in a blue silk turban, his skin as dark as gun-powder, sat before an oaken table, rehearsing a trick that had him filling three crystalline bowls with clear water then tapping each with a glass sceptre. Under the influence of the conjuror's wand, the first measure became a ball of ice, the second boiled as if set upon a stove, and the third acquired a school of tiny crimson fish.

'Allow me to present my old associate in rascality,' Barnaby said to Feizunda. 'Jennet Stearne, formerly the most intelligent girl in East

Anglia, currently the most brilliant woman in the American provinces.'

'*Je suis enchanté*,' Feizunda said, bowing graciously.

'*Et moi aussi*,' Jennet said.

The magician came forward and with a sudden chirping laugh reached behind her ear and drew forth a goose egg. '*Voilà!*'

'*Merveilleux!*' she said.

He smacked his hands together, causing the egg to pop into oblivion like a burst bubble.

Barnaby next brought Jennet to the yellow pavilion, arena of GIBELLUS THE SEER: DESTINIES DIVINED IN CRYSTALS, CARDS, BONES AND PALMS, and introduced her to a squint-eyed wight whose mottled skin and toothless jaw put her in mind of the Turtle of Tewkesbury. Sprawled across a Turkish carpet that he shared with Ptolemy's *Quadripartite*, Guido Bonatus's *Astronomica Tractaus*, John Maplet's *The Dial of Destiny* and a dozen other astrology texts, Gibellus did not bother to rise, but instead offered Jennet a cryptic wink and gummy smile.

'Permit me to cast your fortune,' he said, placing a splayed hand on his chest. He wore a black robe spattered with five-pointed stars. 'I would expect no fee.'

'Alas, I have of late grown unfriendly to all hermetical pursuits,' she said. 'I would be a dissatisfied customer whether I paid you or not.'

'You must not slight my colleague's gift,' Barnaby gently admonished her. 'Through his astrological calculations, Gibellus predicted both the Great Plague of 1665 and the abdication of James the Second.'

'Aye, but did he predict them before they occurred, or after?'

'I assure you, Madam, I am skilled in the diviner's arts,' Gibellus said. 'I can prophesy using ceromancy – that is, by the forms of melted wax in water – as well as lithomancy, by the reflections of candlelight in gems, also halomancy, by the casting of salt into fire, not to mention crominiomancy, by the growing of enchanted onions. In your case, however, a simple palm-reading will suffice. Make a fist and bring it hither.'

Jennet could not forbear a sceptical smirk, but she did as the seer requested. Gibellus unfurled her fingers one by one and studied the hatched plane beneath.

'Five great lines,' he said. 'Every person hath 'em, rays of heart, head, life, fate and matrimony. Their geometry reveals all – the angles and gaps, the arcs and intersections. Let us see what Dame Fortune holds in store for you.'

'Excuse me, Mr Gibellus,' she said, 'but if these lines reveal my future, then logic says they also speak of my past, as I am forty-seven years old, with much of my destiny behind me. I bid you tell Barnaby about my more memorable experiences with love and husbands and the rest, for 'twould make an interesting test of your system.'

'Don't be sly, Jenny,' Barnaby cautioned.

'By Saint Agatha's warts, I shall rise to the challenge!' Gibellus cried. He fixed on Jennet's palm. 'I can see you were once . . . married to a man of . . . nautical bent. A sea captain, mayhap?'

'Aye, 'tis true!' Jennet said, 'My sweet Daniel – Captain Throg-morton to his men, master o'er the man-o'-war *Obadiah*.'

'Ah,' Barnaby said.

'But, alas, he no longer lives,' Gibellus said.

'Dear Throggy went down with his ship in the War of the Spanish Succession,' Jennet said.

'Leaving you with a child . . . a *son*,' Gibellus said.

'My boy, Horatio!'

'Oh, Jenny, I had no idea you'd suffered such a terrible misfortune,' Barnaby said.

'Whilst your son came of age, you pursued your aptitude for horticulture,' Gibellus said. 'Even today your cottage is surrounded by flowers of every description.'

'Hyacinths and jonquils!' She placed a guinea in the seer's hand. 'I was wrong to doubt your talents, sir. Please accept this consideration for entertaining me so thoroughly.'

With the blessing of his associates, Barnaby posted a GONE TO SUPPER sign outside the Cavendish Museum, then guided Jennet across the street to the Pettifog. For two hours they enthralled one other with their respective autobiographies, though Barnaby's account of *Le Cirque*'s ragged rise and imminent collapse paled beside her narratives of the Salem witch-trials, the burning of Haverhill, her Nimacook adoption, Pashpishia's death, Rachel's wanderings and the glorious arrival of Ben Franklin in her bed – and then, of course, there was the previous evening's maddening encounter with Sir Isaac Newton. It took her three separate tellings to convince Barnaby that the man they'd brought to Colchester Assizes was in fact the late Robert Hooke, and just as many to convince him that the real Newton had proven as useless as the impostor.

'I am relieved to learn there is not a tittle of truth in Gibellus's version of your life,' he said. 'I'Christ, I'd always thought him as deft a deceiver as myself – thank goodness I needn't revise my opinion downwards.'

'And now I fear we must endure another parting, for my only hope of toppling my brother is to dishonour him on his own soil.'

'Let me put a proposition to you.' Barnaby puffed on his clay pipe. 'One needn't be Gibellus to see that *Le Cirque* will fold its tents betimes, which sets me to wondering whether my monsters might find an audience in the American Colonies.'

Jennet drank the rest of her coffee and pondered the curator's scheme. Barnaby in Pennsylvania? An excellent idea. If this splendid charlatan joined her company, which already boasted Ben and would soon, God willing, include Rachel too, she would have at her command a kind of Anti-Purification Commission.

'Truth to tell, I've ne'er heard of a prodigy museum in America,' she said.

'So the field belongs to Barnaby Cavendish?'

'Entirely.'

'Reserve me a berth on your ship, dear Jenny, that I might gain renown as the man who brought the Knightsbridge Hermaphrodite to the New World!'

As dusk dropped its soft grey surtout upon the city, she left the Pettifog and set off for Drury Lane, her brain seething with visions of Barnaby, Rachel, Ben and herself assembled in some secret Philadelphia cellar, candles flickering all about them as they whispered their conspiracies against the New-England cleansers. She reached the King's Theatre at half past seven. Ben awaited her in the foyer, dressed lavishly in a chestnut periwig and a gold-trimmed suit of purple silk.

''Steeth, you're more gaudily attired than an Istanbul whore-master,' she said. 'My daughter will be impressed.'

'God's truth, Jenny: I wear this finery to please you, not young Rachel.'

Whilst he queued up to purchase their tickets, she descended to the supporting players' dressing-chamber. For a full minute she studied the hurly-burly. Five actresses in various states of *déshabillé* rushed about the room, putting on their costumes and painting their faces, but Rachel was not amongst them.

A buxom woman with luxurious lips and a beauty spot on her cheek approached Jennet and flashed an equivocal smile.

'Mrs Crompton, perchance?'

'Aye.' With a pang of despair she realized that the woman wore the same dress in which Rachel had portrayed the waiting-maid.

'This is for you.' From the vale betwixt her breasts the actress produced a sealed envelope.

Jennet snatched the packet away and with trembling fingers extracted Rachel's letter.

23 July 1725

Dear Mrs Crompton:

Unhappy Circumstances prevent me from offering my Farewell in Person. Last night, upon enduring yet another salacious Entreaty from Mr Quince, I quit the Drury Lane Company for ever. Gaston says that my Competence in French is most excellent (the one Boon bestow'd upon me by my repugnant Step-Mother), and so I have resolv'd to seek my Fortune in the Comédie Française. By the time you read this, I shall be well across the Channel. Please understand that no Argument you might devise could ever induce me to come with you to the American Colonies.

Regards,
Rachel Crompton

Jennet read the letter a second time, but the words refused to rearrange themselves into a different meaning. She read it a third time. The cruel message remained. On her fourth perusal, the characters grew blurry with her tears.

'If you decide to stay tonight,' the actress said, 'you'll see me play both Betty and Mrs Marwood.'

Jennet dried her eyes, then climbed the stairs to the foyer, where Ben was examining a broadsheet advertising a forthcoming 'Newgate Pastoral' by John Gay, *The Beggar's Opera*. Upon reading Rachel's letter he said, 'Oh, darling, for all you may have slighted her, you do not deserve such thorns as these.'

'Shakespeare knew whereof he spoke,' she said. 'A child's ingratitude is sharper than a serpent's tooth.'

'I shall return our tickets anon.'

She grabbed his decorous sleeve, massaging the lacy filigree. 'Nay, Ben, for I feel *The Way of the World* may be the very physic I require.'

'Then lead the way, my love.'

They stepped into the stalls along with a gaggle of latecomers, finding their seats just in time to behold the shameless and predatory Mr Quince recite the Prologue. As the comedy progressed and the players enacted their roles, Jennet realized that her decision to attend the performance was felicitous indeed. For there, right there, up on the King's Theatre stage – there stood Aunt Isobel. The actress was Alice Shuter; the character, Mrs Millamant – the most magnetic, intelligent and sophisticated of all the fine ladies in London.

Mrs Millamant could match the men around her epigram for epigram. 'One no more owes one's beauty to a lover than one's wit to an echo. They can but reflect what we look and say.' Like Isobel Mowbray, she allowed no person to take her for granted. 'Though I am upon the very verge of matrimony,' she told her future husband, 'I expect you to solicit me as much as if I were wavering at the gate of a monastery, with one foot over the threshold.' Unless she enjoyed certain freedoms within their marriage, she informed this same groom, she simply wouldn't have him. 'As liberty to pay and receive visits to and from whom I please; to write and receive letters without interrogation or wry faces on your part; to have no obligation upon me to converse with wits that I don't like because they are your acquaintance, or to be intimate with fools because they may be your relations.'

Beyond her comeliness and her cleverness, Mrs Millamant possessed another arresting quality. This was a woman with a will. In her view compromise was defeat, and those who moved counter to the way of the world must be numbered amongst its benefactors.

Jennet squeezed Ben's hand and said, 'There was probably ne'er a Newtonian disproof in the first place.'

'Agreed,' he whispered.

'Be quiet, both of you,' said a wan woman to Jennet's left.

'So we've made a kind of progress,' Jennet said. 'At least we're now at the starting line and not behind it.'

The man seated in front of her, a Redcoat captain in a white peruke, turned around and glowered. 'Shut up, you driveling cow.'

She stopped talking. The patrons were right. She was being rude. Once back in America, however, she would raise her voice again, and if her enemies turned Jacobean, cutting out her tongue, she would pick up a pen instead, and if they sliced off her hands, she would hold the pen betwixt her teeth, and if they removed her teeth, she would search out some wise and audacious physician, a Newton amongst surgeons, and bid him reassemble her, tongue and hands and teeth, and a strong new heart as well, the heart of a mare or lioness, and it would not stop beating until Reason reigned in the souls of men.

PART III

Reason's Teeth

CHAPTER THE NINTH

An Interlude of High Adventure, Including
a Shipwreck, a Marooning, a Preternatural Magnet,
and a Perilous Encounter with a Pirate Band

On the eve of their scheduled departure, Jennet returned to *Le Cirque de la Lune* and helped Barnaby pack up his museum. They filled two sea-chests with rags and straw, then laid each bottled prodigy to rest, five per cushioned compartment. For Jennet the task felt like midwifery in reverse. They were restoring the foetuses to the womb, so that Nature might fashion them anew, fixing their asymmetries, excising their scales and feathers.

So familiar was she with the monsters' reputation as good luck talismans, it never occurred to Jennet that anyone might cast them in a sinister light. She was therefore greatly astonished when, after inspecting Barnaby's sea-chests for rats and opium and finding instead the stillborns, the first mate of the *Berkshire*, the squat and obstinate Archibald Eliot, declared that Captain Fergus would 'rather ship out with Jonah himself than this load o' frightful cacodaemons.' The mate's prediction proved correct. Arriving on the quarter-deck later that morning in the company of Ben, Captain Fergus glanced at the prodigies, turned to Barnaby and said, 'Sir, methinks thou art a necromancer, for I see no other reason a man would accumulate such hellspawn. I shan't have 'em on my ship.'

'My dear Captain,' Barnaby said, 'I'm surprised that so well-travelled a person as yourself knows not the therapeutic value of foetal marvels. In Persia or Cathay no self-respecting physician will visit a sickbed without first placing a prodigy in his satchel.'

'My friend speaks the truth,' Jennet said, reprising their ancient chicanery. 'No sooner did I rub the bottle of the Knightsbridge Hermaphrodite than my backache flew clear to Heaven.'

It took Ben but a moment to grasp the game. 'This Tuesday past, simply by giving the Smethwick Philosopher a fraternal hug, I caused my fever to vanish with the morning dew.'

'Therapeutic?' sneered Captain Fergus. 'We shall see about that. Methinks I'll put your claim to the test.' Reaching inside the nearer sea-chest, he caressed the Tunbridge Wells Bloodsucker. 'On my last trip to the Azores, I endured a dreadful attack of the gout, and two years later I can still feel its fire and throb, as if the Spanish boot were clamped 'round my foot.'

'You must understand, sir, the healing effect doesn't always happen instantly,' Barnaby said. 'Oft-times the sufferer must wait till sunrise.'

Jennet said, 'In many cases a full two days will pass ere—'

''Stears!' the captain cried. 'Do I deceive myself? Nay! The pain's starting to fade!' He stroked the stillborn more vigorously. 'My foot feels as fit as when I first kicked my brutish brother in the cods!'

'The Bloodsucker's always been singularly antagonistic to gout,' Barnaby said.

Captain Fergus lifted the Bloodsucker from the sea-chest, bringing its gargoyle ugliness into the sun's unflattering glare. 'Marry, such a hideous pill, and yet so potent.'

Jennet wasn't sure how to explain the abrupt abatement of the captain's pain. She suspected that his cure represented yet another Newtonian desire of the mind, not unlike her experience thirty years earlier of seeing, under Okommaka's persuasion, her mother and grandmother encamped in the sun's corona.

'Very well, Doctor, you may cart along these freaks of yours.' The captain restored the vampire to its brethren. 'I'Christ, we shall deploy 'em against whate'er plagues of flux and scurvy lie before us!'

Two hours later the *Berkshire* caught the tide, received the wind, and started down the Thames. In contrast to their departure from Philadel-phia, no lawyer or businessman arrived to displace Jennet and Ben from their private cabin, and so they passed the afternoon in one another's arms. As always, she found herself pitying any woman obliged to settle for the flaccid passions of an ageing lover, as opposed to the endless ardour of a nineteen-year-old. Did she provide Ben with reciprocal satisfactions? Yes, she decided, though doubtless he occasionally longed for the bloom of youth. Saddened though she was by her daughter's flight to France, at least she would never have to witness Ben casting one eye on his perfection-matrix whilst the other strayed towards Rachel's comely frame.

'Oh, Ben, how my forty-seven years do pull upon me,' she lamented. 'My bosom droops under gravity's persuasion.'

'Only because 'twas such a robust specimen of bosomhood to begin with,' he said.

'And my neck hath acquired many a wrinkle.'

'But see how easily my tongue lays them smooth.'

'And my legs are all shot through with veins.'

'Lodes of perfect turquoise, enriching the precious flesh in which they lie.'

Honourable and well-meant sentiments, unquestionably – and yet she feared that he was not so much speaking from his heart as mouthing the words she wanted to hear. Still, if he must bend the truth, better these blandishments than any outright lie. Flattery was such a noble sort of sin, a pilgrim vice wandering forever homeless betwixt the kingdom of mendacity and the country of kindness.

Three days into the crossing her usual *mal de mer* arrived, but this time they were prepared, for Ben had spent the previous Friday visiting the apothecaries of Tavistock Street. Many swore by ginseng, others favoured mulberries, some endorsed dried silkworms, and a few recommended rose-hip tea. Unable to appraise these competing claims, Ben had acquired all four remedies, amalgamating them into a stinking and thoroughly repellent syrup. Strangely enough, the mixture proved efficacious – not by its merits, she decided, but simply because her stomach, unable to choose betwixt ordinary seasickness and the more complex distress induced by Ben's nostrum, had entered into a state of paralysis.

Jennet had always imagined that Ben and Barnaby would become good friends, and as the voyage progressed this expectation enjoyed extravagant fulfilment. Both were natural philosophers at heart, though of a distinctly pragmatic bent, each hopeful of converting Nature's secrets into contrivances of great utility. Ben had of late grown obsessed with the potential applications of electricity, a force he believed manifested itself in Von Guericke sparks and lightning-bolts alike. 'The day is not far off,' he insisted, 'when Heaven's fire shall become domestic as the ox and compliant as the horse, readily harnessed to illuminate our houses, warm our beds, and cook our food.'

For Barnaby, meanwhile, it was the chemical processes that promised to mitigate human misery. His work with foetal preservation had made him knowledgeable concerning alcohol and other vegetable liquids, and he was evidently near to concocting 'that invaluable elixir sought by all the world's surgeons, a universal insensibility drug'. If his next round of experiments proved successful, posterity would remember him as 'the man who'd raised up amputations and ablations from the bloody bowels of Hell and carried 'em into the sunlight of rational medicine'. This same Barnaby Cavendish, he added with a sly wink, 'had grown rich as Croesus into the bargain'.

As the sixth week of the voyage began, the ocean gradually thickened around the *Berkshire*'s waterline like butter coagulating in a churn. Vast mats of algae pressed against her hull, conjoined to swaying rafts of seaweed. Everyone took heart at this development, for such greenery most probably heralded the American continent, and the ship's cook, a garrulous German named Friedrich Schwendemann, was particularly delighted. In his experience the seaweed would contain an abundance of that red-shelled shrimp known as the brine-berry – an eminently edible creature, succulent and delicious as the plum. Upon considering the cook's claim, Captain Fergus ordered a longboat lowered, and two hours later a mound of newly harvested seaweed rose from the main deck like a haystack in a farmer's field.

Herr Schwendemann had spoken truly. Thousands of brine-berries wriggled amidst the grassy tufts. Beguiled by visions of shrimp cakes, shrimp pies, shrimp stews and shrimp chowders, the crew set about the task at hand, and soon the ship's larder was filled to bursting with the raw material for a dozen feasts.

Observing the hungry sailors at work, Ben and Barnaby found themselves formulating rival theories concerning the genesis of brine-berries. Whereas Ben supposed the shrimp were indeed an aquatic equivalent of fruit, issuing from the seaweed as did apples and pears from trees, Barnaby contended that the vegetation functioned merely as a dwelling-place for the shrimp, which, in the manner of so many ocean creatures, came from eggs. At length Jennet fell upon a method for resolving the dispute. All they need do was fill a tub with a clump of seaweed devoid of shrimp, set it on the quarter-deck, and note whether any brine-berries appeared amidst the strands. Both the printer and the curator appreciated the elegance of her test, and they quickly agreed on its parameters. If the seaweed yielded no shrimp within ten days, Ben would concede the superiority of Barnaby's hypothesis.

During the subsequent week the cook wrought banquet after banquet from the aquatic crop, but Jennet and her friends were concerned less with gustatory matters than with the great shrimp experiment. Every morning they climbed to the quarter-deck and inspected the liquid nursery. On the evidence of their first seven observations, it seemed that the seaweed *per se* possessed no procreative powers.

'Are you ready to admit that the court of Nature hath ruled unfavourably on your claim?' Barnaby asked Ben.

'Mayhap the shrimp will burst forth later today,' Ben replied. 'Mayhap they've already hatched, but they're much too small to see without aid of a microscope.'

Jennet scowled and said, 'Do you really believe that?'

'In sooth – no,' Ben said. 'But since my perfection-matrix contains no grid for graciousness, methinks I'm free to be as stubborn in this matter as I wish.'

The great shrimp experiment: day eight – a day that began like those before it, with Jennet, Ben and Barnaby ascending to the quarter-deck whilst the *Berkshire* cruised through the Atlantic as smoothly as a child's toy sailboat navigating the Serpentine. Bending over the tub, they fingered the seaweed, examining each strand in the morning light, when suddenly a vehement wind seized Ben's hat and carried it out to sea. Other winds followed, equally ferocious, swooping across the decks with a force sufficient to topple the binnacles, steal the oars from the longboats, and set uncoiled lines to dancing like East India cobras.

Instinctively the philosophers retreated to the open stall beneath the quarter-deck, where they huddled like a family of cave-bears taking refuge from a flood. By ten o'clock the brigantine lay in thrall to a thunder-gust.

'Surely there's no stronger power in the universe!' Jennet cried as a lightning-bolt arced across the ashen sky like a filament of divine thought. 'I'Christ, I am sceptical that such a terrible flame' – a thunder-clap shook the air – 'could share a heritage with Von Guericke sparks!'

'You have common intuition on your side, Miss Stearne,' Barnaby shouted over the shriek of the storm, 'and yet methinks Mr Franklin's hypothesis is true!'

'Sparks and holocausts, mites and moose – they're all the same to God!' Ben yelled.

The *Berkshire* rolled from side to side in cycloids so erratic their description would have defied even Newton's fluxions. Whitecaps bloomed everywhere, and the rain descended in vast silvery sheets, like a gigantic curtain demarking the finish of some epic but demented opera. Once more the angry sky brightened with Heaven's fire, and a second later the expected explosion rattled the ship.

'I must lash down my prodigies!' shouted Barnaby, backing deeper into the stall.

'You are a true father to your children!' Jennet cried.

'A true father, aye,' he said, lifting the cover from the hatch, 'even if I do sell one of 'em off now and then!'

Shortly after Barnaby went below, Jennet glanced towards the rigging, where an astonishing sight greeted her gaze. Most of the sailors had climbed aloft and were busily setting the royals and topsails.

'Have they gone mad?' she shouted. 'They should be reefing all that canvas, not putting it in the wind!'

'I would guess our captain hath sensed an even greater storm brewing to the east!' yelled Ben. 'He means to stay ahead of the tempest, lest it catch and smash us!'

No sooner had Ben voiced this conjecture than it received unsolic-ited substantiation. Lurching into the quarter-deck stall, rain-water spouting from his coat-sleeves, Mr Eliot reported that in Captain Fergus's view an unequivocal hurricane was chasing the *Berkshire*, and their only hope was to fly so fast and far that the beast could never overtake them.

'I must ask a favour of ye,' Mr Eliot told Ben. 'With all my men occupied in settin' the canvas and bracin' the beams, we're short on souls to purge the hold! If ye'll work the larboard pump, the boatswain'll take its companion to starboard!'

'I shall happily lend my back to our salvation!' Ben replied.

'And I shall do likewise!' Jennet informed Mr Eliot.

''Tis not a task for a person of your sex!' the mate insisted.

'Compared to the tribulations of childbirth,' she said, 'I would judge the job about as arduous as baking bread!'

Prompted by either desperation or chagrin, Jennet couldn't tell which, Mr Eliot offered a deferential bow. Ben took her by the arm, and together they quit the stall and ventured into the gale. The main deck was a veritable river, the breaking waves and the driving rain washing tumultuously across boards sleek as glass and slick as ice, but at last they reached the larboard pump. In tandem she and Ben grasped the lever and set to work – down, up, down, up, down, up, stroke upon stroke. The wind screamed. The waves rose high as battlements. The rain slapped Jennet's face, drenched her hair, and saturated her dress so thoroughly it became as heavy as chain-mail. To steady her nerves and rouse her spirits she imagined she was operating a Blaeu press in Keimer's Printing-House, churning out copy after copy of an imperially persuasive *argumentum grande*.

After twenty minutes of struggling to keep the *Berkshire* afloat, Jennet suggested to Ben that they were caught in a Sisyphean loop, and soon Mr Eliot appeared and corroborated her pessimism. The hold, he reported, was filling with water as quickly as the machines could empty it.

'Shall we keep to the task?' Ben asked.

'Aye, if ye own the strength, sir!' Mr Eliot replied.

'I do!' Ben said. 'And you, Jenny?'

'Turn on, turn on, Ben!' she said. 'We shall make it glitter by and by!'

As noon came to this wild and sunless sector of the Atlantic, an unnerving sound arose from the rigging, the low guttural croak of the wind cleaving the mizzen-royal in twain. Seconds later the main top-gallant succumbed to the slashing storm, and next the fore-royal was torn asunder.

''Twould seem our captain hath lost his contest with the hurricane!' Jennet shouted to Ben.

'He'd best pop the sheets, else we'll capsize!'

Evidently Captain Fergus had reached the same conclusion, for the crew now descended from the rigging, set their hands to the belaying pins, and yanked them loose. Set free of the fife rails, the sails snapped and fluttered like the banners of a goblin army on the march.

While the captain's failure to outrace the storm was ominous on the face of it, Jennet decided to concentrate on a felicitous implication: the crew, praise God, would soon assume the pumps. Gasping like a beached flounder, she gave the lever an especially energetic push, whereupon a burst of Heaven's fire disclosed a long green island rising from the white ocean. So lush a landmass being foreign to the New-Jersey coast, she leapt to the conclusion that the hurricane had dragged the helpless brigantine well off its course.

'Look, Ben! Caribbean island to starboard!'

'Island?' he shouted. 'I see no island!'

''Tis a Caribbean island!' she cried.

'Caribbean? We cannot be so far south! You saw but a water-mirage!'

'We're in the Caribbean!'

'Your eyes deceive you!'

She was about to assert the probity of her eyes when an enormous wave rolled across the deck, smacking both Jennet and Ben off their feet and pitching them over the larboard rail. Briefly they arced through empty space and, filling their lungs with Caribbean air, plunged into the sea.

Jennet had descended barely ten feet when buoyancy's blessed law sent her in the opposite direction. With the exuberance of an eaglet smashing free of its egg she broke the frothing surface, then expelled several ounces of saltwater from her nose and a full pint from her throat. She blinked madly, squeezing the brine from her eyes. Staring into the troughs betwixt the waves, she beheld the relentless rain, next a bobbing Ben, and then, many yards beyond, the *Berkshire*. Shreds of sail flapped madly on their spars. Uncleated sheets flailed about like the tentacles of a deranged kraken. The hurricane battered the ship merci-lessly, hurtling passengers and crew alike into the ocean with the crude indiscriminate power of an orang-utan shaking down its breakfast from a banana plant.

'We're swimmers, Ben!' she cried. 'This storm can ne'er kill us!'

'Swimmers!' he agreed, spewing out a mouthful of seawater.

Stripped of her company, the *Berkshire* made a final stand against the gale. A more thorough dismemberment could scarcely be imagined. Like a philosopher preparing a hare for micrographic scrutiny, the storm anatomized the ship. Foremast snapped free of fo'c'sle. Mizzen-mast and quarter-deck parted company. Spritsail abandoned bow. Shrouds tore loose from deadeyes. Braces, foretops and crosstrees vanished into the squalls.

'Where is that isle of yours?' Ben called.

'I'm all turned 'round!' she shouted. 'I can only pray some guardian angel will point the way!'

'I'll do the praying, you do the pointing, and by God's grace we'll soon feel sand beneath our feet!'

Shedding their boots and outer garments, the Philadelphians swam in tandem, riding each mountainous swell as if it were Poseidon's wildest horse, until at last they encountered a solid mass – not a beach, but a ten-foot section of the poop-deck bulkhead. Heaving themselves aboard this accidental raft, they sprawled atop its flooded surface, Jennet prone and coughing, Ben supine and shivering.

Having demolished the *Berkshire*, the hurricane gradually departed the scene, exporting its chaos to a higher latitude leaving only a light shower to mark its memory. The Philadelphians looked in all directions, hoping to spot additional survivors, but the storm had evidently borne away every other relic of the wreck.

'Mrs Crompton, a strange phenomenon is upon me,' Ben said, teeth chattering. 'Here I find myself facing either a slow and painful extermination by thirst, or else a quick and gaudy devouring by sharks, and yet I have but one desire.'

She rolled on her back and said, 'Ben, I'm too distracted to think on carnal matters.'

'Dearest, you've read my thoughts. My great yearning is to join with you in erotic embrace.'

'Even as we confront our deaths?'

'*Carpe diem.*'

Like Mrs Millamant taking over the stage in Scene Two of *The Way of the World*, the sun made a resplendent entrance from behind a rose-coloured cloud. 'Tell me, my brave gallant,' she asked, 'are there any conditions under which you might *not* heed the call of concupiscence?'

'None that come to mind.'

'What if a cannonball had shorn off your leg?'

'My lady's touch would ease my agony.'

'What if ants were eating you alive?'

'I would avail myself of whate'er comforts lay at hand.'

The rain stopped. Seagulls circled high above. Golden sunlight washed across the raft, drying the Philadelphians' underclothes and warming their bodies as they exchanged frightened kisses beneath the wide West-Indies sky.

Jennet's island, thank Heaven, was no mirage. Shortly after Ben gave their raft a name – the *Prodigy*, in tribute to poor Barnaby Cavendish – a rank of forested hills appeared in the distance, its silhouette suggesting a many-humped camel fording a river. The wind augmented the Philadelphians' good luck, as did the current, both forces pressing the *Prodigy* steadily towards the landfall, and by late afternoon the raft had run aground in a cove ringed by mangrove trees and dotted with clusters of brilliant white coral.

After praising Providence for their deliverance – Jennet extolling her 'most glorious Creator', Ben lauding the Deist Clockmaker – they disembarked and staggered through the surf, dazed, shocked, sapped and above all enchanted by the fact that they were not dead.

They gained the beach, advancing barefoot across silken sand punctuated by vacant crab-shells, and forthwith entered the forest, soon discovering that their respective deities were watching over them yet, for the storm had deposited pools of sweet rain in dozens of rock crevices and tree clefts. No Pierian Spring could have pleased them more completely, no Well of the Saints, no Fountain of Youth.

'How goes it with you, Mr Franklin?' she asked, sucking down the delicious liquid bounty.

'I am entirely miserable, Mrs Crompton. And you?'

'Completely wretched. I mourn our drowned curator.'

''Tis in sooth a dark day. And yet methinks we have no choice but to embrace optimism, cultivate hope and aspire to make the best of our circumstances.'

'Cock an ear to the breeze, Ben. Listen. Do you hear it?'

'Hear what?'

''Tis the sound of Dame Fortune, laughing as she plays lanterloo with our lives.'

Thirst slaked, throats soothed, they resolved to catch a measure of sleep before exhaustion dropped them in their tracks. Returning to the beach, they dragged the *Prodigy* to the edge of the forest, then set the bulkhead fragment diagonally against a boulder and equipped the resulting enclosure with a mattress made of kelp and heliconia leaves. They yawned, stretched and took up residence in this rude but serviceable lean-to.

'A veritable palace,' he said.

'And so to bed,' she said.

Like serpents slipping free of their skins, they shed their spinning thoughts and muddled fears, then fell asleep to the harsh whisper of the retreating tide.

An avian concerto heralded the dawn — parakeets, Jennet guessed, complemented by several trilling, warbling and cooing kinds unknown to her. Shafts of amber sunlight pierced the lean-to. For an indeterminate interval she lay and listened to the surf, absorbing the rhythmic growl like a foetus attuning itself to the rush and thump of its mother's blood.

'Ah, 'twas no mere nightmare then,' Ben said, rousing himself from his dreams. 'We have truly joined the fellowship of the marooned.'

'The castaway's normal stratagem, I've heard, is to write his coordinates on a scrap of paper, then place the message in a bottle and toss it into the sea,' Jennet said. 'But, alas, we have no bottle.'

'Mayhap some *other* castaway's bottle will reach these shores. We'll uncork the vessel and add our message to its cargo — explaining, of course, that we're but second in the queue to be rescued.'

They passed the morning foraging for breakfast amongst the reefs and tide-pools. So intense was their hunger, they easily convinced one another that eating uncooked shellfish would do a human no harm, then set about harvesting the dozens of pale sand-crabs, brine-berries, conch-snails, and mussels that inhabited the glossy rocks.

'Tell me, Ben, do you perchance share my shame o'er yesterday's panegyric to Providence?' Jennet prised a snail from its shell, setting the animal on her tongue. 'In the cold light of morning, I judge my devotions an insult to Barnaby, Mr Eliot, Captain Fergus and every other wretch who went down with the *Berkshire*.' She chewed the rubbery flesh, which was subtly flavoured, like a mushroom. 'I'd rather believe in no God at all than one who is so capricious in His mercy.'

'My dear Mrs Crompton, you've surely picked the wrong time and place to start experimenting with atheism,' Ben said. 'Whether God be fickle or fair, 'tis only by His intervention we shall e'er see Philadelphia again.'

'No doubt you're right. But in the future I shall forbear to praise the Creator in question.'

Ben scooped a mussel from its shell and popped it into his mouth. 'Are you not acquainted with Monsieur Pascal's brilliant deduction? 'Tis far more sensible to be a believer than an atheist, for the latter hath his immortal soul to lose, the former only his illusions.'

'Aunt Isobel once told me of Pascal's celebrated wager. She concluded that any Supreme Being worthy of the name would scorn the believer for his complacency, even as He rewarded the atheist for his bravado.'

Ben intertwined his fingers and raised the fleshy configuration skywards. 'Forgive my friend her impieties, Lord, whether thou existeth or not. Along with these shellfish she hath ingested a great quantity of salt, and 'tis making her brain go dry.'

From her years amongst the Nimacook Jennet knew that, for all the island's apparent fecundity, their survival was a matter of complete indifference to Nature. They must not take their next full meal, warm night or tranquil moment for granted. Ever the cheer-monger, Ben at first laughed at her fatalism, but then came three successive days in which they failed to extract a single morsel from their habitat, and thereafter he counted himself an eager student of Algonquin arts.

For their initial task Jennet had them erect on the lee shore a wigwam framed by candelabra-tree branches and covered with bull-horn acacia bark. A split-log dwelling would have been preferable, of course, but without an iron axe or a long Damascus knife such a project was unimaginable. Under her tutelage Ben learned how to turn animal skins into moccasins, fashion clothing from grass and reeds, start a fire with a bow-drill, trap grouper in a reed weir, tolerate the taste of roasted katydids, appreciate the flavour of boiled tree frogs, and snare the harelike agouti that proliferated throughout the forest.

At first Ben was distressed to be violating his vegetarian principles so blatantly, but then he noticed that, whenever they cleaned a grouper for roasting, they found a smaller fish within its stomach. 'If a big fish may eat a small fish,' he argued, 'I don't see why I mayn't eat a big fish.'

'A sturdy piece of logic,' Jennet said.

''Tis so convenient being a *reasonable* creature,' he said, 'for it enables a man to find a reason for everything he hath a mind to do.'

With a nod to Francis Bacon's political allegory, they named their isle New-Atlantis, and over the next several months they explored its inner reaches, catalogued its abundance, and ascertained its form – an irregular oval along whose primary axis ran an L-shaped ridge perhaps fifteen miles long. Each expedition proved more productive of wonders than the last, from purple butterflies swarming like fleets of faerie kites to sea turtles with shells suggesting Byzantine mosaics; from ants building great formic cities in the forest's heart to spiders spinning webs as intricate as doilies; from twin waterfalls echoing through the jungle in crystalline duet to troops of nimble monkeys, their tails looped around the uppermost branches, swinging back and forth like antic church bells. A plenary Paradise indeed – though like Adam's primordial estate it harboured a despoiler.

The serpent's name was boredom. There was nothing on New-Atlantis by which a Baconian experimenter might sharpen his wits, no psychic whetstone, no mental flint. Unlike their literary counterpart, Robinson Crusoe, Jennet and Ben took no satisfaction in their cast-away condition. Whenever Mr Crusoe had engaged in yet another act of ingenuity – growing barley, making furniture, taming goats – he'd experienced an unequivocal delight. But the Philadelphians were of a different disposition. They craved salons and seminars, troubadours and telescopes, allegories and air pumps. To condemn such sensibilities to a West-Indies isle was like banishing a herd-dog to a nation without sheep.

For a brief interval they brought to their tedious Eden the salutary artifices of theatre. Ben conceived a cycle of one-act comedies, so thin of plot and broad of theme there was no need to write them down. He had but to toss out the premise, and the New-Atlantis Players would improvise their way to the end. For Jennet, the jewel of their repertoire was 'A Sense of Proportion', all about a lord and lady who resolved their petty domestic disputes – what colour to paint the drawing-room, which cat to allow in the parlour – by hiring two commoners to fight lethal pistol duels, one man representing the obverse of the controversy, the other the reverse. She was also fond of 'Crowned Heads', concerning a king and queen who, eager to spend their every waking hour at gaming and falconry, had the Royal Alchemist fashion a pair of Doppelgängers gifted in handling the quotidian demands of despotism. Offended by the arrogance that had given them birth, the Doppelgängers set about issuing repressive edicts, and ere long the true king and queen found themselves kneeling before the chopping block.

The satisfactions of emoting for an audience of uncomprehending monkeys were few, and the Philadelphians eventually sought other, less cerebral ways to relieve their ennui, so that Ben's Moderation grid – he'd managed to reincarnate the perfection-matrix by marking scraps of acacia bark with a burnt twig – was soon a mass of black dots. While the bounty of New-Atlantis did not extend to Belgian adder-bags, Jennet assumed that their sport would involve no procreative consequences, for she was beyond the age when a woman might expect to conceive, and during the past twenty months she'd bled not at all. She experienced an extreme dismay, therefore, to realize that she was once again with child, for how else to account for her swelling contours and terrestrial *mal de mer*?

'I'll come right out and say it,' she told Ben one balmy afternoon. They were repairing their hut with patches of mud and clay, its roof having leaked profusely during the morning's thunder-gust. 'The third and final offspring of Jennet Stearne Crompton is but six months from daylight.'

'Dearest angel, do you seek to amuse me?' he asked, massaging his scraggly beard.

'My announcement's no more a joke than this wigwam's a cathedral.'

'Pregnant? Really? A woman of your years?'

''Steeth, Ben, do you think me some dry and withered Sarai? Do you imagine I could ne'er quicken my lover's seed unless Jehovah himself injects me with a heavenly egg?'

He scowled and twisted a viscid brown bung into place. 'This all seems most uncanny to me.'

'Uncanny? *Uncanny?* There is no cause to posit a virgin conception here, sir. I needn't remind you of *that.*'

Breathing suddenly became for her swain an activity requiring his complete attention. 'Oh, my dear Mrs Crompton, methinks I am too *young* for fatherhood.'

'As I am too *old* for motherhood.'

'Truth to tell, I feel cozened by this news. 'Tis as if Nature and Dame Fortune and you yourself have all conspired against me.'

'Cozened?' she snarled. 'Cozened? How durst you accuse me of such?'

'If not cozenage, then a malign sort of carelessness. A conscientious woman knows her fertile days and constrains her lover accordingly.'

'Faugh, Ben, no witch-court e'er reached a judgment so unjust! *Nummusquantum!*'

'What?'

'I am angry!'

Pivoting abruptly, she stalked away from the wigwam, her patience stretched to its snapping-point. She would rather hear Gunny Slocum brag about catching counterfeiters, or even Cotton Mather opining about America's Satanic tawnies, than endure another instant of this twaddle.

As the sun arced towards its tryst with the sea, she walked south along the rumbling surf. She vowed to spend the night alone, sleeping atop a pile of heliconia leaves. Alas, no sooner had she made this promise than the sky grew dark as dried blood, releasing a cold, fierce, unsalutary rain. Shivering in the squalls, her grass mantle growing soggier by the minute, Jennet decided that pleurisy was too high a price to pay for dignity. She slogged back up the beach and silently entered Ben's vicinity. For a full minute the castaways stared at each other, shedding rainwater, saying not a word.

'The more I think on it,' he muttered at last, 'the more happily I anticipate teaching our splendid young son the printer's trade.'

Jennet took his wet hand, separating the thick fingers as a coquette might spread the blades of a fan. 'This son of ours could very well be a girl.'

'Then she shall follow her mother into the wilds of modern geometry. Marry, I see this junior Jennet teaching the fluxions at the Philadelphia Friends School. Long before she's born, I shall advantage her by reciting the multiplication tables well within her hearing, over and over and over.'

They flashed one another weary smiles, exchanged mistrustful frowns, and, crossing the threshold of their rehabilitated wigwam, took shelter from the storm.

Printer, philosopher, playwright, and – now – *paterfamilias*, Benjamin Franklin spent the first week of his son's life setting agouti snares in the heart of New-Atlantis, noting their locations on a map he'd made by embedding pebbles in a mud pie. On the morning of the eighth day he took up his woven-seaweed sack and began an inspection tour, feeling a bit like a country squire making the rounds of his estate. Snare number one was unsprung, likewise number two, but the third trap indeed held an agouti, the confused animal dangling like the lead plumb on a carpenter's twine.

Until the moment of his son's birth, Ben had always regarded himself as well experienced in matters of ecstasy. Catching Saturn's rings with his telescope, making electricity with his sulphur-ball, joining with his true love in carnal embrace – surely such activities defined the bounds of rapture. How wrong he'd been, for all these wonders paled beside William Franklin's arrival in the world.

Jennet had delivered in the upright position favoured by her Nimacook kin, her arms locked around two adjacent mangrove trees.

The spasms still caused her much pain, however, and Ben found himself wishing for a supply of Barnaby Cavendish's imagined insensibility drug. Disoriented though he was by Jennet's distress, he ultimately became what she called 'a not incompetent midwife', soothing her during the pangs, guiding the infant free of the womb, pronouncing authoritatively on its gender, and cutting the cord with a stone knife. On Jennet's orders he gathered up the gelatinous afterbirth – it was both fascinating and repellent, like one of Cavendish's monsters – and buried it in the sand. When finally satisfied that the mother had survived her ordeal, he bore their son to a tide-pool and gave him his first bath, gently sponging the bloody, wrinkled flesh with a crumpled heliconia leaf.

While 'William' was clearly the correct name for this astonishing soul, they could not agree on the reason. For Jennet the name evoked the dramatists she most admired, Shakespeare and Congreve. Ben preferred the political connotations, for many a friend of liberty had called himself William, including William Penn, champion of religious toleration, William Wallace, heroic Scottish rebel, and William of Orange, the first British monarch to rule wholly at Parliament's behest.

Cautiously Ben crept towards his prey. Even as it struggled to right itself, the agouti looked him in the eye. He paused, took a step, whereupon the gravity of New-Atlantis forsook its traditional Newtonian allegiance and acquired a disconcerting independence of mind.

''Sbody!'

Ben's captive ankles flew upward, his torso plummeted, his head descended. At last he came to rest, arms hanging downward, fingers brushing the dirt. His first thought (quite ridiculous, he realized) was that a troop of vengeful but clever agouti had fashioned a trap of their own. His second thought (much more rational) was that he'd tripped an agouti-snare laid by some other castaway. His third thought (utterly terrifying) was that the snare had been set specifically for him by a cannibal like those who figured so memorably in Mr Crusoe's adventures.

For an hour he endured his inverted condition, the puzzled blood filling his cranium and clogging his ears. His field of vision was confined to the similarly ensnared agouti, a berry bush, and a mangrove root as gnarled as Newton's shillelagh. When at last two brown leather boots entered the scene, his heart surged with hope, for such footwear was surely beyond a cannibal's budget.

'Look!' a male voice cried. 'We have catched ourselves a most peculiar beast.'

A second pair of dark boots, oiled like a Belgian adder-bag, materialized within inches of Ben's nose. Their owner, likewise male, spoke next. 'God was in whimsical mood when he made *this* creature. The toes are where the head should be.'

'The knees are where the heart should be.'

'The cods are in the stomach's place.'

'Ben Franklin, you are one befuddled animal.' The owner of the unoiled boots leaned over and showed his face to Ben. He was a muscular Negro, dressed in tanned leather breeches and a blue linen shirt, his features fixed in a scowl. 'Have no worries' – he pulled a knife from his belt – 'for I shall free you!'

The blade flashed in the midday sun, and the next thing Ben knew he'd executed an involuntary cartwheel and collapsed on the ground. As Ben's wits returned to him, the owner of the oiled boots – also a Negro, smaller than his companion and dressed only in agouti-skin trousers and a red neckerchief – extended a helping hand.

'How do you know my name?' Ben asked, climbing free of the snare.

'Your name is the least thing we know about you,' the knife wielder said. 'Since you drift ashore, we watch you every day.'

'We keep silent, listen carefully, learn much,' the other said. 'Your little play called "A Sense of Proportion" is most delightful.'

The thought that these two trappers had been spying on him for over a year set Ben's brain reeling once again.

'Call me Njabulo, the name my mother gave me,' the knife wielder said, 'and here is my younger brother, Kanisho, though to our white master in Carolina we were Jedidiah and Oswald.'

'Do I surmise you are slaves?' Ben asked.

'We *were* slaves,' Kanisho said. 'Today we live as free citizens in Ewuare-Village, named after our ancestors' greatest king.'

'Village?' Ben said, flabbergasted. 'You've got a whole village tucked away here?'

'Ruled by our Grand Oba, Ebinose-Mbemba, and his Queen, Ossalume,' Njabulo said. 'Let us tell you a story, Ben Franklin.' He approached the suspended agouti and deftly broke its neck. 'Six months ago, Ebinose-Mbemba and Ossalume call their councillors together and ask them what should be done about the castaways in our midst. All five vote to remove your head, and your woman's head as well. Lucky for you, the Grand Oba and his Queen reject this verdict.'

Kanisho added, 'He says there is no report of Jesus Christ ever removing anyone's head.'

'If your rulers have elected to spare my life, why did you set a trap for me?' Ben asked.

'We ensnare you by accident,' Njabulo said. 'The jungle conceals many such devices, laid for the slave-catchers.' With his knife he cut down the agouti, offering the limp little mound of fur to Ben. 'Go ahead. Take it. Dead agouti don't bite.'

After retrieving his woven-seaweed sack and stuffing his prey inside, Ben told the fugitive slaves that he wished to thank the King and Queen for their clemency. Kanisho explained that the monarchs had more important tasks to accomplish that day than accepting a white man's gratitude. Ben said he would still like to accompany them back to Ewuare-Village, that he might exhibit himself as the harmless printer and innocuous philosopher he was. The brothers assented to this proposition, but only after Ben agreed to make the trip blindfold.

For the next two hours Njabulo and Kanisho guided their quarry through the pungent jungle, Kanisho's neckerchief fitted across Ben's eyes as if he were awaiting execution by a firing squad. All during the journey – up the central ridge, over the crest, and down again – the brothers related the story of their arrival on New-Atlantis, which they called Amakye-Isle.

Born into slavery on Peedee Willows, a Carolina rice plantation, Njabulo and Kanisho had come of age hearing about a very different world, the West African kingdom of Benin, where their great-grandmothers had grown yams and kola nuts before the Portuguese slavers arrived and sent them in chains across the sea. A Bini farmer knew many hardships, many disasters, but such travails were as milk and honey compared with the endless toil of sowing and reaping a rice crop. And yet for other Carolina chattel, things were evidently much worse. If Satan's agents came in degrees of depravity, then the master of Peedee Willows, Andrew Larkin, whose father had won the plantation from the Earl of Clarendon in a game of whist, was amongst the more enlightened of his kind, a devout Anglican who believed it his Christian duty to save whatever percentage of a soul an African Negro possessed. Thus it was that Njabulo, Kanisho, and their fellows were instructed in the Anglican *Book of Common Prayer* and baptized into the Church of England. Though routinely whipped, regularly beaten, frequently starved and sometimes mutilated, the Peedee Willows slaves would in all probability be spared the fires of Perdition.

After three successive failed crops, Larkin concluded that the Almighty did not intend him to be a rice farmer. He sold the plantation and auctioned off the slaves, subsequently heading to Connecticut with the aim of entering the beaver-hat trade. The best bid for Larkin's chattel came from faraway Jamaica, whose sugarcane industry required a continual supply of stout black bodies. Late in July of 1720, Njabulo, Kanisho, and ninety-six other Bini were loaded into the British carrack *Sapodilla* and sent south to the Caribbean.

Shortly after her passage around San Salvador, both of the *Sapodilla's* compasses mysteriously ceased to function, and the next morning the carrack entered a region of stagnant air and fiendish heat. As the languorous days elapsed, the captain was forced to ration water by the teaspoon and hardtack by the ounce, with the slaves' allotment dwindling to zero. But then, in the third week of the becalming, an unlikely Moses emerged from amongst the Bini, the nimble-witted Ebinose-Mbemba, Andrew Larkin's former footman and librarian. Exploiting the epidemic of despair that had infected the ship's company, Ebinose-Mbemba led the other slaves in an improvised revolt that ultimately obliged them to drown the captain, strangle the first mate, debrain the boatswain, and slit each crewman's throat.

Washing the blood from their hands, the Bini implored their ancestors' spirits to blow them home to West Africa, but these prayers were answered only by feeble currents and anaemic breezes. After nine days adrift, the *Sapodilla* ran aground in the shallows surrounding an uncharted isle. Ebinose-Mbemba forthwith ordered his followers to strip the carrack of every valuable artifact: not only such obvious choices as knives, axes, muskets, nails, bulkheads, timbers, planking, rope, sailcloth, telescope and compass, but also Thomas More's *Utopia*, John Bunyan's *The Pilgrim's Progress* and the King James Bible. At Ebinose-Mbemba's command, the *Sapodilla*'s gutted remains were set aflame and reduced to ashes, so that a slave-catcher happening upon Amakye-Isle would never guess that a ship had touched bottom in these waters.

'The longer we live here, the more fortunate we feel in finding this place,' Njabulo told Ben. 'Most West-Indies isles are but swatches of desert, friendly to Spanish pigs, wild onions, and little else.'

'You must approach Ewuare with the proper expectations,' Kanisho warned. 'Though the Grand Oba keeps Thomas More by his bed, our village is not a perfect world.'

'But we do claim this,' Njabulo said. 'You will find no chains in Ewuare.'

Within minutes of regaining his eyesight, Ben decided that, Utopia or not, Ewuare was a splendid and convivial place, at least compared to his wretched little homestead by the sea. Folded into an obscure glade at the bend of the ridge, the village boasted a defensive moat hedged by a stockade wall, its pickets poised to impale marauding slave-catchers. Passing through the gates, the brothers led Ben along a dirt square flanked by private dwellings, each comprising five mud-huts arranged in a semicircle. Children darted from yard to yard, kicking a wooden dodecahedron according to the rules of a Bini game that Njabulo identified as *uhranwi*. Felicitous fragrances rode the breeze, released by the action of cooking fires on agouti stew and grouper soup.

In the middle of the square, evidently occupying a place of honour, rose an object resembling an immense lump of coal, large as an equestrian statue. As Ben paused to inspect the stone – a Bini deity? a monument to the *Sapodilla* mutiny? – a dozen curious Ewuareans clustered around him. They did not desire a closer look at the stranger, Njabulo explained, so much as 'a good view of the spectacle should the King and Queen change their minds and order you beheaded'. Njabulo then laughed uproariously, evidently to indicate he was joking, though Ben had never regarded anyone's beheading, particularly his own, as a proper locus of levity.

'Here is why the *Sapodilla* becomes lost, and your own ship as well.' Kanisho rapped his knuckles on the lustrous black stone. 'She is Orishanla – the Confounder.'

'Place a magnetic-compass within five miles of her, and she seizes the needle and doesn't let go,' Njabulo said.

''Tis belike the mightiest lodestone in the world,' Ben gasped. He caressed the mineral, so massive it bid fair to make the Earth a three-poled planet.

As the crowd dispersed, having concluded that no beheadings were in the offing, Njabulo revealed that the Queen was off supervising the construction of a watch-tower on the lee shore, but the King was currently in residence. The brothers brought Ben to the royal palace, a hulking dome of clay and bark, featuring seashells of every hue – blue, violet, pink, crimson, white – embedded in its walls like numinous barnacles clinging to Saint Brendan's ship. The Grand Oba occupied the atrium, seated on a locally made Yorkshire chair, reading Hobbes's *Leviathan* whilst his prepubescent son sharpened a cutlass on a whetstone. Njabulo spoke to Ebinose-Mbemba in the Bini language, apparently explaining that the intruder desired an audience, and despite Kanisho's prediction the proposal proved agreeable to the King, who now jumped to his feet, entrusted Hobbes to Njabulo, and invited Ben for a stroll about the palace grounds.

'You have a handsome son,' Ebinose-Mbemba said.

'And you as well, Your Majesty,' Ben said.

'Your Majesty,' echoed Ebinose-Mbemba, amused. He was tall, lithe and pleasingly proportioned, arrayed in a crumpled tricorn hat and a blue cloth greatcoat brocaded with gold threads, both presumably salvaged from the *Sapodilla*. 'I've ne'er been addressed in that manner before.'

'Are you not a king?'

'They call me a king, yes, and my wife a queen besides. But what king hath only one hundred and thirteen subjects?'

'The ratio's normally more extreme,' Ben said, nodding.

Ebinose-Mbemba swept his muscled arm through the air, a gesture that seemed to embrace the whole of Amakye-Isle. 'For the Bini, there must always be a Grand Oba. They cast me in the part, and so I play it – but I believe this sad and sorry world has seen kings enough already. From your satire entitled "Crowned Heads", might I infer you agree?'

'Quite so.'

The Grand Oba thrust his hands into his bullion-trimmed pockets. 'My master, Mr Larkin, owned many books on government, each championing a different system of rule. I have read them all, and now I must ask myself, which philosophy is best? If I follow the prescription of Mr More's *Utopia*, I shall ban all personal possessions from Ewuare and replace them with common goods. Are you familiar with this idea?'

'I have not read Mr More, but I know he looked askance on private property.'

'Then you may also know he allowed slavery in his earthly Paradise. Tell me your opinion of slavery, Ben Franklin.'

'My opinion?' He inhaled a mouthful of moist Caribbean air, transferring the agouti sack from his left shoulder to his right. 'My fellow passengers on the *Berkshire* included a man who made his living exhibiting foetal monsters in bottles,' he said at last. 'Slavery, I would argue, is of a similarly freakish nature. Misshapen, rejected by God, loved only by those to whom it brings wealth.'

'A very pretty answer. Ah, but what man dares insult the lion to its face?' Ebinose-Mbemba loosed a smile that hovered disconcertingly betwixt facetiousness and menace. Removing his hat, he fanned his brow until the bright gems of sweat evaporated. 'Having found in Mr More a lamentable lapse, we now move on to Mr Hobbes. According to his *Leviathan*, I must impose on my subjects the harshest despotism imaginable, for all men are selfish beasts at base, and need protection from one another.'

'I am acquainted with the Hobbesian outlook,' said Ben as he and the Grand Oba began their second circuit. 'The eternal war of all against all. But I do not view our human species that way.'

'Nor do I, despite the many cruelties I have witnessed in my life. And so we put Mr Hobbes aside and turn finally to Mr Locke. Were I to heed his *Second Treatise of Civil Government*, I would grant my councillors more power than I enjoy, for only a strong legislature can secure every citizen's natural right to life, liberty and property. In

Locke's society, a monarch sits upon his throne only to execute the contract a community has made with itself.'

'I've always found much reasonableness in Locke.'

'And yet he, too, permits slavery, allowing victorious armies to make chattels of their prisoners. I promise you, Locke would view slavery differently had he sailed with my grandmother to the Carolinas.'

Ebinose⁄Mbemba restored his hat, easing it downward until the shadow of the brim obscured his face. He cleared his throat, lowered his voice, and bid Ben imagine two hundred Africans pursued like game animals by men with muskets and nets. To the Portuguese slavers it mattered little whose parent, wife, husband, or child died during the hunt – and many did die – for the slave trade enjoyed both the sanction of Scripture and the imprimatur of profit. Upon their capture Ebinose⁄Mbemba's maternal grandmother and her fellow prisoners were chained naked to their berths aboard the brigantine *San Jorge*. For ten weeks they lay crushed against each other, rolling about in their own waste whilst the ocean's frigid waters seeped into the hold, the weaker Bini inevitably perishing of fever, flux, scurvy and distemper. Halfway to the Carolinas, the captain of the *San Jorge* realized that he'd failed to stock enough provisions for the remainder of the voyage. His solution, so simple, so efficient, was to bring twenty Africans on deck and hurl them bodily into the sea – chained together, of course, with the leading Bini affixed to a great stone: far be it from the captain to place unearned guineas in the purse of a passing slave⁄master.

'In short, I must argue that no white man has yet imagined a government likely to benefit any race save his own,' Ebinose⁄Mbemba said.

A draining sensation overcame Ben, as if a demon had slit his side, affixed an air pump, and started sucking out his vitals. 'I shan't dispute the point.'

Abruptly the African halted and stomped his left foot in the dirt. He seized Ben's shoulder and laughed as heartily as an Englishman enjoying a Congreve comedy. 'Ah⁄hah, Ben Franklin! Ah⁄hah! Ah⁄hah!'

'Something amuses you?'

'A marvellous idea grows in my head! Follow me!'

330

Ebinose-Mbemba guided Ben into a thatched-roof hut shaped like one of Isaac Newton's meat pies. A dozen clay pots lined the walls, filled to overflowing with seeds, nuts and berries, flanking a massive sea-chest. The instant the Grand Oba drew back the lid, Ben experienced the sort of coursing thrill he normally felt only from swiving and philosophizing. Top to bottom, front to back, the compartment bulged with gold coins.

'Pirate treasure,' Ebinose-Mbemba explained. 'We found it whilst digging our moat. But for the absence of markets, shops and bazaars on Amakye, our village would be awash in worldly goods.'

'These doubloons are worthless to you,' Ben said in a commiserating tone.

'Worse than worthless — a curse. You are not the first white man to visit our island, Ben Franklin, nor will you be the last.'

'You believe the pirates will return?'

'Doubtless they have marked Amakye on their chart, a reckoning they are certain to favour over their distracted compass. On noting that a Bini village has arisen where they buried their gold, they will sell this information to the slave-catchers. Now. Hear my idea. The instant the pirates appear, you will drag the sea-chest into plain sight, thereby making an inland expedition unnecessary. And so Ewuare remains hidden, secret as a leopard's lair!'

Exhilarated by his scheme, Ebinose-Mbemba cavorted about the treasure chest like a fop breaking in a pair of boots.

''Tis an ingenious plan, though I must ask you a question,' Ben said. 'Once I give the buccaneers their gold, what's to keep them from putting me and my family to the sword?'

'Your reputation for cleverness precedes you. Before the pirates come back, you will have devised a solution to this problem.'

'I'm flattered that you would trust your village's fate to me,' Ben said, his head aching as if recently employed in a game of *uhranwi*.

'I have your word then? You will misdirect the buccaneers on our behalf?'

'You have my word.'

'My spies inform me you are an honourable man.'

Ben closed the sea-chest, positioning himself atop the gold like an Italian prince employing a chamber-pot wrought by Cellini, and tried

to picture his Honesty grid. As far as he could recall, it contained only
a fourth as many blotches as Thrift, and only a sixth the number that
marred Moderation. He told Ebinose-Mbemba that in most matters
he was as weak and sinful as any other mortal, and a bit of
a coward to boot. But he would say this for
himself: He was a man
who kept
his

*

Promises
are prime amongst
those commodities to which we
books accord an almost supernatural respect.
When *Poor Richard's Almanack* implored me to present
its author's relationship with Jennet Stearne Crompton in the most
tasteful terms imaginable (for this would be the first time the world
learned of their intimacy), I did not assent immediately, for I knew that
my pledge, once given, could never be broken or even slightly bent.
'Naturally I intend to exercise discretion,' I assured my colleague,
adding, 'but I shall neither truncate the truth nor abridge the facts.
Agreed?'

'Agreed,' said *Poor Richard's Almanack*.

Even today, certain historians perpetuate a rumour first floated
by Ben's political enemies when, at age fifty-eight, he ran for the
Pennsylvania Assembly. This falsehood asserts that William Franklin's mother was Ben's maidservant Barbara, that she was once a
prostitute, and that upon her death two years earlier he'd buried her in
an unmarked grave. I am happy to report that within my species the
only creatures ever to credit this nonsense are *The Bridges of Madison
County* and *The Celestine Prophecy*. Unfortunately, the Pennsylvania
voters of 1764 were a gullible lot, and Ben lost the election, though his
party maintained a majority and subsequently renewed his appointment
as the Assembly's agent in London.

Franklin scholars will note that I have *en passant* cleared up a second
mystery. Thanks to my memoirs, historians need no longer marvel at
Ben's famous enthusiasm for older women, as it traces unequivocally to
his conjugal education at Jennet's hands. He made his appreciation

explicit in an essay called 'Advice on the Choice of a Mistress', the body of which comprises eight reasons a man would do better selecting an older paramour over a nubile one. ('Because they have more Knowledge of the World', runs the first reason. 'Because they are so grateful!' runs the last.) I heartily recommend this amusing piece, which you will find in any substantive Franklin omnibus.

You have perchance noticed that my reminiscences illuminate a third mystery regarding Ben. How did he come to advocate the abolition of the slave trade in an era when the average intellectual wholly endorsed that institution? To answer the question we need look no further than his 1726 interview with Ebinose-Mbemba (an episode Ben omitted from his *Autobiography* lest he inspire the slave-catchers to go looking for Amakye). Now, I cannot say that he left that fateful meeting prepared to join the first abolitionist society he happened upon; indeed, during his years as editor of *The Pennsylvania Gazette* he rarely declined to list an upcoming slave auction or post notice of a runaway. But the seed was sown on that Caribbean isle, and eventually the tree took root.

Ben's abolitionism is a story to make any book proud of its author, though *Poor Richard's Almanack* can be positively insufferable on the subject. In 1758 he wrote a last will and testament providing manumis-sion for the two slaves in his possession, then freed them outright in 1766. Among the earliest of his abolitionist writings is his reaction to a highly publicized 1772 British legal case that culminated in the emancipation of a fugitive slave named Somerset. In a letter to *The London Chronicle*, he reprimanded his fellow Englishmen for celebrating the court's decision while simultaneously ignoring the plight of 'eight hundred and fifty thousand Negroes in the English Islands and the Colonies'. This evil would never be rectified by freeing the occasional fugitive, he insisted, but only by making African slavery itself illegal, whether its victims harvested Virginia tobacco, Carolina rice or Jamaica sugarcane. 'Can sweetening our Tea with Sugar be a Cir-cumstance of such absolute Necessity? Can the petty Pleasure thence arising from the Taste compensate for so much Misery produc'd amongst our fellow Creatures, and such a constant Butchery of the human Species by this pestilential detestable Traffic in the Bodies and Souls of Men?'

I should also note, lest *Poor Richard* chastise me for neglecting the fact, that Ben's last public essay, a letter to *The Federal Gazette* published on 23 March 1790, was a withering riposte to a pro⁄slavery speech recently given in Congress by James Jackson, a Georgia senator. Ben's counterblast took the form of a similar address supposedly delivered one hundred years earlier by a Muslim legislator, Sidi Mehemet Ibrahim, explaining why the Islamic nations must never free their Christian chattels. By turning Jackson's argument on its head, Ben produced a satire commensurate with Swift's 'A Modest Pro⁄posal', Voltaire's *Candide*, or — a work that will soon enter this story — the Baron de Montesquieu's *Persian Letters*.

If we cease our Cruises against the Christians, how shall we be furnish'd with the Commodities their Countries produce, and which are so necessary for us? If we forbear to make Slaves of their People, who in this hot Climate are to cultivate our Lands? Who are to perform the common Labours of our City, and in our Families? Must we not then be our own Slaves? And is there not more Compassion and more Favour due to us as Mussulmen, than to these Christian dogs? We have now above 50,000 Slaves in and near Algiers. This Number, if not kept up by fresh Supplies, will soon diminish, and be gradually annihilat'd. If we then cease taking and plundering the Infidel Ships, and making Slaves of the Seamen and Passengers, our Lands will become of no Value for want of Cultivation; the Rents of Houses in the City will sink to one Half; and the Revenues of Government arising from its Shares of Prizes be totally

*

Destroyed
by a sudden gale,
the wigwam in which Jennet,
Ben and William pursued their uneventful
lives was not initially missed by the castaways. It had
been a forlorn and uninviting structure, 'homely but not homey' in Ben's words. For the first two nights following their loss, they slept contentedly under the stars, William snugged betwixt them like the fleshy band fusing congenitally joined twins. On the third night another storm broke over New⁄Atlantis. Huddled beneath a sailcloth borrowed from the Bini, the wind driving pellets of rain against their

faces as the cold seeped into their bones, the Philadelphians soon concluded that a new wigwam was essential.

Ben set the acacia-wood framework in place, then went off to check his agouti traps, leaving Jennet to fashion the walls from bark and fronds. Although the task seemed at first the paragon of monotony, its wearisome rhythms gradually combined with the pounding sun and the booming surf to put her in a rarefied state of mind.

How mysterious it all was, this planet Earth, this glittering sea, this unknown island: especially the island – Amakye, the fugitive slaves called it – not merely the queerest of places but also the most pristine, a world whose objects were as yet unnamed, and now it was her job to put a word to everything that met her gaze. She cast her eyes across Amakye's multifarious substances, solid and fluid, grainy and slick, wondering what to call them.

William lay prone on the beach, amusing himself by poking his fingers into the saturated sand. A fiddler-crab lurked near his left foot. She approached the animal and lifted its clawed and wriggling body from gravity's embrace, fully intending to throw it into the sea ere it could scratch her son. But instead something moved her to place the fiddler-crab on her palm, as she might set a locust's wing on a microscope stage.

What manner of creature was this? To a Cartesian, of course, the crab was a machine, insensible to pain, incapable of thought, its rowing legs powered by some unseen entity. The crab in turn belonged to a larger machine, the world, its motions supplied by those nebulous presences that Descartes variously called genies, spirits and vortices. Complementing the world-machine was an entirely different domain – the mind – hooked to the bodily realm via the divine pineal gland, or so the Frenchman had taught.

But today this whole system struck Jennet as woefully flawed, an affront to both fiddler-crabs and common sense. Just as Newton's apocryphal apple had inspired him to discern the continuity betwixt heavenly and earthly motion, so did the creature twitching in her hand now proclaim to Jennet an equally momentous link, a tie binding the thinking brains of men to the sentient flesh of beasts. She restored the crab to its native sand, picked up her son, and kissed him on each plump cheek.

In the days that followed her disenchantment with Descartes, she grew convinced that the key to the demon disproof lay right here on New-Atlantis — not concealed like the pirates' gold, but plainly displayed. For to inhabit a Caribbean isle was to know Nature in a fashion not available to a Sorbonne professor or a Fellow of the Royal Society. Standing on a high limestone bluff and observing a violent storm break over the sea, Jennet decided that a lightning-stroke was surely something other than a theatrical prop hurled by a meteorological goblin. Walking the midnight shores beneath a sky unpierced by any church steeple or bell tower, she came to see the wheeling moon and the wandering stars as phenomena quite different from dead matter in thrall to Cartesian vortices. Picking her way along a narrow coral spit whilst contemplating the majestic rollers as they exploded against the rocks, she concluded that the tides could never be fruitfully understood as the toys of invisible genies. Experimenting with the Bini's magnetite block, she apprehended that a lodestone obeyed a principle of its own, caring not a whit for the commands of supposed spirits.

'The world is *alive*!' she told Ben. 'Pole to pole, this swirling planet's *alive*!'

They were wading through the shallows of Copernicus Cove, Ben clutching William to his breast, Jennet inspecting the fish weirs.

'Aye, I suppose that's the case,' he said.

'The Cartesians say 'tis dead, but 'tis *alive*!'

'A reasonable hypothesis, though wanting in precision.'

'The details will come in time. For the present we must irrigate the Earth with all the blood Descartes hath drained away, that a demon disproof might flower on its breast.'

Ben shifted William from his left arm to his right. He frowned. 'I believe I hear Waequashim of the Nimacook talking.'

'But for my years as a savage Indian,' she replied, nodding, 'I would ne'er have hit upon this proposition.'

'Alas, darling, you'll not convince Parliament to strike down the Witchcraft Act merely because the Nimacook religion argues against it.'

'In the Nimacook religion lies but half of my idea,' she retorted, netting a grouper. 'Oh, Ben, how do I make myself clear? 'Tis an insult to the tides to say they cannot turn without some genie's gesture, for in the tug of moon and sun lies explanation enough.'

His frown remained in place, though it now acquired a pensive cast. 'An insult to the tides — well spoken, Mrs Crompton.'

''Tis an aspersion on the lodestone to ascribe its power to spirits, for Mr Gilbert's magnetism is fully equal to the riddle.'

'And 'tis likewise a slur against the lightning to say that demons make it flash,' he noted, 'for in truth such strokes are Von Guericke sparks writ large.'

'To wit, we need no unseen agents, fair or foul, to explain the world. We need only the world itself — its ways and principles and manifest sensibleness.'

'This planet's a place of great abundance.'

'If not abundance then certainly sufficiency. Aye, Ben! The suffi-ciency of the world, *that's* the demon disproof lying hid in the bowels of the *Principia Mathematica*, whether Mr Newton knows it or not. When Aunt Isobel cried out from the pyre, screaming of Aristotle's elements, she meant only that I must look closely, so very closely, at everything my senses embrace. She was instructing me to scrutinize the universe, Nature with her winds and tides and lodestones and sunbeams — her air and water, earth and fire.'

He brushed his lips across their son's brow. 'You have wrought an ingenious conjecture, dearest. Though I fear your enemies will say that in making Creation sufficient, you have rendered the Creator super-fluous.'

'If I must murder God to save a Marblehead hag, then that is what I shall do.'

Ben massaged his unimpressive beard. 'Mrs Crompton, you shock me — a pleasurable sensation, I daresay, though the English legislature is unlikely to be similarly amused.'

'I frame no theologies, sir, merely an *argumentum grande*. So long as we make our purpose clear, we shan't be accused of impiety.'

The more they discussed her sufficiency hypothesis, the deeper their affection for it grew. If this idea took hold in Europe, the Continental Cartesians as well as the Cambridge Platonists would be obliged to see Nature anew. These philosophers would stop slandering the lightning, libelling the tides, traducing the comets, and depriving fiddler-crabs of their wondrous little minds. Inevitably Jennet recalled Newton's claim to be but a boy playing on the sea-shore, diverting himself occasionally with 'a smoother pebble or a prettier shell'. What a splendid event was a pretty shell, and an average shell too. A shell was a thing complete unto itself.

Two weeks later, as Jennet and Ben sat down to Sunday dinner at the royal palace – roasted candelabra nuts, acacia-thorn bread, boiled snails, agouti stew – she unfurled the new *argumentum grande* for Ebinose-Mbemba and his queen.

'According to many Christian thinkers, Satan contrives to control the spirits that make possible all actions and movements,' Jennet explained, dandling William on her knee. 'Nothing pleases the Dark One so much as to deploy the worst of these spirits, the demons, on behalf of his disciples.'

'In Europe and America,' Ben said, 'many magistrates believe 'tis their religious duty to exterminate such disciples – the witches – ere Satan's hordes spread wrack and ruin everywhere.'

Ebinose-Mbemba devoured a handful of snails. 'We Bini have our devils too, but none so strong as could cause such a calibre of havoc. I do not much like this Satan of yours.'

Now Ossalume spoke up. She was a stately woman, dark and comely as the sun-scorched Shulamite towards whom Solomon had directed his affections in the Song of Songs. 'Our mightiest sorcerer might command a million spirits, and still the world would come to its own defence, using the soul of every beast and tree to crush the maleficent host.'

'Ah, but here's the rub,' Jennet said. 'In recent days I have fallen upon an argument whereby the universe operates without benefit of any spirits whatsoever.'

'No spirits?' said Ebinose-Mbemba.

'No spirits.'

'Then what is it that makes one thing happen rather than another?' Ossalume asked.

'The sufficiency of the world,' Jennet said.

'The laws of Nature,' Ben added.

'The *laws* of Nature?' the Queen said. 'Nature's a kind of parliament then?'

'In a manner of speaking,' Ben replied.

'If Nature's a parliament, this makes God the monarch?' the King asked.

'You might look at it that way, aye,' Jennet said.

'I believe my Philadelphians confuse the divine order with the philosophy of John Locke,' Ebinose-Mbemba said.

'Mayhap,' Jennet said, taking a swallow of candelabra-root tea. But better the philosophy of John Locke, she thought, than the demonology of Exodus 22:18.

To maintain their sanity in the months that followed the birth of the *argumentum grande*, the castaways took to devising improbable and reckless schemes for getting themselves off the island. Initially Jennet imagined building a raft, though neither she nor Ben had the skills necessary to navigate it to Jamaica. Ben meanwhile envisioned a flying machine consisting of a lightweight acacia coach slung beneath an immense candelabra-leaf balloon that, when filled with hot air, would ascend into the clouds and carry its passengers to civilization. After ten days of experimentation he forsook the idea, all nine of his scale-model airships having remained stubbornly earthbound.

As the third summer of their Caribbean exile ended, an interval not appreciably different from autumn, winter, or spring in this unseasoned latitude, Jennet came to believe that the key to their deliverance lay with the pirates. When the buccaneers returned for treasure, she and Ben must be prepared to offer them a unique artifact, something so manifestly useful in freebooting that to obtain it they would gladly give the philosophers and their child safe passage.

'Beyond gold, silver, and pearls, what doth a pirate captain most desire?' she asked Ben.

'Mayhap a kind of artificial skin, that he might change his face and thereby elude capture,' he ventured.

'Alas, we lack the resources to produce such masks.'

'Or a superior variety of prosthesis, for I've heard that dismemberment's a common side-effect of freebooting.'

''Tis unlikely our local trees yield a better grade of wooden leg than ordinary.'

'Or an iron helix mounted on his ship's prow,' he said, 'poised to puncture any vessel dispatched by His Majesty's Navy.'

'Your cleverest suggestion so far, and the least practical.' She was about to abandon this entire line of speculation when a luminous notion flashed through her brain. 'Bless me, Ben – I see the answer!'

'Aye?'

'A buccaneer wants a machine that will tell him whether the galleon he's just spotted carries gold!'

Ben offered her a grin of approbation. 'Such a device would spare his crew many a needless skirmish.'

'And here's the pretty part. We can fashion this detector ourselves – by which I mean we can turn the Africans' magnetite into a facsimile, fraudulent at its heart but persuasive enough to hoodwink a pirate.'

'I'faith, Jenny, you've wrought a passing bold plan. 'Twill either take us to Port Royal or send us o'er the plank.'

Ebinose-Mbemba required but an instant to grasp the scheme, whereupon he willingly donated the necessary salvage from the *Sapodilla* – a door-nail, wine cork and clay bowl. Next he used his axe to cleave a fist-size piece from Orishanla, delivering it to Jennet. At the Philadelphians' insistence the Grand Oba instructed his subjects to dig an immense pit on the windward side of the island, bear Orishanla thither, and secure her deep within the earth, lest the mother rock cancel the coming hoax through her own Gilbertian force. Jennet now magnetized the door-nail, stroking it repeatedly across the chunk of Orishanla, after which Ben carried the ore fragment to the sea-chest and buried it beneath the gold.

It was time for the vital trial. Jennet filled the clay bowl with saltwater, pushed the nail through the wine cork, and set the contrivance afloat. The nail pivoted in its miniature lagoon and, true to Mr Gilbert's principle, pointed towards the chest.

'Most impressive,' the Grand Oba said.

'Most lawful,' Ben said.

'I can smell the stench of Port Royal already,' Jennet said.

As Dame Fortune arranged the matter, however, a full seven months would elapse before Jennet again dared to imagine any Jamaican fragrances on the wind. The pirates returned to Amakye on a balmy March afternoon. Peering through the Bini telescope, Jennet watched their two-masted shallop emerge from a fog bank along the western horizon – sails luffing, banners snapping – then drop anchor near Huygens Reef.

Not unexpectedly, the mainmast flew a flag depicting a skeleton holding in one bony hand a cutlass and in the other a glass of rum. Someone had screwed a plaque onto the upper larboard rail, rechristening the shallop *Judas Tree*. Whatever her original name, this once honest packet-ship had evidently been the scene of a mutiny, her officers now probably decomposing at the bottom of the Caribbean.

The Philadelphians bore William to the royal palace, entrusting him to the King and Queen, whereupon four imposing Bini males hoisted the great sea-chest onto their shoulders. As Jennet and Ben fell in behind them, the bearers brought the treasure to the edge of the jungle, secluding it beneath a heliconia tree. The Bini melted back into the forest. Jennet secured the doubloon-detector inside her hempen sack and availed herself of the telescope, raising it to her eye as six buccaneers in ratty shirts and patchwork breeches rowed away from the shallop.

'I cannot say whether they're entirely unacquainted with civilization,' she reported, slipping the telescope under her belt, 'but they dress far more crudely than my Nimacook kin.'

Whilst the buccaneers guided their longboat into the cove, Jennet and Ben pulled the sea-chest free of its hiding place and dragged it across the beach.

'Ahoy, there!' Jennet cried. 'We've found your gold for you!'

The pirate captain vaulted out of the boat and, cocking a silver pistol, marched towards the castaways. He was a hulking Moloch whose most conspicuous feature was his want of a lower jaw. In its place he wore a wooden prosthesis attached to his head by leather thongs and driven by steel springs fitted to wooden cogwheels.

'Unhand my treasure, ye stinking eels!' the captain ordered. The prosthesis reduced his powers of insolence considerably, turning *stinking eels* into *thtinking eelth*.

Moving synchronously, Jennet and Ben honoured their visitor with gracious bows. We look as harmless as a rabbit, she told herself.

'You are addressing Jennet Stearne Crompton, museum curator and natural philosopher,' she said. 'I was marooned here with my infant son after a hurricane tore the *Berkshire* to pieces.'

'This man was but an *infant* when your ship went down?' the captain said, nodding towards Ben. 'You've been here twenty years?'

'Not even four,' she said. 'The child of whom I speak, my dear and gentle William, sleeps peacefully in a nearby glade. Allow me to present my fellow survivor, Benjamin Franklin, a brilliant scholar and the most talented printer yet born in the American Colonies.'

'My friend exaggerates,' Ben said, forcing a smile.

A second pirate appeared, a short dusky man with no left ear and hair like electrified algae. The others remained by the longboat, presumably awaiting an order to come forward and massacre the castaways.

'I'Christ, this man and his mother must've found a copy o' Bonner's map!' the one-eared pirate declared.

'I'm not Ben Franklin's mother!' Jennet shouted. 'Could we all please agree on that without delay?'

'Your associate is understandably curious as to how we came upon the treasure,' Ben said to the captain. 'You will find the answer most enchanting.'

'Arms in the air!' the pirate leader snarled, brandishing his pistol.

Jennet and Ben did as instructed. Whilst the captain kept his weapon trained on them, the one-eared pirate opened the sea-chest — cautiously, by degrees, as if it might be rigged with a petard. The bright tropical sun caught the doubloons, so that the chest now seemed a great chalice filled with a golden nectar.

''Twould appear they've not plundered our booty,' the one-eared pirate said.

'We're castaways, not idiots,' Jennet replied.

'Be ye truly a printer, young Franklin?' the captain asked, thought-fully stroking his wooden chin.

'Aye,' Ben said.

'Ye print books?'

'Books, pamphlets, broadsheets.'

'Then ye'll be interested to know I recently finished me memoirs, *The Amazing Exploits of Hezekiah Creech, Scourge of the Spanish Main.*' The captain uncocked his pistol, slammed the lid closed, and turned towards the one-eared pirate. 'Mr Baldwin, row back to the *Judas* and fetch the manuscript from my desk. 'Tis under the parson's head.' In consequence of his synthetic jaw, *Judas* came out *Judith*.

'Aye.' The mate glowered and started away, obviously frustrated that Captain Creech had not ordered any butchery.

'What establishment employs ye?' the pirate leader asked Ben.

'Of late, Palmer's in London. Once back in Philadelphia, I shall seek a foreman's position with Samuel Keimer.'

'How's this for an arrangement? Your Mr Keimer gives me a thousand pounds sterling, and I allow him to publish me memoirs and keep a full fifth o' the profits.'

'That's not exactly how the man does business. In truth, *you* would pay *him*.'

'In a tart's twat I would! I've written the best adventure book since *Robinson Crusoe*!'

'If such be the case, then I'm sure some London house would relish the chance to print and sell it,' Ben said.

'Ye think so?' Captain Creech's simulated jaw permitted smiles of twice the normal span.

'Verily.'

'And now we would like to show you how we happened upon your gold,' Jennet said. 'The demonstration requires that we use our hands.'

Creech gave her a tepid nod. She dropped her arms, reached into the sack, and removed the clay bowl and its skewered cork.

'Amongst the items we rescued from the *Berkshire* was this, the most useful invention yet contrived by Mr Franklin and myself.' She sidled towards the rolling surf. ''Tis an Albertus Magnus Goldfinder. Behold.'

Stooping, she filled the bowl with seawater, then set the cork adrift. Instantly the door-nail swung towards the chest.

'It seeks the doubloons?' Creech asked, his factitious jaw descending.

'Like a compass hungering for the northern pole,' Ben said.

'Marry!' Despite himself, Creech giggled. 'A pirate with such a device need ne'er chase down a brig only to discover she's full o' naught but linen and tea!'

'Conduct us to Port Royal, and the trinket's yours to keep,' she said. 'The secret's in the needle. It appears an ordinary door-nail, but 'tis actually a sliver from the philosopher's stone Mr Franklin and I recently refined in our Philadelphia laboratory.'

'I've heard o' these philosopher's stones, but I ne'er knew a person that could make one,' the pirate said. 'Do they not turn lead into gold and grant immortality into the bargain?'

'Alas, the one we fashioned performs only the function you've observed,' she said.

Captain Creech announced that he would now determine exactly how much distance might separate the doubloons and the goldfinder before it ceased to work. For his first test, he carried the bowl fifty yards from the chest. The device performed splendidly, as Jennet expected it would. He increased the gap to a hundred yards. Again the finder did its job. Three hundred yards. Success.

Still sceptical, he fished the cork free of the bowl, then bid Jennet and Ben join him in ascending a towering limestone cliff to the south. The climb took the better part of an hour, but at last they all stood two hundred feet above the surf, Creech poised to perform his *experimentum crusis*. The treasure lay a half-mile away, a mere speck on the beach even when viewed through the Bini telescope.

Before Creech could refloat the cork, the mate appeared on the bluff clutching *The Amazing Exploits of Hezekiah Creech*. The pirate captain transferred the manuscript from Mr Baldwin to Ben, who proceeded to peruse the first page.

'Chapter Six tells how I lost me jaw to a Dutch cannonball,' Creech said.

'A diverting anecdote, I'm sure,' Ben replied. He passed the manuscript to Jennet. 'An auspicious beginning, Mrs Crompton, would you not agree?'

BY WAYE OF PROLAWG. Heerin the Reeder will fynde narrat'd the most fantasticul Advenchures yet written down by any mortul Hande. Those book Buyers who enjoye to hear Tales of Daring by the Whorled's Buccaneers shan't be disappoint'd by these Payges, but furst I must recounte something of my Mother's Familee, my uncommun Childehood, and my earlyest Years at Sea.

'I'm favourably impressed,' she said.

'Be truthful now,' Creech warned.

'I note certain orthographic lapses.'

'I suspected as much. Any other defects?'

'Mayhap a whit less bombast would please the London publishers,' Jennet answered.

'Bombast's out o' favour?' Creech asked.

'In recent seasons, aye.'

Turning away from the Philadelphians, the captain offered Baldwin a prolix discourse on Albertus Magnus Goldfinders, then cast the cork adrift within the bowl. For a tense and protracted interval the door-nail pointed out to sea, but then Mr Gilbert's principle joined forces with the inverse-square law, and the dial swung landward and fixed on the doubloons.

'I'Christ, 'twill save us many a fruitless pursuit!' exclaimed Baldwin.

'Take us to Port Royal,' Ben said, 'and we shall afterward make you a present of this machine.'

'I saved the best news for last.' Jennet set Creech's dreadful manuscript on the ground, securing it beneath the telescope. 'Mr Franklin and I have forsworn any further such inventiveness. Of all the buccaneers cruising the Spanish Main, you gentlemen alone will possess a doubloon-detector!'

'Mrs Crompton and Mr Franklin are clearly two of the world's great brains,' Creech said to Baldwin. 'When you slit their throats, do it quickly, so as to minimize their discomfort.'

A tremor passed through Jennet's frame, vibrating every bone. 'Faugh!'

'My Lord Captain, you cannot mean what you say!' Ben wailed.

In Jennet's opinion Creech had meant every syllable – and so she did what the situation required: she reached towards the clay bowl, disassembled the compass, and hurled the door-nail over the cliff. Briefly the little spike sailed on the wind, then fell into the surf.

'Swine-swiver!' Baldwin cried, raising his cutlass.

''Sbones, Jennet!' Ben wailed.

'How dare ye thwart me?' Creech screamed, his jaw flapping like a tavern sign in a hurricane.

'Surely a man so intelligent as yourself can fathom my motives,' she said to the pirate captain. 'You must now bear Ben and me and little William to Philadelphia, that we might extract a *second* detector from our philosopher's stone.'

'Shall I run 'em through?' Baldwin inquired.

Creech said nothing. He rubbed his timber chin. A cloud drifted past the sun, casting a shadow on his already gloomy face.

'What manner o' man is the Pennsylvania Governor?' he asked Ben. 'Will he welcome my crew graciously? Like all buccaneers, we're known to give local economies considerable stimulation, for we buy our rum and sundries exclusively with silver and gold. What's the man like?'

'William Keith is innately indolent, bereft of scruples, and prepared to sell his own mother for political gain,' Ben said.

'Aye, but doth he have any flaws?' Creech asked.

'None whatsoever. Best of all, he hath been like a father to me. 'Twas Sir William sponsored my recent trip to England. Upon our arrival in Philadelphia, I shall see to it that he grants you freedom from harassment.'

Creech retrieved his manuscript and clutched it to his chest. For two full minutes he paced back and forth on the cliff, lost in thought, an experience to which he was evidently unaccustomed.

'The Governor's in sooth your friend?' he said at last.

'We're thick as thieves,' Ben replied. '*Honourable* thieves, I mean.'

'Then the three of ye may board the *Judas Tree* at dawn,' Creech said, 'for we sail on the morning tide.'

With Nimacook stealth and vulpine subtlety, Jennet and Ben made their way through the nocturnal forest, speaking not a word and snapping not a twig, until at last they reached the village gates. As arranged, Ebinose-Mbemba and his wife were waiting for them, Ossalume cradling the sleeping William whilst gently stroking his brow. It occurred to Jennet that her son was having far too eventful an infancy. Once back in Philadelphia, she must somehow arrange for his life to remain free of maroonings, buccaneers, and Utopias for runaway slaves.

Despite the considerable distance separating Ewuare from the pirate shallop, Ebinose-Mbemba feared that even the quietest colloquy might betray their whereabouts, so he proceeded to guide the party along a jungle trail painted in pale lunar hues. In time they reached an outcropping of limestone sheltering a convivial pavilion framed in acacia wood and roofed by heliconia fronds.

'This is where I do my thinking,' Ebinose-Mbemba explained. ''Tis also quite suitable for conversation. Speak to me of the buccaneers.'

Jennet and Ben began chattering in tandem, words flying from their mouths at peregrine velocities, so that their African listeners were oft-times obliged to ask for reiterations, but eventually the whole story came out. The goldfinder ploy had worked. Creech had been fooled. Ewuare was safe for the nonce.

'Even if I could talk as quickly as you,' Ossalume told the Philadelphians, 'I would need until noon to voice all the gratitude in my heart.'

'You have lifted a great cloud from our lives,' Ebinose-Mbemba added. 'And yet one tittle of mist remains, and I would have us discuss it before we part company.'

'If I can burn away the last of the vapour, I shall,' Ben said, receiving William from Ossalume.

'I speak of Creech's map,' the King said. ''Twould be desirable to destroy it, lest it one day lead a slave-catcher to Ewuare.'

'Destroy the map?' Ben said. 'I'faith, Your Majesty, as we continue to gain the pirates' trust, I shall use every means short of martyrdom to bring about that result.'

'Mr Franklin, you are a saint,' Ossalume said.

'Oh, he's hardly that,' Jennet said, 'but he does own a passing impressive perfection-matrix.'

With his free arm Ben gestured broadly, a flourish encompassing the entire pavilion. 'And what does the Grand Oba think about when he enters his sanctuary of late?'

'Carnal comforts,' Ebinose-Mbemba replied, flashing his wife a moonlit smile. 'Also Hobbes, More and Locke.' He sighed prolifically. 'Every day our Bini grow more difficult to govern.'

Elaborating, the King explained that since his last political con-versation with Ben, nearly a year ago, the tribal and temperamental differences amongst the ex-slaves had fractured the community into three sub-villages, each with its own vision of the future. The inhabitants of North Ewuare, the Orishanlists, believed that the general welfare lay in maximum obscurity, and hence they urged a combination of isolationism and reproductive restraint. The people of East Ewuare, by contrast, insisted that fertility control was precisely the policy their former white masters would have wanted them to pursue, and therefore these Uhranwists – the name derived from the Bini kick-the-dodecahedron game – advocated exploratory voyages in quest of hospitable islands to which their descendants might migrate. Even more radical were the South Ewuareans, the Barabbasians, who hoped to make Amakye-Isle the birthplace of a mighty African army that would one day sweep through the New World's rice plantations, tobacco farms and cane fields, breaking chains and smashing shackles.

'I'Christ, how e'er will you reconcile these philosophies?' said Ben.

'Ossalume and I have drafted a constitution,' Ebinose-Mbemba said. 'The parliamentary component of our government will comprise two separate assemblies.' He unfurled his left index finger. 'A lofty upper house consisting of two elected agents per sub-village.' He extended his right index finger. 'And a less exalted lower house in which each sub-village enjoys representation proportional to its size.'

'Tell us your opinion of this scheme,' Ossalume said.

'A cumbersome compromise,' Ben said.

'Quite so,' Ebinose-Mbemba said.

'As unwieldy as my ill-starred Franklin Typesetter,' Ben said.

'I don't doubt it.'

'But preferable to any alternative I can imagine.'

'Indeed.'

At the first intimation of dawn, Jennet, Ben and the Africans once again gave themselves to silence. Ebinose-Mbemba and Ossalume escorted the Philadelphians and their slumbering child back to the village gates, where the Grand Oba, much to everyone's surprise, broke his own rule and spoke.

'Fare thee well, Ben Franklin,' he whispered. 'Fare thee well, Mrs Crompton.'

'This constitutional republic of yours – 'tis a most noble experiment,' Jennet murmured.

'The whole business may end in chaos and carnage,' Ebinose-Mbemba said. 'But this I swear. 'Twill be an entirely illegal chaos and a most unlawful carnage. I shall allow no sanctified slaughter on Amakye-Isle.'

Firming his grip on little William, Ben lowered his head in a gesture of respect. Ebinose-Mbemba and Ossalume deserved such deference, Jennet concluded, for by their own account they were arranging to put themselves out of business, which was not how royalty normally behaved. And so it was that, before joining Ben on his walk back to the beach, she too bowed before the monarchs, humbled by their humility, awed by their modesty, and speculating that they prefigured the brave and canny meek who would one day inherit the earth.

CHAPTER THE TENTH

At Great Risk to Her Person Our
Heroine Inaugurates a Scheme to Rid the World
of Several Unnecessary Delusions

Abetted by favourable winds and congenial currents, the *Judas Tree*'s northward voyage should have taken a mere eleven days, but in fact it lasted twice that long, for Hezekiah Creech insisted on attacking and looting every merchant ship that blew his way. This violent agenda proved unremunerative. Of the seven carracks and brigs he boarded that month, only one carried a treasure chest, and it contained silks and spices, not doubloons. If there were indeed such a thing as an Albertus Magnus Goldfinder, Jennet mused, this sorry pirate could certainly have done with one.

According to their original plan, which she regarded as both elegant and practical, when the *Judas Tree* reached port Ben would arrange for the pirates to deliver her and William to the Chestnut Street townhouse. Once confident that his family was safe, Ben would lead Creech and Baldwin to his Market Street garret, chip a splinter from his 'philosopher's stone' (his most potent specimen of magnetite), run the fragment through a cork, and bid Baldwin bear the new doubloon-detector back to the *Judas Tree* for testing. Whilst the mate was confirming the device's authenticity, Ben would present Creech to Sir William Keith and, after graciously forgiving Keith his failure to provide the letters of credit, gleefully reveal that a band of spendthrift pirates stood ready to disperse their brightest coins amongst the local merchants, at which juncture Keith was certain to promise Creech that his buccaneers would find Philadelphia to be a pirate-friendly city.

By the time the *Judas Tree* dropped anchor, however, Ben had become enamoured of a more elaborate scheme, intended not only to rescue his loved ones but to bring Creech and his band to justice, though Jennet did not learn of this egregious emendation until it was a *fait accompli*. The new plot hinged on Ben's entirely accurate assumption that the pirate captain would not imagine his prisoners to be swimmers. (Monsieur Thévenot's art was largely unknown amongst seafarers, who held that a shipwreck ought always to entail a simple death by drowning, never the more agonizing alternatives of terminal thirst, lethal exposure or carnivorous fish.) Shortly after midnight, Ben slipped furtively from his berth. He laced his sturdy torso into his agouti-skin suit, climbed down the anchor chain, swam a mile to Market Street Wharf, and dashed a dozen blocks west, shivering and dripping, to the largest mansion in Broad Street. Upon entering the foyer, he was informed by the servants that William Keith no longer occupied the Governor's post, but Ben did not allow this development to diminish his resolve. After rousing Keith's successor, a swaggering British major named Patrick Gordon, Ben convinced the new Governor to ignore his visitor's wild beard and strange wet garment, focusing instead on the propitious fact that a pirate shallop lay in the harbour. If Major Gordon acted quickly, he could capture the most abominable buccaneer ever to terrorize the Spanish Main.

Within the hour a raiding party of Redcoat soldiers was bearing down on the *Judas Tree*, one boatload commanded by Ben, another by Major Gordon, the third by Captain Wilcox of the Philadelphia garrison. They circled the shallop and came at her from the east, thereby acquiring the advantage of surprise. And so it was that, slightly after dawn, Jennet awoke to a cacophony of clanging swords, discharging pistols, cracking bones, falling bodies, screams, shrieks, cries, oaths and the scything sound of musket-balls burrowing into wood and flesh. She took William in her arms, pressing his face to her bosom that he might be spared the sight of the skirmish. As the boy wept tears of fright and confusion, she peered through her cabin window and beheld a tumult nigh as terrible as the Indian attack on Haverhill. This time, however, the chaos culminated not in a loss of freedom for Jennet but in its very opposite – her safe delivery, together with Ben and William, onto Market Street Wharf in a longboat rowed by two lobsterback corporals.

'You addlebrained cavalier!' she seethed as Ben clambered onto the pier. 'You ninny-pated knave! 'Tis a miracle we weren't killed!'

'You flatter me, Mrs Crompton, for I know naught of working miracles,' Ben said, clutching Hezekiah Creech's map to his breast. At the height of the hurly-burly he'd managed to appropriate the document, in accordance with his commission from Ebinose-Mbemba. 'Howbeit, I did calculate, quite correctly, that our fifty soldiers would easily o'erpower the sixteen buccaneers.'

'Mark me, sir – you will ne'er again put our child in the vicinity of a pirate battle!'

He folded the map neatly and slipped it into his coat. 'All's well that ends well.'

'But it *didn't* end well, for today you have proved yourself a reckless rogue!' she cried. 'You should take your Moderation grid and blacken every box! *Nummusquantum!*'

In the days immediately following the skirmish, *The American Weekly Mercury* devoted many acres of ink to the subject of freebooting in Philadelphia, with a particular emphasis on Governor Gordon's foray against the *Judas Tree* and his subsequent delivery of Hezekiah Creech's gold to the Crown. The most gripping such story related the fate of Creech himself. By the *Mercury's* account, as the soldiers were leading the buccaneer and his fellow blackguards to Walnut Street Prison, Captain Wilcox indulged in an especially abusive variety of literary criticism, smearing Creech's autobiography with cow dung. Somehow the outraged author broke free of his captors and wrenched the manuscript from Wilcox's grasp. A startled corporal, misreading the situation, shot Creech betwixt the eyes.

They buried the pirate captain in an unmarked grave, on unhallowed ground, along with his orthographically impaired memoir.

Was there a moral to be gleaned from Creech's demise? Jennet wasn't sure. She knew only that, against conventional expectations, the pirate now belonged to that tiny minority of human beings who had died in defence of a book.

While thinking fondly of Creech came naturally to her these days, thinking well of Ben did not. 'To err is human, to forgive divine,' Alexander Pope had declared in his *Essay on Criticism* – two interconnected principles towards which Jennet felt considerable sympathy.

If only Ben weren't so emphatically human, and she so far from divine. After much conscientious effort, she managed to stop berating him whenever the subject of the *Judas Tree* skirmish arose, though other points of disputation emerged to fill the void. They quarrelled about the efficacy of the new smallpox inoculations (Jennet favouring the procedure, Ben urging caution), about the value of lightning-rods (she judging them unproven, he arguing for their immediate and ubiquitous deployment), about the nature of God (she regarding the Almighty as an Aristotelian Prime Mover without knowable attributes, he cleaving to the infinitely clever Deist Clockmaker), and about the need for greater political unification amongst the Colonies (she opposing the notion, largely because he supported it). They even bickered about whose dwelling to make their permanent abode. Whereas he wanted them to occupy his Market Street lodgings, she thought they should live in her townhouse, which was cleaner, roomier and more private. A month after their return to Philadelphia they were still essentially living in both places at the same time, a circumstance that felt to Jennet like living in neither place at any time.

'You must try to understand that I feel *comfortable* in my garret,' Ben said. 'I'm a wight who must be hemmed by his philosophic instruments.'

'Then we need but pack up those instruments and carry them two blocks south,' she said.

'They might break.'

'Then we shall cushion them in straw, as we did Barnaby's monsters,' she said.

'A procedure fraught with risks,' he said.

'I'Christ, Ben, why is it we cannot breach a topic — which roof to call our own, whether it should have a lightning-rod — without squabbling?'

After pondering the mystery for a fortnight, she fell upon a simple but sobering solution. In their minds' most subterranean tiers, they wished to be free of one another. Whether he knew it or not, Ben was suffocating. No doubt his overt desire to be 'hemmed by his philosophic instruments' was real, but it paled beside his unspoken desire *not* to be hemmed by an infant he'd never meant to father and a woman more than twice his age — a woman who might soon become incapable of negotiating a soup-spoon or chamber-pot without his assistance. But Jennet, too, was feeling oppressed, labouring under an onus she could not abide, the burden of being a prospective burden.

When she first told Ben that they'd each become a millstone about the other's neck, he declared that his love for her was ripe and real as a field of Nimacook maize, and he would never assent to a rupture such as she proposed. The second time she offered this diagnosis, he sobbed like a child, so profoundly did the thought of losing her distress him. The third time she spoke to him of millstones, he found merit in the metaphor and consequently broke her heart.

'Alas, I must assent to your argument,' he said, heaving a sigh. 'For years our lives were of necessity intertwined, braided like the threads of a Persian carpet, but now the strands must come unravelled.'

'Ne'er to be rewoven into their former splendour,' she said, her throat swelling like a sprained ankle.

They were browsing through the bins in Gerencer's, searching without success for Newton's promised treatise on invisible particles. Either the tome didn't exist, or it hadn't yet crossed the Atlantic. A few yards away William played with the proprietor's cat, swinging a bit of kite-string through the air, thereby prompting the animal to walk on its hind legs.

'Oh, Jenny, why must we be so *reasonable* in this matter?' Ben said. 'Prithee, talk some nonsense into my head.'

'Nay, dear Ben, I shan't,' she said, drying her eyes with her sleeve.

'I implore you.'

'The time hath clearly come for us to relinquish one another. 'Twould be a generous gesture on both our parts.'

'Not generous — merely practical,' he rasped. 'We must sever our connection whilst we own the strength to do so.'

From the nearest bin she retrieved a dusty quarto of *Romeo and Juliet*. 'Come, my gallant, let us take hold of Shakespeare's great love-tragedy and pledge ourselves to an eternal separation.' She pressed Ben's right palm against the book, then set her own right hand on top. 'I do solemnly swear to give the world its due measure and deserved dose of Benjamin Franklin . . . say it, sir.'

'I do solemnly swear to give the world its due measure and deserved dose of Benjamin Franklin . . .'

'. . . who hath before him gardens to plant, experiments to perform, sages to impress, monarchs to harry and dragons to slay . . .'

'. . . who hath before him gardens to plant, experiments to perform, sages to impress, monarchs to harry and dragons to slay . . .'

'. . . in the name of all I hold sacred and dear.'

Haltingly he echoed her words, then moaned quietly, turned away, and slunk off to sport with William and the bipedal cat.

The new arrangement went into effect the next day: two individual lives, two separate domiciles, with little William inhabiting his mother's townhouse all through the week but visiting his father's garret on Saturdays and Sundays. Occasionally she and Ben joined in connubial embrace, but these episodes became less frequent with each passing month. Gradually Jennet's sobs grew softer, her tears fewer, her dreams longer. She realized that, for the first time since her journey to Trinity College in quest of Newton, she'd done something unequivocally noble, and the novelty of it saw her through many a miserable night.

The sweltering summer of 1728 found both philosophers struggling to avoid bankruptcy, the remainder of Jennet's fortune having gone down with the *Berkshire*. By autumn their prospects had brightened. Bitter over Ben's secret alliance with the former Pennsylvania Governor, Samuel Keimer had at first rebuffed him, but then a formidable commission came Keimer's way – printing paper currency for New Jersey – and he realized that he would meet the deadline only by availing himself of Ben's quick mind, unflagging industry and London training. Jennet, meanwhile, designated her front parlour a classroom and advertised herself as a tutor, and soon several of the city's wealthiest families were entrusting her with their children's minds. She taught them what she'd learned from Aunt Isobel – penmanship, astronomy, geometry, optics, Latin – though rarely with the forbearance that the mistress of Mirringate Hall had so consistently displayed. Of her nine pupils only one evinced uncommon intelligence, Lucy Rooke, a Quaker girl who could draw the micrographic world, especially gnats, mites and pond-water animalcules, as enthrallingly as Dunstan had rendered the horse-head promontory.

Her teaching efforts consumed half her day, William the other half, and yet she found time to collaborate with Ben on the great work, which she'd decided to call *The Sufficiency of the World: A Treatise of How Witchcraft Is an Impossible Crime*. Although she still believed devoutly in her demon disproof, she took little pleasure in its composition, and Ben was likewise uninspired. Despite the book's provocative thesis and pithy prose, they could not imagine the average Parliamentarian sitting down and poring over every page. Most likely the Lords and their counterparts in the Commons would pawn the treatise off on the Royal Society, where it would devolve not to the estimable Dr Halley – he was seventy-four, after all, and doubtless defensive of his time – but to some bright young demonologist all eager to find its faults and savage its lapses. And yet Jennet and Ben persisted in their labours, straight through Christmas and well into the new year, goaded by *Bible Commonwealth* reports that Dunstan and his band were 'campaigning against the Wampanoag and Narragansett Pagans that infest our Massachusetts Coast'.

Late in June there arrived at Keimer's shop a bundle containing over a hundred back issues of *The London Journal*, some as old as two years. Prominent amongst the headlines for the third of April 1727 was the news that Sir Isaac Newton – Knight of the Realm, Master of the Mint, President of the Royal Society – had died thirteen days earlier in Kensington, subsequently receiving an elaborate entombment ceremony at Westminster-Abbey. A dozen eulogies filled the pages, including epitaphs by Dr Halley, Dr Pemberton and the celebrated French *philosophe*, Jean François-Marie Arouet de Voltaire. Mr Pope honoured the late geometer with one of those impeccable couplets Jennet found so annoying: 'Nature and Nature's Laws lay hid in Night. God said, "Let Newton be!" and All was Light.'

Newton's passing instilled mixed emotions in Jennet. As a disciple of Reason and the inventor of the sufficiency hypothesis, she mourned the loss of Creation's keenest intellect, but she was happy to be forever rid of any obligation to return to England, solicit the madman once again, and beg that he go before Parliament with his endorsement of her demon disproof.

Her final flurry of effort on the manuscript had less the effect of elaborating her argument than of multiplying her grievances against

Ben. Contrary to the pledge he'd once made – 'Franklin and Crompton, united against the Conjuring Statute!' – his principal goal these days was not to defeat the witchfinders but to transform himself into America's most celebrated printer. Already he had much to show for his ambition: a rapid, conspicuous and well-deserved rise that was the mirror opposite of Samuel Keimer's rapid, conspicuous and well-deserved slide into ruin. Although the New-Jersey currency project had netted Keimer a handsome profit, he'd managed to squander it in a matter of weeks. For a time he revived his fortunes by publishing a weekly newspaper, *The Pennsylvania Gazette*, but ultimately this venture failed too, and when Ben proposed to purchase both the paper and its parent shop for three hundred pounds sterling, the broke and broken Keimer readily assented. Ben borrowed the specified sum from the father of his high-born friend Hugh Meredith, whereupon Keimer absconded to Barbados, the better to avoid his legions of creditors.

Beyond his obsession with the *Gazette* Ben had also grown pre-occupied with the Junto, a self-improvement and mutual aid society he'd formed with a dozen like-minded young men. Although Jennet scorned the Junto for its deleterious effect on *The Sufficiency of the World*, she decided that its advent was not entirely catastrophic, as the membership happened to include John Tux, née Naanantux, a chestnut-brown Indian whose pensive countenance reminded her of Okommaka in his prime. Astonishingly, John Tux was a Nimacook. More amazing yet, he hailed from her own adoptive clan, the Kokokehom.

On first meeting John Tux, Jennet was hard pressed to persuade him that, her abduction notwithstanding, she did not abjure her savage past. Indeed, but for her devotion to the *argumentum grande*, she might yet be living in the woods, wearing feathers and skins. Convinced at last that she bore him no malice, John Tux proceeded to tell his story, delighted to be once again conversing in the Algonquin tongue.

Not surprisingly, the narrative whereby Naanantux had come to Philadelphia was only slightly less brocaded and bizarre than the adventures that had landed Jennet in the same metropolis. When he was but nine, a *skishauonck* epidemic had claimed both his parents. The orphan fell under the patronage and persuasion of the latest missionary to have insinuated himself into the village, Pierre Dumond, S.J.

Observing in the bereft Naanantux a mind of singular intelligence, Father Dumond convinced him to abandon his tribe, abbreviate his name, embrace Roman Catholicism and join the priest in bringing the One True Religion to receptive Indians everywhere. For the better part of five years, Father Dumond and John Tux had roamed the Algonquin lands south of the Merrimack and west of the Shawsheen, baptizing not only Nimacooks but also Pocassets, Sakonetts, Nipmucks, Abenakis and Wampanoags, a period during which the Jesuit instructed his young charge so ably in the languages of antiquity that before long he could negotiate Saint Thomas Aquinas in the original Latin.

John Tux's career as a latter-day Saint Paul ended abruptly when an Abenaki sagamore took violent exception to Father Dumond's project, subsequently dashing out the priest's brains with a hatchet and threatening to treat John Tux in the same fashion if he failed to mend his Papist ways. Having acquired from his late sponsor a morbid fear of the fiery damnation that awaited all who forsook Holy Mother Church, John Tux lost no time fleeing the Abenakis and heading for Boston. Although he reached the city without mishap, he soon found himself destitute, for while his erudition made him competent to tutor the children of Puritan affluence, the parents of those same children could abide neither his Nimacook blood nor his Catholic faith. Fortunately rumours of the Philadelphia ethos eventually reached his ears, compelling tales of quaking Christians who placed a premium on toleration, and so he made his way south to the City of Brotherly Love. Falling in with Ben and the Junto, he quickly ascended to the position of assistant foreman at Franklin and Meredith's Printing House, even as he shed his Catholicism under the influence of his associates' rational and capacious Deism.

In recent years John Tux had elected to reforge his bond with the Kokokehom, regularly exchanging letters with his grandmother, Quannamoo, sister to the late Miacoomes and now the clan's chief sagamore. According to Quannamoo, hard times had befallen the tribe. Pushed ever westward by the dreams and deceptions of the European settlers, the Nimacooks had most recently established their plantations in the Hoosic River valley. Of the original six clans, only three remained, the Kokokehom, the Moaskug and the Wautuckque.

Evidently there was nothing in Quannamoo's letters about the medicine-woman, Hassane, about Jennet's adoptive cousin, Pussough, or about Kapaog, the one to whom she'd given her milk after the smallpox took his birth-mother. And yet, felicitously enough, Quannamoo occasionally mentioned the Indian of whose fortunes Jennet was most anxious to learn, her first husband, Okommaka. By Quannamoo's report, Okommaka's rage against the white race had lately increased to the point of mania. So far he had failed to rally a war party to his side, but the squaw-sagamore feared that one day soon Okommaka would lead a raid on an English town, an action certain to spark disastrous retaliation.

'In your next letter to your grandmother,' Jennet told John Tux, 'I should like you to convey a sentiment from a footloose plantation maid.'

'*Cowaunckamish.*' I am at your service.

'The message is this. "Pray tell Okommaka that his Waequashim remembers him with great fondness, and she hopes that he will not be so foolish as to make war on the English settlers."'

'In all candour, I doubt that your words will succeed in cooling Okommaka's ire,' John Tux replied. 'And yet I shall happily relay your words. 'Tis the least I owe to one who battles the pricking persecutors of my kind.'

By the end of the year it had become woefully clear to Jennet that *The Sufficiency of the World* was now her responsibility alone. When she chastised Ben for his unannounced decampment, he replied that the final draft would 'boast a greater aesthetic integrity if written solely in your unique and piquant style'.

'Then methinks 'twould also boast a greater aesthetic integrity if your name appeared nowhere on the cover-page,' she said.

'As you wish,' he replied. 'The thesis sprang full-blown from your brow, the words flowed largely from your quill. I can make no claim upon this tome.'

Although Jennet deeply resented Ben's withdrawal from the *argumentum grande*, she could not quarrel with his offer to publish it for free. He could well afford such philanthropy now. Under his guidance, Franklin and Meredith's Printing-House was flourishing, the *Gazette* having transmuted into a daily newspaper boasting hundreds of subscribers in

Pennsylvania, Delaware and New-Jersey, plus several score in Mother England. As with her earlier *A Treatise of How the Four Aristotelian Elements May Serve to Convince There Are No Elementals*, Jennet decided that she would need three hundred copies, though she still could not imagine by what breed of cunning or species of deceit she might induce a Parliamentarian to read one.

On the fifteenth day in April 1730, the first proof of the first signature emerged from Ben's new Blaeu press. Jennet scanned the cover-page, her spirit revelling in its stately appearance even as her eye searched for typographical errors.

THE SUFFICIENCY
OF THE WORLD:
a Treatise of How
WITCHCRAFT IS AN
IMPOSSIBLE CRIME
as Demonstrat'd by
SIR ISAAC NEWTON'S
MATHEMATICKAL LAWS OF NATURE
Including
EXPERIMENTS
Such as the Curious Reader May Himself Perform,
This Being the Personal Investigation
of the Author,
J. S. CROMPTON,
Natural Philosopher

'Have I o'erreached myself, using Newton's name in this way?' she asked Ben. 'Does my action smack of desperation?'

'Aye,' he said with a soft groan. 'But better desperation in the service of Reason,' he quickly added, 'than Reason in the service of desperation.'

He proceeded to expound upon this newly minted maxim, but she failed to hear him, for her brain was now ablaze with an idea, the sort of momentous stratagem she normally conceived only whilst swimming in the Schuylkill or walking the shores of Amakye-Isle.

'''Steeth, I see it!' she shouted, pulse racing. 'I see how we'll get both Lords and Commons to heed my book!'

'How, friend? Tell me.'

''Tis a devilish clever plot.'

'Out with it!'

'We shall arrange for a witch-trial, with my damnable brother at its core. Not one of those travesties he enacts along the frontier, but a full and public test of the demon hypothesis, conducted right here in Philadelphia.' Her heart had not ascended to such an altitude since her invention of the Albertus Magnus Goldfinder. 'Now, Ben, listen to the nexus of my scheme. Every day of the trial, you will report on it in the *Gazette*, narrating each twist and turn in a manner calculated to enthral your London subscribers. After the jurymen issue their verdict, each Parliamentarian will want to know how I convinced them I was innocent, and he will forthwith consult his *Sufficiency of the World*.'

'I must have a plug of beeswax in my ear, Mrs Crompton, for I heard you say 'twould be *you* in the dock.'

'Of course 'twill be me, playing the part of an enchantress.'

'You upbraid me for crossing swords with Hezekiah Creech, and now you wish to cut cards with the Devil himself?'

'Quite so, sir, but aside from the dangers involved, have I not wrought a most wondrous plan?'

Lifting the signature from her grasp, he strode into the drying-room. She followed directly behind, inhaling the pungent and authoritative fragrance of printer's ink.

'Wondrous?' he wailed. '*Wondrous?* 'Steeth, 'tis wondrous insane and naught else. Nay, Jenny, I shan't let you so imperil yourself.'

'I must do this, sir.'

'Will you not understand that I cherish your life even more than mine own?'

'And will *you* not understand that ne'er a month goes by without Dunstan and his demented bride killing some blameless New-England savage? 'Tis my duty to thwart them. My soul demands it.'

For five silent minutes Ben occupied himself in removing a dozen dry signatures from the line — the opening pages of a grammar-school primer — thus making room for *The Sufficiency of the World*.

'Your soul,' he echoed.

'My soul.'

Sighing and snorting, he clipped the first signature of Jennet's treatise to a string. 'Very well, darling. Put on your darkest dress, mount your swiftest besom, and summon a thousand serpents to your door. But take care lest your ruse carry you straight to the gallows. I'll not have you gaining your soul and losing the world – there is no bargain in that.'

As Jennet drew her plans against the Massachusetts cleansers, she inevitably thought of the innumerable animal traps she and Ben had laid during their marooning. More than once she imagined treating Abigail Stearne like a snared agouti, peeling away her hide, boiling the flesh from her bones. Each time the reverie surged up in Jennet's mind, she recoiled from its violence, even as she revelled in its crude justice. 'Keep your object always in view, dear philosopher,' she told herself. ''Tis not to extinguish Abigail's person but rather to eradicate her profession.'

Although the New-England prickers were craftier than any agouti, Jennet's plot was more cunning than any snare. The opening gambit had her shipping thirty copies of *The Sufficiency of the World* to King George's councillors and the remaining two hundred and seventy to prominent Parliamentarians. (The idea of handing out books *gratis* so unnerved Ben that he immediately printed another three hundred, arranging for both Mr Efram and Mr Gerencer to sell them at eight shillings per copy.) Her next move was to turn herself into another person. Her new name, Rebecca Webster, took but a moment to contrive: 'Rebecca' to honour the unfortunate Rebecca Nurse of Salem-Village, 'Webster' to salute John Webster and his bravely sceptical though philosophically impoverished *Displaying of Supposed Witchcraft*. For a base of operations she selected Manayunk to the north-west, a farming community situated on the fertile wedge betwixt the Schuylkill River and the Wissahickon Creek.

Specialists in raising flax, a crop whose proper cultivation they'd learned from the inhabitants of nearby German-Town, the yeoman planters of Manayunk were an unsophisticated bunch, peasants by another name, which made them ideal for Jennet's purposes. As she gauged the character of the village, if a newly arrived widow exhibited coarse manners, asked rude favours, grew strange flowers, and appeared to worship heathen gods, it would not be long ere her neighbours cried her out.

After a full week's search she found an ideal venue in which to enact the great ruse, a decrepit and deserted poultry farm at the intersection of Hermit Road and Sumac Lane. The barn had already become a haven for stray cats, easily cast in the role of animal familiar. Even more felicitous was the dark loamy soil adjacent to the house, a tract well suited to the growing of monk's hood, thorn-apple, mandrake, henbane and other plants certain of arousing local suspicion.

'You have found a tenant,' she informed the farm's owner, a retired Welsh sea-captain rumoured to have made and lost several fortunes importing rum from Barbados.

Obviously William must now live with Ben, lest he awaken one morning to witness his mother being carted off to gaol. At first Jennet had no idea how she might prepare William for her imminent disappearance, but then John Tux reminded her of *pittuckish*, the duty of every wayward Nimacook to visit his clan at regular four-year intervals, an obligation that soon he himself would be fulfilling. Because the boy had always regarded Jennet's Indian past with fascination and delight, she decided to tell him that the time was nigh for her to practice *pittuckish*: betwixt now and early spring she would be away in Massachusetts, living with the Nimacooks, harvesting maize and weaving sleeping mats. So plausible did this narrative sound when she presented it to William, she did not hesitate to circulate the same falsehood amongst the families of her nine pupils. 'Such a rare privilege it hath been to teach your progeny,' she told each mother, even those who'd whelped porridgeheads, 'but now my blood beckons and my heritage calls.'

Naturally the idea of their child inhabiting Ben's unhealthy garret troubled Jennet, and so she experienced a great relief upon learning that the resident landlord, Thomas Godfrey, had resolved to move his family to New-Jersey and rent the entire dwelling to Ben. Rather less soothing to Jennet was the news that a certain Miss Deborah Read, whose widowed mother ran a boarding-house in Spruce Street, would be living at the Market Street mansion as well. While Jennet was prepared in spirit for this event — why had she surrendered Ben if not to let him find the woman who would share his dotage? — the fact of it made her miserable. No doubt Miss Read was a worthy soul, but she had probably never determined a parabolic orbit or launched a war against irrationality.

Jennet signed the lease on a Friday afternoon, moved into the farm the following Monday, and set about presenting herself to the people of Manayunk as the village's most sinister eccentric. She had barely embarked on this masquerade when she realized that Rebecca Webster's paganism must occupy a middle ground: the widow could enact uncanny rites, but she ought never to engage in manifest Devil-worship, lest the jury feel bound to convict her whether they subscribed to the demon hypothesis or not. And so it was that, walking home each evening from their fields and shops, Mrs Webster's neighbours witnessed her performing wild Dionysian dances around a high cairn. They observed her flying kites in thunder-gusts, rehearsing incantations before her barn cats, and tending a garden of consummate grotesquery; but they never saw her sacrifice a goat to the Dark One or pour libations on a Satanic altar.

Even before the first stories of the Widow Webster's peculiarities surfaced in Manayunk, Ben had drafted *The Pennsylvania Gazette* into the charade. For the immediate future, he furtively informed his employees, the paper would pursue a policy of amity towards the Royal Governor, periodically lauding his courage in attacking the pirate shallop. Beyond its praise of Patrick Gordon, the *Gazette* would publish each week a letter from the nonexistent Ebenezer Trenchard. Jennet judged this hoax a true Franklin masterpiece, his most impressive deception since Silence Dogood. She read Mr Trenchard's inaugural epistle straight through without once relaxing her smile.

19 September 1730

To the Authors of the Gazette*:*

I write to acquaint you that I, an ageing Philosopher who learn'd more of Nature's Ways from sailing the World's Oceans than from his Years of

Study at Harvard College, have lately reach'd certain Conclusions pertaining to so-called Witchcraft. Owning no Inclination to write a full Tome on the Subject, I shall instead purvey my Opinions through your excellent Newspaper.

Before the courteous Reader replies that Philadelphians traffic not in Old-World Superstition, let me report that in Manayunk-Village today there are Whisperings of how a certain Widow living in Sumac Lane hath covenant'd with the Devil. To wit, our Province may soon see its first Witch-Trial, sanction'd by the very Parliamentary Act that saw Nineteen supposed Satanists hang'd at Salem in 1692, an Event whose tragickal Nature did not deter the Pennsylvania Assembly from ratifying, to its everlasting infamy, the Statute in Question a Dozen Years ago.

My own Views concerning the 'Demon Hypothesis' have lately alight'd atop the highest Pinnacle to which a reason'd Scepticism might aspire, a Circumstance I credit largely to J. S. Crompton's estimable Book, The Sufficiency of the World. *If my Recommendation prompts even one* Gazette *Subscriber to acquire this remarkable Work (on sale at 8 s. the Copy at Gerencer's, Ephram's as well, and obtainable by Mail from those same Vendors), this brief Missive will have been well worth the Composition thereof.*

Your most humble Servant,
Ebenezer Trenchard, Esq.
Seaman Scholar of Front Street

After five full weeks of portraying Rebecca Webster, Jennet at last received indications that her neighbours were growing fearful: a mysterious fire in her barn, a dead opossum gibbeted from her largest chestnut tree, an aggressive scrap of Scripture nailed to her front door. (*The Soul that turneth after such as have familiar Spirits, and after Wizards, to go a-whoring after them, I will cut him off from amongst his People.*) And yet, alas, not one villager undertook to lodge a formal complaint. While nobody felt any affection towards the Witch of Manayunk, evidently nobody wished to see her in gaol either.

The instant she apprised Ben of the village's complacency, he sought out the Junto's second cleverest member, the poet and surveyor Nicholas Scull, whose aptitude for trickery fully equalled Ben's. On the first

Monday in November Mr Scull rented a room from a Manayunk tallow-chandler named Lawrence Eddings, and by evening he'd convinced the credulous dunderhead to regard his gout as an instance of *maleficium*. Two days later Mr Scull visited Mr Eddings's first cousin, Elizabeth Jarrett, soon persuading the dressmaker that her baby's colic traced to wicked spirits. On Friday Mr Eddings and Mrs Jarrett betook themselves to the local justice of the peace, Herbert Bledsoe, and offered up their reasons for suspecting Mrs Webster of demonic compact, and that very afternoon Jennet's farm-house shook with the insistent clamour of the newly appointed magistrate pounding on her door.

'Do you know what brings me here?' he asked as she gestured him into the parlour. Mr Bledsoe was a sallow and phlegmatic man of not more than twenty-five years, with a thin moustache sitting atop his upper lip like a dormant caterpillar.

'Nay, I cannot imagine,' she said.

'Your neighbours call you a sorceress' — his tone was almost apologetic — 'and so I am bound to arrest you.'

'I know naught of such arts,' she protested.

'Your accusers say otherwise.'

Mr Bledsoe permitted her to bank her cooking-fire, extinguish her hearth, latch her casements, close her shutters and lock her door. He clamped iron manacles around her outstretched wrists and, like a Nimacook taking a white woman captive, led her down the garden path. So far the drama was playing out exactly as she'd written it, and yet she experienced a dim disquieting presentiment that her control over this *pièce bien faite* had reached its zenith. She had awakened a sleeping dragon, the antique fear of *maleficium*, and God alone knew what consequences would soon befall her.

Located on the eastern shore of the Schuylkill, Manayunk Gaol-House was a rude stone structure consisting of Mr Bledsoe's offices on the ground floor and, delved deep into the riverbank like a mass grave, the dungeon itself. The magistrate handed Jennet over to the turnkey, the ursine Matthew Knox, his face aflush with gin, his breath laden with the same substance. Upon removing her manacles, Mr Knox presented her with a burlap smock, then gestured towards a folded muslin screen and instructed her to avail herself of whatever privacy it afforded.

Once attired in prison garb, Jennet followed Mr Knox in a clockwise path down a spiral staircase, their journey terminating in a torchlit grotto containing three iron-gated cells separated by brick partitions. Such heat as the space enjoyed came from an enclosed brazier and its concomitant brick chimney, the contraption dominating the corridor like a great Cartesian heart throbbing within an immense clay golem. In the left-hand cell stood a runty man of middle age, his rheumy eyes and ruddy nose dribbling with the Danish chill. The right-hand cell held an elderly woman of the dilapidated sort frequently apprehended for Satanism – though surely, Jennet reasoned, there could not be a second witch-trial in the offing. Mr Knox placed her in the central compartment, half the size of Billy Slipfinger's hovel in the Fleet, and devoid of all furnishings save a pitcher of water, a chamber-pot, and a pine pallet supporting a straw mattress. Acrid moss clung to the bricks like daubs of green mortar and a huge spider-web spanned the ceiling, two trapped woodworms twitching near the hub.

Shortly after the turnkey locked her in, Jennet learned that, for better or worse, voices travelled easily from cell to cell. Her fellow prisoners introduced themselves as Edith Sharkey and Cyril Turpin.

'So you're the one stands accused o' necromancy,' Mrs Sharkey said.

'Quite so,' Jennet said, itching in her burlap smock.

'Then please know that a witch hath ne'er had a more amiable prison-mate than myself. I'll give ye no cause to make my hair fall out or my skin turn to boils.'

'The charges against me are without grounds,' Jennet said.

'Marry, what a coincidence!' Mrs Sharkey exclaimed. 'They've got no evidence in my case either, save a rumour I came home from marketing one day to find my husband and our serving-maid stark naked in the barn, churning up some love butter. Supposedly I grabbed the plough and furrowed both their skulls with the mould-board. Now I ask ye, Mrs Webster, how could an old wife like me lift all that iron by herself?'

''Tis a mystery, in sooth,' Jennet said.

'Odsfish, ye ladies have me outclassed!' Mr Turpin shouted. 'One of you's indicted for bashing out her husband's brains, the other's accused o' Satanism, and I'm naught but a common thief.' He paused, sneezed twice, and continued. 'Well, not too common, for I've risen far above my station. I started out in the chicken-coop, but soon worked my way up to the goat-pen, and from there to the sheep meadow, and I had my eye on some horses when this outrageous suspicion concernin' Mr Pertuis's cattle fell upon me.'

'I cannot speak very highly of Philadelphia justice,' Jennet said. 'Here we are in gaol, and yet each of us is spotless as Saint Genevieve.'

She eased herself onto the mattress and stretched her frightened bones along its length, the bits of straw jabbing her back and thighs like the nails in a Hindoo fakir's bed. At that moment she wanted nothing more than actually to *be* a witch – a certain kind, of course: not a misbegotten hag with gobber tooth and warty nose, but a full-blooded magus boasting Perdition's every imp as her retainer, each eager to pluck its mistress from her gaol-cell, bear her to little William's side, and fly them both to the warmest and most fecund of Jupiter's undiscovered moons.

As her incarceration progressed, Jennet was pleased to find the rawness of her accommodations counterbalanced by a certain civility in her keepers. Although tradition required Mr Bledsoe to make his prisoners' diet severe, he saw to it that their water was clean, their pease-bread fresh, and their cheese free of mould. He kept the brazier burning around the clock. Best of all, he imposed no limits on visitors, with the result that Jennet and Ben enjoyed one another's company every day.

Mr Knox, meanwhile, provided her with each new issue of *The Pennsylvania Gazette*, as well as daily bulletins on the status of her case. By the turnkey's narrative, Mr Bledsoe had recently enlisted the services of Magistrate Abraham Pollock, his counterpart in Mount-Holly, New-Jersey. Late in October Mr Pollock had tested an accused Satanist, Gabriel Toffey, by standing him on a granary scale and counterweighting him with the town Bible – for it was commonly supposed that wizards and witches contained less physical substance than ordinary mortals, hence their ability to transvect themselves via brooms and pitchforks. Much to Mr Pollock's disappointment, Mr

Toffey's meat and bones elevated the Prophets a full five feet, and so the magistrate was obliged to release him. For reasons not entirely apparent, this episode conferred on Pollock a local reputation as a competent demonologist.

Given what Mr Knox had told her about the Mount-Holly affair, Jennet was hardly surprised when Mr Bledsoe appeared in the dungeon early one morning and declared that his colleague would test her that day. At noon Mr Knox rowed Jennet across the Delaware in his brother's fishing dory, then transported her by hired carriage to Pollock's cramped office, its every surface obscured by deeds, wills and contracts. The magistrate sat behind his desk, signing arrest warrants with such broad gesticulations as to suggest an orchestra *maestro* conducting a tumultuous finale. A choleric man with blotchy yellow skin and a livid scar on his forehead, he seemed to Jennet less an avatar of Themis than a renegade from Hezekiah Creech's pirate band, now posing as a judge.

Throughout the questioning phase Jennet remained unflustered, deliberately arousing Pollock's suspicions whilst simultaneously confounding his expectations. When he asked her why she encouraged so many cats to inhabit her barn, she offered an answer – ''Tis the mice who lure them thither, not I' – that seemed to partake of neither innocence nor insolence but of something in between. When he demanded that she recite the Lord's Prayer, she purposefully switched 'Thy kingdom come' and 'Thy will be done', then calmly explained that she'd learned her *Pater Noster* from an elderly parson who'd routinely scrambled his scriptural clauses. When he inquired whether she indeed grew monk's hood and mandrake in her garden (a rumour to that effect having reached his ears) and whether she intended to mash these plants into flying ointments and libidinous unguents (their most notorious application), she cryptically replied, 'Monk's hood and mandrake boast utilities ne'er dreamt of by a mere provincial magistrate.'

Next Pollock delivered her into the hostile embrace of his three husky sisters so that they might scan her skin, whereupon the impetus of the interview went against Jennet as abruptly as Gabriel Toffey had shot the town Bible skyward. Whilst Knox stared uncomfortably at his boots and Pollock watched in lascivious delight, the sisters stripped off

Jennet's burlap smock, shaved her body – head, armpits, legs, privates – and went to work, their fingers inching across her skin like blind and mindless larva. Just when it seemed she could endure this humiliation no longer, the eldest sister reported a warty protuberance on the suspect's neck. Pollock proceeded to probe the excrescence with a steel sewing needle, betimes declaring it bloodless, which was doubtless true, for Jennet could barely feel the needle's point.

At dusk Pollock and his sisters reclothed her in the burlap smock, bowed her into the posture of a foetus, and lashed her wrists and ankles together with leather thongs. When Knox averred they had no cause to treat Jennet with such cruelty, Pollock plied him with his favourite food, unwatered gin, and the turnkey forthwith found himself on the floor, sprawled across a mattress of documents and singing 'Lillabullero'.

The Mount-Holly witchfinders deposited their trussed prisoner in a horse-drawn cart, conveyed her to the Delaware, and spilled her onto a granite pier as a fisherman might unload a netful of cod. As Jennet lay shivering in the winter air, face down, the damp stone gnawing her bare arms and exposed calves, the sisters hitched a plough-rope around her waist. Without warning, Pollock bent low and swung at her with his balled fist, ramming his knuckles into her stomach and forcing her to exhale. Before she could take more than half a breath, he blithely rolled her over the edge of the pier.

She crashed into the frigid river, the surface shattering around her as if she'd fallen through a cathedral window. Engulfed, she sank, straining and jerking against the unyielding thongs. Water shot up her nose, burning the fleshy cavity beyond. So this was what they'd endured, Isobel Mowbray and Susan Diggens and all the others – this maleficent acid, this liquid fire. She opened her eyes and beheld the Delaware's green swirling murk. Her windpipe spasmed. Her chest grew tight as a brick. And still she sank, deeper, deeper. A noise like muffled cannon-fire boomed in her skull, a phenomenon she soon recognized as the pounding of her heart.

Suddenly the rope went taut, and now she was rising, ever higher, until at last she felt a breeze upon her brow. She devoured the evening air, sucking it down as forcefully as Ben's vacuum-pump drawing the atmosphere from a bottle.

370

'The Delaware hath spurned thee,' Pollock declared, pulling her shoreward, 'a fact I am bound to share with the grand jury!'

'I nearly drowned!' she cried, teeth chattering. ''Twas the rope caused my ascent!'

The witchfinders dragged her onto the pier. 'Nay, Mrs Webster,' Pollock insisted, 'Thy buoyancy comes from Beelzebub!'

''Twas the rope!'

Four days later Pollock offered his findings to the *ad hoc* grand jury. The hearing unfolded with an inevitability that would have made the transit of Venus seem optional by comparison and the inverse-square law a mere matter of opinion. Indeed, Jennet would have counted the whole show a farce but for its occasioning Ebenezer Trenchard's best essay to date.

10 March 1731

To the Authors of the Gazette:

This Tuesday past I again visit'd Manayunk, where I witness'd a Grand Jury return a Billa Vera *against Rebecca Webster following Testimony by her Neighbours and a Presentation by the Mount-Holly Magistrate. Throughout the entire Hearing Mrs Webster sat respectfully beside the Bench, Head bow'd, as if in Prayer.*

In this Week's Epistle I am mov'd to present a Fact not universally known. For nearly forty Years now His Majesty's Privy Council hath charter'd within Massachusetts Bay an Organization styling itself the 'Purification Commission', consisting of a 'Witchfinder-Royal' named Dunstan Stearne and his three fellow Prickers. Far from performing the Godly work the word 'Purification' implies, these Varlets have to date executed over two Hundred innocent Souls, most drawn from the local Indian Population.

How might the good People of Pennsylvania protest this violent Mangling of Justice by Mr Stearne's unholy Company? I answer as follows. We must call upon Governor Gordon to petition his Massachu- setts Counterpart for the Loan of these dubious Demonologists, that they might come to Philadelphia and prosecute Rebecca Webster, in the Doing of which their fallacious Methods will, I am sure, stand expos'd as sheer

Chicanery. Should Mr Stearne and the Others refuse to take the Case, then methinks all reasonable Men will be forc'd to a Conclusion that this 'Purification Commission' hath Much to conceal and More to fear.

Your most humble Servant,
Ebenezer Trenchard, Esq.
Seaman Scholar of Front Street

On the second Sunday following the issuance of the *billa vera*, Ben gleefully recounted for Jennet a recent conversation with Major Patrick Gordon. A practical man who took a dim view of metaphysical matters, the Governor had been vaguely antagonistic to the Conjuring Statute even before the *Gazette* cast him as the hero of the Creech affair, and now he wished to reward Ben's blandishments by becoming a devout crusader on Rebecca Webster's behalf. Assenting to the logic of Ebenezer Trenchard's last letter, Gordon had already asked Governor Belcher of Massachusetts to send his Purification Commissioners south and make the Crown's case against the Witch of Manayunk. The nascent Court of Oyer and Terminer, specially appointed by Gordon to try the defendant, would be administered by the famously even-handed Judge Malcolm Cresswell. In contrast to the Salem protocols, the jury would hear not only the evidence against the accused but also an argument for her innocence. Moreover, Cresswell would allow Mrs Webster to speak on her own behalf, provided her statements were elicited by a skilled and circumspect barrister.

Jennet could not help noticing that despite these victories an uncharacteristic gloom clung to Ben, palpable as a frock coat.

'What ails you, sir?'

'Jenny, dearest, 'tis not too late to end this perilous game,' He pressed his chest against the bars of her cell, printing their grime on his white Holland shirt in four vertical columns. 'Let us tell Magistrate Bledsoe you've merely been *playing* the enchantress – you did it to set Trenchard's pen scribbling against the New-England prickers – but now the hoax hath run its course, and you wish to rejoin human society.'

'What possible good could that accomplish?'

'The greatest good imaginable. 'Twould keep you off the gallows.'

372

She pulled a handful of stuffing from her pallet, closing her fingers as if to mash the straw to flour. 'Hear me, bonny Ben. My whole life I've chased after the abominable Conjuring Statute, and I shan't know peace till it is torn to bits.'

Ben released a dissenting sound, something betwixt a bleat of anger and a groan of woe. 'I did not sleep well last night, Mrs Crompton, nor the night before.'

'I cannot accept a speckled axe.'

'I wonder if I shall e'er sleep well again.'

On the last afternoon in April, as Ben sat in the press-room making ready to draft the newest Ebenezer Trenchard essay, it occurred to him that he'd developed a peculiar habit of living his life in reverse. The normal procedure followed by a person starting a business was first to obtain the funding and then to acquire the tools, but Ben had gone about it backwards, sailing off to buy printing equipment with no capital beyond the ethereal endorsement of a known scoundrel. Another such sequence had a man taking first a wife and only later a mistress, yet here too Ben had inverted the usual chronology, enjoying amorous relations with Jennet long before pledging his troth to Deborah Read. As for the marriage itself, once again he had defied tradition. Convention dictated that, upon winning a woman's love, a man should let her annul any existing marriage contract before wedding her himself. Having absconded to the West-Indies, however, Deborah's ne'er-do-well husband, the potter John Rogers, wasn't available for signing a divorcement decree, and so she and Ben had simply set up house together.

Although he felt an abiding fondness towards his common-law bride, he would admit that his sentiments fell short of adoration. The Helen of his heart's own Ilium would always be Jennet Stearne Crompton. But Jennet was a madwoman, a pagan Fury, her eyes locked on some self-consuming star that she alone could see, whereas he merely wanted to become an accomplished printer and a competent philosopher, ambitions that Deborah stood ready to support in full.

Ben inked his quill and touched nib to paper, but no words flowed forth. The major news of the day was Governor Belcher's announcement that he would instruct his Purification Commissioners to hie themselves to Pennsylvania and expose Rebecca Webster as a Satanist, a development that the imaginary Ebenezer Trenchard would logically disclose in terms of unqualified triumph. Trenchard's fleshly creator, however, was utterly distraught by the bulletin from Massachusetts. Dunstan Stearne's entry into the case, the very circumstance that Jennet so deeply desired and Ben so greatly feared, now seemed inevitable. He set down his pen and brooded.

The brass bell tinkled, the door flew open and a young man strode into the pressroom, liveried in purple silk and swirling a furlined cape, his head crowned by a powdered peruke. Marching up to Ben, he announced that his master wished to speak with the proprietor of the shop — or such was the interpretation that accrued to Ben's limited command of the French tongue.

'*Je m'appelle Delvaux. Êtesvous bien Monsieur Franklin?*'

'*Oui, c'est moi,*' Ben said.

'My master, CharlesLouis de Secondat, Baron de la Brède et de Montesquieu, wishes to have an audience with you. He awaits your response in his carriage,' he said in French.

It was generally a good idea to receive barons, Ben believed. Yes, hereditary aristocracy ranked high amongst his least favourite institutions, but potential patrons were always welcome at Franklin and Meredith's PrintingHouse. 'Inform your master that I would be happy to meet with him but that I hope he speaks English,' Ben replied.

'He indeed speaks English,' Delvaux said with an oblique sneer. 'Also Italian, German, Hungarian and Turkish.'

As Delvaux headed for the door, Ben realized that his caller must be the same Baron de Montesquieu who'd written the scandalous novel *Lettres Persanes*, published anonymously a decade earlier but finally appearing under the author's name during Ben's sojourn in London, for surely there could not be two different Frenchmen labouring under the appellation CharlesLouis de Secondat, Baron de la Brède et de Montesquieu. On the surface a chronicle of Oriental customs, notably that endlessly fascinating institution known as the harem, *Lettres Persanes* was in fact an indictment of the follies infesting French society, framed as a series of letters to and from the courtier Usbek and his young friend Rica, fictive Persians travelling through Europe.

Such a delicious conceit! What in Heaven's name had prompted this accomplished author to seek out the obscure editor of *The Pennsylvania Gazette*?

The instant he clapped eyes on his visitor, an elegant man in his early forties with a breaching stare and a hawk's beak of a nose, Ben nodded respectfully and said, 'Let me declare at the outset, my Lord Montesquieu, that *Lettres Persanes* is quite the most caustic satire I've read since the *Decameron* of Signor Boccaccio.'

A crescent-moon grin spread across Montesquieu's face. '*Monsieur Franklin, je vous remercie*,' he replied, sauntering towards the new Blaeu press. 'But I must confess, I do not think of you Americans as enthusiasts for *les belles-lettres*.' Compared to his valet, the Baron dressed less ostentatiously, spoke less haughtily and comported himself more humbly. 'I regard you rather as the unpretentious inhabitants of a New Eden.'

'For better or worse, we shed our jungle manners and bear-skin leggings several generations back,' Ben said. 'Of course, I still keep an Iroquois hatchet in my desk, should a wild boar or an unruly Tory come charging down Market Street.'

Montesquieu untied his perfumed neckcloth, employing it to sop the sweat from his brow. 'You truly found amusement in my trifling novel?'

'My mouth grew sore from smiling.'

The Baron proceeded to explain that, though he did not disavow *Lettres Persanes*, he hoped his future works would address subjects of greater import than his countrymen's foibles. Towards this end, he had undertaken a grand tour of Europe and the New World, recording such observations and collecting such artefacts – codices, trial transcripts, letters from repentant criminals, even a few torture instruments – as might one day enable him to write a great book on law and government. Already he'd visited Austria, Hungary, Italy and England, and now here he was in America.

'While living in London,' Montesquieu said, 'I became enamoured of two American writers – the natural philosopher J. S. Crompton and also Ebenezer Trenchard, champion of the accused sorceress Rebecca Webster. As you are the publisher of both men, I hope you might point me in their direction.'

'May I trust you to keep Trenchard's location a secret?' Ben asked.

'*Je serai très discret.*'

'To find the journalist in question, you need look but a yard beyond your nose, for Ebenezer Trenchard is my *nom de plume.*'

'*Formidable!*' Montesquieu offered a bow of admiration, nearly losing his peruke in the process. 'Ah, Monsieur Trenchard, I am so honoured to make your acquaintance.' His gaze alighted on a dozen copies of *The Sufficiency of the World* stacked atop the scrubbing counter. 'And here we have the divine Monsieur Crompton!' He removed the topmost volume and brought it to his bosom. 'Nature's laws truly refute the demon hypothesis.'

'I must insist that you ne'er reveal certain facts, concerning J. S. Crompton.'

'*Naturellement.*'

'Is this your sacred promise?'

'*Oui.*'

'Then I shall tell you that Crompton is a woman.'

'*Sapristi!*'

'She is also my dearest friend.'

The Baron's eyebrows ascended to an altitude such that they nearly touched his wig.

'Moreover, she is sister to Dunstan Stearne, the likely prosecutor at the Webster trial.'

'*Mon Dieu!*'

'Most provocative of all,' said Ben, retrieving the broom from its customary corner, 'J. S. Crompton and Rebecca Webster are the same person.'

'*Incroyable!*'

Fixing his attention on the clusters of debris beneath the press, Ben systematically whisked them into the coal-scuttle whilst simultaneously describing Jennet's foolhardy plan. He did not forbear to offer his opinion that she was 'toying with her own life', a circumstance that was causing him 'more anguish than I can calculate'.

'*Une femme courageuse.*' Montesquieu returned the demon disproof to the pile. 'I sincerely hope her trial will deal the tyrannical prickers a fatal blow. You see, Monsieur Franklin, I am a great lover of the concept called freedom, *la liberté* – as are you yourself, *oui*?'

'*Oui*,' said Ben, wielding his broom against the cobwebs beneath the scrubbing counter.

'Though I also believe – and here I suspect we are likewise in accord – that every man's freedom must be constrained by the statutes his nation deploys against despotism.'

Ben stopped sweeping and bobbed his head. 'I would usually trust a congress o'er a king. And yet, even as we shape our statutes, do not these same statutes shape us? Are we not the creatures of our laws?'

'*Exactement!* Good laws make good men. Bad laws harm everyone – not only those who break them, but those who obey them as well.' Montesquieu explained that he'd reached these conclusions during his years as *Président à Mortier* in the High Court of Justice at Bordeaux.

'So you're a jurist as well as a satirist?' Ben said.

'A jurist, *oui*,' Montesquieu replied. 'I am adept at writing statutes – though even more adept at writing about them, *si vous comprenez*. What I so admire about your English form of government is how it honours the reign of law. Three separate parts, each holding the other in check. A parliament to fashion the canons, an executive to administer them, and a judiciary to interpret them.'

In point of fact, the English system was far messier and murkier than that, but Ben had no wish to lecture his visitor on the defects of the British Constitution. Another idea now preoccupied him, quite possibly his greatest since his realization that lightning was electricity's celestial twin.

'*Monsieur le Baron*, I have a proposition for you. Let me make bold to suggest that the perfect lawyer for the remarkable Mrs Crompton is at this moment standing before me.'

'You wish me to defend your friend?'

'*Oui.*'

'*Ce n'est point possible.* In two days I sail for La Brède, to be at last reunited with my family.'

'You say you're skilled at making laws, but I'm offering you something more momentous – an opportunity to make *history*!'

'Or an opportunity to appear ridiculous,' Montesquieu said. 'Your Madame Crompton is intelligent, but juries are not. She could easily lose.'

Humming his favourite ballad, 'The Knight of Liddesdale', Ben made an ellipse about the room, the blacking table at one focus, the scrubbing counter at the other. 'Baron, you have many enemies in France . . .'

'How did you learn this?'

'No man writes a book as barbed as the *Persian Letters* without other men accusing him of treachery against Church and State. I ask you, sir, what better way to prove yourself a loyal Frenchman than to run a wicked English law to earth?'

'Monsieur Franklin, you are quite the logician,' Montesquieu said. 'Perhaps you should argue Madame Crompton's case yourself.'

'Sir, there is but one jurist on these premises.'

A prodigious sigh escaped the Baron's lips. He removed his peruke and rubbed the ball of his thumb across his brow. 'Do you know what my uncle once said to me? "We live in unprecedented times, Charles, and our sacred obligation is to occupy them fully." Very well, Monsieur Franklin. I am persuaded to take up your friend's cause.'

'*Vous ne regretterez pas cette decision.*'

'It occurs to me that in moving against the English Witchcraft Act, we might *en passant* destroy other such laws throughout Europe,' Montesquieu said, 'for never before has the world been so prepared to cast off disastrous ideas.' If good men everywhere rose to this occasion,

he elaborated, posterity would consider itself well served.

Grateful descendants would call the present

century an era of courage, an

epoch of innovation,

and an age

of

*

Reason,

I don't doubt,

will always hold an

honoured place in my affections.

And yet I must admit that the more I think

about it, the less certain I become what Reason actually *is*.

Everyone agrees that Montesquieu's *Persian Letters* and Voltaire's *Candide* epitomize something called the Age of Reason (even though these novels can't stand each other, and neither could their authors), but this doesn't stop Reason from being among the most bedevilling ideas yet visited upon Western civilization.

Is the *Malleus Maleficarum* an unreasonable book? Many conscious entities would say yes. But if by Reason we mean an orderly presentation that cleaves to a kind of perverse Aristotelian logic, then the *Malleus Maleficarum* is an imperially reasonable tome. Was the Third Reich an unreasonable enterprise? When you consider its grounding in neo-paganism, occultist malarkey, blood-and-soil folderol, and crackpot eugenics, yes, indubitably. And yet the Nazis went about their agenda in a manner I can only call rational.

You know what I'm about to say. Whatever the stains on Reason's résumé, Revelation has much to answer for as well. Even were I to agree that Reason has been tried and found wanting (and I'm not convinced that such is the case), I would still applaud the Enlightenment for noticing that Revelation had rather too much blood on its hands, and it was time to contrive a different metaphysic.

And yet I concede that the apotheosis of Reason is a wretched idea. The *Principia Mathematica* will never file a brief on behalf of Reason per se – Reason unchecked, Reason unchained, Reason for Reason's sake. I am the first to insist that rationality disconnected from decency, deliberation, and doubt – a triad that, were I human, I would call humanism – leads not to Utopia but to the guillotine.

In the summer of 1794, some sixty years after the climactic events of this narrative, I decided that, being an honest sort of masterwork, I would observe first-hand the fruits of unfettered Reason. Willing myself to Revolutionary France, I climbed into the consciousness of Benoit Clément, a Catholic priest whom the Committee of Public Safety had recently found guilty of being a Catholic priest. Over two centuries have passed since that horrid day, but I can still recall the details: the suffocating heat of the dungeon, the frightened faces of my fellow prisoners (many of them children), the press of the shackles on my ankles and wrists.

It's the twenty-fifth of June. The Terror is at its height. In recent weeks the Committee has abandoned all pretence of due process. The mere circumstance of appearing before Robespierre's tribunal proves that you harbor Royalist sympathies and have plotted against the Revolution.

I have just finished saying Mass, using stale water for the blood and a rotten pear for the flesh, but no one has drawn much comfort from it. Six guards appear, armed with pistols and pikes. They have a list. My name is on it, along with nine others.

The guards herd us outside and shove us into a tumbrel, then scramble aboard themselves, their pistols trained on our chests. With a crack of his whip the driver urges the horses forward. As we approach the Place de la Révolution, our nostrils burn with the stench of human blood. Soon we hear the peasants singing drinking roundelays as they urge the executioners on in their murderous work. Now another sound reaches our ears, the rushing roar of the guillotine blade.

My *Principia Mathematica* self is appalled. Is this what the love of Reason comes to in the end? Was my Jennet wrong to embrace the Enlightenment dream of eternal rational discourse? Is there any funda-mental difference between a witch-court and the Committee of Public Safety?

We enter the fetid square. Because I am the only cleric scheduled to die that afternoon, the mob demands that I go first. 'Kill the priest' they cry. 'Kill him now!' A guard pulls me from the tumbrel. As I mount the scaffold, the executioner turns the crank, sending aloft the steel blade and its collateral lead weight. My captors set me chest-down on the trestle and insert my head in the yoke. The lunette is slick with blood. I stare into the woven basket, likewise blood-soaked. Lifting my gaze, I see a horse-drawn cart crammed with headless bodies and bodiless heads. A fat man in a brown leather apron stands beside the horse, waiting to receive my remains.

'The Directors of the Lottery of Saint Guillotine are pleased to announce the latest winner – Father Benoit Clément!' the executioner tells the crowd. They've heard the joke a thousand times before, but still they laugh.

I make my confession to myself, then vomit into the basket. The executioner presses the release button. The scaffold trembles as the blade thunders down the groove. I feel a sudden coldness against my neck, as if someone has dropped a snowball on the nape, and for one astonishing instant, at once impossibly brief and supernaturally

protracted, I know the horrors of quadriplegia. Strangely enough,
I'm aware of my head's tumble into the basket, an indescribable
feeling – a falling sensation? – no, this is not an Isaac Newton
moment, because to experience gravity you need
a body as well as a brain: you need
bones and limbs and
muscles
and

*

'Flesh
is as grass,'
the Apostle Peter
had noted in his stirring First
Letter, 'and all glory of Man as the flower
of grass.' The truth of Peter's words became especially
clear to Dunstan Stearne each time the Purification Commission
switched off a Satanist through fire rather than the noose. How little
effort it took to vaporize a witch's grassy flesh. You chained her to a
stake, lit the pyre, and within an hour there was nothing left but bones.
'The grass withereth, the flower thereof falleth away, but the word of
the Lord endureth for ever.'

He gave the signal, and the Commission went to work, foiling the
Devil with clockwork precision. As Samuel Parris checked the thongs
securing the Wampanoag woman's wrists, Abby lifted a steel axe and
dealt her a blow to the skull. The instant the witch lost consciousness,
Abby and the minister carried her carcass to the mound of hay and
deposited it on the summit.

Whenever Dunstan perused a newspaper these days, he realized he
was living in an era of unprecedented ingenuity: Fahrenheit's mercury
thermometer, Lombe's thrown-silk machine, Réaumur's steel-making
formula, Harrison's grid-iron pendulum, Hadley's quadrant. This
cataract of cleverness depressed him. Man did not live by Baconianism
alone. When the Massachusetts Assembly wrote to the Witchfinder-
Royal urging that in the name of decency he should strangle his
prisoners ere burning them, he had instinctively resisted the idea,
averring that the blind embrace of innovation was a pernicious impulse. Only after Jonathan Corwin had bid Dunstan recall that such

chokings boasted a tradition stretching back centuries – that, indeed, Dunstan's own aunt had nearly received this courtesy at her famous Colchester execution – did he relent and adopt the suggested policy.

Poor old Jonathan, dead over two months now, another victim of pleurisy and diabolism. The funeral was still fresh in Dunstan's memory. Reverend Parris had read the judge's favourite piece of Scripture, the Song of Songs, that pious love ballad through which Christ had catalogued the manifold virtues of His Church. 'Thy teeth are like a flock of sheep that are even shorn, which came up from the washing.' For the Church had marvellous jaws indeed. 'Thy lips are like a thread of scarlet, and thy speech is comely.' And a splendid mouth. 'Thy two breasts are like two young roes that are twins, which feed amongst the lilies.' And an excellent bosom.

Pulling on his cowhide gloves, Dunstan marched towards the hay mound and closed his fingers around the throat of the dazed Wampa-noag. For a count of two hundred he deprived her heathen lungs of air. The witch grew still. He released his grip, received the burning torch from his wife, and jammed it into the mound as if inserting a ramrod into a cannon's muzzle. The hay took but a moment to transmute into a bonfire, spewing smoke and spitting sparks.

'An idea of some merit occurred to me this morning,' Abby informed Dunstan. 'I found myself envisioning an exchange of witchfinders 'twixt ourselves and the Kirkcaldy Cleansing League. They would send us their ablest demonologist, and we would export my uncle to Scotland.'

''Tis a worthy scheme, Goodwife Stearne. I shall commend it to our Caledonian brethren anon.'

Evidently Dunstan had not applied sufficient force during the strangulation. Such, at least, was the conclusion he drew when the witch hurled herself off the hay, her clothing aflame, her hair a blazing bonnet, and ran screaming through the woods towards her village. Her fellow pagans would have experienced some difficulty recognizing her at that moment, as she'd lost all particularity and become instead an ambulatory conflagration of vaguely human form.

'I'Christ, we've got a runner!' Abby yelled.

'Oh, how I wish Jonathan could be here!' Mr Parris cried. 'The sight of a runner ne'er failed to stir his blood!'

An absorbing spectacle, but Dunstan did not enjoy it. He could think only of the packet he'd received that morning from Boston, twenty-eight depositions collected by a Philadelphia grand jury whilst interrogating an alleged witch named Rebecca Webster (chief amongst them the report of Abraham Pollock, a New-Jersey magistrate), plus a letter from Governor Belcher exhorting the Commissioners to take the Crown's part in Mrs Webster's forthcoming trial. In principle Dunstan was willing to lease his genius to Pennsylvania, but he had many questions about the case and was glad of the Governor's suggestion that the two of them meet in Boston come Monday.

With characteristic compassion, the Almighty now arranged for an armed Wampanoag deer-slayer to appear from behind a tree and assess the situation. The brave unshouldered his musket and, drawing a bead on the witch, sent a bullet into her brain. Tumbling over the bank of a creek, the dying Indian crashed into the water and extinguished herself in a hissing cloud of smoke.

Dunstan had met Jonathan Belcher on only one previous occasion. The Witchfinder-Royal was delivering a sack of severed thumbs to Belcher's private secretary, the priggish Mr Peach, when the Governor himself had entered the foyer, an unlit church-warden pipe clenched betwixt his teeth. He asked Mr Peach for a tinderbox and, receiving the desired artefact, returned to his duties without giving Dunstan so much as a nod. From that brief encounter Dunstan had judged the Governor a cold and self-absorbed man. He was greatly pleased therefore when Mr Belcher began their Monday meeting by grasping his hand amicably and speaking in an almost deferential tone.

'His Majesty's Privy Council hath requested that I commend you for your long and loyal service to the Crown,' the Governor said, leading Dunstan into his Treamount Street office, an airy space featuring mullioned windows and a parquet floor. With his wide face and bulky frame, Belcher looked rather like the manatee Dunstan had spotted two weeks earlier whilst a-cleansing on Martha's Vineyard. 'The Boston clergy is similarly grateful. More than once I've heard a Puritan minister aver that our province's prosperity traces in the main to your work amongst the savage Indians. I must confess to a certain ambivalence towards your profession, but that needn't concern us this morning.'

Heeding the Governor's gesture, Dunstan assumed an ornate chair cushioned in red velvet. He opened his valise and removed the newest proof of his industry, a baize bag containing four charred Wampanoag thumbs. 'The Puritan divines value my services, and yet they would have me spend a month in Pennsylvania?'

'I gave them no choice in the matter, for the Webster case hath grown complex of late,' Belcher said. 'There are factions in America who would exploit it to raise a cry against the Conjuring Statute. King George will not have a great Parliamentary tradition assailed in this fashion. Is that understood?'

'Aye, my Lord Governor.'

'Even as we speak, a cabal of atheists and freethinkers conspires to bring down the law in question. I allude to an upstart newspaper, *The Pennsylvania Gazette*, that each week prints letters attacking witch-courts everywhere. What is more, Governor Gordon hath appointed Judge Malcolm Cresswell to the case, a man notorious for ceding to defendants the benefit of far too many doubts.'

'An appalling situation.'

'Appalling's the word' – Belcher settled onto a plush divan – 'which is why I now offer you a trump card. I hope you'll see fit to play it.'

Six months earlier, Belcher explained, Governor Gordon had led a military action that culminated in the apprehension of the infamous West-Indies buccaneer Hezekiah Creech. According to Belcher's agents, Gordon had gifted himself with a portion of Creech's treasure before delivering the remainder to the Crown.

'A troubling accusation,' Dunstan said.

'Troubling, but also fortunate,' Belcher said. 'These days a man need but utter the words "Tucker affidavit" within earshot of Mr Gordon, and he will grant that person almost any boon.'

' "Tucker affidavit"?'

'A particularly damning deposition came from a Redcoat corporal named Noah Tucker. The Governor is frantic to keep this fact in the shadows.'

' "Almost any boon"? Such as, for example . . . replacing Cresswell with a jurist less sympathetic to Lucifer?'

'You have a nimble mind, Mr Stearne. Now it so happens Judge

John Hathorne of Salem-Town is recently gone to Philadelphia, that he might convince his nautically inclined nephew to abandon the sea and enter the ministry.'

'Do you perchance speak of the same Judge Hathorne who presided at Salem alongside our dear departed Mr Corwin?'

'The very man.'

'Is it possible Hathorne still practises the law?'

Belcher nodded, smiling extravagantly. 'He hath eighty-nine years, yet his wits remain as sharp as Gideon's sword. When I apprised him of the situation, he insisted he was hale enough to wrestle the Dark One to the ground.'

'I feel a great exhilaration at these developments.' Dunstan reached forward and set the baize bag on the Governor's maplewood desk.

'You will find the good judge at Mrs Crippin's Rooming-House in Callowhill Street.' Belcher, rising, approached Dunstan and slapped his back with the virtuous vehemence of a physician eliciting a new-born's first breath. 'In my next dispatch to Kensington Palace, may I assure His Majesty that the Philadelphia Court will find against Mrs Webster?'

'You may.'

'Your efforts will not go unrewarded. The Privy Council hath directed me to pay your Commission two hundred pounds sterling should the case end happily.'

'We do not cleanse for money, sir, though I would ne'er deny that money's a useful appendage to the hunt.'

Belcher frowned and gestured suspiciously towards the baize bag. 'What's that?'

'Thumbs, my Lord Governor.'

'Come again?'

'Witches' thumbs. Four of 'em.'

'What are they doing on my desk?'

''Tis not obvious?'

'No.'

'They are the basis on which you compute the Commission's salary.'

'Get them out of here.'

'As you wish.'

'Right now.'

'Of course,' Dunstan said, whisking the sack away.

'I'm a worldly man, Mr Stearne. Don't e'er put thumbs on my desk again.'

On the afternoon of May the twentieth, Dunstan and his fellow demonologists donned their darkest Puritan cloaks, secured the door of their Framingham salt-box, and betook themselves to Boston. The following morning they boarded a southbound sloop, the *Ignis Fatuus*, captained by one Angus Morley, a garrulous Calvinist and devoted *Bible Commonwealth* reader who gave the New-England cleansers the same calibre of regard he might have awarded travelling royalty or an itinerant troupe of Shakespearean players. Captain Morley's largesse knew no bounds. He arranged for the demonologists to receive the best berths, fed them fresh scrod for breakfast and boiled beef for lunch, and gifted them with two pounds of Barbados sugar.

After four days at sea, following a stopover on Manhattan Isle and a harrowing storm of possibly demonic origin, the *Ignis Fatuus* sailed up the Delaware and put to port. Dunstan was the first cleanser to disembark, guiding Abby and Mr Parris into the malodorous burbling stewpot known as Chestnut Street Wharf. Studying the people's clothes and overhearing their polyglot conversations, he concluded that Philadelphia swarmed not only with the expected Quakers but also with the dregs and dross of a dozen European cities. Unsavoury Scots abounded here, as did sordid Germans, shady Welsh, seamy Dutch and renegade French. Were it not for his duty to the Witchcraft Act, he would have quit this undeclared penal colony post-haste and led his band back to Boston.

Their initial order of business, he decided – more important even than securing lodgings, locating Judge Hathorne or blackmailing Governor Gordon – was to visit Rebecca Webster and corroborate the signs of Satanic covenant reported by the New-Jersey magistrate. How lamentable if the Widow Webster had been falsely accused! Not only would such a development dash Dunstan's hopes of widening his campaign into Pennsylvania, it would mean that the three cleansers had sailed to this unseemly city for naught.

They passed an open-air vegetable market, traversed a similar emporium selling fish, and entered a tavern called the Friar's Lanthorn. A stifling vapour hung in the air, a cloud compounded of beer fumes and sot-weed smoke mingled with human gas. Rapidly the demon-ologists consumed their lunches – fried halibut and boiled turnips washed down with cider – then climbed into a day-coach heading north. By three o'clock they were in Manayunk Gaol-House, presenting themselves to the magistrate.

At first the youthful Herbert Bledsoe did not believe that these sweaty and exhausted travellers constituted the famous Massachusetts Bay Purification Commission, and his scepticism remained intact even after Abby opened the calfskin tool-kit and withdrew the Paracelsus trident and the mask-o'-truth. His suspicions dissipated only when Dunstan produced the newest edition of the organization's charter, which bore the Privy Council's seal as well as Governor Belcher's signature.

At Dunstan's urging, Bledsoe summoned his gaoler, a corpulent drunkard named Knox, and ordered him to fetch Mrs Webster. Knox descended to the dungeon, appearing betimes with the prisoner – a tall, shorn, handsome woman of middle years, wearing a tattered burlap smock cinched about her waist with a plough-rope.

'Good afternoon, dear brother,' she said.

'T'faith!' Reverend Parris exclaimed.

''Steeth!' Abby cried.

A barbed and bitter chill washed across Dunstan's skin, as if a thousand apprentice prickers were probing his every pore. He shud-dered and winced. A tracery of wrinkles had appeared upon her skin since that distant day when she'd denounced him on the Shawsheen River Bridge, and she'd lost most of her hair to Abraham Pollock's shaving razor, but Dunstan did not for an instant doubt the prisoner's identity. Thundering Christ! By what plan of inscrutable Jehovah or scheme of iniquitous Mephisto did he now find himself face-to-face with Jennet?

'God is not mocked!' he screamed. Snatching the trident from Abby, he waved it around as a cleric might deploy a crucifix against a goblin. 'God is not mocked!'

'This woman who calls herself Rebecca Webster is in sooth my husband's sister,' Abby explained to Bledsoe.

'His *sister*?' gasped the magistrate. 'What say you to this accusation?' he asked the prisoner.

'I say that, being ashamed to bear the name of Stearne, I have cheerfully altered it to Webster,' Jennet replied.

'Then this demonologist is truly your brother?' Bledsoe asked.

'We issued from the same mortal womb,' the prisoner said, 'much as I wish 'twere otherwise.'

Abby flashed Jennet the sort of slanted smile she assumed whenever the angel Justine vouchsafed her the name of a witch-infested village. 'You may spin your spider-web from now till Doomsday, heathen wench, but the Purification Commission shan't become entangled. Husband, I suggest we go apprise Governor Gordon of this farce and then return to Boston.'

Back to Boston? No, Dunstan thought. The Lord might work in mysterious ways, but the Devil trafficked only in plain ones. By selecting Jennet Stearne and not some other freethinking heretic as his principal agent in Pennsylvania, Lucifer had obviously sought to constrain the famous and formidable demonologist Dunstan Stearne from attending whatever courtroom proceeding Jennet's *maleficium* might ultimately inspire – for surely this pricker, like any pricker, would refuse to prosecute his own blood-sister.

'Foolish Lucifer!' Dunstan cried.

'Foolish Lucifer!' echoed Mr Parris.

Foolish Lucifer. How poorly the Devil understood his enemy's mind – how feeble his comprehension of the Witchfinder-Royal's heart!

'Goodwife Stearne, this is no farce,' Dunstan said, 'for by Abraham Pollock's testimony my sister hath truly signed the Dark One's regis-ter.' He paused, waiting for the prisoner to contradict him, but she simply rolled her eyes towards the ceiling beams. Tightening his grip on the trident, Dunstan stepped to within inches of the witch. 'Mr Pollock notes a diabolical excrescence on your neck. I would now confirm his finding.'

Jennet replied with a low, noxious grunt, but she obligingly tilted her head to the side, exposing the mark to Dunstan's gaze. He pressed the trident's middle tine against the blotch. Within five ticks of the clock his hand started shaking.

''Tis Lucifer's kiss – I can feel it!'

'You feel naught but the natural twitchings of your aged fingers,' Jennet insisted.

Abby brushed her palm across the reddish stubble on the suspect's head. 'Whate'er became of your tawnie husband? Did he expel you from his harem?'

'Mr Pollock also reports that the cold-water ordeal indicted Mrs Webster,' Dunstan said, still maintaining the seal betwixt trident and blemish. 'Mr Parris, will you assist me in repeating the experiment?'

'The Schuylkill should serve our purpose,' the minister said, nodding.

But before they could lead Jennet away, an unexpected and utterly profane intervention occurred. Herbert Bledsoe reached out and, like a goshawk catching a pigeon on the wing, plucked the trident from Dunstan's grasp.

'I fear the blood-tie 'twixt prisoner and prosecutor will make for a muddy sort of justice in this case,' Bledsoe said, locking his tiny pale eyes on Dunstan. 'Mr Stearne, you will forbear to test Mrs Webster further. 'Tis apparent the Court must replace you with another.'

'Do you imagine I would decline to cleanse a witch merely because she's kin to me? Hah! My father once brought evidence of Satanic compaction against his own sister-in-law!' Dunstan grabbed the trident and jerked it from Bledsoe's hands. 'You needn't fret, young jurist. When I meet with Governor Gordon on the morrow, I shall happily reveal the blood-tie of which you speak.'

'At which juncture the Governor will instruct you to resign from the case,' Bledsoe said.

Not if I inaugurate our interview with the words 'Tucker affidavit', Dunstan thought. 'This meeting goes on too long,' he told Bledsoe, then swerved towards his sister, fixing her as fiercely as he would any other bride of Lucifer. 'Mark me well, Mrs Webster. You will not avoid the gallows even if pagan Socrates himself ascends from Limbo to prepare your defence.'

'I need no sage for my solicitor, for I have Reason on my side,' Jennet said.

Dunstan turned to his companions and guided them towards the door, tapping each cleanser gently with the trident. 'What is Reason?' he said in a tone of measured ridicule.

'Scripture doth not speak of it,' Reverend Parris replied.

'Reason's a habit of mind that enjoyed great favour with the Papist Scholastics of old,' Abby said evenly. 'But today no person remembers their names.'

The New-England cleansers' clamorous and eventful visit to Man-ayunk Gaol-House aroused in Jennet an optimism quite opposite to the intimidation that had been their aim. All three demonologists had obviously offended Herbert Bledsoe, and it seemed logical to suppose they would likewise offend the jurymen appointed to determine her fate.

'I must confess, Mrs Webster,' the magistrate said, 'ere your brother descended upon us, I thought it possible you'd consorted with the Dark One. But I sense scant holiness in the Purification Commission. From this day forward, I intend to make your cell a hospitable place.'

'Do you mean I might have a true bed?' she asked.

'With a feather mattress,' Mr Bledsoe said.

'A linen shift instead of this rag?'

'If you like.'

'Ink, quill, paper and a writing-desk?'

'Verily.'

'Whene'er a person comes to visit me, I would have Mr Knox let him inside my cell.'

Mr Bledsoe nodded and said, 'I shall accord your callers every comfort within my authority.'

Over the next four days the magistrate made good his promises, civilizing her circumstances as much as he could without provoking public speculation that she'd bewitched him. A pair of Derbyshire chairs arrived in time for her first meeting with her advocate.

The encounter was not long underway when Jennet decided that Charles de Montesquieu had managed to rise above his aristocratic birth to embrace the world in all its earthy particulars. Despite his plumed hat, silk vest, perfumed neckcloth and landed lineage, he seemed at ease in these squalid surroundings, and she believed he would have adapted equally well to the previous, unappointed version of her cell.

'You have written a brilliant book, Mrs Webster, and I am

persuaded to make it the centrepiece of our case,' he said, removing *The Sufficiency of the World* from his portmanteau. 'When interviewing you before the Court, I shall prompt you to speak of acceleration, oscilla-tion, refrangibility and other such principles. Thus will the jurymen learn that the universe obeys Nature's laws, not Satan's wraiths.'

'Monsieur, 'twould seem you have grasped my argument in full,' she said, pacing the length of her stone-and-iron cube: twelve feet wide, only twelve — a fact that Mr Bledsoe's good intentions could never redeem.

'Acceleration, osculation, refrangularity,' Mrs Sharkey chanted from her cell. 'When my case comes to trial, I'll tell the judge I could ne'er have bludgeoned my husband with a ploughshare, for Nature's laws do not permit it.'

'I'm inclinin' towards the same strategy,' Mr Turpin said. ' "Ye think I stole Mr Pertuis's cattle, Excellency? 'Tis obvious ye know naught o' refrangularity." '

'Eavesdroppers, I shall thank you to keep silent,' Jennet said.

'If 'twould be no inconvenience' — Montesquieu pressed his *Sufficiency of the World* into her hands — 'I hope you might inscribe this copy to me.'

She approached her writing-desk, dipped quill into ink-pot, and, opening the treatise, decorated the cover-page with the bold looping hand she'd learned from Aunt Isobel. *À Charles Louis de Secondat . . . avec toute ma considération et ma sympathie . . . Jennet Stearne Crompton.* 'I'Christ, 'tis the first time I e'er wrote my name in a book.'

'Except, of course, when you signed the Devil's register.' Mont-esquieu issued a succinct but merry laugh, then immediately turned sombre. 'I bring good tidings and bad.'

'Tell me the bad straight away.'

'Three days ago, for reasons that remain mysterious, the jurist Malcolm Cresswell recused himself from the case.'

'Faugh!' Jennet said. 'Who hath replaced him?'

'None other than John Hathorne.'

'Hathorne of the Salem trials?'

'The same knave.'

The quill in her hand seemed suddenly as grotesque and sinister as a Paracelsus trident. 'Our enterprise hath sustained a deep wound.'

'Deep, *oui*, but not deadly.'

'I would now receive the good tidings.'

'By the report of Mr Franklin's band of youngbloods, the whole of Philadelphia stands behind you,' Montesquieu said. 'Should Hathorne attempt to abridge your defence, the cries from the gallery will set the courthouse to trembling as when Joshua's trumpets shook down Jericho.'

'A most opportune development.' She laid the quill aside, blew the ink dry, and returned the book to Montesquieu.

From the shadows atop the staircase a man called out, 'Nor hath Dame Fortune yet run short of smiles, darling Jenny' – a familiar voice, coarsened by age yet still ringing and resolute – 'for it seems an old friend is lately come to Philadelphia!'

In the centre of the descending parade marched Mr Bledsoe, brandishing an uncocked pistol. Behind him tramped Mr Knox, grasping a ring of iron keys, and first in line, dressed in a torn and dusty surtout, stepped – Jennet blinked once, twice, then swallowed audibly – Barnaby Cavendish!

'This beggar insisted on seeing you,' the magistrate said.

Astonishment and joy rushed through her like a surge from a Von Guericke sphere. 'He's no beggar, sir, but the treasured companion of my youth! Oh, Barnaby, dear friend, you have once again returned from the dead!'

''Tis a habit I intend to cultivate for the rest of my life,' he said.

Receiving the magistrate's nod, Knox unlocked the cell door and ushered Barnaby into Jennet's presence. For a full minute she and the mountebank embraced. He exuded a bracing scent, a pungent and oddly pleasant mixture of sweat, hay and mildew.

'When last I saw this man,' she told the befuddled Montesquieu, 'he was about to go down with the wreck of the *Berkshire*.'

''Twas a truly fearsome gale.' Barnaby adjusted his spectacles, which had somehow survived the nautical catastrophe. 'But by freeing the Lyme Bay Fish-Boy and the Bicephalic Girl from their sea-chest and wrapping an arm 'round each, I stayed afloat amidst the froth and tumult. Twenty thirsty hours upon Neptune's bosom, and then a Portuguese brigantine delivered us from certain doom.'

'Dr Cavendish curates a prodigy museum,' Jennet explained to Montesquieu.

'My life was saved by two of the most amazing freaks e'er to drop from a woman's womb,' Barnaby elaborated.

'They reside in bottles,' Jennet noted.

'Then you were rescued by Mr Boyle's law of buoyancy,' Montesquieu told Barnaby, waving the *Sufficiency* in his face.

'No doubt, my lord,' Barnaby said.

'Howbeit, some would aver his benefactors were in sooth the prodigies,' Knox said. 'Such a foetus once cured my grandfather's shingles.'

'Mrs Webster, when you address the Court next week, you will avoid all mention of Dr Cavendish's monsters, *je vous en prie*,' Montesquieu said. 'We must distance our arguments from peasant superstition.'

'Your attitude's sensible, *Monsieur le Baron*,' Barnaby said, 'though I for one can't speak too highly of peasant superstition, for it hath kept me gainfully employed these past fifty years.' He lifted the treatise from Montesquieu's grasp. 'If I am to believe Ebenezer Trenchard, Jenny, you've wrought a demon disproof to beat the one that Newton ne'er devised. Ah, but doth the world in fact *want* a demon disproof? That's the question I now put to you wights.'

'Most men are indifferent to metaphysics,' Bledsoe said with a sigh.

'My own taste runs more to pirate tales,' Knox confessed.

'Most men are indifferent,' Montesquieu echoed, 'but their canons are not. I assure you, Dr Cavendish, that even as we speak, our civilization's greatest law books reach out and press Mrs Webster's *argumentum grande* to their collective breast.'

'For a person chary of superstition, you seem passing eager to credit books with minds and souls,' Barnaby said.

'I have lived so long amongst books,' Montesquieu said, 'I cannot but believe they *do* have souls.'

'You strike me as a clever fellow' – Barnaby returned the *Sufficiency* to the Baron – 'and I'm sure you mean to save my Jenny, but I hope you know your enemy. These cleansers are made of iron.'

'I'll wager they've never battled a French jurist,' Montesquieu said.

Barnaby touched his right temple. 'If my Bicephalic Girl were here, her dexter head would say, "I have every faith in Jenny's lawyer."' He pointed to his left temple. 'But then the sinister head would reply, "I have every fear of Jenny's brother."'

''Tis not Dunstan we should fear, but rather his malevolent wife,' Jennet said, lifting the quill from her desk. 'For whilst my brother hath his Paracelsus trident and his pricking needles and his other pretensions to philosophy, Abigail heeds only the madness in her skull.' She blew upon the feather, wondering what sort of equation might describe the vane's exquisite ripple. 'I'faith, good sirs, I have seen this woman's brain at work, and I say it traffics less with rational discourse than doth flint with flour.'

'Then may God help you, Monsieur,' said Bledsoe to Montesquieu.

'Then may God help Mrs Webster,' the Baron corrected him.

CHAPTER THE ELEVENTH

A Metaphysics Debate Captivates Humankind,
or at Least that Portion of Humankind Owning
Subscriptions to *The Pennsylvania Gazette*

Charles-Louis de Secondat, Baron de la Brède et de Montesquieu, stepped out of his hired coach, bid his footman adieu, and presented the driver with a one-pound note and a dip of his plumed hat, the worthy Herr Strossen having steered them a smooth course along the pocked and pitted length of Ridge Road. A kind of carnival was unfolding amidst the hills surrounding Manayunk Courthouse, every knoll a-swarm with Philadelphia rustics chattering in a half-dozen tongues as they read that morning's *Pennsylvania Gazette* and patronized stalls dispensing German-Town lager, meat pies, roasted potatoes and apple tarts. The Baron screwed his hat in place, fastening it to his bewigged head, and started towards the *Maison de Justice*. Weaving through the boisterous, earthy mob, he felt the same vague discomfort he'd endured earlier that year upon seeing, in the Mayor of Antwerp's mansion, Pieter Breughel's painting of a peasant wedding. Montesquieu was a man who believed the world's common people deserved political freedom and personal sovereignty – he endorsed this ideal with every atom of his being – and yet he would admit to a difficulty in extending the principle to the sorts of excessively common people who populated Breughel paintings and attended witch-trials.

It took him four attempts, each louder and angrier than the last, to convince the marshals stationed outside the courthouse that he was Rebecca Webster's advocate and must therefore be granted immediate entry. He pulled his portmanteau tight against his chest and, working his elbows in the manner of a fledgling attempting flight, jostled his way through the foyer. The main hall was packed front to back, side to side, and, if you considered the score of ill-scrubbed youths perched on the rafters, top to bottom. Numerous spectators sat in the aisles, so that Montesquieu had to advance gingerly, like a man crossing a brook by stepping from stone to stone.

Moving past the journalists' desk, he nodded towards Benjamin Franklin, who was too busy scribbling to notice the gesture, then proceeded to the defence table and set down his portmanteau. Along the opposite wall loomed the three Purification Commissioners, black of dress, sour of face: ravens contemplating a carcass. Beside them rose the jury-box, crammed with twelve men whose principal qualifications for determining the defendant's fate were that each held title to twenty acres and had nothing better to do before Sunday.

'Oyez! Oyez!' The bailiff banged his pike against the floor as if cracking the ice-cake on a cistern.

The spectators grew silent. Bedecked in a dark frock coat and a ludicrous periwig spouting white curls, the ancient John Hathorne emerged from his alcove at the languid velocity of a pallbearer. Solemnly, awkwardly, he ascended to the judge's bench, then cleared his throat with a reverberant rasp.

'The Court is now in session,' he said, punctuating each syllable with a tap of his wooden mallet. 'Mr Broom, you may arraign the defendant.'

'Rebecca Webster will come before the bench!' the bailiff declared.

The antechamber door flew open, and the prisoner strode into the hall, attired in her linen shift and accompanied by four marshals holding pikes. An iron chain arced betwixt her wrists like a pur-gatorial watch fob. She brought her lean body to its full height and approached Judge Hathorne. For the first time since pledging himself to her cause, Montesquieu realized that he was in love with Jennet Stearne Crompton. The sensation was at once uplifting and con-founding, like a good law in need of an especially subtle interpretation.

'State your name,' the bailiff commanded.

'Rebecca Webster,' she replied tonelessly.

'Rebecca Webster, the Crown sayeth you have committed the abhorrent crime of sorcery, and this Court doth thereby charge you with heresy against the Christian faith, according to the Witchcraft Statute of King James the First as ratified in the year 1718 by the Pennsylvania Assembly. How plead you, guilty or nay?'

'There being no such crime as sorcery, I must perforce assert my innocence.'

'The jury will disregard all rogue opinions from the defendant,' Hathorne said.

'The Court proposed that you solicit its leniency by forthwith signing a confession of Satanic compact,' the bailiff informed Madame Crompton. 'Will you do this?'

'If you put the thumbscrews to me I might,' she said, 'but mayhap not even then.'

'His Majesty's witch courts have ne'er resorted to torture, Mrs Webster,' Hathorne said, 'a fact with which you are well acquainted.'

The marshals escorted Madame Crompton to the defence table, where Montesquieu greeted her by clasping her manacled hands betwixt his palms.

'How felicitous that you mentioned thumbscrews,' he said.

'Felicitous?' she said, assuming her chair.

'Torture is more relevant to this case than *Monsieur le Juge* imagines.'

Hathorne directed a trembling finger towards the Purification Commissioners. 'The Crown will offer a preliminary argument.'

Securing a thick mouldering Bible under his arm, Dunstan Stearne stepped towards the jury-box and bowed to the foreman, Enoch Hocking, a gnarled rustic with high cheekbones and hair the texture of corn silk. 'Good landholders, I shall begin by confirming a rumour that flits about this courtroom like a mayfly,' the pricker said. 'The defendant was indeed born Jennet Stearne, and she is truly my blood-sister.' He caressed the Bible. 'Should my role as Crown's advocate therefore strike you as paradoxical, let me evoke our Saviour's admonition from Luke Chapter Fourteen. "If any man come to me, and hate not his father, and mother, and wife, and children, and brethren . . . and *sisters* . . . yea, and his own life also, he cannot be my disciple."'

Montesquieu was pleased to observe an expression of perplexity claim every juryman's face. The verse in question evidently bespoke a species of Christianity with which they were unfamiliar.

'The case before you is mayhap the most important yet tried in His

Majesty's American provinces,' Monsieur Stearne continued. 'If you read *The Pennsylvania Gazette*, you will know that Mrs Webster seeks not only to deliver herself from the gallows but to destroy the Parliamentary Witchcraft Act, thus unleashing a deluge of Sadducism, Hobbism, Deism and atheism throughout His Majesty's realm.'

The jurymen's expressions shifted from bewilderment to shock.

'Sadducism?' whispered Madame Crompton. 'Atheism? Is he allowed to speak such lies?'

'I fear your brother thinks them facts,' Montesquieu replied.

'Make no mistake, landholders,' Stearne said. 'Mrs Webster will not rest till she hath hacked off the witch-fighting arm of the Christian religion. Were Satan to grant her the power, she would amputate all demonology from Holy Writ, impounding every Bible in Europe and America and tearing out Leviticus page by page.' He flung open his Scripture, leafed his way eastward from Eden, and declaimed with a passion worthy of a Molièrean player. ' "A man also or woman that hath a familiar spirit, or that is a wizard, shall surely be put to death." ' He snapped the Bible shut and pivoted towards the bench, black cape swirling. 'The Crown would now make its case in the particular.'

'Proceed,' Hathorne said.

'We call to the witness-stand Mr Abraham Pollock, magistrate of Mount-Holly.'

Rage boiled up in Montesquieu's every vein. '*Pardonez-moi*,' he said, rising abruptly. 'By your leave, Judge Hathorne, the defence will make an opening argument.'

'Mr Stearne hath provided the jury with all the preamble it requires,' Hathorne said. 'Find your chair, Baron, that the trial may continue.'

Montesquieu resumed his seat, moving with a sluggishness that aspired to impertinence. 'In France I would be heard,' he muttered.

'If you wish to return home, Monsieur, the Court will not stop you,' said Hathorne.

As Abraham Pollock climbed onto the witness-stand, the audience snorted and grumbled its discontent with Hathorne's ruling. We have sustained a Pyrrhic defeat, Montesquieu thought. If we lose many more such battles, we shall surely win the war.

Stearne and Pollock now commenced a protracted dialogue,

demonologist to demonologist, during which interval they established why four particular tests – swimming an accused Satanist in a pristine current, pricking her suspicious excrescences, noting her commerce with dumb beasts, and requiring her to recite the Lord's Prayer – enjoyed such prestige amongst witchfinders.

The luncheon recess followed. Montesquieu marched directly to the food-stalls, purchased a mutton-pie as puffy and fragrant as a courte-san's pillow, and delivered it to Madame Crompton. Despite her dire circumstances, she retained a hearty appetite, devouring her portion in less than a minute.

At one o'clock the demonologists renewed their conversation. Pollock discoursed extensively on how the Delaware River had spurned Rebecca Webster's body, how his pricking needing had failed to bloody her Devil's mark, and how the *Pater Noster* had crumbled on her tongue. Beyond this plethora of evidence lay the fact that a half-dozen cats currently inhabited the defendant's barn, each displaying intimations of Satanic ancestry.

Hathorne thanked Pollock for sharing his expertise, then offered Dunstan Stearne a conspiratorial smile. 'I realize that the Crown hath barely begun to construct its case, and yet the hour grows late. Might we defer your next witness till the morrow?'

Stomach twitching, Montesquieu leapt to his feet. 'Before the Court adjourns, I would question Mr Pollock.'

'His testimony hath been discussed in full,' Hathorne replied. 'Mr Pollock, you are excused.'

Heedless of the crowd's indignant murmurs, the Mount-Holly magistrate left the witness-stand and strode out of the hall.

'Charles, we must not let this moment pass,' Madame Crompton muttered.

'Have no fear, *mon amie*.' He lingered briefly at the defence table, long enough to give his client's shoulder an obliquely amorous squeeze, then dashed towards the jury-box. 'Good Philadelphians, I beg that you consider Magistrate Pollock's testimony in the light of Reason. If you study the bailiff over there' – he gestured towards the man called Broom – 'you will note a black wart on his left nostril.'

Jurors, journalists and spectators engaged in a collective con-templation of the bailiff's nose. The man turned scarlet and cringed.

'Baron, you seem unaware that we are about to adjourn,' Hathorne said, reaching for his mallet.

A hissing spread through the hall, as if the trial had attracted an audience of vipers.

Hathorne stayed his hand and scowled. 'Lest a cry of favouritism be raised against the bench,' he said to Montesquieu, 'I shall permit you to waggle your tongue for a short interval.'

The hissing ceased.

'I was speaking of the bailiff's wart,' Montesquieu continued. 'Tell me, honourable landholders, do we now apprehend Mr Broom and prick that suspect blot? For such is our sacred duty by Mr Pollock's logic.' He returned to the defence table and, opening his portmanteau, dumped out a bronze basin, a tin flask, and a leather bottle bulging with water. He seized the flask and struck it with his knuckles, producing a hollow bong. 'Consider this container. Empty as a drunkard's mug. I bid you now imagine that my vessel' – he filled the basin with water – 'is the lung of an accused sorcerer.' He stoppered the flask, set it afloat, and carried the demonstration to the jury. 'See how it swims? Do we therefore call this vessel bewitched? Or do we simply admit that it obeys the law of buoyancy, the same principle as raised Rebecca Webster from the Delaware?'

'Baron, you will finish this absurd presentation within one minute,' Hathorne said.

Montesquieu retrieved the flask and laid it on the floor. 'Now watch how easily I make the enchantment disappear, a mere matter of purging the lung in question.' He inflicted his boot heel on the flask, rendering it as flat as a *centime*, then picked up the squashed vessel, held it over the basin, and dropped it in the water. The flask sank instantly. 'Look, gentlemen, the vessel founders! The spell is broken!'

'And hence the Court is adjourned!' Hathorne shouted, hammering on the bench.

'Each time a supposed witch is launched upon a river,' Montesquieu yelled over Hathorne's frantic cadence, 'we learn little about the condition of her soul and much about the status of her lungs. Purged, she sinks! Full, she rises!'

'Purged, she sinks!' echoed Ben Franklin. 'Full, she rises!'

'Adjourned!' John Hathorne cried.

'Purged, she sinks!' shouted Barnaby Cavendish from the front row. 'Full, she rises!'

'Adjourned!'

'Purged, she sinks!' insisted the tallest of Franklin's youngbloods, the Indian John Tux. 'Full she rises!'

Now the whole gallery took up the cry. 'Purged, she sinks! Full, she rises!'

Montesquieu experienced a sudden rush of admiration for Pennsylvania's yeomen. They might lack the nuances of a civilized people, but their instinctive love of *la liberté* was most inspiring.

'Adjourned!' roared Hathorne.

As Montesquieu strode back to the defence table, Franklin stood up, blotted his scribblings with a sponge, and came forward. 'Congratulations, sir,' he said, clasping the Baron's hand. 'Despite Judge Hathorne's sophistry, you have carried the day.'

Montesquieu said, 'Tomorrow Dunstan Stearne interviews Rebecca Webster's supposed victims – a marvellous opportunity to acquaint the jury with the sufficiency hypothesis.'

'And an equally marvellous opportunity for Ebenezer Trenchard to declare that the mirage called *maleficium* is passing from the world,' Franklin said, 'so 'tis time we blamed our troubles on ourselves.'

By goading his mare to her swiftest gallop, Ben managed to reach Philadelphia as twilight fell upon the city, covering Market Street in a caul of mist and murk. No sooner had he reined up before the printing-house than his writerly imagination wrought from the surrounding gloom the opening sentence of Ebenezer Trenchard's next essay. 'At the start of the Webster trial, the Baron de Montesquieu disclosed how our species might finally escape the shadowy slough of superstition to sport upon the sun-drenched plain beyond.'

He entered the shop. Characteristically, he was the first man on the scene, but as the hour progressed the other journalists arrived, and soon the collective scratchings of five pen nibs filled the press-room, none moving faster than Ben's. Beyond the Trenchard letter, the incipient edition of *The Pennsylvania Gazette* would feature William Parson's unsympathetic report on Dunstan Stearne's preamble, Hugh Roberts's scalding critique of Abraham Pollock's witch tests, Philip Synge's paean to Montesquieu's tin flask, and John Tux's general lament over the toll the cleansers had taken on his Indian brethren. Only Nicholas Scull's quill was unemployed, for he had elected to set his article — an attack on Hathorne's irrational rulings — directly in type, so pure was his outrage and supreme his self-confidence.

At eight o'clock the shop's foreman, Ned Billings, arrived with his six journeymen, each eager to assume his respective duty as compositor, framer, inker, washer, breaker and spindle-man. Ben handed his essay to the trusty Billings, bid his colleagues farewell and headed home, happy in the knowledge that, like two great ovens baking loaf upon loaf of nourishing bread, the Blaeu presses would that night yield five hundred copies of the *Gazette*, as they had done each night for the past eighteen months.

Though normally an early riser, Ben experienced difficulty quitting his bed the next morning, as this meant trading a pleasant reverie about Amakye-Isle — he was catching eels in Copernicus Cove — for the waking nightmare of Jennet's trial. The more alert he became, the lower his spirits fell. He wished he owned some sort of time-travelling carriage, crowning product of his philosophic pursuits, that he might vault across the remainder of the week and land unscathed in Sunday.

Through a sudden surge of will he abandoned the sheets and, leaning over the warm cavity from which he'd emerged, kissed his drowsy Deborah on her cheek. He shuffled to the dresser, surprised his face with a splash of cold water, and climbed into his breeches. Almost as useful as a time-travelling carriage, he mused, would be a machine that ejected you from your bed and prepared you for the day ahead.

He stepped into the nursery, expecting to find William asleep, but the boy was sitting on the floor playing with his birthday present from Barnaby Cavendish, a mahogany Noah's Ark cradling a cargo of ten animals whittled from fir blocks. In theory William knew only what he'd been told — his mother was standing trial on a false accusation of witchery, the best lawyer in the world was defending her — and yet he seemed aware of more than these raw facts. It would be pointless to mislead William, painting Jennet's future in rosy hues, for the prism of his mind was aligned to pierce all such adult deceptions.

'Be thee well, son,' Ben said, embracing the boy. 'I'm off to Manayunk.'

From his little ark William removed a wooden tiger and placed it in Ben's hand. 'For Mother.'

''Tis a bonny gift.'

'Tigers are brave,' William said.

'Indeed,' Ben said.

'Tigers are strong.'

'Quite so.'

As if she'd fallen victim to a melancholia of the very sort that afflicted Ben, the mare transported him at a torpid pace, and he arrived in Manayunk later than he'd intended, entering the courthouse just as the marshals were seating Jennet. He noted with satisfaction that two jurymen and at least thirty spectators were reading that morning's *Gazette*. Pulling the tiger from his pocket, he approached the defence table, mysteriously spread with a microscope, a horseshoe, a Von Guericke sphere, a dish of phlox petals, a phial of milk, a bowl of grain and, most peculiar of all, a wire cage containing a distressed rooster.

'William presents you with his bravest beast' — Ben pressed the tiger into Jennet's palm as respectfully as he would Isaac Newton's epochal apple — 'that you might draw courage from it.'

'Tell our son I've ne'er received a better token.'

'Pray call your first witness,' Hathorne instructed the Purification Commissioners.

Abigail Stearne rose from the prosecution table and, black cape billowing like a window-drape in a thunder-gust, glided towards the judge's bench. 'The Crown summons Michael Bailey,' she said.

After settling behind the journalists' desk, Ben opened his valise and retrieved his writing supplies. He trimmed his quill, transmuted into Ebenezer Trenchard, and made ready to report on the day's events.

Mr Bailey, a gorbellied, turnip-cheeked harness-maker, heaved his bulk into the stand. Questioned by Mrs Stearne, he lamented his decision to slam the door in Rebecca Webster's face one evening when she'd come begging for a jug of cider. His regret traced not to his uncharitable behaviour, however, but to the fact that Mrs Webster had evidently retaliated by afflicting his wife with dropsy.

Spurious Connection 'twixt Webster and Wife's Illness, Ben wrote.

As the morning progressed, sufferer after sufferer stood before the Court, each attesting to how he'd spurned the defendant – apparently she'd habitually sought to share her neighbours' victuals and borrow their tools – and consequently endured some hardship or other. The jurors heard of butter that declined to come, dough that neglected to rise, hens who failed to lay, a baby who rebuffed the breast, a wound that wouldn't heal, and flax turned rotten in the field.

Feeble Attempt to cast Misfortunes as Maleficium, Ben wrote.

The first seven witnesses occasioned no reaction from the defence, but then Mrs Stearne interviewed Bethany Fallon, a comely but morose goose girl who told how, two days after she'd refused to let Mrs Webster roam through her pens collecting eggs at will, twenty of her flock had died of an enchantment. When Miss Fallon added that the birds' death throes included running in circles and pecking at rocks until their beaks shattered, Jennet and Montesquieu sat up straight and exchanged urgent whispers. The instant the Crown finished with the witness, Montesquieu proposed to cross-examine her.

'The Court hath heard quite enough of this girl's benighted geese,' Hathorne replied. A sound emerged from the gallery, a shrill moan like the synchronous whimperings of a hundred ill-treated dogs. 'Howbeit, let it not be said I failed to accord the defence every leeway.'

Montesquieu now approached the witness-stand carrying his bowl of grain. 'Mademoiselle Fallon, may I offer a conjecture concerning your geese? I believe they succumbed not to bewitchment but to a natural illness.'

'Aye, a natural illness contrived by the Widow Webster,' Bethany Fallon said, gesturing vaguely towards Jennet.

'More likely your geese grew sick from eating rye seeds such as these.' Montesquieu thrust the grain before the witness. 'You will note that some are brown and normal, though others appear black as tar, a sign of fungal infection. This corrupted food sickened your geese with the disease called ergot, also known as St Anthony's fire and *infernalis*. Its cause was established fifty years ago by my countryman Monsieur Dodart, a Paris doctor with a special knowledge of moulds and mushrooms. Speak truly – did you feel your flock on rye seeds?'

'I have always given them such.'

Ergot caus'd by Fungus not Fiends, Ben wrote.

Montesquieu revisited the defence table, seized the wire cage, and bore the unlucky rooster towards Miss Fallon. Never before had Ben beheld so sorely afflicted a creature; his thoughts turned to Jennet's accounts of *skishauonck*, the smallpox, murderer of her first child. When not throwing itself against the walls of its pen, the rooster bobbed its head in all directions and tore out its own feathers. Unless it died first, the wretched fowl would by day's end be as naked as if plucked for roasting.

'Last evening I fed this rooster contaminated rye seeds, and now it displays a manifest case of the ergot,' Montesquieu said. 'Tell me, *s'il vous plaît*, whether my bird perhaps reminds you of your own stricken flock.'

'Aye, 'tis so,' the girl said. 'But did not Mrs Webster mayhap bid Lucifer taint my grain with the mould of which you speak?'

'Any experienced farmer will tell you that a fungus may thrive without benefit of occult powers. *Écoutez-moi, Mademoiselle*. To save your geese from future plagues, you must purify their food. Use a sieve to filter out the larger black bodies, then drop the remaining seeds in a tub of saltwater. The lesser black bodies will rise to the surface, where you may easily skim them off.'

'Thus sparing my birds this madness?' she asked, pointing a milk-white finger towards the dying rooster. 'Then verily I shall do it.'

'*Vous êtes très intelligente*. I have no more questions.'

Montesquieu returned to the defence table, whereupon Hathorne decreed a recess for the midday meal. As the interval began, Jennet prevailed upon Ben to put the rooster out of its misery. He carried the cage behind the courthouse, removed the bird, and grasped its tattered body by the neck. Closing his eyes, he twisted the head round and round as if removing the cork from a wine bottle.

A brief trip to the Wissahickon Creek yielded two bucketfuls of stones, which he piled one by one atop the feathered witness, and soon the cairn completely obscured the rooster's earthly remains. He set the final stone in place, then offered up a succinct but sincere eulogy, for such commemoration was surely due any creature sacrificed to the cause of demonology's defeat.

Later that day, cued by Abigail Stearne, a fresh parade of *maleficium* sufferers told their stories. After disregarding the initial four victims, Montesquieu elected to cross-examine a wizened flax-planter named Zebulon Plum, whose crop had sustained a blast of Heaven's fire and subsequently burned to the ground. The Baron began by cluttering the stand with the horseshoe, the Von Guericke sphere, the dish of phlox petals, and a copy of *The Sufficiency of the World*. He turned the crank, set his palm against the equator, and thereby made a squall of petals fly to the sphere and stick to its surface like ants mired in a trickle of sap.

'Mr Plum, I show you the force called electricity, supreme amongst those energies with which God has suffused the world.' Montesquieu halted the sphere, causing it to shed the petals. 'Now observe what happens when I cause an electric charge first to accumulate within my body and then to find release in iron.' He gave the ball a vigorous crank, placed his left hand against the sulphur, and extended his right index finger, bringing the pad to within an inch of the horseshoe. A tiny crackling thread shot forth. The Baron flinched. 'Tell the jury what you saw, Monsieur.'

''Tis hard to describe. A kind o' thin, cold spark.'

'*Exactement*. Just as the great Sir Isaac Newton discerned a general gravitation stretching to the very edge of Creation, so has Philadelphia's own Benjamin Franklin postulated a universal electricity.'

Ben blushed to hear his name mentioned in the same breath as Newton's, though he allowed that the parallel was not without merit. *Montesquieu advocates for Universal Electricity over Unseen Elementals*, he wrote.

Flourishing Jennet's book, the Baron faced the jury-box and locked his eyes on Mr Hocking. 'To the curious amongst you I recommend the account of Mr Franklin's work found in J. S. Crompton's admirable treatise, *The Sufficiency of the World*,' Montesquieu said. 'If the Franklin hypothesis is correct, the spark I made leap between flesh and metal just now differs only in degree' – he turned and fixed his gaze on Mr Plum – 'from the celestial torch that destroyed your flax.'

'A spark is not a lightning-bolt,' Mr Plum protested. 'A whelk is not a whale.'

Montesquieu answered the witness's complaint with an insouciant flip of his hand, then strode towards the twelve landholders, staring at each in turn. 'Perhaps these fiery blasts come forth as our planet rubs against its envelope of aether. Perhaps they form in the arcane depths of maelstroms and then ascend to the clouds, returning to Earth during thunder-gusts. But I swear to you, good jurymen, there is no more devilry in a lightning-stroke than in the blooming of a daffodil or the hatching of a swan's egg.'

To Ben's great satisfaction, Montesquieu now employed the very tactic the situation demanded. He approached the witness-stand, cranked the sphere and instructed Plum to unfloor his feet, explaining that otherwise the planter might receive a nasty jolt. He set Plum's palm against the spinning sulphur. The remaining petals hurled themselves against the ball.

'Behold!' Montesquieu cried. 'Zebulon Plum is a Christian man who has ne'er once met Lucifer, and yet he fashions the electric force with his very hands!'

'No devilry in lightning!' Barnaby Cavendish yelled.

'No devilry in lightning!' Nicholas Scull echoed.

'No devilry in lightning!' insisted the thoughtful young magistrate Herbert Bledsoe.

'Silence!' Hathorne screamed, pounding the bench with his mallet.

Von Guericke electrifies the Courtroom, Ben wrote.

The next two witnesses – a glass-blower who held Rebecca Webster responsible for his last eighty bottles turning brittle, a cordwainer convinced that she'd ensorcelled his gladadder–inspired no cross-examinations from Montesquieu. But then Stearne put Wilbur Bennet on the stand, a swart dairyman who'd declined to lend the Widow Webster his plough horse, that she might clear a tree-stump from her property. Two days alter, he'd lost forty gallons of milk to curdling.

Upon receiving Hathorne's permission to question Mr Bennet, Montesquieu marched to the stand bearing the microscope and the milk phial. 'Can you tell me the purpose of this instrument?'

'Methinks 'tis a kind o' magnifier,' Bennet said.

'*Vraiment.*' Montesquieu placed a white droplet on the stage, directed Bennet to peer through the eyepiece, and bid him describe what he saw.

'It looks to me a herd o' worms,' the witness said, scrutinizing the specimen, 'itchin' and twitchin' like they've contracted the chorea.'

Montesquieu told the Court that the microscope's optical components were the handiwork of Anton Van Leeuwenhoek, the legendary linen-draper who could grind lenses so powerful they revealed 'the very stitchery God employed in sewing the fabric of the world'. In his letters to the Royal Society, the Baron continued, Van Leeuwenhoek had described, amongst other wonders, the tiny creatures he'd seen swimming about in pond water, tooth scum and fecal matter. By the lens-grinder's report, sweet milk was free of these animalcules, while sour milk contained them in abundance.

'Would you not agree that Van Leeuwenhoek's beasties account for your ruined milk far better than does the demon hypothesis?' Montesquieu asked the witness.

'I would not,' Bennet said, giving the specimen a second glance. 'Your microscope tells me only that Mrs Webster implored some demon to spoil my milk with foul-tastin' wrigglers.'

'But if they're like other creatures – the ant, the moth, the field mouse – then these wrigglers generate themselves, and we need not posit wicked spirits to explain their propagation.'

'The wrigglers generate themselves!' Barnaby Cavendish shouted, and instantly his cry was taken up and chorused, first by Nicholas Scull, then by the rest of the Junto, then by scores of spectators.

'You will be silent!' Hathorne demanded.

Bennet stole a third peek at the animalcules. 'Baron Montesquieu, you do not study the evidence closely enough. This puddle swarms with the squirmin' progeny o' the very serpent who deprived us all o' Paradise.'

'You have a vivid imagination,' Montesquieu said, packing up the milk phial and the microscope.

'These be the Devil's descendants, I swear it.'

'I should be astonished to find in Europe even one natural philosopher who might corroborate that conclusion. You are excused, Mr Bennet.'

Lens-grinder sees through Witchfinders, Ben wrote.

'The dinner hour is upon us, and so we shall adjourn,' Hathorne said. 'Prithee, *Monsieur le Baron*, I would examine that milk myself.'

Montesquieu glowered but obediently bore the microscope and the phial to the bench, setting them before Hathorne. The judge closed one eye and with the other peered into the milk's darkest reaches. He turned the focus knob, clucked his tongue, and let loose the least spontaneous laugh Ben had ever heard.

''Tis just as Mr Bennet claims!' Hathorne told the Court. 'A hundred tiny demons cruise these white currents! All praise Anton Van Leeuwenhoek, whom history will remember as the man who brought Satan's invisible empire to light!'

The next morning the autumn sun burned with an unseasonable intensity, warming the air and inspiring the larks to praise the world's sufficiency in song, but to Jennet that same world seemed bleak, sterile and unworthy of such music. Making her fettered way to the defence table, she endured a queasiness in her stomach, as if she'd just consumed a quart of Ben's revolting nostrum for sea sickness.

By the Baron de Montesquieu's reckoning, the Commissioners would attack her from two sides today, indicting not only the odd behaviours she'd exhibited whilst living on the Sumac Lane farm, but also the presumed blasphemies entailed in her denial of demons. The odd behaviours were easy to explain. As for the blasphemies, she hoped to answer them by drawing upon the previous evening's tutorial with Montesquieu, during which he had offered up his illuminating trans-lations of those Old Testament verses in which that most horrible of heresies, the willing substitution of Lucifer for Christ, was supposedly anticipated and then denounced by the Hebrew prophets.

Invited by Hathorne to continue the Crown's presentation, the Reverend Samuel Parris bestirred his creaking bones, stretched himself into wakefulness and contemptuously discarded that day's edition of *The Pennsylvania Gazette*. Ebenezer Trenchard's column had begun with an observation Jennet thought especially pithy. 'Just as Rye Seeds infect'd by Fungus must be cast aside lest they afflict Geese with *Infernalis*, so must Statutes infest'd with Superstition be struck down before they send more Innocents to the Hangman.'

'The Crown calls Rebecca Webster,' Mr Parris said.

A chorus of sympathetic murmurs filled the hall as, wrist chains clanking in a discordant carillon, Jennet assumed the witness-stand. She reached into her pocket as far as the manacle permitted and closed her hand around William's wooden tiger.

'Mrs Webster, this Monday past the Court heard from Abraham Pollock, Magistrate of Mount-Holly,' Mr Parris said, hobbling towards the stand bearing the same fat Bible that Dunstan had employed during his opening address. 'He attested to the presence of six cats in your barn.'

''Tis as natural for a widow to solicit a community of innocuous cats,' she asserted, 'as for a marooned sailor to befriend a troop of wild monkeys.'

'I did not ask you to opine upon the character of your cats – that is the jury's prerogative.' Mr Parris offered the landholders a laboured wink and sly grin, then faced Jennet again. 'As Foreman Hocking's worthies go about their job, I know they will recall the scriptural passage Mr Stearne read to us on Monday: "A man also or woman that hath a familiar spirit, or that is a wizard, shall surely be put to death."'

'When next you return to the original Hebrew,' she said, employing what she hoped was a scholarly tone, 'you will notice that the phrase "a woman that hath a familiar spirit" is best translated as "pythoness" – a seer, that is, such as the Oracle at Delphi. The word "wizard", meanwhile, should be rendered as "diviner" or "knowing one". 'Tis baldly obvious the author of Leviticus speaks not of Satanism.'

'Ah – we have a philologist in our midst!' Parris sneered.

'I'm no philologist, Reverend, but I say there is far less demonology in Scripture than the King James translation leads a person to believe.'

'And have you likewise refurbished Exodus 22:18 for us? "Thou shalt not suffer a witch to live."'

'The problem with the usual rendering of Exodus 22:18 is that it makes a hash of the distinction betwixt executing a person and denying him a livelihood. A superior translation of that notorious verse would read, "Thou shalt not patronize a fortune-teller."'

'Superior in *your* estimation,' noted Parris in a caustic voice. 'Alas, Mrs Webster, I fear you give us but the dabblings of a dilettante – and thus I am obliged to put your erudition to the test. Tell me, how do you translate the Hebrew word *kaphar*?'

Jennet blenched. Neither she nor the Baron had imagined that Parris himself might be competent in Hebrew. 'I don't know.'

'It means *atonement*. Now will you please translate *eliyl* for the Court?'

She squeezed the wooden tiger so hard she felt the vein throbbing in her thumb. 'My vocabulary lacks that word.'

'It means *idol*. What are the English words for *zanah*, *goy*, and *asham*?'

'I've ne'er made a formal study of Hebrew,' she said, trying not to wince, and wincing in consequence of trying.

'*Zanah . . . goy . . . asham* – what do they mean?'

'I cannot say.'

'*Whoredom*, *heathen* and *guilty*. The Crown is disappointed in your Hebrew, Mrs Webster. Now let us consider your Greek. By your lights did the framers of the King James Bible abuse the Gospels as badly as they did the Torah?'

'My knowledge of Greek is minimal, Mr Parris. Howbeit, I am not alone in my opinion that our Saviour hath no sympathy for the cleansing trade.'

'Do you say we encounter no wicked spirits or fallen angels in the New Testament?'

'We encounter no wicked spirits of the sort you prickers imagine you're fighting.'

'Truly now?' Parris flung open the Bible. 'Mark 1:34: "And he healed many that were sick of divers diseases, and cast out many devils, and suffered not the devils to speak, because they knew him." Luke 4:33: "And in the synagogue there was a man, which had the spirit of an unclean devil—"'

''Tis one thing to speculate that diabolism may cause disease, and quite another to say Christ bids us murder every midwife who garbles her *Pater Noster*.'

'I am not finished, Mrs Webster. "Which had the spirit of an unclean devil, and he cried out in a loud voice, 'What have we to do with thee, Jesus of Nazareth?'"'

For the next two hours the minister assaulted her with the New Testament. He employed not only the Gospels for his truncheon but also Acts, Galatians, Ephesians, Second Thessalonians, First Timothy and Revelation. As interpreted by the Reverend Samuel Parris, Christ's biography was essentially a chronicle of war: the Messiah's beatific brigades versus Lucifer's demon legions.

At noon Parris unleashed his final quotation, Matthew 25:41: 'Then shall the Son of Man say also unto them on the left hand, "Depart from me, ye cursed, into everlasting fire, prepared for the Devil and his angels." ' He slammed the Bible shut and pivoted towards Foreman Hocking. 'Good jurors, I bid you recall Mrs Webster's statement of earlier this morning: "Our Saviour hath no sympathy for the cleansing trade." Evidently she believes the Gospels want for accuracy. She thinks Matthew a mountebank, Mark a charlatan, Luke a liar, and John a fraud.'

A tremor of unease, subtle but palpable, rumbled through the courthouse.

'Reverend, you must not put words in my mouth.' Jennet said, glancing every whichway. The twelve jurymen and a score of spectators all wore emphatic frowns.

'Even as *you* put words in the *saints'* mouths?' Parris retorted, facing the witness-stand. 'This interview hath ended, Mrs Webster, for I can no longer abide the presence of one who smears offal on Holy Writ.'

Jennet, Ben and Montesquieu spent the lunch recess tallying the morning's losses. It was now clear, the Baron conceded, that they would never win their case on Scripture. Whether rendered in Hebrew, Greek, Latin or English, the Bible belonged to the enemy. Instead they must rely on a concept with which the Hebrew prophets and the Christian saints were apparently unfamiliar.

'Nature,' Montesquieu said.

'*Exactement*,' Ben said.

'We must plant in each juror's brain a vision of Nature so rich and rarefied as to make demonic influence seem the silliest of ideas,' Montesquieu said.

'I fear we do not address the twelve brightest men in Pennsylvania,' Jennet said.

'Jesus had a similar problem,' Ben replied. 'Oft-times his disciples found his parables opaque, and yet those poor bewildered pilgrims finally grasped his message.'

When Jennet returned to the witness-stand, she saw that Dunstan would now assume the Inquisitorial role. He came at her flourishing a stack of papers as a Northman gone a-viking might brandish his battle-axe.

'The Crown hath collected sixteen depositions from your Man-ayunk neighbours,' he said. 'Four such reports tell that your grounds are congested with monk's hood, thorn-apple, henbane, and other such hideous growths, all tumoured and deformed as if sprung from Eden's malignant opposite.'

Jennet raised her arms, separating them as far as the chain allowed. 'I have cultivated my garden as a philosophic laboratory, that I might learn what plants will breed one with the other. 'Tis but simple curiosity waters their roots. I seek to investigate those laws of Nature that have lately inspired so many valuable Baconian treatises' – she gestured towards Montesquieu, who flourished the demon disproof as proudly as a crusader advancing his king's banner – 'such as J. S. Crompton's *The Sufficiency of the World.*'

'Methinks this curiosity of yours is not far removed from necro-mancy,' Dunstan said, pitching his voice towards the jury-box. 'As for the entity you call Nature, it seems to me a peculiar locus for a woman's religious devotions.' He stroked the depositions. 'Another six honest citizens aver that you have oft-times launched silk kites during thunder-gusts.'

'Had my neighbours spied more closely, they would have noticed how, after leaving the kite, the fly-line descends to Earth, coils about a mooring-post, and enters a glass collection jar.'

'A philosophic experiment?' Dunstan asked haughtily.

Jennet nodded. 'I share Mr Franklin's supposition that Heaven's fire, once captured and caged, will reveal itself as a variety of electricity.' She gesticulated in the ragged pattern of a lightning-stroke arcing betwixt sky and ground. 'After the initial explosion, the collateral sparks converge upon a stiff pointed wire atop the kite, then travel unimpeded along the wet twine – water, you see, facilitates the electric flow, an important finding of Mr Franklin's. Finishing their journey, the sparks spill down the mooring-post and enter the jar.'

'And what amount of lightning have you harvested in this fashion?'

'Thus far . . . none.'

'None?'

'Aye. None.'

'Evidently God would keep His fire from the hands of self-appointed sages.' Dunstan slapped the depositions. 'According to six upright men of this community, you are given to building stone mounds and dancing around them in a lascivious manner. Enacting such a spectacle doth not strike me as befitting a Christian woman.'

'And *watching* it doth not strike me as befitting a Christian man,' she said, thereby eliciting sniggers and guffaws throughout the hall.

Dunstan rubbed the scar on his forehead. 'Tell me what manner of philosophy is served by your Dionysian dancing.'

'My dancing's no experiment, kinsman. 'Tis merely how I express my awe as I contemplate Nature's glory.'

Under her brother's relentless and protracted questioning, she now reiterated the purposes behind her gardening, kite flying and dancing, carefully explaining how each endeavour differed categorically from the worship of fallen angels and the solicitation of obscene agencies.

'Mrs Webster,' he said at last, 'I believe there is but one name for your attitude to so-called Nature. Can you imagine what name I mean?'

'I cannot.'

''Tis paganism.'

'I would ne'er use that word to describe my enthusiasms.'

'Pray inform the jurymen, yea or nay, whether you practise pagan rites.'

She shut her eyes and again grasped William's wooden tiger, rubbing her thumb across its backbone. 'Kinsman, I am here to tell the Court how o'er the past three centuries many a blameless person hath gone to noose and stake for activities no more nefarious than growing herbs, delivering babies and leaping in adoration of the universe.'

'I shall ask the question once again. Do you practise pagan rites?'

'I believe God hath gifted His creatures with two great books, one called Scripture, the other Nature. As you cleansers would have it, Scripture admonishes against the manipulation of demons, but when we study the *Codex Naturae*, we find that these demons don't exist.'

'Demons don't exist?'

'Save in the human mind.'

Dunstan released a triumphant cackle and swerved towards the jury-box. 'Faithful Philadelphians, you heard the words fall freely from her lips. Mrs Webster hath just branded herself a Deist at best and a heretic at worst.' Turning, he fixed his gaze on Jennet. 'This interview is ended, sister – likewise the Crown's presentation. May our Saviour forgive you for renouncing him.'

'I have not renounced Christ! I have not!'

Hathorne brought his hammer down hard against the bench. 'Enough, Mrs Webster! Enough! You are finished!'

Jennet stood and trudged back to the defence table, her fingers still clamped around William's tiger. She glanced towards the jury-box. The landholders looked variously sodden with sleep, benumbed by ale, and transfixed by boredom. It seemed fair to suppose they'd under-stood nothing of what she'd meant by Nature's laws. Instead they'd found in Rebecca Webster a woman so impious and arrogant that she'd routinely attempted to make Heaven's fire submit to her

*

Will
the war of
the worldviews eventually
cease? Will the Armageddon of ideas in
time run its course? I doubt it. Since my advent I've been waging my lonely little campaign against rationalized irration-ality, day and night, rain and shine, all seasons, all epochs. The *Principia Mathematica* versus 16th-century astrology . . . 17th-century demonology . . . 18th-century Gothicism . . . 19th-century spirit-ualism . . . 20th-century New Age hogwash . . . 21st-century apocalyptics.

Now, it would be disingenuous of me to claim I have no taste for the fight. Over the centuries my struggle against the *Malleus Maleficarum* has provided me with an exhilaration that my more pacific endeavours – my steam locomotives, suspension bridges, geosynchronous satellites, moon landings – could never rival. When I learned three nights ago that my recent truce with the *Malleus* had disintegrated, I shed no tears. Instead I sallied forth to the vacant Manhattan lot we'd selected as our battlefield and took command of my bibliophagic army.

By the terms of our agreement, should my enemy's troops triumph tomorrow, I must permit them to invade the University of California Press warehouse in Ewing, New Jersey, and devour all three thousand copies of my thirtieth paperbound printing. By contrast, should my soldiers carry the day, they will advance unharried to the Dover Publications warehouse in Mineola, New York, there to consume the seven hundred copies of the *Malleus* currently on the shelves. Not since the Achaeans sailed off to Troy has a war promised its victor such desirable spoils.

As I write these words, twilight descends. Our armies face each other across a terrain strewn with cigarette butts, sweet wrappers, beer cans and broken bottles. Beyond his two divisions of silverfish and three regiments of bookworms, the *Malleus* has recently acquired an air force – five tactical groups of paper-eating Cambodian wasps summoned to the scene by the collected works of Deepak Chopra. I have allies as well. At the beginning of the week, *On the Origin of Species by Means of Natural Selection* joined my side with three companies of pulpchiggers, and the following day *The House of the Seven Gables* showed up with a brigade of termites. Alas, even after I add these reinforcements to my two regiments of booklice and my dozen squadrons of Indonesian moths, Revelation will still outnumber Reason by a factor of two to one.

Last night I read *The House of the Seven Gables* for the first time, seeking to learn exactly why it has come to my aid. I already knew that its author, the estimable Nathaniel Hawthorne, great-great-grandson of John Hathorne, was so ashamed of his ancestor's role in the Salem Witch Trials that he'd severed the connection with a strident *W*. Only upon negotiating the text, however, did I realize that among its several villains is a 19th-century judge named Jaffrey Pyncheon, clearly meant to evoke the 17th-century Salem magistrate.

The story unfolds in 1850. The opening pages disclose that Judge Pyncheon's family tree includes the unsavoury Colonel Pyncheon, who built the seven-gabled house on a Salem property he'd confiscated from Matthew Maule, a poor man executed as a wizard during the notorious persecutions. At the moment of his death, Maule called down a curse upon the Pyncheons, saying that God would give them blood to drink. Before the novel ends, Judge Pyncheon dies of apoplexy, blood pouring from his mouth – the same fate suffered by two previous Pyncheons.

We subsequently learn how thirty years earlier this depraved jurist tampered with the evidence surrounding his uncle's death, sending his kinsman Clifford Pyncheon to prison for murdering their relation (though the uncle actually died of natural causes), then claiming the entire inheritance for himself. The baroque plot comes to a happy conclusion when Mr Holgrove – a lodger in the seven-gabled house and fiancé of young Phoebe Pyncheon – reveals himself as a descendant of the murdered wizard. To wit, Phoebe and her children will bear the name of Maule. The Pyncheon line is dead.

On the whole, I thought it was a pretty good novel, and a long time will pass before an author gives us a more unflattering portrait of John Hathorne. It's too bad the judge never lived to see himself so famously skewered, but the bastard was a hundred years dead when the first edition of *The House of the Seven Gables* rolled off the press.

We attack at dawn. Fear throbs in my soul. Terror creeps along my spine. Part of me, I must admit, wants to take possession of a human pyromaniac. In this guise I would rush to the Dover warehouse and put the *Malleus* inventory to the torch. But that is not how we decided to settle our differences – and, anyway, should I stoop to incarnation, my enemy would do the same. Still, if a box of wooden matches suddenly appeared on the battlefield, I would be tempted to appropriate New York City's most accomplished firebug, wherever he now resides.

Given my heritage, of course, I can hardly imagine the mind of
such a man, so easily enthralled by the sight of flame, so
readily aroused by the crackle of combustion,
so reliably excited by
the smell
of
*
Smoke
rose from
John Hathorne's
clay pipe, spreading outward in
gossamer curls as he seized his mallet and
called the Court to order. The tobacco stench made Montesquieu sneeze. If there were any actual devils in the New World, he decided, one of them was the man behind the bench, Hathorne with the acrid

fire fixed in his jaw and the hot vapours pouring from his nostrils. 'This Boston Judge is hardly the Reincarnation of King Solomon,' Ebenezer Trenchard had noted in that morning's *Gazette*. 'If a newborn Babe were to be brought before Mr Hathorne along with two distraught Women, each claiming to be the Mother, I shudder to imagine how he might rule. Mayhap Hathorne would bisect the Infant with an Axe, then turn to the Women and declare, "Now let me observe who's the more aggriev'd, for she shall have both Halves!" '

'*Monsieur le Baron*, you may open your case,' Judge Hathorne said.

Montesquieu stretched to full height and gestured towards the Purification Commissioners. 'The defence will interview Dunstan Stearne.'

Gasps of surprise and murmurs of dismay reverberated through the hall.

'Sir, I cannot permit you to abuse the Crown's advocate in this fashion,' said Hathorne to Montesquieu.

Monsieur Stearne gained his feet, fired by an eagerness all too familiar to the Baron: the day before, the cleanser had shown a similar zeal in making Madame Crompton admit to Deist sympathies. 'By your leave, Excellency,' Stearne said, 'the Crown's advocate will submit to the proposed interrogation. This Frenchman hath no power to perturb me.'

'Would that I could say the same,' Hathorne grumbled.

As Stearne settled into the witness-stand, Montesquieu flashed him the most sardonic smile in his repertoire. 'Monsieur, if you had to give the Court two reasons why demons exist,' the Baron asked, 'may I assume that the first would be scriptural?'

'Verily,' Stearne said. 'Ephesians 6:12, First Timothy 4:1, and a plethora of other passages.'

Portmanteau in hand, Montesquieu approached the Crown's advocate. 'And the second reason – what might that be?'

'I know that demons exist because, over the years, hundreds of divinely empowered courts have found thousands of witches guilty.'

' "Over the years." "Thousands of witches." Might we attempt a greater specificity? Do you agree with me when I say the epic European witch-cleansing lasted nearly three centuries, an era that saw upwards of eight hundred thousand persons burned, hanged or beheaded as Devil-worshippers?'

'That's quite possibly the total thus far,' Stearne said. 'The great hunt's not yet done.'

'And would you also agree that most of those eight hundred thousand persons admitted to Satanism shortly before they were executed?'

'Aye.'

'Then would it be correct to say that, biblical passages aside, demonology derives its authority from eight hundred thousand signed confessions of heresy?'

'It would.'

'If those documents did not exist, might not a reasonable man question both your prosecution of Mrs Webster and your aggression against the Massachusetts aborigines?'

'But those documents *do* exist.'

'Indeed they do, Monsieur. Indeed they do. Something puzzles me, however. Since a confession was unlikely to save his life, why would any self-respecting Satanist give his persecutors the satisfaction of a signature?'

'By putting his name to a confession, the heretic seeks to purge his soul of the blackest sin imaginable.'

'Mr Stearne, is it not true that the majority of sorcery confessions were elicited under torture?'

'As Judge Hathorne remarked on Monday, torture hath ne'er been used in an English witch-court.'

'Let us disregard England – a mere two thousand cases at best. I speak of the momentous Continental cleansing.'

''Tis a pity that pricking and the other reliable tests of Satanic allegiance have enjoyed so little favour outside His Majesty's realm,' Stearne said. 'Continental law frames witchcraft as an invisible phenomenon and hence a *crimen excepta*, an exceptional crime, so difficult of proof that the ordinary rules of evidence must be suspended.'

'And the ordinary rules of civilization as well?'

Stearne shuddered, temporarily dismayed, then mocked the question with an audible snort. 'Because the Devil himself would ne'er appear in a courtroom and testify against his own disciple, my Continental counterparts have reasoned that torture is the best way to expose a witch.'

'I'm sure you are aware, Monsieur, that in most Continental sorcery cases the executioner continued the torture well past the moment of confession. Can you explain this seemingly irrational practice?'

''Tis well known that Satanists perform their execrable rites in assemblies. Through torture, an executioner induces a witch to name her accomplices.'

Montesquieu asked, 'Is your education such that you might describe for us the five stages of torture employed during the Continental cleansing?'

'I have indeed studied the traditions underlying my profession,' Stearne said. 'The first stage was called preparatory torture.'

'What did that involve?'

Before Stearne could answer, the Reverend Samuel Parris scrambled to his feet and cleared his throat. 'Excellency, the Crown's advocate hath already stated that English witch-courts eschew torture. The Baron's questions enjoys no relevance to this case.'

'I cannot make a proper defense of Mrs Webster,' Montesquieu retorted, 'unless I demonstrate what the witness means when he avers that his enterprise rests on eight hundred thousand confessions.'

Hathorne scowled fiercely before making his pronouncement. 'In the name of fairness, we shall allow a brief discussion of this unhappy topic.'

'We were speaking of preparatory torture,' Montesquieu reminded the witness.

'This required the executioner to squeeze the prisoner's thumb or toe in a metal vice,' Stearne said.

As Parris settled back into his seat, Montesquieu opened his portmanteau and removed a device that to a naïve eye might have seemed intended for cracking walnuts. 'While visiting the European capitals last year' – he held the machine before Stearne – 'I found myself moved to collect and catalogue several dozen torture instruments of the sort once used by Continental executioners. Would you call this a typical thumbscrew?'

'I would.'

'I have heard that the executioner often supplemented the thumb-screw with a larger vice—'

'The Spanish boot, aye.'

'—using it to pulverize the prisoner's foot until the marrow spurted forth.'

The Reverend Parris leapt free of his chair. 'Excellency, I see no merit in this line of inquiry.'

'Eight hundred thousand confessions!' Montesquieu shouted.

'Eight hundred thousand confessions!' Ben Franklin echoed.

Hathorne sucked contemplatively on his clay pipe. One puff, two puffs, three. 'The bench will graciously permit a display of torture instruments, but only the most *pertinent* torture instruments.'

'I would like you to tell the Court about stage two, ordinary torture,' Montesquieu said to the witness.

'Also known as *strappado*, "to pull",' Stearne said. 'The prisoner's feet were hung with weights and his hands tied behind him with a rope threaded through a pulley on the ceiling.'

From his portmanteau Montesquieu retrieved a great iron pulley, large as a melon. 'A pulley such as this?'

'Aye. The executioner ravelled up the rope, lifting the witch into the air. After several such hoistings, the prisoner became highly inclined to confess his diabolism and name his confederates.'

'And if he remained stubborn . . .?'

'The executioner proceeded to stage three, extraordinary torture, accomplished through *squassation*.'

Elaborating, Stearne revealed that, as with *strappado*, the accused witch's hands were tied and his feet weighted. After hoisting him to the ceiling, the executioner would release the rope, then abruptly grab it when the prisoner was within inches of the floor, causing him to jerk violently. With repeated applications, *squassation* normally dislocated a person's arms, hands, legs, and feet.

'I am told that the agony of *squassation* is beyond imagining,' Montesquieu said.

'Hellfire is far worse,' Stearne said.

Montesquieu spun the rollers of the pulley, sending a high barbed screech coursing through the hall like the cry of an enraged cock. 'Far worse. No question. *Oui*. But may I surmise that whereas *strappado* sometimes failed to produce a confession and a list of accomplices, *squassation* nearly always turned the trick?'

'Quite so.'

'Then what purpose was served by the *next* two stages?'

'Stage four, additional torture, figured in cases where a judge wished to punish a witch for a particularly horrific act of *maleficium*.'

Returning the pulley to his portmanteau, Montesquieu removed his steel pincers, fanged like a serpent, then waved them before the witness. 'Punish him, for example, by ripping out his fingernails?'

'For example.'

'Stage five, occasional torture: was that likewise punitive?'

'Punitive, but uncommon. 'Twas inflicted only on a witch of the worst sort, one who could ne'er be called back to Christ.'

For the next hour Montesquieu prompted Stearne to present the particulars of additional torture, which was subject to regulation, and occasional torture, which knew no limits. The jurymen learned of gouged eyes, severed limbs, flesh torn apart with tongs, bowels dislocated by ribbons of swallowed cloth, feet slit open and immersed in boiling lime, and diets of salted herring unmitigated by even one drop of water. Throughout the witness's testimony, Montesquieu surveyed the courtroom. With the exceptions of Judge Hathorne, Samuel Parris, Abigail Stearne and a handful of depraved rustics in the audience, everyone seemed on the point of either fainting dead away or breaking into hives.

Hathorne now declared a luncheon interval, though Montesquieu doubted that anyone felt favourably disposed towards a hearty meal. His intuition proved accurate. Although most of the jurymen and spectators patronized the food stalls, they returned with portions far smaller than ordinary. Ben Franklin brought Mrs Crompton an apple tart, which she succeeded in consuming only on her third attempt.

'Hear me now, Charles,' she said. 'For all you have made a potent presentation, I believe 'twould be unwise to continue spoiling the jurymen's appetites.'

'Have no fear. The Court has seen the last of my vices, pulleys and pincers.'

At one o'clock Hathorne reconvened the trial and publicly forbade the Baron to solicit any more grisly particulars concerning torture.

'I am pleased to comply, Excellency, for the real issue before the Court is how we should *interpret* the use of torture in the classic witch-trials.' Montesquieu turned and gestured towards the mottled white mass on Stearne's brow. 'I see your face is scarred, Monsieur. I hope you've not been tortured.'

'Many years ago I rushed into a raging fire set by Nimacook savages, that I might rescue my father's cleansing licence. The pain of my burns was severe' – Stearne bobbed his mutilated head towards Mrs Crompton – 'but not so severe as to make me repudiate God.'

'Do you say that if accused of witchcraft you would cleave to your innocence no matter how terrible the torture?'

'I do.'

'Most admirable.' Montesquieu enacted a wince. 'I promise you, Monsieur, if you subjected *me* to *squassation*, I would confess to sorcery and name my confederates not because I was a wizard, but simply to stop the pain.'

'Stop the pain!' Franklin cried.

'Stop the pain!' the spectators echoed.

'Silence!' Hathorne screamed.

'Consider this narrative,' Montesquieu said to the witness. 'I arrest a woman on a false charge of Satanism and torture her until she names seven accomplices. Next I apprehend these supposed witches and torture each into naming another seven. By torturing the forty-nine, I acquire three hundred and forty-three new names. I perform the operation once again, flushing out an additional two thousand four hundred and one presumed heretics, and still once again, bringing in a harvest of sixteen thousand eight hundred and seven. In short, my Lord Witchfinder, the question is not, "How could the courts have elicited eight hundred thousand false confessions?" but rather, "Why did they not elicit *ten times* that many?"'

'I have ne'er heard such specious reasoning,' Stearne said.

'Your quarrel is not with me, Monsieur, but with the multiplication tables.'

'I can compute as well as you.'

'Then tell me if I am correct when I compute that your organization makes an annual profit of two hundred and forty English pounds.'

''Tis not so.'

'*The Pennsylvania Gazette* reports that you indict and execute twenty supposed witches each year at twelve pounds a head.'

'The Baron confuses profit with income.'

Having broached the subject of Stearne's finances, Montesquieu now faced the jurymen and proceeded to argue that cleansing could not be understood apart from its economics. Because the courts were empowered to seize the property of convicted Satanists, he explained, witch-hunting had until recently ranked amongst the world's most lucrative industries, commensurate with ship-building, rum-running, and the slave trade. The enterprise was as circular as it was remunerative. As the number of trials increased, the more the courts needed money, and the more the courts needed money, the more they needed witches.

'Money for the judges, money for the lawyers, money for the bailiffs,' Montesquieu chanted, glancing from one juror to the next, 'money for the constables, money for the gaolers, money for the torturers.' He swerved towards the stand, reached into his waistcoat and, like an apprentice ambassador practising a bow, made a great show of pulling out a scrap of paper. 'During my recent European tour I came upon a German document dated 24 July 1628, which I copied by hand from the original, then translated into French and English. Right before he was burned for a wizard, Johannes Junius, Burgomaster of Bamberg, wrote his daughter a letter, which the gaoler agreed to smuggle out of the prison. I would ask that you read the passages marked in red.'

'I assumed the stand to belie your philosophy, Baron, not to become your puppet,' Stearne said.

'As you wish,' Montesquieu said, slipping on his spectacles. He unfolded the transcription and positioned it a foot from his nose. 'Herr Junius beings, "My dearly beloved daughter Veronica, innocent I have entered this prison, innocent I have been tortured, innocent I shall die." Junius proceeds to recount the testimony of the prosecution's witnesses, one of whom claimed she heard him abjure God as he danced upon the moor. "And then came also the executioner, and he put the thumbscrews on me until the blood spurted from the nails, so that for five weeks I could not use my hands, as you can see by my writing." Junius goes on to describe his ordeal of *squassation*. "I thought Heaven and Earth were at an end. Eight times did they draw me up and let me fall again, so that I suffered terrible agony." Next the prisoner reports on a remarkable conversation between himself and his tormentor. "Sir, I beg you, for God's sake, confess something," the executioner says, "even if it be false, for you cannot endure the new tortures to which you will be put. And even if you do bear them, still the judges will not free you, but one torture will follow upon another until you say you are a witch." After pondering his hopeless situation, Junius accepted the executioner's logic and confessed. He told the judges how he fell under the enchantment of a succubus named Füchsin, who appeared to him first in the guise of a dairymaid, later as a goat, and persuaded him to reject Christ, worship Satan and participate in Sabbats. "Now, sweet daughter, here you have the story of my confession, and it is all sheer lies and fabulation, so help me God. Fare thee well, dearest child, and remember me in your prayers, for you will never see your father Johannes Junius again." '

Montesquieu refolded the transcription, slowly, deliberately, and returned it to his waistcoat. A ponderous silence descended upon the courtroom.

'Monsieur, might you tell us your reaction to Johannes Junius's letter?' the Baron asked the witness.

''Tis probably a forgery,' Stearne replied. 'Or if this Junius truly wrote the thing, then he lied to call his confession a fraud. A succubus named Füchsin who is also a were-goat – that's certainly not something a person could simply invent out of his head. I believe this Junius was a wizard.'

'*Merci*, Mr Stearne. I have no more questions.'

On the morning following Dunstan's testimony, the local readership of *The Pennsylvania Gazette* opened their newspapers to find an essay by Ebenezer Trenchard that in Jennet's opinion easily eclipsed everything the Seaman Scholar had written thus far. Trenchard asserted, 'The Crown's Case turns on the Assumption that an innocent Man would never confess to Witchcraft even if you tore out his Fingernails.' He concluded, 'The Baron de Montesquieu hath shown the whole Witch-Cleansing Industry to be a corrupt Castle built upon degraded Sand.'

The rising sun sent shafts of light through the courthouse windows, each beam as glorious and golden as a flying buttress pressed against the weightless wall of a Heavenly palace. Hathorne puffed languidly on his clay pipe, removed the stem and coughed.

'*Monsieur le Baron*, you may interview your next witness.'

'The defence calls Rebecca Webster,' Montesquieu said.

Opaque as stones, phlegmatic as clay, the twelve landholders collectively returned Jennet's gaze as she crossed the hall and settled into the witness-stand. What she wanted most at that moment was a mechanics of human consciousness, a *Principia Mentis* by which she might study each juror's deportment and consequently learn his thoughts.

'My first question is simple,' Montesquieu said. 'Mrs Webster, are you a witch?'

'I am not.'

'Have you ever met the Devil or written in his alleged register?'

'I have not.'

'*Très bien*.' From his portmanteau the Baron obtained his copy of *The Sufficiency of the World*. 'As a devotee of J. S. Crompton, I was gratified to hear you evoke his formidable treatise when Mr Stearne interviewed you on Wednesday.'

'I find Mr Crompton's book to be an irrefutable disproof of demons,' Jennet said.

'A provocative statement, Madame. Your lawyer would have you elaborate upon it.'

Cued by Montesquieu's questions, Jennet spent the next three hours explicating the sufficiency hypothesis. She began by arguing that English experimental philosophy was of a largely Neo-Platonist bent. Because various preternatural beings logically lurked behind Plato's famous Veil of Appearances, this perspective went hand-in-hand with the demon hypothesis. On the Continent, meanwhile, René Descartes's followers had cast the world as a vast clocklike machine. But here, too, spirits both benign and malign were permitted, nay, *required*, since the universe's dynamic phenomena – magnetism, acceleration, elasticity, and the rest – necessarily employed immaterial entities as their agents, many doubtless corresponding to the demons, devils and fallen angels of biblical revelation.

Both views, she explained, suffered from the defect of being untrue.

Poised against Platonism was William of Occam's famous parsimony postulate: God had situated his creatures in a real universe, not the shadow of a real universe, and there was no need to muddy this circumstance with Eternal Ideas and Perfect Forms. As for the dead Cartesian planet, J. S. Crompton had persuasively replaced it with a pulsing, blooming, sufficient world. Why posit genies and vortices when Nature's algorithms could account for all the motions that matter enacted, all the shocks to which flesh was heir?

Hathorne decreed a recess, whereupon Jennet consumed an enormous luncheon. She could recall no time in her life when rabbit pie had tasted more delicious, cheese more savoury, pease-bread more filling, ale more satisfying. Despite everything – despite Bella's death and Rachel's abduction, Dr Halley's reproof and Tobias's reproach, the rout of Aristotle and the wreck of the *Berkshire* – she had finally brought forth an *argumentum grande* and given it to the world.

Fortified, she threw herself into the labours of the afternoon. Thus far she and Montesquieu had provided but the bones of the sufficiency hypothesis. Now they must give it muscle, meat and skin. Under the Baron's direction, the marshals dragged the defence table to within ten feet of the jurymen, then erected on its surface a six-foot inclined ramp scored with two parallel grooves. Though handicapped by her chains and manacles, Jennet grasped a pair of spheres, one of lead, the other of straw, and set them on the starting line.

'Intuition says the heavier object wins the race,' she told the jurors, 'but behold what happens when I perform the experiment.' She released both spheres, rolling them along the grooves. 'Your eyes did not deceive you, gentlemen. Lead and straw reached the finish line at the same instant.' Twice more she demonstrated Galileo's law of uniform acceleration, first pitting a ball of wire against a ball of yarn, then a ball filled with cider against one containing grass. Victory eluded each and every sphere. 'As you have seen, good jurymen, Nature cleaves to her own rules, heedless of our petty expectations.'

No sooner had Montesquieu flourished his lodestone than a cry of uncertain origin and uncanny timbre shot through the courtroom, a piercing 'Aaaaiiiieeee!' A second such scream sent scores of faces turning towards the prosecution table, where Abigail Stearne was rocking to and fro like a victim of the ergot.

'The witch sends forth her demons!' Abigail released a third shriek, lurched to her feet, and vaulted into the aisle. ''Tis Hell's worst minions make those spheres move so contrarily!'

The spectators began chattering amongst themselves, a cacophony admixing confusion with fright.

'I send forth no demons,' Jennet insisted, managing an outward tranquillity even as she seethed within.

'Silence, spectators!' Hathorne commanded.

'I'Christ, her goblins are loose within me!' Abigail cried, limping towards the judge's bench. 'They gnaw upon my stomach and bowels! Call them back, witch! Call your demons back!'

'Oh, my dearest wife!' Dunstan wailed.

'Darling niece!' Mr Parris yelped.

From Abigail's throat came a sound like the death rattle of a rabid lynx. 'Her demons choke me! They rob the breath from my lungs!'

It was the same old Abigail, Jennet realized. The decades since Salem had not weakened her powers of prevarication by one whit.

Arms outstretched in a pose of crucifixion, Abigail halted before the judge. 'Excellency, there is but one way I may lift this curse.' Like a Roman conspirator preparing to assassinate Julius Caesar, she slid a glittering silver bodkin from her dress. 'I must release a drop of the witch's blood.'

'This woman plays you false,' Jennet calmly informed John Hathorne. 'She played you false at Salem, and now she plays you false again.'

Twirling around like a weathercock in a gale, Abigail sprang upon Jennet and embraced her as she might a lover. The bodkin flashed in the afternoon sun. Abigail snarled, and suddenly the blade was glancing along the edge of Jennet's jaw, leaving in its wake a stinging wound.

'Lying slush-bucket!' Jennet cried. 'Filthy vixen!'

The spectators' jabber grew louder yet.

'Be quiet, all of you!' Hathorne ordered.

'The spell is broken!' Abigail shouted with manufactured exuber-ance. She restored the bodkin to her dress and made her way to the prosecution table, slowly, uncertainly, like a lost traveller staggering through a blizzard. 'Broken,' she gasped, collapsing into her chair. She folded her elbows, rested her head on the fleshy pillow, and appeared to fall asleep. 'Broken . . . broken . . .'

'Good Philadelphians, you must not believe Mrs Stearne's play-acting,' Montesquieu said, placing his handkerchief in Jennet's grasp.

'*Merci.*' She raised her manacled wrists and pressed the white silk against her bleeding jaw.

The Baron turned his palms outward and beseechingly approached the jury-box. 'She hath merely mimicked a woman possessed.'

'*Monsieur le Baron*, 'tis not your place to tell these dozen worthies what they may and mayn't believe,' Hathorne said. 'I pray you, finish your dumb show, that the jury might begin its deliberations on the morrow.'

'Mrs Webster, do you feel prepared to continue, despite this outrageous attack upon your person?' Montesquieu asked.

'Aye,' Jennet said, passing the Baron his blood-soaked handkerchief.

She proceeded to illustrate the law of magnetism, making first a watch-fob, next a key, and then a musket-ball fly across the table and adhere to Montesquieu's lodestone. Abigail slept soundly through all three collisions, but stirred slightly during the fourth: the noisy meeting of the magnetite and a steel stirrup.

'The Gilbertian force is woven into the very tapestry of Creation,' Jennet told the jurymen. 'Magnetism follows its own God-given principle, unimpressed by human will or demonic desire.'

For the next presentation she charged the Von Guericke sphere and drew a range of substances – eider-down, sot-weed granules, wig powder – to its surface.

'Though natural philosophers still have many questions concerning universal electricity,' she said, 'they know better than to give their ignorance the name of *demon*.'

Her climactic presentation had her placing a pentahedral glass prism on the defence table. She allowed the setting sun to strike the prism and send a full spectrum, red to orange to yellow to blue to indigo to violet, cascading across the jury-box, then employed a second prism in restoring the rainbow to a stream of purest whiteness.

'The phenomenon of refraction belongs to Nature alone. 'Tis not the play-thing of hypothetical spirits. And God said, "Let there be—"'

'Aaaaiiiieeee!' screamed Abigail, leaping up like a boulder launched from a catapult. 'I'Chirst, her devils find me! Her refraction demons pound a prism into my heart! Aaaaiiiieeee!'

The spectators abandoned their benches, their collective mutters reverberating off the walls and rattling amongst the rafters.

'Sit down, every one of you!' Hathorne cried.

To a man, to a woman, the spectators remained standing.

'Her electric imps set my bile aboil! Her magnet-spirits fill me with Golgotha's nails!' Abigail ran towards the defence table, gathered up the philosophic tools – ramp, lodestone, sulphur ball, prisms – and hurled them in all directions. 'Sayeth the witch, "Let mine enemy eat of the iron that locked Christ to his Cross!" The nails! The nails! I must purge myself of the unholy nails!'

'Darling Abby, methinks this bride of Lucifer means to murder you!' Dunstan shouted.

Bending in two, Abigail clutched her stomach, slapped her cheek, and opened her mouth. Four iron nails spewed from her gullet, clanking and clattering as they rolled across the table.

'Heaven protect us!' Foreman Hocking shrieked.

'I cannot believe it!' Hathorne gasped.

'Deliver me, Lord!' Abigail spat up two more nails. 'God have mercy!' Another nail came forth. 'Aaaaiiiieeee!'

It seemed to Jennet that a tremor of unease now passed through Montesquieu. For one small second, the sliver of an instant, he apparently thought he might actually be defending a witch.

'Spectators, find your seats, or I shall have the marshals drag you from the hall!' Hathorne shouted.

Regaining his wits, Montesquieu bounded towards the jury. 'Honourable landholders, heed not this woman's mendacity!'

'Oh, my Saviour!' Abigail strode away from the spiky vomitus and, lurching upright, spat an eighth nail into her open palm. She rushed to the jury-box and held the nail before Mr Hocking. 'Good sirs, you must refuse to set yon witch upon the world!' She pivoted towards an open window and hurled the nail through the aperture. 'In Christ's name, you mustn't loose her!'

Now Barnaby joined the tumult, quitting the gallery and dashing towards the judge's bench. 'Excellency, these seeming wonders are but an illusionist's tricks!'

'The raven!' Abigail cried. 'The raven! She torments me with Beelzebub's spectral bird!'

Ducking and cringing, she gestured as if to catch and crush a pesky midge, when suddenly a large black raven feather materialized in her grasp. She swatted the air a second time, thus plucking another feather from the invisible bird.

'More tricks!' Barnaby shouted.

'She shan't defeat me!' Abigail snatched a third feather from the aether. 'I love Christ even more than the witch adoreth Satan!'

'Abby, save yourself!' Dunstan insisted.

'Scratch the witch!' Mr Parris advised.

'Save myself, aye!' Abigail dropped all three feathers and pulled the bodkin from her pocket. She stepped towards Jennet and froze abruptly, whereupon her bodkin arm jerked outward, twisting and twitching like the tail of a storm-tossed kite. 'Oh, sweet guardians of grace, she turns my dagger against me!' Her bodkin arm reversed direction, pushing the blade deep into her side, directly below her rib cage. 'The thrusting lance! Our Saviour's precious hurt!'

'Damn you, Jennet, you shall cease this assault upon my wife!' Dunstan, rising, pounded his fist on the prosecution table. 'Desist! Desist!'

Abigail yanked the bodkin free. A thread of blood jetted from the lesion, staining the floor with a sinuous red line. Her eyes crossed, her tongue snaked forward, and she drove the blade into her left breast.

'Witch, thou canst not conquer me!' she screamed, lactating blood. 'Christ's mercy is my armour and shield!'

'Sit down, spectators!' Hathorne shouted. 'Sit down!'

Barnaby dropped to his knees, pressing his right hand against Abigail's shed blood as if sealing a seed within a furrow. He lifted his palm and licked it clean.

'Excellency, this gore be sweet, not salt like true blood!' he informed Hathorne. 'I swear 'tis naught but cherry pulp!'

Abigail tore the bodkin from her breast and, dashing towards the defence table, cut an invisible slit in the air and then a palpable gash in Jennet's scalp.

431

'She seeks to fool us with cherry pulp!' Barnaby shouted.

Again Jennet availed herself of Montesquieu's handkerchief. Even as the wound stopped flowing, Abigail pocketed the bodkin and strutted down the crowded aisle, the perplexed mob parting around her. With a final ghastly shriek Abigail entered the foyer, kicked open the front door, and leapt into the gloomy dusk.

'The Court is adjourned!' Hathorne cried.

'Cherry pulp!' Barnaby screamed.

'Are you deaf, sir? Adjourned!' Hathorne pounded the bench so violently that his tool snapped in half. The disembodied mallet-head spun like a child's top. 'Adjourned! Adjourned!'

Matthew Knox supplied Jennet, Montesquieu and Barnaby with a splendid meal that night, a succulent fellowship of roasted pork, boiled cabbage and Syracuse salt, then capped the feast by rolling a cask of ale into the gaol-cell and pouring full tankards all around. As he made to leave, the turnkey mentioned, diffidently but earnestly, that he'd heard rumours of a bewitchment in the courtroom, whereupon Jennet invited him to join their colloquy. If Barnaby could convince this simple gaoler that Abigail's antics did not portend Satanic intervention, it followed that he might convince the jury as well.

She downed her portion of ale in one colossal gulp, thereby achieving considerable relief from the lacerations in her jaw and scalp. 'Good curator, do enlighten us,' she instructed Barnaby.

'My knowledge of the magician's art goes back some twenty years, when I joined forces with a crystal-gazer and an illusionist to create *Le Cirque de la Lune*,' Barnaby told his audience. 'The latter wight, one Feizunda, taught me the rudiments of legerdemain — the same rudiments as were employed against our Jenny this afternoon.' He turned to Mr Knox. 'Friend, did you know your brain is home to a member of the insect race?' No sooner had a frown gathered on Mr Knox's face than Barnaby reached forward and retrieved a large black cricket from inside the gaoler's left ear. 'Behold the source of the music you hear each night as you fall asleep.'

'Monsieur Cavendish, your dexterity astounds me,' Montesquieu said.

''Tis a magnificent trick,' Mr Knox said.

'The same trick by which Abigail Stearne seemed to pluck feathers from a spectral raven today,' Barnaby said. He presented the cricket to Jennet, who set it on the floor that it might hop to freedom. 'As you may have heard, Mr Knox, the Stearne woman also vomited forth eight iron spikes. Speaking of which, I am reminded that my noonday meal was an uncommon tart, filled with . . .' He pressed one hand against his stomach. 'I'Christ, those acorns confound my digestion! 'Twould seem a purgation's in the offing!'

Clamping his free hand across his mouth, Barnaby staggered groaning and retching towards Jennet's writing-desk, then abruptly disgorged five greenish-brown acorns. They bounced off the brass ink-pot with short, sharp reports.

''Steeth!' Knox exclaimed.

'I would imagine such sleight-of-hand demands many hours of practice,' Montesquieu said.

'Aye,' Barnaby said, 'but once he's mastered the illusion, a person can appear to purge himself of everything from hickory nuts to Christ's own nails.'

'*Hélas*, Madame Webster, I must confess that when I beheld Abigail Stearne spew that iron, a wave of faithlessness washed over me,' Montesquieu said.

'I saw it in your countenance, Charles,' she said. 'But know that I absolve you, for I have ne'er seen so persuasive a deception.'

'For her third trick the insidious Abigail stabbed herself with a bodkin,' Barnaby informed the turnkey, 'just as I now stab myself with my own digit.'

He unbuttoned his day-shirt and, pulling back the placket, drove his thumb deep into the flesh beyond. A dollop of blood rolled down his naked chest.

'Marry!' wailed the turnkey.

'Be not alarmed, Mr Knox,' Barnaby said. 'This blood's mere cherry pulp, burst from a leather pouch concealed within my hand.'

''Twould appear you've poked your thumb into your heart!' Knox gasped.

'A simple matter of folding it into the palm of the same hand.' Barnaby yanked the digit free of his chest, then wiped away the mock blood with his handkerchief. 'Were we to examine Abigail's bodkin, we would discover that on encountering resistance the blade slides into the shaft. No doubt the flick of a lever converts it to a normal dagger.'

'A question, Mr Knox!' Cyril Turpin cried from the adjoining cell. 'When this conjuror finishes entertaining you, might he bring his tricks to *my* abode? I would be a most appreciative audience.'

''Tis not my job to arrange amusements for chicken thieves!' shouted Knox.

'I'm a horse thief, sir, and I shall thank ye to address me as such!'

The turnkey gathered up the residue of their meal – platters, utensils, tankards – and let himself out of the cell, locking the door behind him. By way of a parting remark, he proclaimed that Barnaby's magic would surely dazzle the judge, flabbergast the jury, and set Mrs Webster free. Montesquieu and Barnaby were less confident, however, and for the next two hours they rehearsed their presentation.

At ten o'clock, yawning and bleary-eyed, Barnaby shuffled off to his lodgings in Mount-Airy Lane. Montesquieu lingered, writing out his final remarks to the jurymen, a moving and cogent paean to Nature's laws, nine pages long. He performed it aloud for Jennet. Her body felt wholly depleted, but her brain remained alert as, sprawled on her mattress, she savoured the Baron's eloquence and drank in his sagacity.

It was not enough, of course. How could it be enough? What breed of eloquence could nullify Abigail Stearne's numinous crucifixion nails, what species of sagacity could prevail against her preternatural feathers?

'Compared to Abby's phantom raven,' she told the Baron, 'Reason's a feeble fowl indeed, wings clipped, tail shorn.'

'And yet come morning we shall make it fly,' Montesquieu declared, rolling his address into the semblance of a telescope. 'We shall send it soaring clear to Heaven.'

Although her mattress was soft and her fellow prisoners quiet, sleep eluded Jennet that night, and the next morning she entered the courtroom in a benumbed and bedraggled state. Someone had restored the defence table to its former location, but the aftermath of Abigail's

434

rampage, the bits and pieces of the previous day's philosophic demonstrations, still lay scattered about the hall like corpses on a battlefield. Montesquieu sat hunched over the nine pages of his speech, shielding them with the fervour of a biblical scholar protecting a newly unearthed Gospel. He seemed no less dazed than she, peruke askew, eyes bloodshot, waistcoat only half buttoned, but he managed an energetic smile, and in receiving her from the four marshals he briefly lifted her, chains and all, off the floor.

Settling into her chair, she apprehended that an atmosphere of dread now permeated the courtroom, not unlike the palpable terror that had suffused Haverhill prior to the Nimacook attack. Each time she looked towards the gallery, most of the spectators glanced away, as if they feared bewitchment. Only the Franklin faction – the journalists and the Junto members – willingly returned her gaze. At the prosecution table Dunstan studied his notes whilst Mr Parris read his Bible. Abigail was evidently still at the prickers' inn, nursing her illusory lesions.

'*Voilà!*' Montesquieu said, unfurling that morning's *Gazette* before Jennet. 'Ebenezer Trenchard at his finest.'

Her eyes alighted on the last paragraph. 'Watching Abigail Stearne pretend to expel iron Nails from her Stomach this Friday, I thought of Exodus 7:11, wherein Pharaoh commands his Masters of Legerdemain to make Serpents of their Sceptres in mocking Imitation of the divine Miracle the Courtiers have just witnessed: the one true God transforming Aaron's Rod into a slithering Reptile. But Jehovah has the last Laugh, for the holy Snake immediately devours those of the Egyptian Magicians.'

Hathorne seized his mallet, now repaired with spirals of copper wire, and smacked it against the bench. In a striking deviation from their customary contrariness, the spectators grew instantly silent.

'Yesterday in this hall we beheld a frightening wonder,' the judge began. 'We saw Mrs Webster's demons attack Abigail Stearne with crucifixion nails, a spectral raven and, deadliest of all, a steel bodkin. Mr Stearne informs me that, thanks be to God, his wife will not die, though her wounds are sufficiently grievous to keep her abed.'

'Excellency, the defence knows a second way to interpret this so-called attack on Mrs Stearne,' said Montesquieu, rising.

'Sit down, *Monsieur le Baron*,' Hathorne said. He faced the jury-box, slamming his mallet repeatedly against his palm like a cook tenderising a mutton chop. 'We cannot doubt that the Court of Oyer and Terminer is now under siege from Lucifer himself. I must perforce instruct you worthy landholders to begin your deliberations anon, that this trial might cease before all Hell's agents come against us.'

'The defence calls Barnaby Cavendish to testify,' Montesquieu declared.

Barnaby jumped to his feet.

'Your memory fails you, *Monsieur le Baron*,' said Hathorne, 'for you examined your last witness yesterday.' He slid his clay pipe from his robe and pointed the stem towards Mr Hocking. 'Good Foreman, you will take your eleven to the antechamber.'

Hocking abandoned his chair, removed his felt hat, and gestured the jury to a standing position.

'Your Honour, you must permit me to address the Court!' Barnaby cried, storming the judge's bench. 'I am the very Dr Cavendish whom the Baron wishes to interview!'

'Then you are the very Dr Cavendish who will not be heard today,' Hathorne retorted.

'Give me but a moment's preparation, Excellency, and I too shall make hobnails fly from my mouth!'

'Be seated, sir.'

Barnaby flourished his blood-pouch. 'I can show the Court how Abigail Stearne seemed to stab herself! 'Twas all legerdemain!'

Hocking led his colleagues out of the jury-box in a solemn parade.

'Dr Cavendish, the Court can no longer abide your noxious interruptions!' Hathorne set the unlit pipe betwixt his lips and blew into the stem as if playing a fife. A staccato, birdish *tweet* emerged from the bowl. 'Marshals, you will escort this demented spectator into the yard!'

'Abigail Stearne hath deluded you!' Barnaby cried.

The four marshals lurched out of their niches and, rudely taking hold of the curator, bore him down the central aisle.

'Tell your minions to unhand that man!' Jennet screamed towards the bench. 'He's but a frail and harmless philosopher who will not survive a mauling!'

'Mrs Stearne vomited no nails!' Barnaby shouted as the marshals dragged him towards the entrance hall. 'No nails! No nails!' And suddenly he was gone.

'Excellency, you must at least suffer the Crown's advocate and myself to make our closing arguments!' Montesquieu protested.

The jury foreman halted his eleven before the antechamber door.

'Mr Stearne,' said Hathorne to Dunstan, 'what think you of the procedural issue the Baron hath raised?'

'In the interests of delivering this Court from the Dark One, the Crown relinquishes its privilege of a summarizing speech,' Dunstan replied.

'Then it seems only fair for the defence to relinquish that privilege as well,' Hathorne said, 'and I so rule.'

Montesquieu dashed across the hall and, planting himself before Hocking, made a heroically hopeless attempt to distil his nine-page address into a handful of compacted clauses. 'Good landholders, this day you can bring low the odious Witchcraft Act of James the First! In framing your verdict, you must remember that God allows no demon to confound His design!'

Mr Hocking shepherded his eleven jurors out of the hall, the last juror slamming the door in Montesquieu's face. The bailiff inserted his key and activated the lock.

'Call those jurymen back!' Nicholas Scull demanded.

'Call them back!' Ben cried.

'This Court is adjourned!' Hathorne shouted, punctuating the pronouncement with his mallet. 'When the jury hath reached its verdict, the tower bell will ring seven times!'

Jennet's mind became a fractured scrying-glass, a shattered gazing-crystal, each shard reflecting a facet of the commotion. John Tux stomping his feet and screaming 'Call them back!' Montesquieu shouting his abridged address at the antechamber door. Hathorne crying 'Seven bells!' whilst hammering madly on the bench like a man shingling a roof in a hurricane. Ben brandishing the *Sufficiency* and challenging all within his hearing to read it. The spectators rising in clusters and stumbling towards the entrance hall, doubtless headed for the food stalls.

'Nature does not submit herself to Satan!' Montesquieu cried.

'The day is at hand when Occam's razor will cut the noose from the neck of every convicted witch!' Ben insisted.

'Mr Hathorne, you are no friend to justice!' Herbert Bledsoe declared.

Montesquieu projected a final sentence towards the antechamber – 'Insult not the world with fables of wizardry!' – then returned to the defence table and explained to Jennet that any further unsolicited oratory would do their case more harm than good.

'You made a noble effort, Charles,' she said.

'Against an ignoble judge,' he muttered.

Adjusting his opulent wig, Hathorne gained his feet and lit his pipe. He puffed twice, stepped into the alcove behind the bench, and vanished through the door, a twist of smoke coiling behind him like a boar-pig's tail.

The great waiting stretched from ten o'clock till eleven, and then from eleven till noon, Montesquieu, Ben and Jennet huddled together at the defence table like wayfarers gathered before a tavern hearth. Jennet's lawyer attempted to alleviate his anxiety by contriving chapter titles for his projected *magnum opus*, which he planned to call either *The Essence of Civil Government* or *The Spirit of the Law*. Ben passed the time by drafting potential headlines for the next morning's *Gazette*. Evidently his choices failed to please him, for he'd crossed them all out, including JUSTICE CRUSHED AT WEBSTER TRIAL and JUDGE HATHORNE'S SHAME and PILATE IN PENNSYLVANIA.

Jennet decided that she could best endure the immediate future by contemplating the ruins of her philosophic apparatus. Before the jury-box sat the Galilean ramp, now split down the middle. Nearby lay the lodestone, broken in two. Wrapped in shadows, the Newtonian prisms rested forlornly beneath the prosecution table; the little glass wedges seemed peculiarly alive – a species of marine creature, she imagined, spawned in a luminous sea but now tossed upon a nocturnal beach, where they lay suffocating for lack of light. Fissured but still whole, the sulphur-ball cast its shadow on the floor. The black oval evoked for Jennet one of Aunt Isobel's favourite stories from the history of natural philosophy.

'Some eighty generations ago the great Eratosthenes, director of the Library of Alexandria, joined two facts that had ne'er been yoked before. What were they, dear child?'

'At noon each year on June the twenty-first,' Jennet told her tutor, 'a stick set upright in the ground casts no shadow at Syene, whereas in Alexandria on the same date, at the same time, such a vertical post throws a substantial shadow.'

'Eratosthenes made an inference from this seeming impossibility . . .'

'He concluded that the Earth could not be flat. He decided 'twas in fact a sphere.'

'And then?'

'And then he measured the length of Alexandria's noontime shadow. One of Euclid's finest theorems, the equality of alternate interior angels, told Eratosthenes that the distance from Alexandria to Syene must be seven-point-two degrees of the Earth's circumference: the fiftieth part of a circle. Because Eratosthenes knew that four hundred and eighty miles lay betwixt Syene and Alexandria, the simplest arithmetic revealed that a bird encircling our planet would make a trip of some twenty-four thousand miles.'

'Darling Jenny, you have learned your lesson well!'

Shortly after striking one o'clock, the tower bell tolled again – seven times. Judge Hathorne reassumed the bench. Foreman Hocking led his fellow landholders to the jury-box. The spectators pushed and shoved their way back into the courtroom, packing it from wall to wall.

'Oyez! Oyez!' the bailiff cried, bringing his pike against the floor with the pounding regularity of a Newcomen steam pump.

A hush settled over the hall.

'Mr Hocking, hath the jury reached a verdict?'

'Aye, Excellency.'

'How goes it with the defendant? Be she guilty or nay?'

Jennet recalled Aunt Isobel's old *experimentum magnus*, the teacher and her pupils searching for microscopic diabolism in the tissues of supposed familiars. To minimize its suffering, Isobel had ordered each animal be strangled prior to dissection. But in a witch-court no such compassion obtained. Mr Hocking slid – 'By way of preventing further *maleficia*' – his knife into Jennet's side – 'such as were visited upon Abigail Stearne' – firmed his grip on the shaft – 'we are decided that the defendant' – and twisted the blade – 'is guilty.'

A strange wind blew through the courtroom, a howling amalgam

439

of outrage and incredulity, and now the separate *No*'s burst forth, a 'No!' from Ben, a 'No!' from Montesquieu, a 'No!' from Mr Scull, a 'No!' from Mr Bledsoe, a 'No!' from John Tux. A score of Manayunk spectators likewise expressed their dismay, unleashing sounds such as Jennet had not heard since the whooping tawnies had descended on Haverhill.

The marshals hauled her quivering body before the bench. She struggled to stand up straight, commanding each relevant part of herself to make a proper contribution to the effort, neck and shoulders, spine and hips, knees and ankles, and by the time Hathorne spoke again she had achieved a dignified posture.

'Prisoner at the bar, have you anything to say before sentence is passed?' the bailiff asked.

'May God strike down the Witchcraft Act of James the First,' she cried, 'and all its abominable brethren!'

'Let the record show that in her final statement the prisoner added sedition to her list of offences,' Hathorne said. He paused briefly whilst the bailiff outfitted him with the black silk cap. 'Rebecca Webster, the jury hath found that you did sign a pact with the Devil, a crime for which no punishment may be considered too severe. Come Wednesday morning a company of His Majesty's soldiers will bear you to Walnut Street Prison, where at the noon hour you will be brought into public view, stood upon the horse-cart, and hanged by your neck until you are dead.'

'*Eppur si muove*,' she said.

'What?'

'Still, it moves.'

The judge glowered and took up his mallet one last time. 'The Court of Oyer and Terminer is hereby dissolved.'

CHAPTER THE TWELFTH

In Which Truth Acquires the Clothes of Science, Justice Assumes the Shape of Lightning, and the Narrator Finally Runs Short of Words

As she lay atop her pallet, inhaling the stench of the straw and shivering whilst the dungeon's chill invaded her flesh, it came to Jennet that above all else she wanted to see the stars once more. She'd been without them for two months, her trial having occurred entirely by day and her incarceration beneath Manayunk Gaol-House being in essence an entombment. A glimpse of Orion would satisfy her, or Cassiopeia, Lyra, Gemini – or even a bright planet: scintillating Venus, crimson Mars, banded Jupiter, locked in their Keplerian ellipses.

It had not been Herbert Bledsoe's idea to make her final three days on Earth a Draconian ordeal of cold, hunger, encumbrance and solitude. He enjoyed no choice in the matter – or so he claimed. Shortly after the jury delivered its verdict, Governor Gordon had informed Mr Bledsoe that any coddling of the Satanist would probably cost him his appointment. Thus it was that the magistrate appropriated Jennet's feather mattress along with her wool blanket. He removed her writing-desk, impounded her books, reduced her suppers to stale bread and grey beer, and forced her once again to wear the burlap smock. To Jennet each such privation seemed as harsh as the sting of a scourge, but one cruelty in particular she found intolerable: Bledsoe's decision to allow her just one visitor per day, one hour per visit.

On Sunday afternoon she expended her allotted interval with Montesquieu. Standing outside her cell, the mournful aristocrat leaned against the dormant brazier and poured out his heart whilst her fellow prisoners pretended not to eavesdrop. He pledged that upon his return to La Brède he would commend her treatise to every Continental court and legislature, so profound was his respect for her, so deep his adoration.

'*Vraiment, Madame*, the British Conjuring Statute has found a new adversary,' Montesquieu said, 'a weasel-faced male satirist this time rather than a beautiful female *philosophe*, but a person no less dedicated to the fight.'

For all the Baron's passion, his oath sounded hollow to her, artificial as Hezekiah Creech's jaw. She hoped that her analogous promise of forty-two years earlier had not chimed so untruly in Aunt Isobel's ear.

'*The Sufficiency of the World* will outlive you,' he continued. 'It will outlive us all. Your masterwork is destined to join Dante and Chrétien amongst the world's imperishable things.'

'If only my soul could make the selfsame boast,' she said.

He ran a gloved finger along the brazier's clay chimney. 'Do you not believe in the promise of eternal bliss?'

'I would not wager Pascal's last thruppence on that possibility, and neither – let us speak candidly, Charles – neither would you. Like Shakespeare, we hold death an undiscovered country, if 'tis even a country at all.'

It occurred to her that she'd managed to invent a novel sort of martyrdom. Jesus Christ, Saint Stephen, Giordano Bruno and Jeanne d'Arc had all sacrificed themselves because in their various white-hot opinions the world was not sufficient. By Christ's calculation, the given required a supplementary phenomenon called the Kingdom. For Stephen, it needed an organized Christian Church. For Giordano, the world must have endless mystic duplicates of itself. For Jeanne d'Arc, the world became complete only upon intersecting the plane of Heaven, the better to bring the voices of departed saints within earshot. But until the Passion of Rebecca Webster, no one had ever martyred herself to the idea that God had got it right the first time. Until the Webster hanging, nobody had used her own execution to argue against popu-lating the universe with angels and spirits and other immaterial entities, so miraculous was the accessible, so wondrous the mundane.

442

'How I wish you could behold the commotion outside the gaol-house,' Montesquieu said. 'All sixteen prosecution witnesses are collected on the lawn, screaming for vengeance against Rebecca Webster as an opium-eater might cry for his next phial.'

'Why would I want to see such a spectacle?' she asked.

'Because your sympathizers are gathered on those same grounds, and their number is twice as great, their voices thrice as loud. Believe me, Madame, when the executioner shows himself on the scaffold this week, the hisses and howls will deafen him.'

'And will your own hisses and howls be amongst them?'

He bobbed his head, saying, 'Forty pounds sterling has persuaded the captain of the *Fleur de Lys* to keep his ship in port another week.'

'Then I shall ask a boon of you. In my life I've witnessed two public executions. My aunt died screaming at the stake. Giles Corey kept crying, "More weight!" I do not fear the undiscovered country, but I dread the painful portal by which I shall enter it. When the noose closes 'round my neck, you and Ben must come forward and ally yourselves with universal gravitation, pulling me earthward that my end might come more quickly.'

'*Mon Dieu!* I cannot imagine committing such violence against you.'

'You must.'

'*Ce n'est point possible.*'

'Please, Charles. Tell me you'll do it.'

The dungeon reverberated with Matthew Knox's boots clomping down the spiral staircase.

'Monsieur,' the turnkey said, 'I fear your hour hath elapsed.'

Montesquieu abandoned the brazier and, reaching through the bars, squeezed Jennet's hands betwixt his own. 'I promise to intervene as you desire. But know this. Should the rope break, I shall forthwith carry you to safety.'

'Spoken like a true cavalier!' Mrs Sharkey called from her cell.

'Baron, you have the soul of a knight!' Mr Turpin shouted.

'Give no thought to heroism, Charles,' Jennet said, 'for it can only end in a storm of musket-balls.'

'Monsieur,' said Mr Knox again.

'*Au revoir*, my brilliant advocate,' Jennet said.

'*Au revoir*, my mad and glorious friend,' Montesquieu replied.

He turned away and, one measured step at a time, mounted the stairs, wheezing and moaning as would an accused wizard chafing against the mask⁄o'⁄truth.

Jennet's hour with Ben occurred on Monday morning. He arrived bearing sorrowful but entirely expected news. The previous afternoon Major Patrick Gordon had summoned him to his office in Broad Street and explained that his administration was obligated to reject *The Pennsylvania Gazette*'s latest attempt to influence Rebecca Webster's fate – a formal petition, signed by over two hundred citizens of the colony, requesting that she be pardoned.

'He said to me, "Mr Franklin, you must realize that His Majesty's statutes apply as forcefully in the Provinces as in Piccadilly." '

'How are we to explain such callousness from a man whose star your journal did so much to brighten?' Jennet asked.

'I cannot prove my suspicion,' Ben said, 'but I believe your brother hath fallen upon a means of blackmailing Mr Gordon. And hence we are forced to pursue some other path to your reprieve.'

'There is no other path.'

'Then we shall hack one out.'

'Do not entertain false optimism, dear Ben.'

'Do not embrace specious despair, sweet Jenny.'

They passed the remainder of the visit discussing their son, until at last they reached a wrenching decision: there must be no final reunion betwixt Jennet and William. Seeing his mother in a dungeon cell, shackled like a West African slave, jaw scarred, scalp shorn, whilst outside the gaol⁄house a mob of her supposed victims wailed for her blood, William would immediately understand that she was destined for the gallows.

'Tell him I died of a prison⁄fever,' she instructed Ben. ''Tis a plausible narrative, with naught of the shame that attaches to having a witch for a mother.'

'Splendid idea!' Mr Turpin shouted.

'Let the boy remember ye as ye were!' Mrs Sharkey called.

Punctual as always, Mr Knox came tromping down the staircase.

Ben seized a bar in each hand, as if making ready to bow the iron and pull Jennet through the gap. 'Brave lady, I fear I'm about to lose my wits.'

'You foresaw this disaster,' she said. 'You would be within your rights to look me in the eye and say, "If only you had listened to me . . ."'

'I would ne'er be so ungracious.'

She continued briefly on the subject of Ben's prescience, then bound him to the same pledge she'd extracted from Montesquieu. The moment the horse-cart pulled away, leaving her to dangle, he must come forward and lovingly abet the breaking of her neck.

'My arms and legs shall honour thy wish,' he said, 'though my mind and heart will fight them every inch of the way.'

The turnkey cleared his throat conspicuously. 'Mr Franklin.'

Ben climbed the stairs backwards, that his gaze and Jennet's might stay fused as long as possible.

On Tuesday afternoon Barnaby Cavendish descended into the depths of Manayunk Gaol-House. He arrived bearing his latest acquisition, preserved in an alchemist's flask, which he set on the floor outside her cell.

'The Globe-Boy of Baltimore,' he explained.

'No other epithet would do,' Jennet said, for the foetus was marked with lines suggesting meridians and blotches resembling continents.

'A rumour hath reached me from German-Town. It tells of a stillborn babe with a brow so ridged as to resemble a crown of thorns. On the morrow I shall acquire this wondrous Christ-Child, and when I combine him with my Baltimore Globe-Boy, then add the two freaks who survived the shipwreck, I'll have the matrix of the Jennet Stearne Crompton Museum of Wondrous Prodigies.'

'I am flattered by your choice of name – but now let me ask of you another beneficence.' She gestured towards the thing in the jar. 'I would have the loan of yon Globe-Boy, for I believe he will succour me in the hours ahead.'

'The sufficiency of the world?'

'Indeed.'

'I shall instruct him to watch o'er you most tenderly.'

For the balance of his visit Barnaby told tiresome and protracted tales drawn from the nonexistent archives of the Jennet Stearne Crompton Museum of Wondrous Prodigies. She didn't mind. Only by playing the role of carnival charlatan might her friend manage to endure this

445

final reunion without dissolving into a blubbering puddle of woe. He related how the Lyme Bay Fish-Boy had once foiled an assassination plot against the Spanish king, how the Bicephalic Girl had become trapped in an endless disagreement with herself concerning the Eucharist miracle (Papist transubstantiation versus Protestant consubstantiation), and how the Baltimore Globe-Boy had recently rolled all the way to Florida and there discovered the Fountain of Youth. No sooner had Barnaby finished recounting the contrarian ministry of the German-Town Christ-Child than Mr Knox began his descent.

'I'm told the babe's palms have tiny holes at the centres,' Barnaby said. His face was so time-ravaged that the tears reached his jaw only after trickling through a labyrinth of wrinkles, groove and wens. 'Being a doubting Thomas, however, I'd have to see the marks myself ere I called them crucifixion wounds.'

After Barnaby was gone, Jennet sprawled on the cold stone floor and stared at the Globe-Boy. Catching the feeble torchlight, the foetus's lidless green eyes glinted like sunstruck emeralds. The stain below his left shoulder distinctly resembled Great Britain: each nation was there, even little Ireland, circumscribed by seas of skin.

'All flowings and fallings, all flappings and snappings, all swingings and springings, all splittings and flittings . . .'

Her chains scraped against the bars of her cell as she extended her hand, caressed the frigid glass, and prayed to the bottled monster that she might again behold the stars.

Throughout the demonologists' homeward voyage on the *Ignis Fatuus*, the Son of Man and the Father of Lies battled one another, each seeking to determine the future of American witchfinding. The fact of Christly intervention became apparent to Dunstan when, shortly after the sloop dropped anchor off Manhattan-Isle, Abby removed her dress and permitted him for the first time to cast an eye on those places – left breast, right side – where Jennet's demons had inserted the dagger. The lesions were completely healed. It was as if they'd never existed.

'Praise God, I see no sign of the bodkin,' he said, pulling off his day-shirt.

'Our Saviour's lips have kissed my wounds away,' Abby said.

He removed his breeches. ''Tis a miracle, plain and true! Now let me put my own lips to those very spots, that my passion might complete your cure.'

But Lucifer, too, had reserved a berth on the *Ignis Fatuus*. As the sloop blew across Long-Island Sound, a raging fever took hold of Mr Parris, causing him to convulse as violently as any were-wolf or epileptic. For thirty-five terrible hours he thrashed about in his bunk — haemorrhaging from his mouth and nose, spitting up bile, screaming like a victim of the Spanish boot — until at last he lay quiet in his niece's arms.

Within minutes of the minister's death, Captain Morley came to Abby and Dunstan, all grief-struck as if he too were kin to the deceased. After bemoaning the loss of 'a tireless and brilliant general in the war against demonic insurgence', the captain regained his stalwart self and addressed a practical matter. Mr Parris's body, he explained, might harbour the seeds of a contagion, and prudence demanded that they cast it over the side.

The burial ceremony occurred at noon, the entire ship's company standing silently on deck whilst Dunstan read from the Book of Ezekiel. Balanced on the larboard rail, the corpse lay inside a canvas sack weighted with a length of anchor chain. ' "And when I looked, behold, a hand was sent unto me, and, lo, a roll of a book was therein," ' Dunstan recited. ' "And he spread it before me, and it was written within and without: and there was written therein lamentations, and mourning, and woe." '

' "Lamentations, and mourning, and woe." ' Abby echoed.

'Oh, Goodwife Stearne, my heart goes out to you.' Captain Morley tipped the sack towards the waves until it slid free of the rail. The bagged corpse drilled through the surface of the sea and vanished.

'He was ne'er a particularly loving uncle,' Abby said, 'but as a witchfinder he'll prove difficult of replacement.'

'May God rest his soul,' Dunstan said.

'Before I became a woman,' she noted, ''twas his wont to beat me nightly with a willow wand.'

The *Ignis Fatuus* put to port the following morning. Although Dunstan had vaguely hoped that a welcoming committee organized by the Calvinist clergy might greet them, no one amongst the scurrying

447

multitudes on Clark's Wharf took much notice of the cleansers as they disembarked. Perhaps the news of their victory had not yet reached Boston — perhaps the *Bible Commonwealth* reporters were still in Philadelphia, their quills poised to set down the visual, auditory and olfactory particulars of Rebecca Webster's gallows dance.

Eager to collect their two hundred pounds, and more eager still to tell their sponsor of the jurymen's verdict, Dunstan and Abby proceeded directly to the Governor's mansion in Treamount Street. Splendidly attired in a red silk waistcoat and feathered turban, a manumitted Negro named Simeon ushered them past the snootish Mr Peach and into Governor Belcher's august presence.

''Tis my sorrowful duty to report that yesterday the eldest amongst us, the Reverend Samuel Parris, died of a fever,' Dunstan said, addressing the Governor with a deferential bow. 'Our bereavement is somewhat compensated, however' — he lifted his head and grinned — 'by the felicitous outcome of the Philadelphia trial. To wit, Excellency, Rebecca Webster meets the hangman two days hence.'

'Pray accept my sympathy on the death of your fellow pricker,' Belcher said, clucking his tongue. 'Concerning Mrs Webster's imminent execution, 'tis not exactly news 'round here, as this office subscribes to six different provincial journals.'

Dunstan strained to purge his voice of pride. 'Ah, but did you know the jury deliberated a mere three hours?'

'I did,' Belcher said with an inamicable snort.

The Governor's manner perplexed Dunstan. Surely the salvation of the Parliamentary Witchcraft Act, once a matter of imperial concern to Belcher, merited a greater show of enthusiasm. 'In my letter to the Privy Council,' Dunstan said, 'I shall fully credit you with the deft manoeuvres by which John Hathorne replaced Malcolm Cresswell as chief jurist.'

'Your scheme was a masterstroke, my Lord Governor,' Abby added. 'Hathorne displayed even more theological acuity in Philadelphia than at Salem forty years ago.'

From the tea-chest beside his desk Belcher retrieved a half-dozen issues of *The Pennsylvania Gazette*. 'Both *The New-England Courant* and *The Bible Commonwealth* reported on the case, but 'twas Mr Franklin's pithy periodical supplied the fullest account. For all I hold it a seditious paper, methinks there is wisdom in these essays by Ebenezer Trench-ard.' He tapped the topmost issue with his index finger. HATHORNE COERCES GUILTY VERDICT FROM JURY, ran the headline. 'Mr Stearne, I am sorely vexed. Why did you neglect to tell me that the Baron de Montesquieu, not to mention Mrs Webster herself, would make such puissant points against the demon hypothesis?'

'There is no more truth in Trenchard's narratives than in sailors' tales of selkies and sea serpents,' Dunstan said.

'If milk will curdle in consequence of animalcules,' Belcher said, 'and geese go made from ergot, 'twould seem the world hath need of neither demons nor demonologists.'

'Every word Mr Franklin prints is a falsehood,' Dunstan said.

Propping his elbows on the desk, Belcher made a steeple of his fingers and leaned towards Abby. 'According to Mr Trenchard, you pretended Mrs Webster unleashed a band of wicked spirits against you.'

'That was no pretending, my Lord,' she said. 'Her goblins drove a dagger into my side.'

Belcher set his palm atop a ragged stack of papers. 'Yesterday I received a petition from our House of Representatives. They, too, admire the Trenchard letters, and so they ask that for the present I restrict your Commission's activities—'

'Restrict them?' Abby said.

'Restrict them, aye, until such time as His Majesty's advisers have sorted through the arguments advanced in Mrs Webster's favour.'

Dunstan stared out the mullioned windows. Sheets of rain descended on Boston, thick as the smoke from John Hathorne's pipe, heavy as the fumes of burning Haverhill. 'I did not realize our Governor was so beholden to his legislature.'

'Every so often I must lend an ear to the rabble,' Belcher said. 'It makes me appear fair-minded.'

'I beg your pardon, Excellency,' Abby said, 'but the Massachusetts House enjoys no power o'er the Purification Commission, and neither – forgive my bluntness – and neither do you.'

'Wrong, Madam, wrong – for your charter hath no validity without it displays the signature of the man who occupies this mansion. B'm'faith, I cannot recall setting my name to any such paper.'

'You did sign it, sir, three days after you took office.' Opening his valise, Dunstan withdrew the Commission's charter from its customary place betwixt Question Five and Question Six of the *Malleus*. He passed the paper to Belcher. 'See how your name adorns the bottom, plain as a button.'

The Governor grunted, smiled obliquely, and proceeded to perform an action so audacious that in Dunstan's view it would have shamed even the Baron de Montesquieu. Removing a pair of scissors from his desk drawer, Belcher blithely punctured the charter and clipped out a rectangular fragment bearing his signature. The snippet drifted free of the blades and, as the Witchfinder-Royal gasped and shuddered, glided to the floor like an errant autumn leaf.

'Examine your charter more closely, and you'll see it wants for ratification,' Belcher said. He smoothed the gelded document across his desk, and for an instant Dunstan imagined he intended further mutila- tion – but instead the Governor folded the paper in half, securing it beneath his ink-pot. 'You may now follow Simeon back to the antechamber, where Mr Peach will present you with your two hundred pounds. As for your charter, I stand prepared to sign it once I hear that the Privy Council hath found no merit in Mrs Webster's case. But until I take up my quill for such purpose, you must not imagine that you enjoy the slightest authority to hunt so-called witches in this province.'

Dunstan said, 'Had you seen Abby vomit forth those iron nails, you would not be thwarting us so.'

'Trenchard insists 'twas legerdemain made the nails appear,' the Governor said. 'He compares the event to the trickery of Pharaoh's court magicians.'

'They were Christ's own nails flew from my mouth,' Abby said.

'Demon-carried through time and distance, all the way to Philadel- phia,' Dunstan added.

'Demon-carried?' the Governor said.

'Aye,' Dunstan said.

'Through time and distance?'

'Indeed.'

'Spend your two hundred pounds wisely, Mr Stearne, for many a year will pass ere I suffer you or any other witch-pricking mountebank to draw a single shilling from the Royal Purse.'

They took a room at the Red Parrot in Hannover Street, a wretched establishment presided over by a bovine woman who, upon learning that her customers were Rebecca Webster's prosecutors, treated them with a deplorable surliness. They rose the next morning at eight o'clock, discovering to their dismay that the rain had not slackened, then broke their fast with eggs and salted veal in the tavern. All during the meal Abby ministered to Dunstan's melancholy, reminding him of the difficulties his father had faced during the dark days following the Salem hunt, when Sir William Phipps had presumptuously reprieved nearly fifty convicted Satanists.

'The Province's original Witchfinder-Royal did not allow Phipps's defection to discourage him,' she said, 'and I know you will endure Belcher's treachery with equal fortitude.'

'Your faith is most gratifying,' he said, heaving a sigh.

At two o'clock they boarded a day-coach heading west, sharing the compartment with a wig-maker off to visit his sister in Natick and a tallow-chandler seeking to borrow money from his uncle in Marl-borough. The rain continued to fall, drumming on the windows with a monotonous cadence that set their fellow passengers to dozing.

'Our next course of action is clear,' Abby whispered in Dunstan's ear.

'How so?'

'Let us grant the nefarious Governor Belcher six weeks in which to collect and ponder the Privy Council's findings,' she said. 'If he ratifies our charter, we shall bless him and return to our trade. But if he withholds his signature, we must betimes cry him out.'

A vile discomfort spread through Dunstan, as if, in digesting the morning's meat, his stomach was now encountering a poisonous green morsel. 'Cry him out? Can you mean . . . for sorcery?'

'Aye.'

'I'Christ, 'tis the boldest proposition I've yet heard from your lips,' he said, pressing a hand to his belly. 'Do you truly believe Belcher practises the dark arts?'

'He reeks of perdition.'

'But the man's a governor.'

'And Lucifer's a prince. I was ne'er a person to be dazzled by rank.'

The rain went soft in Needham, turned to a swirling mist in Natick, and vanished completely by the time they reached the Merry Alewife in Framingham. They collected their valises and headed south down Badger Road, moving into the teeth of a frigid wind.

Dunstan had imagined that their crossing of Waushakum Pond might be impeded by ice-floes, but so far the freezing air had wrought upon the water only a delicate crystalline crust. They removed the pine-bough cloak from their dinghy and dragged the craft into the shallows. After retrieving his fishing-pole from the stern, Dunstan upended a flat rock and took hold of the large gluey slug beneath. They clambered aboard. As Abby worked the oars, Dunstan impaled the slug and tossed the hook into the pond. The iron easily pricked the ice, bearing the slug netherward. A crisp and sanguine sun cleaved to the horizon, tinting the pond the colour of a ripe pumpkin, but he took no pleasure in the vista. He was cold, and weary, and worst of all nauseated, as if a regiment of Van Leeuwenhoek's wrigglers were mustering in his stomach.

Dusk descended, leaching the world of its nuances and hues. By the time Abby had rowed them to shore, Dunstan had hauled their supper from the pond's murky bottom, a corpulent catfish with long elegant whiskers. Docking, they disembarked and followed the dirt path towards the house, Dunstan holding the fish suspended before him so that it oscillated on its line like a Satanist dangling from a swimming-rope.

Two ragged pieces of paper lay nailed to the front door. The top fragment read, HEREIN DWELLETH THE MURTHERERS OF BLAMELESS SALVAGES. On the lower scrap was sprawled a familiar Gospel verse. O GENERATION OF VIPERS, HOW CAN YE, BEING EVIL, SPEAK GOOD THINGS?

'Mayhap we could be doing a better job of explaining ourselves to our neighbours,' Dunstan said.

'"A prophet is not without honour,"' Abby recited, '"save in his own country."'

The demonologists passed the next hour in silence, stumbling about the house like exhausted beasts of burden whilst they lit the candles, ignited the lanthorns, swept the floor, aired out the bed-chamber, and set a fire in the hearth. Presently Dunstan's thoughts turned to preparing the catfish. He searched through the utensil box and, finding no knife of suitable sharpness, opened his wife's valise and retrieved her dagger.

'I mourn him, truly I do,' Abby said as she greased the great iron skillet. 'I did not love my uncle, but I mourn him.'

Dunstan winced. How might he speak to her of his apprehension? What words would make sense? After testing a dozen preambles in his mind and judging none adequate to the task, he finally blurted out his succinct but anguished opinion. 'Goodwife Stearne, methinks you bring too much ardour to your designs against Mr Belcher.'

'You perplex me.'

'You name Belcher a wizard, and yet we've not submitted him to a single proof.' He laid the drowned fish on the dining table, brought a lanthorn close, and made ready to remove its head.

'Lucifer hath beguiled the Governor,' she said. ''Tis as blatant as blood on snow.'

He set the tip of her dagger an inch behind the fish's unblinking eye, then pushed. The blade failed to pierce the scales but instead retreated into the shaft. 'We've neither swum him, nor pricked him, nor – i'Christ, Abby, your bodkin doth break!' He lifted the dagger free of the fish. The blade shot forward. What sorcery was this? Again he pressed the knife-point against the scales, and again the blade retreated, leaping outward as he jerked it away. 'There be some imp within!'

'Can it be you've ne'er held a pricker's bodkin before?' Abby said.

'Pricker's bodkin?'

'To secure the blade, you need but throw the lever in the shaft.'

'Pricker's bodkin?!' His heart crashed against his ribs like a pent and raging beast. Lurching towards Abby, he held the dagger before her gaze. 'Speak truthfully. Is this sham blade the same as pierced you Friday?'

''Twas clever of you to wheedle Hathorne to our side' – she lifted the skillet to her breast as a Christian knight might raise his shield against a Turk – 'and no less clever of me to seal our victory with my gift for legerdemain.'

'Legerdemain? So Trenchard spoke the truth? Legerdemain? Is this why your flesh bears no wound?'

'"Tis time you cleaned our fish.'

'Raven feathers, our Saviour's nails — illusions all?'

'When you married Abigail Williams, you espoused a most artful cleanser.'

'My sister goes to the gallows in consequence of *tricks*?'

'Nay, Goodman Stearne, she goes in consequence of signing Satan's ledger. Now let us curtail this dreary discussion and prepare our supper.'

It seemed that all his earthly possessions had surrendered their solidity. The hearth stones, door hinges, window panes, wall planks, floor boards, roof beams — these things were fluid now, molten, pouring into one another like metals roiling in a crucible. When he attempted to speak, Dunstan could find no words save the pronouncements of Saint John Chrysostom, most renowned of the Desert Fathers and prime amongst the objects of his own father's secret admiration for the Roman Church.

' "What else is woman but a foe to friendship, an inescapable punishment, a desirable calamity, a domestic danger, a delectable detriment, painted in fair colours?" '

'Husband, you are exceedingly spleenful this night.'

The manner of her departure, he decided, must be biblical yet abrupt, dramatic yet merciful. With an anguished howl he tore the skillet from Abby's grip and, raising its iron mass high, smote her on the brow. Samson battering the Philistines. Jael spiking down Sisera's head. Her skull broke open like an egg, and she fell insensible to the floor.

' "No wickedness approaches the wickedness of a woman!" ' he cried, quoting the Book of Ecclesiasticus. ' "Sin began with a woman, and thanks to her we all must die!" '

Later, after he'd set down the skillet and prayed for her soul and mopped up the matter of her intellect, he took the Commission's tool-kit in hand and walked through the damp woods until he reached the dock. Crickets and cicadas sang all about him. The pond soughed against the shore. Opening the calfskin satchel, he retrieved the short pricking needle and hurled it towards the dark pond. Next he rid himself of the long needle, next the magnification lens. He tied the mask‑o'‑truth to the shaving razor and threw them both in the water.

As the night thickened there descended upon the former witchfinder a tranquillity such as he normally experienced only when drawing landscapes or reading Scripture. Each second followed upon the next like the divine and perfect strokes of an angel's wing. He wished that he might just then take hold of Heaven's pendulum and bring it to a halt, stopping time for ever.

What was a deposed cleanser to do with his life? How could he put his wisdom to use? Who might his next sponsor be?

Slowly a strategy congealed in Dunstan's brain. On the morrow he would slip into the forest, deeper, ever deeper, beyond Framingham, beyond all the English settlements, and from that day forward he would live as had Chrysostom and the other Desert Fathers, sustaining himself on fried locusts and raw honey.

All five implements remained submerged – testament to their holiness, proof of their kinship with martyrs' bones and saints' fingers.

Dunstan of the wilderness. But that would not be the end of him, for on certain rare occasions he would quit the forest and appear before his fellow Calvinists, heralding the Great Antisatan, Suedomsa – Asmodeus inverted – the angel whose shoes he was unworthy to loosen and whose hem he was unfit to kiss: Suedomsa, supreme pricker, divine cleanser, descending upon Massachusetts Bay in a chariot of fire and driving Lucifer from the New World for ever.

He reached into the tool‑kit one last time, drew out the Paracelsus trident, and flung it into the night. The device followed a lovely flowing arc, as perfect a curve as any a geometer might inscribe, and as it reached its apex the moonlight glinted off the tines, so that the trident became a skyborne lanthorn, a celestial beacon, an Oriental comet, pointing the way towards Bethlehem.

On Wednesday at six o'clock, as two raw‑faced, ill‑scrubbed lobster‑backs brought her out of the dungeon and into the dawn, Jennet saw that the Baltimore Globe‑Boy had received her petition favourably. She would not die before seeing a stellar object. Directly ahead lay the morning star, Venus, coruscating above Martsolf's Mill.

Crimson coats muted by scrims of fog, a full company of soldiers encircled the tumbrel, each man keeping an uneasy watch on the two factions in the prison-yard. She recognized the commanding officer, the same gaunt and ashen Captain Wilcox who'd led the attack on the West-Indies pirates. The crowd had apparently changed its disposition since Montesquieu's report, for while her admirers indeed outnumbered the sixteen prosecution witnesses by a factor of two, the latter group was much the noisier. On seeing their nemesis, Jennet's putative victims showered her with imprecations and rotten vegetables. Michael Bailey, the harness-maker who blamed her for his wife's ague, hurled a turnip. The root's decayed matter spattered against her forehead. Daniel Morris, the glass-blower who imagined she'd bewitched his bottles, attacked her with a squash. The sloshy spheroid struck her shoulder and disintegrated. From Wilbur Bennet, the dairyman who believed she'd soured his milk, came a cabbage, its putridity exploding across her chest.

A solitary horse, grey and stippled as the moon, stood ready to bear Jennet to the gallows. Hunched in the driver's box, Matthew Knox offered her a flaccid smile. As the rising sun glinted amongst the trees, washing Venus from the sky and igniting the dew on the dormant lilac bushes, Herbert Bledsoe stepped from his office. He grasped her chain, guided Jennet into the tumbrel, and seated her directly behind Mr Knox. After easing himself onto the opposite bench, he applied his handkerchief to her brow and cheeks, then wiped away the vegetable residue. From his coat he procured a glittering object that at first she thought was a pocket-watch.

'Every drop's for you.' Mr Bledsoe passed her the small copper flask. 'Brandy nauseates me.'

'Thank you.' Accepting the flask, she made a mental effort to forgive the young magistrate his part in making her last days of imprisonment so gratuitously miserable, but her labours came to naught – under present circumstances, evidently, such magnanimity was beyond her. 'Thank you kindly, Mr Bledsoe.'

She pulled out the stopper, tossed back her shaved head, and pressed the flask to her lips. Her wrist-shackle clanked against the copper. The fiery stream trickled down her gullet and spread across her stomach. In a matter of seconds the brandy entered her brain, but instead of producing the desired insensibility it merely made the people swirling around her seem as swollen and grotesque as anything Barnaby Cavendish had ever put in a jar.

Captain Wilcox shouted incoherently, and the Redcoats fell in on both sides of the tumbrel, twenty men per file. The drummer pulled two mahogany sticks from his belt, set them against the sheepskin head, and rattled out three tight rolls followed by two single beats. He repeated the cadence. A second shout from Wilcox, and the soldiers began to march, even as the horse, feeling the bite of Knox's whip, released a tremulous whinny and set off towards Walnut Street Prison.

Whilst the prosecution witnesses rushed to the head of the parade, Jennet's admirers clustered around the tumbrel, their ranks as ragged as the Redcoat formation was orderly. She gulped down a second dose of brandy, then a third. Her brain seemed to rotate on its axis. To spare herself the noose, she realized, she would gladly burn all the existing copies of *The Sufficiency of the World* – burn them then and there, burn them into oblivion, burn them as resolutely as John Flamsteed had immolated his pathetic *Historia Coelestis Britannica*.

The procession advanced down Ridge Road. An expansive farm rolled by, its hills a-swarm with bulbous and oblivious sheep. Apple trees raised skeletal branches towards a sky the grey of the Globe-Boy's pickled flesh.

After perhaps a half-hour the tumbrel reached the edge of Man-ayunk and drew within view of the Wissahickon Creek Bridge, a graceful arc of sandstone. Reaching into her smock, shuddering as the wrist-shackle touched her breast, Jennet retrieved the wooden tiger. She passed the carving to Mr Bledsoe and secured his promise to return it to her son on the morrow, whereupon a wholly unexpected event occurred.

With the suddenness of a thunder-clap the woods flanking Ridge Road erupted with a noise she'd not heard since the burning of Haverhill: Nimacook battle cries – if not Nimacook, then some equally contentious tribe. Scores of Indians plummeted from the trees and landed on the backs of the Redcoats, two braves for each soldier, dragging them down with the predictably lopsided success of wolves falling on lambs. The drum cadence stopped. Knox halted his team. Bledsoe yelped in fear. Jennet steeled herself and drained the brandy, soon finding within the depths of her bewilderment a lucid thought: a quick death at the hands of a tawnie was far preferable to slow strangulation on the gallows.

In the mêlée now unfolding, the Indians did not scruple to press their advantage. The instant Captain Wilcox freed his sword from its scabbard, his collateral savages knocked him senseless with their tomahawks. Every time a soldier attempted to fire his musket, his appended Indians thwarted him by wrapping thongs around his wrists and ankles. Soon the entire Redcoat company lay rolling about on the ground, trussed and disarmed, so that a wayfarer coming upon the scene might have surmised that a committee of witchfinders was about to swim forty accused Satanists *en masse*.

A second commotion drew Jennet's attention to Wissahickon Creek Bridge, where the Rebecca Webster faction and the *maleficium* sufferers were assaulting each other with improvised armaments – rocks and clods, sticks and fists, feet and teeth. The impetus clearly lay with her apostles, and the prosecution witnesses soon retreated bleeding and moaning into the forest.

She surveyed the victorious Indians. There was something most peculiar about them. With their silly feather headdresses and ridiculous war-paint, they would have looked more at home in the King's Theatre than here in a Pennsylvania woodland.

A barrel-chested savage clambered into the tumbrel and offered Bledsoe an amicable nod. 'Pray hand over your prisoner to my stalwart Junto clan,' the Indian said, repositioning his cockeyed feathers, 'that we might bear her to a less hostile clime.'

'Mr Franklin?' the astonished magistrate groaned. ''Tis really you?'

'My name's Chief Ephemeron,' Ben said.

'Dearest Ben,' Jennet gasped.

'Chief Ephemeron,' he corrected her.

Bledsoe pulled an iron key from his coat and, sliding the blade into the lock above her left wrist, popped open the shackle as efficiently as a serving-wench might turn the tap on a keg, then with equal dexterity uncuffed her right wrist. The bracelets thudded against the tumbrel floor, quite the most agreeable sound Jennet had heard since William first took suck at her breast.

Now Nicholas Scull, the youngblood through whose initiatives the citizens of Manayunk had been moved to demand Mrs Webster's arrest, appeared from out of nowhere, sporting an Indian disguise only slightly less outlandish than Ben's. He scrambled into the driver's box and snatched the reins from Knox. Addressing the turnkey in a morbidly jocular tone, Scull informed him that if he wished to avoid 'the piquant unpleasantry of a scalping' he must surrender his seat forthwith. With the frightened agility of an adulterer responding to the cuckold's unexpected return, Knox leapt from the tumbrel and sprinted north along Ridge Road.

As far as Jennet could tell, the sham Indians' raised tomahawks and flashing knives were keeping the Redcoats in check, and it gradually came to her that she probably wasn't going to Walnut Street Prison this morning, or the next morning, or any morning in the immediate future. Dame Fortune and the Junto had plucked her from the gallows.

'Mrs Crompton, I wish you Godspeed.' Bledsoe placed the wooden tiger in her palm, then jumped to the ground and rushed to join Knox.

Scull urged the speckled horse forward. The wagon rattled across the bridge and continued down Ridge Road, Jennet's partisans all the while celebrating her deliverance by applauding like satisfied play-goers.

'Oh, Ben,' she said, 'I've ne'er seen such a marvellous display of derring-do – but I cannot imagine the next step in this audacious caper.'

'You will be spirited to safety,' he responded.

'Over two hundred miles as the crow flies, three hundred as the carriage rolls, till you reach the Hoosic River,' Scull elaborated.

'To wit, you are escaping to the bosom of your Kokokehom kin,' Ben said. ''Tis high time you filled your *pittuckish*.'

At the Hunting-Park Road intersection, Scull set the horse on a north-east path, in eternal divergence from Walnut Street Prison with its expectant crowd of public execution enthusiasts.

'Three hundred miles,' Jennet sighed. 'You may call it an escape, but it sounds more like an exile.'

Ben scratched both cheeks simultaneously, his war-paint having evidently begun to itch. 'As a woman convicted of witchery and suspected of sedition, you shall not this day elude the noose without antagonizing many an agent of the Crown, from Governor Gordon taking bribes in Locust Street to the Lord Chancellor shooting quail in Marylebone Park.'

'To put it crudely,' Scull added, 'instead of a rope around your neck, you will soon acquire a price upon your head.'

'Believe us, darling Jenny, the Nimacook village is your one true haven,' Ben said.

'Your reasoning's persuasive, but you must suffer little William to come with me,' she said.

'I think not,' Ben said, 'for such a gambit would surely place him in deadly peril.'

Betimes the tumbrel reached the Henry Road intersection, where the Baron de Montesquieu's coach loomed out of the morning mist, the driver's box occupied by another Junto youngblood, the brawny Philip Synge, dressed in tawnie trappings. The Baron's team of matched black geldings anxiously stomped the ground, tossing their heads, steam gushing from their nostrils. As Scull pulled back on the reins, halting the tumbrel, Montesquieu and his footman stepped out of the coach. Jennet half expected to see them disguised as Indians, but instead they wore their usual powdered perukes, silk waistcoats and perfumed neckcloths.

'*Madame Crompton, vous êtes sauvée!*' an exultant Montesquieu cried.

At Ben's urging, Jennet vaulted free of the tumbrel, regaining her balance as a second coach came clattering out of the fog. Juxtaposed with Montesquieu's lordly equipage, this newly arrived conveyance was a shabby affair, lamps broken, curtains torn, paint as mottled as the Turtle of Tewkesbury's skin, and yet it seemed roadworthy enough, pulled by as sturdy a team as Jennet had ever beheld. Commanding the horses was Montesquieu's customary driver, the phlegmatic Herr Strossen, and no sooner had he decelerated the coach than the passenger door flew open to reveal the first real Indian of the day, John Tux, who promptly hopped to the ground.

Now Ben abandoned the tumbrel. 'Herr Strossen hath agreed to transport you and Mr Tux safely to the Hoosic,' he explained to Jennet, 'a task for which he will receive two hundred guineas plus this venerable coach, both incentives supplied by *Monsieur le Baron.*'

With a snap of his whip, Nicholas Scull got the tumbrel moving again. He continued down Hunting-Park Road, vanishing anon into the spectral embrace of the fog.

'We shall travel the entire western shore of the Delaware,' John Tux said, 'thence to New York and finally to Massachusetts – a six-day journey by my calculation.' He pointed to his bulging purse. 'Thanks to your French patron, we are supplied with funds sufficient to sleep in whatever inns suit our fancy, trade up our horses should an injury befall them, and seal the lips of any magistrate who looks upon our party askance.'

Jennet approached the Baron and kissed his brow. '*Mon cher Charles*, 'twould appear I am profoundly in your debt.'

'I merely financed this madness,' Montesquieu said. 'The scheme itself was entirely of Monsieur Franklin's design.'

John Tux extended his fluttering hand and gestured towards the open compartment. 'The faster we leave Philadelphia, Waequashim, the greater our chances of seeing the morrow's sun rise up.'

''Twill not be long before the Redcoats break their bonds and come charging onto the scene,' Ben added urgently. 'I shall give you till the count of five.'

'How can we know the Kokokehom will take me back?' Jennet asked John Tux. 'My long-ago departure was accomplished most discourteously.'

'One!' Ben cried.

'They will take you back,' said John Tux with prodigal confidence. 'The rules of *pittuckish* require it.'

'You must tell William his mother will always love him,' Jennet instructed Ben.

'Two!' he barked. 'You have my word,' he added.

'*Mon ami grand*,' she moaned, throwing her arms around the Baron.

'*Hélas*, we've no time for farewells, Madame,' Montesquieu said.

'Three!'

She turned and hugged the love of her life. 'My bonny Ben.'

'Four!' he shouted. 'My dearest Jenny,' he gasped. 'Five!'

Uncoiling her arms from Ben's heroic rotundity, she allowed John Tux to hoist her into the decrepit coach. As the Indian climbed up beside her, the Baron's footman slammed the door, Herr Strossen cracked his whip, and the wheeled monstrosity lurched onto Henry Road and headed

north. Leaning out the window, Jennet stole a final glance at Ben standing beside the Baron's equipage, enshrouded by the dust of her departure.
His absurd feather headdress was all askew, its cockeyed angle evoking
Newton's periwig or perhaps a drunken earl's peruke. Her sweetest
swain. Her bonny Ben. One day that remarkable young man would
be known throughout the Colonies, for surely fame must touch
a person so skilled at scheming and adept at
deception, even though he
made a thoroughly
preposterous

*

Indian
disguises were by
far the most common subterfuges
employed by dissident American patriots during
the Colonial era. The stratagem through which Ben rescued
Jennet foreshadowed the halfdozen pseudoMohawk and faux
Algonquin raids that occurred as the winds of insurrection blew from
Boston down to Charleston. As far as I can determine, the Colonists'
goal was not to implicate any actual Indians but rather to lend a general
mood of chaos and indeterminacy to the struggle against British rule.

A typical such action was the *Gaspée* affair. In 1772, while chasing
a smugglers' ship, this British customs schooner ran aground at
Namquit Point near Providence. At nightfall a wealthy Rhode Island
merchant named John Brown led eight boatloads of patriots dressed
as Indians out to the *Gaspée*. They shot the captain, routed the crew,
and burned the vessel. The official inquiry failed to identify a single
perpetrator.

Then, of course, there was the legendary Boston Tea Party, sparked
by the Royal Governor's refusal to let the *Dartmouth* and her two sister
ships leave for England with their unwanted tea until the Colonists
paid a duty on the entire cargo. On the evening of 16 December
1773, several dozen 'Mohawk braves' rowed out to the vessels, ripped
the lids off 342 crates filled with the vexatious leaves, and dumped the
containers into the bay. 'Many Persons wish that as many dead
Carcasses were floating in the Harbour,' John Adams wrote at the
time, 'as there are Chests of Tea.'

As we all know, Jennet was right about Ben. He did become famous, not only in America but throughout Europe, largely in consequence of his 1751 treatise, *Experiments and Observations on Electricity made at Philadelphia in America*, and its two sequels. (Among their many insights, Franklin's electricity papers clarified that lightning bolts do not descend from the sky like hailstones – even Jennet, as we have seen, laboured under that common misconception – for these flashes manifest a reciprocal discharge between cloud and ground.) Now, I can't really blame my father for treating Franklin so cavalierly during the four hours they spent together in 1725. How was Newton to know that this cheeky kid from Philadelphia, who seemed almost as unbalanced as his demented half-sister, would amount to anything? How could he guess that, by the turn of the century, scientists would be routinely referring to Franklin as 'the Newton of electricity'?

Naturally I'm more interested in Ben's genius for experiment than in his talent for expedience, but let me here acknowledge the man's political gifts. A loyal British subject at heart, he was truly aggrieved to see the Empire sundered, but when the time came to consecrate the American Declaration of Independence, he signed it with the same species of aplomb Jonathan Belcher had displayed invalidating Dunstan's witchfinding charter. 'We must all hang together,' Ben said, taking pen in hand, 'or assuredly we shall all hang separately.'

Whenever I ponder his many diplomatic achievements, I am especially moved by Ben's success in convincing the French government to supply the American patriots with firearms, foodstuffs, ships, troops, officers and, above all, money. Consider his inauspicious circumstances. He lands in Auray on 3 December 1776, proceeds to Paris, and in secret meets the French Foreign Minister, the Comte de Vergennes, three days after Christmas. Our hero is seventy, exhausted and still mourning his Deborah, now three years dead. He has come to Paris as the envoy of a dubious rabble in rebellion against a legitimate European king, and somehow he must persuade an absolute Catholic monarch, Louis XVI, to aid the very sort of Protestant insurgents who, for a century and a half, have been his country's worst enemies in the New World. It's like inviting Francis of Assisi to go duck hunting. And yet, through a combination of wit, charm and bald propagandizing, not to mention his *je ne sais quoi* with the ladies (who wield considerable influence in French government circles at this time), Ben pulls it off. In February 1778 a treaty is signed at Versailles, and soon afterward millions of *livres* are flowing into the Yankee treasury. I would not claim that Ben won America's war of independence with that treaty – we must not overlook George Washington's military prowess, Thaddeus Kosciuszko's knowledge of fortifications, and Baron von Steuben's ability to mould brigades from bumpkins – but I cannot imagine the Colonists' victory without the Franco-American alliance.

Yesterday my own war of independence, my lifelong struggle to rid myself of the *Malleus Maleficarum*, likewise received a boost from Benjamin Franklin. Throughout the long and bloody Battle of Fortieth Street, the pendulum of victory swung to and fro. The first engagement found my booklice outflanking and subsequently decimating the *Malleus*'s silverfish, but then his Cambodian wasps strafed my termites, sending them into retreat. When my Indonesian moths retaliated by firebombing the *Malleus*'s bookworms, his remaining silverfish grew so enraged that they massacred my pulpchiggers. But then, suddenly, like Blücher at Waterloo, *Poor Richard's Almanack* swooped onto the scene leading a corps of Madagascar papyrus beetles, and the tide turned in my favour. Once I'd hurled those five thousand carapaced berserkers into the fray, the *Malleus*'s doom was sealed.

My arthropod mercenaries were quick to claim their prize. Shortly after two o'clock they departed a field strewn with legs, wings, antennae and proboscises, subsequently crossing the East River in a coal barge, hitching a ride to Mineola in a garbage truck, and marching into the Dover Publications warehouse. At 4.30 p.m. the rationalist bacchanal began. With the same calibre of zeal the Colonial dissidents brought to the Boston Tea Party, the insects descended buzzing and singing upon the nearest carton of Witch Hammers, chewed off the lid, and sunk their mandibles into the eschatological obscenities.

Only after my soldiers were well into the second carton did I perceive, and immediately repent, my error. My God, I thought – my God, I've become that vilest of creatures, a biblioclast. I am no better than those misguided Greeks who consigned the works of Protagoras to the flames; no better than Diocletian building a pyre from any and all volumes pertaining to Jesus Christ; no better than the Emperor Shih

Huang-ti ordering the destruction of every book published before his ascension (so that human history would appear to begin with his reign); no better, even, than Joseph Goebbels supervising the incineration of more than 20,000 volumes – Freud, Steinbeck, Zola, Hemingway, Einstein, Proust, Wells, Mann, London and Brecht among them – in the streets of Berlin on 10 May 1933.

'Cease!' I told my insect hosts. 'Cease and desist!'

But, alas, I no longer controlled the bibliophages. Instead of heeding me they continued feasting, and by dawn Dover's entire *Malleus* inventory lay in their digestive systems, the air filling with the sound of burping pulpchiggers and cooing booklice. And so I must beg your sympathy, gentle reader. Now that I've regained my senses, I see that the best counter to a malicious idea is a *bon mot*, not a bonfire; I see that the correct reply to a
corrupt text is a true one, not a termite corps; I see that the proper
way to defeat the agents of darkness is not to burn down
their houses but to rip away their
shutters, open their doors,
and let in
the

*

Sunlight
dancing on the
mist above Cutshausha Falls,
fashioning a rainbow even as it corroborated
refraction's eternal laws. Snowflakes sifting down from the
winter sky, each crystalline wheel a marvel of Euclidian precision.
Rivulets rushing along the thicketed slopes, eager to feed the swollen river in accordance with ancient hydraulic principles. *Nux*, yes, no question: here on the shores of the Hoosic, here amongst its beasts and fish and fowl, the sufficiency hypothesis obtained in full.

An ample valley, a robust forest, a place in which she'd found – not happiness exactly, not bliss, nor even satisfaction: the word, she decided, was *tranquillity*. For the first time since receiving her commission from Aunt Isobel, Jennet enjoyed an inner equipoise, her soul's pendulum describing an arc neither too long nor too short. Her body grew firm and muscular. Her barren scalp, so brutally shaved by Abraham Pollock's sisters, again yielded its shock of hair, the auburn now inlaid with silver. Her curiosity became keener than ever, eventually finding a worthy object in the countless species of spider thriving near the Indian village. Why didn't these daughters of Arachne get tangled in their own threads? Were they Platonists at heart, spinning their webs in reference to an unseen ideal? Was a spider's bite always a calamity or might the poison be some secret medicine? The Kokokehom had noted her obsession. Waequashim Ashaunteaug-Squaw, they called her. Waequashim the Spider-Woman.

Owing largely to John Tux's correspondence with his sagamore mother, Quannamoo, an exchange in which he'd cast Jennet as the heroic enemy of the Indian-killing witchfinders, her return to the clan had occasioned much festivity. Shortly after Herr Strossen's coach had clattered into the village, Quannamoo arranged a welcoming ceremony, a *wopwawnonckquat*. In form the custom was rather like running the gauntlet, though in spirit it was the opposite: instead of assailing the initiate with whips and cudgels, the assembled Nimacooks honoured her with praise and caresses. As Jennet moved down the line, familiar faces appeared before her, each a bloated, shrunken or otherwise unfaithful reflection of the memory she'd been carrying in her head. Thus did she experience a grand reunion with Hussane, no longer a rascally young medicine-woman but a middle-aged *taupowau*, well on the way to cronehood. Likewise waiting to greet her was Kapaog, the brave she'd suckled as a babe following his mother's death from the flogging sickness, his frame now towering over six feet, his legs as strong as saplings, his broad hands holding a bead necklace: a gift, he explained, offered in gratitude for her milk. But the acme of the *wopwawnonckquat* was the moment in which Pussough, her Lynx Man appeared and, cupping his hands beneath her jaw, tilted back her head until their eyes met.

'*Askuttaaquompsin?*' he asked.

'*Asnpaumpmauntam,*' she replied. Yes, I am well.

From the pocket of his deerskin coat Pussough withdrew the largest raven feather Jennet had ever seen, larger even than the specimens Abigail had disgorged during the trial, a quill that, crisply trimmed and dipped in venom, would have been worthy to record her most wicked thoughts and scandalous fancies.

'I found it in the wayside cavern to which we guided you after the Haverhill raid,' he explained.

'A strange place for a bird to shed its plumage,' she said.

He slid the feather along her scalp, lodging it in the thickest of her nascent locks. 'Perhaps it comes from the very raven who blessed us with the first maize seed.'

'Then I shall wear this token with great respect, and never let it far from my sight.'

After the *wopwawnonckquat* celebrants had dispersed, Jennet's Nima-cook mother-in-law stepped forward, the ancient Magunga, now dry and shrivelled as a corn husk, bearing the news Jennet most dreaded to hear. The rumours were true. Okommaka had been sorely wounded whilst leading a foolhardy raid on the English settlement at Springfield. Taking Jennet's hand, Magunga guided her towards the square, where two more Nimacooks joined their company, nimble young braves whom Magunga introduced as her grandsons, Wompissacuk and Chogan. The solemn procession continued to the village's largest wigwam, its walkway planted with trilliums – his favourite flower, Jennet remembered.

'*Pausawut kitonckquewa*,' Magunga said, pausing at the threshold. He cannot last long.

'One bullet he carries in his side,' Wompissacuk elaborated, 'another in his chest.'

'At first the battle went our way,' Chogan added, 'but then a company of lobsterbacks arrived.'

Jennet stooped before the doorway and, stepping forward, abandoned the blazing sunlight for the gloomy wigwam. It was a foetid place, foul and swampy. Speckled with sweat, taut with pain, her *wasick* lay on a sleeping mat, eyes closed, mouth gaping, his quavering flesh swathed in a woollen blanket. A woman of middle years crouched beside him, the lissome mother of his strapping sons, soaking a wad of sphagnum in an earthenware bowl filled with water.

Okommaka's two wives exchanged hasty glances. 'I am glad of your arrival,' Maansu told Jennet. 'He speaks of you often.'

As the squaw rubbed the dripping moss across Okommaka's brow, Jennet dropped to her knees and took his fevered hand in hers. His eyes flickered open. He smiled.

'Waewowesheckmishquashim?'

'Aye, my husband, 'tis your wayward Waequashim, home at last.'

467

'I am sensible of the destiny that took you from us.' A sudden spasm rippled through his frame. He clenched his teeth and groaned. 'Your noble war on the witchfinders.'

'Methinks we are not the luckiest of persons, you and I,' Jennet said. 'The bold Okommaka lost his battle with the Redcoats, and the benighted Waequashim failed to defeat the demonologists.'

'But we fought well, did we not?'

'Aye, husband. We fought well.'

'Then perhaps we are not so unlucky.'

She bent towards him and kissed his lips. 'Do you think of her?'

'*Nux*. Yes. Almost every day.'

'I am much inclined to visit the mound beside the Shawsheen,' she said, 'but I fear there would be naught left of it.'

Once again Maansu saturated the sphagnum. She caressed her husband's face with the cool spongy mass.

'Has the night come?' Okommaka asked.

'Not yet,' Maansu said.

'Ere the moon rises,' he said, 'I shall fly to the mountain of Kautantouwit, who will then bear my soul to Keesuckquand. And after I am gone a month, dearest wives, you must look to the sun, and you will see Pashpishia and her father, sitting by the council-fire.'

Okommaka did not die that night. Instead he lingered for three more days, succumbing to the bullets on a drear and drizzly afternoon, Thursday by the English calendar. At first Jennet felt nothing at all, and then she felt entirely too much, a knife in her heart, a nail in her gut. It was only through the greatest effort that she succeeded in applying a mask of soot to her face, paddling a canoe across the Hoosic, and joining the circle of mourners.

From noon until dusk the grieving Indians sat around the grave, and for even the most stoic warrior there was no shame in letting his tears fall like rain. When at last the weeping was accomplished, Hassane came forward and erected the soul-chimney, the *cowwenock-wunnauchicomock*, atop the mound. Carefully she canted it to the south-west, so that Okommaka's spirit might more easily find its way to Kautantouwit's abode, whereupon Jennet's thoughts turned to the inevitable day when, lifting her eyes to the blue and cloudless Hoosic Valley sky, fixing on the sun's corona, she would see them both,

Okommaka and Pashpishia, laughing together and warming themselves by the council fire.

Okommaka's remains were not a week in the ground when Wompissacuk and Chogan embarked upon a scheme by which they hoped to ameliorate their grief whilst simultaneously bestowing a boon on Waequashim. Their intention was to build her a private wigwam, siting it in the enormous oak tree that flourished on the lee shore of the Hoosic. Completed in the space of a month, the dwelling proved a veritable mansion, a splendid assemblage of birch bark and cedar planks, subdivided into four discrete rooms, rather like the Market Street garret in which Jennet had first frolicked with Ben. The northwest chamber she devoted to dining, whilst the adjacent area became home to her spider experiments and rock specimens. In the south-east sanctum she erected her sleeping platform, an amenity that she oft-times shared with the passionate Pussough. Most sacred of all was the remaining space, the one in which she gathered and read and lovingly stroked her books.

The source of this literary abundance was Ben. Every spring and again in the fall John Tux would employ Herr Strossen to bear him to the Hoosic, the young Nimacook having decided that he owed his mother such constancy, and he always hauled along a gift-crate from the ambitious editor of *The Pennsylvania Gazette*. By the end of her third year in exile, Jennet had accumulated a substantial library. Her trove included an especially nourishing shelf of Shakespeare, a credible collection of Milton, and a half-dozen quartos from Alexander Pope. 'All are but parts of one stupendous whole, whose body Nature is, and God the soul' – a reasonable enough sentiment, though she preferred Rica's evocation of Spinoza in Chapter Twenty-nine of *Lettres Persanes*: 'If triangles had a god, it would have three sides.'

Beyond its bibliographic treasures, each Franklin crate included a hodgepodge of clothing, tools and news-clippings. In the accompanying letter Ben would offer amusing accounts of William's adventures, and he also narrated his own accomplishments – his election as Grand Master of the Masons, his establishment of a public subscription-library in Philadelphia, his inauguration of America's first German-language newspaper, his definitive demonstration, via kite and collection jar, that lightning-bolts and Von Guericke sparks were in essence identical – but he always began by reporting on the aftermath of the Webster trial, which had evidently wrought a greater measure of justice upon the Earth than Jennet would have dared imagine. 'As you can see by the enclos'd Clipping from *The New-England Courant*,' he wrote in the spring of 1733, 'Governor Belcher hath depriv'd the Purification Commission of its Charter, quite clearly in Consequence of your Testimony.' Six months later: 'According to this Day's Issue of *The Bible Commonwealth*, quote "His Majesty's American Witchfinders have temporarily ceas'd their Activities, mayhap pursuant to Governor Belcher's ill-conceived Injunction, more probably that they might mourn the Passing of their guiding Light, the Reverend Samuel Parris."' The spring of 1734 brought the most heartening news of all: 'I scour the Pages of every Colonial Journal to reach the Printing-House,' Ben wrote, 'and I find no Evidence that your Brother and his Wife are abroad in the Land. Is it too much to hope we have seen the Last of them?'

Not every message from Ben was cause for celebration. Scarcely a month went by in which Governor Gordon neglected to declare that he still regarded Rebecca Webster as a convicted Satanist and fugitive from justice. A bounty of fifty pounds sterling lay upon her head, and Gordon fully intended to prosecute her the instant she was brought before him. Another unhappy dispatch detailed the attack of pleurisy, attended by a suppurating lung, that Ben had suffered in the summer of 1735. Still another sad bulletin disclosed the demise of *Das Philadelphische Zeitung*. But the most terrible letter from Pennsylvania concerned Deborah and Ben's first-born son, Francis Folger Franklin, dead of the smallpox aged four. 'Shortly after we interr'd that good and loving Boy in the Yard of Christ Church,' Ben wrote, 'I was mov'd to reverse a long-standing Prejudice of mine, and in consequence our William is now inoculat'd against this Pestilence.'

When not contemplating the mysteries of arachnid architecture, Jennet pursued a construction project of her own, an enclosed veranda extending along one side of her tree-hut. She took a particular pride in the window curtain, which she'd made by attaching colourful pebbles and shiny snail-shells to three-foot lengths of twine. It was shortly after she'd hung the last curtain-strand, on a congenial August afternoon, that a loud greeting came wafting through the branches of her oak. 'Hallo, Jennet Stearne!' John Tux? No, this was a different sort of voice, less musical, more hearty. 'Hallo, dearest friend!' Nor could her visitor be Pussough, whose tongue boasted a distinctly Nimacook cadence.

'Hallo!' she called back.

'Is it true a brilliant philosopher dwells up there, and will this same sage entertain a wayfarer from Pennsylvania? For he brings most glorious news!'

'Oh, my bonny Ben!' she cried, unfurling her rope ladder.

Five minutes later they stood together on her veranda, locked in a protracted embrace, at the end of which she stood back, pressed Ben's hand betwixt her palms, and offered her condolences on the death of little Francis.

'This life oft-times seems to me a squall of scalding tears,' he said, 'and they ne'er burn deeper than when a parent must bury his own child.'

'I know too well the despond of which you speak,' she said.

He brushed his fingers along the curtain, wringing a soft carillon from the pebbles and shells. 'Let us think on happier matters, dearest. I cannot say what miseries the morrow may bring you, but *today*, J. S. Crompton — *today* every rose in Christendom blooms in your honour, every lark warbles your praises, and Dr Halley's comet dances to an air called "The Song of Jennet".' Dipping into his waistcoat he withdrew a news-clipping. 'Behold an article from *The London Journal* of this past July the First concerning a Parliamentary act to be henceforth known as the Witchcraft Statute of George the Second.'

Jennet snatched away the clipping. She rushed past the introductory paragraphs, lingered briefly on a sentence identifying the new law's initiator as an alderman named Heathcote, then plunged into the heart of the matter.

I. Be it enact'd by the King's most excellent Majesty, by and with the Advice and Consent of the Lords spiritual and temporal, and Commons, in this present Parliament assembl'd, that the Statute made in the first Year of the Reign of King James I, entitl'd 'An Act against Conjuration, Witchcraft, and Dealing with Evil and Wicked Spirits,' shall, from the 24th day of June next, be repeal'd and utterly void and of non effect.

II. And be it further enact'd that from and after the said 24th of June, the Act pass'd by the Parliament of Scotland in the ninth Year of Queen Mary entitl'd 'Anentis Witchcraft,' shall be and is thereby repeal'd.

III. And be it further enact'd, that from and after the said 24th of June, no Prosecution, Suit, or Proceeding shall be commenc'd or carried on against any Person or Persons for Witchcraft, Sorcery, Enchantment, or Conjuration, in any Court whatsoever in Great Britain.

' "Repealed and utterly void and of non effect," ' she said, her voice trembling. ' "Repealed and utterly void . . ." ' Her tears hit the clipping with soft silent collisions. 'Oh, Ben, you must promise me these words come not from the pen of Ebenezer Trenchard, for I could ne'er abide such a hoax.'

'Even Ben Franklin places certain matters beyond jocularity. Read on, Jenny. The best is still to come.'

She dropped her gaze to the final paragraph, scanning it through the watery veil.

In voting to overturn the Conjuring Statute of King James I, some several Parliamentarians allud'd to a Treatise with which we Journal *Editors were heretofore unfamiliar, Mr J. S. Crompton's* The Sufficiency of the World. *In the Words of Randolph, Earl of Somerset, 'This noble Tome offers a Rationale, rooted in the most rigorous Newtonian Experimentalism, whereby ev'ry thoughtful Christian might see how the suppos'd Crime of Witchcraft is an Impossible Thing.'*

'My book's been read by Somerset himself!' she cried.

Now Ben was weeping too. 'Some several Parliamentarians, it says. *Some several.*' He patted his eyes with a corner of his handkerchief, then passed the cloth to her. 'And now I must tell you of yet another blessing. Right before John Tux and I departed for the Hoosic, Governor Gordon made public his intention to lift the bounty and pardon you in full. To wit, my dearest love, you are a free woman, heir to the same rights enjoyed by all British subjects this side of the Atlantic Sea. Shall I save you a place in Herr Strossen's coach?'

'On first principles, the answer requires no thoughts.' She twisted the handkerchief into a taut cord of silk. 'And yet there are riches on these shores.'

As if cued by Jennet's remark, a red-tailed hawk took flight from a nearby chestnut tree, gliding past the veranda in a majestic parabola.

'The grandest telescope in America hath lately come into my possession,' Ben said.

'I have my lofty house and my humble library. My industrious spiders and my beauteous rocks. I have my tranquillity.' She returned the handkerchief to Ben. ' "Repealed and utterly void and of non effect." Did a Lutheran hymn e'er boast a more beautiful refrain?'

'Certainly not,' he said.

'Did Shakespeare e'er write a better line?'

'Not more than once or twice in his whole life.'

'Bear me to Philadelphia, bonny Ben, that I might peruse the *Codex Naturae*, study the Galilean satellites through your new telescope, and watch our son grow to manhood!'

Foreseeable as the phases of the moon, predictable as the pull of charged sulphur on chaff, Pussough's reaction to the news of her imminent departure involved no surprises, few nuances and much lamentation. He moaned and keened and stamped his moccasined feet. He declared that he wanted to die. They spent the night together, alternately arguing and swiving, and by morning her Lynx Man had found within himself a proper measure of gallantry. Of *course* she must return to Mr Penn's province. No question. *D'accord.* Her child needed her, and moreover she was a philosopher at heart, far less Waequashim of the Kokokehom than J. S. Crompton of the *argumentum grande.* She belonged in Philadelphia.

And so it was that Rebecca Webster, née Jennet Stearne, ended her exile, allowing Herr Strossen to bear her and Ben back to the Colonial capital.

It was not long after their arrival that a typically Franklinesque obsession took hold of Ben. He wanted the reading public of America and Europe to know that the author of *The Sufficiency of the World* was in fact Rebecca Webster, vindicated witch, who was in turn Jennet Stearne, natural philosopher, a revelation he imagined making in either

The Pennsylvania Gazette or his newest publishing venture, *Poor Richard's Almanack*. Once Mrs Webster's true identity was known, he argued, Jennet might earn a handsome income touring the great cities of Europe, lecturing on how she'd brought the English Parliament to its senses.

But Jennet had no interest in eminence. She wanted only to pursue a modest philosophic life, designing and executing experiments spun from her intuition that magnetism and electricity, like lightning-bolts and Von Guericke sparks, shared a common heritage. Though it was not at first obvious how she might support herself during these investigations, she eventually solved the problem by selling the Chestnut Street townhouse to a Dutch shipbuilder named, strangely enough, Van Leeuwenhoek, a distant relation to the father of microscopy.

A succession of brief visits to Ben's residence in Market Street convinced her that her son's real family consisted of his distractible but doting father and his dull but affectionate stepmother. If she wanted to serve William's happiness most fully, she would play a role analogous to that which Aunt Isobel had assumed in her own upbringing. She would become the child's secondary nurturer, his deputy mother, introducing him to Newton's optics and Virgil's epic, to Shakespeare's lovers and the Nimacooks' lore, to the glories of geometry and the satisfactions of swimming – but, alas, she would not be the one to dry his tears, wipe his nose, prepare his supper, bandage his abrasions, tuck in his bed-clothes, or comfort him when phantoms troubled his sleep.

Ignoring the counsel of Ben, Barnaby, John Tux, Nicholas Scull and everybody else she knew in Philadelphia, she seized the opportunity to purchase, for a fraction of its worth, the Sumac Lane farm, a property that, owing to its reputation as the home of a convicted sorceress, had found no tenants since her flight to the Hoosic Valley. Her friends all agreed that the Witchcraft Statute of George II, with its unequivocal rejection of the demon hypothesis, had implicitly turned the Manayunk villagers into objects of ridicule, which meant they were certain to variously shun and harass the woman who'd brought this humiliation upon their heads. And yet something like the opposite occurred. Not long after her return to the farm a delegation of her neighbours, some twenty in all, gathered outside her door bearing home-brewed ales and piquant apple pies. This committee of the contrite owed its formation to Bethany Fallon, the goose-girl who'd once fed contaminated rye seeds to her flock, though now she was Mrs Markley, a brewer's wife with a brewer's child in her belly.

'We have sinned against you, Mrs Webster,' she said, stepping onto Jennet's stoop. 'We wronged you no less than Judas wronged our Saviour.'

'My trial brought to light a wicked judge and three corrupt prickers, but I see no such malefactors here,' Jennet said.

'We always remove the black bodies from our seeds before we feed 'em to our geese,' Mrs Markley said, 'and so far our flock's been free o' the ergot.'

Next to speak was Mrs Plum, the flax-planter who'd told the Court how a lightning-bolt had burned his crop. 'Now that Parliament hath endorsed Mr Crompton's opinions,' he told Jennet, 'I am pleased to call electricity and Heaven's fire the selfsame substance.'

'Sir, you must ne'er accept a scientific principle simply because it boasts the weight of authority,' Jennet said. 'Accept it rather because it enjoys the blessing of evidence.'

The blessing of evidence. As her neighbours drifted away, the euphoric phrase lingered in her brain, mocking her aspirations. The blessing of evidence was exactly what her magneto-electric hypothesis could not claim. It was just that, a mere hypothesis, trapped in the foggy valley of conjecture, miles below the towering crag of fact.

Throughout the spring of 1738, whenever a thunder-gust seemed about to break over Manayunk, she would assemble and launch a silk kite surmounted by an upright wire. The fly-line terminated in a lean-to sheltering a collection jar in which stood an iron horseshoe, the surrounding area ringed by twenty hobnails laid flat on the grass. To guide the wire directly into the clouds, she always detached the kite from the mooring post and steered it by hand, but only after putting on boots outfitted with paraffin soles and equipping the fly-line with a water-repellent leather bridle.

By the summer solstice she'd seen a dozen storms rip apart as many silk handkerchiefs, and still not a single lightning-bolt had found its way to the collection jar. But then, one turbulent evening in July, she managed to pilot a kite directly into a burst of Heaven's fire. As the collateral sparks contacted the wire, electrified the wet twine, and entered the jar, the hobnails stirred and shivered – but they did not leap towards the encased horseshoe. Did the hobnails' agitation trace to a brief moment of magnetism, she wondered, or had they moved simply in consequence of the celestial explosion itself?

She retrieved the horseshoe and passed it over the hobnails. No movement. Not the slightest quaver. The shoe was evidently inert. Ah, but did this mean that her magneto-electric hypothesis was wrong, or merely that the collection jar had not stayed charged long enough to magnetize the iron? She couldn't decide.

The following Sunday, whilst Ben, Deborah and William attended their dreary little Presbyterian church in Pine Street and Jennet with equal devotion pruned her cherry tree, the vivid noon sun vanished abruptly behind a mantle of slate clouds. A thunder-gust was coming, she surmised – a new opportunity to imbue a horseshoe with the Gilbertian force.

Methodically she set the stage for the experiment, positioning the horseshoe inside the collection jar and encircling it with hobnails. This time she rested the jar on a slab of paraffin in hopes that the glass would thereby remain charged for a significant interval. She rushed into the house and laid out the necessary materials – handkerchief, cedar sticks, pointed wire, tail-cloth, skein of twine, leather bridle – on the parlour worktable. Within ten minutes she'd fashioned the wooden cross and affixed the wire. A thunder-clap rolled across Manayunk, and then came another. She glanced through her front window. Myriad chestnut leaves vibrated on their twigs. The rosebush shivered as if experiencing dread. It was going to be a magnificent hunt.

As the thunder boomed a third time, her front door reverberated with a frenzied, desperate pounding. Her immediate thought was that, contrary to her wishes, Ben had revealed the Widow Webster's identity as J. S. Crompton, and now some local oddfellow wished to waste her time expounding on the moon's inhabitants or presenting his disproof of uniform acceleration.

She abandoned the worktable and marched to the door, her humour worsening with each step. 'Who goes there?' Silence. 'Tell me your name!' More silence, then renewed pounding. 'I receive no visitors today!'

'You will receive *me*!'

The door swung open, and a rangy man of some sixty years lurched through the jamb, clad in a shredded linen smock and, about his legs, pieces of blanket tied with thongs. He shoved past Jennet and scuttled into the parlour. It took her several seconds to recognize the intruder, so broken was his form and weathered his face. Bits of dead leaves and flecks of moss clung to his arms and shoulders. He'd lost a third of his weight, much of his colour, and most of his teeth.

''Sbones,' she muttered.

As if no longer yoked to one another, Dunstan's eyes flickered madly behind his brass-framed spectacles. 'Hallo, Jennet Stearne.'

'I am Rebecca Webster.'

'Thou art Jennet Stearne, convicted witch, whom Providence saw fit to deliver from the gallows. As for your brother, he is now a voice crying in the wilderness, preparing the way for the divine cleanser Suedomsa.' He darted to the couch and, doffing his torn felt hat, eased himself onto the bolster. Splotches of dirt covered his fire-scarred brow, making each wrinkle look like a wheel-rut. 'When the messenger heard of your reprieve – he sees a newspaper rarely – but when he heard, he was glad in his heart. He started south betimes. That was . . . two months ago, three mayhap.'

'If you aim to rekindle our affection for one another, you will not succeed.' She sidled towards the worktable. 'I'll show you no hospitality beyond a piece of cheese and a night's lodging in my barn.'

' "Leave there thy gift before the altar, and go thy way," ' he quoted. ' "First be reconciled with thy brother, and then come and offer thy gift." '

'I am sensible of the sermon you evoke. 'Tis my recollection the Saviour was reproaching those who spurn their siblings without cause. I have cause, Dunstan. I have cause.'

'Suedomsa's messenger saw you draw down the lightning-fire. Why hobnails? The hobnails are perplexing.' Reaching into the deerskin pouch on his belt, he filled his palm with bits of stale acorn-bread. He brought his hand to his open mouth as if concealing a yawn, then jammed the crumbs inside. 'Explore your western woods – you'll find the messenger's hut, his cooking pots, the bones of twenty hares. So many bones in the world. Bones upon bones. Abby's bones still lie in Massachusetts.'

'Abby's bones?'

'The messenger's wife. Abigail Stearne. Her bones.'

'Were I a better Christian, this news would sadden me.'

'Murdered.'

She released an involuntary moan. 'Murdered?' Swallowing hard, she smoothed out the green silk handkerchief, then laid it atop the cedar cross.

'Murdered, aye.'

'As she nearly murdered me with her mendacity.'

'Murdered by parties unknown.' Dunstan devoured another handful of bread crumbs. He jerked up from the couch and limped to the worktable, casting the handkerchief aside as he might a filthy nose-rag. He seized the cedar cross, and, bringing it to his mouth, kissed the axis. 'The messenger acknowledges but one authority in the matter of demonology, and 'tis not the English Parliament. This day Suedomsa will either press the cup of martyrdom to his prophet's lips, or he will allow that cup to pass.'

'To give the name of martyr to your hideous little life is to soil a noble word.' She took the cross from him and, retrieving the hand-kerchief, tied each corner to a separate node.

Now the rain arrived, large steady droplets pelting the chestnut leaves and making them crackle like spitted meat on a slow fire. Dunstan rushed to the hearth and, for reasons not immediately ap-parent, removed the glass-chimneyed lamp from its peg. ' "Every valley shall be filled, and every mountain and hill brought low," ' he quoted, tearing the cork stopper from the fount. He lifted the lamp high, inverted it, and – much to her astonishment – showered his head with the fuel, so that the glistery beads rolled down his cheeks like tears. Whale-oil fumes wafted through the parlour, raw and briny, layered like Barbados rum. 'The messenger needs another draught.'

'Dunstan, you mustn't do this.'

'Another draught of chrism.'

'I shan't permit it.'

'Another draught.'

A familiar voice broke upon the scene, rising unbidden through the strata of her brain. 'Pray do as he commands,' Isobel Mowbray said.

At first Jennet wondered if the voice might indeed be her aunt's, drifting in from some hinterland of Heaven, but she soon decided the spectre enjoyed no reality beyond her skull. Marching into the kitchen, she resolved to revel in this felicitous ability to delude herself, and so she bid other ghosts join Isobel's.

'Bring him what he wants,' Susan Diggens's shade commanded.

'I shall,' Jennet said, approaching the pantry.

'The man needs his chrism,' said Bridget Bishop of Salem-Village.

'God forgive me,' Jennet said.

'Baptize him with fire,' Rebecca Nurse said.

Jennet took down the earthenware jug. 'I did not imagine it would end this way.'

'More oil,' Giles Corey said.

'As you wish,' she replied.

'Do it in remembrance of my father,' said Veronica Junius, daughter of Johannes.

An uncertain interval elapsed. Perhaps she lived amongst the *revenants* for a minute, perhaps a month – she couldn't say. She experienced a flying sensation, as if astride an enchantress's besom, and the next thing she knew she was back in her parlour, clutching the earthenware jug.

Dunstan still stood by the hearth.

'Whether a man be Papist or Protestant,' she said, setting the jug before him, 'self-slaughter's a sin.'

He unstoppered the jug, flung the cork to the floor, and, like a priest of Apollo pouring a libation on an altar, drenched himself with the rendered blubber. ' "Thou anointest my head with oil." ' The dark flashing rivulets spilled down his arms and soaked his frock. ' "My cup runneth over." ' Stinking of whale juice, he returned to the worktable and attached the tail to the kite.

'If you mean to fly that thing, you must add the leather bridle and put on paraffin boots.'

'When the messenger and his sister were but children, seven years old, eight years old, their father took them to a splendid fair in Ipswich.' He tied the twine to the juncture of the sticks, then bore the kite into the anteroom. 'A harlequin had come up from London, bringing with him a trained African baboon.'

479

'I remember. You drew the ape's portrait.'

'It danced for all the children. You laughed most joyously.' He opened the door and stepped into the rain. 'I'faith, Jenny, your brother loved you that day. He loved you more than love allows. He thanked the Almighty for giving him a sister.'

She followed him across the lawn, the wind whipping her hair, the rain peppering her cheeks and brow, then rooted herself near the mooring post. He continued another twenty paces, stopping beside the lean-to. She shut her eyes and attempted to revive Aunt Isobel's voice, Susan Diggens's spectre, all the desires of her mind. Apparently the urge to contact occult entities and do other witchy things lay deep within every person's soul – even those who knew such communion to be impossible.

She blinked, staring towards the lean-to, until at last a legible image emerged from the blur. Defying the elements, scorning the odds, Dunstan had managed to get the kite aloft, his hands wrapped around the saturated fly-line. With icy determination he aimed the device at an immense storm cloud.

' "And now also the axe is laid unto the root of the tree"!' quoth Dunstan as the kite dived into the nebulous black mass. ' "Every Tree therefore which yieldeth not good fruit is hewn down and cast into the fire"!'

A blinding white bolt came forth, cleaving the innermost of Aristotle's crystalline spheres. Dunstan fell to his knees, fingers interlaced in prayer, the wet twine still locked betwixt his palms. A second bolt cracked the celestial dome. The great Aristotelian globe shattered. Contacting the pointed wire, the sparks jumped to the fly-line. All along the twine, the hempen filaments stood erect like the fur of an enraged cat.

Dunstan laughed. The sparks spilled into his praying hands. He simultaneously cried his Saviour's name, released the kite, and burst into flames. The kite shot away like an arrow. Jennet moved to cover her eyes, but the tableau transfixed her. For a full twenty minutes she studied the oily, burning, screaming heap, the raindrops hissing as they met the fire, the fleshy embers orbiting the lean-to, until the last of the sodden ashes settled to earth, and she saw that all the goblins were gone, all demons dead, all spirits fled, and there were no more witches in the world.

Three days later, as Jennet meandered through her garden uprooting weeds and trimming vines, she was startled to observe a squat man in a grimy tan surtout making his way towards the farm-house, a leather valise protruding from his spine like Robert Hooke's hump. She intercepted him at the midpoint of the flagstone path. Their transaction took but a minute. The mail-carrier strode away whistling, a half-crown gratuity in his pocket.

She scurried back into the house, shredded the envelope, and, scattering the bits of paper across the floor like a grass-maid seeding a park, unfolded the letter from Paris.

4 June 1738

Ma Chère Maman:

As you well know, my sweet pathetic Father view'd Postal Carriers as the most heroic of Persons, and so I shall honour his Memory by assuming my Words will reach you ere Autumn comes to Pennsylvania.

This letter is occasion'd largely by my Acquaintance with a remarkable Englishman, Jonathan Belcher, former Royal Governor of Massachusetts Bay. Upon retiring from his administrative Post, Mr Belcher spent several Years touring the European Capitals, and his Fondness for Tragedy and Comedy inevitably brought him to the Théâtre Français, where he oft-times observ'd my Portrayals of Corneille's Heroines and Molière's Ingénues. Shortly after seeing me in Le Médecin Malgré Lui, *Mr Belcher became the Patron of my Career, supplying me with such Funds as I required whilst awaiting a new Role. Lest your Imagination run to lascivious Fancies, let me assert that my Dealings with this Gentleman have been altogether free of improper Conduct. Our Connection is essentially in the Nature of a Friendship, Nothing more, though surely Nothing less.*

'Twas through Mr Belcher I learn'd of your Part in the Philadelphia Witch-Trial, which at the Time was much discuss'd here in Paris. Not

long into his *Account of the Proceeding and its Aftermath*, Mr Belcher mention'd that the Defendant was Blood-Sister to the Prosecutor, one Dunstan Stearne. Knowing Stearne to be your Maiden Name, I soon deduc'd that the Crown's Advocate was my Uncle Dunstan, the escap'd Enchantress my own Mother. As you are mayhap aware, your Testimony in Philadelphia inspir'd Mr Belcher to enjoin the Massachusetts Cleansers from practising their Trade, which Action doubtless prevent'd the unjust Executions of many heathen Savages.

And so it happens that my Attitude to you hath of late undergone a Revolution. I cannot forgive your Treatment of me, but neither can I shake my Admiration for you. You are still my Nemesis, and yet you are also my Idol. Mr Belcher avers that such Ambivalence is not a terrible Thing. He says 'tis better to go through Life in thrall to Paradox than indentur'd to Regret.

For the Moment this is All I have to say, chère Maman. I harbour a fond Hope that you will wish to continue this Correspondence, as I am curious to learn just how astonishing we might become to one another.

Tous mes amitiés
I remain your affectionate
Rachel

It was a good letter, she decided, as pleasing a product as might ever issue from the Great Jovian Storm that was their relationship. True, she would rather have achieved the status of *mother* in Rachel's eyes than the designation *idol*. But idol was adequate. Idol would do.

The following morning she slipped her daughter's letter into her jacket pocket and took the day-coach to Philadelphia, subsequently consuming a noontime meal of broiled shad and fresh-water mussels at the Black Horse Tavern. At one o'clock she ambled down Market Street to Franklin and Meredith's Printing-House.

No sooner had she stepped into the shop, her entrance heralded by the famous brass bell, than Ben and William, huddled over the older Blaeu press, together pulled the spindle lever, rolled back the bed, and peeled the fruit of their industry from the type-form. The boy waved the wet broadsheet through the air as exuberantly as an explorer about to plant his nation's flag on a newly discovered continent.

482

'Mother! Mother! Look what I made!'

'Ah, I see you've taken up your father's trade,' she said.

'I did it all on my own,' he said. 'Compositing, framing, inking, printing. Father helped only a little.'

'This man pursues the noblest calling in the world,' Jennet said, kissing Ben's cheek. 'I think of a remark once spoken by our friend the Baron de Montesquieu. "I have never known any distress that an hour's reading did not relieve."' She passed Ben the pages from Paris. 'Look at this.'

As Ben unfolded Rachel's letter, William placed the broadsheet in Jennet's hands.

'Take care not to smear it,' the boy admonished her.

WANTED
by
His Majesty King George II:
WILLIAM FRANKLIN
Age 12 Years,
for
- Piracy on the High Seas
- Daring Mail-Coach Robberies
- Forgetting to Wash Hands
- Neglecting to Study Multiplication Tables
£100 REWARD
for such Information as may lead
to the Capture of this most
NOTORIOUS CRIMINAL

'I've heard of this fugitive Franklin,' Jennet said. 'Is he not the lad who robbed the Royal Mint last year, making off with two kings' ransoms and a sack of shillings?'

'That he did, ma'am,' William said.

'My son, you are surely the second most skilful printer in Pennsylvania.'

With the back of his hand Ben gave Rachel's letter an emphatic swipe. ''Tis the very rock on which a reconciliation 'twixt mother and daughter might be built,' he told Jennet. 'You must reply anon.'

The midday sun blazed like a hearth-fire, sending trickles of sweat down everyone's temples and raising red blotches on their cheeks. 'I shall draft a letter to Rachel this evening,' she said, fanning herself with William's broadsheet. 'However, I am sceptical concerning the ultimate efficacy of such a correspondence.'

'You've ne'er shared my affection for optimism,' Ben said.

She cupped her palm around William's shoulder. 'Son, methinks the two of us should go down to the Schuylkill, that we might gain some relief from this uncivilized heat.'

A smile as wide as Hezekiah Creech's, and high as the Maw of Folkestone's, appeared on the boy's face.

They arrived at the riverbank shortly after two o'clock. William stripped himself down to his underclothes, and then Jennet guided him along a ramp of sand and into the water, one cautious step at a time. The current lifted her skirt to the level of her hips, fanning it outward like the petals of a lily.

Placing one hand against his neck, another under his rump, she gradually tilted his body backward – a Deist baptism, she mused, observed with regal apathy by the Cosmic Clockmaker – until the Schuylkill lapped at his sides and touched his ears. When he voiced a fear that he was about to sink, she proceeded to instruct him in Mr Boyle's buoyancy principle, explaining that if a swimmer kept his head low and his lungs nearly full, he could not but remain on the surface. Heartened by this knowledge, William inhaled, held his breath, arched his back, and, sensing that he was waterborne, asked his mother to step away. She withdrew her hands, and he found himself afloat, ready to embrace the aquatic life as joyfully as any otter.

'And now you are evermore immune to drowning,' she said.

''Twas considerably less painful than becoming immune to the smallpox,' he said.

For the balance of the afternoon they played at nine-pins and fished without success for perch and suckers, then watched the westering sun dip towards the unseen reaches of the wild continent. The waters evaporated from her skirt, leaving behind subtle dots of mud and delicate threads of moss that, depending on one's attitude to fashion, looked either appallingly untidy or appealingly primeval.

As dusk settled over the Schuylkill, mother and son started east towards the Godfrey mansion, eating their way from one Market Street stall to the next. William stuffed himself with venison pasties, gooseberry tarts, almond puddings and corn fritters, washing it all down with apple cider and unfermented syllabub.

At seven o'clock she delivered the satiated boy to his door. Sour and stubby Deborah Franklin greeted her stepson with an extravagant smile and a firm hug, a ritual that evidently drained her reserves of cordiality, for she neither asked after Jennet's welfare nor invited her into the house.

'Fare thee well, dear William,' Jennet said. 'Next time I shall teach you how to swim beneath the water.'

'*Beneath?*'

'Holding your breath.'

'How far might I go before I must have air?' he asked.

'From one bank of the Schuylkill to the other,' she replied.

'Hurrah!' His face glowed like a night-crier's lanthorn.

'That sounds dangerous,' Deborah said.

'Young William was born to the beat of the tide and the crash of the surf.' Jennet stepped off the stoop and started into the darkening mist. 'He shall always count the water his friend!'

The coming of night failed to cool Philadelphia, and so once again Jennet went down to the river. Betimes she came upon a willow tree, as stately as the one that marked Pashpishia's grave, and there she shed her garments, securing them beneath a stone. She followed the shore to a place where the Schuylkill ran deep. She pressed her palms together and, leaning over the bank, bent her knees and jumped. The water received her. Rolling onto her back, she worked her legs in a flutter kick, her arms as if making an angel in snow. She moved against the flow. How far north, exactly, might she travel via this medium? To New York? Unlikely. To Massachusetts? Certainly not. And yet her great desire that night was to swim to the Kokokehom, seek out Pussough, and take him to her bower by the Hoosic.

A full moon rose over Philadelphia, the great Quanquogt *wampumpeag* bead. In nine hours the Delaware would be at flood, and the high-masted ships would leave for Port Royal, Havana, Bridgetown, Bristol, Gravesend, Lisbon and a dozen other cities. She spun around, surrendering to the current. Her gaze roamed from Venus to the other

planets to the fixed stars beyond and . . . was it possible? Had a nomad entered the summer sky? She couldn't be certain, of course, not until she'd caught the object in Ben's telescope, but it seemed that a soft glimmering comet lay just below Orion, due east of the Great Dog. Perhaps Giordano Bruno was right. Perhaps the cosmos throbbed with an infinity of worlds, which meant there were surely other thinking creatures in the heavens, pursuing their lives, charting their dreams, devising their sciences. And if you believed in the laws of probability, as Jennet did, then one of these creatures had recently dived
into a soothing river, and she was at that moment
happily contemplating distant
constellations whilst
swimming

*

Naked
came I from
my author's brain, I,
Principia, a quivering precipitate of
heretofore unthought ideas, a plasma compounded
of geometry and inspiration, celestial mechanics and lucky guesses.
The midwives of my advent, those skilled printers and diligent binders, incarnated me with their ink, fixed me with their paper, secured me with their adhesives, and clothed me in their leather. And somewhere along the line I acquired passions commensurate with your own.

You will not be surprised to hear that my Jennet spent her remaining years endeavouring to establish a connection between magnetism and electricity. Early in these investigations she concluded, quite correctly, that to magnetize a horseshoe she must subject it to a steady electric stream, not simply jolt it with lightning sparks. Her attempts to wring a continuous flow from static Von Guericke discharges proved bootless, however, and after six months she had nothing to show for her labours except the largest collection of sulphur balls in the New World.

Eventually it came to her that she was going about the problem backwards. Rather than trying to generate first electricity and then magnetism from a rotating Van Guericke sphere, she must instead start with a lodestone, spinning it via a Newcomen steam engine. A coil of copper wire placed near such an apparatus would soon, logically enough, become home to an electric current. Alas, my goddess never realized that she should have put the coiled wire *inside* the spinning lodestone, thereby exploiting its magnetic field – or else she could leave the surrounding stone alone and spin the wire instead. And so it was that the principle of electromagnetic induction had to wait another seventy years for its definitive demonstration, which occurred courtesy of Joseph Henry in 1830 and Michael Faraday in 1831.

Throughout this period of futile experimentation, Jennet wrote long letters to Rachel, and her child reciprocated, but the exchange failed to have the effect the women desired. Rachel never managed to comprehend her mother's obsession with lodestones and copper wires. Jennet was equally confounded by her daughter's liaisons with a series of French writers both famous and obscure. At one point Rachel even attempted to fill the void that was visited upon Jean François-Marie Arouet de Voltaire by the premature death of his dear friend, the talented young actress Adrienne Lecouvreur, but she soon tired of vying with a ghost, and Rachel and Voltaire went their separate ways.

Although both electromagnetic induction and maternal satisfaction eluded Jennet, her final years were far from empty. One bright and brittle October morning Pussough appeared at the farm, accompanied by a large wolfish dog whose sienna coat suggested a patchwork quilt made of periwigs. A woman living alone might do without a birch canoe, her Lynx Man explained, or a stewpot or even a sleeping platform, but a guard dog – never. She gladly accepted the gift. The dog's name was Ahanu. He Who Laughs.

Before old age carried him off, the ebullient Ahanu watched over Jennet for seven years. Pussough stayed for roughly the same interval, learning about steam-powered magnets to a degree that far exceeded his curiosity, until a winter chill turned to pneumonia and took him to the mountain of Kautantouwit.

The longer she lived, the more the sufficiency hypothesis became for Jennet not simply an abstract principle but a personal creed, and in time her neighbours realized that a wise-woman dwelt amongst them. They appeared on her doorstep at odd hours, and unless they'd awakened her from a particularly diverting dream, she always received them courteously. While her clients had never heard of either Hassane or Isobel Mowbray, in truth she'd become at once a rationalist edition of the Kokokehom medicine-woman and a philanthropic version of Mirringate's mistress. My goddess set broken bones, lanced boils, delivered babies, dispensed herbs for preventing pregnancy, prescribed simples against quinsy and the gout, bent young minds towards contrariness and doubt, and convened philosophy salons in her front parlour: Jennet Stearne, the Witch of Manayunk.

I must decline to provide the details of her death. How could I bear to set them down? Let me merely state that she lived to the impressive age of eighty-three, whereupon her heart's Cartesian mechanism ceased to function. Lying abed in her farmhouse, she slipped into the undiscovered country on 4 July 1761, watched over by Ben, William, John Tux, Nicholas Scull, Bethany Markley and Zebulon Plum, exactly fifteen years before Ben would sign the Declaration of Independence. Among her Philadelphia friends, only Barnaby Cavendish did not help Jennet out of the world, for two decades earlier he'd collapsed and died while lecturing on his newest acquisition, the Argus of Providence.

Jennet had never joined a church, and so Ben buried her behind Manayunk Courthouse, scene of her astonishing presentation of the sufficiency hypothesis, not far from the tomb of the ergot-ridden rooster. Six months later, Ben, William and the Junto conducted a memorial service in Nicholas Scull's drawing-room, temporary home of the Free Library of Philadelphia. Rachel sailed all the way from France. Montesquieu did not attend, having died in 1755, his deathbed utterance baffling all who heard it: '*La vermin se reproduit*' – the wrigglers generate themselves. At the climax of Jennet's funeral Ben recited the whole of Milton's *Lycidas*. 'Yet once more, O ye Laurels,' he read, 'and once more, ye Myrtles brown, with Ivy never-sere, I come to pluck your Berries harsh and crude, and with forc'd Fingers rude shatter your Leaves before the mellowing Year . . .'

I think about her every day. I think about her intelligence, her energy, her impatience with consecrated nonsense. Naturally I retain fond memories of her struggles to comprehend me, and also of our lovemaking, which I accomplished by inhabiting Pussough during her exile among the Kokokehom. My soul bleeds for Jennet Stearne. I grieve for her now, and I shall grieve for her when my Four Hundredth Anniversary edition rolls off the presses in 2087.

Ben ultimately attained Jennet's age, then added one more year, succumbing in 1790 to yet another attack of pleurisy. He lived to see the birth and ratification of the American Constitution, surely one of our planet's worthier documents. (Vibrating with mutual if qualified respect, *We the People* and I play contract bridge in cyberspace every Saturday night, partnered respectively with *Poor Richard's Almanack* and *L'Esprit des Lois*.) Throughout his entire adulthood, Ben never stopped being rational. One month before his death, he wrote to the Reverend Ezra Stiles: 'As to Jesus of Nazareth, my Opinion of whom you particularly desire, I think the System of Morals and His Religion, as He left them to us, the best the World ever saw . . . but I apprehend it has receiv'd various corrupting Changes, and I have, with most of the present dissenters in England, some Doubts as to His Divinity.'

Concerning William Franklin, the less said about that creepy little Tory bastard the better. Most historians would concur that he inherited neither his mother's breadth of vision nor his father's generosity of spirit but received instead his maternal grandfather's mediocrity. On 4 September 1762, William married Elizabeth Downes in London, and five days later he accepted a commission as Royal Governor of New Jersey. Throughout the pre-Revolutionary period, William strove mightily to thwart the dissidents' cause, alternately breaking his father's heart and arousing his wrath. At the risk of sounding vain, I would say that, while disagreeing with my illustrious progenitor on many points, ethical and theological, I have been a better son to Isaac Newton than William Franklin ever was to Ben.

I cannot take leave of you without mentioning another actor in Jennet's life, her great legacy, the Witchcraft Statute of George II. To be sure, that glorious law cannot be called the beginning of the end for European witchfinding. The *Zeitgeist* was radiant with scepticism long before the British Parliament weighed in against the demon hypothesis. It was more like the end of the end. And yet I count its passage a triumph. As late as 1768, the English evangelist John Wesley, founder of the Methodist Church, wrote in his journal, 'The giving up of witchcraft is in effect giving up the Bible,' and two years later he publicly complained that 'The infidels have hooted witchcraft out of the world.' Were it not for the Act of George II and the *argumentum grande* that inspired it, Wesley might very well have found an audience for his lament.

After 1740 there is almost nothing for a witch reporter to report. Yes, in May of 1749 the Inquisition determines that Sister Maria Renata Sänger von Mossau, a Würzburg nun, has signed the Devil's book and bewitched the other members of her convent, but it's a throwback case, and everybody knows it. Sister Maria is nevertheless beheaded the following month and her corpse tossed onto a bonfire of tar barrels. Four years later a vigilante mob in Hertfordshire swims a suspected witch named Ruth Osborne, performing the test so crudely that she chokes to death. But times have changed, and at the next assizes the ringleader, Thomas Colley, is convicted of wilful murder and condemned to the gallows. And then at long last, on 11 April 1775, the final legal execution for witchcraft occurs in the Western world, when a deranged serving woman named Anna Maria Schwägel is decapitated in Kempten, Bavaria, having confessed to copulation with Satan. And suddenly it's over. *Finis.* The infidels have hooted witchcraft out of the world. In 1821 even the pious country of Ireland succumbs to the Enlightenment, and its lawmakers repeal the Conjuring Statute of 1587.

The optimists among you will argue that the witch universe is gone for ever. You're probably right. Still, let me take this opportunity to detail the diaspora of *The Sufficiency of the World*, quite possibly the rarest published treatise on our planet. Forget about the Internet. The rare-book websites won't know what you're talking about. At present two copies reside in the British Museum, one in the Bibliothèque Nationale, one in the New York Public Library, and two in the Library of Congress, whilst a seventh graces the Franklin collection of the American Philosophical Society in Philadelphia. True, it's unlikely that Western Civilization will ever again have need of Jennet's remarkable work, but I thought you ought to know where to find one, just in case.

Before we part company, I invite you to journey with me to the convivial community of Maplewood, New Jersey, for I have just now discovered an opportunity to connect – obliquely but meaningfully – with my goddess. Join me as I climb inside the mind of Inez Maldonado, an idealistic educator, sauntering towards fifty, who teaches eighth-grade arithmetic from an historical perspective. The postulates of geometry were not handed down from Olympus, Inez tells her students. They were devised by human beings. When Pythagoras's nose itched, he scratched it. When Euclid heard cicadas thrum their abdomens, he revelled in the music.

On Tuesday afternoons Inez meets the eleven members of the Rocket Club in Room 332 of Maplewood Middle School. She would prefer coaching the chess team, but Fred Maltby, an ageing geography teacher, has captained that activity since time immemorial. Nevertheless, in recent years Inez has developed a fondness for the Rocket Club, which so obviously nourishes the socially inept young-sters it tends to attract.

It's Saturday morning – launch day. The spacious grounds of the soccer field swarm with the rocketeers, many of their parents, and several students too cool to have signed up but too curious to have stayed at home. The April sun is warm and mellow. Bluejays, robins and bumblebees are on the wing.

At the moment, the main object of Inez's concern is twelve-year-old Juliet Sorkin, who has designed and built a sleek, magnificent rocket named the Golden Comet. A prodigy of sorts, Juliet has a bad habit of lecturing to her classmates using big words, and in consequence they pick on her. Our teacher's pet is sweet-tempered, easily distracted, and like many bright people mildly dyslexic, her cherubic face sprinkled with freckles and three ripe pimples. Although Juliet has recently won second prize in the Maplewood Science Fair – for an exhibit about human cloning centred around her cousin's discarded collection of Barbie dolls – she remains an outsider.

From the viewpoint of my *Principia* self, one fact about Juliet Sorkin eclipses all others. She is a direct descendant of Jennet Stearne, Hammer of Witchfinders. Were Juliet to become curious about her ancestry, she might succeed in tracing her line back ten generations to Stéphane Crompton, born 11 November 1746, the bastard son of Rachel Crompton and René Duvic, a professional cad specializing in

Voltaire's former lovers. But Juliet doesn't strike me as harbouring a genealogical bent. She's a forward-looking sort of misfit.

The Golden Comet is ready for its maiden flight: parachute secure, igniter snug against the propellant, alligator clips in place. At a signal from my Inez self, the students draw back from the launch pad – fifteen feet, that's our rule. Juliet takes the controller and inserts the safety key, arming the system. The warning bulb lights up.

'What engine?' asks Danny Ginsburg, who is forever sneaking his chameleon into school.

'A D12-9,' Juliet replies proudly. Most of the kids still use pathetic B's and C's.

'That means twelve Newtons of thrust, huh?' says Danny's best friend, Raoul Pindar, who has a crush on Juliet but doesn't quite know it.

'Eleven point eight, actually,' says Juliet with a touch of pedantry, then counts down from ten to zero.

She presses the controller button. At the speed of electricity the current rips along the wires, charges the alligator clips, and heats the igniter. Now comes that delicious micro-instant between the igniter combusting – you can tell by the smoke, the sizzle, the little flame – and . . . lift-off! A circumscribed explosion spews sparks and cinders onto the steel disc, and Juliet's ship rides up the launch rod, leaves the pad, and zooms skyward with a thick emphatic hiss. The spectators clap and cheer. Twenty Newton-seconds elapse as the Estes engine and my father's Third Law carry the vessel five hundred – eight hundred – twelve hundred – fifteen hundred feet into the heavens! In the entire history of the Maplewood Middle School Rocket Club no ship has ever risen fifteen hundred feet.

Propellant spent, the Golden Comet glides for nine seconds, a tiny apostrophe in the sky, and then the ejection charge detonates. The nose cone pops off, the shock cord pays out, and the parachute opens like a blossoming orchid.

But now disaster befalls the flight. The ship is soaring so high that the wind gets under the chute and bears the whole assemblage far beyond the soccer field. With sinking heart and foundering spirits, we all watch as the Golden Comet floats towards the pine groves of

Memorial Park and passes from view. I glance at Jennet Stearne's descendant. She is wincing. Her lower lip trembles. When gravity reasserts itself and the ship plummets, the chute lines will catch in the treetops, and Juliet will lose her masterpiece.

'I'm going to get it back!' she informs her teacher.

'Good luck,' my Inez self replies.

But it is my *Principia* self who empathizes most fully with poor Juliet. For a protracted moment we stare into each other's eyes, and, romantic that I am, I allow myself to imagine that my goddess has been restored to me.

Oh, yes, it's she all right. We are back in Colonial Salem. Crouching by the banks of the Merrimack, she removes the iron hook from the trout's mouth, then glances across the river. A beautiful young Indian brave gathers marsh marigolds on the far shore, oblivious to my presence in his mind and body.

This time Jennet and I enjoy a brief conversation. In halting English, I tell her that she will come of age not in Salem but in a Nimacook village. This heritage, I insist, will figure crucially in her demon disproof.

'How can you possibly foresee such a thing?' Jennet asks.

'I don't know.' I set the marigolds on the shore, a gift for my goddess, then slip into the New England woods. 'It's just one of those secrets of the universe.'

As my reverie evaporates, Juliet, Raoul and Danny go sprinting across the field and disappear into the pine groves. Inez Maldonado admires their ambition, their optimism. She wishes she could be like them. This is not a good time in her life. Her cholesterol count is too high. Her husband has mentioned a divorce.

We are helping Hejong Kim and Peter Gorka prepare their ships for launch when suddenly the recovery team bursts out of Memorial Park, and we've never seen a more entrancing tableau. All three youngsters are jumping up and down, and there – there in the lead – there strides Juliet Sorkin, cradling the Golden Comet, nose cone and parachute included. Her smile is as big as a boomerang. Reaching the launch site, she tells her teacher that Raoul spotted the rocket at the base of a pine tree. This makes little sense to either Inez or me. Why didn't the branches snag the chute lines? For a full minute we ponder the question, and then we resolve to worry about it no longer. We give Juliet a hug. It's simply a mystery, we tell ourselves. It's just one of those secrets of the universe.

ACKNOWLEDGEMENTS

This book about books draws its historical framework and thematic tissue from dozens of volumes. Of particular value to my project were *Masks of the Universe* by Edward Harrison, *Thinking with Demons* by Stuart Clark, *Malleus Maleficarum* by Heinrich Krämer and James Sprenger, *Witchcraft in Europe: A Documentary History*, edited by Alan C. Kors and Edward Peters, *Religion and the Decline of Magic* by Keith Thomas, *The European Witch-Craze* by H. R. Trevor-Roper, *A Trial of Witches* by Gilbert Geis and Ivan Bunn, *Les Sorcières: Fiancées de Satan* by Jean-Michel Sallman, *A Delusion of Satan* by Frances Hill, *The Devil in the Shape of a Woman* by Carol F. Karlsen, *Age of Enlightenment* by Peter Gay, *The Unredeemed Captive* by John Demos, *Women's Indian Captivity Narratives*, edited by Kathryn Zabelle Derounian-Stodola, *The First American: The Life and Times of Benjamin Franklin* by H. W. Brands, *Franklin of Philadelphia* by Esmond Wright, *Isaac Newton: The Last Sorcerer* by Michael White, *A Portrait of Isaac Newton* by Frank E. Manuel, *Franklin and Newton* by I. Bernard Cohen, Benjamin Franklin's *Autobiography*, and, last but not least, *Mathematical Principles of Natural Philosophy* by Sir Isaac Newton.

The Algonquin words and phrases in *The Last Witchfinder* are generally authentic. My characters normally speak the Narragansett dialect as recorded by Roger Williams in his remarkable linguistic treatise of 1643, *A Key into the Language of America*, the first of its kind published in the New World. Williams is better known as the founder of the settlement that became Rhode Island, an enterprise that consumed him following his expulsion from Massachusetts in 1635 for 'new and dangerous ideas'.

I would like to thank those friends, relatives, colleagues and Benjamin Franklin impersonators who offered me their reactions to the novel as it evolved: Joe Adamson, Linda Barnes, Michael Bishop, Ginger Clark, Shira Daemon, Margaret Duda, David Edwards,

Gordon Fleming, Merrilee Heifetz, Nalo Hopkinson, Philip Jenkins, Michael Kandel, Kirk McElhearn, Bill Meikle, Carolyn Meredith, Gregory Miller, Christopher Morrow, William Pencak, Alis Rasmussen, Elisabeth Rose, Bill Sheehan, James D. Smith and James Stevens-Acre.

My gratitude also goes to my wife, Kathryn Morrow, for her endless emotional and intellectual inspiration, to my agent, Wendy Weil, for so skilfully navigating the shoals of contemporary publishing, to my editors, Jennifer Brehl (USA) and Kirsty Dunseath (UK), for befriending a formidable manuscript, to my neighbour Londa Schiebinger for her insight into the Royal Society's female skeleton, and to my cousin Glenn Morrow for offering me many fruitful challenges and supplementing my research with dozens of compelling facts.

AUTHOR'S NOTE

If my experience in composing *The Last Witchfinder* may be counted typical, then the writer of historical fiction derives no less delight from adhering to the facts of his chosen era than he does from bending those facts in pursuit of some presumed poetic truth.

There was indeed a 1604 Parliamentary Witchcraft Act, and it remained the law of the empire until 1736. The date of England's last legally sanctioned execution for sorcery I have advanced slightly, from 1685 to 1689. My presentations of the Glorious Revolution, the Salem Witch Trials, the Abenaki Indian raid on Haverhill (carried out in these pages by my fictional Nimacooks), Samuel Sewall's campaign against *The New England Courant*, the Baron de Montesquieu's antipathy towards the Conjuring Statutes, and Johannes Junius's confession of Satanism are as free of falsehoods as my research efforts and thematic preoccupations allowed.

The young Benjamin Franklin, visiting London for the first time in 1725, formally requested, through the physician Henry Pemberton, an audience with Sir Isaac Newton, though nothing came of Franklin's plea. Chapter Eight offers my speculations on what might have transpired at this meeting had it occurred. In 1730 Franklin devoted several column inches of *The Pennsylvania Gazette* to his eyewitness account of a witch trial in Mount Holly, New Jersey. Although most historians regard this article as a lampoon, I decided to take Franklin at his word.

Finally, while the problem of witchcraft held no particular fascination for Newton, he did in fact go on record as believing that evil spirits were mere 'desires of the mind'.

Creative
destruction

More praise for *Creative destruction*

'In the tradition of *Beat the Market* and *A Random Walk Down Wall Street, Creative Destruction* blows holes in the conventional wisdom about management, corporate cultures, and the underpinnings of a successful corporation. It argues a whole new paradigm for survival and growth which hopefully will have a far-reaching effect on the actions of boards, management, and investors going forward. Foster and Kaplan are on to something profound.'

— Frank Biondi, Senior Managing Director, Waterview Advisors

'A provocative wake-up call for leaders.'

— Mike Masin, Vice-Chairman and President, Verizon

'As this book with its long-term analysis makes clear: A successful past is but an opportunity to build the future. The only true winners are those that relentlessly drive innovation and change and continually challenge organizational practices and culture.'

— Linda Robinson, Vice-Chairman, Young and Rubicam

'A compelling road map for management to strike a necessary balance between operational excellence and creative destruction. Those who do not heed its advice to challenge conventional mind-sets aggressively do so at their peril.'

— John Hagel, co-author of *Net Worth* and *Net Gain*: *Expanding Markets Through Virtual Communities*

'Offers a clear blueprint for how corporations can modify their thinking in order to remain competitive.'

— Pamela Thomas-Graham, Executive Vice President, NBC, President and CEO, CNBC.com

'Reading *Creative Destruction* was like the scales were falling off my eyes. I had had a mental cataract operation.'

— Robert McKinney, former US Ambassador to Switzerland

'I spend a good deal of every week listening to business leaders and economists from around the world discuss their writings and experiences. This is the single most informative account of the eternal battle between managers and markets, and it explains with intellectual force and hard research why managers must prune their corporations in order to survive the remorselessness of the market. '

— Leslie H. Gelb, President, Council on Foreign Relations

Creative destruction

From 'built to last' to 'built to perform'

RICHARD N. FOSTER AND SARAH KAPLAN

FINANCIAL TIMES
Prentice Hall

An imprint of Pearson Education

London · New York · San Francisco · Toronto · Sydney
Tokyo · Singapore · Hong Kong · Cape Town · Madrid
Paris · Milan · Munich · Amsterdam

PEARSON EDUCATION LIMITED

Head Office:
Edinburgh Gate
Harlow CM20 2JE
Tel: +44 (0)1279 623623
Fax: +44 (0)1279 431059

London Office:
128 Long Acre
London WC2E 9AN
Tel: +44 (0)20 7447 2000
Fax: +44(0)20 7240 5771
Website: www.business-minds.com

First published in the United States in 2001 by Currency Doubleday

First published in Great Britain in 2001

© Mackinsey & Company Inc., United States

The right of Richard N. Foster and Sarah Kaplan to be identified
as authors of this work has been asserted by them in accordance
with the Copyright, Designs and Patents Act 1988.

ISBN 0 273 65638 4

British Library Cataloguing in Publication Data
A CIP catalogue record for this book can be obtained from the British Library

10 9 8 7 6 5 4 3 2 1

Design by Claire Brodmann Book Designs, Lichfield, Staffs
Typeset by Pantek Arts Ltd, Maidstone, Kent
Printed and bound in Great Britain by Biddles Ltd, Guildford & King's Lynn

The Publishers' policy is to use paper manufactured from sustainable forests

To my youngest son, Thomas William Foster, for his energy, inquisitiveness, sparkle, amd infinite patience; to my wife Catherine for her unending, unshakeable and enthusiastic support, confidence and patience; to my older sons: Doug for his market insight and practical understanding, and Lucien for his wisdom and counsel.

RNF

To my parents who set me on my path and to my sisters who have travelled with me along the way.

SK

Contents

About the authors

RICHARD FOSTER is a Senior Partner and Director at McKinsey & Company, a leading global management consulting firm. He joined the firm in 1973, was elected Partner in 1977 and Senior Partner in 1982. In his primary client service role within McKinsey & Company, he has worked in more than 50 industry segments, but primarily in the medical products, pharmaceuticals, imaging, electronics, chemicals, consumer products, retail, and asset-management industries. He has focused special attention over the past 25 years on improving the growth and innovative performance of large organizations.

Mr Foster has written articles on innovation and business performance for *Business Week*, *The Wall Street Journal*, and *The Harvard Business Review*. His 1986 book, *Innovation: The Attacker's Advantage*, was voted one of the five best business books of the year in a *Wall Street Journal* CEO poll.

A Trustee of the Santa Fe Institute, he is also a board member of the Keck Foundation and serves on the Advisory Board of the Whitehead Institute. He received his BSc, MSc, and PhD from Yale University in Engineering, and Applied Science. He lives in New York City with his wife and has three sons.

SARAH KAPLAN was an Innovation Specialist at McKinsey & Company consulting for more than a decade with firms around the world in industries as diverse as pharmaceuticals, medical devices, airlines and consumer products on issues of growth and renewal. She received her BA from UCLA and MA from Johns Hopkins School for Advanced International Studies. She is currently pursuing a PhD in Management of Technology, Innovation and Entrepreneurship at the MIT Sloan School of Management and resides in Cambridge, MA.

Acknowledgements

'Creative destruction' is the result of over a decade of research, sponsored by our colleagues at McKinsey & Co. and our clients. First and foremost, we would like to thank all of them for their support and counsel during this period.

While many colleagues have contributed time and thought to the arguments put forth in this book, some deserve special mention. First on the list is Peter Walker, the Managing Director of our New York Office. Pete has been a steady supporter of the effort since it earliest days. His path remained steady, even when it was not clear that we were still on the scent. Without his long-term support, this enterprise would not have succeeded.

As the work has moved along, others have played key roles in keeping the effort alive and the standards high. They include Rajat Gupta, Herb Henzler, Ian Davis, Bill Meehan, David Meen, John Bookout, Steve Coley, Mike Nevens, Bruce Roberson, Ron Hulme, Tim Koller, Bill Fallon, Ron Farmer, Peter Freedman, Anton von Rossum, Andreas Beroutsos, Eric Lamarre, Michael Silber, Jessica Hopfield, Endre Holen, Hugh Courtney, Kathleen Hogan, Bill Pade, Peter Bisson, Larry Kanarek, Suzanne Nimocks, and Kevin Coyne.

Several of our friends in academia have made strong and steady contributions to our thinking over the years. They include Tim Reufli from the University of Texas, David Campbell from the University of Illinois, Martin Shubik, Will Goetzmann, and Stan Garstka from Yale, Ronel Elul from Brown, Joe Bower, Clay Christensen and Teresa Amabile from Harvard Business School, Ron Heifetz from Harvard's Kennedy School of Government and Mihalyi Csikszentmihalyi formerly of the University of Chicago (now at Claremont Graduate University).

Early readers and advisors included Brian Arthur and Eric Beinhocker, both of whom took enormous time to think through and comment on the strengths and weaknesses of our ideas.

Early McKinsey contributors to the effort included Karen Barth, Vince DePalma, Carl Hanson, Anna Slomovic, Bro Uttal, and Lily Zaidman. They helped in taking the earliest ideas and turning them into something tangible. Chip Hughes and Kenneth Bonheure conducted early explorations into the practical implications of our work as they turned our abstract ideas into useful tools for day-to-day life.

On the operating level, Shishir Shroff began working on the Performance Database that forms a critical part of our analysis while a graduate student at NYU Stern School of Business in the early 1990s. Little did he suspect that the task might turn into a career, but it has. To this day, there is no one who understands more about the database and its construction than Shishir, who now is a Practice Specialist with our Corporate Finance and Strategy practice in our New York Office. In the early days Shishir worked under the guiding hands of Michael Allison and Mike Ghenta. Robin Tsai, one of the best statistical analysts that either of us ever have known, provided expert advice on what was knowable and what was not, along with insightful early statistical analyses. Later we had sustained contributions from Larry DiCapua, Tom Ball, and Ravi Chanmugam.

Ajay Shroff, now at Harvard Business School, undertook the job of rebuilding and updating the McKinsey Performance Database after the first efforts clearly showed that it would be valuable. Ajay brought enormous clarity to the effort. After the data were clearly portrayed, Christopher Baldwin and Robert Reffkin came on to write the key case studies which put a human face on the data. Their deep digging, unimpeachable standards for completeness, and strong writing skills will be seen in many chapters which follow. In the early days Anne Biondi provided expert bibliographic summaries and catalogues. Cara Davis provided continual facts for all phases of the book's preparation, gave us expert literary advice, and found accurate answers and arcane facts to address our endless questions. Without Cara there would be no book.

As we worked out the details, many colleagues have made substantial contributions. Steven Abernethy, now chairman of Transecure, and Qiang (John) Feng did yeoman's work interpreting the early results of the database four years ago. Paul Brown-Kenyon, Jurgen Kaljuvee, Rajini Sundar, and Antony Blanc did early case studies. After the initial data showed some surprises, Christian Weber and Stephan Leitner from our German offices provided intellectual leadership in interpreting why the anomalies occurred. Their early work found clues to future interpretations that proved reliable. Subsequently, Toshi Moghi and Nick Robinson did strong work in developing automated ways of displaying the data so that mere mortals could understand almost four decades of data for over one thousand companies. Somu Subramaniam was a constant guide to when we were on the right and wrong tracks.

Our work to understand the long-term record of company performance grew out of our practical experience with our clients. One client in particular stands out as the foremost source of our insights, Johnson & Johnson. We would like therefore to recognize our debt to our clients and friends, Ralph Larsen, Robert Wilson, Roger Fine, Bill Weldon, Jim Lenehan, Russ Deyo, Bob Darretta, Christian Koffmann, JoAnn Heisen, Brian Perkins, Bill Nielsen, Jim Utaski, and Bernie Walsh for all their guidance to us over the years.

As the analytic work came together, Stephen Fenichell helped to turn our initial thinking into the first draft of *Creative Destruction*. This draft showed us how far we had come, and how far we had to go. Amanda Urban from International Creative Management gave us much needed encouragement and expert guidance so we continued on. Erik Calonius, a skilled writer for *Fortune* and the *Wall Street Journal* then came on to guide the final draft. At the point the draft was ready for other eyes, Roger Scholl, president of the Currency Books Division of Doubleday, took pen in hand and led us to the final product that follows. Roger's experience and judgement have made the book both more readable and to the point. Our assistants throughout this process, Heidi Smith, Lin Sierzenga, and Loreta Kelly, have unfailingly delivered the goods on time and to very high-quality standards, despite the press of daily business. Of these, the job has fallen to Heidi to complete the task. She has delivered with enormous energy, patience, wit, and style in the last two years of preparation.

The Fosters' good friends Kelly and Robert Day also provided critical shelter, quiet, and unending friendship when book writing overlapped house refurbishment. Carole and Arthur Broadus have been faithful and encouraging friends throughout the exercise. Many others have quietly supported this effort as the authors laboured away including Parker Merrow, Sarah and Bill Manson, Jude and Eric Boass, Patricia Henry, and Ulda Calderon

Throughout this effort, one is constantly reminded of old, yet fresh lessons in life: these kinds of enterprises are impossible without family support. Richard Foster has received more support from his wife Catherine than any one should be able to expect. Through years of 'just one more chapter to go' stories, she tirelessly and enthusiastically supported the effort no matter the personal cost to her. Foster's six-year-old son Thomas has his mother's understanding for his father's long absences. He is mature beyond his years. If Dad needed to do it, it was OK with Thomas. His understanding is quite remarkable for any age. Foster's older sons, Douglas and Lucien, have continued to be both great companions and helpful readers and advisors on this project as well.

Sarah Kaplan extends a debt of gratitude to her parents, Meredith McGovney Kaplan and Hesh Kaplan; to her sisters, Esther, Sharon, and Rachel; and to her close friends and supporters, David Ashen, Laurie Blitzer, Joe Haviv, Chip Hughes, Sylvia Mathews, Noah Walley, Kristina Wollschlaeger, and the late Joe Merolla, for their unfailing encouragement through all of the peaks and valleys that come with such endeavours.

It is standard, but necessary, to say that all those mentioned above have made their efforts to help us. To the extent they have succeeded, the success is theirs, to the extent they have not, the responsibility is ours.

New York, NY
January 2001

Introduction:
The game of creative
destruction

In 1986, Richard Foster published a best-selling book titled *Innovation: The Attacker's Advantage*, which explained the limitations of long-term corporate performance, based on the inevitability of profound changes in the way business is conducted (which we call 'discontinuities'). The conclusion reached in the book was that during technological discontinuities, attackers, rather than defenders, have the economic advantage. Although they often lack the scale associated with low costs, neither do they have the psychological and economic conflicts that slow, or prevent, them from capturing new opportunities.

Foster drew these conclusions from a study of about a dozen companies. But as the years passed, he found them to be true of hundreds of other companies as well. Yet the attacker's advantage did not seem to last. Once a company attacked, it began to act suspiciously like a defender, with all the associated weaknesses. In fact, as the 1980s passed and we made our way through the 1990s, both of us observed that almost as soon as any company had been praised in the popular management literature as excellent or somehow super-durable, it began to deteriorate. Searching for excellent companies was like trying to catch light beams: they were so easy to imagine, but so hard to grasp.

Was this just a peculiarity of the companies we knew, or was something more fundamental taking place? Keeping in mind an admonition attributed to Winston Churchill, 'The farther backward you look, the farther forward you can see,' we began to examine the long-term record of some of the country's leading companies and their competitors to gain a better understanding of long-term performance.

To our amazement, we found that it was not easy to gather this data. No one, it seemed, had assembled a data set comprehensive enough to determine which companies really were the strongest performers over the long term.

Undaunted, we set out to gather the missing data on corporate performance and its determinants. We selected more than sixty variables to examine, including sales growth, margins, return on invested capital, debt and debt ratings, R&D spending, and total return to shareholders (defined as the increase in stock price per year plus any dividends or special payments made). We wanted to look back far enough to ensure that we had included the major events that had occurred in companies, industries and the economy as a whole over the past 38 years. We wanted to be able to see what role discontinuities played in the economy, in individual industries, and within companies. We wanted to see the patterns of the economy, to determine what was regular and routine, and what was irregular or periodic (for example, major technological shifts or major changes in federal regulations, or changes in industry structure owing to entry and exit of competitors). We wanted to be able to measure the pace and the extent of these changes.

In particular, we wanted to objectively measure 'good' and 'poor' performance as it appeared in the economy at different times (for example, during the expansionist period of the 1960s and the inflationary period of the 1970s). We wanted to use these standards to recognize 'normal' performance when we saw it, as well as exceptional performance – whether exceptionally good or exceptionally bad. We wanted to look over a long enough period of time, and across a wide enough range of industries, that we could tease out the forces at work – to see the contextual changes and their causes. We wanted to be able to test the conventional wisdom of the day: 'it's all about technology,' or 'it's all about macroeconomics,' or 'high multiples presage low returns,' or 'it's all about growth,' or 'it's all about profitability,' or 'it's all idiosyncratic' or 'excellence is …'

After more than a decade of effort, and with the assistance of more than 50 of our McKinsey colleagues, we had successfully built a database of the performance of more than 1,000 companies in 15 industries over almost four decades in order to model capital markets in the US economy. We will refer to this database from here on as 'The McKinsey Corporate Performance Database.'

Our McKinsey Corporate Performance Database is built entirely of US companies. It includes longtime competitors like Exxon and Chevron, and new-economy companies like Cisco and Dell. It includes such slow-moving industries as electric utilities and such 'hot' industries as software and semiconductors. It includes such low-tech industries as paper and trucking and such technologically sophisticated industries as medical and pharmaceutical products. It includes such regulated industries as airlines and such unregulated industries as specialty chemicals. It includes the oil industry with its ups and downs, and the defence industry with its steady dependence on the US government.

The McKinsey Corporate Performance Database differs from the real economy only in that it does not include all the industries or companies represented in the real economy – although it does offer a detailed history of 1,008 companies, which as far as we know is the largest study of its kind. These companies represented, at the end of 1998, $2.1 trillion in sales and $5.2 trillion in market cap.

All the companies in the McKinsey Corporate Performance Database are more or less 'pure' plays, that is, more than half of their sales come from the industry of which they are a part. The database does not track 'complex' companies, like General Electric or Johnson & Johnson, that compete in many different industries. Nor does it track industries with a small number of players (e.g., automobiles or razor blades), because without a larger number of competitors we have no standard for 'normalcy.' (Nonetheless, we have used the McKinsey Corporate Performance Database to 'synthe-size' what a 'model' J&J would look like, and then compared this model to the real thing. Assembling the components of our database economy in the same way, say, as J&J assembles its business, yields a pattern of return that very closely matches the actual observed patterns.)

We allowed new companies to 'form' (i.e., enter the database) when they were large enough to be part of the largest 80 per cent of US companies, as measured by market capitalization (a number that the University of Chicago Center for Research on Security Prices provided for us). These companies are referred to later in this book as 'new entrants.' The year of 'entry' refers to the year these companies qualified to enter the database, not the year they were formed.

A definition of markets and corporations

Let us be more specific about what we mean when we say 'market' and 'cognitive structure'. To us markets, including capital markets, are 'informal aggregations of buyers, sellers, their owners, and other intermediaries, who come together for the purpose of economic exchange.' The 'capital markets' are markets where capital is exchanged, for example, money for equities and debt. The buyers and sellers are usually corporations, and they may or may not list their shares in an equity market for the purpose of establishing a current value of the enterprise.

These informal aggregations, and the processes they employ, set the balance between continuity and change in the economy. The rules of the capital markets govern entrance, conduct, and exit (including bankruptcy) of the players in the markets. In our economy, it is the consumer who makes the individual decision about whether to continue with the present products and services or to change to new ones. The capital markets provide the cash to serve up the options for the customer, but the consumer sets the rate of change.

Clearly, capital markets are very different from corporations. Corporations have a 'cognitive superstructure'. They have a chairman and a board of directors. They plan and they control. Their people take their responsibilities very seriously, as the law requires them to. Their executives have trained their entire life for their positions, and they have gone through exceptionally rigorous selection processes. They are not administered by distant committees, as the capital markets are.

A major purpose of corporate planning and control is to eliminate surprise or risk:

Control, which essentially means 'keeping things on track', ranks as one of the critical functions of management. Good control means that an informed person can be reasonably confident that no major, unpleasant surprises will occur.

As Robert Simons, the Charles M. Williams Professor of Business Administration at Harvard Business School, says, 'Measurement focuses on errors of commission (mistakes) and shortfalls (negative variances) against goals. Control systems are negative feedback systems. Control reports are used primarily as confirmation that everything is "on track." Surprise is the enemy.'

Capital markets, because they are designed to provide for admission of new competitors and the elimination of weak ones, perhaps increase the chances of surprise. While capital markets do 'control', they control process and adherence to standards, not results. Nor do capital markets establish 'goals'. The Federal Reserve comes as close as any institution to attempting to 'control' the economy through some sort of target setting and adjustment policy, but this is not at all similar to a corporate control process.

With the exception of the Federal Reserve, capital markets do not 'think' about improving their overall levels of performance. Administrators think about how well the markets are functioning, but they do not influence their performance levels. While capital markets are controlled by regulators, judges, police, court systems, and the Federal Reserve Bank, no one would confuse any of these with the management tasks of a corporation.

Because of this lack of managerial control, the capital markets, when properly performing, introduce new options and adaptations more quickly than do corporations. Efficient capital markets eliminate the old without reflection or remorse – or the delay that remorse brings about – and when government policy contravenes these simple objectives, such as in state-owned companies, the positive effects of capital markets often are lost.

We also allowed companies to die when they were acquired (most 'dying' companies are acquired) or went bankrupt (which only a few do). These companies are referred to later in this book as 'departures'. When a company leaves or 'departs' the database, all prior data relating to that company is retained in the database. We also captured companies in the database that both entered and left during the period covered by the database, such as Rolm. Finally, of course, there are a few companies that were captured in the first year of the database (1962) and remained until the final year of the database (1998). We refer to these companies as 'long-term survivors'. Only 160 of the 1,008 companies we tracked fell into this category. Our database is like a videotape (taken with a hidden camera) that followed individuals around as they awakened, bathed, ate, worked, returned home, relaxed and slept. But rather than track individuals, we tracked companies. The McKinsey Corporate Performance Database allows us to trace to specific industries such macro-effects as the great decline in stock prices in 1974 and 1975 (almost all declined, with the exception of oil and computer hardware stocks), as well as trace the effects to specific companies (Champion International and International Flavors and Fragrances, for example, were clobbered). Our database allows us to ask questions about cause and effect – and get the answers quickly – without the need to build a new database for each new question. It gives us the range and scope to understand both the core and the periphery of the economy simultaneously, and in a way that relates to the overall performance of the economy (since our database faithfully tracks the macromeasures of the economy that others have put together – for example, the S&P 500 total return to shareholders indices).

Our research shows us that the McKinsey Corporate Performance Database mimics the real economy with exceptional fidelity. If an event took place in the real economy – for example, the stock market crash of 1974 and 1975 – it shows in our database. We can track both the event and the nation's recovery from the event. In the 1970s, the economy was enriched by the computer hardware and oil industries, and our database reflects that. Defence and pharmaceuticals gained leverage in the 1980s, and our database shows that, too. The chart below compares the annual returns to investors, as measured by our databases, with the returns to investors, as measured by the S&P 500. As one can see, it is nearly a perfect match. One can see quite easily the cycles of performance in the US economy.

How total return to shareholders (TRS) in the McKinsey Database compares with total return to shareholders in the S&P 500

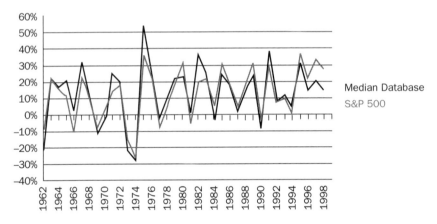

Again, the data that underlies our analysis of creative destruction is based on our analysis of the McKinsey Corporate Performance Database, which has been built from the real experiences of 1,008 US companies. Our findings and analysis have also been bolstered by our personal relationships with some of the largest and most successful companies in the United States. As advisors, we have worked to uncover what works and what does not. We hope our findings will allow other companies to improve their performance – more quickly and with more assurance than they might have had otherwise.

16 October 2000

1

Survival and performance in the era of discontinuity

This company will be going strong one hundred and even five hundred years from now.

C. JAY PARKINSON, PRESIDENT OF ANACONDA MINES
statement made three years in advance of Anaconda's bankruptcy

I n 1917, shortly before the end of the First World War, Bertie Charles (or B.C., as he was known) Forbes formed his first list of the 100 largest American companies. The firms were ranked by assets, since sales data were not accurately compiled in those days. In 1987, *Forbes* republished its original 'Forbes 100' list and compared it to its 1987 list of top companies. Of the original group, 61 had ceased to exist (see Figure 1.1).

Of the remaining 39, 18 had managed to stay in the top 100. These 18 companies – which included Kodak, DuPont, General Electric, Ford, General Motors, Procter & Gamble, and a dozen other corporations – had clearly earned the nation's respect. Skilled in the arts of survival, these enterprises had weathered the Great Depression, the Second World War, the Korean conflict, the swinging 60s, the oil and inflation shocks of the 1970s, and unprecedented technological change in the chemicals, pharmaceuticals, computers, software, radio and television, and global telecommunications industries.

They survived. But they did not perform. As a group these great companies earned a long-term return for their investors during the 1917–87 period 20 per cent less than that of the overall market. Only two of them, General Electric and Eastman Kodak, performed better than the averages, and Kodak has since fallen on harder times.

Fig. 1.1 Long-term survivor performance

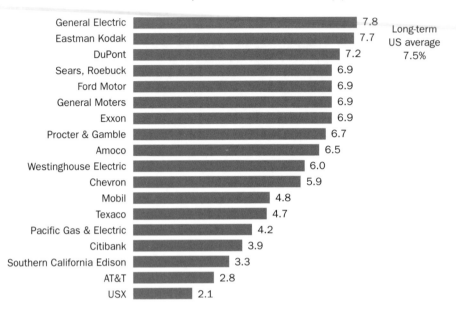

Growth in market capitalization CAGR 1917–1987 (%)

General Electric	7.8
Eastman Kodak	7.7
DuPont	7.2
Sears, Roebuck	6.9
Ford Motor	6.9
General Moters	6.9
Exxon	6.9
Procter & Gamble	6.7
Amoco	6.5
Westinghouse Electric	6.0
Chevron	5.9
Mobil	4.8
Texaco	4.7
Pacific Gas & Electric	4.2
Citibank	3.9
Southern California Edison	3.3
AT&T	2.8
USX	2.1

Long-term
US average
7.5%

Source: *Forbes*, July 1987

One reaches the same conclusion from an examination of the S&P 500. Of the 500 companies originally making up the S&P 500 in 1957, only 74 remained on the list through to 1997. And of these 74, only 12 outperformed the S&P 500 index itself over the 1957–98 period. Moreover, the list included companies from two industries, pharmaceuticals and food, that were strong performers during this period. If today's S&P 500 today were made up of only those companies that were on the list when it was formed in 1957, the overall performance of the S&P 500 would have been about 20 per cent less *per year* than it actually has been.

> Of the 500 companies originally making up the S&P 500 in 1957, only 74 remained on the list through to 1997.

For the last few decades we have celebrated the big corporate survivors, praising their 'excellence' and their longevity, their ability to last. These, we have assumed, are the bedrock companies of the American economy. These are the companies that 'patient' investors pour their money into – investments that would certainly reward richly at the end of a lifetime. But our findings – based on the 38 years of data compiled in the McKinsey

Corporate Performance Database, discussed in the Introduction – have shown that they do not perform as we might suspect. An investor following the logic of patiently investing money in these survivors will do substantially less well than an investor who merely invests in market index funds.

McKinsey's long-term studies of corporate birth, survival, and death in America clearly show that the corporate equivalent of El Dorado, the golden company that continually performs better than the markets, *has never existed*. It is a myth. Managing for survival, even among the best and most revered corporations, does not guarantee strong long-term performance for shareholders. In fact, just the opposite is true. In the long run, markets always win.

THE ASSUMPTION OF CONTINUITY

How could this be? How could a stock market index such as the Dow Jones Industrial average or the S&P 500 average – which, unlike companies, lack skilled managers, boards of experienced directors, carefully crafted organizational structures, the most advanced management methods, privileged assets, and special relationships with anyone of their choosing – perform better, over the long haul, than all but two of *Forbes's* strongest survivors, General Electric and Eastman Kodak? Are the capital markets, as represented by the stock market averages, 'wiser' than managers who think about performance all the time?

The answer is that the capital markets, and the indices that reflect them, encourage the creation of corporations, permit their efficient operations (as long as they remain competitive) and then rapidly, and remorselessly, remove them when they lose their ability to perform. Corporations, which operate with management philosophies based on the assumption of continuity, are not able to change at the pace and scale of the markets. As a result, in the long term, they do not create value at the pace and scale of the markets.

It is among the relatively new entrants to the economy, for example, Intel, Amgen, and Cisco, where one finds superior performance, at least for a time. The structure and mechanisms of the capital markets enable these companies to produce results superior to even the best surviving corporations. Moreover, it is the corporations that have lost their ability to meet investor expectations (no matter how unreasonable these expectations might be) that consume the wealth of the economy. The capital markets remove these weaker performers at a greater rate than even the best-performing companies. Joseph Alois Schumpeter, the great Austrian-American economist of the 1930s and 40s, called this process of creation and removal 'the gales of creative destruction'. So great is the challenge of running the operations of a corporation today that few corporate leaders have the energy or time to manage the processes of creative destruction, especially at the pace and scale necessary to compete with the market. Yet that is precisely what is required to sustain market levels of long-term performance.

The essential difference between corporations and capital markets is in the way they enable, manage, and control the processes of creative destruction. Corporations are built on the assumption of continuity; their focus is on operations. Capital markets are built on the assumption of *discontinuity*; their focus is on creation and destruction. The market encourages rapid and extensive creation, and hence greater wealth-building. It is less tolerant than the corporation is of long-term underperformance. Outstanding corporations do win the right to survive, but not the ability to earn above-average or even average shareholder returns over the long term. Why? Because their control processes – the very processes that help them to survive over the long haul – deaden them to the need for change.

THE REALITY OF DISCONTINUITY

This distinction between the way corporations and markets approach the processes of creative destruction is not an artifact of our times or an outgrowth of the 'dot.com' generation. It has been smouldering for decades, like a fire in a wall, ready to erupt at any moment. The market turmoil we see today is a logical extension of trends that began decades ago.

The origins of modern managerial philosophy can be traced to the eighteenth century, when Adam Smith argued for the specialization of tasks and division of labour in order to cut waste. By the late nineteenth century these ideas had culminated in an age of American trusts, European holding companies, and Japanese *zaibatsus*. These complex giants were designed to convert natural resources into food, energy, clothing and shelter in the most asset-efficient way – to maximize output and to minimize waste.

By the 1920s, Smith's simple idea had enabled huge enterprises, exploiting the potential of mass production, to flourish. Peter Drucker wrote the seminal guidebook for these corporations in 1946, *The Concept of the*

Corporation. The book laid out the precepts of the, then, modern corporation, based on the specialization of labour, mass production, and the
efficient use of physical assets.

This approach was in deep harmony with the times. Change came slowly
in the 1920s, when the first Standard and Poor's index of 90 important US
companies was formed. In the 1920s and 1930s the turnover rate in the
S&P 90 averaged about 1.5 per cent per year. A new member of the S&P 90
at that time could expect to remain on the list, on average, for more than 65
years. The corporations of these times were built on the assumption of continuity – perpetual continuity, the essence of which Drucker explored in his
book. Change was a minor factor. Companies were in business to transform
raw materials into final products, to avoid the high costs of interaction
between independent companies in the marketplace. This required them to
operate at great scale and to control their costs carefully. These vertically
integrated configurations were protected from all but incremental change.

We argue that this period of corporate development, lasting for more than
70 years, has come to an end. In 1998, the turnover rate in the S&P 500 was
close to 10 per cent, implying an average lifetime on the list of 10 years, not
65! Drucker predicted the turning point with his 1969 book *The Age of
Discontinuity*, but his persuasive arguments could not overcome the *Zeitgeist*
of the 1970s. The 1970s were, for many managers, the modern equivalent of
the 1930s. Inflation raged, interest rates were at the highest levels since
before the Second World War, and the stock market was languishing. Few
entrants dared risk capital or career on the founding of a new company based
on Drucker's insights. It was a fallow time for corporate start-ups. As the long-
term demands of survival took over, Drucker's advice fell on deaf years.

The pace of change has been accelerating continuously since the 1920s.
There have been three great waves (see Figure 1.2). The timing and extent
of these waves match the rise and fall of the generative and absorptive capabilities of the nation. The first wave came shortly after the Second World
War, when the nation's military buildup gave way to the need to rebuild
the consumer infrastructure. Many new companies entered the economy
at this time, then rose to economic prominence during the 1940s and
1950s, among them Owens-Corning, Textron, and Seagram.

The second wave began in the 1960s. The rate of turnover in the S&P
90 began to accelerate as the federal defence and aerospace programs once
again stimulated the economy, providing funds for the development of

Fig. 1.2 Change in the S&P 500: 7-year moving average

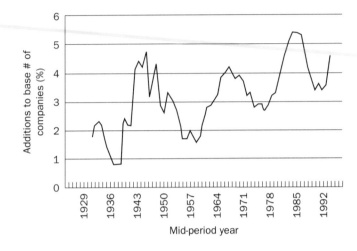

logic and memory chips, and later the microprocessor. They were heady days – 'bubble days', in the eyes of some. The hot stocks were called 'one-decision' stocks: buy them once and never sell them, and your future fortune was assured.

The bubble burst in 1968. The New York Stock Exchange, which had risen to almost 1000, did not return to that level again until the early 1980s. During this absorptive, or slack, period, when the country was beset with rising oil prices and inflation, and when bonds earned returns substantially greater than equities, few new companies joined, or left, the S&P 500. Interestingly enough though, despite the worst economic conditions the United States had endured since the Depression, the minimum rate of corporate turnover did not drop to the low rate of turnover seen in the 1950s. The base rate of change in the economy had permanently risen.

Paul Volcker, chairman of the Federal Reserve Bank, finally led the charge that broke the back of inflation, and the number of new companies climbing onto the S&P 500 accelerated. In the 1980s, once again the S&P began substituting new high-growth and high-market-cap companies for the slower-growing and even shrinking-market-cap older companies. The change in the S&P index mix also reflected changes in the economic mix of business in the United States. When the markets collapsed in the late 1980s and a short-lived recession hit the American economy in the early 1990s, the rate of substitution in the S&P 500 fell off. But again, even at its lowest point, the rate of turnover was higher than it was during the 1970s

Fig. 1.3 Average lifetime of S&P 500 companies

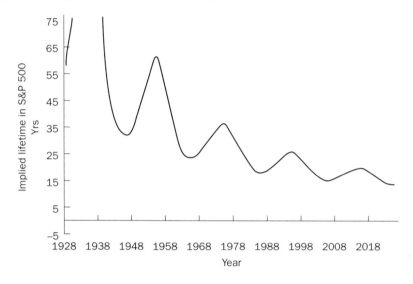

decline. The minimum level of change in the US economy had been quietly building, and was increasing again. This was even more evident as the technology-charged 1990s kicked into gear, accelerating the rate of the S&P Index turnover to levels never seen before. By the end of the 1990s, we were well into what Peter Drucker calls the 'Age of Discontinuity'. Extrapolating from past patterns, we calculate that by the end of the year 2020, the average lifetime of a corporation on the S&P will have been shortened to about 10 years, as fewer and fewer companies fall into the category of 'survivors' (see Figure 1.3).

THE GALES OF DISCONTINUITY

The Age of Discontinuity did not arrive in the 1990s by chance. It arose from fundamental economic forces. Among these are:

- the increasing efficiency of business, due to dramatic declines in capital costs – as industry shifted from goods to services, there was a concurrent decline in interaction and transaction costs; these costs declined because of the advent of information technology and the steady rise in labour productivity due to advances in technology and management methods

- the increasing efficiency of capital markets, due to the increasing accuracy (and transparency) of corporate performance data

- the rise in national liquidity, due to the improved profitability of US corporations, and a favourable bias, unparalleled anywhere else in the world, toward US equities
- strengthened fiscal management by the federal government, including an effective Federal Reserve, and reduced corporate taxes.

These forces have helped to create the likes of Microsoft, with a market capitalization greater than all but the top 10 nations of the world (Microsoft's real assets make up about 1 per cent of its market value). Computer maker Dell has virtually no assets at all. Internet start-up companies begin with almost no capital. For these companies, returns on capital are unimaginably large by previous standards. Productivity is soaring. The pipeline of new technology is robust. There are more than 10,000 Internet business proposals alone awaiting evaluation at venture capital firms, even after the Nasdaq collapse in March and April of 2000. By all reports, the number (if not the quality) of these proposals is increasing all the time. Information technology is not nearing its limits. The effectiveness of software programming continues to grow; communications technology is just beginning. The global GDP will double in the next 20 years, creating approximately $20–$40 trillion in new sales. If, through the productivity improvements the Internet enables, the world can save 2 per cent of the $25 trillion now produced, the market value of those savings will run into the trillions.

Incumbent companies have an unprecedented opportunity to take advantage of these times. But if history is a guide, no more than a third of today's major corporations will survive in an economically important way over the next 25 years. Those that do not survive will die a Hindu death of transformation, as they are acquired or merged with part of a larger, stronger organization, rather than a Judeo-Christian death, but it will be death nonetheless. And the demise of these companies will come from a lack of competitive adaptiveness.

> If history is a guide, no more than a third of today's major corporations will survive in an economically important way over the next 25 years.

To be blunt, most of these companies will die or be bought out and absorbed because they are too damn slow to keep pace with change in the market. By 2020, more than three-quarters of the S&P 500 will consist of companies we don't know today – new companies drawn into the maelstrom of economic activity from the periphery, springing from insights unrecognized today.

The assumption of continuity, on which most of our leading corporations have been based for years, no longer holds. Discontinuity dominates. The 100 or so companies in the current S&P 500 that survive into the 2020s will be unlike the corporate survivors today. They will have to be masters of creative destruction: built for discontinuity, remade like the market. Schumpeter anticipated this transformation over a half century ago when he observed: 'The problem that is usually being visualized is how capitalism *administers* existing structures, whereas the relevant problem is how it *creates* and *destroys* them.'

THE NEED TO ABANDON THE ASSUMPTION OF CONTINUITY

How can corporations make themselves more like the market? The general prescription is to increase the rate of creative destruction to the level of the market itself, without losing control of present operations. As sensible as this recommendation is, it has prove difficult to implement.

Hundreds of managers from scores of US and European countries have told us that while they are satisfied with their operating prowess, they are dissatisfied with their ability to implement change. *How do the excellent innovators do it?* they ask, presuming that excellent innovators exist. *What drives an innovation breakthrough?* Others question how one grows a company beyond its core business. And most fundamentally of all: *How do we find new ideas?*

The difficulties behind these questions arise from the inherent conflict between the need for corporations to control existing operations and the need to create the kind of environment that will permit new ideas to flourish – and old ones to die a timely death. This may require trading out traditional assets, challenging existing channels of distribution, or making dilutive acquisitions. But whatever the challenges, we believe that most corporations will find it impossible to match or outperform the market without abandoning the assumption of continuity. Author James Reston, in his book *The Last Apocalypse*, observed Europe's fear that the first millennium would end in a fiery conclusion:

When the millennium arrived the apocalypse did take place; a world did end, and a new world arose from the ruins. But the last apocalypse was a process rather than a cataclysm. It had the suddenness of forty years.

The current apocalypse – the transition from a state of continuity to a state of discontinuity – has the same kind of suddenness. Never again will American business be as it once was. The rules have changed for ever. Some companies have made the crossing. Under Jack Welch, General Electric has negotiated the apocalypse and has seen its performance benefit as a result. Johnson & Johnson is moving across the divide quickly, as we will see later. Enron has made strong progress by transforming itself from a natural gas pipeline company to a trading company. Corning has been successful in shedding its dependence on consumer durables and becoming a leader in high-tech optical fibre. In France, L'Oréal seems to be on the right track, having found a new way to organize itself and transfer beauty concepts from one economy to another. But these are the exceptions. Few have attempted the journey. Fewer still have made it to the other side successfully.

CULTURAL LOCK-IN

For half a century, Bayer aspirin drove the growth of Sterling Drug until Johnson & Johnson introduced Tylenol. Out of fear of cannibalizing its Bayer aspirin leadership, Sterling Drug refused to introduce its leading European non-aspirin pain reliever (Panadol) to the United States. Instead, it tried to expand its Bayer line overseas. This failure ultimately led to its acquisition by Kodak. Sterling Drug had become effectively immobilized, unable to change its half-century-old behaviour out of fear. Its strong culture – its rules of thumb for decision making, its control processes, the information it used for decision making – blocked its progress and ultimately sealed its fate. It had locked itself into an ineffective approach to the marketplace despite clear signs that it needed to act in a new way.

Cultural lock-in – the inability to change the corporate culture even in the face of clear market threats – explains why corporations find it difficult to respond to the messages of the market place. Cultural lock-in results from the gradual stiffening of the invisible architecture of the corporation, and the ossification of its decision-making abilities, control systems, and

Cultural lock-in dampens a company's ability to innovate or to shed operations with a less exciting future.

mental models. It dampens a company's ability to innovate or to shed operations with a less exciting future. Moreover, it signals the corporation's inexorable decline into inferior performance. Often, as in the case of Sterling Drug, cultural lock-in manifests itself in three general fears – the fear of cannibalization of an important product line, the fear of channel conflict with important customers, and the fear of earnings dilution that might result from a strategic acquisition. As reasonable as all these fears seem to be to established companies, they are not fears that are felt in the market. And so the market moves where the corporation dares not.

Cultural lock-in is the last in a series of 'emotional' phases in a corporation's life, a series that mirrors remarkably that of human beings. In the early years of a corporation, just after its founding, the dominant emotion is passion – the sheer energy to make things happen. When passion rules, information and analysis are ignored in the name of vision: *We know the right answer; we do not need analysis.*

As the corporation ages, the bureaucracy begins to settle in. Passions cool and are replaced by 'rational decision making', often simply the codification of what has worked in the past. Data is gathered, analysis is performed, alternatives are postulated, and scenarios are developed. Attempts are made to avoid the game of information sculpting. Only when rational decision making is in vogue does all the relevant information flow to the right decision maker, at the right time, and in the right form to be easily analyzed and interpreted. Rational decision making is triumphant, at least for a while. This stage is often pictured as the normal state of the corporation, although in our experience, particularly as the pace of change increases, rarely does this ideal state accurately describe how the company actually operates.

Eventually, rational decision making reveals that the future potential for the business is limited. Often at this point, threatened by the prospects for a bleak future, the corporation falls back on defensive routines to protect the organization from its fate, just as defensive emotions emerge in our lives when we sense impending trauma. Management now sees the future filled more with trouble than with promise. Decisions are made to protect existing businesses. The fear of discarding the old for the new (product cannibalization), the fear of customer conflict and the fear of earnings dilution through acquisition paralyze acts of creative destruction, and often effectively shield the corporation from the perception of future trouble, as well as the need to act, for a long time. Cultural lock-in is established, thwarting the emergence of a leader or team that might save the day.

THE CAUSES OF CULTURAL LOCK-IN

Why does cultural lock-in occur? The heart of the problem is the forma-tion of hidden sets of rules, or mental models, that once formed are extremely difficult to change. Mental models are the core concepts of the corporation, the beliefs and assumptions, the cause-and-effect relation-ships, the guidelines for interpreting language and signals, the stories repeated within the corporate walls. Charlie Munger, a long-time friend of and co-investor with Warren Buffet, and vice-chairman of Berkshire Hathaway, calls mental models the 'theoretical frameworks that help investors better understand the world'.

Mental models are invisible in the corporation. They are neither explicit nor examined, but they are pervasive. When well crafted, mental models allow management to anticipate the future and solve problems. But once constructed, mental models become self-reinforcing, self-sustaining, and self-limiting. And when mental models are out of sync with reality, they cause management to make forecasting errors and poor decisions. The assumption of continuity, in fact, is precisely the kind of disconnect with reality that leads corporations into flawed forecasting and poor decisions.

Mental models manifest themselves in corporate control systems. These systems are designed to ensure predictable goal achievement, whether it be cost control, the control of capital expenditures, or the control of the deploy-ment of key personnel. Effective control means that an informed manager can be reasonably confident that unpleasant surprises will not occur.

Unfortunately, control systems can also create 'defensive routines' in organizations, including the failure to challenge the status quo, the failure to encourage a diversity of opinions, failure to disagree with superiors (thereby displeasing them), communicating in ambiguous and inconsistent ways, and making these failures, even when known, 'undiscussable'. Change becomes impossible.

Corporate control systems also undermine the ability of the organiza-tion to innovate at the pace and scale of the market. Under the assumption of continuity, for example, the arguments for building a new business can be turned back, since its probable success cannot be proven in advance. Under these circumstances, it is more likely that ideas based on the incremental growth of current capabilities and mental models will be encouraged.

Corporate control systems limit creativity through their dependence on *convergent thinking*. Convergent thinking focuses on clear problems and provides well-known solutions quickly. It thrives on focus. Order, simplicity, routine, clear responsibilities, unambiguous measurement systems, and predictability are the bedrock of convergent thinking. Convergent thinking is tailor-made for the assumption of continuity. Convergent thinking can be effective at handling small, incremental changes and differences, but transformational changes completely flummox the system.

Discontinuity, on the other hand, thrives on a different kind of thinking, *divergent thinking*. Divergent thinking focuses on broadening, i.e., diverging, the context of decision making. It is initially more concerned with questions than getting to the answer in the fastest possible way. Divergent thinking places enormous value on getting the questions right, then relinquishes control to conventional convergent thinking processes.

Divergent thinking thrives as much on the broad search as on the focused search. It focuses as much on careful observation of the facts as on interpretation of the facts. It focuses as much on the skills of reflection (which requires time away from the problem) as on the skills of swift decision making (which seek to avoid delay). We refer to these three skills – conversation, observation, and reflection – as the COR skills of divergent thinking. Unfortunately, conventional corporate control systems, built on the assumption of continuity, stifle the COR skills of divergent thinking, or kill it outright.

When mental models are out of sync with reality, corporations lose their early-warning system. Leaders with genuine vision are suppressed. As Ron Heifetz, director of the Program on Leadership at the Kennedy School of Government at Harvard, observed: 'People who lead frequently bear scars from their efforts to bring about adaptive change. Often they are silenced. On occasion, they are killed.'

> 'People who lead frequently bear scars from their efforts to bring about adaptive change. Often they are silenced. On occasion, they are killed.'

Abbott Laboratories, for example, flush with the success of their strategy to build strong positions in the medical diagnostic and test equipment business, was anxious to avoid the shocks to the pharmaceutical industry posed by the emergence of Medicare and Medicaid in the early to mid-1970s. Yet it found itself with an incumbent CEO who squelched three potential successors seeking to change strategy.

Once cultural lock-in guides a company's decisions, in the absence of some great external shock, the corporation's fate is sealed.

HOW THE MARKETS ENABLE CHANGE

Markets, on the other hand, lacking culture, leadership, and emotion, do not experience the bursts of desperation, depression, denial, and hope that corporations face. The market has no lingering memories or remorse. It has no mental models. The market does not fear cannibalization, customer channel conflict, or dilution. It simply waits for the forces at play to work out – for new companies to be created and for acquisitions to clear the field. The markets silently allow weaker companies to be put up for sale and leaves it to the new owners to shape them up or shut them down. Actions are taken quickly on early signs of weakness. Only when governments are brought in, as with a bailout, does the market mimic a probable corporate response. Most of the time, the market simply removes the weak players, and in removing them, improves overall returns.

Lacking production-oriented control systems, markets create more surprise and innovation than do corporations. They operate on the assumption of discontinuity, and accommodate continuity. Corporations, on the other hand, assume continuity and attempt to accommodate discontinuity. The difference is profound.

REDESIGNING THE CORPORATION BASED ON DISCONTINUITY

The right of any corporation to exist is not perpetual but has to be continuously earned.

ROBERT SIMONS

The market has pointed the way to a solution. In response to the tension that builds between the potential for improved performance and the actual performance of large businesses, in an era of increasing pace of change in the economy, there are certain kinds of firms, particularly private equity firms, as we discuss in Chapter 7, that have demonstrated the ability to change at the pace and scale of the market, and they have earned sustained superior returns for doing so. The two kinds of private equity firms – principal investing firms and venture capitalists – are quite different from each other, but each looks somewhat like the holding companies of the late nineteenth century. It is possible to imagine that they will form the seeds of the industrial giants of the twenty-first century.

These newly important firms have been able to outperform the markets for the last two to three decades, longer than any other company we know of. The difference between these partnerships and the conventional corporation is in their approach to organizational design. These financial partnerships have discovered how to operate at high levels of efficiency and scale while engaging in creative destruction at the pace of the market, exactly as Joseph Schumpeter envisioned. Created around the assumption of discontinuity, they have then determined how best to incorporate or fold in the requirements of continuity.

These firms never buy any company to hold for ever. Rather, they focus on intermediate (four- to seven-year) value creation. Corporations, in contrast, concentrate on the very short term (less than 18 months) for operations and the very long term (greater than eight years) for research.

Private equity firms make as much money by expanding the future potential of their properties as they do from increasing the properties' operating incomes. When a private equity firm invests in a company, or buys all of the equity, it buys it with a 'take-out' strategy in mind: management knows what it must do in the next four to seven years to build the property so that it has long-term value for the next buyer.

Finally, private equity companies think of their business as a revolving portfolio of companies in various stages of development. They realize they will sell some of their properties each year and buy others. They keep the pipeline full of new properties at the front end and supplied with buyers at the back end, cultivating both simultaneously (a skill at which they excel).

These firms differ from conventional corporations not only in their divergent thinking, but also in the depth and speed of their research activities. Moreover, private equity firms allow each of the companies they buy to retain their own control systems. This allows the private equity firm to concentrate on creation and destruction to a far greater extent than traditional corporations do, and to an even greater extent than their own wholly or partially owned subsidiaries do.

THE ROAD AHEAD

Long-term corporate performance has not matched the performance of the overall markets because corporations do not adapt as fast as the markets do. This is because of the way they evolve, not because of the way they accomplish their day-to-day work. For historical reasons, as we have discussed above, corporations have been designed to operate, i.e., to produce goods and services, rather than to evolve. In order to evolve at the pace of the markets, they have to get better at creation and destruction – the two key elements of evolution that are missing.

Redesigning the corporation to evolve quickly rather than simply operate well requires more than simple adjustments; the fundamental concepts of operational excellence are inappropriate for a corporation seeking to evolve at the pace and scale of the markets. One cannot just add on creation and destruction; one has to design them in. And only if the corporation is redesigned to evolve at the pace and scale of the market will long-term performance improve. Markets perform better than corporations because markets allow new companies to enter more freely, and they force the elimination of those companies without competitive prospects more ruthlessly than corporations do. Moreover, markets do these things faster and on a larger scale than corporations.

We believe that corporations must be redesigned from top to bottom based on the assumption of discontinuity. Management must stimulate the rate of creative destruction through the generation or acquisition of new firms and the elimination of marginal performers – without losing control of operations. If operations are healthy, the rate of creative destruction within the corporation will determine the continued long-term competitiveness and performance of the company. Today's financial partnerships give us confidence that this realignment can work. They also suggest a way to do it.

Corporations must be redesigned from top to bottom based on the assumption of discontinuity.

To create new businesses at a faster rate, corporations also need to ponder the details of divergent thinking. Divergent thinking is a prelude to creativity. Many divergent thinkers possess apparently opposing traits: they may be passionate and objective, or proud and humble; they may be both extroverted and introverted; in negotiations they may be flexible and unyielding, attentive and wandering. They possess what Mihalyi Czikszentmihalyi, one of today's leading thinkers on creativity and the author of *Flow*, has called 'a sunny pessimism'. F. Scott Fitzgerald described it in this way:

The test of a first-rate intelligence is the ability to hold two opposed ideas in the mind at the same time, and still retain the ability to function. One should, for example, be able to see that things are hopeless and yet be determined to make them otherwise.

Managing for divergent thinking, that is, managing to ensure that the proper questions are addressed early enough to allow them to be handled in an astute way, requires establishing a 'rich context' of information as a stimulus to posing the right questions. It requires control through the selection and motivation of employees rather than through control of people's actions; ample resources, including time, to achieve results; knowing what to measure and when to measure it; and genuine respect for others' capabilities and potential. It also requires the willingness to remove people from responsibility when it becomes clear they cannot perform up to standard. In the end, both divergent and convergent thinking must successfully coexist.

Next, to improve long-term performance, the overall planning and control processes of the corporation need to be rethought. The conventional strategic planning process has failed most corporations. As practiced, it stifles the very dialogue it is meant to stimulate. New ways of conducting a dialogue and conversation among the leaders of the corporation and their inheritors are needed.

Finally, corporate control systems must be built that can manage both to control operations and increase the rate of creative destruction. Control what you must, not what you can; control when you must, not when you can. If a control procedure is not essential, eliminate it. Measure less; shorten the time and number of intermediaries between measurement and action, and increase the speed with which you receive feedback.

The point is to let the market control wherever possible. Be suspicious of control mechanisms – they stifle more than they control. Let those who run a business determine the best mix of controls for their business (they know the system best) and shift the burden of integration to the corporate level, rather than designing uniform systems that have to be implemented throughout a corporation independent of the business. When such changes are implemented, the focus of the corporation will shift from minimizing risk, and thereby inadvertently stifling creativity, to facilitating creativity – and that is what is needed to strengthen long-term performance.

To implement these ideas, the role of leadership must be rethought. Ron Heifetz of Harvard says:

> The adaptive demands of our societies require leadership that takes responsibility without waiting for revelation or request. One may lead perhaps with not more than a question in hand. A leader has to engage people in facing the challenge, adjusting their values, changing perspectives, and developing new habits of behaviour.

If these steps are taken effectively, they will help prevent the emergence of cultural lock-in.

This book offers a clear storm warning to dot.com companies. You have been born at a special time – one where all the elements of the ideal creative environment exist simultaneously. By focusing on 'getting the product out' and 'building the website', you are following in the footsteps of millions of companies since the time of Adam Smith. You are blessed to exist at a time of rapid change, which gives you the opportunity to peer into the future and design your corporation accordingly. But after the early heady days of growth, your challenges will be the same as those of other companies of the past: to grow and avoid being trapped by cultural lock-in.

A NEW BEGINNING

The agenda outlined above is substantial. Not all companies will be willing to take it on. The first step is to recognize the description of the business world as an increasingly *discontinuous* place. In the following pages, we will lay out in more detail why we see the world as a place of discontinuity, and outline the specific problems, and solutions, corporations must address if they are to break the paradigm of underperformance over the long term and truly act as companies built on excellence. Building a company to last – managing to survive – is no longer enough in an age of discontinuity. The chapters that follow will help point the way.

2 How creative destruction works:

The fate of the East River Savings Bank

Some things are hurrying into existence, and others are hurrying out of it. And of that which is coming into existence, part is already extinguished. Motions and changes are continually renewing the world . . .

Roman Emperor Marcus Aurelius
Meditations (AD fourth century)

Driving up West 96th Street from the Henry Hudson Drive on the way to Central Park, one approaches a venerable-looking bank at the corner of Amsterdam and West 96th. The building is not large, but it is impressive. It has been built to last.

Monumental in design, it is one huge storey tall (with double-height windows), built solidly of limestone, and about half a block long. It has five very permanent Ionic columns guarding its main entrance. The dates '1849–1926' are etched in the stone of the frieze. Aphorisms about the virtues of saving, authored by Thomas Jefferson and Abraham Lincoln, grace the frieze on each side of the dates. As one approaches the building, the thought occurs: 'I would like to have my money in that bank. It will be there for ever.'

But as you cross Amsterdam you realize that this bank is not a bank at all. Today it is a CVS pharmacy. The bank's history serves as a reminder that what seems strong and permanent in this world can easily be swept aside. And the more venerable an institution appears, the more vulnerable it is likely to be.

The East River Savings Bank as a drugstore in 2000

The East River Savings Institution was founded in 1848 and prospered quietly as the city of New York grew. Darwin R. James, the eighth president of the bank, often said that the savings bank atmosphere seemed to him to be quiet – that it required little energy or activity on the part of the president.

This pattern was not to last, however. In 1925, James changed the bank's name to East River Savings Bank and set off on a series of innovations: advertising its services to the public and sponsoring legislation to permit local savings banks to open branch offices.

Located in the limestone and marble monument at Amsterdam Avenue and 96th Street, the first branch of the East River Savings Bank opened its doors in 1927. It was designed by the well-known architectural firm Walker & Gillette, which had created many of New York's fashionable town houses, as well as the New York Historical Society, the Greenwich Country Club and the entire town of Venice, Florida. 'Since savings banks relied on the small deposits of large numbers of patrons, their buildings were often impressive structures that would attract the attention of local residents, and draw them into the spacious and richly appointed interiors,' explains Andrew Dolkart of Landmark West! 'Here, they could open an account with the assurance that in such a grand building their money would be safe.'

As the Great Depression took hold across the United States, banks everywhere in the country failed. But the East River Savings Bank continued to prosper. In 1932, it acquired both the Maiden Lane Savings Bank, a bank established for German immigrants working mainly in the jewellery industry, and the Italian Savings Bank of the City of New York. These banks, though not built with the structural elegance of the East River Savings Bank, for the next three decades provided the bank with the savings of New York's immigrants.

But the 1970s proved perilous for the East River Savings Bank. Interest rates soared, and home and multi-family loans fell precipitously as a result. In a bid to diversify, East River acquired two upstate New York S&Ls. It also took advantage of new laws that permitted S&Ls to invest 5 per cent of their assets in real estate. That move, however, attracted a real estate developer, who bought East River and changed its name to the River Bank of America. The new name reflected the 'nationwide real-estate, corporate lending and capital markets activities of the company'.

But the River Bank began going downstream fast. Management invested in advertising and new consumer products, but bad loans overcame them. In 1991, the Federal Deposit Insurance Corp. ordered River Bank to 'cease and desist'. By 1992, non-performing assets had risen to $575 million, or 29 per cent of all assets. In 1995, the branches of River Bank were sold to Marine Midland.

In 1997, Marine Midland Bank (before it itself was acquired by the Hongkong and Shanghai Banking Corporation) decided to sell the bank branch. Local residents were alarmed. 'The Marine Midland Bank on the northeast corner of Amsterdam Avenue and 96th Street is the sort of solid, stately presence that nearby residents have come to *assume is permanent*,' *The New York Times* opined. But despite the reservations of local residents, Essex Capital Partners, a real estate firm specializing in urban retail space, bought the branch office in early 1998. Six months later, residents learned that Essex would lease the bank to CVS, a nationwide pharmacy chain with 36 stores in New York.

And so the bank became a drugstore. It is the way creative destruction works.

THE ACCELERATION OF CREATIVE DESTRUCTION

The demise of institutions like the East River Saving Bank branch at West 96th Street may be unfortunate, but it's not unusual. The turnover in our institutional giants is not a consequence of the Internet or of the New Economy. Rather, it is a phenomenon that has been building slowly since the 1920s, long before the beginning of the end for the East River Savings Bank.

Today, the rates of change can be seen in the rapidity with which powerful new companies climb onto the S&P list, and the equal pace with which older, venerable companies tumble off. This turnover, which would have been unimaginable in the 1920s, was almost as surprising just 25 years ago. Yet in the light of the number of new companies admitted to the S&P list, it has been accelerating for the past 70 years.

This accelerating rate is important, because these new companies generate higher levels of total return to shareholders than the older survivors do. Without them, the overall performance of the markets, and arguably, the economy, would have been far less than it is. For example, if the S&P 500 were today made up of only those companies that were on the list when it was formed in 1957, the overall performance would have been significantly less, as seen in Figure 2.1.

> If the S&P 500 were today made up of only those companies that were on the list when it was formed in 1957, the overall performance would have been significantly less.

The McKinsey Corporate Performance Database, which tracks data over the last 38 years, reflects these changes as Figure 2.2 demonstrates. More insight into the nature of the changes shows that many of the companies that played a significant role in the US economy have ceased to exist, and many others have come into the economy.

The new entrants to the database over time represent an increasing proportion of the total number of companies included, while the survivors represent a decreasing proportion. Unlike the S&P 500, the number of companies in the McKinsey database is not fixed. And in fact, the number has grown from 249 in 1962 to 696 in 1998, and the rate of growth of such new companies into the database has accelerated from 1.6 per cent per year in the 1960s to 4.6 per cent today. The acceleration has occurred in

Fig. 2.1 Total return to shareholders of S&P 500: Long-term survivors versus median for the S&P 500

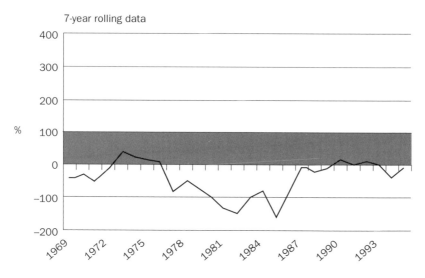

Fig. 2.2 Change in S&P 500 versus net new companies index

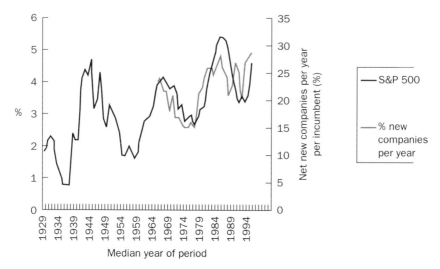

Net new companies median excludes regulated industries: oil, electric energy, trucking, airlines, and defence since these are overweighted in the PDB relative to the S&P 500

waves, as has been true of the S&P 500. (These numbers would be even more dramatic if the electric utility industry, representing about 100 companies in the sample, and which has not been subject to the same market disciplines as other companies, had not been included.)

Fig. 2.3 Companies by category

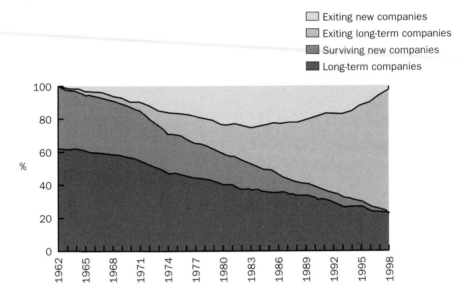

Individual industries, such as computer hardware, telecommunications, or medical devices show even more rapid rates of change, sometimes exceeding the overall averages by factors of two or three.

The robustness of the process of creative destruction in the American economy has directly underpinned the strong long-term performance of the American capital markets. The US economy is now dominated by companies that were not large enough to qualify in the top 80 per cent of the US in 1962. It is quite possible that in 36 year's time, the new US economy will be dominated by companies that are now not large enough to qualify in the top 80 per cent of US corporations.

Schumpeter captured the spirit of this change in 1938 when he noted:

. . . the . . . process of industrial mutation . . . incessantly revolutionizes the economic structure from within, incessantly destroying the old one, incessantly creating a new one. This process of Creative Destruction is the essential fact about capitalism. It is what capitalism consists in and what every capitalist concern has got to live in.

PORTRAITS OF CONTINUITY

The S&P Index clearly tells the story of the acceleration of change and the growth of discontinuity in the overall economy. But what of individual industries? How do they track over time? How does creative destruction really work?

To answer these questions in a transparent way, we have to simplify the complex patterns of performance seen in the capital markets. We need to be able to understand what proportion of the changes we see can be attributed to the overall economy, to individual industries, and to individual companies.

To accomplish this purpose we have developed the performance chart. The performance chart allows us to visualize the past patterns of creative destruction: to determine when it began and when it stopped; to determine how normal or abnormal it appears; to compare an industry to the economy; and to compare one industry with another.

The performance chart is a portrait of long-term performance. It transforms the complexities of annual changes in total return to shareholders into a simple, yet accurate, picture that abstracts the essential details of industry or company performance from the noise of annual variation.

There are two kinds of performance chart: one that compares the performance of an industry, say pharmaceuticals, to the performance of the overall economy (the collection of all the industries in the McKinsey Performance Database) and one that compares the performance of a company, say Merck, to its industry.

The core of each industry chart is the 'normal' range of the economy; the core of the company charts is the 'normal' range of performance of each industry. In each chart, the top of the normal range is represented by 100 per cent and the bottom by 0 per cent. The exact position of the industry or company line relative to the normal range depends on the industry or company's performance in a given year relative to the performance of the overall stock market in that same year. To make the charts even more transparent, rather than plot individual years, we have plotted seven-year rolling averages. This process 'filters' the annual 'noise' from the data, and leaves only the tell tale underlying traces of true performance levels and changes. If the industry has exactly the same performance as the economy, it will lie halfway between the top and bottom, at 50 per cent. As long as the industry or company performance is within the 'normal range', that is between 0 per cent and 100 per cent, its performance is statistically indistinguishable from the performance of the economy or industry. When the results are either greater or less than the normal range, then creative destruction may be at work and an explanation for the exceptional (either positive or negative) performance is required.

Many industries – specialty chemicals, for example – perform within the 'normal' range of US markets. The performance for the specialty chemicals industry is shown in Figure 2.4.

Fig. 2.4 Specialty chemicals: 7-year rolling total return to shareholders (TRS) versus economy

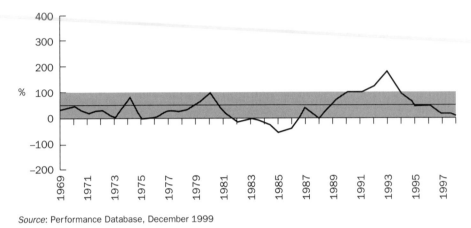

Source: Performance Database, December 1999

Other than a brief period in the late 1980s, which, it might be argued, offset a weak period in the late 1970s, there has never been a period of exceptional performance in the specialty chemical industry. The market has priced it 'fairly' in all periods. In each period this industry has tracked the US economy. In fact, for most of the periods we have examined, the specialty chemical industry was below the median, although the difference is not statistically significant. Individual companies within the specialty chemical industry offer a different story, as we will see later. The same conclusions can be reached for five other industries: commodity chemicals, paper, electric utilities, toiletries, and, with the exception of a brief time in the early 1960s, the trucking industry. These industries account for about one-third of the sales in the McKinsey Database and represent the forces of continuity. It is an important force, but, according to our database, not a dominant force in the US economy.

A similar pattern holds for individual companies, particularly long-term survivors. As a general rule, companies that have survived over the long term do not outperform their industries. In medical products, for example, Becton-Dickinson has been an enduring and important

As a general rule, companies that have survived over the long term do not outperform their industries.

company. While Becton-Dickinson has had some very good years in an absolute sense, it did not outperform its industry, as Figure 2.5 shows.

Fig. 2.5 Medical supplies: Becton-Dickinson & Co.

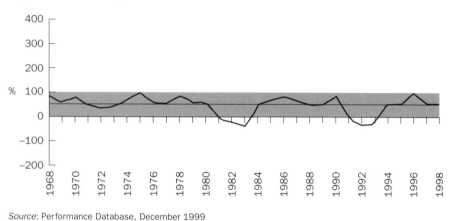

Source: Performance Database, December 1999

Becton-Dickinson's fate was interlocked with the fate of the medical products industry as a whole.

Rohm and Haas, for example, has risen above and fallen below the mean of its industry, but while one can find periods when Rohm and Haas has done better than the industry, there are an equal number of periods when it has done worse. Other companies, such as Raytheon and International Flavors and Fragrances, follow this same basic pattern. These companies arguably have more real risk than close competitors that stay within the range of their industry. It is one thing to expect a down cycle to be met with an up cycle in a year or two. It is quite another to have to wait a decade or two for a reversal.

This is true of other companies in other fields, as well: Rockwell and General Dynamics in defense; Westvaco and Mead in paper; American Home Products and Bristol-Myers Squibb in pharmaceuticals; Texas Instruments in electronics; AMR, the parent company of American Airlines, in air transport.

Some companies, like Delta Air Lines, have had great performances in the past, but for the most recent two or three decades have stayed within the 'normal' range of performance for their industry. Other such companies include Air Products and Chemicals, Dow Chemical, Ethyl Corporation, and Baxter International.

Not all long-term survivors necessarily performed at the median of their industry, however. A small group of companies consistently underperformed their industries year after year. An example is Champion International (see Figure 2.6), although it recently came back into the

Fig. 2.6 Paper: Champion International Corp.

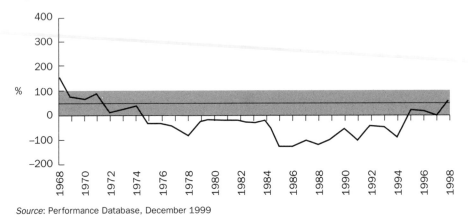

Source: Performance Database, December 1999

'normal' performance range just before being acquired by International Paper. Gates Learjet is another example, as is NL Industries. Compared to their peers they have sustained substandard performance.

There is a small, select group of companies that have been able to sustain their long-term performance above the average level of their industry – even if it has not exceeded the 'normal' range. Among them are Hewlett-Packard (see Figure 2.7), Medtronic, Abbott, Merck – and for the last 10 years or so – Warner-Lambert. It is interesting that all the companies in this group participate in industries where there is a great deal of change in the normal course of events. Their results may be the best results possible for companies that don't move into new industries (which, as we will see shortly, will have higher levels of total return to shareholders because of the performance of the industries in which they participate). The companies that succeed in these industries do so because they are able to continually outpace the expectations of analysts. This is a tall order.

> The companies that succeed do so because they are able to continually outpace the expectations of analysts

There is also a small, select group of companies that have been on a long-term march to superior performance in their industry. Among this group are Kimberly-Clark and Sherwin-Williams. Kimberly-Clark was in the commodity paper industry until the early 1970s, when it decided to move into the consumer paper business, which had stronger long-term performance than the commodity paper business. It chose to compete with

Fig. 2.7 Computer hardware: Hewlett-Packard Co.

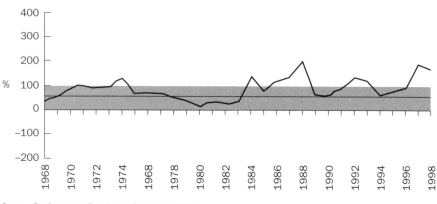

Source: Performance Database, December 1999

Fig. 2.8 Paper: Kimberly-Clark Corp. – 7-year rolling TRS relative to industry

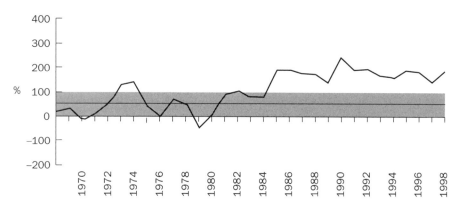

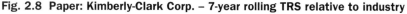

Procter & Gamble in the paper diapers business and successfully created the Huggies brand, which, while producing results that were normal for the consumer paper business, were superior to the results in the commodity paper business. Unable to break the pattern of the commodity paper industry, the company moved into an adjacent and more rewarding field. As a result, Kimberly-Clark began an era of greater performance for its shareholders (see Figure 2.8).

Sherwin-Williams offers a similar story. It switched its focus from making paints to multi-channel paint distribution, and it opened more than 2,000 stores during the 1980s. These important moves have rewarded the shareholders of these companies.

In general, however, companies rarely escape the gravity of their industries. They play by the rules, and their performance is determined more or less by those rules. They achieve what the industry achieves. This too was the fate of the East River Savings Bank. The industry was dying and the bank could not escape its downward pull. The building, despite its marble columns and ornate plinth, built to reflect the bank's permanence, was closed up – and reborn as a drugstore, just as Schumpeter would have predicted. It is the way creative destruction works.

PORTRAITS OF DISCONTINUITY

Continuity is not the only story in the capital markets. In fact, discontinuity plays a far more crucial role when industries and companies outperform the market.

Within industries

In some industries, performance differs from that of the general economy for sustained periods of time. For example, the US computer hardware industry, from its early days in the 1960s until the beginning of the 1980s, steadily outperformed the general market.

The 1960s and 1970s were a time of substantial innovation. IBM dominated the industry, and there was plenty of technological headroom. By the early 1980s those conditions did not hold any longer. Apple and DEC were challenging IBM. Meanwhile, software companies like Microsoft were beginning to emerge; computer hardware underperformed the overall market, vanquished by a pair of powerful technological discontinuities, the personal computer and software. Only recently has the computer hardware industry recovered (see Figure 2.9), but with an entirely restructured industry focused on personal computers and client servers, not the large mainframe hardware that generated the strong returns in the 1960s and 70s. The computer industry was more difficult for the analysts to price consistently. There were periods where they underestimated what the price should be and were pleasantly surprised, driving returns up. And there were other periods where they overestimated what the price would be, and were unpleasantly surprised, driving returns down. A more detailed description of the evolution of the computer hardware industry is given on pages 37–9.

Fig. 2.9 Computer hardware: 7-year rolling TRS versus economy

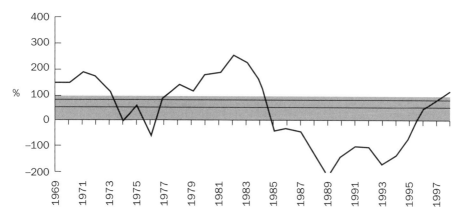

Source: Performance Database, December 1999

Computer hardware industry evolution

In 1962, there were eight companies in the computer hardware industry: IBM and the seven dwarfs (Burroughs, Sperry, etc.). In 1967, IBM accounted
for more than 55 per cent of all sales in the sector. It was not until 1988 that
IBM fell to below 50 per cent market share in McKinsey's database for that
sector, and even in 1995 IBM accounted for over a third of the total sales. Even
more significantly, IBM earned 80 per cent of all net operating profits within the
industry in 1967; by 1995, that figure was near 40 per cent.

Because IBM practically defined the computer industry in the late 1960s and
early 1970s, (when computers were still considered part of the office equipment
industry, along with adding machines, dictating equipment, and typewriters), most
of the new entrants to the field were competing against IBM in some part of the
market. The early successes of Digital Equipment and Wang Laboratories in finding market segments for their computers brought more computer makers into the
market. Storage Technology, for example, was created in 1972 with the simple
plan of making tape and disk drives that were interchangeable with IBM's offerings and selling them for 10 per cent less.

Storage Technology and similar companies with an 'as good as IBM, for less'
strategy discovered an underserved market, and were rewarded with rapid sales
growth and large returns to shareholders. Generally, these small companies were

able to compete on price, and so began to erode IBM's market share. Strong demand coupled with improvements in production technology allowed profit margins and earnings to rise appreciably. While a number of new companies were entering the market, their entry rate was actually slower than the rate of sales growth, allowing companies to enjoy growing sales and growing margins. This situation was a positive one for shareholders, as the computer industry generally outperformed the economy during the decade.

But the impressive returns led even more companies to enter the market. A flush of mainframe and workstation companies like Amdahl, Floating Point Systems, Intergraph, and Stratus challenged IBM and Digital Equipment in the market for larger systems. With computer manufacturers entering the market faster than the market grew, margins started to drop by 1982, a trend that continued through the decade, causing many shareholders to reevaluate the profitability of their investments, pushing total return to shareholders, or TRS, in a downward direction through the 1980s. Hardware ended the decade well below the rest of the economy.

The high rate of entry into the hardware market in the late 1970s and early 1980s is an indication of how easy it had become to join the party. Any computer scientist with a garage could build a low-cost system that was comparable to many products on the market. New companies like Apple, Compaq and (later) Dell, along with component makers like Seagate, Western Digital, and Quantum, went after the desktop market, which had grown up from home hobby computers sold by Tandy and Commodore.

IBM legitimized and ultimately standardized the desktop computer with its PC. Simultaneously, the number of companies in the market grew dramatically. Interpreting these potentially conflicting trends, Standard and Poor's speculated in 1985 that it was unlikely that anyone would even bother to try to 'clone' IBM's latest personal computer, the AT, based on Intel's 286 processor and sporting 256k of RAM and no hard drive, presumably since IBM had such a commanding lead. Clearly, young Michael Dell missed the report.

In fact, many of the entries into the market continued to grow at the expense of IBM. Although its market share declined from its peak in 1970, it was still able to hold on to its profit margin until 1982, when it finally recognized the difficulties that it faced from competition. At that time, IBM announced that it expected the industry's sales to grow at a rate of 15 per cent, and that IBM intended to grow faster than the industry. In reality, the industry's growth actually slowed from 15 per cent in 1984 to 7–10 per cent over the 1990s. IBM's expectations of its own growth proved even less accurate. To drive its growth, it ramped up spending on R&D to $4.2 billion (9 per cent of sales) in 1984. Unfortunately for IBM, its investments were not sufficient to fuel growth.

IBM's business was built around large, proprietary systems that left them vulnerable to the new entrants in the field. IBM did not adapt to the development of standardized computer components, and only a few years after the introduction of the IBM personal computer, it began losing the battle for the burgeoning market.

By the mid-1980s, the hardware industry was suffering, and yet new companies continued to be formed. With margins falling and hardware companies underperforming the market in 1983, there seemed little incentive for new companies to join the fray. Yet the number of companies continued to grow through the rest of the 1980s.

Fig. 2.10 Semiconductors: 7-year rolling TRS versus economy

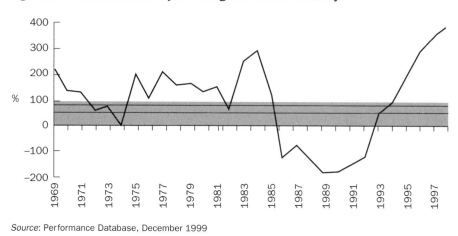

Source: Performance Database, December 1999

The same is true in other industries. For example, the semiconductor industry had superior performance for investors in the 1970s, reflecting not only the growth of computer hardware but also the growth of telecommunications, particularly the Internet (see Figure 2.10). Like the computer hardware industry, the semiconductor industry has gone through major technological discontinuities. The economic implications of these discontinuities were apparently difficult to forecast, as shown by the long periods of over and under performance of the semiconductor industry. In this case the discontinuity was the result of the switch from memory chips to microprocessors, but the effects for shareholders were the same as they were during the transition in computer hardware from 'big iron' to personal computers and software. It was difficult for the analyst and investor community to properly price the equities of semiconductor companies in the face of the technological risk and the aggressive actions of Japanese manufacturers to expand their share in the United States.

Software, the wunderkind of the late 1980s and early 1990s, has had two major periods of outperformance since it came into existence (see Figure 2.11). The ability of the software industry to develop and deliver products that apparently 'surprise and delight' its customers on a continuing basis for two decades now has exceeded everyone's expectations. In many ways the patterns in software appear to be similar to the early patterns in computer hardware and semiconductors. The future will tell whether this industry is able to sustain its above-average performance. A more complete description of the changes in the software industry is given on pages 43–4.

> The ability of the software industry to develop and deliver products that apparently 'surprise and delight' its customers on a continuing basis for two decades now has exceeded everyone's expectations.

Fig. 2.11 Software: 7-year rolling TRS versus economy

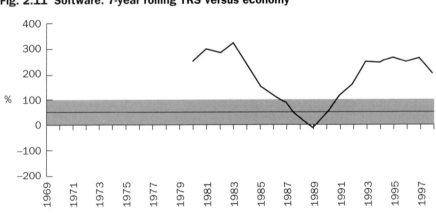

Source: Performance Database, December 1999

The oil industry has, quite by chance, shown a pattern that is similar to that of the computer industry, but for quite different reasons (see Figure 2.12). It proved difficult to accurately forecast, due to the difficulty in predicting the price of oil. The late 1970s afforded the industry a period of outperformance, since all the surprises were positive. But, like computers, it eventually substantially underperformed the economy. These changes directly reflect the formation and subsequent demise of OPEC and its control of the world's oil supply and pricing.

The pharmaceutical industry provides another example of forecasting difficulties (see figure 2.13). Pharmaceuticals performed well in the 1960s and

Fig. 2.12 Oil: 7-year rolling TRS versus economy

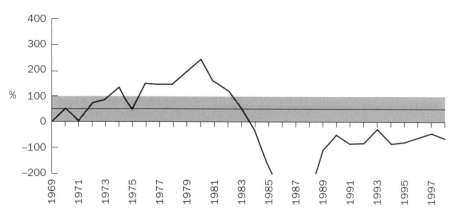

Source: Performance Database, December 1999

Fig. 2.13 Pharmaceuticals: 7 year rolling TRS versus economy

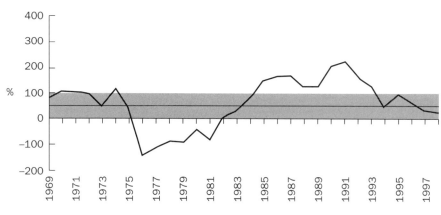

Source: Performance Database, December 1999

early 1970s, then hit a bump as Medicare and Medicaid legislation threatened to pop the balloon. This industry has come back, however. It benefits from exceptionally strong drug discovery and marketing skills, and strong patent protection of what it discovers. It is still delighting analysts and investors alike.

The medical products industry faced similar issues, but has rebounded, benefiting from the rapid advance in technology (see Figure 2.14).

The US defence industry, controlled entirely by the strategic needs of the nation rather than raw market forces, shows a pattern different from that of either the computer hardware or semiconductor industries, but is nevertheless as difficult to forecast as was the flowering of *glasnost* and the demise of the Soviet Union (see Figure 2.15).

Fig. 2.14 Medical supplies: 7-year rolling TRS versus economy

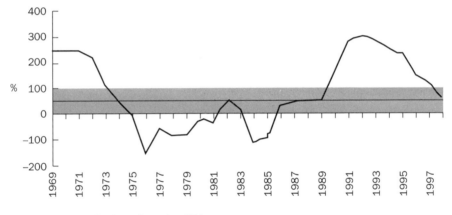

Source: Performance Database, December 1999

Fig. 2.15 Defence: 7-year rolling TRS versus economy

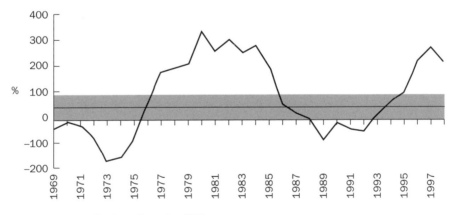

Source: Performance Database, December 1999

Software industry evolution

The computer industry first began to separate into the hardware and the software industries in 1970, when IBM made the decision to charge separately for the software that ran on its mainframes. Although companies like Ross Perot's Electronic Data Systems had been around since the 1960s, selling specialized data processing software for mainframe systems, the move by IBM created an opportunity for companies to build generic, 'packaged' software applications that could compete with some of IBM's offerings. The industry's fate didn't truly begin to diverge from that of the hardware industry until the arrival of the personal computer in the early 1980s. At the end of 1981, the software industry remained small. Software is primarily purchased for an installed base of computers, rather than for computers that have just been released, so the transition from mainframes to PCs that occurred in the mid-1980s wasn't fully reflected in the software industry until six years later. In fact, in 1990, the top two software companies in the world were IBM and Unisys. IBM's software sales reached nearly $10 billion, about as much as the remaining top 10 companies combined.

The potential of the PC, however, brought companies into the industry at an incredible rate, with each year between 1982 and 1986 finding as many new entrants in the industry as existed in the industry at the beginning of the year. Earlier in the decade, while software sales were growing rapidly, an influx of new entrants reduced the average size of software companies, increased competition, and lowered expected profitability. As a result, the median return to shareholders fell, bottoming out in 1986. Since then, however, total return to shareholders in the software industry has improved substantially, and has remained significantly better than that of the economy as a whole.

In 1987, the prospects for software companies brightened with the buildup of an installed PC base. Improvements in PC hardware (the introduction of the Intel 286 chip and a broader adoption of hard disk drives) allowed software companies to offer more complex and useful tools to PC users. Spreadsheet and word-processing packages became ubiquitous (if antiquated by today's standards). Improvements in PC operating systems, first with Apple's Macintosh and later with Microsoft Windows, enabled users to interact with computers through a standardized graphical interface, giving them access to complex features without needing to memorize a host of new keystrokes.

As computer usage increased, so did users' need to share files with others. This helped drive consolidation around particular applications. In 1985, for

instance, five of the top 15 business applications were word-processors (including Wordstar, Microsoft Word, and WordPerfect). By 1990, the number was down
to two, and by the mid-1990s, Microsoft Word was the only dominant player.

In many ways, software companies have reaped the rewards of innovation in
the hardware industry, even when hardware companies have not been able to
benefit themselves. A faster hard drive with greater capacity has little utility to
consumers unless it enables them to actually do something better or faster – and
that requires software. Since personal computer components (except, perhaps,
computer processing units, or CPUs) are interchangeable with the products of
other hardware manufacturers, companies in that industry have had to rely on
price to gain market share, whereas software companies have not. In fact, competition in the hardware industry enables more customers to purchase greater
computing for less, leaving more resources to spend on new and improved software to utilize the excess capacity

Investors in the defence industry benefited from both the intensification of
the cold war and its demise. The period of outperformance was substantial,
but like all other periods of outperformance, it had a beginning and an end.

There also have been industries that have more or less continuously
underperformed the markets, proving to be continually disappointing to
investors and analysts alike. The airlines industry stands out in this regard
(see Figure 2.16). Underperformance in that industry can be blamed on
any number of things – regulation or deregulation, increasing or decreasing fuel prices, the power of airframe manufacturers or engine

Fig. 2.16 Airlines: 7-year rolling TRS versus economy

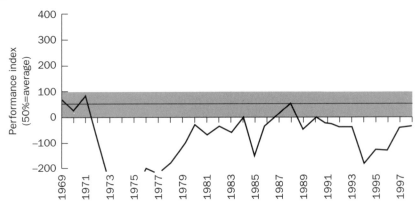

manufactures, or just blind, and unfulfilled, optimism on the part of investors. It shows, however, that it is possible to underperform the economy for sustained periods of time.

The sources of discontinuity vary greatly, as we have seen. Some are due to technological change, as is true of computer hardware and software; some are due to international competitive changes, as in the oil industry; others are due to the changing attitudes and policies of government, as we have seen with the defence industry or in telecommunications. And in some industries there are several causes. In pharmaceuticals, for example, both technological change and changing government policy play a part. In all cases they are very difficult to forecast accurately, and thus open the window to 'abnormal' returns. Try as we might, we have not found a single example of an industry that has continuously outperformed the overall market over this period of time. What the data shows is that outperforming the market is possible at the industry level, but it is almost always temporary.

> Outperforming the market is possible at the industry level, but it is almost always temporary.

Within companies

With regard to individual companies, we did not find any long-term survivors that had significant sustained outperformance. Nonetheless, we did find many (though certainly not all) new entrants that had stronger performance than that of their peers. The period of exceptional performance for these entrants varies, just as the period of exceptional performance for a newer industry varies, but ultimately it always comes to an end.

Storage Technology, a maker of computer storage devices (which we describe in more detail in Chapter 4), is a typical example (see Figure 2.17). Founded in the early 1970s, the company enjoyed exceptional performance in its first few years – better, in fact, than could be explained by the stellar performance of the computer industry itself during those years – by offering customers IBM-compatible mainframe components for a price that IBM was unwilling to match. Ten years later, however, the industry had eroded Storage Technology's lead, as the following exhibit shows.

Fig. 2.17 Storage Technology: Initial year, 1972 – 7-year TRS performance chart

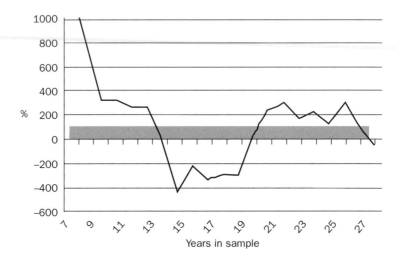

Years in sample

Storage Technology was forced to think 'bigger and bigger' to try to stay ahead. It even began to try to produce a mainframe to battle IBM head-on. After a couple of costly missteps, sales, earnings growth, and return on invested capital declined, its stock price finally collapsed, and the company found itself in Chapter 11 – before resurrecting itself once again by returning to its core business.

What does this indicate? As Richard Foster pointed out in *Innovation: The Attacker's Advantage*, new entrants into an industry have the upper hand in competing with older companies. To be sure, some, like Exabite, International Rectifier, and Unitrode, underperform the industry and there are circumstances in which new entrants fare worse than long-term survivors do (particularly in monopolies such as defence or electric utilities, or in industries such as pharmaceutical and medical products where research and product licensing discourages entrepreneurial efforts). But in most industries, new entrants, or 'attackers', have the advantage. That is not to say that all attackers are winners. That is certainly not the case. But it is the case that most winners are attackers.

In most industries, new entrants, or 'attackers', have the advantage.

In fact, if one looks at companies in all the industries we examined in the way described above, the results, while less dramatic, are quite similar. As Figure 2.18 shows, it is the new entrant that performs in a superior way.

Fig. 2.18 Eventually the edge wears off . . .

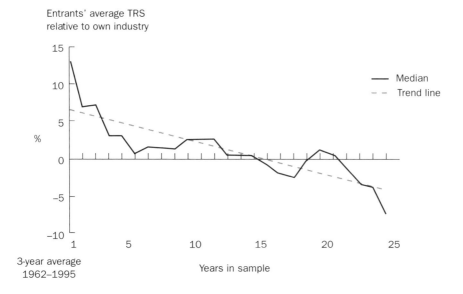

Eventually, its performance deteriorates to the industry average, and then below. There are three reasons for this pattern, which we will elaborate on in later chapters. First, the original innovation that the entrant brings is imitated or bested in the market, often by even newer entrants, leaving little excess profitability or growth available for the original innovator. Second, the market learns how to properly value the company, and returns accordingly approach the cost of equity for the industry. Third, the new entrant falls prey to cultural lock-in and can no longer create innovation on the scale that brought its original success.

Companies that outperform the market are temporary members of a permanent class. Many of these companies are in pioneering industries, or are pioneers in their own industry. During their period of outperformance they bring something new to the economy, either as an entire industry or as an individual company. Their 'excellence' is a result of their newness and utilitarian novelty rather than their enduring managerial skills. We have found that very few companies attempt to change at the pace and scale of the market. Yet only this kind of broad-based change can assure such corporations that their long-term survival will not result in long-term underperformance of the market. Excellence as such has been transitory rather than permanent; it has been episodic. Corporate 'excellence', like the exceptional performance of an industry, does not last for ever. It is always crushed by the forces of creative destruction.

DISCONTINUITY AND CREATIVE DESTRUCTION

The relationship between 'newness' and performance within companies and industries is vital. Newness within an industry is represented by the net rate of companies' entry and exit from the industry. The newer an industry is, the fresher it is. Turnover in industries is similar to turnover in a grocery store. The faster the turnover, the fresher the food. Newness is a measure of the pace and scale of creative destruction in an industry.

Newness is a measure of the pace and scale of creative destruction in an industry.

To see the details of how the processes of creative destruction work, we have created a new company index, or Newness Index. The Newness Index is an index of the pace and scale of net new companies entering an industry. The Newness Index is similar in spirit to simply measuring the rate of change among the companies listed in the S&P 500 index.

The Newness Index simply subtracts the number of companies leaving an industry over a seven-year period from the number of companies entering during those same seven years. To better allow us to compare between industries, we then divide that difference by the starting number of companies in the industry.

In our sample, the ratio of net entrants (entering companies minus exiting companies) relative to the number of companies in the industry has been increasing over the past 36 years, from about two net new companies for every 10 companies in the economy in the early 1960s, to about three in 1998. These rates of change can be thought of as the base rate of change for the economy. They are the rates of change that we will use later to judge corporate rates of change.

Just as market indexes are bolstered by new entrants, so are industries. New entrants are drawn into areas of opportunity by the potential for strong returns. Not all the new entrants succeed, of course. But the more successful among them are able to find a way to conduct their business with much higher rates of return than that of the incumbent survivors.

A few industry examples may help make the point more clearly. During the 1970s, the medical products industry had a rate of net entry lower than that of the economy overall. While the economy was adding two companies for every 10 companies in existence over a seven-year span, the medical products industry was actually losing companies through consolidation and contraction. At the end of the 1970s, however, this period of contraction reversed itself. The fear of adverse effects from Medicare and Medicaid had abated, and spurred by the potential of new technology, new companies began to enter into the medical products field. By the early 1990s, the medical products industry was adding more than five companies for every 10 that existed over a seven-year period (see Figure 2.19). That is an enormous rate of change.

Fig. 2.19 Net rate of new-economy entry: medical

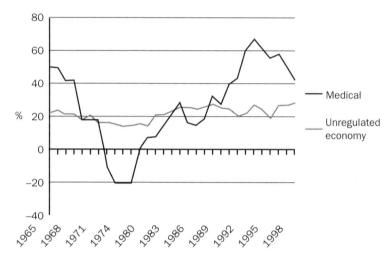

Fig. 2.20 Medical supplies: TRS versus net rate of new-company entry

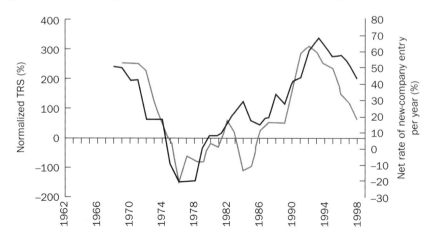

The rates of change are closely related to the returns investors received, as Figure 2.20 shows.

The same pattern is observed in other industries. In the oil industry, during the price boom of the 1970s, the net rate of entry increased.

So, too, did the return to shareholders.

Moreover, the return to shareholders was highest during the period of rapid entry. During periods of price collapse and economic pressure, the industry contracted, as can be clearly seen in Figures 2.21 and 2.22.

In the telecommunications industry, with the breakup of AT&T in the early 1980s, new spin-offs were formed, and the industry took on a dynamic

Fig. 2.21 Net rate of new-company entry: oil

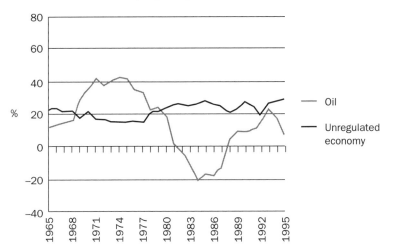

Fig. 2.22 Oil: TRS versus net rate of new-company entry

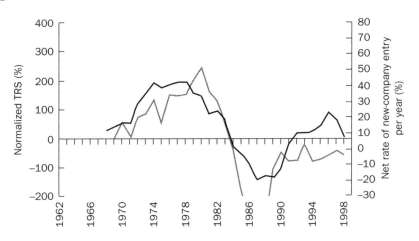

character. With the breakup, new customer services were founded, and new opportunities for cost and asset reduction were identified. Industry performance blossomed.

While it might not be surprising that these relationships exist, it is surprising that they are so strong. Many factors affect industry profitability and growth, as well as investor expectations about profitability and growth in the future. Such a strong correlation between total return to shareholders and the Newness Index of change suggests that these relationships are among the strongest in these industries.

Fig. 2.23 Net rate of new-company entry: telecommunications

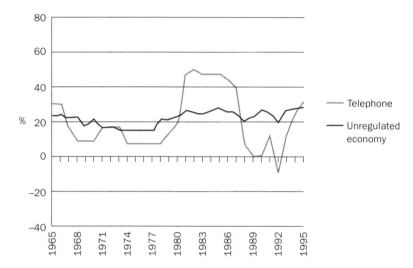

Fig. 2.24 Telecommunications: TRS versus net rate of new-company entry

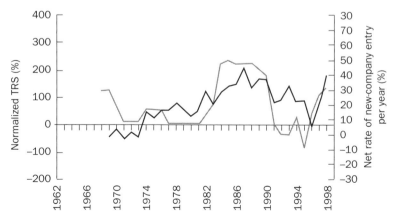

Source: Performance Database, December 1999

WHY NEWNESS WORKS

Why does newness correlate with shareholder returns? The missing link so far in our discussion of companies and newness is the role and influence of the investor. It is, after all, the investors' views about the long-term future value of the company's equity that count. It is investors who must be convinced that the value is there, or they will sell the equity. If enough investors sell, price pressure will drive the stock down. On the other hand, if enough investors feel that the prospects for the company are better than implied in the current price of the stock, they will buy it. If more investors seek to buy the stock than sell it, the price will go up until the demand of buyers is once again in balance with the supply from the sellers.

How does the investor, or a group of investors large enough to affect the price of a stock, decide what it's worth? How do they know what the future will be? As we saw earlier, some industries have been characterized more by continuity than by change. The forces at work kept the rates of entry and exit rather low. The game changes only slowly. To the astute observer, rather regular patterns of variation became clear. Under these circumstances, over time 'rules of thumb' can be developed. As long as the industry continues to operate within the limits that existed when the rules were established, the rules work.

Forecasts of the future are often made, as a practical matter, by analogy with the past. If continuity provides the general economic context, history will be an adequate guide to the future. In this case, one would expect the prices of stocks to be reasonably 'fairly' set, increasing only by the amount required to cover the cost of equity, as prescribed by well-known financial theory.

However, the markets are made up not only of industries characterized by continuity but of industries characterized by change, such as the computer hardware and software industries; the oil industry in the 1970s; pharmaceuticals and medical products during the age of managed care; and now industries affected by the Internet. How does one's forecast change? The answer, it appears, is only with great difficulty.

In the presence of discontinuities, the old rules of thumb do not work. Surprise events throw off traditional forecasting, such as the unfolding of the Medicare and Medicaid plans by the government in the early 1970s; or the increase and then decrease

> In the presence of discontinuities, the old rules of thumb do not work. Surprise events throw off traditional forecasting.

in oil prices due to the formation of OPEC in the early 1970s; or the over-supply of DRAMs in the semiconductor market in the early 1980s followed by the proliferation of microprocessors; or the technological transformation of the computer industry in the 1980s; or the breakup of AT&T and the gradual deregulation of the telecommunications industry in the 1980s; or the emergence of the Internet in the 1990s.

G. K. Chesterton, the late-nineteenth-century British novelist, social commentator, and the man who inspired Gandhi to work to bring national-ism to India, captured the conundrum of valuation during creative destruction when he said:

The real trouble with this world of ours is not that it is an unreasonable world, or even that it is a reasonable one. The commonest kind of trouble is that it is nearly reasonable, but not quite. Life is not an illogicality; yet it is a trap for logicians. It looks just a little more mathematical and regular than it is; its exactitude is obvious, but its inexactitude is hidden; its wildness lies in wait.

It is not hard to understand why, when markets are rapidly changing, they are difficult to forecast and their 'wildness lies in wait'. As a practical matter, one can't decipher the structure, determine how it works, and fast forward to see the future, as the East River Savings Bank discovered. The conventional model works in limited cases, but these cases will be less frequent in the future.

If one could foresee these discontinuous events, proper price adjust-ments could be made, but this appears to be a difficult task in practice. Moreover, discontinuities, and periods of rapid change, can trigger a major shift upward or downward. Outperformance occurs because an industry or company is able to surprise the investment community.

Nonetheless, the initial surprise cannot by itself explain the periods of excep-tional performance, either on the high side or the low side, that extend far longer than the duration of the discontinuity. How can this be? We think the reason for the extended period of outperformance is the failure of analysts and investors to reset future expectations of the industry or company rapidly enough. Because analysts are anchored to the past, they are unable to weigh the anchor and accurately reset their scenarios for the future at a sufficient pace.

There is a great deal of evidence that suggests that when people, for example, investors and managers, are taken out of a familiar environ-ment – an environment of continuity – their ability to deal with the future deteriorates rapidly. John Sterman, J. Spencer Standish professor of management and director of the System Dynamics Group of MIT, who has studied the ability of managers to learn over long periods of time, says that in complex environments, the more experience people have the more poorly they perform. Here is a distillation of Sterman's findings:

- 'Even in perfectly functioning markets, modest levels of complexity cause large and systematic deviations from rational behavior.'

- 'There is little evidence of adaptation of one's "rules" as the complexity of the task increases.' When the environment is complex, people seem to revert to simple rules that ignore time delays and feedback, leading to lowered performance.

- Individuals 'forecast by averaging past values and extrapolating past trends. [They] actually spend less time making their decisions in the complex markets than in the simple ones.'

- The lowered performance people exhibit as a result of greater complexity does not improve with experience. People become 'less responsive to critical variables and more vulnerable to forecasting errors – their learning hurts their ability to perform well in the complex conditions'.

- Most individuals do not learn how to improve their performance in complex conditions. In relatively simple conditions – without time delays or feedback – people 'dramatically outperform the "do nothing" rule, but in complex situations many people are bested by the "do nothing" rule'. Attempts individuals make to control the system are counterproductive.

Markets that are undergoing rapid or discontinuous change are extremely complex. Economic systems are highly networked and involve substantial feedback. Given Professor Sterman's findings, it is not surprising that forecasting deteriorates in the face of rapid change.

THE DIFFICULTY OF FORECASTING DISCONTINUITY

We believe investors deal with the complexity of the future by adopting a sceptic's bias in the face of good prospects – and an optimist's bias about poor prospects. It would not be unreasonable to attribute the deep cause of this 'bias' to

Investors deal with the complexity of the future by adopting a sceptic's bias in the face of good prospects – and an optimist's bias about poor prospects.

risk aversion. However, there is another, more compelling, reason for this bias: the use of forecasting algorithms that are anchored in the short-term (e.g., two-year) past of the industry or company, rather than analogies and patterns of industry evolution drawn from other sectors of the economy.

The McKinsey Corporate Performance Database shows that after a discontinuity, industries and the products and services that constitute them evolve slowly at first until they are established in the eyes of their customers. Then they evolve more quickly, until they have reached nearly all the customers they can, at which point the evolution slows down again. The pattern can be seen in Figure 2.25

We refer to this common pattern as an S-curve. While this pattern may vary somewhat for sales or earnings, for example, near the top of the S-curve it is not uncommon for sales to go into a cyclical period, or turn down rather than stay constant, it is a reasonable approximation in all industries we have studied. For example, in the US commodity chemical industry, which is probably in its mature state, the evolution of sales has followed the pattern shown in Figure 2.26. Often these patterns are difficult to detect for those in management or in the investment community focused only on the last few, and the next few, years, since the patterns are revealed only by a long view. The implications of the S-curve evolution of industries on traditional forecasts based on reasonable extensions of the past are significant.

Fig. 2.25 Typical evolution of industry earnings

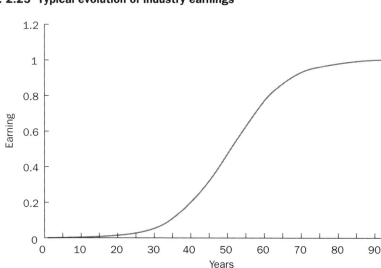

Fig. 2.26 Sales evolution

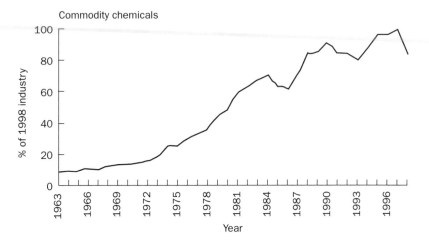

Commodity chemicals

First, early forecasts of long-term sales or earnings of a given company will be too low – too conservative – and will have to be continually adjusted upward as new data is accumulated. As these upward revisions are made, the stock price will rise and returns to shareholders will increase. In addition, later-stage forecasts will be too high, as analysts' predictions, based on previous quarters' growth, eventually outstrip actual performance as the growth curve begins to flatten (see Figure 2.27). Analysts find themselves continually adjusting their predictions lower, reducing returns to shareholders. In this way, discontinuities give rise to periods of a company's stock outperforming and underperforming the market.

This is exactly what happens in fast-moving industries like computer hardware. During the period from 1962 to the mid-1970s, both the total return to shareholders and the price-to-earnings ratio of the computer industry were above the corresponding levels in the US economy as a whole. This proved to be a nightmare for value investors who shunned this industry waiting for a better time to invest. When the 'better time' came, the companies were underperforming the market, and both TRS and price-to-earnings ratios fell below the level of the economy – until a new group of leaders took over in the market and drove performance up again by riding the new S-curve of personal computers and eventually the Internet. Of course, this flies in the face of a model of the capital markets that assumes high price-to-earnings ratios are associated with the probability of low returns. Figure 2.28 illustrates this.

Moreover, analysts and investors tend to be sceptical that companies can sustain high levels of growth for low levels of investment for long periods of

Fig. 2.27 Forecast errors

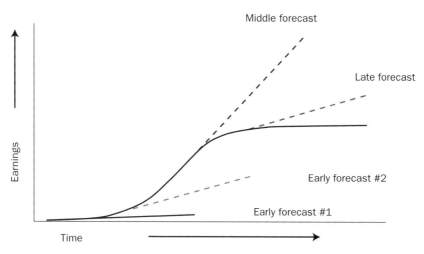

Fig. 2.28 Consequences of forecast errors for P/E and TRS

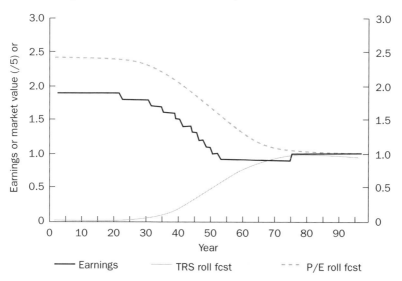

time. When managers confound these expectations, as Microsoft, Cisco, and Dell were able to do throughout the 1990s, they are richly rewarded, as we pointed out earlier. Some companies have shown that they can confound the markets for a decade or more if they are skilled in the arts of creative destruction.

Some companies have shown that they can confound the markets for a decade or more if they are skilled in the arts of creative destruction

HOW CREATIVE DESTRUCTION WILL WORK IN THE FUTURE

One implication of this understanding of how the processes of creative destruction work is that as the speed of change accelerates, the relative mis-forecasting can be expected to increase. Readers who have been following the 'dot.com revolution' know this can be the case. As the speed of change hits very high levels, there will be times when the estimated short-term value of the company will be several times (e.g., five times) in excess of any sustainable long-term model. As the forecasting errors are realized, market capitalizations come crashing down, as do price-to-earnings multiples and returns. A sad consequence of this phenomenon, which is nothing more than the application of the errors we have described above, is that total returns to shareholders can become substantially negative and can remain there for years, waiting for reality to catch up with forecasts. The inadequacy of forecasts is to blame for the 'bubbles' one sees in the market. And while the bubble begins at just about the mid-point of the earnings evolution, it reaches its peak before the earnings growth slows. This is generally far earlier than most analysts expect.

There are several implications for management:

- The opportunity for investments are more attractive in earlier years than one may have thought. Companies should take these effects into account when considering acquisitions.

- The risks of substantial reductions in price and total return to shareholders (albeit from very high levels) will increase as the pace of industry and company evolution increases.

- As the pace of industry and company evolution increases, there will be less connection between the quarter-to-quarter performance of the company and its stock price.

- Market volatility is likely to increase as the speed of industry and company evolution increases.

THE IMPORTANCE OF FOSTERING CREATIVE DESTRUCTION

Creative destruction underlies the realities of performance to this day – perhaps more than ever, as the Schumpeter quotation earlier in the chapter noted.

No company has demonstrated an ability to outperform its industry for long periods of time. The markets are simply too competitive to let one company get ahead and stay ahead. And analysts are too quick to try to match a company's share price to its rate of change and growth. Despite strong companies like Hewlett-Packard, GE, J&J, and comeback stories such as Kimberly-Clark, Colgate-Palmolive, DuPont, and Sherwin-Williams, in general the only companies to achieve and maintain above-industry-average returns are new, emerging companies. And even they earn their returns for a limited period, often less than a decade. They do well for a period of time

> The company that lasts for ever and performs in a superior way, rewarding its investors continually over time at above-average rates – is a myth.

because they are able to grow for longer periods of time at higher levels of profit than analysts expected. This combination of results surprises the analysts and results in strong total return to shareholders. The conventional notion of excellence – the company that lasts for ever and performs in a superior way, rewarding its investors continually over time at above-average rates – is a myth. The assumptions on which it is based simply don't hold up.

But perhaps the markets that excel at the arts of creative destruction suggest a model for stronger long-term performance: mastering continual change. It is the markets that set the standard for pace and scale of change. As we've seen, specific industries can sustain significantly higher levels of performance than that of the economy as a whole, and it is the industries that have faced and managed change the most that have had the best sustained levels of performance. The message is clear: only companies that change at the pace of the market can hope to match or exceed the overall market's performance. Unless companies change at the pace and scale of the market, their performance will almost inevitably slide into mediocrity.

The key for corporations is to mimic the pace and scale of change in the markets, without losing control of the operations they oversee. The markets, of course, do not have to worry about operations. Corporations do. Blending the creative destruction of the markets with operating excellence is an extremely tall order. Nonetheless, it is essential, for the pace of creative destruction in the economy is increasing. Over the past 70 years, hidden from general view, there has been a relentless acceleration in the introduction of newness to the US economy.

Our studies suggest that the pace of creative destruction will probably continue to accelerate in the decades ahead, albeit in cycles, putting substantially increased strains on corporations, many of which today continue to operate under the assumption of continuity. The reasons for a corporation's lack of willingness to change are deep, as we will see in the next chapter, and the problems are exceptionally difficult to address. But they *can* be addressed – if strong leadership can be found. New systems of management will have to be developed to capitalize on the 'wildness' of creative destruction, despite the difficulty of this task. For those who do not learn the lessons of discontinuity and creative destruction, the fate of the East River Saving Bank may well be their own future.

3 Cultural lock-in

> Things should be made as simple as possible, but not simpler.
>
> ALBERT EINSTEIN

For many years, IBM was everyone's favourite company. It represented technological virtue: innovation; an aggressive American spirit; the essence of American competitiveness. Yet, under John Akers, the company fell hard in the 1980s, and for a time its very survival seemed in question. As *The Economist* noted in 1993:

> When John Akers took over as chairman of IBM in 1985, it looked as if he had won the best job in American business. Still only 50, Mr. Akers had had a meteoric rise through the ranks. He seemed set for a secure tenure at the top of a great company whose technological and managerial prowess was both admired and feared throughout the world. Mr. Akers himself thought that IBM was poised for explosive growth. So did most other people. Instead, it has plunged into huge losses, and a chorus of critics is demanding his head.

When IBM failed, it failed in a major, dramatic, and public way rather than the slow, Alzheimer's-like way that many imagine to be the fate of large companies. It did not, like MacArthur's old soldier, simply fade away. It went with a crash, taking John Akers and many of his top managers with it.

What happened to this 'excellent' company? Could it have avoided its fate? How did so many intelligent executives misread the company's situation so completely? Why did they fail to take corrective action for so long? How could a dynamic leader like John Akers not see what was coming? Did IBM simply become too big? Did it become too bureaucratic? Did its technology lose its edge? Did its marketing become anaemic? Did it lose touch with its customers?

In our view, none of these things, in and of themselves, were responsible. Rather, the company's collapse was a collective failure of the mental processes, or the 'mind,' of the corporation. IBM's failure was the failure to see the present for what it is, a failure to see the rich mosaic of possibilities for the future. It was a failure of hubris – thinking that one company, no matter how powerful, is more powerful than the collective forces of the market. It was a failure to understand the context for decision making in the corporation. It was a failure of dialogue among the most senior managers, who preferred to review programmes and make decisions within the context of the view that IBM, and only IBM, was in charge of the pace of change of the computer industry. It was a failure to recognize that continuity – business as usual – is a fallacy.

In the 1980s, IBM was not facing 'business as usual'. IBM, in fact, was in the midst of a *market discontinuity* as personal computers came of age. Market discontinuities change and contort almost every aspect of managerial perception, rendering old ways of seeing and describing the world obsolete. Discontinuities challenge the most basic assumptions of continuity that companies create for themselves. In IBM's case, the company's thinking was based on the assumption that 'we should continue to invest in mainframe computers, where there is much more room for productivity improvement'. This may have been true, but it missed questioning whether even greater productivity improvements could be achieved with investments in personal computers. (Perhaps this second question was not asked with force within the company because of an implicit fear of cannibalizing its mainframe business.) Discontinuities of this sort present management with an almost unending stream of enigmas, dilemmas, paradoxes, puzzles, riddles, and mysteries, which remain unsolved until the mental context of the viewer changes. They present management with a maelstrom of disorder.

For many CEOs, being caught in a discontinuity is like falling into an Alice in Wonderland-like nightmare, where familiar people play vastly different roles, where the weak become strong and the strong are made weak. Would John Akers have guessed in 1983 that his successor at IBM would have virtually no knowledge of the computer businesses, and be drawn from the managerial ranks of tobacco and cookie companies? Would he have imagined a CEO with a background in credit cards and consulting who would one day be recognized as the saviour of the corporation? Would John Akers have imagined that a little start-up software company that had been an insignificant contractor to IBM would one day have a market capitalization several times as large as IBM's? Clearly not.

For many CEOs, being caught in a discontinuity is like falling into an Alice in Wonderland-like nightmare, where the weak become strong and the strong are made weak.

The reason IBM stumbled was that something was wrong with John Akers's view of the world – with his mental model. Akers believed in continuity, in gradual, incremental change. But the world had become discontinuous. The world Akers and IBM knew was shifting under their feet as the dominance of the mainframe computer faded. Discontinuities present management with an almost hallucinogenic trip through territory that they think they know but are suddenly incapable of navigating.

John Akers was not alone. The seismic shock that ran through the computer industry at the time was merely representative of shifts in other markets. The drug industry collapsed in the mid-1970s; defence rocketed up and then down; semiconductors went on a roller-coaster ride; airlines never escaped the gravitational pull of their markets, and sometimes dived to the bottom of the financial Marianas Trench. Discontinuities bring fundamental shifts in the way competition interacts in the marketplace (resulting in changes in companies' underlying performance) and the way in which investors infer possible future patterns, and therefore demand changes in mental models. As we shall see, mental models are often useful and necessary constructs. The world would be too complex to comprehend without them. Unfortunately, however, more often they feed the assumption of continuity than of discontinuity, for reasons we will describe later in this chapter.

MENTAL MODELS

The originator of the concept of the mental model was Kenneth Craik, a Scottish psychologist who in 1943 proposed that mental models are the manipulation of a vast variety of internal representations of the external world:

If the organism carries a 'small-scale model' of external reality and of its own possible actions within its head, it is able to try out various alternatives, conclude which is the best of them, react to future situations before they arise, utilize the knowledge of the past events in dealing with the present and future, and in every way to react in a much fuller, safer, and more competent manner to the emergencies which face it.

We form mental models of just about everything – cars, aeroplanes, corporations, ballet, opera, markets and their evolution, competition, operations, customer loyalty, consumer marketing, innovation, operational excellence, knowledge development and management, and so on. Forecasting, in particular, is an exercise in applied mental modelling. Some of these models may be static, while others, frequently the most useful ones, are dynamic. Some are quite real; many are symbolic. Some may be visionary. Some may have multiple legitimate interpretations, which depend on the perspective and context of the viewer.

Few business strategies are elaborated today without recourse to mental models, which depict the corporation and its role in the market, the economy, the competitive landscape, and the world as a whole. More often they are implicit and inarticulate, and often hidden or invisible. But they are there nonetheless. We cannot function without them. They are essential to reasoning. Anton Pavlovich Chekhov, the Russian playwright and poet who wrote hauntingly about the inability of people to communicate with one another, maintained that one must 'snatch at small details, grouping them in such a manner that after reading them one can obtain the picture on closing one's eyes'. Mental models are the mechanism by which we 'snatch the small details' and group them. As Albert Einstein observed, 'Man seeks for himself a simplified and lucid image of the world.'

Philip N. Johnson-Laird, a cognitive psychologist at Princeton University, notes: 'Small scale models of reality need neither be wholly accurate nor correspond completely with what they model in order to be useful.' In other words, there is some give and take. The painter, the poet, the speculative philosopher, and the natural scientist, each in his own way, make mental models of the world they intend to represent to others. So, too, with great investors or great managers, like Charlie Munger. John Akers, we could safely say, needed to apply more effort to the creation and use of mental models.

There are many examples of how models simplify the world without ignoring useful information. In the physical world, the science of data compression is focused precisely on this task. Data compression is an essential art in the computer and telecommunication industries. The mechanism for the compression is the removal of all non-essential data. What is non-essential information? Non-essential information is defined as all the information between two points that does not change – the white spaces on a page, for example. If all the white spaces – the areas where there is no information – are removed, while an accurate, but short, note is made of which white spaces were excised, where they began and where they terminated, one would have a shorter but accurate 'model' of the page. In this way, the message is simplified without losing its exact character. This is essentially the way mental models work.

Virginia Woolf once said: 'If there is one gift more essential to a novelist than another, it is the ability to develop single vision.' The concept of 'vision' is clearly a mental model of the future order of things. In business, visions are simplified representations of what the corporation stands for, where it is going, and which actions are acceptable and unacceptable. Members of the organization need to understand management's vision in order to assess whether their rewards are sufficient to justify their participation in it.

Of course, corporations have more than one mental model. There are, indeed, many mental models within a corporation. The mental model at a traditional manufacturing company, for example, may be built on the image of the company as a manufacturing process, with billing, receivables, and payables. A computer company may see itself as a network of interconnected nodes.

Whatever the specific representation, the mental models formed at the highest levels of the organization filter down to the divisional level. Lower-level models may be smaller versions of the corporation's larger mental model, or they may be different. But in either case, they must fit compatibly with the overarching model of the corporation if the corporation is to function smoothly.

The power of mental models

Craik would agree with Charlie Munger that mental models help investors and managers better understand the world, since they simplify an incomprehensibly complicated world. The need to simplify arises from our limited cognitive capacities. Our mental capacities, cognitive psychologists tell us, are quite limited compared to the complexities of life. We have limitations in our attention span, memory, recall, and information processing. The human mind's solution to the overwhelming complexity of today's world is to form mental models.

Johnson-Laird elaborated on the usefulness of this in his 1983 book *Mental Models*:

> Mental models play a central and unifying role in representing objects, states of affairs, sequences of events, the way the world is, and the social and psychological actions of daily life. They enable individuals to make inferences and predictions, to understand phenomena, to decide what action to take and to control its execution, and above all, to experience events by proxy; they allow language to be used to create representations comparable to those deriving from direct acquaintance with the world; and they relate words to the world by way of conception and perception.

Mental models are useful to the extent that they edit the world around us down to what we perceive as the essentials. 'A tight analogy or model permits us to know more about the world with less work,' notes Dean Keith Simonton, cognitive psychologist, historiographer, and noted researcher on the process of creativity at the University of California – Davis. As such, mental models can facilitate success or, if inaccurately shaped, bring failure. They help us determine how to take advantage of opportunities and how to hedge risks. They help us spot problems and work out solutions. Mental models and the rules of conduct generated from them, whether explicit or implicit, are at the core of most managers' reasoning processes.

Mental models aid managers in problem solving as well, particularly the complex problems that corporate decision makers face. Without recourse to mental models, our cognitive systems would be too overloaded with data to function successfully. The great virtue of mental models is their ability to simplify complex situations and distribute decision making so that thousands of people in a company can make decisions day in and day out without having to coordinate each of them with everyone else in the organization. However, there is great risk as well, since inaccurate mental modelling can leverage a myriad of decisions.

Mental models also facilitate dialogue and discussion. They allow us to interpret the language and acts of others. Language is essential to the construction of mental models. As James March, a professor of political science and sociology at Stanford University, noted: 'Language is used to create new meaning out of old, to make metaphorical leaps, to discover what a person might come to understand.'

John Akers had a mental model of IBM, but it was wrong. Bill Gates, too, had a mental model, which was right for a while, until he recognized it had to be changed. George Soros, Warren Buffet, and Charlie Munger all had mental models that worked very well for a while and now are under stress. As Brian Arthur, a professor at the Santa Fe Institute and, in the eyes of many the 'chief economist' of the New Economy, has noted, competition is competition within an 'ecology of mental models'.

The limits of mental models

As useful as mental models are for a while, they clearly have a dark side, as John Akers discovered. When faced with discontinuous conditions, the mental factors that people generally favour, based on experience, expertise, knowledge, and learning, become liabilities. The very mental models that are at the heart of managerial strength are also at the heart of managerial weakness in an age of discontinuity. This is precisely the environment that has been increasingly prevalent in today's market, one that will become even more common in the future.

When accurate, of course, mental models can help predict the future, and offer a distinct competitive advantage. But as appealing as they are, managers must remain vigilant, because mental models can be fraught with uncertainty, ambiguity, and errors. Inaccurate mental models can propagate errors in judgment and system design, result in errors of action, and, finally, result in poor performance. Shifting mental models requires real work. Because so many of our mental models lie hidden beneath the fabric of corporate life, shifting course can be difficult.

There are four general problems associated with mental models and their use: first, they can be wrong because they are limited by the simplifications that made them useful; second, they can be improperly used; third, they can lead to wrong answers if fed by incorrect information; and fourth, their effectiveness is rarely assessed. We will cover each of these points in turn.

They can be wrong

The effectiveness of mental models can be limited by the very simplifications that underlie them. Oversimplification can lead to systematic errors of judgment, logic, and forecasting. For example, an online marketer who assumes that consumers are going to continue to provide data about their habits, practices, and desires for free is making an assumption that could easily turn out to be incorrect. Already, some marketers are beginning to see that for relatively small fees they can circumvent major potential privacy liability.

Professor Kurt Gödel (1906–1978) of the Institute for Advanced Study at Princeton proved in the 1930s that no system can be both complete and consistent and that the errors inherent in mental models are inevitable. That is why those using mental models must be aware of their potential limitations and find ways to reduce the consequences of those limitations.

They can be improperly used

When the environment becomes truly complex, decision makers fail to respond appropriately by constructing new mental models. Instead they seem to revert to older, simpler models, as John Sterman suggested. Sterman observed that decision makers, for example, often forecast by averaging past values and extrapolating past trends rather than rethinking the forces at work in the industry and imaging how they might play out. Yet such complex relationships are increasingly common in the wired world of the Internet.

To the extent that mental models are inaccurate, they lead directly to risk (although it is often hidden risk, since the model does not alert the modeller to it). For example, in the last chapter we discussed the disastrous collapse of semiconductor returns in the early 1980s. The surprise in this was that no one anticipated it, even though it was well known that the Japanese were building new semiconductor plants at a large enough scale to swamp the industry with chips and cause prices to collapse. This is exactly what happened. But the mental models American semiconductor companies used led them to believe that prices could not decline as much as they did. The collapse took several companies with it, including Mostek, one of the leading players at the time. Mostek completely missed the impending collapse – and paid for that flawed mental model with its corporate life.

Require correct and timely information

Mental models are only as strong as the information they are based on. That information can be wrong, late, incomplete, distorted through emotion, ambiguous, or irrelevant, or it can be the result of inept measurement due to selection or other cognitive biases. Such imperfect information will inevitably misrepresent reality. If one does not have accurate and timely input, one will never get an accurate or timely output.

Require assessment

The construction and use of mental models, as Piaget pointed out, is often a process generally hidden from view, rather than a managerial process that is open to debate and challenge. Yet, as we've seen, the fact that mental models exist does not mean they are correct.

Rarely are 'quality control' processes used to check and test the validity of a mental model before it is put into use, or when it is in use to see if it is still accurate. Among the testing used to verify the effectiveness of other products, such as pharmaceuticals, are the use of 'double-blind' procedures to ensure that the absence of negative effects is not confused with the confirmation of a positive effect; actively seeking contradictory evidence, rather than seeking only evidence that confirms effectiveness; and searching for and considering alternatives to help ensure that the best alternative is selected rather than simply selecting an alternative that works. Without such quality control, the modelling process is open to error. Yet rarely are any of these procedures used, or even considered.

The need for new mental models can be obscured by contradictory data and incremental fixes to existing models. Changes in context should trigger re-examination of one's mental model, but often they do not. Since the mental models decision makers use specify the information they require, decision makers frequently reject information that challenges the relevance of the model itself. As the context changes, there is a strong preference for a leader to retain the existing model – for example, as the case of John Akers's insistence on relying on 'big iron'.

Loyalty to a flawed model can be costly. If a mental model becomes outmoded – in the sense that it no longer provides an accurate simplification or rendering of reality – then any conclusions or predictions derived from it will be distorted as well. There is a reluctance on the part of managers to change models because there is no guarantee that the new models will be more effective than the ones they are replacing. Consequently, if the existing models seem to be working, managers are reluctant to abandon them.

Decision makers seek data that confirms existing mental models, rather than data that contradicts such models.

Moreover, the leaders who created the existing mental models often have a vested interest in protecting them. They are unlikely to abandon them unless a change in leadership of the organization ushers in a new, more appropriate mental model. Studies show that decision makers seek data that confirms existing mental models, rather than data that contradicts such models. There is a natural human bias toward confirmation.

James March offers a telling illustration of the difficulties in changing mental models in his report about the accidental discovery of the hole in the Antarctic ozone layer:

> The NASA scientists' belief that low ozone readings must be erroneous (because they knew the ozone layer existed) led them to design a measurement system that made it impossible to detect low readings that might have invalidated their models. Fortunately, NASA had saved the original, unfiltered data and later confirmed that total ozone had indeed been falling since the launch of Nimbus 7. Because NASA created a measurement system immune to disconfirmation, the discovery of the ozone hole and the resulting global agreements to cease CFC production were delayed by as much as seven years.

Richard Foster had a similar experience in 1987 in China, while visiting a preeminent hospital there. When he asked the head of the hospital's diagnostics lab about the incidence of AIDS in China, the hospital administrator replied, 'We have no AIDS in China.' Amazed, Foster pressed further. 'In all your blood testing in China, you have never found a single case of AIDS?' he asked. 'Oh, no,' the administrator replied, 'we know we don't have AIDS in China, so we don't test for it.' As James March observed, 'Experience is edited to remove contradictions.'

Dean Keith Simonton offers a possible reason for this potentially dysfunctional cognitive behavior:

> To give up one's intellectual framework willy-nilly simply to accommodate the confusion of random events is to risk expanding psychological disorder, with a corresponding loss in behavioral adaptiveness.

The ability to dismiss disconfirming data is an ancient art. One way that people do it is through 'issue avoidance', by simply avoiding threatening or negative data. Chris Argyris, the James Bryant Conant Professor of Education and Organizational Behavior at Harvard, calls this form of avoidance a 'defensive routine'. Defensive routines may result in avoiding alternatives, or denial. 'You're wrong. We *are* innovating, changing, and keeping up with the markets, perhaps now more than ever,' an executive might argue when, in fact, all the innovation is incremental.

In a more contemporary example, when former McDonald's chairman Mike Quinlan was asked by *Business Week* whether, in view of McDonald's flagging performance, they needed to change their approach, Quinlan replied, 'Do we have to change? No, we don't have to change. We have the most successful brand in the world.' His admission was apparently so starkly wrongheaded in the eyes of the company's board that they fired Quinlan and found a new CEO.

The evidence is overwhelming that mental models, built to assist in decision making, once constructed often become the single most important barrier to change. We believe this problem will become increasingly pervasive as discontinuous shifts occur in industry after industry. The move to the Internet is just the first in a long series of what are likely to be confusing changes in context that will face most business leaders.

In this era of rapid change and increasing complexity, mental models represent a tool of tremendous promise – but also of tremendous risk. *To the extent they are built on the assumption of continuity, they are more of a liability to the user than a benefit.* We cannot avoid using mental models, however. It is the way we are wired. Our only choice lies in deciding which one to use, and how to use it. This means recognizing the need to change mental models, and finding a way to change them that is less costly than holding on to mental models that do not work. The executives at Mostek could compellingly discuss the costs of remaining with an inaccurate mental model.

CREATING AND CHANGING MENTAL MODELS

Piaget's research showed that we unconsciously create mental models from our earliest days. As we age we learn, from both formal and informal processes. Learning is one way of characterizing the process of changing mental models. 'The most powerful learning comes from direct experience,' says Peter Senge, author of *The Fifth Discipline*. We use our experience to change our mental models.

Jay Forrester, well-known inventor of magnetic-core memory storage, a precursor to today's RAM technology, and father of 'system dynamics', a systematic method of modelling complex structures, commented in 1971 on the simplicity of the mechanisms for changing our mental models:

A mental model changes with time and even during the flow of a single conversation. The human mind assembles a few relationships to fit the context of a discussion. As the subject shifts so does the model. Each participant in a conversation employs a different mental model to interpret the subject. Fundamental assumptions differ but are never brought into the open.

James March agrees. Mental models are often changed through the extended and informal process of corporate dialogue. This happens through 'myths, symbols, rituals, and stories. They are the ligaments of social life, establishing links among individuals and groups across generations and geographic distances.' March says elsewhere: 'They give context for understanding history and for locating oneself in it.'

During the dialogue process, mental models are adjusted to reflect local context. These adjustments are then fed back into the mental models of top management. In this way, the mental models change. As March noted about 'visions' – mental models in the process of formation 'cannot be established in an organization by edict, or by the exercise of power or coercion. It is more an act of persuasion, of creating an enthusiastic and dedicated commitment … because it is right for the times, right for the organization, and right for the people who are working in it. By focusing attention on a vision [mental model], the leader operates on the emotional and spiritual resources of the organization, on its values, commitment, and aspirations.'

Sterman also attests to the power of informal processes to change mental models:

Active modelling occurs well before sensory information reaches the areas of the brain responsible for conscious thought. Powerful evolutionary pressures are responsible: our survival depends so completely on the ability to rapidly interpret reality that we long ago evolved structures to build these models automatically.

Forrester's, March's, and Sterman's comments on the importance of conversation as a tool for aligning different mental models offer an important insight into how corporations can change mental models in a visible way, which we will explore in more detail in Chapter 11.

But more than conversation and dialogue is required to change a company's mental models. 'The constructive process is guided by contextual cues and implicit inferences based on general knowledge,' says Johnson-Laird. Contextual clues provide the puzzle edges that let us know where we are going – but only if we can interpret them (i.e., the

More than conversation and dialogue is required to change a company's mental models.

context) correctly. Often the culture of the organization sets the context. Language, visual imagery, beliefs and behaviour are the primary carriers of the culture and thus set the context.

Johnson & Johnson's response to the Tylenol crisis in the mid-1980s provides an example of the power of context for establishing new mental models, in this case a mental model of the right approach for dealing with the crisis. The crisis presented a complex problem for J&J because the causes were not clear, the consequences of not dealing with it were enormous (seven people in the Chicago area died after taking the pills), and the cost of stopping and fixing the problem was very large – large enough to jeopardize the market value of the corporation.

But one of the beliefs underlying Johnson & Johnson is its Credo, crafted by Robert Wood Johnson, which is still used as a guide to decision making and behaviour today. The Credo establishes the hierarchy of values at J&J: mothers first, employees second, community third, and investors fourth (the assumption is that if the first three are done well, the fourth will follow). The clarity of the Credo, and the dedication of the management and staff of J&J to the Credo, allowed Jim Burke to easily and rapidly decide what to do and how to act. His immediate decision was to recall Tylenol from drugstore shelves across the nation when there was a threat that the widely used pills were tainted. The incident cost J&J a reported $100 million that year, but the decision was made in hours when the threat to consumers became clear. In other corporations, recalls are not handled as quickly and perhaps not as effectively as they are at J&J because they do not have J&J's Credo. The Credo is a key element of J&J's culture, which plays a strong role in establishing the company's mental models when it faces a new situation, or in deciding when old ones are in need of repair.

Rarely do companies say they are 'setting out to build a new mental model'. But they do say they will 'develop a strategy to capitalize on the new opportunities in electronic commerce,' or that they will 're-examine the principles on which our organizational structure is based to compete more effectively in the future'. These are examples of statements of intent to create new mental models. Once built, mental models are enormously powerful in determining how the corporation responds to opportunities and challenges.

HOW MENTAL MODELS AFFECT CORPORATE BEHAVIOUR

Mental models have an impact on four primary areas of conventional 'corporate architecture': information systems, decision-making processes, executional capabilities, and control systems.

Information systems

The amount, type, quality, form, and frequency of data are effectively determined by senior management's mental model, whether that model is explicit or implicit. For example, many corporations believe that their performance is more dependent on sales margins than on capital employed. In these companies, the monthly profit and loss statements therefore capture information on sales and cost of goods sold (so that margins can be calculated), but do not reflect the capital employed in the business at all, despite the fact that investors are very much concerned with how much capital a corporation will need in the future.

Decision-making processes

The major decision-making processes of the corporation – planning systems, calendar management, agenda setting, decision criteria, and all the rest – are designed to be compatible with the mental models of the corporation. Needless to say, these decision-making systems are fed by, and therefore have to be compatible with, the information systems of the corporation. If the corporation feels that it is driven by the product-development cycle, as semiconductor manufacturers like Intel and Texas Instruments are, then this cycle drives the key decision-making processes (e.g., the decision to start the design of a new chip, or the decision to begin considering construction of a new plant, or the decision to switch suppliers for the next product offering), the executive calendar, the agendas of the major management meetings, and the strategic planning process. For a consumer retailer like Saks Fifth Avenue or The Gap, the calendar is driven by the major seasonal merchandising decisions, as well as very close monitoring, often day by day, of store sales to determine when a holiday sale (that is, selling their merchandising at lower prices to reduce inventories of already purchased products) should be started, stopped, or have its terms changed.

Executional capability

Third, the mental model must be compatible with the executional capability of the organization. The human resources processes, staffing, evaluation procedures, and so on, are determined within the context of the mental models of the corporation. For chemical companies like DuPont, international experience may be seen as key, since they see themselves very much as global players; indirect experience of, say, the business practices in China will not be sufficient. Direct line experience is preferred. For airline companies such as AMR, the parent of American Airlines, customer experience may be considered key, and those who have had frontline experience are seen as the most valuable.

Control processes

Last, the control processes – whether they be the operational control processes, the compensation systems, or the capital allocation processes of the corporation – all are determined by the mental models of the corporation. A company that has slim margins, such as an electric utility like Con Edison, will value those people most who know how to control costs on a day-to-day basis. A pharmaceutical company like Merck, Pfizer or Johnson & Johnson, which values the transformational innovation required for the discovery of new drugs, will not look at cost control as the most important control process, but will focus much more on finding the right scientists and giving them the freedom of time and resources necessary to maximize the chances that they will discover the new chemical entities that will be the key to more effective treatment of disease.

These four elements, as well as the mental models that determine how they interact, constitute what we call the architecture of the corporation. We call this corporate architecture 'MIDAS' – Models, Information, Decisions, Actions, and Systems of control – to make it easier to remember. The elements of the corporate architecture change as the corporation matures and the mental models change. And it is the evolution of corporate architecture – with the mental models steering the direction – that determines the competitiveness of the corporation. Thus the process of building mental models, whether these processes are explicit and examined or implicit and unexamined, is the core managerial process of the corporation.

> It is the evolution of corporate architecture – with the mental models steering the direction – that determines the competitiveness of the corporation.

THE NATURAL EVOLUTION OF CORPORATE ARCHITECTURE

As companies grow and mature, the five core elements of the corporate architecture, or MIDAS, and the relationships between those elements evolve in response to changing resources (including talent), competitive pressures, the culture of the organization, and prospects for the future.

We believe it is the nature of the evolution of the corporate architecture that accounts for the declining innovativeness of the typical corporation, leaving it more vulnerable to attack from smaller companies. Unlike older companies, newer companies, steered by different mental models, use different information sets, decision-making approaches, and systems of measurement and control. When those mental models are more accurate than older models, newer companies gain a huge competitive advantage.

Consider Transecure and General Motors, to take two extreme examples. Transecure is a very small Internet start-up focused initially on the resolution of legal conflicts that arise on the Internet. Transecure has experienced some early success and is rapidly building its business. Its mental model has evolved several times since Steve Abernethy and Ahmed Khaishgi founded the company in mid-1999. Early on in the process of starting the company, it was called WebLaw. WebLaw intended to offer legal services over the Web. As time went on, this notion was transformed into the present focus on dispute resolution, and the name was changed to Transecure. Having clarified its focus, at least for a time, it began to market the concept to other Internet companies that could build an inventory of disputes to resolve. There was no information system in place other than a list of people Abernethy and Khaishgi knew, or could get to know at Internet portals and auction sites. Decision-making systems were simple and aimed at getting the right people on their board to establish credibility and to find initial customers. The control processes were put into place by angel investors, who put up the initial funds to allow Abernethy and Khaishgi to eat while building Transecure. Most of this control stems from the right of investors to take over Transecure if things do not go as they should. There are very few other control systems in place. There are no 'strategic planning' systems, although there are frequent meetings to determine where to go next. There are no elaborate employee evaluation and feedback systems. That is more or less done on the fly, but with care. Abernethy and Khaishgi were fuelled by the pure passion to create something new; to change the world for the better with something they themselves had built. They were willing to risk everything to make it happen, and they were highly energized by the challenge and the risks involved. Transecure is not based on the assumption of continuity – quite the opposite. Transecure is based on the assumption of discontinuity. Abernethy and Khaishgi intend to create discontinuity, and they are comfortable with the assumption that Transecure itself will undergo several discontinuous transformations in its own development.

Contrast this architecture with that of a large established company, like General Motors. General Motors is clear about what it intends to do, and has been doing it for a long time. The key elements of its mental models were established by Alfred Sloan in the 1920s. To make decisions and communicate among its thousands of employees around the world, and among its many different kinds of transportation businesses, it has well-developed information systems based on huge investments in computers and communications. GM's decision-making systems have been honed for decades; many are now routine. Planning and control processes, including human resource processes, have been in place for decades, and are well fed by the information systems, which are tailored to the needs of these decision-making and control systems. Major investments have been made in enterprise resource management systems (ERPs) to help evolve the control systems in the most cost-effective way, and to integrate them as seamlessly as possible into the purchasing and supply chain systems, as well as the marketing and sales departments. It would be hard to say that General Motors is fuelled by passion. The senior management group is a very experienced and competitively oriented group dedicated to doing the best they can for General Motors, its customers, its employees, and its investors. But passion is not the hallmark of that system.

At one time General Motors was the size of Transecure, and it probably was ruled by passion then; but that was long ago. The architecture of General Motors today has as little similarity with the architecture of Transecure as it does with its own original architecture. The architecture of General Motors has changed over time, often with great purpose and forethought, but sometimes with consequences that were difficult to see in advance, including the emergence of the assumption of continuity, and the narrowing of the range of possible decisions, at least at the intermediate levels of the corporation.

The comparison between Transecure and General Motors illustrates the differences between the early architecture and the mature architecture of corporations. It is the assumption of continuity, when discontinuity rules the marketplace, that shapes the mental models of long-term corporations, and these mental models affect the rate of adaptation of the corporate architecture. It was the inadvertent – and unmanaged – evolution of IBM's corporate architecture that resulted in John Akers's difficulties. Akers was not able to see the need to transform his mental model of the computer hardware business; he was more comfortable operating with the model that had brought him and his colleagues success within IBM. With this understanding, there was no need to change information systems (say, to more closely track the progress of smaller competitors that were selling different products to IBM's clients, products that these customers in some cases liked very much), decision-making systems, implementation approaches, or control systems. In fact, there was no need, in Akers's mind, to change much other than the effectiveness of the sales force. They should just get out and sell more, and the 'problem' (i.e., the enormous earnings decline) would be solved.

It was the wrong analysis, and it led to the wrong answer. It also led to Akers's removal. While Akers's model was based on the assumption of continuity, the industry was going through one of the most significant discontinuities in its history. It was a discontinuity that was effectively hidden from the view of IBM's management committee at the time, as incredible as it seems. They could not see it because their mental models would not allow them to accept the validity of the information they were receiving. Defensive routines had silently crept into the corporation, unannounced and unnoticed.

Unmanaged, the evolution of the corporate architecture proceeds in a predictable way, which inevitably leads to cultural lock-in – a state in which the corporation is effectively frozen in place by three fears: the fear of cannibalization of the existing product line, the fear of moving into businesses that will conflict with its customers', and the fear of acquiring companies that will result in the short-term dilution of the company's earnings and therefore a potential decline in stock price. Unable to act in the face of these three fears, the corporation sets the context for its own underperformance, just as IBM was doing until its board of directors acted by replacing John Akers with Lou Gerstner. There are four key stages in the evolution of an industry. We present a light sketch of each to give the reader some sense of how cultural lock-in occurs within intelligent, thoughtful corporations despite the best efforts of managers.

STAGE 1 – FOUNDATION (ATTACK)

In any new industry, many new companies are drawn to capitalize on the opportunities. We saw in Chapter 2 how this had routinely happened in computer hardware, computer software, medical products, and several other industries. Many of these companies are very much like Transecure, created and led by a few people in their twenties or thirties who are fueled by their passion to change the world. They are willing to work all day and all night. Their mental models are still fluid. Decision making is ad hoc, or at best, guided by the structure imposed by investors and board members. As Robert Simons says:

In the start-up phase, there is little demand for formal control systems. Because employees are in constant face-to-face communication with each other, it is possible to control key aspects of the business without formal reporting structures. Internal accounting controls to ensure that assets are secure and accounting information is reliable are the only formal control systems needed.

During this phase, success either happens or it does not. There is little reflection about why. The day-to-day work is all-consuming.

Outsiders might consider these companies creative, but, in fact, the creative stage, the stage where the idea is first laid out, is largely finished. Abernethy and Khaishgi did not formulate the original idea for WebLaw when they were at Transecure. In fact, they developed it while they were at McKinsey working as hard as they could for their clients during the day, and at night working as hard as they could to figure out how to start WebLaw. This is often the way it is, whether the new entrepreneurs are at McKinsey, a university, or another corporation. The creative ideas are often revealed during the off hours of the day. Once the business starts, there is little time left for anything other than making it work.

At this stage, many of the competitors in the sector are not able to survive. Frequently they are purchased by other larger companies in their field. Some go bankrupt. A few, however, survive, and advance to the next stage.

STAGE 2 – GROWTH

The second stage in the evolution of a new industry is characterized by rapid growth. Frequently this is at the lower knee of the S-curve, as we explained in Chapter 2. Many Internet companies are in this stage now, as are a number of biotech companies. Having passed the first test of survival, with a few hundred people to manage (which is a typical number at this stage), some of these companies begin to reflect on the causes of their success. Often, they will attribute their success to their 'unique' blend of market insight, technological strength, and managerial methods and culture. In fact, their success may have been due to good fortune rather than good management, although it can be difficult to sort out. They believe they have done well – that is, grown from a few people to several hundred people – because of their intelligence and the actions they have taken, the quality of the people they have hired, and the managerial systems they have built.

In this stage the company tends to operate in many locations and in multiple markets. Formal training systems have been implemented in an effort to make sure that new employees are told about the corporate culture, why it is successful, and how it works, regardless of where they work or for whom. Mission statements are created and distributed. Managers have been told that certain activities are taboo. Decision making is increasingly delegated to lower levels. Measurable goals are established. Diagnostic control systems are implemented to meet the information and control needs of senior managers. Performance incentives are tied to the achievement of measurable targets. Once in place, these formal systems and additions to the invisible corporate architecture become difficult to change. The original passion has given way to the superiority of rational decision making. There wasn't time for it in Stage 1; there was too much to do.

The growth prospects of such companies are typically as strong as, or stronger than, ever. There are many opportunities to pursue extensions of their existing strategy, and these still make money and do not require changes in the skill base. Management is aware that the markets and competition are constantly changing, so they look outside for evidence of competitive threats to determine the need to do something more radical, but often they don't find anyone doing 'just what we are doing'. There is no crisis looming. The present course can be stayed without risk, although today companies in this stage are perhaps more sober about their success and prospects than they were a year ago.

At the end of Stage 2, a few more of these companies are acquired by competitors, although often at a premium price. In communications, for example, Cisco is a likely acquirer today, as is Lucent. Despite the premium they have to pay, they see these companies as attractive complements to their current product lines, and a valuable resource for the future.

STAGE 3 – DOMINATE

Those companies that survive to Stage 3 have come of age. A few have risen to dominate their industries and become models of managerial acumen. They have scale, resources, talent, and insight. It seems as if they will last for a long time. Ariba, Commerce One, Broadcom, and others are examples of such companies today. They have become the 'excellent' companies that reporters, academics, consultants, and executives drop by to see. When asked how they did it, they often respond with details about their corporate architecture – the systems, their information, their ability to execute, and their control processes.

The frequent implicit objective at this stage is to refine and extend their successful system of management, often by acquiring other companies and indoctrinating them into the parent's successful culture. Everything and everyone runs like clockwork. Robert Simons describes this stage as follows:

In mature firms, senior managers learn to rely on the opportunity seeking behavior of subordinates for innovation and new strategic initiatives. At this stage, they begin to use selected control systems interactively. Belief systems, strategic boundaries, diagnostic control systems, and interactive control systems now work together to control the formation and implementation of strategy. Finally, businesses' conduct boundaries are imposed any time that a crisis demonstrates the costs of errant employee actions.

The company has become a real machine. There is little surprise – as long as continuity prevails.

But surprise is often lurking at this stage, out of view of the newly large and successful company. Stage 3 companies often have difficulty identifying threatening Stage 1 companies because these companies exist on the periphery of an industry and often look different than what Stage 3 companies are used to. Perhaps they base their oblique attack on insights from a dissatisfied group of customers, or a potentially risky or potent new technology, or just on the slow reaction speed of the Stage 3 company. If a credible attack forms, it will be aimed precisely at the weakest spots of the current market leaders. Nothing else will have a chance of success, due to the scale and market power of the leaders. It is generally virtually impossible to predict which of the would-be attackers will be successful, but it is easier to assess whether the attack itself will be successful. The outcome is a matter of economics and timing, and more attacks fail than succeed. Nevertheless, some do succeed, and these reach prominence in the market outside the vision of the successful Stage 3 company. These attackers are the carriers of discontinuity.

Amazon.com is an example of the impact a Stage 1 company can have on a mature company, in this case, Barnes & Noble. How could Amazon, a start-up company with few resources, compete with established superstore chain Barnes & Noble? As everyone knows, Amazon had a new idea – that literate people would be great users of the Internet, and that they would buy more books that way than in the store. Amazon took this simple idea and executed it well. Within two years, people were asking, 'How can Barnes & Noble compete with Amazon?'

Barnes & Noble didn't take Amazon seriously at first because it was so locked into the assumption of continuity (as well as the traditional myths about advantages of scale, market power, consumer knowledge, and financial resources). It could not imagine that discontinuity could so rapidly alter the bookstore landscape. Barnes & Noble has since gotten the message, but it allowed Amazon to gain an enormous online advantage because it was so focused on the assumption of continuity.

Not surprisingly, many new companies fail. Most end up being bought by another company, or end up in bankruptcy court. The markets are simply not big enough to hold all the companies that want to capitalize on the opportunity they see. Unsuccessful competitors either entered the market too early or too late, or could not implement their ideas successfully, or didn't offer enough of a competitive advantage over existing companies. A few new companies survive, however. The handful of new entrants that survive will have found some weakness to exploit in the existing order. The market will reward them by boosting their stock at every surprising advance.

Finally, there comes a time when a younger attacker goes for the jugular. It has gained the upper hand. The attack almost always comes as a 'surprise' to the incumbent. Was Time Warner prepared to be acquired by AOL in 2000? Was IBM prepared for the strength of Ariba and Commerce One, or earlier, the strength of the younger Microsoft Corporation?

STAGE 4 – CULTURAL LOCK-IN: THE EMERGENCE OF THE THREE FEARS

In this final stage, the formerly dominant company finds itself in a fight for its very survival. Often, the only real defence a company has at this point is to cut prices. There are many ways to do this that do not appear to be price cutting, such as increasing the value of the product offered. But in the end, most companies resort to price cutting. If the prices can be cut far enough, and fast enough, the attack may be postponed, at least for a while. But the problem is unlikely to end there. One or two attackers may be turned back, but new competitors will continue to come if they perceive a business opportunity. Eventually one will break through.

In such fights, emotions sway both combatants. The attacker will use passion, conviction, and other 'hot' emotions. Incumbents often slip into dark denial, first denying that the attack is imminent, then that it is under way or that it is having a significant impact. The battle constitutes an assault on the mental models of the corporation, the foundation beliefs upon which decision making is based. Just as the human mind recoils, first in denial and then in anger, from the suggestion that its assumptions are wrong, so, too, does the corporation.

Just as the human mind recoils, first in denial and then in anger, from the suggestion that its assumptions are wrong, so, too, does the corporation.

Psychologist Elisabeth Kübler-Ross has discovered that the human mind shuffles through five distinct phases as it deals with trauma and other negative information: denial, anger, bargaining, depression, and, finally, acceptance. Each stage is interwoven with bouts of hope, followed by despair. These are normal and natural progressions in corporations as well as individuals, as the mind attempts to shield itself. But each step in this natural process slows or blocks incoming information. Accordingly, the need to change mental models is blocked, and disaster is courted; defensive routines appear. At IBM in 1989, for instance, John Akers boldly announced: 'I don't think there were fundamental changes in the market conditions.'

In 1991, as everything came crashing down around him, Akers angrily sent out what he thought was an internal memo denouncing the sales force – which immediately found its way to *The New York Times*: 'Everyone is too damned complacent, and it makes me goddamned mad.'

Where you see anger among top management, look for the signs of denial.

As psychologist Priscilla Vail notes, in discussing how children learn:

We know from common sense, experience, and now neuro-psychological research that positive emotional stances enhance a child's capacity for learning, just as negative ones – some of which become habitual – deplete intellectual energies.

The same is true of corporations.

The cycle of denial and disconfirmation in a corporation manifests itself in the fear of cannibalization, the fear of customer conflict, and the fear of dilution.

Cannibalization

In the business world, cannibalization is the act of introducing products or services that compete with the company's existing product line, as Richard Foster explained in *Innovation: The Attacker's Advantage* and as Clayton Christensen elaborated on in *The Innovator's Dilemma*. When companies decline to cannibalize their own products, they are operating under the delusion that if they don't introduce the new product, no one else will either. Thus, they reason, prices will remain firm, and profits will be protected. Companies further support this rationale by pointing to their strong market share, and the high costs that consumers would suffer if they switched to a competing product.

The fallacy in this thinking is that new competitors *do* enter markets (unless a company has a monopoly, which is rare). Furthermore, the value of the incumbent's market share is actually minimal, since the new product, if it is a serious contender, by definition offers substantial new benefits. Customers, taking the long view, may decide to switch to the new product, despite the near-term costs of switching.

The decision not to cannibalize, then, can lead to a loss of share and deteriorating performance. In some cases it can lead to permanent market losses. IBM's decade-long inattention to the software market is a case in point. Had Lou Gerstner not taken over as chairman, IBM might not have survived.

Competing with your customers

The second fear, competing with your customer, can be as fatal as the failure to cannibalize. Companies resist doing anything to jeopardize their relationships with customers, particularly when the company has a small number of important customers. Unfortunately, the customers realize this, and use that leverage to keep the company from expanding its distribution channels.

As with cannibalization, the error is in assuming that a new set of companies will not emerge to compete for a share of the market, skipping wholesale channels and selling directly to end customers. Dell, for example, does not deal with Wal-Mart. They went directly to the customer. Other companies, such as Compaq, could have gone the same route, but they were afraid of alienating their existing customers. This was the market opening that Dell charged into with such astounding success. Cisco, the supplier of routers and hubs, has shown the same courage in its distribution system, but not without some conflicts. The Internet and e-commerce have accelerated this trend. (CEO John Chambers cemented customer loyalty by introducing the Internet as a direct distribution channel.) Cisco's dedication to customer satisfaction subsequently has been exemplified by this use of the Internet to lower customer costs through efficient transactions and provide comprehensive customer support. This decision ultimately resulted in huge savings ($535 million in 1998) and deepened relationships with customers. Shipments were accurate and on time 98 per cent of the time, and 60 per cent to 80 per cent of questions were handled online. In 1998, Cisco reported dramatic on-line growth: almost 1 million log-ins per month, with a 25 per cent increase in customer satisfaction.

Earnings dilution

The third fear is the fear of dilution. The fear of dilution makes it very difficult, if not impossible, for incumbents to purchase companies on the periphery – those that are pursuing a potentially superior business strategy, or that have access to unique talent or other assets. The argument (based on traditional financial analysis) is that if one dilutes one's earnings per share, the market will simply apply the same multiple to the new combined company that it used before the acquisition. Stock prices will decline and value will be destroyed.

Today, dilution is the argument many incumbents use to explain why they have not acquired Internet start-ups. Unfortunately, this argument also blocks them from entering vigorous new markets. In the end, it could destroy more value than what is risked in the acquisition. Moreover, this analysis assumes that the market cannot be convinced that the acquisition will improve the long-term prospects of the incumbent. Dilution analysis also assumes that the growth of the acquired company will not more than offset the dilutive effect of the purchase in a reasonable period of time. In the early days of biotech, most of the major pharmaceutical companies could have bought Amgen but did not, for fear of dilution. Now Amgen earns more per quarter than the entire acquisition price would have been a decade ago (regardless of the multiple at the time). Clearly, conventional economic thinking led to the wrong conclusions. The right way to look at this problem is to develop a point of view on what the future value of the company will be, as we showed in Chapter 2, and then decide if it is worth it to pay that price.

These three fears of corporations, which amount to the fear of making contrarian strategic decisions, determine whether or not a corporation has the courage to position itself well for the future. The market, we have seen, has no fear. The market will cannibalize; it will compete with customers, and it will encourage the growth of high-multiple companies. The market does not suffer from denial. *To achieve the success of the market, corporations have to change their mental models at the pace and scale of the market. They will have to overcome the disconfirmation biases and the defensive routines that sustain it.* Unless the corporation can learn to overcome the natural bias for denial, it will, in the long term, fail, or at best underperform. Such fears culturally lock corporations into inaction. Survival may be assured, but so is a company's underperformance. The assumption of continuity hurts or inhibits a corporation's future. In the fifteenth century, Machiavelli advised leaders to ignore discontinuities:

When a problem arises either from within a republic or outside it, one brought about either by internal or external reasons, one that has become so great that it begins to make everyone afraid, the safest policy is to delay dealing with it rather than to do away with it, because those who try to do away with it almost always increase its strength and accelerate the harm which they feared might come from it.

Such advice may have worked in fifteenth-century Italy, but it will not work in the twenty-first century global economy. The solution, today, is to recognize and embrace the prospect of discontinuity.

THE MIND OF THE CORPORATION; THE MIND OF THE MARKET

We began this chapter with a story about IBM and the difficulties John Akers faced. The question that we raised was: Why do the indices of the capital markets over the long run outperform all but a handful of even the best individual companies, despite the fact that markets have no intelligent executive committees, boards of directors, CEOs or CFOs to lead them? The capital markets are not 'managed' in the conventional sense of the word. They are merely 'administered'. Moreover, the markets have no performance objectives. No one at the SEC is 'controlling' the total return to shareholders of the New York Stock Exchange. We administer markets, we don't manage them. Attempts at the opposite approach have failed, as any Russian can attest.

The question, then, is: Why should an unmanaged system achieve a level of long-term performance that is matched only by a few companies in the managed system? Why does a system lacking a centralized cognitive superstructure consistently prevail over a system richly equipped with one? The answer, as we outlined in Chapter 1, is that the capital markets are naturally more robust and adaptable than our corporations. Adam Smith noted in *The Wealth of Nations*:

> Every individual is continually exerting himself to find out the most advantageous employment for whatever capital he can command . . . [and] is led by an invisible hand to promote an end which was no part of his intention.

Smith's invocation of the invisible hand was the first attempt to explain the superior performance of the unmanaged system against a conscientiously managed one. The much-sought-for 'sustainable competitive advantage' is an unattainable ideal. It does not exist. It is continually and inexorably carved away by the relentless winds and tides of the capital markets. Many managers and executives have a deep, presumptive belief in the success of rational thinking. It is a belief psychologists are increasingly challenging.

Many managers and executives have a deep, presumptive belief in the success of rational thinking. It is a belief psychologists are increasingly challenging.

Markets effectively 'reason' through social process; corporations use 'rules of inference'. Daniel Kahneman, a psychologist at Princeton, and Amos Tversky, a psychologist at Stanford until his death in 1996, who had extensively studied the psychology of decision making, questioned the assumption that 'only rational behavior can survive in a competitive environment, and the fear that any treatment that abandons rationality will be chaotic and intractable'. The effectiveness of orderliness in a discontinuous world must be questioned.

One would not say that the markets are necessarily orderly, although the rules they live by are orderly and rational. The rules of the market do not prevent discontinuity; rather, they encourage it. Our inadvertent reliance on stable, often invisible, mental models may have worked in previous decades, when the future was more or less like the past. But it does not work today, with the markets' current rate of change, nor will it work in the future, as the rate of change continues to accelerate, in line with long-term historical trends.

The fact is that capital markets embrace creative destruction more effectively than corporations do. Moreover, markets engage in creative destruction at a greater pace than ever before. Operational excellence will continue to be essential for competitiveness. But it simply will not be enough. The assumption of continuity and its intimate link to operational excellence must give way to the more complex assumption of discontinuity and its intimate link with creative destruction. That is the challenge to management in the coming decades.

In the following chapters, we will lay out the nature of these changes and describe what is required for the corporation to act more like the market.

4 Operating versus creating:

The case of Storage Technology Corporation

The data storage company Storage Technology was founded in 1969 by four IBM engineers who believed they could build disk and tape drive systems for IBM computers at a lower price than their former employer did. Storage Technology was one of the first companies to spin off from IBM with the explicit idea of challenging IBM. After reporting its first profit in 1972, Storage Technology grew dramatically, exceeding $1 billion per year in sales in 1982.

After reporting its first profit in 1972, Storage Technology grew dramatically, exceeding $1 billion per year in sales in 1982.

Jesse Aweida, founder of Storage Technology and CEO until 1984, was convinced that a high level of operational management and 'just enough' innovation would keep the company ahead of IBM. Transformational innovation, he decided, was not necessary. 'To compete with IBM,' Aweida said, 'a small company has to focus down and concentrate on a very narrow market, such as tape drives. In that market, you have to commit to technological innovation.'

Aweida implemented this strategy by investing in highly focused R&D that minimized manufacturing costs and yet enabled Storage Technology to match new IBM products within six months of their arrival in the market. This became the company's strategy for accommodating operational effectiveness *and* innovation. Aweida knew that he could not take on IBM directly, so he limited innovations to a specialized area, attempting to keep the company ahead through manufacturing cost reductions. Aweida's objective was to operate and manage the process of creative destruction in parallel. Implicitly, he was attempting to overcome the assumption of continuity.

Initially, Aweida's strategy worked. Throughout the 1970s, it sold its products at a 15 per cent discount to IBM's products. Storage Technology's market share rose, and it won a reputation for providing components of equal or better quality than IBM's. Sales surged at well above industry average growth rates (see Figure 4.1).

The stock market responded to Storage Technology's success, giving the company a high multiple and rewarding its long-term shareholders with higher returns than were being earned in the computer industry in general (which itself was above the capital markets averages).

Innovation played its part in the company's success. Storage Technology's first tape drive not only matched IBM's newest release but even surpassed it, since it could read tapes of an earlier IBM format (a feature the new IBM devices did not offer). Moreover, when IBM developed disk drives with non-removable disks in the 1970s (called hard drives today), customers were no longer able to create data backups simply by

Fig. 4.1 Storage Technology 1972–1981: Sales growth versus industry

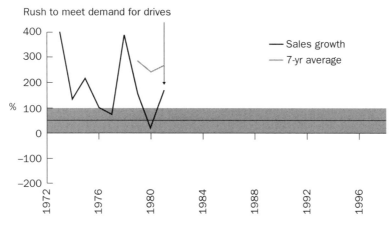

Source: Performance Database, February 2000

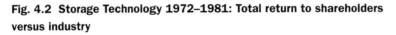

Fig. 4.2 Storage Technology 1972–1981: Total return to shareholders versus industry

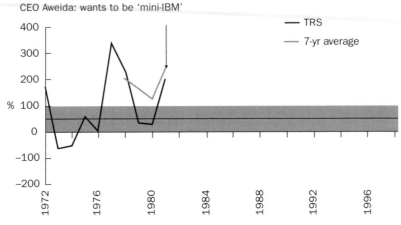

Source: Performance Database, December 1999

inserting a second disk. This was manna for Storage Technology, which had been looking for a way to expand into disk drives. By 1981, Storage Technology had made the transition from a Stage 1 company to a Stage 2 company. It was an early survivor, and the shareholders were greatly rewarded for it.

As Storage Technology continued to grow, however, the delicate balance between operational excellence and innovation began to destabilize. Seeking more growth, Aweida shifted his vision for the company. His new goal was to make Storage Technology a 'mini-IBM' (see Figure 4.2).

The first step of this journey was to expand Storage Technology's original narrow vision (focused on dominating hard drives) to a grander vision to compete with IBM in mainframes. Discovering that it would be difficult to match IBM with only its own research, Storage Technology pursued the acquisitions of Amdahl Corporation (headed by former IBM chief engineer Eugene Amdahl) and Magnuson Computer – small companies trying to produce IBM-compatible mainframes and minicomputers. Ultimately, Storage Technology spent $120 million in collaboration with limited partners to develop its own mainframe. Aweida's second step was to

> Storage Technology believed that optical storage drives would leave magnetic media in the dust. The vision was pure creative destruction.

spend heavily on the development of optical storage drives. Storage Technology believed that optical storage drives would leave magnetic media in the dust. The vision was pure creative destruction. But in trying to develop optical storage drives, operations at Storage Technology had taken second place. The balance was about to become unbalanced.

Because IBM experienced delays in its new 3380 line of disk drives and had none to sell, Storage Technology had an opportunity to sell all the drives it could produce. But Storage Technology tripped on its own operational shoelaces. 'We said to ourselves, "Boy, here is an opportunity to really double up the market," so we tripled production. That was a big mistake,' Aweida later reflected.

In order to triple production, Storage Technology accepted component parts from suppliers that did not meet specs. Within a year, 10 per cent of the drives the company produced were faulty. Storage Technology's excellent reputation was tarnished. With Storage Technology preoccupied in fixing its operations fiasco, IBM finally introduced its new drives, recapturing the market and leaving Storage Technology with a suspect reputation and excess capacity. IBM had out-operated and out-innovated Storage Technology.

With Storage Technology reeling, IBM decided to compete with the company on price. Initially, IBM had resisted reducing its margins because it was being challenged in court by the Justice Department. But in 1982, after the Justice Department dropped its decade-old charges against IBM, IBM cut the price of its latest disk drive by 15 per cent.

The repercussions were felt in 1983, when Storage Technology's disk drive sales fell by $200 million, leading to a $40 million loss. Storage Technology reacted in early 1984 by cancelling plans to produce its mainframe and by beginning to cut costs; nonetheless, by October 1984, Storage Technology had announced that it would report a quarterly loss of over $20 million. The loss violated loan agreements that the company had made with 10 banks for a $125 million credit line. In a last-ditch effort to avoid bankruptcy, Storage Technology announced the layoff of 10 per cent of its workforce and a 10 per cent pay cut for management.

On 31 October 1984, Storage Technology filed for Chapter 11 bankruptcy. By this time, the estimated quarterly loss had tripled to $60 million. Compounding its troubles, Storage Technology's 70 per cent market share in the tape drive business was eroding rapidly, as customers began to fear Storage Technology's demise. After failing to obtain an additional line of credit to continue operations, CEO Jesse Aweida resigned. The balance between creative destruction and operational excellence had completely collapsed. Stage 3 proved to be much more difficult than Stage 2. As Aweida said later: 'Maybe that [growth in sales in the late 1970s] made us a little cocky.' Aweida discovered that the balance between operational excellence and substantial innovation is not easy to maintain.

By January of 1985, the board had found a successor to Aweida, former IBM engineer Ryal R. Poppa, who stepped down as CEO of BMC Industries in Minneapolis to take over running Storage Technology. Poppa had made his name as a turnaround guru by tripling sales at BMC during his three years there. His goals for Storage Technology were less visionary than they were driven by the bottom line: 'I want to bring the same profitability to Storage Technology creditors and shareholders that Lee [Iacocca] brought to Chrysler.'

Poppa flew around the country to convince customers that the company would cut costs dramatically, refocus itself on its core business, and survive bankruptcy. He cut the workforce by another 30 per cent, killed the optical storage research (which was still years from producing a marketable product), and even sold the $6 million corporate jet. He also sold off chip fabrication and circuit board assembly units that had been purchased to fulfil Aweida's dream of producing his own computers. Creative destruction had taken a backseat. Operational excellence was given top priority. The assumption of continuity was all that mattered.

Poppa's approach didn't facilitate his relationship with some in the company (his nickname, 'the Ayatollah', followed him from BMC; as if to underscore this, his decision to kill the optical device unit was announced on Christmas Eve). Still, his approach was quick to generate results. By January 1986, Storage Technology had recorded its first profitable quarter since 1983. The market responded by more than doubling the stock price.

With costs now under control and sales starting to grow again, Storage Technology was able to reach agreements with its creditors, handing over more than 85 per cent of the company's equity to settle most of its $800 million in liabilities. By 1987, Storage Technology had emerged from bankruptcy.

Staying in business, however, would require more than settling claims against its assets. It required maintaining operational excellence – and taking up innovation again. The computer industry was in full bloom. The pace and scale of innovation in computer hardware was stunning (especially measured by the rate at which new companies were crossing the 'small company threshold'). But to play the game, a company had to innovate. Creative destruction had to be reinstalled. Fortunately, Poppa had maintained research in magnetic media because it did not challenge the basic business model he was pursuing. By 1986, Storage Technology had caught up with IBM in disk drive technology, matching a new technique developed by IBM that could provide twice the storage capacity of earlier products.

Moreover, Poppa thought he could attack the old-line tape business, which, while mature, was still large ($10 billion). IBM had regained the upper hand in technology and market share after the Justice Department's decade-long antitrust case against it had ended. But Storage Technology thought it had the skills and resources it needed to challenge IBM in this segment and win.

Storage Technology did come up with a new innovation in the tape drive market. Prior to 1986, tape storage systems consisted of reel-to-reel machines that required considerable manual effort to switch from one tape to another. Both IBM and Storage Technology offered their own versions of tape drives that used hand-size cassettes that could store substantially more data in a more convenient format.

Storage Technology went one step further, however, bundling the cassettes into a library system. The library could hold up to 6,000 cassettes, which were shelved circularly around a robotic arm that could grab a selected tape and insert it into the tape drive. This allowed the entire data system to be accessible within eleven seconds. While this was quite slow by disk drive standards (which could do the same job in milliseconds), disk drives cost about 35 times more per megabyte than tape storage. Compared to manual retrieval, which would take several minutes, tape storage was a dramatic innovation. In fact, the robotic tape library system allowed Storage Technology to become the market leader for mainframe tape storage.

Poppa also focused his attention on the rapidly growing mainframe disk storage market, where IBM had regained market dominance (90 per cent share in 1987) during Storage Technology's troubles. To innovate, Storage Technology (along with several other smaller companies) began to develop a new type of disk drive system. The new concept was to replace the hard disks that were being sold for mainframes with a group of smaller hard disks that would act in unison to provide a single, large storage space. The system was referred to as a RAID system (for redundant array of inexpensive devices). Not only did it allow small and relatively inexpensive hard disks (originally designed for personal computers) to replace the costly mainframe disks, but it allowed data to be replicated over the array, so that any given disk could fail without a complete loss of data. RAID systems promised far larger disk storage at appreciably lower prices than those of the traditional hard disks.

By 1990 Storage Technology had begun discussing its new RAID product, called Iceberg, with its customers. By January 1992, CEO Poppa had secured $150 million in orders and was ready to start discussing the project publicly (even though it was still far from completion). Poppa was so impressed with Iceberg that he even claimed it could make Storage Technology the 'IBM of the 90s'. The market was suitably impressed. But Poppa's words were eerily reminiscent of Aweida's announcement – exactly a decade earlier – that Storage Technology would become a 'mini-IBM.'

Storage Technology's first shipment of test units had been delayed by bugs in the computer code. Meanwhile, another small disk supplier, EMC, had entered the market with a RAID product two years earlier. Still, Poppa remained enthusiastic about Iceberg: 'I told Dick Egan [EMC's chairman and founder], "You've got a tricycle compared to our Cadillac",' he said.

Despite Poppa's sunny pronouncements (classic Stage 4 denial behavior), the balance between operational excellence and innovation at Storage Technology had once again been broken. Delays continued, pushing Iceberg's delivery dates back. And that was just the tip of Iceberg's problems. The capital markets, sensing problems, became jittery. Their nervousness was reinforced in May 1992, when Poppa and 14 other Storage Technology executives sold more than 90,000 shares of company stock following Iceberg's announcement. The resulting sell-off cut Storage Technology share value by half in just four months; shares finished the year 76 per cent below their high. By mid-1993, Iceberg was still more than six months from shipment. The conflicts between innovating and operating had dealt a second death blow to Storage Technology.

By the time Iceberg reached the market in 1994, the computer industry was once again in the midst of a dramatic market shift. With the proliferation of personal computers in the 1980s, computing power no longer needed to be centralized in a mainframe system. New approaches were proliferating; new companies were racing into the market, sensing the opportunity in the Internet and truly distributed computing. Companies were turning to enterprise-wide networks that used servers to share data and files between individual client computers.

While this transformation was a potential boon for data storage device makers, it meant that Storage Technology needed to re-focus, readapting its products from being purely IBM mainframe compatible to being compatible with such open systems as UNIX. This change of focus led to a merger with Network Systems.

As Storage Technology worked to extend its product line to open systems and build market share with Iceberg, the company's growth remained flat. In 1995, after pressure from the board of directors, Poppa agreed to retire at the end of 1996. David Weiss, who had spent 23 years at IBM before joining Storage Technology in 1991, was named president and COO (and in May 1996 assumed the position of CEO). Storage Technology had given up trying to be an outperformer for investors, and was now operating at average levels, in what we have seen in previous chapters as the classic slow downward spiral.

Weiss realized that Storage Technology did not have the infrastructure necessary to adequately market Iceberg. He needed a partner. He also realized that IBM was no longer the dominant player in the disk storage market. Rather, EMC, with its 'tricycle' of a RAID product, had captured the mainframe disk storage market that Storage Technology had planned for Iceberg.

So Weiss negotiated with IBM. In June of 1996, IBM not only agreed to stop making disk storage subsystems but to resell Storage Technology RAID systems to its customers through 2000. Weiss extended his partnering efforts with NCR, which agreed to resell Storage Technology tape drive products. Partnering helped Storage Technology gain market share for mainframe disk sales. Unfortunately, the real game was in the open systems of the Internet, an area dominated by EMC and other competitors.

Storage Technology tried to get into open systems with some of its mainframe storage innovations, such as instantaneous virtual backup software. In August 1999, their efforts appeared to be paying off: Sun Microsystems, a top supplier of Internet servers, agreed to resell Storage Technology tape libraries. That good news was countered, however, when IBM announced that it would re-enter the data storage market in 2000 with new products that would compete head-to-head with Storage Technology.

As sales growth continued to stagnate, and with little obvious forward progress, shareholders again became frustrated. In February 2000, Weiss announced that he would step down as CEO as soon as a successor was found.

After starting as a high-technology, fast-growing company, Storage Technology, unable to master the art of balancing operational excellence and creative destruction, now finds itself the main player in a stagnant market (tape storage for mainframes). (See Figures 4.3 and 4.4 for graphical summaries of the Storage Technology story.) Today, it continues to seek ways to expand into the open systems market and find new routes to expand shareholder value. It has fallen far short of its goals and aspirations.

> After starting as a high-technology, fast-growing company, Storage Technology, unable to master the art of balancing operational excellence and creative destruction, now finds itself the main player in a stagnant market.

Fig. 4.3 Storage Technology: Sales growth versus industry

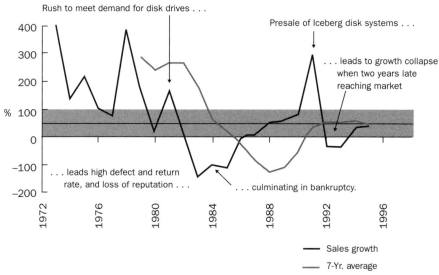

Source: Performance Database, December 1999

Fig. 4.4 Storage Technology: Total return to shareholders versus industry

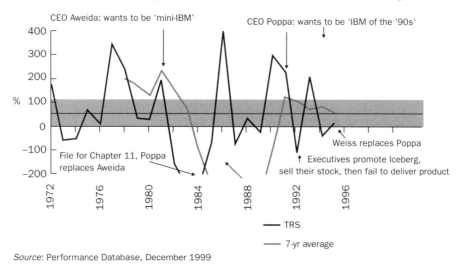

Source: Performance Database, December 1999

THE INCOMPATIBILITY OF OPERATIONS AND CREATIVE DESTRUCTION

There are hundreds of cases like Storage Technology's. The facts differ, but the patterns are the same. From the days of Adam Smith's pin factory, the central purpose of the corporation has been production, logistics, selling, and billing. Aided by the elements of the corporate architecture – systems of information, decision making, and measurement and control – the company is expected to run smoothly, anticipate problems, and avoid risks. These are the activities that allow corporations to create wealth and deliver on its promises to its customers. It is an operational system based on the presumption of rational thought, and it is implicitly deterministic. The presumption is that 'if these things are done, the results will be as expected'. Doing these things constitutes the daily life of most corporate employees.

In reality, of course, the system does not always run as it is supposed to run. Despite its rational expectations, the system stumbles all the time. This is what operational excellence seeks to avoid, and it is in *operations* that every business, large or small, must succeed before it can even begin to think about the future.

> It is in *operations* that every business, large or small, must succeed before it can even begin to think about the future.

In a recent series of meetings, we talked with more than 50 managers from large and small companies in the United States and Europe. They ran the gamut from high-tech to daily consumer-staples firms. We asked them to characterize what it took to be successful in their particular business. Their answers were remarkably uniform, given the vast differences in their corporate purposes, size, and nationality.

Of all the attributes that business leaders saw leading to success, operational excellence was highest on their list. Operational excellence included best-in-class design, manufacturing excellence, logistics and sales skills, adept execution, personal drive, and an obsession with the customer. In addition they felt that strong systematic planning, effective operational controls, ability to leverage their assets over wide geographic areas, and the ability to maintain low overhead were all required to be competitive these days. That is a full boat.

Whether European or American, whether in packaged goods or high tech, these executives and managers felt that operational excellence was the price of admission today. It is 'operational excellence that lets you reap the synergies of all the other elements of your business', they routinely explained.

But many of these executives felt the standard they had set for themselves was difficult to achieve. Difficulties in execution were on the top of this list, starting with the failure to execute at all. Some companies, for example, were not able to integrate acquisitions, largely because of enormous cultural differences between the companies. Others failed to integrate functional skills or transition to a new skill base.

The failure to execute effectively was more common than the failure to execute at all. The executives we talked with cited cases where execution was excessively costly, or where a company failed to get products to market on time or misjudged the level of investment required.

Finally, more than a few of the executives we surveyed said they had trouble focusing execution. They were not tough enough in determining at an early stage what would make a difference in the overall performance level of the enterprise – or what projects needed to be cut out of development to avoid starving the remaining projects or bankrupting the company. There were many variants of operational failure. The decision processes of these corporations were simply not up to the tasks before them.

As a consequence, these senior executives wanted to know what the best techniques for ensuring execution were; what practical advice there was to help individuals stay focused; what the best performance measures and control processes were – ideas that would keep everything moving along smoothly – and how to cope with these challenges as the size and complexity of the corporation grow.

Yet there was an irony in their questions. As concerned as they seemed to be with operational effectiveness, they were actually more concerned with creative destruction (although they did not call it creative destruction). They were adamant about discussing the difficulties they had with innovation and the tendency of their companies to stay too long in old product lines. The executives we talked to did not equate innovation and R&D, or even innovation and technology change; they saw innovation as a broader topic – doing new things whatever their origin or doing old things in new ways. Their concerns included R&D, of course, but they were broader than that topic alone.

We are sympathetic to that view. We see innovation as the development of new products and services that meet customer needs cheaper, faster, and better than current alternatives do. Innovation to us also means retooling business processes to develop new products and services. In this sense, innovation can refer to changing approaches to sales and services, or to the structure of large transactions, or to the migration paths customers follow to move from one computer system to another, or to skills for diversification, or to the development of technologies that enable the sales of other products, or to the development of new business models themselves.

Despite the importance of innovation to them, the executives said they had difficulty pulling it off. They cited the inability to grow beyond the core, the lack of ideas compelling enough to change customer behaviour, slow product development, and the failure to establish an 'innovative culture' (although none could really define what that meant). They are many of the same problems that Storage Technology faced and failed to resolve.

Regarding the elimination of product lines that no longer had potential or fit within the concept of the corporations, many cited their tendency to 'ride the wave too long'; even the best of the innovators had a problem with this, and were willing to admit it. Again, their problems are not dissimilar to the experience of Storage Technology.

When asked what stands in the way of better change management in their companies, these executives cited several barriers. The most common complaint referred to problems that stemmed from 'rational' analysis – the kind of analysis that markets collectively do not perform. The top reasons cited for lack of change in the corporation was that they had become too financially focused; that the kind of analyses used to justify projects killed them; the inability to move into new areas with sufficient force; the refusal to stand up to unpleasant realities: 'If they did not like the characteristics of new technologies, they ignored them.' Several told us, 'Whenever you find a division of a company that

> **'Whenever you find a division of a company that failed because it could not change, look to the parent. That is where the problems are.'**

failed because it could not change, look to the parent. That is where the problems are.' It was a point that this group of executives generally agreed upon. Parental control, they feel, is the kiss of death for competitiveness. For each of these blockages, our executives would like to have answers.

These executives had three kinds of questions about innovation. The first centred on their confessed inability to develop innovative strategies:

- 'How do the excellent innovators do it?' – which presumes, of course, that excellent innovators exist.
- 'What drives breakthrough innovative ideas?'
- 'How should we determine an innovation strategy' – meaning, particularly, how do we set the balance between evolutionary and revolutionary innovation?
- 'How can we avoid riding the curve too long?'
- 'How can we develop more compelling ideas to change customer behaviour?'

The second kind of question centred on managing the flow of innovations into the corporation:

- 'How do we grow beyond the core business?'
- 'How do we bring products to market faster – including prototyping, scaling up, engineering, and launch?' (One executive asked, 'How do we handle the bottlenecks caused by four divisional CEOs who have to be involved in most innovation decisions in order to review product line overlapping, brand overlapping, and geographic overlapping?')

- 'How do we create a culture within the organization that supports innovation?' (Specifically, 'How do companies keep the innovative spirit alive as they grow larger and more complex?')
- 'How do we ensure that innovators are listened to – despite the pressure of the day-to-day business and the resource constraints that come with it?'
- 'How do we deal with the cultural differences between units working on incremental and those working on transformational innovation?'
- 'How do we deal with risk?'
- 'How do we evolve skills?'
- 'How do we prioritize between different great ideas that the organization develops?'

The third, and perhaps most basic, kind of question was centred on how to discover and manage new ideas:

- 'How do we find ideas?'
- 'How do we transform ideas into businesses?' ('How do great innovators think about "easier, faster, better"?')
- 'How can we better leverage what we have done?' ('How do we overcome the "not-invented-here" syndrome in some of our third country markets?')
- 'How do we get companies that are totally integrated around centralized computer systems to become more innovative? The computer systems are strangling us!'

Everyone pointed out that as size and complexity increase, changes become harder. As one executive said: 'The question is then how do we create a favourable environment in a big organization?' Another executive asked, 'How sustainable is this process which has tremendously increased the number of SKUs?' And another turned the question inside out: 'How do you manage product complexity that is generated by intense flow of innovation?' These executives could not figure out how to run their corporations in such a way that they could achieve operational excellence *and* creative destruction at the pace and scale of the market. Failing to find a way to address this issue, they simply placed most of their attention on operational excellence. This can work for a while, as we saw with Storage Technology. But not for ever. The system of operational excellence is consistent, but it is not complete.

LIMITATIONS OF THE OPERATING ORGANIZATION

What are the origins of this dilemma? First, organizations based on the assumption of continuity do not work well when faced with discontinuity. Three factors, all part of the architecture of the organization, or MIDAS, stand in their way: decision-making systems, managerial control systems, and information.

Organizations based on the assumption of continuity do not work well when faced with discontinuity.

Decision-making systems

Decision-making systems that support the day-to-day life in many corporations work well only when:

1. History is a good guide to the future, and uncertainty and its risk are at a minimum.
2. The context is simple and unambiguous rather than complex and ambiguous.
3. The decision-making process is balanced and calm, rather than erratic and subject to stress.
4. The competitive, technological, and regulatory environment is stable, rather than in a period of rapid change.
5. Information is standard, unambiguous, and complete, rather than uncertain or difficult to interpret.
6. Decisions can be handled in a hierarchical fashion, with little information distortion.
7. There is a consistency of preferences, such as a common set of beliefs, among decision makers.
8. Mental models match anticipated conditions (when systems are self-referential, analysis of future risks is quite difficult).

Needless to say, these conditions are rarely met.

Measurement and control systems

Measurement and control systems, which are intended to keep the organization on course once decisions are made, suffer from similar weaknesses. The purpose of control systems is to help achieve an organization's objectives. They do this by identifying key control variables, determining standards against which results can be compared, measuring the results, diagnosing deviations from the standards, correcting deviations from standards, and adjusting the standards as appropriate. As we mentioned in the Introduction, Robert Simons says: 'Measurement focuses on errors of commission (mistakes) and shortfalls (negative variances) against goals. In fact, control systems are negative feedback systems. Control reports are used primarily as confirmation that everything is "on track." Surprise is the enemy.'

Measurement and control systems, like decision-making systems, perform most effectively in routine functions and processes. Used inappropriately they can thwart the recognition of key, non-standard issues and even undermine management's intent. When designing control systems, for example, the designers select only a few variables, from the many possibilities, to control. Once the variables are selected, disproportionate attention is placed on them, drawing attention away from potentially important new concerns or problems. In this way, control systems filter out warnings of 'disruptive environmental change', as Simons terms it.

Information systems

Finally, information systems suffer from a variety of limitations. These include the high cost of changing them, limited access, and erroneous, irrelevant, or missing information (and the assumption that it will be used by decision makers if it is available). These assumptions are violated frequently. Among the most common errors:

1. Decision makers gravitate to familiar information. They know how to use such information and how to assess its quality; they know the tricks buried in such data. Decision makers are more likely to seek the confirmation of existing information than to look for disconfirming information.

2. When faced with inconsistent data, decision makers tend to rely on the first cue that captures their attention – and exclude all others from consideration.

3. Decision makers prefer certain kinds of information delivered in a certain form. For example, decision makers prefer vivid information to *pallid* information; that is, they prefer stories to systematic information, and they prefer information about specific cases to information about abstract statistics. Most decision makers would prefer to see a chart than a table, or a real product rather than a description of a product, or to see a person who represents a particular class of people – say, those with colds – than read statistics about colds.

Psychologists have found that decision makers are like everyone else: They tend to pay more attention to dramatic events (though they may be low in real significance) than they do to routine events that have a high probability of affecting their lives and that of the corporation. Such information may be perfectly delivered, but it is less than perfectly perceived!

> Decision makers tend to pay more attention to dramatic events than they do to routine events that have a high probability of affecting their lives and that of the corporation.

These elements of the operating organization are 'sticky.' That is, they are usually designed to support a single competitive environment and conform to a single model of competition. They are based on the assumption of continuity. They do not function well in discontinuous times. When the assumption of continuity is undermined, they cannot help to create an effective response. In fact, they hinder it.

REQUIREMENTS OF THE INNOVATING ORGANIZATION

The second reason that one cannot easily answer the executives' questions, and deal with the kinds of problems Storage Technology faced, is more complex. It deals with the fundamental difference between the corporation that operates on the assumption of continuity and one that is built on the assumption of discontinuity. Innovation is at the heart of the concept of discontinuity.

Industries are more innovative than the companies in them, since by definition the market consists of all innovations and a single company can lay claim only to their own. For example, in cellular telephony, Motorola has been a leader. It introduced a wide range of products, from the transformational MicroTAC® handheld cellular phone to the incremental VibraCall® ringing technology. Nevertheless, even a company as innovative as Motorola contributes only a portion of the overall innovation of the entire industry. There are many other competitors in this industry, including Nokia and Ericsson, that have also introduced important innovations. In addition to innovation in phones, there was also innovation in cellular services. AT&T's 1999 announcement of the combined handset and One Rate Plan, which allowed a customer to pay a flat rate of 10 cents a minute whether using a landline, a cell phone, or a calling card, changed the model of industry pricing.

As innovative as individual companies have been, none of them can claim to have dominated innovation in cellular technology. The industry has a life of its own. Over time, the *industry*, rather than any individual company, sets the standard for innovation. The continuous cycle of learning, developing insights, selecting ideas and developing concepts happens faster and more comprehensively in the market than in any one company. In the market, many competitors are simultaneously working on new ideas that could result in growth businesses – large companies, small companies, and entrepreneurs. Conflicting ideas are being pursued simultaneously. Many will not succeed. The competitive standard, therefore, more than any single company, is the market.

Types of innovation

As the cellular telephone industry illustrates, there are many kinds of innovation. Innovation can be thought of as occurring at three levels. First is *transformational* innovation, which matches Schumpeter's concept of a 'historic and irreversible change in the way of doing things'. The second level is *substantial* innovation, which offers less surprise and scope than Schumpeter's concept but still significantly upsets the conventional order. Often substantial innovations follow transformational innovations, as aftershocks follow the main earthquake. The third level is *incremental* innovation, which is the everyday engine of change of most corporations.

Organizations rarely distinguish between the kinds of innovation, and that leads directly to trouble. At Storage Technology, for example, founder Aweida made two mistakes because he failed to understand the differences between what he had demonstrated he could do (incremental innovation) and what he wanted to do (substantial and transformational innovation). His first mistake was to attempt to develop a new mainframe (a substantial innovation) to compete head-on with IBM. Basing his estimates on what it would take to compete with IBM on his experience with incremental innovation, he underestimated greatly the magnitude of the challenge of developing a new mainframe. Storage Technology fell far short of market requirements. Moreover, his timing was terrible, since at the same time he chose to compete with IBM in mainframes, the computer industry was beginning a transformational shift away from mainframes and to personal computers. Aweida's second mistake was to attempt to develop optical storage systems years before the underlying technology was ready. Again, Aweida's experience in incremental innovation was not an accurate guide to the requirement of transformational innovation.

Later, President Poppa's success with incremental innovation led him to believe he was capable of beating EMC in RAID storage systems by developing Iceberg, a substantial innovation. Poppa tried to use the same processes that had succeeded in delivering incremental innovations to support transformational innovation, but they were inadequate to meet the tougher technical development standards of Iceberg.

By failing to distinguish between the kinds of innovation and managerial requirements, Aweida and Poppa failed to foresee the demands and challenges in front of them. Their gut instincts, based on their experience with incremental innovation, was an insuffcient guide to the rigours and timing requirements of substantial and transformational innovation. Consequently, they mismanaged three major projects and derailed Storage Technology. These errors directly led to their removal.

Two factors determine the level of innovation: how new the innovation is and how much wealth it generates. Incremental innovations are not very new to either the customer or the producer and generally have slight impact; substantial innovations are quite new to either the customer or the producer and can have greater economic impact. And transformational innovations, which can invoke entirely new designs, or manufacturing processes, or uses, have the greatest impact of all. Turned around, if an innovation is very new and creates an enormous amount of wealth, we call it transformational because it transforms the industry. If the innovation is not very new and does not create a lot of wealth, then we think of it as incremental. Substantial innovation falls between the two. You'll never forget a transformational change, while incremental changes go unnoticed all the time.

We believe that the scale of innovation is logarithmic rather than arithmetic. Substantial innovation is often 10 times greater than the change that results from incremental innovation, and offers 10 times the rewards (and invokes 10 times the uncertainties). Moreover, substantial innovation is often generative: once established, the innovation leads to other innovation (sometimes called *positive returns*).

Transformational innovation is 10 times greater than substantial innovation. Transformational innovations tear at the social fabric (and that of the economic markets) far more than incremental innovations do. Based on our experience and the analysis of the innovation portfolios of several large companies, the frequency of innovations is logarithmic, as well. There are perhaps 10 substantial innovations for every 100 incremental innovations, and perhaps one transformational innovation for every 10 substantial innovations.

The 'newness' and wealth creation of an innovation can be drawn on a graph like the Richter scale (see Figure 4.5).

Fig. 4.5 Types of innovation: Richter scale of innovation

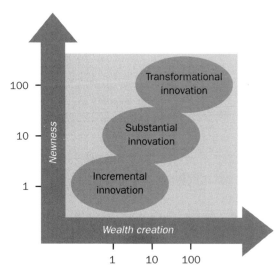

Many businesses, of course, are built on an idea that is not very new, and they can still do very well. At Storage Technology this included the line of tape drives that Poppa had developed. Other examples range from Palm Pilot imitators like Handspring, to new frozen yogurt versions of popular ice cream flavours, to the next generation of Microsoft Word. These are not transformational innovations, but examples of operational excellence – the continued pursuit of ordinary business. Innovations that are very new (remember the Apple Newton, or Snapple beverages?) but do not create wealth are not transformational, in our opinion. Such products are better termed *inventions*.

Each level of innovation – incremental, substantial and transformational – requires a different managerial process and is managed by a different level of the corporation. Incremental change can be handled by frontline people. Transformational change can be enacted only by senior management. Each presents a different challenge, as well: incremental change challenges current strategy without challenging the firm's traditional controls; and transformational change challenges the corporation's strategy and controls. Managing innovation is impossible without understanding which layer of innovation one is dealing with. Both Aweida and Poppa at Storage Technology did not understand the differences; it cost them the leadership of the company, not to mention shareholders' returns.

Incremental innovation

Incremental innovation is characterized more by what has *not* changed than what *has* changed. While incremental innovations are not very new and they do not create much wealth, they must be pursued in order to maintain one's competitive position.

Incremental innovations are attractive because not much has to change to assure their implementation. They offer more or less the same value to the customer as does pre-innovation value. They use more or less the same manufacturing equipment. They are sold through more or less the same channels, with the same sales terms, as the pre-innovation product or service. They are improvements over what has preceded them – but not vast improvements.

The *Glenavlon*

Incremental innovations are the red blood cells of the economy. Without them, existing corporations could not survive. They are the product of countless total quality management and reengineering programs. They can be accomplished by the rank and file. They are well understood. They do not challenge the existing business model or strategic plan. Senior management participation is not required.

One way to understand incremental innovation is by looking to the past, to the evolution of sailing ships. In the 1880s, clipper ships like the *Glenavlon* were often seen on the horizon (see photo). These swift-sailing vessels carried cargo between the major ports of England and the United States. They were the FedEx carriers of their time, having been perfected through hundreds of years of incremental improvement. (In fact, FedEx CEO Fred Smith has an extensive collection of clipper ship models, which he displays in glass cases at FedEx headquarters.)

But by 1870, ships powered by steam that had been around for nearly seventy years were challenging the leadership of the clippers. In the beginning, steamships were not at all effective (since the steam engine itself was not terribly efficient in 1820). Most of the cargo-carrying capacity of the steamship was consumed by fuel storage. By 1890, however, steam engines had improved to the point where they could overtake the cost advantage of clippers. The handsome clipper ships began losing market share to the steamships (or, more often in the early days, to a steam-and-sail hybrid).

The *France II*

But the owners of the sailing vessels, and the naval architects who supported them, were not ready to relinquish control of the seas. They fought
back by incrementally improving their ships. The drawing of the *France II*,
shows one of those ships:

This was a much-improved vessel. It had one more mast than the *Glenavlon*,
and was also longer at the waterline. It was a faster ship. It also carried more
cargo, and thus was cheaper to operate per ton-mile than the *Glenavlon*.

Thus continued a skirmish of technologies, steam versus sail. The
Preussen (see photo) was the next improvement in sail. It was again an
incremental improvement, with more sail, more length at the waterline,
and a cheaper ton-per-mile operating cost.

Did the *Preussen* stop the progress of the steamships? Absolutely not.
The steamships kept on attacking.

Undaunted, the naval architects struggled for further improvement, this
time with a gaff-rigged design. The *Thomas W. Lawson* was the result (see
photo). The ship had even more sail and waterline, which resulted in even
more speed. But at this point, the incremental change in technology was
reaching its natural limit. On Friday, 13 December 1907, nearing the Scilly
Isle, Captain Turner found he could not control the *Thomas W. Lawson*.
With the winds blowing at 60 knots, the sailing vessel ran into the rocks.
Miraculously, Captain Turner survived. But the rest of the crew was lost –
and so was the age of sail. Incremental innovation had run its course.

The *Thomas W. Lawson*

The *Preussen*

Captain Turner and Presidents Poppa and Aweida of Storage Technology had something in common. They all were unwitting victims of the end of incremental innovation. Captain Turner lost his ship and crew; Poppa and Aweida lost their company.

Alas, incremental innovation is *not* the signature of the marketplace. It is the signature of continuity, of companies clinging to incumbency. Incremental innovation is more a part of operational excellence than it is creative destruction.

Transformational innovation

Transformational innovation can create new markets, turn the tides of commerce, make billionaires, vanquish competitors, and inspire the next generation. While incremental innovation rarely challenges the establishment, transformational innovation *frequently* upsets the conventional concepts of the corporation and its operational systems. Transformational innovations do not spring from 'product quality' programmes. They come from intensely creative people bent on destroying the established order.

Transformational innovations tend to be 'competency destroying'. In other words, the competition must destroy the incumbent products in order to compete. Transformational innovations are often conceived of by senior management, and led by them as well. Often the transformational innovation is the very reason for a new company's existence. Frequently the product, the tooling, the distribution methods, the media campaigns, and the value propositions are new as well. The synthesis of these elements can work surprisingly well, even explosively well, stunning Wall Street analysts. Stock prices can explode, enriching lucky or insightful investors.

Existing companies generally do not create transformational innovations. Markets do by enabling the assembly of an entirely new corporation – people, capital, and technology.

Substantial innovation

Substantial innovations are often the second generation of transformational innovations. These are products or systems that follow the pioneering innovation. One example is the Windows operating system, which supplanted the old DOS system. Huggies to Pampers. Sam's to Wal-Mart. The 747 to the 707. FedEx's SameDay® Service to its Standard Overnight® Service. These are bold new products, but not nearly so bold as the original transformational innovations. What separates these innovations from incremental change is both the extent of the change and the impact of the changes. Windows was not a simple extension of DOS. It was a total rewrite that in the end had a very different look and feel from DOS, incorporating optical interfaces, or 'windows,' which made it easier for consumers to use. (Those who know the two systems will immediately recall the differences.) Windows was meant to compete with the Macintosh operating system. One could 'click' one's way though the various options rather than remembering a seemingly endless series of typed, coded commands.

Substantial innovations offer secure competitive advantage for a time. They tend to build on, and reinforce, the competencies that were required to make the transformational innovation – but they build new core skills as well, differentiating them in an important way from incremental innovations. Substantial innovations stretch the limits of the information and skills of the organization, often requiring outside expertise to pull them off. They are often competency-destroying for the defenders of the old order. They often involve senior management, but mostly in an advisory role.

Substantial innovations generally do not emerge from an accretion of incremental innovations. The intent of these designs is to follow on the heels of the transformation. To stay on the attack. To gain advantage. They tend to be boldly conceived and meticulously assembled. Those companies that think they can achieve substantial innovation by merely stepping up incremental efforts will be sadly disappointed – whether they are an enterprise resources planning system (or ERP, as it has become to be known) designer dreaming of crossing over to the Internet, or a drug maker hoping to evolve its studies of small molecules into genetics. These innovations do not come from the random accretion of small advances. They come from a lofty ambition to do much better in the market coupled with an innovative approach that is different from what has come before (e.g., a new concept for an Internet-based ERP). While the final product will, of course, be assembled from existing subcomponents, lofty goals and a novel approach separate such advances from incremental change.

In failing to recognize the differences between these three different types of innovation – and many managers manage them as one – managers fail to meet the needs of any.

THE CREATIVE FOUNDATIONS OF TRANSFORMATIONAL INNOVATION

The underlying element in all innovation is creativity. Only by understanding creativity can one grapple with what is needed for sustained performance.

Creativity

Most words used in management today have their origins in the fourteenth century. But the word *creativity* is more recent, first cited by Webster in 1875. In the 1880s, William James used the word to support his philosophy of pragmatism. James described the nature of the creative process in this way:

Instead of thoughts of concrete things patiently following one another in a beaten track of habitual suggestion, we have the most abrupt cross-cuts and transitions from one idea to another, the most rarefied abstractions and discriminations, the most unheard of combination of elements, the subtlest associations of analogy; in a word, we seem suddenly introduced into a seething caldron of ideas, where everything is fizzling and bobbling about in a state of bewildering activity, where partnerships can be joined or loosened in an instant, treadmill routine is unknown, and the unexpected seems the only law.

This hardly sounds like the orderliness of the ideal operating organization. It seems more like a state of confusion and disorder, one perhaps waiting for order to arrive.

James believed in the 'great man' theory of creativity, which implied that creativity seethed within the person, but he believed that the environment was also crucial. Modern thinkers stress the environment to an even greater degree. Mihalyi Csikszentmihalyi noted:

To say that Thomas Edison invented electricity or that Albert Einstein discovered relativity is a convenient simplification. It satisfies our ancient predilection for stories that are easy to comprehend and involve superhuman heroes. But Edison's or Einstein's discoveries would be inconceivable without the prior knowledge, without the intellectual and social network that stimulated their thinking, and without the social mechanisms that recognized and spread their innovations.

What is the process of discovery and what are the 'intellectual and social networks and mechanisms' that 'recognize and spread' those discoveries? How do those processes compare to the processes required to run the operating organization?

The process of discovery

The process of discovery takes two paths, which in practice are quite recursive. One is divergent thinking – a matter of opening up. The other is convergent thinking – focusing down. It is the latter kind of thinking that is conventionally practised in the operating organization, where it has been raised to a high art. Divergent thinking is rarely practised in the operating organization, and in fact appears at cross-purposes with its intent.

Divergent thinking

The purpose of divergent thinking is to cast the broadest possible net in searching for solutions, as well as in searching for the proper questions that need to be addressed. The tool of intuitive genius, divergent thinking can readily change the definition of the problem to be solved, or the context in which the problem is solved. It involves the ability to switch from one perspective to another fluently, as well as an ability to pick up on or make unusual associations. Chess masters call this 'zoom-out' thinking – the process of putting all the known information into context, both within the strategic context of the game being played, as well as in the context of other general knowledge the chess player has about his or her opponent and what other great players in the past have done in similar situations.

Zoom-out thinkers are 'wide categorizers'. They exhibit a strong interest in disciplines outside their own specialty area. They are trained in diverse disciplines, and they are often aggressive in acquiring new skills. They tend to surround themselves with diverse stimuli, and they change those stimuli regularly. Renowned Harvard professor emeritus E. O. Wilson, for example, typically works on several projects at once. This is a common pattern among creative individuals; it keeps them from getting bored or stymied, and it produces an unexpected cross-fertilization of ideas.

As Dean Keith Simonton notes: 'It is evident that a person is more likely to see congruence between hitherto isolated elements if that person has broad interests, is versatile, enjoys intellectual fluency and flexibility, and can connect disparate elements via unusual associations and wide categories that force a substantial overlap of ideas.'

Divergent thinking is made up of three highly interlinked, overlapping, and recursive phases – search, incubation, and collision. Collectively, they constitute the unique hub of the discovery process.

Search

During the search phase, individuals seek to define inconsistencies between current theory and new data. 'These anomalies provide the raw material on which the subconscious can work,' Csikszentmihalyi notes.

The creative process starts with a sense that there is a puzzle somewhere, or a task to be accomplished. Perhaps something is not right, somewhere there is a conflict, a tension, a need to be satisfied. The problematic issue can be triggered by a personal experience, by a lack of fit in the symbolic system, by the stimulation of colleagues, or by public needs. Without such a felt tension to attract the psychic energy of the person, the creative process is unlikely to start.

Anomalies – things that don't fit the established order – can serve as precursors to opportunities or problems. A stock may be undervalued, a customer need unrecognized, a new technology not fully used.

Anomalies do not necessarily jump out at management. It takes someone with what Pasteur called a 'prepared mind' to see them. Csikszentmihalyi says:

Fleming was not the first bacteriologist to see a petri dish spoiled by a mold contamination, yet he was apparently the first to notice the far-reaching implications of the clear ring around the little fuzzy spot on the gel. Similarly, Archimedes was not the first to have seen a bathtub overflow, Newton the falling of an apple, or Watt the steam escaping from a tea pot, but these three did notice the broader implications of these trivial, almost everyday occurrences.

'Seeing the broader implications' often requires the observer to 'suspend disbelief' – and to use substantial diligence until a new pattern appears. These skills are seldom nurtured in operating organizations. Yet they are essential for transformational innovation. As Kuhn observed in 1962: 'The accumulation of anomalies – findings that cannot be assimilated into any framework or tradition – prepares the way for revolution.'

There is a fine line to walk here. Lingering too long on a bit of data may lead to wasted work, or it could be the prelude to discovery. Who can make that call? Even those who have been right previously are not necessarily infallible the next time around. In fact, one could argue that as one gathers expertise, he or she becomes less accepting of new data. This, in fact, is a classic characteristic of mature organizations. They fail to innovate because they fail to recognize the fact that they have been rejecting data that does not support the company's mental models. One can't search for anomalies through reading and study alone, although reading and study can trigger creativity. In business one often learns from being mentored, from apprenticeships, through meetings with customers, or from visits to 'world-class' corporations, manufacturing sites, distribution centres, or laboratories.

> Lingering too long on a bit of data may lead to wasted work, or it could be the prelude to discovery

Incubation

The incubation stage is the most mysterious of the three stages of divergent thinking. Sometimes it appears as if the problem-solving process has stopped altogether.

Incubation is the absolute opposite of the normal business processes of the operating organization. It is often totally unpredictable. But since it is also the heart of the creative process, it creates a dilemma for the business executive who wants to support innovation but has little patience for unfocused activity. In the incubation period, observations stew on the edge of consciousness until something clarifies. As Newton observed: 'I keep the subject constantly before me, and wait until the first dawnings open slowly, little by little, into the full and clear light.'

There is no way to plan 'enough' incubation time. What, then, can one do to improve the productivity of this period of incubation? One useful tool is what psychologists call 'suspending disbelief' – suspending judgment on data or observations that seem to make no sense. It allows time for the rearrangement of data, allowing one time to find new images that explain or illustrate how things might work. Suspending disbelief is essential to avoiding premature closure on an issue, or entrenchment in existing ideas and approaches. Suspending disbelief helps to improve one's chances of finding a fresh view of the universe. It is an unnatural act for an operating organization, but an essential trait for an innovative organization.

A second useful tool is to deconstruct the problem so that you can recombine elements of it and gain fresh insight. Sir James Black, Nobel Prize winner for the discovery of histamine antagonists, suggests that one 'turn the question around'. Dr. Black prefers an 'oblique attack' to a problem rather than a direct one.

One way to change context, Csikszentmihalyi observes, is to position yourself at the intersection of different cultures or disciplines: 'where beliefs, lifestyles, and knowledge mingle and allow individuals to see new combinations of ideas with greater ease. In cultures that are uniform and rigid it takes a greater investment of attention to achieve new ways of thinking. In other words, creativity is more likely in places where new ideas require less effort to be perceived.'

Collision

The end of the incubation stage is achieved when a good idea is recognized, a process we call *collision*. Collisions of different information or perspectives often emerge instantly, but the process can drag on as problem definition evolves and solutions emerge. There is often a dialectic between the 'irrational and the rational aspects; between passion and discipline'. The resolution usually can't be predicted in advance. In the passage that follows, Csikszentmihalyi illustrates this point with a description of the creative writing process:

What is so difficult about the process is that one must keep the mind focused on two contradictory goals: not to miss the message whispered by the unconscious and at the same time force it into a suitable form. The first requires openness, the second critical judgment. If these two processes are not kept in a constantly shifting balance, the flow of writing dries up. After a few hours the tremendous concentration required for this balancing act becomes so exhausting that the writer has to change gears and focus on something else, something mundane. But while it lasts, creative writing is the next best thing to having a world of one's own in which what's wrong with the 'real' world can be set straight.

These three phases – search, incubation, and collision – define the divergent-thinking process. Divergent thinking is the headwater of the creative process. Unfortunately, these skills are rarely well developed even in the well-run and well-operating organization. As a result, it is often starved for substantial and transformational opportunities, at least compared to the general market.

Convergent thinking

The second part of the creative process is convergent thinking. Convergent thinking, the key to analytical genius, is the thinking measured by IQ tests. It involves solving well-defined, rational problems that have a single correct answer. Chess masters call this thinking 'zoom-in' thinking. Zooming in is the act of understanding the microdetails of the present situation – where all the players are situated, what the most recent moves have been, and so on. Zooming in is similar to deductive thinking.

Convergent thinkers do their work by focusing in on the essential details, screening ideas for relevance, and exercising their knack for simplifying problems just enough to capture their essence – but without excluding the significant details. Screening is an essential skill, one where the practitioner, according to Teresa M. Amabile, the Edsel Bryant Ford Professor of Business Administration at Harvard Business School, combines a 'constricted scan that screens out all but essential information, a narrow focus on bits of information, and a compulsiveness that permits slow mastication, digestion and storage of large amounts of information'.

> Convergent thinkers do their work by focusing in on the essential details, screening ideas for relevance, and exercising their knack for simplifying problems just enough to capture their essence.

Whereas divergent thinking requires breaking down a problem into smaller bits, convergent thinking depends on 'reassembly' and reduction. It is a two-step process involving decision and trial. Most corporations have mastered convergent thinking. It is the *divergent* processes that are strange to the focused corporation.

Observing the creative process in corporations as a whole, one notices that it involves a very complex web of problem definition and solution, during which new information is being generated, analyzed, and interpreted.

Fig. 4.6 The act of creation

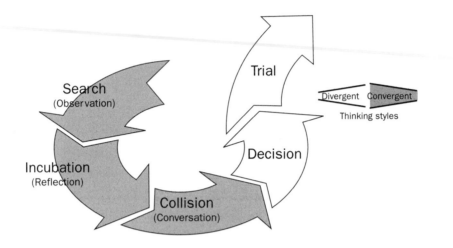

These processes are so complex, and operate at such different speeds – sometimes almost instantaneously (as in the case of insight), and sometimes ponderously slowly (as ideas incubate) – that it is often difficult to calibrate where one is in the process, and whether the process will have a productive end. This is the risk, the tension, and the energy of the creative process. It is not at all like a normal operating process. It is far messier. We can represent the process simply, as a crudely interrupted circle, as shown in Figure 4.6.

The fact is, the path toward insight is rarely straight. As David Perkins, a professor and co-director of Project Zero at Harvard's Graduate School of Education, said: 'In many creative endeavors, the goals, and hence end states, evolve along with the problem. The goals may shift as the search proceeds.'

Unlike the 'small motor skills' required to control operations, controlling creativity and discovery requires 'large motor skills' (see Chapter 9) – changing the people, changing the context, and changing the pace. And it may require unforecastable time. One cannot expect to gain immediate results, but one should not be too surprised if they occur. It is very different from controlling operations. The creative process is also deeply human. It can take enormous personal courage to pursue a creative idea.

What makes the creative process difficult for management is that it has no recognizable parallels in the operating disciplines of decision making, measurement, and control found at the heart of today's corporations. We are dealing with entirely different processes. The role and meaning of information is different. The role and meaning of decision making is different. And the role and meaning of measurement and control are entirely different.

Creative people

Arthur Rock, one of the most successful venture capitalists of the twentieth century, and the founder of Arthur Rock & Co., said that 'an idea is simply an excuse for getting a team together to make something happen.' Yet, as we've seen, the skills required to excel in the creative process are different from the skills required to excel in operations.

What are creative people – those who do excel in the creative processes – like? They tend to have high aspirations. They are impatient. They are open to new experiences, emotion, and risk taking – to the point of being risk seekers. They are willing to risk a great deal because of the happiness and deep satisfaction the creative experience brings to them. As Csikszentmihalyi said, creative people come equipped with a 'sunny pessimism', or the ability to have an optimistic sense while looking into the teeth of a negative outlook.

Creative people are willing to face short-term risk to win long-term rewards. Teresa Amabile says, 'While many would be dissuaded by the risk of failure, the creative individual does not see the possibility of failure so much as the possibility of success.'

> Creative people are willing to face short-term risk to win long-term rewards.

Moreover, the risk of failure may actually motivate the creative person. Economist George Steiger noted, 'In innovation, you have to play less of a safe game if it's going to be interesting. It's not predictable that it'll go well.'

Indeed, there are those who actually seek the risk. In a study of lab directors done by Dr Kevin Dunbar, professor of psychology at McGill University, the directors reported that they liked high-risk projects because they had a long time horizon, which provided the freedom to make some substantial or transformational advances.

In short, creative people are different from traditional operating people. They are comfortable with ambiguity, and they are open to new experiences and thoughts.

The COR skills of creativity

The creative process, particularly divergent thinking, depends on three essential skills that are not often required in the operating organization:

- **Conversational skills.** To successfully pass along your ideas to others, you must converse well.
- **Observational skills.** You must be able to look broadly across industries and cultures to absorb relevant information, even when its relevance may not be visible to others.
- **Reflective skills.** During the incubation process, you must be able to reflect on the various data and information you have absorbed, and allow these floating pieces to come together into a meaningful pattern or purpose.

We refer to these three skills as the COR skills of the creative process. We discuss them in more depth in Chapter 9.

No amount of experience in the operating environment can prepare one to perform well in the creative environment, and vice versa. The skills, for the most part, are in opposition to one another. To blend them requires exceptional ability.

This ability is required for the leaders of today's corporations if they are to master the dual demands of operations and innovation. Unfortunately, these creative skills are usually dulled by the architecture of the organization (information systems, decision-making systems, executional focus, and the incentives and control systems). As a result, it is nearly impossible for corporations to move from the assumption of continuity to the assumption of discontinuity. Creativity, and its accompanying transformational and substantial innovation, challenges the basic precepts of the corporation focused on operational excellence alone. This is why corporations struggle when they try to embrace creative destruction while remaining operationally excellent.

The definition of innovation

The word *innovation* first appeared, according to Webster's online dictionary, in the fifteenth century. It was derived from the Latin word *novus*, or new. In modern business terms, newness can refer to anything that affects customers, manufacturing, sales, or service. The extent of 'newness' can, of course, vary from incremental improvements to wholesale change. Innovation can encompass:

- a new product enabling a pioneering approach to surgery, as Johnson & Johnson accomplished in the 1980s with 'keyhole' surgery, or laparoscopy

- a new process for making steel, as Nucor launched in the 1970s

- a new service for the customer, as MCI created with their Friends and Family service

- a new way of doing business, as Enron came up with when they created the natural gas trading market.

Innovations are clearly based on more than just technological change.

While innovation is based on creativity and invention, it is much broader. An invention implies the 'conversion of a creative idea to some communicable and verifiable form, generally to fulfill some need or perform some task'. Innovation is invention that has produced economic value. Without economic value there can be no innovation. Invention *precedes* innovation. It does not presume economic worth. Innovation implies that there is at least an expectation of wealth creation. By such a definition, innovation that does not create value is not really innovation at all. Not every invention is an innovation, because not every invention can be exploited, much less emerge successful in the market.

5 The gales of destruction

Cheyenne Software could not have had a better start in life. It was founded in 1983 by Barry Rubenstein, who had previously started Safeguard Scientifics, where he structured the initial financing of PC networking pioneer Novell. Following Safeguard, Rubenstein realized that the PC networks that were proliferating would need antivirus and backup programs to protect the integrity of their data. In the classic style of a start-up, Rubenstein decided to breathe life into his idea.

The first step was raising money. After contacting three dozen private investors, Rubenstein quickly raised $2.7 million. Next, Rubenstein recruited mainframe veteran Eli Oxenhorn, who was director of computer operations at Warner Communications, to serve as CEO, and ReiJane Huai, a former Bell Labs computer engineer, to lead software development. Although Rubenstein held the position of chairman, Oxenhorn managed the company.

The company initially marketed itself as a custom provider of software for LANs (local area networks), which interconnect PCs. For developing and maintaining its clients' software integration applications, Cheyenne received fees and long-term recurring royalties for its services. Securing clients like Chemical Bank and Fisher Business Systems enabled Cheyenne to go public in 1985.

Soon Rubenstein realized that there was an even bigger market for Cheyenne's custom applications. Most LANs held thousands of gigabytes of critical corporate information, and protecting them was increasingly complex. Responding to that opportunity, Cheyenne introduced ARCserve, a data storage manager for Novell networks that had a much higher level of data management and protection services than any other product.

As Novell boomed, so did ARCserve, which was the only server-based backup product that worked on all Novell platforms. By 1991, Cheyenne's ARCserve software supported more than 90 per cent of the installed base of backup hardware.

By 1993, the company had decided to leverage the widespread implementation of ARCserve by linking ARCserve to InocuLAN, Cheyenne's antivirus software. ARCserve was also linked with Cheyenne's automated server-based facsimile software, FAXserve, which allowed users to send vital reports generated by ARCserve to destinations of their choice.

Despite these additions to the product line, Cheyenne had not been able to expand beyond its dependency on ARCserve sales. In early 1994, Cheyenne stumbled: the latest version of ARCserve shipped late, which led to a failure to meet earnings expectations. The company's stock fell. Fortunately, in April, the new version of ARCserve was released, relieving pent-up demand and allowing Cheyenne to beat estimates. The company also announced that its president, ReiJane Huai, would replace Eli Oxenhorn as CEO. This news reassured wary investors, sending the stock up 13 per cent in a single day.

But the good news didn't last. That June, the SEC announced an investigation of the company based on an allegation that senior executives allegedly had sold shares prior to the missed earnings report. A class-action lawsuit by shareholders followed. Cheyenne's stock price fell by more than 70 per cent. Meanwhile, bugs were being reported in the new version of ARCserve, and some system administrators charged that the company had released its product six months before it was ready. Despite this, Cheyenne bounced back. The bugs were fixed, the suits settled, and profits in 1995 soared.

Cheyenne was still saddled with the need to grow, however. Unfortunately, ARCserve's innovations were not enough. With a highly successful LAN product, but little in the pipeline to expand the business further, Cheyenne became vulnerable to acquisition because it could not both operate effectively and innovate at the pace and scale required by the market to remain competitive. In April 1996, McAfee Associates, a company focused on the market for antivirus software, made an offer of $1 billion in stock for Cheyenne. McAfee CEO Bill Larson was confident that Cheyenne would accept the offer. 'This deal will get done,' he said. He simply needed to 'lay out our options, and enlist the shareholder community to communicate [to Cheyenne's management] that this is a marriage made in heaven'.

But Huai was adamantly opposed, calling the offer 'absolutely inadequate from a valuation point of view, from the point of view of a strategic business'. Huai went on the offensive, questioning McAfee's viability as an antivirus provider. 'The long-term prospects [for antiviral products] are really questionable,' he said.

Cheyenne fought the McAfee offer, implementing a poison pill strategy and filing suit against McAfee and Larson for making 'false and misleading public statements concerning Cheyenne'. For his part, Larson suggested that Cheyenne should fire Huai. Though Cheyenne reported a 33 per cent drop in quarterly profits, Larson was not able to apply sufficient pressure. On 1 May, McAfee dropped their offer. The McAfee bid, however, had signalled the opening of a 'shopping season', and it wasn't long before a suitor more agreeable to Huai and Cheyenne stepped forward: Computer Associates International.

CAI, which was rumoured to be interested in Cheyenne before the bid by McAfee, made an offer of $1.2 billion in cash. 'Sanjay [Kumar, president of Computer Associates] called and said, "It seems like a good idea for us to pool our companies together."' Huai said. Huai accepted the offer. While the deal was a 20 per cent premium on McAfee's offer, the rise in McAfee's stock since its failed bid was announced would have raised its offer value to $1.8 billion, an indication that Cheyenne had paid dearly for its 'white knight'.

Cheyenne was soon acquired by Computer Associates and downsized to generate more profits. By 1996, the flame that burned so brightly in 1983 had been extinguished. Cheyenne had lost its economic purpose and the market responded as Schumpeter had indicated it would. This is the way destruction happens in the marketplace.

Sometimes the destruction process can take decades. The Studebaker was one of the classic cars of the 1950s. Where is the company that made it now? Studebaker's decline began in the Great Depression, after more than 70 years of almost continuous growth and prosperity. Although sales declined to about 36,000 units in 1933 (from more than 84,000 in 1928), Studebaker's management stubbornly refused to trim its common stock dividend and cut other costs. As a result, the company only slowly recovered from the Depression. In the Second World War, Studebaker got a substantial cash infusion from the government. In 1954, it acquired Packard Motor Car Co. But Packard itself was weak; Studebaker killed off the Packard line four years later. By the late 1960s, Studebaker stopped making cars altogether. The company 'reinvented itself' as a component manufacturer but never regained its star status. In 1979, it 'merged' with Worthington of Canada to form Studebaker-Worthington, which was then acquired by a company called McGraw-Edison.

Anaconda Copper is another fallen star. By 1929, the company had amassed a worldwide natural resource empire encompassing copper mines in Chile, Mexico, and the United States; iron ore in Ontario; and vast nickel reserves in Australia. As late as 1968, as we noted at the beginning of Chapter 1, Anaconda president C. Jay Parkinson confidently predicted, 'This company will be going strong a hundred and even five hundred years from now.' Shortly afterward, in 1971, the Chilean mines were nationalized by the short-lived government of Salvador Allende. Weakened to the breaking point, Anaconda sold the remaining assets to Atlantic Richfield, which subsequently sold them on the open market in 1985, and like that, Anaconda was gone.

Another example, American Locomotive, comes from the railway industry, the industry that in its own time came closest to the booming telecommunications market of today. American Locomotive was incorporated in 1901 and quickly turned to 'voracious acquisitions' to take advantage of the explosive growth in railways. In the early years of the century, American became the largest rail equipment manufacturer in the country. However, with the building of a national system of superhighways in the 1950s and the steady progress of the diesel engine, trucking eventually took over much of the railways' market. AL tried and failed to diversify into areas outside their core competencies – heat-transfer equipment and automobiles – but became successively weaker and weaker. In the early 1980s, its remaining fragments were quietly subsumed into Cooper Industries.

As we go through the early years of the Internet transformation, stories like these are certain to continue.

THE EMOTIONAL DIFFICULTY OF DESTRUCTION: THE CASE OF INTEL

There are few things more emotionally upsetting to most people than the thought of killing off a company or a division, or firing a large group of people. Little wonder that within many companies one can find useless businesses, protected by complex accounting systems that 'subsidize' one business through another. Very often, divisions continue to operate even after they have outlived their economic purpose, at least as measured by the returns to investors.

The tension that a decision to close such a business division evokes is evident even in the best of companies. Few companies have been able to ride the turbulent waves created by 'gales of creative destruction' better than Intel. Yet Intel, too, has experienced the emotional *Sturm und Drang* of destruction.

In mid-1985, Andy Grove, then president of Intel, paid a visit to Intel's last remaining DRAM (dynamic random-access memory) manufacturing facility in Hillsboro, Oregon. His message to the staff: Intel would stop manufacturing DRAMs. It was a momentous decision for Intel, which was once the world leader in the DRAM business. DRAMs were its 'heritage' product, the product that got the company going in 1968. But by 1983, the market had become oversupplied. Japanese manufacturers, driven by the determination to dominate world commerce in these vital parts of the information revolution, had virtually destroyed the industry. Had Intel stuck with DRAMs, it would have gone bankrupt. The situation was obvious, but making the obvious decision was agonizing.

At the time of Intel's founding in 1968, semiconductor memory products were overtaking the core memory products of other companies. Semiconductor memories were the new 'gale' of the industry. By 1972, Intel's 1-kilobit 1103 DRAM chip had become the largest-selling integrated

circuit in the world and accounted for more than 90 per cent of Intel's
$23.4 million in revenue. As first mover, Intel commanded nearly 100 per
cent share of the memory chip market. By the end of the 1970s, Andy
Grove was able to say, 'Intel still stood for memories; conversely, memories
meant Intel.'

But in the early 1980s, the large Japanese DRAM producers (e.g.,
Fujitsu, Toshiba, NEC, Hitachi) entered the US market with high-
volume, high-quality, low-cost products. Moreover, since the technology
was still maturing, Intel was forced to spend ever more heavily on R&D to
keep a step ahead of its rivals. As the DRAM approached commodity status,
prices collapsed, and with that came a collapse in return to shareholders. It
was a pure and simple case of oversupply. In a single three-month period
over the summer of 1984, the price of DRAMs fell by 40 per cent, dragging
down industry performance with it. Intel slipped further than the industry
as a whole because of its dependence on DRAMs – and this was reflected
in Intel's total return to shareholders (TRS).

One Monday in January of 1983 (subsequently called 'Black Monday' at
Intel), Karl 'Casey' Powell, Scott Gibson, and 15 co-workers who had
worked as a team to find new applications for the newly developed microprocessor resigned *en masse* from Intel. They left because Intel was still
obsessed with developing and producing DRAMs, and would not provide
the resources that Powell and Gibson felt they needed to develop a wholly
new concept in computer applications: parallel processing. The defecting
Intel employees formed a company called Sequent Computer Systems.

Fig. 5.1 Semiconductors: Return on invested capital versus economy

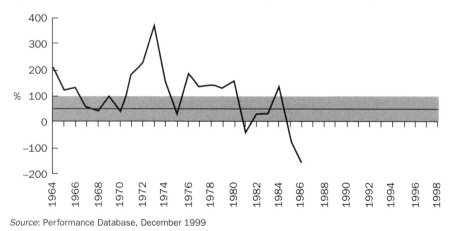

Source: Performance Database, December 1999

Fig. 5.2 Intel's total return to shareholders, 1972–1984

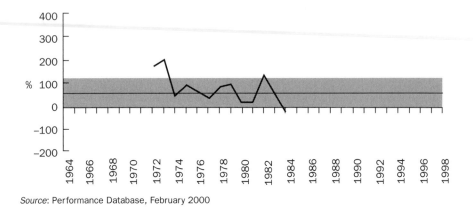

Source: Performance Database, February 2000

By the fall of 1984, Intel was losing money on its declining DRAM business. Intel's CEO, Gordon Moore, and president, Andrew Grove, presided over a series of 'meetings and more meetings, bickerings and arguments, resulting in nothing but conflicting proposals' over the future of Intel's fast-fading DRAM business. As Grove would later recall, making an apparently simple strategic decision – exiting from the random-access memory business – was powerfully blocked by the emotional ties the founders and senior executives had for memory chips, the silicon wafers that had 'made Intel Intel'.

As Grove recalled:

As the debates raged, we just went on losing more and more money. It was a grim and frustrating year. During that time, we worked hard without a clear notion of how things were ever going to get better. We had lost our bearings. We were wandering in the valley of death.

Halfway through that 'grim and frustrating year', CEO Moore and President Grove were standing in Grove's office in Santa Clara, California, gazing dolefully down at the Ferris wheel of the Great American amusement park revolving off in the distance. Grove turned to Moore and asked him point-blank: 'If we got kicked out and the board brought in a new CEO, what do you think he would do?' To which Moore unhesitatingly replied: 'He would get us out of memories.' After a few moments of silence, Grove asked Moore: 'Why shouldn't you and I walk out that door, come back in, and do it ourselves?'

That rhetorical question started Intel's two leaders on a long, painful course of action that eventually eliminated Intel's core business. As Grove later recalled, even after determining the correct strategic direction, implementation proved next to impossible, so deeply ingrained in the mental models of key employees was the role of DRAMs. As Grove said later:

Intel equaled memories in all of our minds. How could we give up our identity? How could we exist as a company that was not in the memory business? Saying it to Gordon was one thing; talking to other people and implementing it was another.

It was a classic case of cultural lock-in (and what Andrew Grove would later dub a 'strategic inflection point'). The 'defensive routines' of data disconfirmation, emotional resistance, and elaborate rationalizations were taking their invisible toll. Not only was Grove 'far too tentative', by his own account, in attempting to marshal the depth of conviction required to exit expeditiously from the memory business, but he found himself 'talking to people who didn't want to hear what [he] had to say'.

As Grove observed:

The company had a couple of beliefs that were as strong as religious dogmas. Both of them had to do with the importance of memories as the backbone of our manufacturing and sales activities. One was that memories were our 'technology drivers', which meant that we always developed and refined our technologies on our memory products first because they were easier to test. The other belief was the 'full-product-line' dogma. According to this [belief], our salesmen needed a full product line to do a good job in front of our customers; if they didn't have a full product line, the customer would prefer to do business with our competitors who did.

Grove and Moore would need to eliminate not merely the memory business itself, but the 'twin dogmas' that had protected Intel for so long and insulated it from reality. In practice, eliminating the prevailing mental model of the corporation, and the emotional superstructure that reinforced it, proved at least as difficult as eliminating the DRAM business itself.

To kill the DRAM business, Intel's VP of Finance instituted a capital-allocation system. This caused capital investment in Intel's memory business to 'gradually and incrementally decline'. By late 1984, DRAM production was reduced to a single fabrication site in Oregon. (R&D investment in DRAM continued to absorb about one-third of Intel's total R&D investment, despite the fact that senior management had already arrived at a decision to cease production of DRAM chips.)

That message, unfortunately, would take a while to sink down to the middle-management level. Grove would later credit a group of aggressive middle managers with gradually starving the DRAM business out of existence – even as more senior managers wavered, hesitated, and publicly and privately anguished over the difficulty of achieving an exit. He would later credit these middle managers with pointing the way for the senior managers, and attributed their ability to act to their being 'closer to the market' and less prone to sentiment than the senior team.

Other middle managers, with a more personal stake in keeping the DRAM business alive, were not about to give up without a fight. One proposal that the DRAM unit managers desperately advanced was a breakup of the company into two separate entities, one providing a commodity product (DRAMs) and the other a 'specialty' business (microprocessors). Although this proposal was never accepted, the company spent time and money on its evaluation.

The conflict continued. At one point Grove replaced the manager in charge of the doomed DRAM unit with another, to whom he clarified his strategic objective: 'Get us out of memories!' Yet the new manager found himself unable to offer anything better than a compromise – he would undertake no R&D on *new* memory products, but would continue to do R&D on products 'already in the works'.

As Grove would later recall, he reluctantly agreed to this request, on the grounds that exiting the DRAM business had to be pursued incrementally. 'I rationalized to myself that such a major change had to be accomplished in a number of small steps,' he recalled. Indeed, as late as mid-1985, Intel was entertaining a request by the general manager of the Components Group (to whom Memory Components reported) that it acquire advanced DRAM 'fabrication facilities in Japan in order to keep Intel abreast of the latest Japanese equipment advances in DRAM manufacture'. Needless to say, the market itself would never have embarked on such equivocation and delay. There would have been no one to make it.

Finally, Grove 'took charge of the implementation of the exit decision'. First, he visited Intel's last remaining DRAM manufacturing facility, in Oregon, and told the staff they would not be making DRAMs there any longer. Once this difficult and momentous decision had at last been made – publicly – there was no turning back. Intel told its sales force to notify the company's memory customers that Intel would no longer be making

DRAMs. The key uncertainties at the time were: 'What will our customers say? Will they abandon us? Will they lose loyalty to our brand?' As Grove recalled, he and his team were pleasantly surprised by their customers' reactions – or rather, lack of one. 'Their reaction was, for all practical purposes, benign,' said Grove.

Indeed, the image of the market held by Intel's senior managers had become severely distorted by cultural lock-in. They feared taking action. Ironically, key customers had long since accepted the fact that Intel was no longer a major factor in the DRAM market. They had already found other suppliers. 'Well, it sure took you a long time,' one customer commented.

As Grove would later philosophically observe: 'People who have no emotional stake in a decision can see what needs to be done a lot sooner.' And this, of course, is the key advantage that markets have over companies.

'People who have no emotional stake in a decision can see what needs to be done a lot sooner.'

While significant managerial energy was consumed by the decision to leave its heritage business, Intel also aggressively pursued a transformational innovation – the microprocessor, which was designed to power the original IBM PC. Soon sales of microprocessors outpaced Intel's highest sales levels of DRAMs.

As Grove himself cheerfully concluded: 'By 1992, mostly owing to our success with microprocessors, we became the largest semiconductor company in the world, larger even than the Japanese companies that had beaten us in memories. By now, our identification with microprocessors is so strong that it's difficult for us to get noticed for our non-microprocessor products.'

So powerful was the influence of the microprocessor that the health of the entire semiconductor industry, in fact, improved (see Figure 5.3). Financial success, and reward for patient shareholders, followed. Intel's total return to shareholders soon climbed above the industry average, as shown in Figure 5.4.

Less than half a decade after the microprocessor victory, Intel faced potential cultural lock-in once again. This time it came in the form of the discontinuity that has been shaped by the Internet. In 1996, in response to this challenge, Intel added a fourth strategic objective to what had been a tripartite program: 'Encapsulating all the things that are necessary to mobilize our efforts in connection with the Internet.' Intel has structured that effort as a venture capital firm would, building several funds that invested

Fig. 5.3 Semiconductors: Return on invested capital versus economy

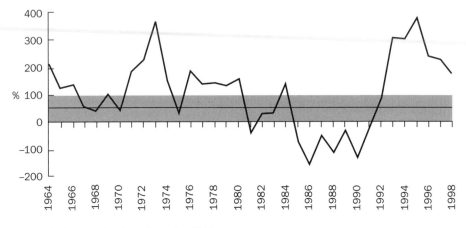

Source: Performance Database, December 1999

Fig. 5.4 Intel's TRS, 1972–1998

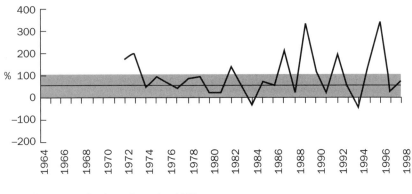

Source: Performance Database, December 1999

some $1 billion in new non-Intel start-ups. By the first quarter of 2000, sales of these investments had added materially to Intel's reported results. The future will tell whether the junior executives at Intel, those who aggressively fixed the DRAM dilemma, will be able to muster the courage to overcome the cultural lock-in regarding the personal computer industry that now sits at the edge of the campfire.

As Intel's history demonstrates, the time it takes to overcome cultural lock-in – to make the destroy decision – can be agonizingly long. The Intel story, however, is typical. There are hundreds of others like it.

How different Intel and other companies are from the market as a whole, which is stripped down to just buyers and sellers, without emotion, and is therefore tougher, more ruthless, more relentless, and less bridled with remorse than corporations. The markets have no sadness about destruction. They simply let it happen. It is a tough standard for any corporation to match.

ESCAPING FROM OLD IDEAS

John Maynard Keynes identified the real problem within corporations more than half a century ago: 'The difficulty lies not in the new ideas, but in escaping from the old ones, which ramify, for those brought up as most of us have been, into every corner of our minds.' Novelist and political writer Arthur Koestler, one of the most articulate observers of creativity, extended Keynes's observation by noting: 'The act of discovery has a disruptive and a constructive aspect. It must disrupt rigid patterns of mental organization to achieve the new synthesis.' As markets, competitive strategies, and regulations change, previously accurate mental models of customers and their needs, competitors and their strategies, rules of the game and the games themselves, change in incremental and most often unrecognized, or undiscussed, ways. As our McKinsey colleague, Peter Winsemius in Holland, summarizes: 'Our organizations tend to be good at what was important yesterday.'

Why is this the case? There are several schools of thought. Arthur Koestler claims it is because 'we learn by assimilating experience and grouping them into ordered schemata, into stable patterns of unity in variety. The matrices which pattern our perceptions, thoughts and activities are condensations of learning into habit.' It is this pattern of converting learning into habit, as well as the unthinking application of habit, that undermines the effectiveness of our past practices. The situation changes, but we do not recognize the changes.

The second school of thought is one that was first described by Elisabeth Kübler-Ross as she studied the reaction of people to life crises (specifically, the reaction of individuals at the moment they learned they were terminally ill). We briefly describe Kübler-Ross's sequence of denial, anger, bargaining, depression, and acceptance in Chapter 3. We believe the Kübler-Ross analysis is a metaphor for the corporate reaction to crisis, and drives to the heart of cultural lock-in. In patients facing a terminal illness the mood swings associated with the Kübler-Ross cycle can be wild and the period of adjustment long – and sometimes unresolved before death. The same happens in business, as senior managers face the potential corporate trauma of separating or terminating a business that has made long contributions to the well-being of the corporation. In life, the Kübler-Ross reaction is a 'normal, healthy one'. But in business, it delays the sense of urgency surrounding the crises, supports the status quo, and makes the afflicted company easy prey for aggressors. The problem, in other words, is not with objective reality but with the distortion of reality.

THE CONCEPT OF DESTRUCTION

Joseph Schumpeter observed in his studies of the pattern of development of markets and economies that destruction and creation were often paired. This is an ancient meld. Egyptian and Greek history are filled with stories of the mythical Arabian Phoenix bird, foster-father of Achilles, which destroyed itself in a pyre and then was reborn every 300 years or so, marking the turning points in Egyptian history. The Phoenix was an early symbol of the cycle of birth, life, death, and resurrection, leading to immortality. In business, that sense of immortality is known as continuity. The Phoenix, in other words, combined both creation and destruction.

The Buddhists have their Phoenix equivalent in the Garuda, a bird, their religious stories say, that was fond of the daily killing and eating of a snake, until a Buddhist prince taught him the value of abstinence. The penitent Garuda then brought back to life the many generations of serpents he had fed upon.

In Chinese culture the Feng, a bird with the head of a pheasant and the tail of a peacock – a structure not unlike the Phoenix or the Garuda – plays a similar role. Hindus have perhaps the most complex theory of creation and destruction: the Hindu trinity of Brahma (the creator), Shiva (sometimes a destroyer), and Vishnu (the arbitrator), which focuses directly on the balance of destruction and creation.

While the origins of creative destruction probably are lost in religious and cultural history, it is clear that Schumpeter was far from the first to focus on the close bond between creation and destruction, birth and death, continuity and change. In fact, he was one of a long line of thinkers who, to this day, strongly affect our ideas. But Schumpeter did apply the lessons of creation and destruction to the economy in a very persuasive way. Destruction is a mechanism that allows the market to maintain freshness by eliminating those elements that are no longer needed. As such, it is an essential feature of capitalism.

Destruction is a mechanism that allows the market to maintain freshness by eliminating those elements that are no longer needed. As such, it is an essential feature of capitalism.

Destruction, of course, is a negative and frightening word, conjuring up images of chaos and disorder. Perhaps without Schumpeter's guidance we would have tried to find a different word to describe the process. But we would have had to have found some word like it – because it *is* what happens in the market. Companies are born and they die or are subsumed. Unlike *creation*, which brings images to mind of a bright future, limitless possibilities, and perhaps personal growth, *destruction* triggers fear and foreboding. One thinks of Al 'Chainsaw' Dunlop, the former CEO of Scott Paper whose alleged callousness was synonymous with destruction.

When Schumpeter coined his phrase, 'gales of creative destruction', he had in mind the fate of collections of companies, old companies being replaced by new ones. The Russian revolutionary Mikhail Bakunin, considered by many to be the most radical of all anarchists, once said: 'The urge to destroy is also a creative urge.'

But this is not what Schumpeter had in mind. His idea was rather the opposite, that the efficiency of the new corporation placed such economic pressure on the old corporation, which did not change its ways quickly enough, that it eventually could not compete, and over time outlived its economic usefulness. Undoubtedly Schumpeter anticipated that even companies in new industries that had lost their edge would over time be eliminated. Schumpeter would not have been surprised by the fate of Cheyenne Software.

Schumpeter was not talking about processes that occur inside a company itself, although he easily could have addressed this issue. He left it up to us to apply what we mean by 'destruction' to individual companies. In Schumpter's sense destruction is 'the end of the economically useful life', whether a part of a corporation or of a company. This does not necessarily mean that this part of the corporation will die, however, or otherwise cease to exist. It simply indicates that the economic rationale for having it as part of the company has ended or is about to end. That could be because the potential of the business has played out, or because the basic economic rationale for the corporation has changed. Thus a division that might be appropriate for destruction at Intel does not necessarily warrant destruction at Fujitsu, which may have different objectives and resources.

In other words, *destruction* does not mean 'death' in the Judeo-Christian tradition, but rather 'transformation' in the Hindu tradition. In this sense, *destroy* really means something much closer to 'trade' than to obliterate. In some instances, *destruction* may, of course, refer to the end of economic life altogether, but that would be a special case of the more general principle. In either case, however, whether in the company or in the economy, the new will drive out the old.

There are various 'acts of destruction' or 'trading'. In a corporate setting the most dramatic acts, as we just mentioned, are the decisions to sell or shut down a group. A milder form might be to spin off groups that could make better use of debt capital if their parent retained only a minority (non-consolidated) share. The point of destruction in these cases is, as Schumpeter implied, to make way for creation, to allow for an increase in the 'freshness' of the corporation.

We do not normally think of restructuring as an act of destruction or trading. Restructuring is a normal part of the operational responsibilities of the corporation. One can restructure for growth or for returns, but the intent is to continue to actively manage the enterprise, rather than spin it out to increase the capacity for creation.

The notion of destruction raises some challenging questions for management. First, how can a company be run as a 'destroyer'? We actually don't know of any companies that are run specifically that way, other than the occasional asset stripper (few of whom exist, and even fewer of which survive). A good many companies are traders, however, and as we discuss in Chapter 7, many of them are private equity investing firms.

There are, of course, ageing companies that generate significant cash flow and yet do not grow. Some of these companies have lost their ability to trade as they have matured. As these companies have aged, so have their employees. Such companies are perfectly comfortable places, but they are not places for one to begin a career and grow. The reality is that recruiting new people is quite difficult for these companies. Over time, despite their strong returns and good dividends, their market capitalization tends to shrink relative to the growth of the economy, because they are not growing. The companies gradually lose relative economic power and simply fade away, as Cheyenne, Studebaker, and Anaconda did. If, along the path, their economic performance deteriorates, they may be bought out or go under even more quickly. But as we pointed out above, such companies can last for quite a long time in this state of 'suspended animation'. It would not be fair to categorize these companies as 'destroyers'. They are not intent on destroying anything; they are intent on merely staying alive. But they eventually expire.

How can managers and executives respond to destruction or trading that occurs at the pace and scale of the markets? Are people emotionally equipped to handle this kind of stress? The answer must certainly be 'no' regarding destruction. People are not emotionally equipped to live a life of destruction. But then again, neither are many called upon to do that. In most ageing companies, the decline is both gradual and relative to the overall market. People gradually move away from the centre of the nation's economic activity. The costs to individuals come more in the form of lost opportunity than real losses. With regard to trading, there are firms that have learned to trade at the pace and scale of the markets, as we describe in Chapter 7.

People who are caught up in overt destruction – for example, bankruptcy or a premature ending like Cheyenne – certainly need to find new jobs. And there will be more of this in the future, if our forecasts are correct. There are at least three broad strategies that such individuals can pursue. The first is to ponder the risk in advance, assess the consequences, and prepare an 'evacuation plan', just as one would if one lived on the coast and faced an approaching hurricane. Second, people can broaden their skills so that they have more options if their fears about their company or division materialize. Being dependent on a single skill set has always been risky, but it will become more risky in the future. Third, one can live in a place where there are ample opportunities if their current job is eliminated. In Silicon Valley or Silicon Alley, or Austin, Boston, or Raleigh-Durham, people are for ever changing positions. When one job ends, another opens up. People become loyal to areas rather than companies. More of this will likely take place in the future. These are not foolproof solutions, nor are they necessarily pleasant. But the reality of destruction is a fact of economic life.

Interestingly, American laws make it more difficult to declare bankruptcy in the United States than in the United Kingdom and many other countries. While this is a plus for US creditors and employees, it comes with an economic cost for the nation as it slows the rate at which our resources can be redeployed and thus our rate of progress. Despite this, we have not heard a single voice in favour of making bankruptcy easier in the United States in order to increase the rate of progress. If there are voices for policy changes in bankruptcy, it is for more stringency, not less.

Nonetheless, destruction is a reality of the market. It signals the end of economic utility for a division or company or industry. It can be postponed but not avoided. It is an inherent part of capitalism. The danger is that if it is not recognized as a normal part of corporate management, progress and performance can be slowed, and change will strike the company unawares. We have seen many examples of this, as Cheyenne, Studebaker, and Anaconda have demonstrated. To ignore destruction is to invite disaster. The issue, then, is how to deal with it. The way to handle it is to recognize destruction for what it is and make an explicit decision to deal with it, to trade dying assets before they have to be destroyed.

LEVELS OF DESTRUCTION

Destruction, like innovation, can be incremental, substantial, or transformational. In the case of innovation, we characterize the processes by the newness of each innovation and the amount of wealth created. In the case of destruction, the level of change depends on the extent of destruction and the amount of wealth at risk if destruction is not carried out.

Virtually all companies go through some form of *incremental* internal destruction each year. Procedures are changed, individual posts or branch offices closed, and so on. This kind of destruction does not challenge the basic mental model of the corporation; indeed, it is essential for the improvement of the operating routine of the corporation. Such change is essential to the concept of continuity. This kind of incremental destruction can be successfully carried out by the front line of the organization, just as incremental innovation is; it goes on day in and day out in a thousand, often unnoticed, ways.

Substantial destruction – the decision to lay off 10 per cent or more of the workforce, terminate a joint venture, kill an area of research or the development of a new product line – is not a decision that can be taken by the front line alone. Senior management must be involved. Such decisions are usually unpleasant to contemplate, plan, and implement. Nonetheless, they are vital to the long-term competitiveness of most organizations. Substantial destruction is warranted when major systems (e.g., corporate planning) get old and encrusted, and need to be replaced by more modern equivalents. Such replacements from time to time can trigger a fundamental change in the mental model of the corporation. Substantial destruction is a process fundamentally different from incremental destruction.

Transformational destruction irreversibly changes the course of the corporation. Closing down a heritage product line – as Intel did with its DRAM business – putting the company into play, and declaring bankruptcy are all examples of transformational destruction. It is transformational destruction that is closest to Schumpeter's meaning when he wrote about 'gales of creative destruction'; he envisioned companies and even whole industries being replaced. Often transformational destruction is triggered by market events, such as the entrance of foreign competition (in the case of Intel's DRAM) or the emergence of oversupply. Transformational destruction is a totally different and far more permanent process than substantial destruction, since the changes are irreversible.

All three kinds of destruction are crucial for corporate health. As corporations grow and mature, they become more complex. The complexities manifest themselves in rules, design manuals, and bureaucratic growth. The corporation becomes encrusted with rules and procedures.

Destruction is the one sure way to eliminate this encrustation. It scours corporate systems clean, keeping them fresh. And the longer one waits to remove the crust, the more dramatic the act of destruction must be, as Cheyenne Software discovered after it was too late.

6 Balancing destruction and creation

I have the feeling that I am sitting at a campfire, late at night, and the embers are slowly going out. I can hear the sounds at the edge of the light, just beyond view, but I don't know what they are or what they mean.

CEO OF A FORTUNE 100 GLOBAL CORPORATION
January 2000

In Chapter 3 we described the natural evolution of the key elements of a corporation's invisible architecture: mental models, information systems, decision-making systems, executional capabilities (actions), and control processes (which we called MIDAS), which can result in cultural lock-in. As we discussed, there is an inevitable evolution of corporations from the early passion of creation through the rational analysis stage and then into the trap of denial. This trajectory describes the great majority of American corporations over their lifetimes. A few corporations, however, have made attempts to break out of this pattern, and a few have succeeded, at least to a greater extent than the others.

The key to their success is the balance they have struck between creation and destruction – between continuity and change.

Often, we see a corporation beginning life as a result of a transformational innovation. As it matures, it begins to focus more on operations. The focus on innovation shifts, as we noted earlier, from transformational innovation to substantial innovation. Most corporations do not begin to focus on their need to destroy at this point. But a few do. Even at these early stages of development, those few companies begin to systematically break down the structures they have just built. If they do this too rapidly, of course, they destroy the basis of their existence – their current cash flow. If they do it too slowly, however, they will perform well in the short term but find themselves stuck in a cul-de-sac of mediocrity as time goes on. The corporation may still enjoy considerable success as it continues to improve through incremental innovation, but over the long term it is not sufficient to drive superior performance.

Eventually one of two things happens: either the corporation's performance begins to slow, or it attempts to revitalize itself. Companies can revitalize themselves by restarting the business, cashing out, simultaneous substantial creation and destruction, or simultaneous transformational creation and destruction. We will describe each in more detail.

One way companies try to revitalize themselves is by attempting to create transformational innovation without changing themselves to any degree. This is a difficult course to follow, and is usually unsuccessful. A second way is what we call 'cashing out', that is, liquidating the corporation through a sale of assets to another corporation, as Cheyenne had to do. This approach rewards current shareholders but clearly leaves the corporation moribund in the long run. It also leaves the company open for acquisition.

> One way companies try to revitalize themselves is by attempting to create transformational innovation without changing themselves to any degree. This is a difficult course to follow, and is usually unsuccessful.

SIMULTANEOUS SUBSTANTIAL CREATION AND DESTRUCTION

A third approach companies can take is to attempt both creation and destruction on a substantial scale. Corning, which moved from cookware and diversified glass products into fibre optics, and Enron, which evolved from a natural gas pipeline company to a trader of natural gas and other commodities, have pursued this course. They demonstrate that management with vision and high executional skill can implement this approach. Both companies resolved not only to 'destroy' their current business but to build the skills to produce new revenue streams. While each destroyed its current business, it was with some confidence that the new business was close enough at hand that the company would be able to survive the crossing. The stocks of both companies plummeted until the markets were convinced they were on the right track.

Corning

In 1864, Amory Houghton, long an investor in glass companies, purchased the Brooklyn Flint Glass Company. Four years later it transferred operations to Corning, New York, attracted by ample coal for fuel and by good transportation. Houghton renamed the company The Corning Flint Glass Company in honour of its new location. The firm, which initially produced consumer products such as thermometer tubing, pharmaceutical glassware, railway signal glass, and tableware blanks, was incorporated in 1875 as Corning Glass Works. In 1879, when Thomas Edison needed a glass bulb for his new electric lamp, he turned to Corning for assistance.

At first, the bulbs created by Corning were made by gaffers working gobs of molten glass on blowpipes, and production was very low. But a team of four glassworkers, capitalizing on the potential of moulds, was eventually able to turn out more than 1,200 bulbs a day. By 1908, the year Dr Eugene Sullivan established one of the nation's first industrial research laboratories at Corning, lightbulbs accounted for more than 50 per cent of the company's business. Corning's bulb marked the beginning of a partnership between glass and electricity that grew broadly over the years and now has taken on increasing importance in the age of electronics.

In addition to its technological prowess, Corning's success stemmed from its joint ventures. Corning formed a glass construction company, Pittsburgh Corning, with Pittsburgh Plate Glass in 1937; a fibreglass company, Owens-Corning, with Owens-Illinois in 1938; and a silicone maker, Dow Corning, with Dow Chemical in 1943. Corning has always understood that performance was the issue – not control, but performance for shareholders. It has provided that continually, although at times its devotion to shareholders has come at the expense of increasing corporate size.

Following the Second World War, Corning expanded globally. The company's laboratories made it the undisputed leader in the manufacture of specialty glass, which it used at the time to develop consumer products. For example, the company developed the first chemically durable glass, borosilicate glass, which could withstand sudden temperature changes, for freezer-to-oven Pyroceram brand ceramic cookware. This glass made the company's products the leading cookware in the market and made Corning a household name.

In 1947, the company's research revolutionized glass-forming methods to mass-produce bulbs, making television affordable for millions. By 1949, the efforts of James W. Giffen, head of the laboratory's newly formed machine research group, had paid off with a new method for centrifugal casting of television funnels. At the same time, Dr William H. Armistead, a Corning research chemist, developed a new lead-free glass composition specifically for television tubes that was both lighter and less expensive to produce. These television products dramatically increased Corning's sales and earnings growth. Investors responded accordingly with approval, bidding their stock to new levels.

But by 1983, James Houghton, the CEO, sensed that after a hundred years of excelling at the manufacture and sales of consumer goods, growth in that field was going to become increasingly difficult. Houghton initiated experiments with many different businesses. He narrowed the company's focus to high-growth industries and began buying laboratory services companies, such as MetPath in 1982, Hazleton in 1987, and both Enseco and G. H. Besselaar in 1989. The company also established international joint ventures with Siemens, Mitsubishi, and Samsung and dropped Glass Works from its name, representing a move away from consumer products and to technology.

> Houghton sensed that after a hundred years of excelling at the manufacture and sales of consumer goods, growth in that field was going to become increasingly difficult.

Along with these efforts, which had only a slim connection with the core ceramic technical skills of the company, Corning began to work on the development of optical-fibre technology, thus entering a completely new arena. For years, the commercial use of optical fibres for voice and data transmission was impossible because of light loss over distance. In 1970, three Corning researchers solved the problem when they created the first optical waveguides – glass fibres made from fused silica – that maintained the strength of laser light signals over significant distances. The invention paved the way for the commercialization of fibre optics for long-distance telecommunications and other uses. In 1993, AT&T chose Corning to provide fibre-optic couplers for its undersea telecommunications system.

To enhance developmental efforts with optical fibres, in 1994 Corning undertook a joint venture with Siemens AG, forming Siecor and Siecor GMBH. Siecor GMBH then acquired several fibre and cable businesses from Nortel Networks, expanding the firms' presence in Canada. Corning also formed Biccor to invest in fibre-optic ventures in Asia.

Then Houghton retired and was succeeded by president and chief operating officer Roger Ackerman. As CEO, Ackerman decided to 'double R&D spending . . . putting it into optical communications'. The next year, demonstrating Corning's commitment to creative destruction, Ackerman tried to sell off the slowly growing housewares unit, Corning Consumer Products, which accounted for 50 per cent of sales and 50 per cent of the employees. He first attempted to sell the unit to AEA Investors, but the sale fell through. But the following year, Corning was able to complete the sale of CCP to Kohlberg, Kravis and Roberts, signalling the end of Corning's involvement with consumer products. By expanding its presence in telecommunication and other technologies and selling off its consumer division, Corning distinguished itself from the vast majority of traditional companies, demonstrating its willingness to actually 'act like the market'. Corning has shrunk to grow several times in its century-and-a-quarter history.

Nor did Corning stop there. In 1999, it bought UK-based BICC Group's telecommunications cable business, and in 2000 the company acquired Siemens AG's optical cable and hardware businesses and the remaining 50 per cent of its joint venture, Siecor Corporation and Siecor GMBH. Also that year, the company acquired a communications components and mechanical control devices company, Oak Industries, and announced plans to spend some $750 million to double its optical-fibre manufacturing capacity. Later in 2000, Corning acquired NetOptix, a maker of optical filters, in a deal valued at about $2 billion.

These acquisitions are proving to be successful. For example, in early 1999, Corning introduced LEAF® Fibre, the first fibre and optical component capable of dramatically increasing the speed and information-carrying capacity of telecommunication networks. In addition, the company developed the first optical amplifier for telecommunication networks; the device can boost as many as 80 wavelengths of light through a single optical fibre. These inventions have enabled the company to dominate the market and rapidly increase sales growth.

Corning is now the leading provider of bandwidth, a market that is growing 30 per cent a year. In 1999, Ackerman said Corning has 'the largest position in the world in this particular technology [ultrahigh bandwidth], and we are continuing to invest aggressively in new plant equipment and, probably more importantly, in innovation'. It has been Corning's steady commitment to creative destruction, without sacrificing its operational excellence, that has placed the company at the forefront of the lightbulb, television, and fibre-optics industries – and in investor returns.

Following this long-standing tradition, Corning is not satisfied in being in fibre optics alone. Ackerman said the company plans to go 'well beyond optical fibre. We're spending a lot of money on R&D and doing very well in what I would call manipulating light information'. Ackerman states that 'Corning leads primarily by technical innovation and shares a deep belief in the power of technology. The company has a history of great contributions in science and technology, and it is this same spirit of innovation that has enabled us to create new products and new markets.'

With more than 50 per cent of sales coming from the fibre-optics unit and 30 per cent of sales from the advanced material unit, which produces a variety of industrial and scientific products, Corning has a bright future based on the assumption of discontinuity, not the comfort of continuity. So far, Corning has been a master of the game.

Enron

When Houston Natural Gas and InterNorth, two giants of the industry, merged to form Enron in 1985, Kenneth Lay, a former Federal Energy Regulatory commissioner, was selected to be the new CEO. Lay was recruited from a competitor to fight off the expected unwelcome advances of corporate raiders, since Enron had substantial debt when it was formed. Lay's first task as CEO was to aggressively eliminate layers of bureaucracy within the company while expanding the company's pipeline network. But even as he expanded the pipeline business, Lay saw that in the newly deregulated US natural gas market, the highest long-term returns were likely to be generated not by selling or transporting gas, but by trading it.

Indeed, when the US government deregulated the natural gas industry in the 1980s, it converted a stodgy, cost-based regulated industry into a competitive market. To supply that market, new companies, new networks, new

New companies, new networks, new financial channels and new products had to be created. The possibilities for innovation were endless – but so were the risks. Sensing a market opportunity in this volatility, in the late 1980s, Enron began to build a gas bank business to serve as an intermediary between producers and consumers of gas. The 'bank' would provide customers with a new form of stability – by custom-tailoring gas supply contracts according to quantity, time period, price index, and settlement terms.

It was Jeff Skilling, a senior partner at McKinsey at the time, who came up with the idea of creating a method to trade natural gas. He first presented his idea to the management committee of Enron Corp., who initially gave Skilling's idea a cool reception. But after further thought and more one-on-one discussions, CEO Lay and President and COO Richard Kinder championed Skilling's idea. In the end, Skilling left McKinsey to join Enron with the charter to create Enron Capital and Trade, now called Enron North America.

ECT was one of the first entrants into the free market for natural gas, operating as a trader, that is, buying gas from producers and selling gas to customers, such as power plants and industrial complexes. Previously, only regulated pipelines could purchase and sell gas, and the customers for natural gas had only one source of supply, their local utility.

When Skilling arrived at Enron, he inherited the old gas purchasing and marketing arm of the regulated pipeline business. Until deregulation, pipelines were engineering-oriented utilities that earned a fixed rate of return based on the amount of capital they had invested. Because the rate of return was fixed, buying smart or selling smart added nothing to the bottom line. Innovation was almost irrelevant. Skilling's first task was to change that.

Skilling rejected the conventional strategy of being the lowest-cost provider of a commodity product in favour of seeking to provide natural gas at the right time and the right price for a particular use. The trading model could not have been further removed from the traditional utility mind-set. In fact, Skilling wanted to change the traditional mind-set of the company from thinking of itself as a pipeline to thinking of itself as an energy store, closely following the approach MCI took when it entered the telecommunications business (deregulating along lines strikingly similar to the energy market). As Lay later commented: '[The energy market] will become just like the competing telephone companies, which offer a full line of telecommunications services today. You'll be able to call up and order all your energy from Enron.'

In 1992, natural gas futures contracts began trading freely on the New York Mercantile Exchange, a discontinuity in which Enron led the pack. Practically from its inception, the new unit provided its parent company with 22 per cent of its operating profits. As Skilling put it, 'Selling natural gas is getting to be a real business, like selling washing machines. We're taking the simplest commodity there is, a methane molecule, and we're packaging and delivering it under a brand name, the way General Electric does.'

To reach his objectives, Skilling dismantled the traditional hierarchy common in bureaucracies and created in its place a relatively flat pyramid with only three levels between the CEO and the lowest worker. He also replaced descriptive job titles with the kind found in professional service firms, titles that indicated the level of competency rather than describing the specific area of responsibility. Finally, Skilling and his team created a very high-risk, high-reward compensation system in which the base salary can be, for top performers, as little as one-third of total compensation.

As one executive said: 'We hire very smart people and we pay them more than they think they are worth.' This 'Enron premium', a combination of higher-than-expected pay and the confidence of ECT personnel that they were continuously developing new knowledge and tech-

'We hire very smart people and we pay them more than they think they are worth.'

niques and improving their skill sets, enabled Enron to retain exceptional people in the face of lucrative offers from competitor companies.

Skilling gave permission to young traders to commit up to $5 million on a deal without being obliged to seek upper-management approval. Performance criteria were broadened from simple revenue figures by establishing a system of 'peer review' whereby teams of up to two dozen employees were given free rein to rank their peers on criteria like 'ability to learn', 'leadership of self and others', 'connecting and leveraging', and, of course, 'innovativeness', in addition to raw revenue figures. These evaluation and compensation systems allowed ECT to turn over the vast majority of the organization in the initial few years – hiring the new talent that would be able to design and negotiate sophisticated contracts, and encouraging those unwilling to shift their mental models and skills to move on.

The environment that management created at ECT bears little resemblance to the one that preceded it in the era of regulation of natural gas. Senior management actively supported new ventures, even when they might cannibalize existing businesses. 'Nothing happens without people being willing to put flesh on the table,' said one manager. For each of their new major ventures, someone in the leadership ranks was willing to put his or her reputation on the line and move away from lucrative activities to make the initiatives succeed. They were willing to do this not only because they believed in the idea, but also because they knew that if they succeeded, they would get major financial rewards *and* have the opportunity to run the new business.

ECT even changed its workplace environment, creating large, open work areas so that people would constantly interact with each other and exchange ideas easily. Since information is key to the success of the business, all information was made available to everyone. The company developed proprietary analytical tools that are available to everyone on a single IT system.

Perhaps the most interesting example of creative destruction was Enron's facility with managing exit – and its myriad consequences. In an attempt to anticipate and even drive the next wave of electricity deregulation (the retail market), the company rapidly spent in excess of $30 million to aggressively pursue first-to-market advantage in California and New Hampshire, two key states that had championed energy deregulation. But just as MCI had learned to launch multiple new business models into the market, with tight strings attached, Enron abruptly pulled back from the consumer market when customer response proved unexpectedly tepid. Rather than punishing Lou L. Pai, the head of that unsuccessful effort, Enron's response was to reward him for a successful management of the exit by promoting him. In fact, timely exit is a key element of the mental model at Enron.

Another variant of simultaneously pursuing creation and destruction can be seen in the efforts of General Electric, Hewlett-Packard, and Johnson & Johnson. At GE, for example, Jack Welch, within four years of taking over as CEO, divested 117 business units – from mines to Light N' Easy irons –

totalling one-fifth of GE's 1981 $21 billion asset base. Welch was determined to mount a massive assault on GE's outmoded identity. The 'new' GE that Welch envisioned would be a high-tech provider of large-ticket products and essential services, from mutual funds to jet engines, credit-card processing, medical imaging, and network television programming. By aggressively moving to sell off the prime symbols of the 'old' GE, Welch advanced his case by years, if not decades. He had unambiguously demonstrated to all concerned that 'nothing was sacred', that 'change would be accepted as a rule, rather than the exception,' and that 'paradox is a way of life'.

The key distinction between this third approach of simultaneously implementing substantial creation and destruction, and the previously mentioned strategies of restarting or cashing out, is that these companies have rejected the assumption of *continuity* and embraced the assumption of *discontinuity* as the primary driver of their performance. They are not trying to achieve excellence in operations, and only later deal with creative destruction as they have the time. They are first and foremost focused on achieving market levels of creative destruction; they then design their operating procedures to be compatible with that constraint.

Achieving this in the proper balance (given their 'inverted' approach) is not simple. In each of the companies named above it raised practical problems (for example, how to redeploy once-productive people without creating so much resistance that the efforts are sabotaged from the start, or how to eliminate businesses that board members consider to be part of the heritage of the corporation). Careful thought and attention was given to these questions. But in the end, with sufficient leadership, these companies addressed and handled them. As a result of getting the balance right, these companies have provided returns to their shareholders that have matched the returns of the S&P 500, sometimes with a little room to spare.

SIMULTANEOUS TRANSFORMATIONAL CREATION AND DESTRUCTION

A fourth option is attempting *simultaneous* transformational creation and destruction. An example is Monsanto. CEO Dick Mahoney started Monsanto's transformation in the mid-1980s by divesting commodity chemical businesses, acquiring pharmaceuticals, and investing in biotechnology R&D. Robert Shapiro took over as CEO in 1995 and further accelerated the transformation. Shapiro understood that the markets wanted growth. As a former patent attorney, he also believed in the power of technological change. Shapiro launched a major growth initiative that led to shaping investments in biotechnology and genomics, in acquisition of seed companies to commercialize the biotech products, and in building a human nutrition business. As an example of Monsanto's technical success, the introduction of transgenic soybean seeds rendered the 'chemical weeding' of fields so easy that in the first year after its introduction (1996) US soybean farmers bought enough mutated soybean seeds to plant 35 million acres, or roughly half of the total acreage devoted to soybean production in the country.

Sensing the potential of Monsanto's invention, Shapiro boldly embarked on a wholesale transformation of the nearly century-old firm from a traditional chemicals-and-pharmaceuticals giant into a biotechnology company. He moved aggressively toward his goal by coupling a 'deal-a-day' acquisition programme for seed and smaller agricultural biotech companies with an exit from Monsanto's traditional core chemical businesses. In December 1995, he sold Monsanto's plastics business to Bayer AG for $580 million, then he spun off the $3 billion chemical company (under the new name Solutia) in 1997.

The idea was to allow the remaining $7.5 billion business to focus on the life science growth pillars: agricultural chemicals, seeds, pharmaceuticals, and food ingredients. On this base, he radically realigned the management structure that existed in the days when Monsanto was a 'chemical company'. Arguing that 'things are moving too fast for traditional management', Shapiro created 'two-in-a-box' management teams that pair relevant technology and marketing managers to make decisions about the business.

In 1999, in a bid to pay down the substantial debt incurred from an unprecedented number of acquisitions, the company put up for sale one of its most profitable products – the artificial sweetener NutraSweet – as well as the rest of its $1-billion-in-annual revenues food-ingredient business. The goal was to generate cash while conveying to shareholders and other stakeholders the sheer depth and conviction behind this massive strategic shift. While seeking to exit from a wide variety of businesses, Monsanto embarked on a cost-cutting programme estimated to remove nearly 4,000 employees from the company payroll of 30,000 worldwide. As Shapiro said:

We're entering a time of perhaps unprecedented discontinuity. Businesses grounded in the old model will become obsolete and die. Years ago, we would approach strategic planning by considering 'the environment' – that is, the economic, technological, and competitive context of the business – and we'd forecast how it would change over the planning horizon. Forecasting usually meant extrapolating recent trends. So we almost never predicted the critical discontinuities in which the real money was made and lost – the changes that really determined the future of the business.

Monsanto's transformation was, instead, built on the belief that they could be the drivers of a discontinuity in their market. But they could do so only if they destroyed what they once had been.

> Monsanto's transformation was built on the belief that they could be the drivers of a discontinuity in their market. But they could do so only if they destroyed what they once had been.

Initially, the market appreciated what Shapiro was trying to do, more than doubling the multiple on Monsanto's earnings. In 1998, however, widespread consumer resistance started to develop to genetically modified foods, particularly in Europe. The prospects for longer-term earnings growth seemed very much delayed. The market lost confidence in Monsanto's vision. In the summer of 1999, Monsanto sought refuge in a merger with American Home Products, whose chairman, Jack Stafford, was, like Shapiro, a lawyer. As the summer progressed, it became clear that the two sides could not get along and the merger had to be undone.

At that time Monsanto entered negotiations with several companies. Ultimately, Monsanto ended up partnering with Pharmacia & Upjohn to become Pharmacia in a merger of equals. Shareholders of both companies were dismayed, at least initially. Both sets of shareholders had been expecting to receive a premium for their companies were they acquired by a larger pharmaceutical player. When the deal was announced, the combined market capitalization of the two companies was $54 billion. Shares of both companies dropped sharply after the announcement, but by the time the deal was complete, the market had recognized the potential synergies, increasing the combined market capitalization to more than $60 billion.

The merger was sold on the prospects of becoming a major pharmaceutical player, not the biotech company that Shapiro tried to create. Pharmacia has already divested several components that defined the company, including its Equal brand sweetener, sold for $570 million to Pegasus Partners, and its bulk NutraSweet business was sold to J. W. Childs Equity Partners for $440 million prior to the merger. Additionally, it spun off the agrochemical division of Monsanto in an IPO. The name of the small spin-off tells us who was the greater of the two merger 'equals' – it is called Monsanto. Shapiro will remain as a non-executive chairman through 2001.

For a while it looked like Monsanto's transformational move was a stroke of genius. But in the end, too many things had to work perfectly for too long. Monsanto stumbled perhaps because the business it attempted to move toward was not yet an assured market. This is hindsight, however. At the time it looked like a reasonable strategy to almost everyone.

BALANCING CREATION AND DESTRUCTION IN PRACTICE: THE CASE OF SEQUENT COMPUTER

The story of the life and death of Sequent Computer shows the full cycle of corporate birth, growth and extinction over a short period of time.

Maintaining the balance between creation and destruction is exceptionally difficult, even for those with exceptional credentials. The story of the life and death of Sequent Computer shows the full cycle of corporate birth, growth and extinction over a short period of time. It gives us a quick movie of what really happens to companies on the ascent, as they reach the summit, and as they head down.

As we mentioned earlier, Sequent Computer was an Intel spin-off born without much foresight in Intel's incubator in 1983. 'We knew we were going to build a computer, we just didn't know what kind of computer it was going to be,' Casey Powell, Sequent's first and only chief executive, said.

A few weeks after Intel's 'Black Monday' in 1983, Sequent Computer Systems decided that it would produce a 'parallel processing' computer, a new type of high-performance computer that used multiple processors manufactured by Intel or its competitors. Despite the technological risk and the uncertainty of an unproven management team, Sequent raised $5.2 million from several venture capitalists within months of Black Monday. Less than two years later, Sequent's first computer, the Balance 8000, was completed.

The Balance 8000 was the first commercialization of a technology referred to as symmetric multiprocessing (SMP), or parallel processing. Previously, mainframes and minicomputers used single central processing units (CPUs) to perform calculations for all of the users connected to the system. To provide greater computing capability, companies like IBM and Digital Equipment Corp. designed and developed their own complex CPUs. Sequent believed that it could design the software and hardware necessary to make several inexpensive, mass-produced CPUs work together as a single unit, cutting the cost of production enormously. In the Balance 8000, Sequent created a machine that could use up to 12 CPUs harmoniously. It was a substantial innovation in the industry.

When Sequent first announced its SMP computer, however, the industry barely noticed. 'Of the six people who showed up at our first presentation, four were [the conference organizers]. They felt sorry for us,' said Robert Gregg, a former chief financial officer of Sequent.

Initially, customers were equally unreceptive. Sequent had created the Balance 8000 to solve scientific and technical problems that required substantial, dedicated computing power. But it found the market small and difficult to penetrate; it sold fewer than 50 machines, capturing only $5 million in revenue in 1985.

Soon, however, the market began to discover Sequent. While the Balance 8000 could outperform much higher-priced computers on technical problems, it was even more effective for business applications that involved multiple users accessing and modifying a large database. In the first half of 1986, Sequent signed four-year deals with Siemens and Amperif to supply $70 million worth of computers to be rebranded and bundled with other office computing products. And Boeing Co., a company that Sequent had hoped to sell to for technical computing, bought a Sequent computer to store and manage a research database instead.

As sales grew, Sequent decided to go public, raising more than $25 million in April 1987. Sequent's product line also grew as it released the Symmetry models, which were based on up to 30 of Intel's new 80386 microprocessors and ranged in price from $85,000 to $800,000. In terms of MIPS (a simple measure of computing power), Sequent's top machine was on par with IBM's 3090 mainframe, which sold for $11.5 million. The Symmetry series led to an operating profit of $4 million on sales of $38 million in 1987, almost double the sales of 1986. This rapid expansion continued through 1990, with profits rising to $16 million on sales of $146 million in 1989.

Most of Sequent's sales were driven by database management needs. In early 1987, Sequent entered agreements with several independent database companies, including Oracle and Informix. It agreed to prepurchase software licences and ship computers with the customer's choice of database. Working directly with software companies, particularly Oracle, helped Sequent draw attention to itself. In 1989, Oracle announced that the Sequent machines were the most cost-effective computers to use with its databases. For similar performance, customers would have to pay twice as much for a Digital Equipment VAX system, or six times as much for IBM's offering.

Sequent computers were an excellent value for database applications, and Sequent continued to sell computers in ones and twos, even to large clients. Coca-Cola, Radisson, and Boeing, for example, were customers, although they bought Sequent for specific database needs rather than for companywide distribution.

To reach customers looking for tens or even hundreds of machines, Sequent entered a five-year agreement in 1989 to supply Unisys with computers that Unisys would bundle with additional software and peripherals and sell under its name. It reached similar, smaller agreements with Siemens and Prime Computer.

While this approach paid off in the short run (original equipment manufacture, or OEM, sales accounted for 34 per cent of revenues in 1989), it also concentrated Sequent's customer base at a time that it needed to be broadened. A year later the agreements unravelled. Prime Computer broke its agreement in order to pursue its own parallel system, and Unisys, which had bought more than 25 per cent of Sequent's computers in the first half of 1990, began facing operational difficulties that led it to announce its intentions of phasing out all OEM agreements. The market distinctiveness, which Sequent had established early on, was being eroded by competitors' imitations.

The pace of imitation accelerated, and Sequent's direct customers began to find that they had growing bargaining power, as several small computer companies such as Pyramid Technology and Teradata followed Sequent into the area of high-performance multiprocessor systems. IBM and DEC started to offer competing systems as well. Additionally, a slowdown in the overall economy resulted in more of Sequent's sales coming from its lower-end, lower-margin products. These events led to a decline in sales in 1991 and an operating loss. The honeymoon was over.

Scott Gibson, one of the company's original founders, who served as president, director, and co-CEO with Powell, attributed Sequent's problems to external causes: 'It's pretty clear that the entire industry is going through a very difficult period. It has also become painfully clear that Sequent is not immune to the industry-wide effects of a severe slowdown in capital spending by end users.' However, the comparison of total return to shareholders relative to industry performance indicates that Sequent's downturn in 1991 was primarily internal. Others within Sequent may have not shared Gibson's publicly stated view; in February 1992, it was announced that Gibson was resigning his positions, which would be taken over by Powell.

Sequent had found that after its original innovation – creating a successful SMP computer – its business relied on working with software builders to provide customers with systems that could address a specific need. This strategy was extended from database management to networking in late 1991. As PCs replaced mainframe terminals in the late 1980s, companies began to shift to a client-server computer structure, where files could be maintained centrally and shared across the company. Novell had captured a sizable share of the networking software market with its NetWare software. Sequent worked with Novell to produce a version of NetWare that took advantage of the capabilities of the multiprocessor environment.

Sequent's file servers began selling immediately, returning the company to profitability in 1992. But its competitors, which had already caught up with Sequent by offering multiprocessor machines capable of running Oracle database software, were not far behind. The software that Sequent helped Novell develop would need only slight modifications to run on other multiprocessor machines, and Novell had a strong interest in licensing to Sequent competitors. Whenever the competition caught up, Sequent drove forward into new territory rather than defending the turf that it first claimed. 'When other people offer the same capabilities, we have to go on to something new,' Powell said. The spirit of substantial and transformational innovation was alive, but little attention was being paid to the right way to deal with the operations of the business, or how to oversee their decline.

The company's head start in the file server market was indeed fleeting, and with little new to offer customers, Sequent saw its growth slow again in 1993, while costs associated with the sales force grew, leaving Sequent with a loss on the year. Sequent's progress was also hampered by the delay of Intel's Pentium processor, which promised to double the speed of Sequent's Symmetry models.

In the wake of 1993, Sequent began to rethink its strategy and started focusing on larger clients, choosing to forgo competing for smaller contracts that they had chased in earlier years. While sales responded well in 1994, Sequent's success was in a larger part attributable to a weakened dollar that led to greater international sales, propelling Sequent faster than most of the industry, which was more reliant on domestic markets than Sequent. In the next two years, Sequent continued to grow and succeed in line with the industry as a whole, but now it faced an innovation challenge.

Until 1996, the increased computing performance of Sequent products was primarily due to improvements in Intel's processors, speeding along at the rate of Moore's Law, which states that the speed of microprocessors will double every 18 months. The number of processors that Sequent had been able to lash together effectively remained capped at 32. Beyond that, the CPUs simply began to get in one another's way when trying to share other components, such as RAM or the main disk drive. Stanford engineers proposed a new type of computer structure called non-uniform memory access, or NUMA, that would enable multiprocessor computers to share memory and disk space more efficiently. Several SMP computer manufacturers worked feverishly to perfect the first marketable NUMA computer, but Sequent was first again with its NUMA-Q system, which could link 64 Pentiums. The system was released for shipment in February 1997. Unlike many companies, Sequent had been able to achieve a second transformational innovation. But the cost was high.

While large customers responded positively to the NUMA-Q, including a $59 million order from Boeing, the stock market was far less responsive to Sequent's breakthrough than it had been to earlier innovation. Essentially, the capital markets did not believe that Sequent's latest advance would lead to higher cash flows for the company beyond the first year or two. In addition, the NUMA-Q emphasized Sequent's focus on the top end of the computer market, rather than the smaller dedicated machines that had been the source of its initial success. Powell was emphatic: 'I'm big, big, big – I'm after the $5m to $40m space. If a [Sequent] sales guy goes to try and sell a four-way [an earlier, smaller system], not an eight-way [NUMA-Q 2000], he hasn't got a job.'

From the start Sequent claimed that the performance of its top machines could rival that of mainframes. With a NUMA-Q built around Intel's next big chip, the Merced, projected for delivery in the middle of 2000, IBM began considering tendering an offer for Sequent. In July 1999, IBM agreed to pay $810 million for the company, which Sequent's board accepted. Sequent was an independent company no longer, although the NUMA-Q brand may well survive with an IBM logo on it.

In its 16 years of independent existence, Sequent had consistently maintained a technological advantage, bringing concepts to market years ahead of other companies. But it was never able to claim and defend the high ground as it moved forward, as Corning and Enron did. Its operations side simply couldn't match its success at innovation. It was not a bad performance for a company, but it was not enough. The right balance between creation and destruction wasn't achieved. In the end, the market did the necessary cleaning.

What can we conclude from this? First, to create at the scale and pace of the market, one has to destroy at the scale and pace of the market. The destruction that is essential to maintain freshness in a capitalistic market economy is also essential within the corporation if it is to extend its prosperity. Yet destruction is as difficult to master as innovation, since it requires overcoming the emotional barriers of denial that are built into the natural evolution of the corporation. As a result, corporations often pay insufficient attention – or pay attention too late – to the task of destruction.

Second, striking the right balance between creation and destruction is extraordinarily difficult. In the popular 1991 movie *Other People's Money*, Danny DeVito was cast as 'Larry the Liquidator', a workout artist who found and scavenged weak companies. Larry realized that his latest prey, New England Wire and Cable, could not survive competition from abroad. Near the end of the movie, Larry comes to town to tell the shareholders (who are also employees and townspeople) that the end is at hand. Larry's final comments are well-argued. 'In the end,' he says, 'market forces will seal your fate, not me.' While Larry does not get the girl (the brilliant lawyer who defended the company), neither does the town get a reprieve – it loses its company. The message of the movie mirrors the lessons of life: the markets always win.

We think back to the unnamed senior executive quoted at the opening of the chapter, who stares out past the light of the campfire and ponders the fate that awaits him. His worries are well founded, his fears are real. Night eventually will deepen, and the embers will cool. Predators do crouch beyond the light. Our only defence is to be well prepared.

7 Designed to change

Don't tell me about the flood. Build me an ark.

attributed to LOU GERSTNER, CHAIRMAN OF IBM

As we indicated in Chapter 1, by the year 2025, the average length of time a company resides on the S&P 500 will be no more than 10 years, compared to 20 years today. The pace of change is accelerating. Survival alone, as we have seen, is no guarantee of performance. Based on the historical record, even those companies that do survive to the year 2025 will likely underperform the markets.

Can the steel link between survival and underperformance be broken? Can today's companies avoid the fate of the East River Savings Bank and other companies that have slipped into obscurity? We believe they can. In fact, the prescription to do so is quite simple to state: 'Act like the market.'

What does 'act like the market' mean? It means that corporations must strive to change themselves at the pace and scale of the market. But how does a company go about 'acting like the market'? How does one, as Lou Gerstner put it, 'build the ark'?

To build the ark, the concept of the corporation must change from the nineteenth-century view that managers must operate a company first and handle creative destruction when they can. It must establish a more dynamic

It is necessary for the corporation to become a creator, operator, and trader of assets, rather than a merely efficient operator of assets.

view that mandates managing creative destruction first and operations second. But it must do so in a highly decentralized way that nevertheless does not sacrifice control. It is necessary for the corporation to become a creator, operator, and trader of assets, rather than a merely efficient operator of assets.

Specifically, companies must:

1. Increase the pace of change to levels comparable with the market.

2. Open up their decision-making processes to make use of the collective talent of the corporation and its partners (and avoid cultural lock-in).

3. Relax conventional notions of control, but not to the detriment of operations.

These are the critical elements of the new corporation – the corporation that will be able to successfully ride the waves generated by Schumpeter's 'gales of creative destruction'.

THE ARCHITECTURE OF CREATE, OPERATE, AND TRADE

In Chapter 2 we discussed the five elements of corporate architecture that shape and drive companies: mental models, information systems, decision-making systems, executional capability (actions), and systems of control (or MIDAS for short). Coordinating these elements is relatively simple in the operating corporation, which has one reasonably stable mental model. The mental model drives the structure of the information systems, which are perfectly stitched into the fabric of the decision-making and control systems of the corporation. Action (or execution) comes as a consequence of the decision-making systems, and is held in check by the control processes. It is all very neat and simple. But because the business environment is constantly changing, the system becomes vulnerable to cultural lock-in and eventually loses its effectiveness.

The increasing pace of change in the markets requires a new model. It is likely that this new model will be more complex, to accommodate the higher pace of change in the future. An operating model will still have to exist, but it will have to be joined by creating and trading, the essential functions of creative destruction. In other words, the five elements of MIDAS will be completely different for companies seeking effective creative destruction and successful operations.

Creation versus operations

Companies seeking to foster creation must support multiple mental models – representing fundamentally different approaches to business – because such models are always present in the marketplace. Rarely is there such uniformity of thought in the marketplace that there is no dissension. That would constitute a monopoly, and there are precious few of those (even monopolies have their opposing interests, as OPEC and DeBeers illustrate). How does such thinking fit in with the mental models of typical companies focused on operations? Let's take a look.

In companies focused on operations, the essential information is known, and is presented when it is needed and in the form it is needed. In companies focused on creativity, it is often not clear what information is necessary or relevant. The information necessary for decision making can be ambiguous, difficult to obtain, or simply missing.

The decision-making processes in companies focused on creativity are equally unclear. Frequently, such processes evolve along with the decision to be made. One may discover problems only as the solutions become obvious. Only after the fact are the methods clear. Accordingly, the real-time measurement of the efficiency of decision making for the creative process is extremely difficult, if not meaningless altogether.

Control also takes on a different meaning in the organization focused on creativity. The precise nature of control systems at the heart of operational effectiveness are useless in the creative process. In the creative process control has more to do with the selection of people with talent, with having some sort of worthwhile objective, and with having a set of warning signals that can shut down the system before harm is done. But these are crude measures of control. More finely tuned control measures run the inherent risk of shutting down the creative process altogether. Here permission is more important to creative output than control.

Execution, too, takes on a different meaning. In companies focused on operations, execution is almost routine, made up of a thousand little tasks, executed one after the other until the job is done. Miss a few of these trivially simple tasks, and the overall operational effectiveness may be jeopardized. In the organization focused on creativity, execution may mean 'thinking the right thought' as much as 'doing the right thing'. Creation is dependent on execution, certainly, but the nature of the process is entirely different.

Trading versus operating

Trading – the 'destruction' part of creative destruction – is more like operations than it is like creation. Yet there are substantial differences in the requirements for effective trading and effective operations as well. For example, in trading, the information needed is not routine. Most trades, at least at the corporate level, are one-time deals and have to be designed each time from scratch. Trading is the final act. There is no presumption of continuing activity. In trading, control also takes on a different meaning. Control implies achieving the desired outcome, then bringing the process to a stop with no loose ends. This is a different kind of control than that exercised in either operations or creation. In trading, the control system has to be designed for the individual trade, unless a routine commodity is being traded. Rarely, however, does the senior level of a corporation face routine trades. When 3M spun off Imation, when Hewlett-Packard spun off Agilent, when Siemens spun off Infineon, or when General Motors spun off Delphi Systems, the transactions were anything but routine.

Not surprisingly the invisible architecture of organizations that foster creation, operations, and trading is very different, and much more complex, than the invisible architecture of an organization focused on operations alone. (See Appendix B for a summary of the different requirements.)

Can any company maintain the balance between continuity and discontinuity as well as the markets? Yes, companies can, although simply trying to adapt the systems utilized in an operating organization will not often work. Rather, one has to start over and create systems built on discontinuity. We now turn to two companies that have successfully ridden 'gales of creative destruction' – Kleiner, Perkins, Caulfield and Byers, and Kohlberg, Kravis and Roberts. These companies can not only claim to have successfully ridden through the gales – they can rightfully claim to have helped create them.

CONTINUOUS CREATION: KLEINER, PERKINS, CAULFIELD AND BYERS

Kleiner, Perkins, Caulfield and Byers is a leading venture capital company. Venture capital firms operate for the sole purpose of helping to launch small companies with new, potentially valuable ideas.

Kleiner Perkins, as it is commonly referred to, was formed in 1972 by Thomas Perkins, the first general manager of Hewlett-Packard's computer division, and Eugene Kleiner, a veteran of Bell Laboratories and a co-founder of Fairchild Semiconductor. Unfortunately, their timing could not have been worse. The United States was slipping into the longest recession the country had seen since the Great Depression. It was a terrible time to form a company for the purpose of funding technology start-ups. Still, the firm managed to raise $7 million. Soon after it raised its initial capital, Brook Byers, a specialist in life science businesses, and Frank Caulfield, a career venture capitalist, became partners, adding their names to the firm.

The firm's combined expertise in computers and biotechnology proved to be its competitive advantage, luring both investors and entrepreneurs to the fund. Its first major success came in 1976 when it decided to invest in Genentech, the first recombinant DNA technology company. Kleiner Perkins provided the capital and appointed Robert Swanson, a Kleiner Perkins associate, CEO. After producing the first human protein and then cloning human insulin, Genentech went public in 1980. Its stock price doubled the first day. By 1992, the $1 million that was originally invested in Genentech in 1976 was worth $372 million. Genentech remains one of Kleiner Perkins' most profitable companies to this day.

Kleiner Perkins also focused on computer companies. In the 1970s, it funded many firms including Tandem Computers and Lotus Development, followed by Sun Microsystems and Compaq. In the 1980s, it funded Intuit and Symantec. By 1982, Kleiner Perkins had become one of the largest venture capital firms in the world, with investments totaling $150 million. By 1998, Kleiner, Perkins, Caulfield and Byers' success had helped it raise more than $1.2 billion, which it had invested in more than a hundred private firms that subsequently offered their shares to the public. The total market value exceeded $80 billion in 1998.

The capital for Kleiner Perkins' funds came from large investors, including the endowments of the University of California, Stanford, Harvard, MIT,

Georgia Tech, Yale, Vanderbilt, and Michigan. More recently Kleiner Perkins has brought in money from the pension funds of General Motors, the Rockefeller endowment, and the foundations of Ford and Hewlett-Packard.

Kleiner Perkins prefers to raise funds from institutions and very wealthy individuals because they can help finance portfolio companies in later rounds. Of the money that is invested, Kleiner Perkins receives a 2 per cent management fee and 30 per cent of all profits. The share holdings are distributed to its investors after the public offerings.

Today, Kleiner Perkins organizes its investment strategy around eight categories, which are divided between the life sciences (medical devices and diagnostics; drug discovery and therapeutics; and health care services) and information sciences (the Internet; enterprise software; consumer media; communications; and semiconductors).

Kleiner Perkins is selective in its investment candidates, and examines their management closely. 'What we do is look for markets that are going to change at least by an order of magnitude, technologies that can make it possible, and great teams – because strategies are easy, it's execution that's everything,' said L. John Doerr, who has served as leading partner since the 1980s. When considering a company for investment, a single 'no' from any one of the 19 partners can stop the investment. In addition, two partners must be willing to sit on the company's board of directors. 'The valuation process is not numbers-crunching. It's really based more on experience,' said Michael Curry, who serves as CFO for Kleiner Perkins. 'If you can't do the math in your head, it's probably not a venture deal.'

Doerr believes that investment strategies should be built around specific market initiatives. 'There are four hundred venture firms, right? So how can any one firm develop significant market share? Only by focusing on initiatives, which means several partners work together to help build companies and opportunities in specific areas.'

Not all of Doerr's initiates have been successful. In the late 1980s, for example, the company invested in several companies that were targeting the mobile computing market, including Dynabook Technologies. Although the market has since proven itself, at the time Kleiner Perkins and Dynabook were too far ahead of the technology and the market. Doerr admits he was slow to pull the plug. 'We didn't execute, and we didn't shut it down,' he recalled. 'We thought the portable market was going to be so big.' By the time Kleiner Perkins was able to off-load Dynabook to Unisys in 1990, it had cost the firm $8 million.

In the 1990s, Doerr was skeptical about the value of the Internet. 'At first, I thought Al Gore was nuts when he talked about information highways, on ramps, off ramps, and roadkill. But I was wrong. We can use networks, not just to lower costs, but to improve communications and build communities.' Now the companies that Kleiner Perkins has funded *define* much of the Internet. They include America Online (which bought Netscape), Amazon.com, and Excite (which merged with @Home).

Kleiner Perkins's 1995 investment in Netscape marked its shift from computer hardware to Internet investments. 'In the 1980s, PC hardware and software grew into a $100 billion industry,' Doerr said in 1996. 'The Internet could be three times bigger.'

The IPOs Kleiner Perkins have founded have been so successful that today the firm receives more investor interest than it needs. One effect of the firm's success has been mergers and acquisitions between companies that Kleiner Perkins started. In 1998, Compaq acquired Tandem Computers for $3 billion in stock, and AOL bought Netscape for $4.3 billion (after rumours that Sun was in talks with Netscape).

More recently, Kleiner Perkins has taken steps to form partnerships of its own, announcing plans in 1999 to join Charles Schwab, TD Waterhouse, Ameritrade, Benchmark Capital, and Trident Capital in an investment bank to underwrite Internet company offerings. In 2000, Kleiner Perkins continued the trend, forming eVolution Partners with Bain & Company and Partners of Texas Pacific Group.

Venture capital firms like Kleiner Perkins show that it is possible to operate a create–operate–trade model very effectively and over long periods of time. They also illustrate how different the 'invisible architecture' of the corporation – the mental models, the information and decision-making systems, the executional capability and the control process – have to be to make the system work. Of course, venture capital companies are not an incremental step away from operating organizations. They are totally different. But they are not the only examples of successful, sustained approaches to the create–operate–trade organization. Principal investing firms are a second example.

> Venture capital firms like Kleiner Perkins show that it is possible to operate a create–operate–trade model very effectively and over long periods of time.

CONTINUOUS TRADING: KOHLBERG, KRAVIS AND ROBERTS

In 1988, Duracell, then a division of Kraft Foods, was a struggling, under-performing company trapped in its own operational processes, unable to break the cycle of cultural lock-in that engulfed it. It was at this low point that the leverage-buyout firm Kohlberg, Kravis and Roberts bought Duracell from Kraft Foods. Leverage-buyout firms such as Kohlberg, Kravis and Roberts buy struggling companies and then seek to dramatically improve their operations through breaking the cycle of cultural lock-in by selling divisions without potential, providing incentives for extraordinary performance, and increasing the penalties for underperformance.

KKR paid $1.8 billion for Duracell ($1.45 billion in debt and $350 million in equity), believing that the company had substantial untapped growth potential, especially in international markets (which comprised 12 per cent of the company's sales).

With help from KKR, Duracell began to transform itself by selling its underperforming divisions and consolidating production (in part to pay off KKR's debt, which had been incurred in making the purchase). Subsequently, Duracell diversified its product line, further decreased production costs, and added new advertising and marketing efforts. Contrary to the exploitative image some critics have associated with KKR, the firm strove to make Duracell stronger than it ever had been. And they were successful. Between 1989 and 1995, Duracell's cash flow increased at an annual compound rate of 17 per cent (under Kraft, Duracell's cash flow had been flat).

Duracell's CEO, Bob Kidder, found that KKR was aggressive about the development of new technologies. 'Not once did Henry [Kravis] or George [Roberts] ask, "How can we cut R&D?"' Kidder recalled. 'In fact, they asked just the opposite, "Should we be investing more in R&D to ensure that we have a technological edge for the long haul?"' Duracell's R&D efforts led to the development of a mercury-free alkaline battery, a rechargeable battery, and a smart battery for laptops. Duracell had to destroy to create, and cultural lock-in prevented that from occurring while the company was owned by Kraft.

More innovation followed: Duracell introduced the freshness date code, battery multipacks and the package battery tester. As a result of such brand-strengthening moves, the company became the market leader. With new advertising efforts and new distribution channels, the company added

500,000 retail outlets to its worldwide distribution network by 1996. Meanwhile, Duracell was able to dominate the European market and expand sales in South America, Africa, the Pacific Rim, and the Middle East. The original five-year plan targeted 15 per cent annual growth, but Duracell was racing far beyond that. It had grown so fast, in fact, that within three years of the buyout, in 1991, KKR decided to take Duracell public.

Duracell introduced the freshness date code, battery multipacks and the package battery tester. As a result of such brand-strengthening moves, the company became the market leader

Five years later, in 1996, Gillette bought Duracell for $2.8 billion in stock (KKR had already made more than $1.3 billion during the previous eight years as a result of Duracell's operations – a 39 per cent annual compounded return on its investment). The $350 million that KKR had originally invested in Duracell had returned $4.22 billion. That was the amount Kraft had forfeited through poor management.

CREATIVE DESTRUCTION AND PRIVATE EQUITY FIRMS

Kleiner Perkins and KKR are both examples of private equity firms. Private equity firms are made up of a set of limited partnerships organized as investment funds. These firms operate under a special set of regulations established by the US government in the 1930s and 1940s to regulate companies that choose not to offer their equity shares to the public. What is interesting to us is that, based on the historical evidence, private equity firms do a far better job of embracing the spirit of discontinuity than do the traditional operating companies that have been the backbone of the productive capacity of the United States.

Private equity has its origins in the Great Depression and against the background of the trusts of the late nineteenth century. Private equity companies were first provided for by the Securities Act of 1933 to protect the public from undue risk (or unscrupulous bankers) from certain financial ventures (e.g., backing newly formed firms). Congress recognized that 'sophisticated' investors were in a better position than the general public to assess the risks of these ventures. The Securities Act provided an opportunity for wealthy individuals, in small groups (fewer than a hundred investors), to invest capital in more risky and less regulated ventures, all overseen by the Securities and Exchange Commission.

Even before the Securities Act was signed into law, venture capital had begun as a family affair with the formation of Venrock, the Rockefeller family venture capital fund and Bessemer, the Mellon family fund. By the early 1950s, other venture capital firms had formed, including American Research and Development, led by visionary investor and Harvard Business School professor Georges Doriot, which backed the formation of Digital Equipment Corporation (absorbed by Compaq Computer in 1998) and many other successful start-up firms. Another venture capital firm, J. H. Whitney, led by Benno Schmidt Sr, invested heavily in the early advances in medicine.

The Securities Act of 1933 was followed by the Investment Company Act of 1940, which established regulated 'investment companies' for small groups of 'sophisticated' investors. Again the purpose of the act was to keep such companies separate to protect less sophisticated investors. The Investment Company Act defines an investment company as any company that has more than 40 per cent of its assets invested in companies that it does not control (that is, does not hold a majority of the stock).

For 40 years after this regulation was put in place, the potential of private equity went largely unrecognized. While some investors did place their funds in regulated investment companies, the amounts of money were not large compared to investments through the public markets. There were probably two main reasons for this. First, there was thought to be a great deal of potential left in exploiting the public equity markets, particularly in the 'conglomerate boom' of the 1960s. Financial entrepreneurs like Jimmy Ling (who built LTV) and Harold Geneen (who built ITT) were convinced that strong management could manage any business well, and that a well-hedged portfolio of tightly controlled public companies was the key to financial success. The idea was to use a combination of debt and ownership control to leverage earnings-per-share growth in initially weak companies. If this approach was successful, there would be no large-scale need to turn to private capital for funds.

The second reason private equity was dormant for so long was that the economy came under severe stress in the 1970s as inflation, created by skyrocketing oil prices, drove the economy into a decade-long period of 'stag-flation'. Stagflation, and the high cost of debt, brought an end to the conglomerate idea. It also brought a significant slowdown to venture capital as the IPO market almost completely stopped. In 1974, there were seven IPOs in the United States; a mere $96 million was raised. The year 1975 saw only six. In 1999, by comparison, there were 527 IPOs, raising $69 billion.

As the United States emerged from the 1970s, however, the conditions were ripe for a significant expansion of private capital. In the early 1980s, as the country turned the corner from a period of high inflation rates and low growth, a new form of corporation was founded: the 'leveraged buyout association,' as George Baker, a professor at Harvard Business School, called it. Having seen what happened to the conglomerates of the 1960s, the LBO association sought to avoid some of the problems that undermined the conglomerate concept from the 1960s.

The LBO association was based on the concept of leverage and decentralized operational control. Moreover, control was based on contracts and the ownership structure of the corporation, rather than on managerial control as Ling and Geneen had practised it. As Professor Baker points out, 'The LBO association is not a *keiretsu*-like system, nor is it a conglomerate.'

The leveraged buyout associations succeeded. At the same time, venture capital was also beginning to flourish. As stated earlier, Kleiner Perkins was formed in the early 1970s, although it really began to be successful in the early 1980s. General Atlantic Partners was another such firm. More established firms like Venrock and J. H. Whitney also were finding new opportunities.

As venture capital investment volume began to build, investors flocked to private equity. In 1999, for example, 4,006 venture capital deals took place, in the United States involving investments of $45.6 billion, or about $135 million per day. Roughly half of that money was invested in start-ups. Another $27 billion was invested in 1999 in companies by 'principal investors' (formerly known as leveraged buyout associations). In fact, Professor Baker claims, 'the principal investing association' movement was one of the most important reasons for the resurgence of the US economy in the 1980s. To put these numbers into context, there were about 11,000 mergers and acquisitions in 1999, accounting for $1.7 trillion. Twenty years ago, mergers and acquisitions would have represented virtually all the financial transactions that took place in the economy. Today, while M&As still dominate the field, for every dollar represented by an M&A deal, 25 cents is traded in private equity markets. Moreover, returns in the private equity market have been substantially above those of the public equity markets since the early 1980s, as Figure 7.1 shows.

Fig. 7.1 Returns by asset category

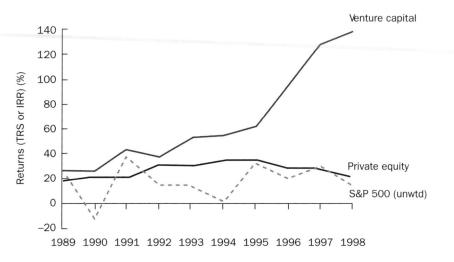

These two kinds of private equity firms, venture capital firms and principal investing associations, although different from each other in their focus, are successfully riding the waves of Schumpeter's 'gales of creative destruction' – venture capital in the area of creation and principal investing in the area of trading or destruction.

How have they done this? Private equity firms are designed for change. They have replaced the traditional assumption of continuity with the assumption of discontinuity. In doing so, they have become critical players in shaping the processes of creative destruction in the US economy. They are increasingly important drivers of change, and have also created enormous wealth for their shareholders. And in doing so, they have evolved a system of management and control that is far more suited to the management of discontinuity.

HOW PRIVATE EQUITY FIRMS OPERATE

Although private equity firms are very diverse, they have many similarities. We will look at their differences, their similarities, and what we can learn from them that can be carried over to public equity firms.

Differences

There are significant differences between the venture capital and principal investing firms. The greatest difference between them is their investment

Fig. 7.2 The S-curve and private equity

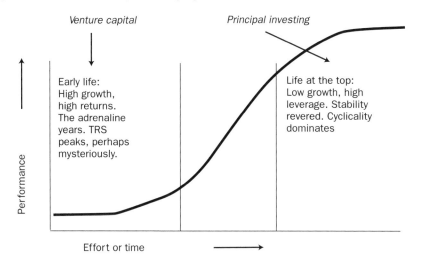

Venture capital

Principal investing

Early life:
High growth,
high returns.
The adrenaline
years. TRS
peaks, perhaps
mysteriously.

Life at the top:
Low growth, high
leverage. Stability
revered. Cyclicality
dominates

Performance

Effort or time

focus (see Figure 7.2). Venture capital firms focus on the early stages of a company's or industry's life, or what we call in Chapter 2 the beginning of the S-curve, where there is substantial growth potential. Principal investment firms, on the other hand, generally focus on companies that are nearing the slower-growth phase of their evolution, where there is substantial potential for restructuring and transforming them through operational and financial improvements.

Venture capital firms distribute money to the companies they own in small amounts, using the process to control the evolution of the company. Principal investing firms, on the other hand, make large single investments (supported by significant debt loads), and subsequently derive profits off the cash flow.

Similarities

While there are clearly major differences between venture capital and principal investing firms, there are also several common features of both that distinguish them from public equity firms. Those features are an adoption of limited life investments, minimal corporate size, control based on contracts and incentives, and an obsession with decentralization. While some of these categories may seem to be similar to practices in public equity corporations, the extremes to which they are carried out by venture capital firms sharply distinguish these firms from most public equity firms. We have found that, collectively, these four differences constitute a superior approach to the management of discontinuity. Let's examine those four differences in more detail.

Limited-life investments

All investments made by private equity firms are assumed to have a 'limited life' – typically 10 to 12 years or less. At the end of that time they are required to sell their investments and return the capital to their fund investors. 'Though the closing of any one limited partnership does not mean the close of the private equity firm, the requirement that it do so constrains the private equity firm to behave quite differently from the typical public equity company.' Private equity firms invest only when they have a clear idea about how and when they will divest.

Private equity firms invest only when they have a clear idea about how and when they will divest.

Many corporations are slow to divest unless forced to do so. As a result, history shows that corporations tend to be opportunistic buyers but reluctant sellers of companies. As long as divisions or companies within the corporation meet minimal performance criteria, they are unlikely to be sold. The private equity firm, on the other hand, not only has to put its equity capital from its funds to work as soon as is feasible (the capital generally has to be fully invested within six years), it also has to realize gains for its limited partners for the sale of the stock of its businesses. As a result, private equity firms have to be both systematic buyers and sellers – creators and destroyers. They are much more aggressive in their creative efforts to identify acquisition opportunities and to find buyers for their 'transformations'.

Moreover, the limited life of the private equity investment focuses the activities of the firm on the change it can accomplish in the next three to seven years (to give it some time to correct mistakes before the divestment occurs), whereas the normal corporation is consumed with either the next quarter's operating numbers or that of the very long term – say, beyond 10 years (for example, in basic research programmes). The intermediate time horizon for investments allows private equity firms more freedom in making fundamental changes to their investments than public companies can currently muster.

Minimal 'corporate' staff

Private equity firms control staff size, and therefore involvement with their investments (due to time constraints), through a fixed management fee that typically runs about 2 per cent per year of the assets under management. In addition, the general partners of the private equity firm share in the profits they make above some minimal level of return, say, 20 per cent. This arrangement creates a clear standard of performance for the management of the private equity firm, so that it can judge its own performance independent of the performance of the companies it has invested in. If the costs of guiding and administering the private equity firm rise above 2 per cent, the private equity general partners lose income. This fixed fee is a powerful incentive to keep the private equity general partnership small. Its small size and the financial structure of the partnership mean that the first priority of the management group has to be creating new investment opportunities and shedding old ones, rather than focusing on the day-to-day management of the companies they invest in.

Methods of control: contracts and incentives

Private equity firms have a very different philosophy of control than most public equity corporations do. The control systems used by private equity firms give up the rights to day-to-day operational control in return for very clear contracts negotiated with the company receiving the investment. Because of the small staff size of private equity firms, they simply do not have the time to control the day-to-day process. The control processes invoked by private equity investors are tailored to the specific needs of the individual company and its future shareholders. Private equity firms do not attempt to control multiple businesses with a single management approach (or a single set of information reports or decision processes).

There are two key methods private equity firms use to control their investments: the contract with the company they invest in, and the incentives they provide to management for fulfillment of the contract. The key feature of contracts between private investment firms and corporations receiving the funds is the *restrictive covenant*. Restrictive covenants specify, and limit, the decisions that the private equity firm must be involved in. Everything else falls under the responsibility of management. The restrictive covenant approach gives the investor the 'right to control', rather than a mandate to control. As such, private equity firms adopt a minimalist approach to operational control: they control what they must when they must, not what they can when they can. If problems arise, a private equity firm frequently has the right to interfere, but, in the absence of problems, they do not interfere.

The requirements for control generally include some of the following: decisions regarding the issuance of new shares; mergers, consolidations, or the purchase or sale of assets; and the award of stock and cash dividends. In addition, these covenants often specify balance sheet requirements (including working capital and net worth); restrictions on encumbrances and indebtedness; levels of managerial compensation; the use of proceeds; the issuance of preemptive rights and the rights of first refusal; mandatory redemption rights, registration rights, and so called drag-along and tag-along rights; charter amendments; and the nature of the business. While this list appears to be quite long, the entrepreneurial managers who accept the conditions set forth in the contract are free to run all other aspects of their business as they see fit. The list does not include any line item budget restrictions or the use of capital. It does not require approval of specific investments. It does not require involvement in the creation or changing of corporate strategy.

The second key method of control is through incentives. Private equity firms permit a much broader range of management incentives than conventional corporations do. While private equity firms seek very high levels of performance, they are also prepared to offer very high levels of rewards. Their target TRS is often at least double that of the conventional corporation. These high targets stimulate a greater sense of urgency. But if market-based performance measures are reached, managers can make many times their annual compensation. The range of compensation and risk is far greater in the private equity firm than in the conventional corporation. 'Everything about the firm's structure and incentives are geared to increasing the long-term financial value of assets,' says Baker.

Perhaps because of their comfort with the contract system and their own persuasive skills, private equity companies are more comfortable with minority ownership and a minority of board seats than are operating companies. Board meetings are often used to convey information, identify issues, and make decisions on behalf of the investors. It is a system based on permission more than tight control. While reporting is frequent and detailed, it is not as overwhelming as that in many traditional operating companies.

Conventional public equity firms depend far more on daily operational control, with a flexible set of criteria for action, than private equity firms do. Perversely, this greater flexibility often saps initiative on the part of the divisions within a large corporation, out of fear of second-guessing. The flexibility intended to provide options actually opens the door to defensive routines and cultural lock-in.

While many public equity corporations feel they see themselves as decentralized, they keep tight strings on strategy decisions, major (and often minor) investments, compensation structures, advancements and promotions, and information flow.

Obsessed with decentralization

Integral to the concept of effective management by private equity firms is the notion of decentralization. Each of the companies that a private equity firm invests in is a legally separate company, with its own management structure and board. Decentralization, of course, has long been a primary organizing principle for many public equity companies. What is novel about private equity firms is the extent of decentralization, which often includes the decentralization of responsibility for the balance sheet as well as strategy and major investments.

Duracell, for example, was fully responsible for the health of its balance sheet, for paying the interest on its loans, and for raising more capital when it was needed. In a large public company, these functions are typically handled by a 'corporate group', based on the argument that the corporation can negotiate better financial arrangements than any single division. That may be true, but it is also true that with the assumption of this responsibility for the balance sheet and additional financings, the corporation narrows the scope of thinking and responsibility of its operating company. For Duracell, these decisions are critical to company performance.

In general, the private equity firm does not make serious efforts to capture potential synergies among its operating companies. Private equity firms, and the companies they invest in, have neither the luxury nor the temptation to engineer the kinds of financial, technical, or talent synergies that are commonly sought in public corporations. Moreover, financial transfers from one company in a private equity portfolio to another are restricted in the United States by the provisions of the Investment

Company Act of 1940. Talent transfers, in the name of information transfer (including technical knowledge transfer), are rarely sought because private equity firms would rather the companies maintain their focus on their goals, rather than be distracted with the effort required to realize profits from potential synergies.

We are not suggesting that private equity firms, because they have embraced the concept of 'limited life', minimal corporate staff, control through contracts and incentives, and obsessive decentralization, have found the path to perpetual excellence. Despite their strengths, venture capitalists do miss markets, enter markets too early or too late, pick the wrong teams, and ride some investments longer than they should. Principal investing firms, too, blunder from time to time. Private equity firms are not infallible. Moreover, when the markets change again, and enough competition emerges, the weaknesses in their approaches may be exposed, and new corporate models will need to be found.

Nevertheless, private equity firms have performed well over the past 20 years, and at a pace that equals that of the marketplace. Moreover, they have evolved a system of management that is quite different in practice from the surviving incumbent publicly traded corporation. With this system of management, private equity firms have done as well as any group we have seen in finding ways to 'create, operate, and trade' simultaneously. Even with their faults and inevitable mistakes, they offer a useful model that companies can turn to when they are seeking guidance in learning how to adopt the assumption of discontinuity.

Private equity firms offer a way to deliver what only the markets have been able to deliver so far. They change at the pace and scale of the market, thrive on creative destruction and thus thwart cultural lock-in, and control through permission without putting operational excellence at risk. And in doing so, they have created substantial wealth for their investors.

CORPORATE EXAMPLES

None of the public equity firms we have examined in the McKinsey Corporate Performance Database 'found the secret' of creative destruction. None has outperformed the market, or demonstrated excellence relative to the overall market over the long haul. As described previously, there are companies such as Enron and Corning that are beginning to demonstrate that they too can adopt some of the mechanisms of private equity investors for the benefit for their shareholders. And there are some diversified corporations that have done much better than most. GE and J&J are perhaps the two best examples. We discuss J&J in Chapter 11. Now we turn our attention to GE.

In a June 1999 interview in *The Wall Street Journal*, GE CEO Jack Welch philosophically observed:

I've talked about all the disadvantages of working at a big company, but there are a lot of advantages to being huge. Last year we made 108 acquisitions for $21 billion. That's 108 swings. Every one of those acquisitions had a perfect plan, but we know 20 or 30 percent will blow up in our face. A small company can only make one or two bets or they go out of business. But we can afford to make lots more mistakes, and, in fact, we have to throw more things at the walls. The big companies that get into trouble are those that try to manage their size instead of experimenting with it.

GE has 'created options' in broadcasting and financial services, to name a few; it has 'traded options' in its sale of GE appliances. It has 'operated' (in its high-performance management style) many businesses, including plastics and jet engines. In doing so, GE has completely reshaped its portfolio and achieved some of the rates of change seen generally only in private equity firms or in the indices of the capital markets themselves. During the past 20 years, GE has remained near the top of the normal performance band of the S&P 500 index.

> GE has completely reshaped its portfolio and achieved some of the rates of change seen generally only in private equity firms or in the indices of the capital markets themselves.

Not all of the 108 acquisitions that GE made in 1998 were start-ups. But they did position GE well within the growth sectors of the economy. The businesses that GE traded, on the other hand, were those that Welch and his staff decided had no 'economic function' within GE.

When Welch took over at GE in 1981, much of GE's management philosophy was based on the idea of 'defend first; attack if you must'. Welch's greatest contribution to GE employees and shareholders, in our view, has been turning this rule on its head. GE today clearly 'attacks first, and defends when necessary'. By engineering such a profound shift in strategic direction, Welch demonstrated that survivor companies can be successful in absorbing and applying the requirement for discontinuity. GE found a way to effectively integrate the functions of creation, operation, and trading close to the pace and scale of the market. In doing so, it went from being a great innovative manufacturer to 'a global services company that happens to make great products'.

In GE's case, the 'create, operate, trade' model is already in place. Copying GE's success is not easy, despite the fact that the company is willing to share its ideas and methods. Still, GE's success shows that such change can be accomplished in public companies, and that the capital markets will reward companies that can do it.

CURRENT EFFORTS

The heady progress of the stock market during the late 1990s has given rise to some new experiments attempting to capitalize on the potential of creative destruction. One of the most famous of these attempts is the 'incubator', a company whose sole function is to generate new successful companies. In many ways, incubators are like venture capital companies, but they provide more than just capital and advice. They supply high-speed telephone lines, computers, office space, and, in many cases, access to executive search resources, accountants, consultants, and lawyers. While venture capital firms are typically partnerships, incubators often see themselves as public companies. Should they be able to do what they hope, they will likely reap substantial stock-market gains.

At this writing, there are at least 700 incubators in the United States, up from 12 in 1980. All of them are attempting a Schumpeterian task – balancing the management of creative destruction with the management of operations.

The new incubators have predictably offbeat, or 'e-centric', names: Devine InterVentures (which has money from Dell and Microsoft); eCompanies (in Santa Monica, California, with money from KKR, Goldman Sachs, the Soros fund, Sprint, and Walt Disney); e-Cubator (formed by investor Scudder-Kemper Investments); eFinanceworks in New York (formed by former principal investment firms CapZ and General Atlantic); eHatchery in Atlanta; Garage.com (founded by former Apple fellow and chief evangelist Guy Kawasaki); I-Group HotBank (the Boston-based partnership between Softbank and the Intercontinental Group); IdeaLab (the Pasadena, California, firm founded by Bill Gross, backers of eBay, Citisearch, GoTo.com, and more than 30 other Internet start-ups since 1997), and Ignition (founded by ex–Microsoft product developer Brad Silverberg).

Among the incubators in Europe are Starthouse and Speed.com, Gorilla Park, antfactory, and Earlybird. Hong Kong has Incubasia, and Japan Softbank.

Some of these high-talent agglomerations already sense a greater destiny. Devine InterVentures, for example, dreams of becoming a holding company on the scale of General Electric.

How many of these young incubators will become important institutions and last over the long term? At this point it is unclear. Many are starting to fail now. But we expect the best of them to last, modified in form and function but definitely different from the traditional survivor. They are attempting to design themselves for creative destruction.

Regardless of the type of company created, however, mastering creative destruction will be a prerequisite for strong, sustained performance. And as we've seen, there are already a few examples to look to. In the following chapters, we will look at what is needed to manage creative destruction in the operating corporation.

8

Leading creative destruction

You implore us: Will you guys make up your minds? One day, it's SG&A. The next day it's top-line growth.The next day it's cost of goods. The next day it's Credo behavior. The next day it's innovation. Will you make up your minds? Well, the answer is no! We are not going to make up our minds, and you don't want us to make up our minds.

Roger Fine

member of the Executive Committee of Johnson & Johnson, 1998

It was a typical late-fall Monday afternoon in northern Germany in the early 1990s. The 10-person internal management committee, known as the *Vorstand*, was an hour into their regular meeting. As usual, no one other than the *Sprecher* (chairman of the management committee), Professor Schultz, had spoken. Schultz was signing capital authorizations. Although the company had more than the equivalent of $20 billion in physical assets to look over, and spent $2 billion per year, no member of the *Vorstand* was able to authorize an expenditure of more than $250,000. Consequently, during the year, several thousand proposals had to be authorized. Each had be scrutinized by the central planning department after it had been thoroughly prepared by the 'responsible' department. With several thousand proposals a year needing the approval of the *Vorstand*, typically 50 to 100 had to be approved each week. The approval process was straightforward. The *Sprecher* looked at each proposal to see if central planning had approved. If they had, he signed the authorization on behalf of the sitting *Vorstand*, unless he had personal knowledge that contradicted the recommendation of the central planning unit (in which case he made a unilateral decision to turn the proposal down). No discussion with the *Vorstand* was needed. None was expected. They simply sat and watched the *Sprecher* sign the requisitions. When he had finished, the great bulk of the meeting had been completed; other topics were briefly raised, and the meeting was adjourned.

Granted, the routine represented in this meeting, coupled with the utter lack of dialogue, is unusual. But the routine it represents is not. In some of the most advanced companies, routine dominates the agenda of the management committee (which is the name we will use for the corporation's most senior management group) meetings. Under the assumption of continuity, many top management groups interpret their primary purpose to be the stewards of operational excellence. They need to assure the shareholders that the operations are going well. The way to do this is to hold a 'review'. We call these meetings 'presentation and response' meetings. Lower-level executives present their bulletproof plans to higher levels of executives to see if they can get them approved. The sessions are spent reviewing the plans of the divisions, reviewing capital appropriations, and reviewing recommendations for advancement. Dialogue is not sought. Winning the case is the objective. It is more like a court drama – with point and counterpoint – than a joint session in problem defining and solving.

In the normal life of many corporations, much of the management committee's time is spent in routine meetings, often at the request of others, rather than as a consequence of their own drive to manage. The management committee is extraordinarily responsive to the requests of others. They see their job as one in which they make decisions based on the options presented to them. It is not their job to generate alternatives. That is the work done by the organization 'beneath' them. Rarely do they enter territory as murky as grappling with the

> In the normal life of many corporations, much of the management committee's time is spent in routine meetings, often at the request of others, rather than as a consequence of their own drive to manage.

balance between creative destruction and operations. It is not even clear how they would do that if they decided they wanted to. Once, when we suggested to a very senior and very talented executive member of a management committee that they eliminate the least important 20 per cent of the routine agenda items from the management committee meetings, the question we received in response was 'Well, then what would we do with our time?' Indeed. What would they do with their time!

Clearly, this system does not work. The failure of a company's leaders to challenge the very premises under which the company operates is the source of much of the long-term lack of competitiveness one sees in corporations. This process leaves too many issues unspoken and too many opportunities unaddressed. The market has a much more robust dialogue, through thousands of 'buy and sell' conversations every day. The market is constantly shaping new options and killing off programmes that are just not progressing rapidly enough.

MANAGERIAL STALEMATE

In Chapter 4 we discussed lengthy conversations we have had with more than 50 executives from more than two dozen companies in the United States and Europe, in fields ranging from consumer products to high tech. All had the same sense of what it took to be successful – operational excellence – and all had problems with the same thing, change management, or what we call creative destruction. They could not do both at the same time. While the German company cited above demonstrates an extreme example of change paralysis, the same general problem, with perhaps milder symptoms, is widely felt.

There are two parts to the problem. The first is understanding the environment well enough to see opportunities, and to anticipate problems, in a timely way. Executives on both sides of the Atlantic have told us that strategic insight is needed for success. One of the most common phrases we heard was 'You have to know where the market is going.' Of course, such insight requires knowing future customer (and consumer) behaviour, future channel behaviour, future technology developments, future supplier capabilities, and future regulatory opportunities and restrictions. The executives found it very difficult to read the industry (very much as analysts have trouble reading the industry, discussed in Chapter 2).

In practice, these executives couldn't predict future customer behaviour patterns. They misjudged competitors' reactions to their own moves, generally underestimating the ferocity of counterattack. Further, they misjudged their timing, either coming in too early (Kodak in electronic imaging) or too late (Pacific Bell and, until recently, AT&T in mobile telephony). They also failed to understand the different levels of skills required between two generations of technology (or between two business models). They found it difficult to generate the sense of urgency that is required to initiate and sustain change. Most of all, the executives found great difficulty in transforming future insights into an attractive business model.

The second part of the paralysis problem stems from the difficulty in implementing change that goes beyond the current mental models. Executives conceded that they found it very difficult to integrate both successful operations – the requirements for strategic management and change management. And most often it was innovation that suffered. The most common sentiment was 'We're okay, but we have vast room for improvement. The incremental things seem to go well, but larger change eludes us; and we are worried about the future.' Here are a few of the things executives said to us that underscore these points:

- 'On a relative basis, and judging by our market success, I believe that we are effective innovators. However, on an absolute basis there is vast room for improvement, especially in meeting schedules. Our biggest issue is that we do not have a culture that values meeting deadlines. We need a more disciplined approach. The engineers would probably say that they are doing a great job, but the sales managers would probably say that they need more new products, and at a faster pace.'

- 'With our hands-on consumer goods characteristics, we are not sufficiently focused on more transformational options.'

- 'Salespeople would probably say that we were not quick enough in introducing new products and engineers would probably say that we don't use the best stuff.'

- 'With regard to our effectiveness at innovation, if we hit 20 per cent we are lucky. It is very hard to guess ahead on what customers will want. It is like leading ducks – they go wherever they want. We need to figure out how to get our products close to customers' specifications and rapidly reach closure. Too often, we are guilty of developing too many products instead of basic technologies. I think that frontline engineers and salespeople would be more charitable in their comments, because they measure success one product at a time whereas I measure it as a business.'

- 'Our effectiveness at innovation troubles me greatly, because I believe that we are less and less innovative, perhaps as a result of size. Innovation for us has less to do with R&D or engineering than with how we serve our customers. Innovation either does not occur rapidly enough or does not bubble up to the resource controllers and decision makers. I guess that there are probably smart people down there seeing stuff, but the ideas are not getting to the point where there is an ability to embrace, adopt, and execute.'

- 'Innovation is important to us, but we are not very innovative because our focus has been too much on the internal rather than on the external. There has been an inherent conservatism about reaching out for the future. Our group is a small and reasonably separate unit within the corporation, so we have had somewhat more success. We were the first of the print publishers to go aggressively to the Internet. If we were not under the constraints of the overall corporation, we could have gone even faster.'

- 'By everyone's standards, we are rated as the best at innovation in our industry. From a development point of view, I worry that in the older parts of the company we are stuck in the past. Getting agreement and then getting them to do something is the challenge.'

It is clear that most executives feel they can do better. But they do not know how to proceed. Their specific questions ranged from 'What will the value proposition be that could be so compelling as to change our behaviour?' to 'What are the first steps?' In some cases, the executives said they preferred to avoid these problems rather than address them, hiding the failure of a core business with acquisitions or even scurrilous accounting (none of which solved the real problem). 'Some resorted to denial: 'Great innovations happen by accident,' one company argued. 'Some individuals come across a great idea and they exploit it. You cannot manage for that. The best you can do is to put

'Some individuals come across a great idea and they exploit it. You cannot manage for that. The best you can do is to put people in touch with one another and see what happens. In our business all innovation is incremental in any case.'

people in touch with one another and see what happens. In our business all innovation is incremental in any case.' (It should be noted that this large company has underperformed the markets for 20 years.)

The irony is that the executives making these comments and asking these questions are the corporate managers that most people would think have all the answers. But they don't. And most are not satisfied with the answers that they have at hand. They simply do not understand how to run their companies at the pace and scale that will match the markets without sacrificing operational control. They are frozen in the headlights.

TECHNICAL WORK VERSUS ADAPTIVE WORK

As we noted in Chapter 1, Ron Heifetz is one of the most reflective and effective thinkers in the country about the nature of leadership. Heifetz has thought extensively about the nature of authority and its relationship to leadership. His work is broadly consistent with the work of earlier pioneers, such as Chris Argyris and Dean Keith Simonton.

Heifetz makes a distinction in companies between technical work and adaptive work. Technical work is the work of experts. It is the exercise of authority, 'a conclusive statement from a person in command'. Adaptive work, on the other hand, is exploratory work. It is work where the answer is not known by the experts – any experts. Adaptive work is often creative work.

To function effectively, management committees must grasp and grapple with the difference between technical work and adaptive work. As Heifetz says:

In a complex social system, a problem will lack clarity because a multitude of factions will have divergent opinions about both the nature of the problem and its possible solutions. Competing values are often at stake. Furthermore, in a large social system the scientific experts often disagree even on the fundamental outlines of a problem, particularly in the early stages of problem definition. The critical strategic question becomes, 'Whose problem is it?' And the answer is not so obvious.

In times of distress, he claims, we turn to authority for:

- direction
- protection – scanning the environment for threats and mobilizing a response
- order – orienting people to their places and roles, controlling internal conflict, and establishing and maintaining norms

Both investors and employees seek answers to the questions of 'direction, protection, and order' from the senior management of the corporation. In those cases where the nature of both the question and the answer is clear, an 'authority' or 'expert' can make pronouncements that will provide accurate direction, protection, and order. For many questions put to them, senior management is a qualified 'authority'. Most operations questions involve 'technical' work, and thus are fully addressable this way. Technical work thrives on the desire to reduce or eliminate ambiguity.

But desire to eliminate ambiguity cannot be fulfilled in real markets. In real markets, authority and expertise are insufficient. Leadership is required. By leadership Heifetz means 'inducing learning by asking hard questions and by recasting people's expectations [in order] to develop their responsibility'. Standard authority will not work in these cases, because there is no precedent yet. The hard work of learning has yet to be done.

Leadership of this type is often required of the management committee and chairman of a corporation. Managing the proper level of creative destruction demands this kind of 'adaptive work'. It requires management to ask expert questions rather than to fall into the more familiar pattern of providing expert answers.

> Managing the proper level of creative destruction requires management to ask expert questions rather than to fall into the more familiar pattern of providing expert answers.

For the executive committee, taking on this task amounts to a role reversal – a reversal for which it is generally not prepared. Most members of management committees are there because they have demonstrated their skill in operations – whether in production, marketing and sales, product development, or finance. They have not reached their position because they have demonstrated great skill at understanding the vagaries of future markets or the processes of capital (financial or human) allocation for the benefit of investors. Their skill is an expert's skill at answering questions, not the leadership skill of asking questions.

Adaptive work requires changing one's mind-set. In the case of a corporation, it is the mind-set of the management committee that has to change; doing so gives permission for the rest of the organization to change its mind-set as well.

When faced with an adaptive challenge, companies have to try to break down the problems requiring adaptive work into components that will yield to authoritative answers. 'Yes, we need more creative destruction. Specifically, we need to invest over the next two years in mobile telephony as it applies to medicine. Moreover, we have to find a way to exit from our traditional hospital businesses without hurting our customers.' These are ideas that can be turned into action plans. In this way the complexities of adaptive work have been reduced to the more familiar territory of technical work.

The evidence suggests that the economic environment will continue to ratchet up the rate of change. If we are right, the adaptive work of the corporation will only increase. As we go forward, then, the purpose of the management committee has to change; its primary responsibility in the future must be to identify the adaptive challenges facing the corporation and focus its attention on these challenges. No other group can do this. Should it fail to do this, the company will inevitably falter or stagnate.

The management committee must also modulate the level of adaptive stress it places on the organization (and it is capable of placing the organization under great stress!). Managing the stress level is closely associated with managing the pace of change. Management cannot randomly select the pace of change that best suits it, since, as we have seen, markets generally change faster than the corporations, leaving weaker players behind. There is a natural tendency to avoid changing too fast. But if management committees give in to that inclination, they place the long-term health of their employees and investors at risk.

The management committee must keep attention focused on the relevant issues until they are resolved, then move on to the next challenge, shifting responsibility for the last challenge to the next level. What is a technical challenge for the management committee, of course, may be an adaptive challenge for the next level of management. But at that point, the process simply repeats itself.

Changing a corporation's mind-set from the assumption of continuity to the assumption of discontinuity is an exceptionally difficult task. It involves moving from the comfort zone of technical work, with its dependency on authority, to the open-endedness of adaptive work and its requirements for leadership. Whether corporations are willing to do what it takes to adopt the assumption of discontinuity – to engage in creative destruction at the pace and scale of the market – is, we would argue, *the* prime test faced by management committees. Can the management committee eschew its traditional role as the monitor of the decisions of others – the challenge of technical work – and embrace the adaptive challenge of becoming the controller of the rate of creative destruction in the corporation?

The questions and issues real markets pose are not clear and certain. Real markets are filled with uncertainty and ambiguity. Old problems rarely present themselves in the same way a second time. The all-important problems are almost always new problems, just as all-important opportunities are new opportunities (as any venture capitalist can attest). In other words, real markets do not cater to problem solvers. They cater to the masters of adaptive work. They cater to leaders.

DEFLECTING THE ISSUES

The pain of dealing with the adaptive work that accompanies the assumption of discontinuity is often more easily avoided than addressed. As Heifetz says:

> Authorities, under pressure to be decisive, sometimes fake the remedy or take action that avoids the issue by skirting it. In the short term, of course, this may quell some of the distress. If the [leader] succeeds in shifting . . . attention to a substitute problem . . . then the problem . . . may cause less discontent. Attention is deflected from the issue, which appears to be taken care of. We readily invite distraction because it lowers distress. In the long run some problems get worse, and then frustration arises both with the problem situation and with those people in authority who were supposed to resolve it. In response to the frustration we are likely to perpetuate the vicious cycle by looking even more earnestly to authority, but this time we look for someone new offering more certainty and better promises.

Heifetz claims that the flight to authority is particularly dangerous because of this avoidance of adaptive work, which occurs in response to the company's biggest problems, and because it disables key personnel and resources needed to accomplish that work.

Faking it

The executives we talked to revealed many examples of 'faking it' or 'skirting' the issue. We offered some examples above. Others include an excessive focus on short-term financial results (when it is quite clear that the short term contributes only in minor ways to the generation of wealth) and denial of the importance of innovation for long-term success (e.g., 'Our brands make us strong. That is all we need.'). A variation on that theme is a general acknowledgment of the importance of innovation, while at the same time only programmes of incremental innovation that do not challenge the established mental model of the business are implemented (such as the clipper ship versus steamship battles of the late nineteenth century, described in Chapter 4). The challenges of incremental innovation are easier to conceptualize and tackle. But genuine long-term competitive advantage comes only from substantial and transformational innovation.

Shifting attention to other issues

Some of the executives we talked to blamed the parent company for the failure of divisions, or blamed failures in their corporations on middle management, when the real culprits were the corporate incentive systems that rewarded the short term and provided no parallel system for rewarding long-term performance. In short, it is quite easy to avoid adaptive work, and few executives really want to do it unless they are clear about its importance and the distinction between adaptive work and technical work.

LEADING ADAPTIVE WORK: 'MIXED SIGNALS'

Roger Fine, General Counsel at Johnson & Johnson, understands the difference between technical and adaptive work as well as anyone we have met. He had the opportunity to comment on this challenge in a speech he gave in 1996 to the top 800 executives of the corporation. Fittingly, it was delivered at an off-site meeting that J&J had dedicated to renewing the corporation's commitment to innovation. Roger Fine's speech crystallizes the challenge to leadership very clearly:

You know, over the past four years new words have crept into our vocabulary at J&J: Words like 'ambiguity' and 'complexity' and 'paradox' and 'multiple mental models'. What these words and what the ideas behind them have given us is an enormous respect for the power of complexity and ambiguity. We need to embrace this. We need to turn this to a competitive advantage.

It's a sign of the maturity of the individuals in an organization, a sign of the maturity of an organization that they welcome complexity, or what some people call 'mixed signals'. I'd rather change mixed signals to complexity and ambiguity to make the point.

> It's a sign of the maturity of the individuals in an organization, a sign of the maturity of an organization that they welcome complexity.

It's a habit of highly successful people that they welcome complexity and ambiguity and mixed signals. They take it as a challenge to be innovative. And what's so great about this company is that we have the experience to handle this better than anybody else.

And why is that? Because we have the greatest example of mixed signals in the history of business, and we call it our Credo, which establishes the basic principles by which we operate. If anybody ever asks us the following question, we all know the answer: 'When are you guys gonna make up your minds? What are your objectives? What are your core principles? Is it the customer? Is it the employee? Is it the communities and society? Or is it the stockholders?'

Our answer is 'Yes, it's all of the above. We refuse to make up our minds.' The great strength of our company is in not making up our mind, but of using our energy and intellect, not just to balance and reconcile those principles of the Credo – that sounds passive – it's to take each one of those and use them robustly. We will infuse each of those abilities to the maximum of our ability and talent.

MANAGING THE CONFLICT BETWEEN ADAPTIVE WORK AND TECHNICAL WORK

How do Roger Fine's 'mixed signals' look to someone seeking direction, protection, and order? They do not look helpful. If Fine's dictum is to be successfully applied, the organization itself has to come to realize that its desire for direction, protection, and order will not be met from above. Fine's message is that the organization has to deliver it to itself. Top management will err if it stands in the way of this realization. By taking the 'expert' road, and thus eliminating the need for others to develop their own sense of direction, protection, and order, the management committee can thwart the accomplishment of the adaptive work it would like to see.

But if the management committee does not provide direction, protection, and order, what does it provide? The fundamental responsibility of the management committee is to ensure that the scope of inquiry of the corporation is sufficient to provide for its future. If the cause of the long-term degradation of performance is cultural lock-in, then it is up to the senior stewards of the business to prevent that from happening.

This is the message to be gleaned from the fall of IBM in the 1980s described earlier. The fault of IBM management at the time was not that they had lost operational control. Quite the opposite. They were the best in the world. What they had lost control of was the scope of inquiry on a scale sufficient to ensure their future. They had become so focused on operational excellence that the process of dialogue about the future had dried up. While the form of the meetings differed from the *Vorstand* meeting described at the beginning of the chapter, in effect, it was almost identical.

Our conventional notions of leadership are deeply rooted in the notion that the leader is able to lead because he is an expert. He or she has a clear vision of the future. But we cannot know the future, particularly today. Perhaps, based on our expertise, we can eliminate some possibilities, but that is all. The executives we talked to confirmed that fact. A general comment was 'It is essential to be able to read our industry, but we don't know how to do that.' All one can do is depend on our adaptive resources.

DESIGNING A PROCESS FOR INCREASING ADAPTIVE WORK

How can an organization accomplish adaptive work without losing control of its technical work, or operations? Over the past decade we have been working with many of our clients to find ways to more effectively achieve this objective. We have also worked intensely with private equity firms over the past decade on the same task. As a result of these experiences we have concluded that there are three responsibilities management must assume.

First, management must assume the responsibility for designing a process that allows adaptive work to flourish without losing operational control. This begins with shaping a broad vision of the processes of adaptive work that accommodates both divergent and convergent thinking and yet does not sacrifice operational control. The goal is to mimic the real-life processes of creativity (as we described them in Chapter 4) as closely as possible in order to maximize the chances of 'mimicking the market'. In carrying out this responsibility, the management committee has to provide sufficient time in the process to allow alternative mental models of the business to be conceptualized, for voices of opposition to be developed and constructively heard, and for a search for new solutions.

More often than not these processes are informal, invoking a series of temporary processes (e.g., meetings, discussions, visits, and 'free time' to think through the implications of the ideas being discussed), involving the part-time activities of many people rather than the establishment of a new department or function staffed with full-time people. In this sense, these processes work at the interstices of the organization, rather than by interfering with existing processes, or by establishing new organization units. There are several ways to reach this objective. We will describe one recent example in depth in Chapter 11.

Second, management has to take oversight responsibility for the conduct of the process so that it reaches a useful outcome that matches the pace and scale of the market, yet does not threaten the loss of operational control or create unproductive levels of stress and conflict in the organization. The key tool management has to achieve this result is the pace at which it introduces new thinking to the organization. If new challenges and ideas are added too quickly, the result will be stress, conflict, and a collapse of productivity. If the pace is too slow, then competitiveness will be lost, as we have seen in many cases in this book. A key task for management is reviewing the pace of the process of managing adaptive work, reaching a judgement about whether it is too fast or too slow, and responding accordingly.

Third, management should take responsibility for several supporting, yet critical, activities in the management of adaptive work. These include: framing issues for discussion, selecting the people to participate in the discussion of the issues, and overseeing the required implementation – specifically, by setting the standards and goals for performance and by assigning responsibility for execution.

Collectively, these three responsibilities are aimed at managing the transition from divergent to convergent thinking, and at managing the balance between thinking and acting.

ADAPTIVE WORK IN PRIVATE EQUITY

As we discussed in Chapter 7, adaptive work thrives within the world of private equity. The leaders of private equity firms have extensive experience in balancing divergent and convergent thinking, and in balancing thought and action, although they rarely call these activities by these names. They also have a great deal of experience in the design (and redesign) and oversight of the processes to achieve these balances. The biggest difference we see between private equity firms and public equity companies is the amount of time and energy senior managers in private equity firms spend on revising their worldviews and thinking through the implications of those changes for companies they should buy and sell, compared with corporate leaders, who spend their time thinking about how to improve their present operations.

The private equity firm, because of the rapid pace of change of the assets it owns, is continually assessing its progress; questioning its fundamental direction; thinking of the next wave of change. As a result, successful venture capitalists become excellent analysts of future opportunities, and principal investing firms become exceptionally talented at tearing apart a business to understand its potential and vulnerabilities. Neither skill is used as often in public equity firms, where new business proposals often come out of R&D rather than out of a new business development function run by partners with personal funds invested. The difference in these two approaches can be astounding in terms of their results. The differences in the capacity for adaptive work can be even more fundamental.

Today there are a number of important early attempts being made to bridge the gaps between the approaches of private and public equity, combining the approaches of private equity with the rigours of public equity ownership (for example, continually having to meet 'mark-to-market' tests, which compare how well these companies are doing relative to the general stock market indices).

It can be rough going, as all these firms have discovered. Many faced extreme financial pressures in the second half of 2000 after the Nasdaq markets collapsed, and their market valuations declined by as much as 90 per cent. Moreover, the market is sceptical that these companies are different from mutual funds and thus are reluctant to offer high multiples for these companies at this writing. Yet, if these companies succeed in their attempts to find practical, sustainable ways to blend the managerial approaches of private equity with the requirements of public equity corporations, they will represent an attractive model that other companies will want to emulate. For the time being, these are interesting companies worth paying attention to given how skilled they are at adaptive work. As one of the oldest of these companies, Safeguard Scientifics provides a detailed study of the processes of adaptive work in the challenging environment of public markets.

SAFEGUARD SCIENTIFICS

In 1953, three years out of college, Warren 'Pete' Musser left his job as a stockbroker to form a $300,000 investment fund called Lancaster. With no specific industry focus, expertise, or investment strategy, Musser initially invested in a wide range of young companies in industries that he believed had long-term growth potential. Investments were made in real estate, office automation, medical services, cable television, robotics, and automobile parts. The results were strong. The company's first investment, for example, was in a cable television firm called Comcast, now the fourth-largest cable company in the United States.

Musser changed Lancaster's name to Safeguard Industries after a successful early investment in a business called Safeguard, which Musser renamed Safeguard Business Systems. SBS made cheque printers that wrote payment amounts by perforating the paper. Benefiting from Safeguard's managerial and financial support, Safeguard Business Systems grew to provide computerized information systems and successfully promoted its services to more than 650,000 small businesses. The Safeguard Industries investment in Safeguard Business Systems became the company's largest source of income, leading to the initial public offering of Safeguard Industries in 1965. Switching from cable companies to cheque-perforating machinery companies to computerized information systems companies began to develop Musser's adaptive work abilities.

Although Safeguard Business Systems was profitable, the concept of Safeguard Industries was vulnerable, as demonstrated by its other holdings, including a remanufactured auto parts business. Losses in the remanufactured auto parts business forced the company into debt.

The financial losses resulting from the slow-growth businesses ultimately spawned a new investment strategy. In 1977, Musser decided to identify and invest exclusively in high-growth businesses. Musser had learned the lessons of the assumption of continuity the hard way.

Nonetheless, the timing of the move was unfortunate. Safeguard Industries' mounting debt forced it to spin off Safeguard Business Systems to its shareholders in 1980. Under the plan, shareholders of Safeguard Industries received shares of Safeguard Business Systems. But by splitting the profitable unit away from the parent, Safeguard Industries was able to transfer some of the burdensome debt of the company to the more profitable entity, thus stabilizing the finances of the remaining businesses and generating capital to invest in new areas of the economy with high potentials for growth. The company renamed itself Safeguard Scientifics, reflecting its intention to invest in high-tech firms.

As a consequence of spinning off Safeguard Business Systems, Musser realized that separating the interests of the companies at an appropriate point led to a tremendous return for the shareholders. 'We noticed that a $4 stock went to the equivalent of $50 if you added up both resultant companies,' Musser said. 'All we had done was split the assets. That left a visible impression on us.' The adaptive strategy that he intuitively pursued was paying dividends.

> Musser realized that separating the interests of the companies at an appropriate point led to a tremendous return for the shareholders.

Musser decided that once an acquired growth company was on solid financial and managerial footing, Safeguard would split it off as a separate public company through a programme that would sell portions of Safeguard's holding directly to Safeguard stockholders. This would be a theme that was to generate superior returns over the years, although the timing and nature of the spin-offs differed considerably. The former investment company would come close to taking over some operating responsibilities, but it never crossed the line to day-to-day operations.

Before Safeguard Scientifics had an opportunity to implement its novel plan on a broader scale, however, the company was nearly destroyed by a totally unrelated event. An Iowa stockbroker, Gary Lewellyn of Des Moines, owner of a small brokerage, in an attempt to manipulate the Safeguard stock to his own benefit, began to accumulate Safeguard stock in late 1981. By November, he had accumulated about 7 per cent of the outstanding shares. Lewellyn had purchased the stock in small daily increments on margin through Swiss American, the US branch of Credit

Suisse. To finance his purchases, Lewellyn misappropriated $2.8 million of government securities from an account he managed for the First National Bank of Humbolt, Iowa, the bank where his father presided.

Over the next five months, he continued to buy the stock, trying to force a run-up (and preventing a call on his previous margins); by March of 1982, he 'owned' 58 per cent of the company. When Swiss American and Merrill Lynch stopped extending him margin, he set up accounts in the names of his Des Moines clients and continued to buy, even from himself, to create an illusion of demand.

On 17 March Lewellyn informed Swiss American that he couldn't fulfil his obligations and went into hiding. After a spending spree in Las Vegas, Lewellyn turned himself in to the FBI.

The results were disastrous for all involved: Safeguard saw its stock price plummet, followed by a 10-day suspension of trading by the SEC. Swiss American and Merrill Lynch found themselves owning the majority of Safeguard; the First National Bank of Humbolt was declared insolvent and was liquidated by the FDIC. Lewellyn received 20 years in prison for embezzlement.

Although Swiss American wanted to sell the 1.6 million shares it was left holding, Musser was able to convince the firm to hold the shares for a year. Musser was also able to assure his other investors that the recent fiasco had nothing to do with the underlying business plan of Safeguard, and in 1983, shareholders agreed to a secondary public offering of the 1.6 million shares to rid Swiss American of its unwanted ownership. Fortunately, Safeguard's first attempt at a rights offering was a blockbuster.

In February 1981, Musser spent $2.5 million of the money Safeguard made for 51 per cent of Novell, Inc., at the time a struggling software maker. By the end of 1984, Novell was growing rapidly as the market for local area networking (LAN) hardware and software developed, and Safeguard decided it was time to spin Novell off. In February 1985, Safeguard stockholders were given the right to purchase a share of Novell for $2.50 for every two shares of Safeguard they held; a total of 2.3 million shares were distributed in this fashion. By allocating stock to its shareholders, Safeguard's ownership of Novell fell to 23 per cent, and it relinquished direct control. Subsequent to the offering, Novell grew by more than 200 per cent in 1985, on its way to a peak value of over $500 a share in the 1990s. By 1990, Safeguard had reduced its ownership of Novell to less than 5 per cent, reaping capital gains of nearly

$100 million over three years. Some of these sells may have been required by the US Investment Company Act of 1940, which would have declared Safeguard Scientifics a mutual fund and exposed it to ordinary earned-income tax liabilities, rather than capital gains, had it not sold its interest. The provisions of the law can help force these companies to value adaptive work even when they do not want to.

While spinning off a company at the height of its achievements might not seem surprising for a financial intermediary, it would be exceptionally surprising for an operating company to take such action. Traditionally, the operating company will hold on to the company rather than realize gains in the public market. The rationale is based on the assumption of the strong link between control and performance. 'We cannot give up control of the enterprise, because if we do, performance may suffer.' Such a decision is based on the assumption of continuity. The opposite logic was used at Safeguard, which was eager to find other new opportunities. It relinquished control, profited from its transaction, and provided a stunning opportunity to investors, freeing Safeguard to move on to the next opportunity.

Unlike the traditional venture capitalist, though, Safeguard was prepared to hold a stake in a company for years beyond the IPO if it needed to strengthen the company. For example, in the late 1980s, Safeguard held a minority 15 per cent block of the stock in Machine Vision, a maker of optical systems for industrial applications. In November 1985, Safeguard reduced its holding from 15 per cent to 11 per cent through an offering at $2.75 per share. Machine Vision performed poorly in its early days. Rather than sell its position, Safeguard decided to increase its ownership to 70 per cent through a warrant that it held in 1985, and by purchasing shares on the open market in order to help Machine Vision through hard times. Working with Machine Vision, Safeguard changed the direction of the company to a focus on reselling computer hardware and software to businesses and institutions, changing its name to CompuCom to commemorate the shift. This proved to be a successful strategy. CompuCom grew by 45 per cent annually from 1988 to 1992, providing substantial returns for Safeguard shareholders. In this case the traditional assumption of the link between performance and control proved to be correct. Safeguard demonstrated its ability to use either assumption to its advantage, depending on the circumstances.

Safeguard did not restrict its investments to only small start-ups. In the late 1980s, as many companies found difficulty in raising the capital necessary to expand, Safeguard provided unsecured credit in exchange for substantial stock warrants. Again, their direct lack of control is notable. Through this mechanism, Safeguard obtained equity in QVC, the television shopping channel, and Infotron, a manufacturer of communications networking equipment. In addition, in 1988, Safeguard formed Radnor Venture Partners, a venture capital group. Radnor and the other venture capital firms that Safeguard started later on were designed to allow Safeguard to invest in companies that didn't meet its strict criteria for joining the Safeguard fold but were nevertheless promising. Safeguard has been relentless at finding new ways to create value through changes in its approach to ownership and control.

In the 1980s, Safeguard Scientifics decided computer hardware and software were the areas with the largest growth opportunities. In the 1990s, its focus began to turn to information technology, showing its determination to change at the pace and scale of the market. It began to develop companies offering consultation and implementation services, such as Cambridge Technology Partners, which Safeguard took public through a rights offering in May of 1993. By buying in at the IPO price of $5 per share for Cambridge Technology Partners, Safeguard shareholders were able to realize a 15-fold increase in their investment over the following three years.

Safeguard's focus on shareholder return drives its involvement with companies that it has taken public. 'We are active in the management of these companies. We aren't just passive investors, so we can influence their strategies and their directions. We can help to pick the management, and that gives us better knowledge on how the company is doing,' said Musser. Each company is assigned a team of experienced Safeguard professionals in the areas of operations, finance, legal, and business development. But Safeguard is focused on giving support rather than establishing standards for control.

In the case of Safeguard Scientifics, less control did not compromise performance or the aspiration for high performance. Quite the reverse was true. Those chosen by Safeguard to serve on the board of directors of partner companies push strongly for high levels of return for shareholders. In July 1999, after Cambridge Technology

After Cambridge Technology Partners failed to meet estimated earnings, Musser disposed of CEO James Sims for failing to move the company forward: 'We asked Jim to excuse himself.'

Partners failed to meet estimated earnings, for example, Musser disposed of CEO James Sims for failing to move the company forward: 'We asked Jim to excuse himself,' said Musser. Days later, Safeguard forced Edward Anderson, a former Safeguard executive, out of his position as CEO of CompuCom Systems (Safeguard still owned 54 per cent).

As the IPO market accelerated with the growth of Internet-related start-ups in the late 1990s, Safeguard realized that its method of rights offering was limiting the potential of its offerings. By allocating all of the shares on offer directly and proportionately to shareholders of Safeguard, small investors, who account for 70 per cent of all Safeguard investors, were able to participate, but investment banks were often unable to offer large blocks of shares to the institutional investors. To provide large blocks of shares to institutions (and thereby increase demand and share price), Safeguard developed a second method of taking companies public, called a *directed shares subscription programme*. With this method, a smaller portion of the shares is distributed to Safeguard stockholders at the IPO price (typically higher than that for a rights offering), allowing those interested to buy at the same rate as larger institutions. The directed shares subscription programme is a recent example of Safeguard's determination to innovate to allow itself the flexibility to move into and out of businesses.

The first company to be offered in this way was the Internet Capital Group, in August 1999. Two Safeguard executives helped form ICG in 1996 as an Internet holding company actively engaged in business-to-business e-commerce through its own network of partner companies. The formation of ICG corresponded to the passing of the National Securities Markets Improvement Act, which relaxed some of the constraints on the number of investors that could participate in a venture capital company.

Providing operational assistance and capital support, ICG intended to maximize the long-term market potential of its partner companies. Safeguard shareholders were allowed to buy a share of ICG at the offer price of $12 for every 10 shares of Safeguard held. The strategy increased interest in the offering and yielded higher returns for initial shareholders, as ICG's stock price ended the year up over 14-fold, making it the most successful IPO of 1999 (although it has since fallen off substantially). Safeguard Scientifics' 13 per cent interest in ICG, bought in two transactions for a total of $29 million, was valued at about $150 million as of December 2000.

ICG's success contributed to Safeguard Scientifics' shift in focus from information technology businesses to Internet businesses. It was the third fundamental shift Safeguard had made in 20 years. And the shift was not at all marginal. When Safeguard changes its spots, it changes them to stripes. The company moved again. In 1999, it announced that it planned to target e-commerce, e-business, and e-communications companies. 'In the early 1990s, we helped define and implement client server architectures in enterprise computing environments through Cambridge Technology Partners. Now, we are helping build the Internet as a new medium for business and consumer interactions and transactions through a number of our partnership companies,' said Musser. Safeguard rides the waves as the gales of creative destruction blow.

This investment strategy is intended to increase shareholder return and optimize the deployment of resources by building on Safeguard's portfolio of high-growth companies while sharpening its investment focus. Safeguard's partner network has grown to 40 directly held partner companies and 210 companies held indirectly through its private equity funds. Musser's decision to focus on Internet companies has enabled Safeguard to build a larger network and take more companies public. Between 1990 and 1998, Safeguard took nine companies public, compared to four companies in 1999 alone. This is adaptive work at its best.

Shareholders of Safeguard are in many ways buying the opportunity to participate in the public offerings of its partner companies. Although Safeguard's stock has not performed above average, the nine rights offerings that have been completed between 1992 and 1998 have on average resulted in a 67 per cent internal rate of return for the Safeguard shareholder, substantially above even the very high levels of return achieved in the public markets. Musser believes that 'shareholders should be evaluating Safeguard on its value creation, not on earnings'. It seems hard to argue.

Safeguard Scientifics is a clear example of how a firm can operate as the creator, operator, and trader of options. It is also a clear example of the power of adaptive work. Safeguard would not have produced the returns it did if it had limited itself to technical work. Musser and the senior people at Safeguard provided the function of the market, but so far have not been caught up in cultural lock-in. While they certainly do not formally talk about managing the rate of creative destruction or about how to innovate and eliminate at the pace and scale of the market, these notions are clearly part of the tacit knowledge of the organization. The essential role of the management committee at Safeguard is to manage the pace and scale of creative destruction, and to do it in a way that does not jeopardize operational control. Management has developed a process to manage the transition from divergent to convergent thinking, and to manage the balance between reflection and action, techniques Musser and his colleagues learned and applied in the markets of the 1980s.

Safeguard's ability to continually generate substantial and perhaps even transformational innovation, while not losing control of its operations, is one of its core strengths. The key is its focus on people and its willingness to tighten up control when things are not working well. Its primary lever for control, once it has made an investment, is people selection (or elimination). Once that is done, control is truly delegated to the (often public) operating company.

Recently Safeguard has had to go through some hard times – some due to misjudgements it have made and some due to the late-2000 Nasdaq collapse. And it will undoubtedly have to go through hard times in the future. But it has made it through these times without sacrificing longer-term performance. In the end the challenge may be for Safeguard to maintain its methods as it goes through the inevitable change in senior leadership. Maintaining as fine a balance as Safeguard has is not easy. Many people can read music, but few can play like Glenn Gould.

L'ORÉAL

The world of American venture capital is a very long way from life in high-fashion France, but L'Oréal and Safeguard Scientifics share a management philosophy of creative destruction. Liliane Bettencourt, as the primary shareholder of the French cosmetics company L'Oréal, is not only the wealthiest woman in Europe (the *Forbes* Richest list, Summer 2000, listed her as the richest woman in the world), but also the beneficiary of one company that for the time being has found the secret of perpetual economic youth.

L'Oréal was started by Madame Bettencourt's father, Eugene Schueller, in the early 1900s. Schueller, a chemist by training, developed a synthetic dye that could be used on human hair and began selling it in the streets of Paris in 1907. Within two years, he was calling the dye L'Oréal, based on the French word *auréole* ('aura of light'), and selling it to local hairdressers.

Schueller extended his product line to include soaps and perfumes, and after the Second World War, he convinced his compatriots to follow the American hair care trend of putting down soap bars in favour of shampoo.

When her father died in 1957, Bettencourt inherited the company, which continued to grow and expand internationally until 1963, when it was taken public. Bettencourt maintained a majority stake until 1974, when she traded 49 per cent of her share to Nestlé in exchange for 3 per cent of the food giant, although she maintained 70 per cent of the L'Oréal voting rights in the exchange. This deal, along with additional stock purchases later, made Bettencourt the largest shareholder of both companies.

Lindsey Owen-Jones became CEO in 1988 when L'Oréal was one of the largest companies in France, with nearly $4 billion in sales. It was a blue-chip company that the market considered unlikely to grow. However, since Owen-Jones took over at L'Oréal, the company share price has risen 10-fold, while the S&P 500 has appreciated sixfold, roughly at the same pace as that of the consumer products industry. L'Oréal has also been paying out consistent dividends over the period, making its return to shareholders even higher.

What did L'Oréal, a large, old company, do to generate such strong performance? Before Owen-Jones, L'Oréal had expanded by acquisition. It had bought Lancôme in 1965, Ralph Lauren and Gloria Vanderbilt cosmetics in 1984, and Helena Rubinstein in 1988. This approach had produced growth, but not high returns to shareholders. In those days L'Oréal was quite restrictive in terms of product and brand territory definition. Owen-Jones saw this restrictiveness as the primary constraint on L'Oréal's performance.

Accordingly, Owen-Jones decided that L'Oréal should adopt a much more expansive mind-set by enlarging the category where it competed and the markets that its key brands had to cover. This mind-set would allow L'Oréal to become a more potent competitor in the marketplace by increasing the pace and scale of change. Owen-Jones decided that there was a very broad market for beauty concepts that came from outside the home market, wherever that was. While Lancôme, for instance, remained closely connected to the concept of French beauty, Georgio Armani perfumes sold to consumers desiring Italian fashion, and Gloria Vanderbilt and Ralph Lauren Polo represented New York style and wealth. Most of the sales of fragrances and cosmetics were outside the country they represented. Polo did particularly well in England, while Gloria Vanderbilt became the top-selling fragrance in Europe only four years after its release.

Under Owen-Jones, L'Oréal accelerated its pace of internationalization, increasing sales by equating different brands with different national identities. 'To me, being truly international is to find a new way in which brands can be extremely coherent internationally and yet in which each country can bring something to the overall international picture,' said Owen-Jones. Given this concept, L'Oréal is constantly looking for a transfer of ideas between regions and businesses, and thus leverage of its innovations on a global scale. For example, its Japanese office developed a hair colour product for teenagers that has become a very significant product line across the world. In addition, this has helped to enhance L'Oréal's skills in the area of hair colours, which the company leverages successfully for women's products.

The engine of this process is creative destruction. First, L'Oréal is 'obsessed' with being more innovative. This is an objective widely shared by the organization. Innovation is at the centre of L'Oréal's most important internal processes. Each global division has to target a certain amount of innovation (share of sales achieved), and over the last 10 years, the percentage of innovation-driven sales has increased significantly. Every brand manager has to be able to define precisely (and present it to the top management) what new product plan they are working on and what potential impact they expect from their efforts. As a consumer goods company, L'Oréal is obsessed with being faster in the marketplace, reducing time to market, and being sure that it presents interesting concepts and not just new products.

> Innovation is at the centre of L'Oréal's most important internal processes. Every brand manager has to be able to define precisely what new product plan they are working on and what potential impact they expect from their efforts.

Second, beyond innovation *per se* is a strategy to let innovations evolve in a way that mimics the dynamics of the market. This is the heart of L'Oréal's creative destruction process. For example, in 1986, before Owen-Jones took over, L'Oréal released a Lancôme-brand liposome cream to hide wrinkles at $50 per jar. When the competition matched L'Oréal's product three years later, L'Oréal added liposomes to its lower-priced Plenitude line, allowing customers to buy the cream for $8. Many companies would not consider this move, fearing the effects of cannibalization. L'Oréal saw it the other way around: Adding liposome to Plenitude was part of mastering the game of creative destruction. Having different brands for different markets allows L'Oréal to introduce new technology to the high-end products first, and over time allows it to migrate to the lower-priced markets and eventually be replaced. In many ways this is the cosmetic equivalent of the 'chip wars' that occurred in the semiconductor industry, with each generation moving down in price performance to allow the next generation to enter.

For this strategy to work, Owen-Jones has to be certain to have a new improvement waiting for Lancôme before it sends its innovations down to the low-price brands. This is the essence of managing the pace of creative destruction. Owen-Jones says: 'Our labs have a basic rule – they're not allowed to let anything trickle down until they've provided something hot which will be the next new thing. That's my call.'

L'Oréal has worked hard to make certain there always is a 'next new thing', increasing research in line with profits and producing more patents on a yearly basis than any other French company. Owen-Jones controls the pace of creative destruction through this process. Needless to say, while Owen-Jones calls the pace, if the pace falls behind the market, if the labs cannot successfully come up with the 'next new thing' at the pace of the market, L'Oréal will fall behind.

This strategy became successful almost immediately after Owen-Jones took over. The company grew sales and, significantly, margins through the late 1980s and early 1990s. In addition, Owen-Jones demonstrates the same savvy in dealing with the capital markets as Bill Gates did at Microsoft, and John Chambers did at Cisco, when he underplays the long-term signifi-cance of short-term performance. In 1990, for instance, after a strong annual performance, the company attributed much of the increase to one-time adjustments. Additionally, L'Oréal typically refused to provide earnings estimates throughout the year, and Owen-Jones dismissed the value of quarterly reports, saying that only an American investor could be interested in such a thing. Nevertheless the performance increases have continued to come, causing continual upward revisions in analysts' esti-mates and delighting shareholders.

The implicit strategy of creative destruction is leveraged by a programme of acquisition. Owen-Jones acquired Maybelline in 1996 for $758 million. Although the acquisition doubled L'Oréal's US sales figures and made L'Oréal the leader in market share, the deal had an overriding global strategic rationale. L'Oréal immediately began to market Maybelline as American urban chic in Europe and Asia. It also served to fill out the lower end of L'Oréal's offerings. With its premier brands like Lancôme being offered in department stores, L'Oréal wanted to extend its cosmetics offerings to drugstores and discount stores such as Wal-Mart, where Maybelline and its major competitor, Revlon, are sold.

Through the mid-1990s L'Oréal continued to grow solidly, always building revenue and usually growing its margin. L'Oréal's new trajectory became apparent to the market in 1991. As Europe began to slide into a recession, revenue and profit growth continued to accelerate. Over 12 months starting in June 1991, L'Oréal's share price doubled. During the period, profits continued to grow, and Owen-Jones continued to explain much of them away, either as fluctuations in exchange rates or as one-time capital gains.

Through the strategy of globalizing its operations while relentlessly engaging in creative destruction, L'Oréal has proven itself to be not only a tough competitor but also a rewarding investment for shareholders. It has demonstrated over the past 15 years that the ability to operate and change at the pace and scale of the market can be accomplished, even in a larger corporation, if the leadership is present and sufficiently visionary.

Moreover, L'Oréal demonstrates that it is possible for a company to change from a focus on operations to a simultaneous focus on operations and creative destruction. As we have seen time and again, however, strong past performance does not imply strong future performance. It only buys the opportunity to make the next step. The pace of change is accelerating and will continue to do so. It has been the secret to L'Oréal's strong economic performance for the past decade and half. L'Oréal knows how to play the game of creative destruction; it knows how to lead adaptive work.

CHANGING THE RATIO OF ADAPTIVE TO TECHNICAL WORK IN THE CORPORATION

Setting the proper, that is, market-based, balance between adaptive work and technical work, as we have said, is the responsibility of the management committee and the CEO. No other group has sufficient scope of authority to both see the need and command the attention to get the job done. The tool for initiating the change in balance of adaptive and technical work is really quite straightforward: it is the annual calendar of management committee meetings, and agendas for each of these meetings. It is sometimes difficult to imagine that the prosaic act of setting the calendar, a task often delegated to support staff, is at the heart of some of the most important decisions management has to make. But it is nonetheless true. The calendar of meetings determines which issues will be addressed, which conversations will be held, who will and will not have a voice in challenging the existing mental models, and who will have a voice in proposing and establishing new mental models. In the end, the pace of change in the corporation can be set by the pace of these meetings and the issues that are accepted for inclusion.

> It is sometimes difficult to imagine that the prosaic act of setting the calendar, a task often delegated to support staff, is at the heart of some of the most important decisions management has to make.

In addition to the calendar, the agendas for the individual meetings are also critical. The more traditional agenda calls for the exchange of information and the ratification of strongly recommended decisions. Generally there is not much dialogue at these meetings, and what dialogue there is centres on the exchange or clarification of information. These meetings usually take place near the end of a convergent thinking process. The agenda setting for these meetings can generally be assigned to staff, with periodic review. No special skill is needed to run the meetings other than that of a convener.

A different type of meeting involves a real conversation, where people exchange 'views of the world' (i.e., mental models) to identify, clarify and resolve issues and to convert general notions of direction into a rough sense of action. These meetings are typically nearer the front end of a divergent thinking process. They are much more open-ended, and correspondingly have rather loose agendas. The sequence of the issues on the agenda is often important as well. It should be designed by someone senior enough to have an overall sense of what is trying to be accomplished, and a hypothesis of how the conversation in the meeting should flow. The idea is to get the best ideas on the table and discussed in an open way. Avoiding premature closure is an important art in these meetings, and often it is useful to assign someone the role of keeping the meeting on track so that it lingers and speeds up at appropriate times.

We are not suggesting that the management committee address itself *only* to adaptive work. That would be a major error and would send an unproductive signal to the corporation. Clearly the management committee does have to continue to review key operating decisions, change-of-ownership decisions, budgets and resources, talent reviews, and external relations. However, it is essential that the committee makes a conscious decision about the balance of time and attention that is spent on each of these issues. This time allocation should not just happen, as it often does. It should be entirely premeditated. If the outcome of premeditation is worse than the unmanaged outcome, it should be seen as an opportunity for reflection and improvement. To abdicate this responsibility is to abdicate responsibility for the balance of adaptive versus technical work, and to abdicate the responsibility for the longer-term performance of the corporation.

SETTING THE STANDARDS FOR MANAGEMENT EFFECTIVENESS

Setting the standards of effectiveness for these tasks helps to establish standards by which management committees should be judged by the CEO and the board. Typically, the CEO is the architect of the activities of the management committee. It is with his or her leadership, and permission, that the management committee sets its agenda, mobilizes the company's resources, carries out its tasks, establishes standards, and evaluates its performance. The CEO is both the chairman of the management committee and a member of that committee. In his role as a member of the committee, he participates in the dialogue along with the others. If the management committee fails to ask and answer the questions about the responsibility for managing creative destruction and operations, only the CEO can be found to be at fault.

The task of setting the proper balance between the company's focus on creation and trading versus operations is at the core of what the management committee and the chairman value. Accordingly, the committee should be evaluated based on its ability to set and adjust this balance properly. In the end, the management committee must take responsibility for both operational effectiveness and managing the rate of creative destruction to match the markets. This is the standard by which it should be judged and to which it should be held.

Throughout this chapter we have been addressing the following questions: What is the role of the management committee when the corporation has to change at the pace and scale of the market? What value does it add? How can it address the requirements of direction, protection, and order? How effective is it? We think these questions are at the heart of long-term future corporate performance. We have come a long way from the *Vorstand* meeting in Germany described at the beginning of the chapter. Often these questions are not asked. Unless a company can answer these questions clearly and pragmatically, performance will ultimately suffer.

9 Increasing creation tenfold

Arun Gupta is the founding entrepreneur of NeuVis, which is one of the newly formed companies currently on the periphery of the decision support software industry, a several-hundred-billion-dollar, rapidly growing industry meeting companies' changing information needs. NeuVis was established five years ago to take advantage of new programming tools (Java Beans) to bring more flexibility to the process of changing corporate decision support systems. Before forming NeuVis, Gupta was the chairman of DataEase International, a successful software developer that was sold to Symantec in 1992. While at DataEase, Gupta had begun wrestling with the problem of how to improve the efficiency of changing major elements of the software that underpins most corporate decision support systems today. Changing a key element of these programmes, say, the programme that manages the general ledger, is a very costly and often time-consuming process, since the software that controls the flow of information across the interface between the general ledger and the systems it interacts with, such as the accounts receivable system, has to be completely rewritten. While Gupta could visualize what needed to be done to cut the time and cost of these switchovers, he could not see technically how to do it. When DataEase was sold to Symantec, Gupta was given a multiyear contract, but he had no real job. However, he was not idle. He took advantage of the two years of free time to develop his ideas for metalevel software language. Based on the ideas he developed during that time, Gupta formed NeuVis in 1994. After five years of development, which Gupta personally financed, NeuVis had successful first-round financing managed by Goldman Sachs.

If you ask Gupta what he did for those two years of 'incubation', he cannot really say, other than that he was playing with ideas and talking with lots of people. In fact, this time was critical in creating his ideas and testing the robustness of his conclusions. Gupta was intensely engaged in the process of divergent thinking, simultaneously drafting problems and solutions until they fit together. The toggling between observation, reflection, and conversation served to juxtapose ideas, until at one point Gupta arrived at the business concept and direction he was searching for.

Gupta's story is typical of those founding new companies. Often the founder starts the new company after years of reflection and preliminary testing. Sometimes the necessary reflection takes place at a university, sometimes on the open road. But it rarely takes place in the corporation. There are simply too many other pressures to allow that kind of reflective time. Whether Gupta and NeuVis will be one of the successful attackers from the periphery is not knowable. But what is certain is that Gupta required the time for conversation, observation, and reflection before he could create his company. This is time that is normally not available in an intense operating environment.

THE REQUIREMENTS FOR DIVERGENT THINKING

As we showed in Chapter 4, the capital markets produce substantial and transformational innovations at 10 times the rate of the established corporation. The story of NeuVis is one of thousands of similar stories that are being played out in the capital markets.

To reach the level of innovative power of the market, corporations that have excelled in operations will have to master the skills of divergent thinking just as they mastered convergent thinking. For divergent thinking, as we have pointed out, is at the heart of the creative process.

Also in Chapter 4, we discussed that the purpose of divergent thinking is to discover new ideas at the pace and scale of the market. Achieving this purpose requires focusing on significant problems (unmet needs) and identifying promising solutions, just as Arun Gupta did. The divergent-thinking process does not require that the solution be developed in detail, nor that the solution be proven effective. These critically important steps, although necessary, are better treated as part of the convergent-thinking process. The purpose of divergent thinking is to define the possibilities and propose a promising solution that can be validated to the point of creating a business plan that will attract external investors. Search, incubation, and collision, as we saw in Chapter 4, are the core elements of divergent thinking. These processes are essential if discontinuity is going to be embraced.

Divergent thinking, as seen through search, incubation, and collision, may seem ungovernable. But our experience has shown us that there are some techniques that can stimulate divergent thinking. To a great extent, however, current corporate processes thwart the pursuit of search, incubation, and collision at the pace and scale of the market.

THE FAILURE OF STRATEGIC PLANNING, RESEARCH AND DEVELOPMENT, AND CORPORATE VENTURE CAPITAL

There are three processes in most corporations that are relied upon to provide a search, incubation, and collision, all resulting in a flow of new ideas: research and development, corporate development, and corporate planning. However, in our view, none of these processes seems to be working particularly well. Collectively these three functions, operating as they have been, have not produced change within survivor corporations at the pace and scale of the market.

Strategic planning

Strategic planning was originally conceived of as a mechanism for identifying major opportunities facing the corporation and developing the plans to capture those opportunities. Today there is widespread dissatisfaction with strategic planning. As one senior manager confided to us about his company's strategic planning processes: 'Our planning process is like some primitive tribal ritual: There is a lot of noise, dancing, waving of feathers, beating of drums, and no one is sure exactly why we do it, but still there is an almost mystical hope that something good will eventually come of it, and it never does.' Another disappointed manager noted, 'Our annual planning process is like the office Christmas party: We feel obliged to have one, even though no one seems to really enjoy it.'

Often today's strategic planning does not attempt to collect information that could challenge existing mental models. It focuses on the re-analysis of the existing businesses and the analysis of similarly sized competitors, rather than attempting to understand what is happening at the periphery of the business and how it might change. Often strategic planning has become a paper exercise, devoid of direct observation in the marketplace. Junior planners are sent off to write plans without much dialogue with the senior executives who might have the necessary insight and perspective to spot real opportunities. The process gathers new information

> Often today's strategic planning does not attempt to collect information that could challenge existing mental models.

infrequently, offers few new experiences, and does not allow time for reflection or conversation among thoughtful people. It has been reduced to a pure numbers exercise, rather than an exercise in thinking. (A self-administered test of the adequacy of a corporation's strategic planning processes is provided at the end of this chapter.) To be successful, strategic planning must be designed to incorporate the principles of divergent thinking.

Research and development

Research and development (R&D), which most people think is charged with the responsibility for renewal, is also often disappointing. An examination of the companies in the McKinsey Corporate Performance Database shows that there is no general correlation between R&D spending (either funding level or growth of resources) and total return to shareholders. The results vary considerably by industry. In the pharmaceutical industry there is a reasonably strong correlation between R&D and total return to shareholders. This is the conventionally assumed relationship. These companies spend on R&D to create new products, which helps maintain growth. In the pharmaceutical industry the process seems to be working.

This same positive relationship is seen in several other industries as well, if to a lesser extent: pulp and paper, commodity and specialty chemicals, aerospace and defence, and oil extraction. But in three of the industries we analyzed – soaps and detergents, medical and surgical equipment, and telecommunications – there is no correlation at all. Perhaps soaps and detergents can be intuitively understood, since they are in a 'low-tech' industry.

But medical products and telecommunications are far from low tech. That is not to suggest that if R&D were stopped the result would not be a loss for the shareholders. One would expect that to be the case, actually, since both these industries depend on new products for their growth. It is just that the R&D expenditures in these industries do not create enough 'surprise' to provide excess rewards to shareholders.

There is a third group of industries, however – computer hardware, software, and semiconductors – where the correlations are actually negative! The more that the companies spend on R&D, the lower are the total returns for shareholders. This occurs because the primary source of new products and innovation in these industries is not internal R&D, but rather technology licensed from the rest of the industry (there is extensive cross-licensing in these industries) or from acquisitions.

On the whole, our analysis indicates that investors expect more from R&D than they actually get. There are two reasons for this. First, technological change is only broadly correlated with total return to shareholders. Total return to shareholders is a result of the corporation's current performance and expectations about its future performance. Technological change is only one of the ways in which either current performance or expectations about future performance can be affected. Other ways include having preferred supplier or customer relationships, holding a unique market niche, or having access to special resources. It would be surprising if technological change were equally important in all industries.

Second, even in those industries where technological change is important, the most important technological advances may come either from inside the company, as a result of R&D, or from outside the company as a result, say, of the purchase of a licence for the use of technology developed by another company, or through an acquisition. We would expect a correlation between R&D and TRS in those industries where cross-licensing of patents is rare, such as in the pharmaceutical industry. But in those industries where cross-licensing is more common, for example, semiconductors or computer hardware, there is not much of a relationship.

The decision whether to use internal R&D to develop the technological information required to create surprising new products or services, or to use licensed technology or to acquire a company that owns the needed technology, is the technological equivalent of a traditional make-or-buy decision, although one does not normally think of R&D in this context. In testimony to the practical nature of this observation, Cisco has penned this credo: 'Most innovations don't happen in your company.'

Corporate venture capital

Perhaps out of frustration over the ineffectiveness of internal efforts to develop important new technologies, many US corporations have recently stepped up their spending on venture capital. The first wave of such spending reached a peak in 1989 at about $1 billion per year, an amount that accounted for more than 20 per cent of all venture capital raised in the United States. By the early 1990s, corporate spending had fallen off to less than $300 million as profit pressure mounted during the recession. Today, however, corporation spending on venture capital has risen to a level in excess of $10 billion per year (compared, however, to about $160 billion on R&D), once again more than 20 per cent of all the venture capital raised. Many leading companies are pursuing this route: AOL–Time Warner, AT&T, Intel and Lucent, to name a few. European companies are also providing venture capital funds; Siemens and Deutsche Telekom are examples. According to Dan Case, CEO of investment company Hambrecht & Quist: 'Of the 100 largest companies in the United States, two-thirds are doing [corporate venture capital], think they are doing it, or are thinking about doing it.'

Corporations are flocking to venture capital because they sense the potential for financial returns and the strategic growth options that venture capital has recently come to represent. As one company executive says: 'Investments of $2 to $5 million are not much, compared to our R&D budgets. But the benefits and insights we get are significant.' The efficiency of using corporate venture capital to gain insight into the periphery may turn out to be substantial, and more effective than traditional R&D.

But for corporations to be effective with these investments, they are going to have to learn to be effective private equity investors, and as we discussed in Chapter 7, there are four reasons why that is difficult. First, corporations often, at least inadvertently, apply the same rules to their venture capital investments as they do to their normal investments, for example, no cannibalization, no channel conflicts, and no dilution. Under these circumstances, they perpetuate their current mental models, rather than wrestle, in marketlike fashion, with new opportunities. Second, corporations often require majority ownership, which is contrary to the general style of venture investing. Third, corporate venture capital groups are often led by individuals without proven venture investing records. Rather, these individuals have strong operating records, and so may find it hard to compete successfully with lifelong investors. Fourth, the compensation for the leaders of many corporate venture capital groups is more like the internal compensation structure of the corporation than that of traditional venture capital firms. Consequently, the corporate groups rarely attract the quality of talent the traditional venture capital firm does. There are exceptions, of course, like Cisco, Dell, or Intel, but such exceptions are rare. Thus it is far from clear that corporate venture capital is going to provide the opportunities necessary to fill the gap left by R&D or strategic planning.

The collective failure of these three processes – strategic planning, R&D, and corporate venture capital – has contributed to the inability of the corporation to match the pace and scale of change in the marketplace. We believe that it is possible to improve all three processes sufficiently to bring survivor corporations more into line with the pace and scale of change in the capital markets. But to do so, the fundamental assumptions underlying these processes will have to change. The old assumption of continuity and the unrivalled importance of operating excellence will have to be replaced by an assumption of discontinuity and the importance of mastering creative destruction.

IMPROVING STRATEGIC PLANNING, R&D, CORPORATE VENTURE CAPITAL

Among the first stars to appear on a winter night are the three that make up Orion's belt. The bright light of these stars does not reveal all that could be seen, however. Near the centre star of the belt is the vast Horsehead nebula, the birthplace of future stars. The nebula of economic activity, however, rather than at the centre, is at the periphery of current industries. It is at the periphery that new companies are forming to exploit unmet customer needs and to capitalize on new capabilities, new technologies, and new ways of doing business. The periphery is a vital part of Schumpeter's 'gales of creative destruction'.

Defining the periphery

The periphery can be visualized as the edge of the vortex of creative destruction, caused, in the simplest case, by competition between a maturing business and a new one. In this vortex, attacking companies, seeking to fulfil hitherto unmet or unknown needs (as in the case of Enron), or to exploit new and potentially valuable capabilities (as in the case of Cisco), occupy the periphery, while the defenders occupy the core of the vortex, focusing on the evolutionary improvement of the existing business.

In some very mature industries, such as airlines or steel, the vortex spins slowly, bringing only infrequent challenges to the existing order. In other industries, such as broadband communications or corporate decision support systems, the vortex spins so rapidly that the periphery is about all that one can observe. Moreover, in some cases the speed of the vortex is dramatically changing as a result of external forces. This is currently occurring in the electric power industry as it is being deregulated.

One pragmatic way to define the periphery is the earliest point in time that private capital can be attracted to support an idea. Arun Gupta is at the periphery of the decision support software business. In a few years, many of the key positions in this round of the decision support software business will be taken. But in a few years there probably will be another major discontinuous change in the decision support software industry, due to advancing computer hardware and software technology and continually changing customer needs. Accordingly, there will be a new periphery.

For now, however, NeuVis is part of what may become the future decision software support business. If Gupta is successful, his approach will change the structure of that industry. If he can establish a pre-emptive position in the periphery, he has a good chance of surviving and prospering for a while in the core. Competitors, unaware of what he is trying to accomplish and how he is going about it, will find themselves defending their positions in the future, if Gupta has it right and if he can successfully execute against his vision.

Understanding the periphery

To understand the periphery one has to understand the unmet needs waiting for fulfilment, as well as the capabilities that may be used to fulfil them. The knowledge itself may be difficult, or expensive, to get and maintain. Moreover, access to the required information may only be available in exchange for access to information that others feel is valuable for them. Accordingly, companies also have to invest to develop their stores of exchangeable information.

Understanding the companies forming at the periphery is necessary to gaining strategic insights into the future possibilities of the industry, but it is also important for revealing the most pressing unmet customer needs. Each of the companies operating at the periphery is selling products, or exploring selling products, to some group of currently dissatisfied customers. It is important to know who they are, what they are dissatisfied about, and what other approaches they are pursuing to meet their unmet needs.

Each of the companies operating at the periphery is selling products, or exploring selling products, to some group of currently dissatisfied customers.

Understanding the periphery can also provide insight into the *actual* cutting edge of corporate capabilities, rather than the theoretical edge. For example, today one reads a lot in the press about new drugs that will come from understanding the genome. However, when one looks on the periphery of the biotech industry, it is virtually impossible to find companies pursuing clinical development of new drugs based on new genomic insights. Companies are pursuing bioinformatics (DoubleTwist, Ingenuity Systems, DNA Sciences, or Spotfire), software products that allow scientists to make sense of the genome, protein analysis that allows scientists to make sense of the proteins that are made by the genome (including Protogene Laboratories, Ciphergen Biosystems, Zyomyx, Mycometrix), new medical diagnoses, and new drug-screening technologies, but almost none are pursuing new drugs at the clinical stage. In a few years it will be different. There will be clinical efforts going on; the periphery will have moved.

Alternatively, by focusing on the periphery one can identify companies that are forming to exploit new opportunities or skills in hitherto unknown ways, as Enron did when it entered the natural gas trading business. There is no better way to understand the cutting edge of new business possibilities than to understand the periphery.

Understanding the evolution of the periphery

While it would have been interesting to know what Gupta was thinking a few years ago, it was not worthwhile trying to replicate it or to invest with him then, because there were so many unanswered questions about his approach. Gupta himself was uncertain about how his efforts would turn out, and in any case he was unwilling to give up some of his control over the pace of development to others. Moreover, a few years ago, the decision support systems business was dominated by a few competitors, including EDS in the United States and SAP in Germany. The conditions were not ripe for entry.

But customer needs have changed, and new technology is available. Support for entrepreneurs aspiring to pursue ideas that may eventually compete in the periphery is provided by universities with government support, or by larger corporations, or inadvertently by companies like Symantec, which house entrepreneurs like Arun Gupta yearning to realize their own dreams. Incubation takes place most commonly in this non-corporate environment. Consequently it is important to understand, as best one can, what is happening in the nebula of new ideas before the ideas arrive at the periphery. By understanding something about what is happening in these places, one can more accurately describe how the periphery might evolve.

At the point that ideas appear to have a chance of becoming economically successful, private capital takes over the support role. Because of the great amount of capital now available for venture investing (aided by the US Department of Labor's 1979 clarification of the Employee Retirement Income Security Act's 'prudent man' rule to allow pension funds more latitude to invest risk capital), this point is moving toward increasingly uncertain ventures.

Implications of evolution

To foresee the economic implications of evolution of the periphery, one has to divorce the idea of company failure from the notion of a business concept failure. In any industry, there will be many companies on the periphery. It is likely that several companies will be pursuing almost identical strategies. They focus on the same customers, with the same value proposition and the same marketing approach. While some of the companies will fail, a few, perhaps only one, might succeed. However, if even one company survives, then the business strategy pursued by that single company will survive, even if most of the companies pursuing that strategy do not. Consequently it is the potential of the business concept, rather than the potential of an individual company pursuing the concept, that should be the focal point for understanding the periphery.

Most business concepts that make it to the periphery will not survive. The point of attempting to understand the implications of the evolution of the periphery, however, is not to find a foolproof way to predict the future. It is to find a way to identify the real possibilities for the future, so that a more intelligent choice can be made about strategic direction, research programmes, venture investments, and acquisition candidates. Cisco, for example, has used its skill in understanding the periphery to decide which companies to acquire to extend its franchise in the hope of gaining a sustained competitive advantage and substantial returns for its shareholders.

Most corporate analysts find it easy to dismiss the power of new approaches because they associate these approaches with a single company, rather than a class of companies all pursuing the same strategy. This error inevitably leads to a more pessimistic assessment of the future possibilities for change than is warranted. This flawed approach is a variant of the defensive routines we discussed in Chapter 3.

The importance of the periphery

In our view, a central focus of a corporation's strategic planning, advanced research, and corporate venture capital activities should be on understanding the evolution of periphery and the potential implications of that evolution for wealth generation. Focusing on the evolution of the periphery helps ensure that the focus of innovative activity within the corporation will be on substantial and transformational change, since these are the dominant types of change found on the periphery. Moreover, focusing on the evolution of the periphery, as Enron did when it conceptualized newly emerging needs in the natural gas business, or as Corning did when it focused on fibre optics, helps ensure that the timing and focus of new business development efforts will be neither too early nor too late. The periphery provides an external market benchmark for the pace of change in the economy. Appropriate use of this benchmark can help focus strategic planning or research efforts so that they don't become too abstract or narrowly focused.

The periphery provides an external market benchmark for the pace of change in the economy.

Because the periphery constitutes a standard being set by thousands of venture capitalists, it is a pragmatic test for the adequacy of corporate focus.

Defining the periphery

Here are a few questions that can help define and interpret the periphery:

1 Which companies define the periphery of your industry today?

2 What business strategies are they pursuing? How are those strategies different from the ones you are pursuing today? Which approaches offer the greatest potential? Which represent the greatest threat?

3 If one examines the periphery from the point of view of the customer, what new benefits do companies competing at the periphery bring to customers? When will it become economically feasible to provide these benefits?

4 If one examines the periphery from the point of view of competitors currently occupying the core, which are most vulnerable to attack? How will the attack take place? When will it occur? What will be the consequences of an attack to key customers? To prices? To profits and value created? To talent? Are there opportunities for retaliation?

5 After examining the implications of the periphery from the perspective of customers and competitors, which competitors from that arena are likely to succeed? Which are likely to lose, and why?

6 What are the economic implications of any changes in the competitive order in terms of your industry market share, prices, profits, talent, and value creation?

7 What are the implications for *your* company? What options do you have?

Answering these questions will require new information. Pondering the implications of the newly gathered information will take time. New concepts will have to be given a chance to flourish. The key question one needs to keep in mind is not which of these new efforts will fail, but which will succeed.

Today, while there is some effort within long-term-survivor corporations to meet this test, the efforts are far too small or sporadic to match change at the pace and scale of the market. For example, today in the United States, about $3 of private venture capital is being spent for every $5 on R&D, yet few of the venture activities of corporations could come close to this ratio.

The need to understand the evolution of the periphery as a basis for change has grown as the pace of change in the economy has grown. As the pace of change accelerates further in the future, gaining the skill to understand the periphery will become even more important. Understanding the evolution of the periphery was much less important in the past, as the current systems of strategic planning, research, and corporate development were being shaped. But it is vital today. Accordingly, it must become a core concept in the restructuring of strategic planning, research, and corporate ventures.

RETHINKING STRATEGIC PLANNING AS EXTENDED DIALOGUE

Strategic planning has too often become a dry, lifeless enterprise in today's corporations, as we indicated earlier. We believe drawing on the evolution of the periphery, combined with a spirit of divergent thinking, can bring it back to life.

A great deal is already known in most corporations about the periphery and its likely evolution. The employees of the corporation already have a great deal of this knowledge, if it could only be brought to light. Rarely, however, is this knowledge gathered or, because the strategic planning process is so rigidly structured and narrowly focused on next year's plans, rather than on the economic long-term implications for the corporation.

> The objective of the redesign of the strategic planning process is to unlock the talent of the organization so that it can identify and address the issues of creative destruction.

Cultural lock-in has inadvertently prevented the talent of the organization from addressing the issues of creative destruction. The objective of the redesign of the strategic planning process is to unlock the talent of the organization so that it can identify and address the issues of creative destruction.

If the corporation were quite small, say, one or two people, the task would not be difficult. The involved people would simply get together for a meal to discuss the options in front of them. In this kind of conversation, nothing is sacred. During this dinner discussion all are equal, limited only by their cognitive and verbal abilities; no inhibitions are respected. Under these circumstances, there is no given order to the conversation. The issues are raised spontaneously. The parallel question to be asked by the senior management of long-term survivor corporations is: If you could assemble the 50 to 100 most talented, thoughtful, and creative people inside or outside your organization, regardless of tenure or position, who would they be, and what would you talk to them about?

Imagine that you can bring these people together, a few at a time, for an intimate conversation similar to one you might have with friends in your living room after dinner. The conversation will run for three hours, but beyond that there are no deadlines, or end products due. The agenda is yours. This is the environment we would like to create for the senior management of the corporation. It is an exercise in divergent thinking. This is the exercise that Arun Gupta went through over a two-year period as he worked on the concept of NeuVis. We will discuss this in more detail in Chapter 11.

Applying divergent thinking

Can the processes of divergent thinking, which are so essential for the generation of new businesses, be replicated in established corporations? What would it have taken to create an environment inside the corporation where Gupta could have succeeded?

From our research and experience we believe there are five requirements to realizing the potential of divergent thinking in matching the pace and scale of the market:

1. **Pick the right people.** Not everyone is capable of divergent thinking. The process of divergent thinking is characterized by the lack of clear goals, inherent ambiguity, and recursive problem solving. Engaging in divergent thinking can frighten and discourage some people who are comfortable only with the proven pathways of convergent thinking. Senior management has to be able to distinguish those with talent for divergent thinking from those who do not have it.

    Divergent thinkers tend to be energetic and have high aspirations. They are passionate, impatient, self-motivating individuals who are complex, smart, and comfortable with ambiguity and risk. One of the most distinctive characteristics of divergent thinkers is their tolerance for (Teresa Amabile would say 'love for') ambiguity and uncertainty. Csikszentmihalyi's people with a 'sunny pessimism' believe that the problems are exceptionally hard (they are pessimists about solving the problems), but they believe that if the problems can be solved, they are the ones to solve them. Divergent thinkers thrive on dialogue, challenge, interchange, new people, new tools, new experiences. Unlike most of us, divergent thinkers believe they can 'fill in the blanks' in the information they are given to solve problems. When they do, they experience the rush of the 'ah-ha!' collision. They seek that rush. Divergent thinkers like risk. They will innovate only when they face risk. Yet while divergent thinkers like risk, they also personalize failure. They need to be in a position where, if they do fail, they will be able to recover. If the dialogue is properly conducted, the collective community offers a hedge against individual risk. That is the kind of corporation divergent thinkers flock to.

2. **Allow adequate preparation time.** As we discussed in Chapter 4, the time required for the divergent thinking process to reach fruition is unpredictable and often rather lengthy, as the story of Arun Gupta's journey to NeuVis illustrates. The unpredictability is a consequence of the complexity of the problem, the need to understand what resources exist, and how these resources might be combined in an effective manner through an iterative process. Often, 'suspending disbelief' is necessary to avoid premature closure, or entrenchment in existing concepts and approaches. Suspending disbelief means temporarily accepting data and observations that do not seem to make sense. The ability to suspend disbelief helps to ensure that the chances for finding a fresh view are maximized. Suspending disbelief is an unnatural act for an operating organization, but essential to an innovative organization. Adequate preparation time is needed to lay the groundwork for ideas to form and be shaped in sufficient detail to allow a credible plan to be developed. As Csikszentmihalyi noted, artists who spent the longest time getting familiar with their materials before they painted, painted the most important works. There must be time in the dialogue process for the artists to become familiar with their materials if important outcomes are sought. Divergent thinkers need time to wander and wonder. The cadence of observation, reflection, and conversation has to be right. Incubation is required for productive divergent thinking.

One of the most valued opportunities management can give to divergent thinkers is the time to prepare and the time to let ideas and insights collide.

3. **Set high aspirations.** Many entrepreneurs, including Arun Gupta, want to 'change the world'. This is what distinguishes them from conventional, or incremental, problem solvers. Divergent thinkers seek tough and important problems to solve, or they will lose interest. We have observed that many times the difference between an incremental and transformational outcome in business is the result of the aspiration level of the leaders.

4. **Provide resources, flexibility, and deadlines.** Divergent thinkers want to work in an environment rich in alternative resources, data, and access to the information and information-processing tools they need to do their work. They do not expect to be controlled in any detailed way. They have trouble with routines and schedules. They want to be free to seek the most interesting people to work with. They dislike being isolated, or having limited access to the resources and people they feel they need. They like to be in environments where they can discover new things. But they also need deadlines, as we will discuss further below.

5. **Provide senior coverage.** Someone in leadership has to be willing to put his or her reputation on the line in order to make the dialogue a success. As one Enron manager bluntly put it: 'Nothing happens without people being willing to put flesh on the table.' There will be many challenges along the way. Senior management has to be available to sort them out.

If the strategic dialogue process can pass these five tests, the chances of success are high.

Designing the strategic planning process

We have used the principles laid out above to redesign the strategic planning process. There are four steps in the redesign process. The first step is for top management to plan the overall process. The second step is to prepare for the first dialogue. This preparation is different from the preparation required in classical strategic planning processes, since it involves more senior management time; is generally longer than the typical strategic planning process, since it is intended to provide time for 'incubation' to take place; and depends on the direct experience of the periphery by top management. The third step in the process is to force the collision of perspectives and develop recommendations for specific action steps to be taken. This step is designed to replicate the process of collision as we described it in Chapter 4. The fourth step is for the results to be summarized for top management, who will then decide which of the recommendations to pursue.

The following sections cover in more detail each of the steps in redesigning the strategic planning process.

Step 1: Overall process design

The first step in reconceptualizing the strategic planning process is to design the overall process. Top management's objective in this step is to select the issues for discussion over the next year or two, pick a leadership team to prepare and lead the discussion, and establish the timing and venue for the first discussion.

Senior management should select the issues after appropriate discussion. We recommend that this discussion does not last more than a day. Each member attending should prepare a list of the most important issues or opportunities facing the corporation over the next five to seven years. They should focus on the pace of creative destruction in some aspects of the business, and on under-standing the economic implications of the evolution of the periphery. (We offer examples of these issues and approach in Chapter 11.) We have found

Trips abroad, or visits to customers, help ensure that the management team adopts an external rather than internally focused mental model.

it productive to conduct this session after members of the senior management have taken a foreign trip, or visited a series of customers, or attended a major trade show or a major industry meeting – some event to help open their thinking to the challenges of creative destruction in their industry. Trips abroad, or visits to customers, help ensure that the management team adopts an external rather than internally focused mental model.

Having selected the issues the company intends to address, the leader of the first dialogue should be chosen. Generally the leader should be selected from among the top management team that developed the slate of issues necessary to ensure continuity of thought and intent. The role of the leader is to select the participants in the dialogue (from the 50 to 100 of the most knowledgeable people), lead the dialogue-development process and chair the dialogue itself, and make recommendations to the senior management group after the dialogue. This process is designed to observe the principles of divergent thinking and to best leverage the insight and judgment of senior management.

Step 2: Preparing for the first dialogue

Observing the requirements for divergent thinking means that sufficient time has to be allowed for the participants in the dialogue to gain a first-hand understanding of the periphery, as opposed to reading the views of others. Nike's senior managers, following in the footsteps of CEO Phil Knight, have developed a keen sense of the importance of direct experience. Nike organizes 'inspirational trips' for key employees and managers charged with the responsibility for a product line, for example, basketball trips. These events give managers an opportunity to visit with pro players to understand what is working and what is not. Often it is the leading customers, like pro players, who see unmet needs first or most clearly. Occasionally these lead customers will also have very good ideas about how to meet these needs. The trips also give managers a chance to hang out at schools, mix with the street ballplayers, and still have enough incubation time to mull over the insights they've gathered along the way.

A second example of Nike's focus on understanding the evolution of the periphery (although they do not call it that) through direct experience is their investment in NikeTown stores. They operate them not as retail profit centres (or as competition with key customers like Champs, Foot Locker, and Athlete's Foot), but as a way to achieve greater insight into consumers' unmet needs. Nike sees NikeTown stores as 'retail laboratories' that provide insight not only into product needs but also merchandising needs. Many credit Nike with leading the way toward branded stores-as-entertainment, an approach now followed by Warner Brothers, Disney, Levi's, Coke, Harley-Davidson, and others. Because NikeTown stores are enormously popular, Nike gets a good sense of the range of emerging customer needs. In fact, Nike's second NikeTown, placed in Chicago, has become one of Chicago's most popular tourist sites.

Preparation on this scale ensures that sufficient new information will be brought to the process to maximize the chances of novel insight. Traditional strategic planning processes, which rehash old or secondhand data, cannot be expected to generate new ideas with the same frequency. While this process takes longer than the conventional process, the costs can be spread out over a longer period of time, and the value of insights created are much greater than those found in the conventional strategic planning process.

Step 3: Design and conduct the first conversation

After the preparation has been completed, the team is ready to begin the dialogue. Generally the dialogue occurs over two days, with a very light agenda to allow ample time for discourse. The only constraint on the dialogue meeting is that a clear set of objectives has to be developed, such as determining the best opportunities to pursue, developing the case for pursuing those and not other opportunities, the sequence of their pursuit, and the details of the next steps to take.

The fact that there is a light agenda for the dialogue does not imply that the dialogue is loose. But the dialogue should be managed by a well-prepared leader rather than follow a pre-arranged agenda. The job of the dialogue leader is to encourage the creative thought of the other participants in the dialogue. At McKinsey, our partners have developed a tool kit of questions for use by the leaders of the dialogue to stimulate better ideas. These questions are drawn from a database of questions developed by 'reverse-engineering' actual innovations with which we have been involved. The questions posed nudge workshop participants out of their usual ways of looking at the world. It is a technique that has been successfully used in more than 125 applications across a broad array of industry sectors and company situations.

As we stand back from our experience with these meetings, we see that there are four tricks we have learned over the years, in addition to the bank of questions that our partners at McKinsey have developed that improve the productivity of the actual dialogue:

1.   **Changing the context.** Mihalyi Csikszentmihalyi observed that positioning an individual at the intersection of different cultures or disciplines can stimulate creativity: 'In cultures that are uniform and rigid it takes a greater investment of attention to achieve new ways of thinking. In other words, creativity is more likely in places where new ideas require less effort to be perceived.'

There are several ways to change the context. The first is to change the social context of the dialogue, say, by providing a rich mix of senior and junior executives, researchers and marketers, Europeans and Americans to improve the productivity of the meetings (as long as all have shared the same preparation steps).

The second way to change the context is to change the mental context of the problem. For example, William McGowen, founder and chairman of MCI, was known for 'reverse thinking', thinking the opposite of what everyone else at the time was thinking. Sir James Black, as we noted earlier, calls such thinking 'turning the question around'. If you believe you need a small molecule to build a new pharmaceutical drug, try a large one, as well. After all, you cannot always anticipate what will work.

An alternative to reverse thinking is to employ the 'zoom-in, zoom-out' approach favoured by some chess champions. Zooming in reveals the fine details of each part of the game and the short-term trends. Zooming out shows the relationship among the parts and how they are changing over long time scales. Juxtaposing the perspectives gained by zooming in and zooming out often results in novel insights, insights that form at the 'intersection' of these two perspectives.

A fourth trick is to change the physical context simply by getting away.

2.   **Visualization.** Visualization – forming a visual image in the 'mind's eye' – can help to stimulate connections. Astronomer Vera Rubin doodled to discover her thoughts on the structure of the universe; Jonas Salk claimed that it was his efforts to visualize the viral process that led

to his discovery of the polio vaccine. Visualization can be used during 'collision' meetings by attempting to draw a picture of the relationships that are being discussed, rather than relying on verbal cues alone. For this reason, it is sometimes helpful to have a graphic designer at some of the meetings, or perhaps an artist, to capture different ways of expressing common thoughts.

3. **Using a muse.** Many creative people need a muse, someone to play off, to converse with, to argue with. Einstein, for example, had Besso in developing his special theory of relativity. 'When Einstein burst in on Besso in May 1905, three and a half years [after their last discussion], it was time, light, and the ether that were on his mind. Sure enough, talking with Besso worked. "Trying a lot of discussions with him," Einstein wrote in 1922, "I could suddenly comprehend the matter. Next day I visited him again and said to him without greeting: Thank you. I've completely solved the problem."'

    As Paul Valéry, the French poet and essayist, said, 'It takes two to invent anything. The one makes up combinations; the other chooses, recognizes what he wishes and what is important to him in the mass of the things which the former has imparted to him.'

    The same technique can be used in dialogue meetings, by having the participants pair up to discuss their thinking: placing a researcher with a marketing expert, or a senior executive with a junior one, or an executive from the hardware business with one from the software business. If the chemistry is right, and the muse relationship develops, the results can be very impressive.

4. **Slowing things down.** We have often observed that the dialogue meeting leader can increase the productivity of the meeting by consciously slowing things down, rather than speeding them up (as one typically does in business). As Valéry said about poetry, 'Poetry is about slowing down, I think. It's about reading the same thing again and again, really savoring it, living inside the poem. There's no rush to find out what happens in a poem. It's really about feeling one syllable rubbing against another, one word giving way to another, and sensing the justice of that relationship between one word, the next, the next, the next.'

    Nothing could be more contrary to the accepted ways of doing business in corporations focused on operations than to slow things down. Yet this may be precisely what is necessary. Allowing long immersion in the details of the data, combined with personal reflection – letting the parts of the business 'rub together' – increases the probability that significant new insight will be born. Using this technique forces the meeting leader to develop a fine sense of when to push and when to hold off, since the final deadline does have to be met, but the most important objective of the session is to develop potentially successful new directions.

Step 4: Post-dialogue reflection and decision making

After the dialogue has been completed, it is the task of the dialogue chair-person or leader to summarize the results for top management, who will decide which opportunities to pursue given the other demands on the corporation. These decisions should be taken rather quickly, within a few weeks of the completion of the dialogue, since it is important for the credibility of the process that the participants know the results of their hard work have been used. Some favour making the decision to proceed on some of the ideas at the conclusion of the dialogue, but we have found that often senior management needs time to reflect on the implications of the recommendations before proceeding.

Once the first issue and dialogue have been completed, the senior executives can proceed to pick the leader for the second dialogue, and then the third, and so on. Since the design of all conversations are conceptually the same, having done one, the others follow in step. The pace can vary according to the needs of the marketplace and the capacity of the organization for change. Controlling the pace of these meetings, as we discussed earlier, is one of the most direct ways management has to control the pace and scale of change in the corporation.

These four steps, taken together, can provide the basis for a new strategic planning process, one that has proven to be much less bureaucratic than traditional processes. The four steps we outlined are not new. They mimic the processes in the marketplace, they focus on the periphery, and they bring the process of strategic planning to the point of application for capital. We have designed several successful processes along these lines for our clients. In Chapter 11 we will discuss in detail the longer-term use of these techniques at Johnson & Johnson.

Reconceptualizing R&D

Given the evidence presented earlier in this chapter, we believe 'R&D' is a dysfunctional phrase. The classic phrase 'R&D' inadvertently emphasizes the unity between research and development, rather than the unity of the need for technical information useful for generating new businesses.

> The classic phrase 'R&D' inadvertently emphasizes the unity between research and development, rather than the unity of the need for technical information useful for generating new businesses.

In the light of our research on the increasing importance of creative destruction, we believe the goal today within corporations should be new business creation – not research and development. Research is one way to acquire some of the information needed for new business formation. Technology licensing is another. The acquisition of small companies, perhaps as part of the job of the corporate venture capital department, is a third. If the objective is to acquire the information needed for business building, then all three of these functions – classical research, licensing, and small-company acquisition through corporate venture capital – may be more productively linked than kept separate. In many ways this is already happening today in an informal way. Acquisitions, particularly of smaller companies, are increasingly a core element of rapidly changing and highly innovative industries. Cisco alone made 51 acquisitions between 1993 and April 2000 in the course of gaining access to technology.

Development, on the other hand, is concerned with the effective use of technical information rather than its acquisition. We feel that 'information acquisition' and 'information application', both in the service of new business generation at the pace and scale of the market, are more useful concepts than R&D.

While the day-to-day activities of research, licensing, and small-company acquisition are totally different, they share the same purpose: providing technical options for the creation of new businesses to the corporation. Linking research, licensing, and small-company acquisition is no different in principle from linking material 'make-or-buy' decisions in the manufacturing department. Research 'makes' the needed technical information, and licensing and acquisitions 'buys' the information. If it is cheaper to make the needed component or subassembly, then it is made. If it is cheaper to buy the needed component or subassembly on the open market, then it is purchased. It is a very efficient system. This logic holds for technology information acquisition as well.

J&J's approach

We can see an illustration of this integrated approach at Johnson & Johnson, a very large manufacturer of pharmaceuticals, medical equipment, and consumer products. J&J has long been skilled in riding the waves of creative destruction, and in doing so it has provided exceptional long-term total return to shareholders. Part of their secret is the close link between research, licensing, and corporate venture capital. J&J did not set out to design the system this way; nonetheless it has evolved in very much the way described above. To complement their internal R&D efforts, J&J has a corporate venture capital group called Johnson & Johnson Development Corp. (JJDC). This is a small group that looks a lot like the venture capitalists of Silicon Valley. They, along with more than 100 vice-presidents of business development (or VPs of licensing and acquisition) around the world in the different J&J operating companies, spend all of their time scanning the market for viable new technologies both in start-up companies and within other major corporations.

Having been in existence now for more than 25 years, JJDC is one of the longest-running examples of corporate venture capital. One of the reasons JJDC was successful is that they were given the time they needed in the early years to get the fund over the investment-stage hump. According to Jim Utaski, who was the president of JJDC between 1990 and 2000: 'Having only two bosses over 25 years who were both very growth-oriented helped. We needed at least a 10-year horizon to realize returns. This patience level does not exist for most corporations.'

Established in 1973 by CEO Jim Burke, JJDC received 'air cover' from Burke's long-term vision. Burke's successor, the current chairman of J&J, Ralph Larsen, has shared this commitment. Utaski says. 'Our cost-neutral position eliminated all critics; it is difficult to dismantle the unit now.'

This freedom has allowed JJDC, with its eclectic team of senior executives, technologists, and lawyers, to pursue an appropriately varied portfolio of technologies (often in competition with each other), provide a window on technology to J&J's operating companies around the world, and measure success according to venture capital-like criteria (Utaski would rank JJDC among the top-performing second-tier venture capital firms). They 'do deals', bringing the technologies into the corporation (usually into one of the decentralized operating companies) to be developed and launched through the highly capable worldwide sales and distribution channel the corporation has developed. Most of these technologies are already in some stage of development.

To make sure that J&J does not miss out on scientific breakthroughs before they become viable technologies, the corporation has another group called the Committee Office of Science and Technology (COSAT). This group of eight to 10 PhDs stays in touch with the top researchers around the world, tapping into breakthrough research and connecting it with the internal R&D efforts around the corporation. They come quite close to a real understanding of the evolution of the periphery as it applies to J&J. Because both of these groups are sponsored at the corporate level rather than in the operating companies, they have the flexibility to maintain longer time horizons on their activities, often nurturing researchers or small start-ups for years before the technology can be licensed or the company acquired.

An acquisition can stimulate a brilliant new idea in its core business, just as an in-house idea can spark an acquisition. Johnson & Johnson is one example of a company that pursues both paths – and reaps the significant rewards. The J&J leaders believe that the only way to act like the market is to be deeply immersed in it.

Reconceptualizing corporate venture capital

Few companies have had the success J&J has had with corporate venture capital. While small investments have been successfully made by a few firms, the great majority of these efforts are insufficient to match the pace and scale of change in the market. One alternative to focusing solely on corporate venture capital is that provided by J&J, but there is another option that has become increasingly well developed in Europe.

This alternative approach – internal 'business plan contests' – capitalizes both on the employees' knowledge of the periphery and on the traditional corporate venture capital strength of understanding the new companies. Together these functions may work in a fashion superior to that of

> At one European electronics firm, a business plan contest led to the identification of more than 180 new business concepts, which resulted in four new start-ups within the corporation.

traditional corporate venture capital, according to the work of our McKinsey colleagues who developed the concept. At one European electronics firm, a business plan contest led to the identification of more than 180 new business concepts, which, after a period of refinement, elimination, and incubation, resulted in four new start-ups within the corporation. The impact was greater than that of long-standing corporate venture capital activities in the corporation that did not leverage the knowledge of the employees.

To begin the process, the company established a cross-functional senior review team that was supported by the corporate venture capital department. The team solicited ideas, emphasizing people in the lower ranks who had traditionally been excluded. The business plans were reviewed and winners were selected. Winners were awarded prizes as well as seed money to move forward. More important, the winners were coached on how to develop and iterate their ideas. Through this process of iteration and staged decision making, the number of quality ideas grew over time.

AddVenture! at Infineon

Other companies have created similar programmes. A clear example is Infineon Technologies, the former Semiconductor Group of Siemens. Infineon launched a business plan/idea generation competition in 1997 – the AddVenture! Program, which was open to all employees.

The programme was structured so that ideas were developed step-by-step into comprehensive business plans. The programme ran over several months, accompanied by workshops and coaching sessions at company locations worldwide. More than 200 teams submitted proposals. Several dozen were developed into detailed business plans. A jury of senior executives and experts on technologies and markets selected a final set of teams that entered into negotiations for funding. The evaluation criteria largely matched those a venture capitalist might look for in a winning start-up concept – but also took corporate strategic interest into account.

Five new growth businesses have taken off so far, all targeting market opportunities of several hundred million dollars each. The Group has established a unit called Infineon Ventures, which nurtures these businesses and helps identify other new business opportunities inside and outside of Infineon. It is more successful than traditional corporate venture capital activities are.

Infineon's experience shows that corporate competitions do more than simply generate ideas. They help change a company's culture by motivating employees to reach outside their daily responsibilities. Competitions also teach employees to think about building businesses around their ideas.

Business plan competitions are now a proven tool. In Germany alone, regional competitions have tapped venture capital of several hundred million euros, and have stimulated thousands of new jobs.

It is not clear whether enough Arun Guptas can be created within the environment of long-term-survivor corporations to make a difference. But the need to do so is clear, as well as the conditions that will have to be met: the need to swap the assumption of continuity for the assumption of discontinuity; the need to balance the focus on operations with the focus on creative destruction; the need to understand the likely evolution of the periphery; and the need to provide time for ideas to incubate if the efforts are going to be successful. If the corporation is going to become an active creator, operator, and trader of options, at the pace and scale of the market, it must learn to mimic the methods of Arun Gupta. Moreover, as we have discussed, there are significant options available for reconceptualizing the key change processes of the corporation: strategic planning, R&D, and corporate venture capital. The key requirement in the end is the will to change. The Guptas of the world, if they can find a way to prosper in the survivor corporation, can give senior management the option to change at the pace and scale of the market. But management still has to make the decisions, as we discussed in Chapter 7. The dilemma is how to accomplish this degree of change without undermining operational excellence. The answer to that dilemma lies in the details of the control processes of the corporation, the focus of the next chapter.

Diagnostic questions to evaluate the quality of a company's strategic planning

Are you satisfied with your strategic-planning efforts?

1 Do you feel that enough good ideas emerge from your strategic-planning efforts?

2 Have your businesses missed opportunities that they regretted?

3 Are you concerned that your strategic-planning process is mainly a paper exercise?

4 Are there two parallel processes in your organization – the effort to develop the plan 'for corporate' and the real planning process in the business?

5 Has the annual planning process become a rote exercise where last year's plan gets updated on the word processor?

6 Are your strategic plans more tactical than truly strategic?

7 Do you tend to be more reactive than proactive in shaping major issues for your business?

8 Are you satisfied with the quality of feedback for your strategic plans?

9 Are your budget, capital allocation, compensation, and succession planning guided by the themes in your strategic plan?

10 Does the strategic-planning process link strategies to an understanding of the future of the industry?

10 Control, permission, and risk

Give us a proposition we can't say yes to.

CEO OF A MID-SIZED HIGH-TECH ATTACKER

If corporations are to be a creators–operators–traders of options, they will have to learn to accommodate and balance the assumption of continuity and the assumption of discontinuity. They will have to accommodate and balance divergent and convergent thinking. To do that, they will have to learn to balance control and permission.

In his classic 1946 work *The Concept of the Corporation*, Peter Drucker commented on the underlying tension at General Motors at the time between freedom and control:

General Motors could not function as a holding company with the divisions organized like independent companies under loose financial control. On the other hand, General Motors could not function as a centralized organization in which all decisions are made on the top, and in which the divisional managers are but little more than plant superintendents.

The tension was resolved, Drucker argued, through GM chairman Alfred P. Sloan Jr's concept of decentralization, which was developed between 1923 and the mid-1940s. Decentralization was:

. . . not merely a technique of management but an outline of a social order. For Mr. Sloan and his associates, the application and further extensions of decentralization are the answer to most of the problems of modern industrial society.

Decentralization ensured the accountability of the organization's operating divisions and, with the tightly specified accounting systems it required, allowed GM's central management to determine which of its divisions was operating well and which was operating poorly.

On the other hand, GM employees told Drucker that their greatest cause of job dissatisfaction was not inadequate pay but excessive interference from senior management in the operational details of their jobs. On balance, Drucker felt that decentralization, as practised, sapped the spirit, independence, and the initiative to be more productive of lower-level managers and workers. Accordingly, he advised GM management that decentralization should be carried to its 'logical conclusion', that is, to enhance the independence and initiative of the workers and foremen. He further recommended that GM's central governing policy should be reoriented toward 'developing . . . a "responsible worker" with a "managerial aptitude" [operating in the context of] a "self-governing plant community".'

GM management rejected Drucker's recommendations, arguing that the decision would abrogate the 'expertise' of senior management. The truth is, the 'top men', as they were known, who ran General Motors during the 1930s conceived of decentralization not as a means of relinquishing control but of extending it over their far-flung empire. Perhaps more surprisingly, the leadership of the United Automobile Workers union also rejected Drucker's recommendations, insisting that financial reward, not psychological gratification, was the only factor worth considering in the compensation-and-control equation. The opinions of workers and foremen were ignored by both management and the unions.

The tension between central control (an assertion of continuity) and local initiative (in the spirit of discontinuity and change) was resolved in favour of continuity.

BALANCING CONTROL AND PERMISSION

As in the 1940s at General Motors, the essential tension between control and the permission to take local initiative continues within many corporations today. To balance control and permission, we will first have to describe the key features of each way of thinking.

Control

Control is the outward expression of convergent thinking. As Kenneth Merchant, dean of the Levanthal School of Accounting at USC, said: 'Control, which essentially means "keeping things on track", ranks as one of the critical functions of management. Good control means that an informed person can be reasonably confident that no major, unpleasant surprises will occur.'

As Robert Simons pointed out, the purpose of control is to eliminate surprise. The purpose of divergent thinking is to create surprise. Control needs a stable environment to work. Divergent thinking fosters a dynamic one. Control systems squelch divergent thinking and creativity. Adaptive, divergent-thinking environments celebrate it.

In the practical everyday world of business, control is valued by investors, senior managers, mid-level managers, and specialists (e.g., scientists, salesmen, planners, controllers, etc.). It is sought out by individuals in their own lives. Formal systems for gaining control include processes for setting standards; collecting, processing, and delivering information; and the design of evaluation and reward systems. Informal control systems, which are often unrecognized as 'control systems', include conversations among managers and subordinates, physical presence, and calendar and agenda setting. In the corporation, control is required at four levels: the corporate level, divisional level, functional level, and project level. Controls are required to help prevent profit shortfalls and the assumption of excessive risk.

In response to these complex needs and processes, most corporations have developed hundreds of subordinate control systems within the corporation. Sometimes they are in conflict. We asked the senior management of one company to name the five most important systems for maintaining control over operations and the five most important processes for ensuring the effectiveness of technology development. Ten systems were identified in all. No system that was identified as being important for controlling operations was also important for controlling the flow of innovation. Moreover, often the systems that were important for ensuring operational excellence (e.g., systems designed to keep the production processes running at high speeds) undermined efforts to introduce innovations (which would require disrupting the existing manufacturing processes).

Conflicts, if they were spotted (and often they were not, since even the recognition of the problem was discouraged), were resolved on a case-by-case basis. Even though these systems were in perpetual conflict, no reasonably enduring solution could be found. The differences were often resolved 'politically', with the victory going to the most senior person. Moreover, control systems, once in place and running, were difficult or costly to remove or change. It was difficult to argue that these systems mimicked the market.

Control systems may not only be in conflict with one another; they can also inhibit performance in a number of ways. They can:

- Distort the information they are meant to interpret, as has been discussed previously. The control system can reject information that does not fit the pre-established requirements of the system (e.g., form, timeliness, or accessibility). Novel information that could offer clues to new opportunities – or risks – is difficult for the system to accept.

- Emphasize issues that are easily understood, rather than issues that may be equally important but less apparent and more complex. 'What gets measured, gets done.' To which we could add: 'What does not get measured, does not get done.'

- Emphasize issues that were important when the control systems were built, rather than those that exist now or those that will exist in the future.

- Inadvertently inhibit adaptive work and dampen creativity and innovation. The more novel the system, the more difficult is the job of designing control systems.

- Contribute to a false sense of security if they are not designed to be adapted to changes in the environment. Control systems are generally self-renewing, and regardless of their gradual ineffectiveness, remain in place because of the cost and complexity of changing them. Once in place, control systems have advocates who are reluctant to change them.

- Can be abused by 'gaming the system'.

As a result, companies that are focused on tight control systems as an integral part of their effort to be operationally excellent risk not being able to anticipate or cope with a changing com-

Companies that are focused on tight control systems as an integral part of their effort to be operationally excellent risk not being able to anticipate or cope with a changing competitive environment.

petitive environment. Realizing the limitations of tightly controlled corporations, Bill McGowan of MCI decided to cultivate a corporate culture based on freedom and flexibility. As McGowan recalled:

> If people have a standard procedure for everything, when does anybody learn to make decisions? Are you supposed to follow the manual all the way to the top and then one day suddenly start thinking for yourself? I used to get up once a year before all the employees, and say, 'I know that somewhere, someone out there is trying to write a manual of procedures. Well, one of these days I'm going to find out who you are, and when I do, I'm going to fire you.'

Capital markets are the opposite. Capital markets do not establish goals, in the performance sense of that word. Moreover, capital markets are silent on the issue of the need to eliminate surprise. Effective capital markets are designed to provide for admission of new competitors and the elimination of weak ones, and thus increase, not decrease, the chances of surprise. Capital markets control the process of entry and exit, not operations *per se*. Capital markets establish standards for the quality and timeliness of information about operations, and they enforce adherence to standards. But they do not control results. As a result, capital markets generally introduce new options more quickly than corporations, and eliminate old and weak ones without remorse.

To foster this kind of discontinuous behaviour within corporations, control has to be balanced with permission to engage in divergent thinking. As our former colleague at McKinsey, Tom Peters, observed in 1991: 'We need to give up control, and lots of it, to stand even a chance of gaining control in these tumultuous times.'

But what controls should be given up? How can they be given up without losing control over operations? What do we replace them with, if anything? Before we move on to these crucial questions, we need to understand the flip side of control: permission.

Permission

In management, the counterpoint to control is permission. For most managers, permission means having the freedom to act without first having to check, and perhaps justify, their actions with higher levels of management. Freedom to act also implies that they are free to do what is right in their eyes to meet the goals of the business. Managers seek freedom from interference from senior management, just as the General Motors workers did. But granting this freedom is difficult for executives who feel an obligation to maintain control. Permission, they argue, is just one step closer to recklessness. Control-oriented executives are like the farmer who pulls the carrots up each morning, 'just to see how they're doing'. Striking the right balance between control and permission has long been a dilemma for management. As the pace of change in the economy accelerates, the importance of balancing the tension between control and permission will increase.

As the pace of change in the economy accelerates, the importance of balancing the tension between control and permission will increase.

Permissions sought

What kinds of permissions do managers seek? There are several. The permission to explore to the same extent that exploration takes place in the capital markets. The permission to pursue their goals without undue interference from the operational control systems, which, by requiring unnecessary information or review cycles, or requiring useful information too frequently, drive up the cost of compliance and drive out the time needed for exploration. The permission to take risks, that is, experiment with new business concepts at the pace and scale of the market, without higher-than-market costs (e.g., bankruptcy, loss of health, loss of job). Finally, the permission to seek external funds for valued ideas if the parent corporation decides not to pursue the idea. If these four permissions were granted, many managers would feel that they have sufficient freedom to 'do what is right'.

Permission is not a decision. It is an enabling concept. If one is granted permission, one is granted an option to act. Permission does not imply a lack of responsibility, or recklessness. Rather, it implies increased accountability.

Permission granted by senior management or investors transfers control to the second group. It is not uncommon for a group that has just received an increase in permission to hoard it by not passing it along to their subordinates (thus re-initiating the unwanted system of control).

Some companies have learned the lessons of permission management very well. At J&J, for example, explicit performance targets are avoided, giving employees in the business units permission to 'do the right thing'. Chairman Ralph S. Larsen says: 'I don't want to set financial targets for the growth of the businesses within J&J. Either I shoot too low and the businesses don't reach their potential, or I shoot too high and they are forced to pursue bad business practices to make the numbers.' To Larsen, company aspirations are not about numbers, they are about generating new growth businesses that will change the face of the health care market. With sales of $27 billion dollars in 1999, J&J is a leading global provider of health-care products. But it did not get to be so big by doing it 'by the numbers'.

Similarly, MCI did not set a growth target and then figure out how to reach it; it focused its thinking on the entire 'opportunity space' it had, then extracted as much value from it as it could. And MCI has grown rapidly as a consequence.

The markets grant enormous permission, of course, to everyone who enters – permission to try, permission to risk, permission to fail, and permission to succeed.

Permission conundrums

The shift within corporations from control to permission is not easy. Giving permission is tantamount to giving up control. One must deeply trust those to whom control is relinquished. In the private equity world, control is relinquished only after long, and often arduous, negotiations. And when it is granted, a 'term sheet' (a short summary of the key provisions of an agreement that is a prelude to a binding and detailed contract) faithfully records the details of the exchange. Permission (granted by the capital holders) for control (received by the operating team) is drafted and signed. Often this term sheet includes 'flip' clauses, specifying that should standards slip, control reverts to the originating party.

Permission without the resources to exercise those liberties, of course, is disingenuous. Permission requires the obligation to provide either the resources (money, talent, equipment, time) or the time and wherewithal to get them.

The failure to grant permission – the collapse of intrapreneuring

At the time of the publication in 1985 of Gifford Pinchot's *Intrapreneuring: Why You Don't Have to Leave the Corporation to Become an Entrepreneur*, 'intrapreneurship' was hailed as 'one of the great social inventions' by *The Economist*. The source of this enthusiasm is not hard to understand. 'Intrapreneuring' appeared to offer a practical solution to one of the most vexing challenges facing the managers of large corporations: how to release the entrepreneurial talent of the organization.

Yet, despite its apparent theoretical soundness, extensive publicity, and a significant degree of interest in putting his provocative notions to work, Pinchot's work has failed to make a dent in how most corporations operate. Pinchot, in an interview with *INC*. magazine, ventured a guess as to why that was the case.

> **INC**.: Perhaps the most surprising suggestion you've made is that [intrapreneurs] be managed the way venture capitalists manage entrepreneurs, right down to offering them the chance to accumulate a substantial amount of corporate money – intracapital, you call it – to spend as they choose. What is it that venture capitalists do right?
>
> **Pinchot**: Venture capitalists tend to be very careful in selecting the people who are to be involved in a business. But having been very rigorous in the selection process, they are then in a position in which it makes a certain amount of sense to trust the entrepreneur to make the kind of lightning maneuvering decisions required in a start-up . . . [O]nce the entrepreneur has the money, he has a great deal of freedom to spend it however he thinks is best.
>
> **INC**.: As opposed to how a typical corporation handles the would-be intrapreneur?
>
> **Pinchot**: Corporations do just the reverse. You ask for two years and they give you a year and a half. 'Couldn't you do it faster?' they ask. 'Couldn't you do it with less money?' But if the intrapreneur is doing his job right, he has already pared his estimates to the bone. And companies tend to have people signing off on each request for a capital expenditure, with each one treated as a separate item. But that extra scrutiny doesn't produce a better investment; quite the reverse. It causes the would-be intrapreneur to pad his budgets and to spend it all right now. After all, if you can't take money out of an engineering budget and put it in marketing, then the intrapreneur has only one solution: overinflate the hell out of every budget, and then, by God, spend it that year, because you may need the slack next year.

So despite the initial enthusiasm about intrapreneuring, it was never implemented. Permission was not granted.

Setting the balance between control and permission

Balancing risk and reward has been one of the most useful and durable principles of economic decision making. But setting this balance requires grappling with the issue of the balance between control and permission, because the decision about who assumes risk and who receives rewards is intimately connected to the questions of who is in control. In this regard, it is important to have a common understanding of the meaning of risk.

The nature of risk

If the future were known, while there would certainly be unfavourable news, risk would evaporate. But since we don't know the future, risk will always be a part of practical decisions. The word 'risk', in fact, comes from the Italian *risco*, a word used by sailors to express the chances of ending up on the rocks.

Risk is not absolute. It implies probabilities. Furthermore, what one person perceives as risk may not be seen as risky by another (who may have special knowledge and experience, or simply a stronger ability to recover from failure). A CEO who risks billions on behalf of his company, but has a long-term contract, is not risking as much as the lower-level project manager who may lose his job if the project fails.

Risk-taking behaviour and goals

How do decision makers choose between alternatives? First, decision makers use 'expected value' to compare alternatives. Expected value refers to the level of benefits (or costs) multiplied by the probability that they will occur. So if there is a 20 per cent chance of a $10 gain, that is the same as a 40 per cent chance of a $5 gain. Both bets have the same expected value: $2. In the first case the expected value is 20 per cent of $10. In the second case the expected value is 40 per cent of $5.

Which choice will most decision makers take? Kahneman and Tversky, two academic psychologists who have made great contributions to our understanding of this question, say the answer depends on how close the return is to the 'target return' that the decision maker has in mind. Richard Bernstein, in his book *Risk*, summarizes Kahneman and Tversky by identifying four different regimes:

1. 'When decision makers are in the neighborhood of their goals and confront a choice between two items of equal expected value, decision makers tend to choose the less risky alternative if outcomes involve gains, and the more risky alternative if outcomes involve losses.'

   If the expected value of $2 is close to what the decision maker hoped to gain, he would chose the less risky alternative; he would choose the opportunity with the $5 gain.

2. 'When individuals find themselves well below the target, if they are falling further and further behind the target, they tend to take bigger and bigger risks.'

   If the $2 was much less than the decision maker wanted, he would take a flier on a 20 per cent chance of gaining the $10, the logic being 'what do I have to lose, I am already so far behind'.

3. 'As [corporations] come closer and closer to extinction, they tend to become rigid and immobile, repeating previous actions and avoiding risk.'

   If, having lost several prior bets, the decision maker is faced with the same choice as above, he will choose whatever he has been choosing previously. He has passed from a rational state into an irrational, emotional state. Some corporations find themselves in this state from time to time, particularly those that have maturing industries and have failed at prior diversification efforts.

4. 'When individuals find themselves well above the target, they tend to take greater risks.'

   In other words, if our decision maker feels the $2 he or she has won initially is so far above what he or she expected to achieve in the first place, the person may next take a shot at the opportunity for the riskier $10 gain. He or she is willing to risk more at this stage.

These results, which have been verified many times since Kahneman and Tversky first published them, are important in understanding risk and the balance of permission and control. When management presents options of uncertain values to either investors or managers, they need to understand how the payoffs compare to the individual's 'targets'. If the payoffs are about what one expects, investors or management will likely choose the less risky venture. If they are a reasonably long way from their targets, on either the high or low side, they will often choose the riskier venture. And if the choices are presented to someone who has experienced a long string of losses, that person will make a decision independent of what the facts suggest, simply responding to prior experience. Management, then, can affect the outcome of a decision by adjusting the risk/reward parameters to fit expectations.

Designing to encourage creation and trading

If change is perceived as more valuable than continuity (often the case in venture capital or principal investing), change will be made. But if change is perceived as bringing in less value (which is often the case in corporations), continuity is chosen.

When the values are perceived as very similar, the choice is more complex. If the corporation and its shareholders are satisfied with its rates of return, for example, making significant change is difficult to justify. This is indeed the situation today for many companies despite the market's gyrations. Today, more than in many periods, we would argue, it's important that senior management make a conscious effort to give permission to the organization to explore options for creating future value.

Leadership is essential in setting the balance between continuity and change. To match the pace and scale of change in the markets, corporate senior management should ensure that the economic and personal rewards for those who take risks finding new business opportunities are at market levels, even if the opportunity is not pursued at the end of the day. This is what the private equity community has done over the past two decades. Through a continuous flow of insights into new opportunities, private equity firms have actually reduced their risk, while boosting the pace of change and their rewards.

Fear of risk; fear of failure

Fear is the sharp edge of risk. Many people and many institutions can't take it – they are risk averse. Their fear of risk restricts the free flow of new information and enhances the natural propensity to disconfirm unwelcome

Fear of risk restricts the free flow of new information and enhances the natural propensity to disconfirm unwelcome data.

data. In one Fortune 500 company we surveyed, we found that fear was the number-one barrier to innovation (see Figure 10.1). At the corporate level the fear is the fear of cannibalization, channel conflict, or earnings dilution as we described. At the individual level, fear is often the fear of unrecoverable economic harm done to one's career.

When asked what the most significant factor in his company's declining performance was, one Fortune 500 CEO replied: 'We lack a culture of risk taking.' Because of this, he explained, the company's engineers and business managers were unable to work together to create innovative products that would succeed in the marketplace.

To understand this issue better, we asked 600 individuals at that corporation, spread across several businesses, functions, and countries, whether the corporation tolerated different ways of thinking. Of them all, 56 per cent felt the corporation did. Then we asked if they felt failing on a project

Fig. 10.1 Perceived barriers to improving innovativeness

% of responses

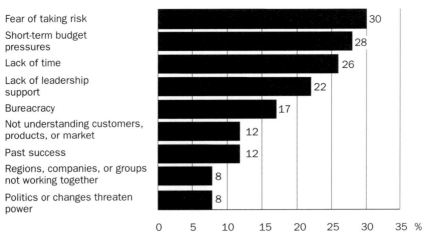

Source: Mckinsey & Company client survey of Fortune 100 Companies
Note: Multiple open-ended responses possible

would set back their careers. Some 57 per cent felt it would. In other words, the perceived cost of failure was relatively high. Finally, we asked employees if they felt they would be rewarded proportionately for the risks they might take. Some 89 per cent said no. The company may have tolerated and even encouraged different ways of thinking, but the low rewards for risk taking, and the unrecoverable costs of failure, explain why so little real innovation emerged from the corporate ranks.

Ideas are fragile things that must be handled carefully. As Michael Faraday, the British discoverer of electromagnetism, once pointed out:

The world little knows how many thoughts and theories which have passed through the mind of a scientific investigator have been crushed in silence and secrecy by his own severe criticism and adverse examinations; that in the most successful instances not a tenth of the suggestions, the hopes, the wishes, the preliminary conclusions have been realized.

Risk aversion kills even the best ideas. As Roy Vagelos, former CEO at Merck, said: 'There is only one sure road to failure that I've seen many wander down: some people become so afraid of failing that they are unable to do a critical experiment or take a first step in a market.'

Permission versus control at Enron

How do the concepts of control, permission, and risk fit together? Enron offers one good example of managing these elements to a favourable outcome. The Enron formula balances control (instituted through its performance evaluation system) and permission (encouraged through employee incentives).

When Jeff Skilling arrived at Enron in 1990, the company fit the traditional gas industry mould. Skilling and Lay had to change the organization dramatically. Through a series of processes they labelled 'facilitators' and 'enablers', they gave aggressive permission to the organization to innovate in new markets and cannibalize existing businesses where necessary. The table below shows the facilitators and enablers created at Enron.

FACILITATORS

- Initiated a compensation system that provided monthly compensation of only one-third of expected annual compensation but provided potential for higher-than-normal annual compensation if risks were assumed and results were achieved.

- Created a performance evaluation system driven by a committee of peers that used the same criteria for everyone in the organization.

- Cut back the control system to a few key variables that were closely monitored. The rest of the activities ran without intensive involvement from top management.

- Established open-plan work areas to allow people to constantly interact with each other, thus removing some uncertainty about what was happening.

ENABLERS

- Cut organization layers, and eliminated specific job titles and delinked job titles from job responsibilities, making titles more like those in professional service firms.

- Removed career staff positions and created an associate pool to do needed analytical work.

- Hired large numbers of exceptionally highly qualified people.

- Changed information flow so that everyone had ready and easy access to all information.

- Made information access free.

Almost immediately, there was a great deal more energy at Enron among its employees. As one junior manager described it, this was due to:

1. Support from upper management.
2. Loose organizational structure. 'People take a lot of ownership because no one is telling you what to do.'
3. The personnel review process. 'It is more than the monetary reward. It is reassuring that a consensus was developed about you and that you are getting good feedback.'
4. Investing significantly in recruiting and hiring smart people.
5. Being nimble and able to quickly adapt to change.

Enron sought out employees willing to take control of their own careers and that of the company. To help promote this attitude, technical and corporate information is available to everyone throughout the organization through a proprietary IT network, one configured for loose distribution. Moreover, as was pointed out in Chapter 6, Enron uses compensation as another lever to encourage creativity.

Enron North America has even reinforced the message in the design of its executive offices. At its headquarters, you will not find the cubicles of a conventional energy company, but a great open space that not only tells the visitor this is an energy *trading* company, but also that it is a place where people can gather and communicate. The office of the CEO is glass-walled and placed near the action. Passers-by are likely to be invited into Jeff Skilling's office for an impromptu chat.

Through its actions, Enron has dramatically changed the balance of permission and control. While this is only part of Enron's story, its impact on the creative productivity of the corporation is clear. Enron has transformed itself from an operating organization into an organization dedicated to create-operate-trade.

Permission run amok: Thermo Electron

Permission, however, doesn't always work. The story of Thermo Electron, one of the most interesting experiments in corporate design to emerge over the past two decades, is a case in point. After a rocky start, for much of its history Thermo looked like it might become the new model of the modern organization. The corporation was almost entirely based on what we have called 'permission'. But the particular way Thermo chose to grant permission contained a time bomb, as we will explain.

> Thermo looked like it might become the new model of the modern organization. But the particular way Thermo chose to grant permission contained a time bomb.

Thermo Electron was founded in 1956 by George Hatsopoulos with $50,000 borrowed from a friend, in an attempt to capitalize on his PhD research in the field of thermionics, a method of converting heat to electricity. In 1965, natural gas producers contracted with Thermo Electron to develop industrial equipment that ran on gas rather than electricity, and in

1968, Ford Motor Company provided funds to build a low-emission auto-mobile engine. Thermo Electron's growth as a research lab allowed it to go public in 1967.

Thermo Electron's first major financial success was in supplying chemical-analysis equipment to auto companies in the United States. In 1971, Congress passed a law requiring car makers to report the amount of nitrogen oxides their cars were emitting. Ford, with whom Hatsopoulos was still working, was scrambling to find a supplier since there were no such devices on the market. Hatsopoulos seized the opportunity: 'I said, "Give me an order for ten instruments and we will deliver." They said, "What instruments? You don't make instruments." I said, "We'll develop it."' Thermo Electron was able to produce the instruments a year ahead of the competition, prompting orders from the other automakers. 'Then all hell broke loose,' he recalls. 'Then you don't need a marketing force. You need a telephone operator to take orders.'

By 1980, the Waltham, Massachusetts, company was registering about $200 million in annual sales, generating $7.5 million in net income for its shareholders. But the lingering effect of the 1970s recession began to take its toll on large equipment orders from industry, and Thermo Electron's profits declined to $2.5 million in 1982 and fell to $50,000 in 1983. At the same time, Thermo Electron was investing heavily in R&D, building new applications for its existing technology.

With Thermo Electron having grown into a mid-sized corporation, man-agement issues began to appear. In order to fund some of its development, Thermo Electron decided to partially spin off one of its divisions, Thermedics, which held patents for medical applications, to the public. Hatsopoulos referred to the partial spin-off as a 'spin-out'. In August 1983, the spin-out was completed, raising $4.7 million for the new company. Thermo Electron maintained an 80 per cent stake in the new company, but the spin-out did provide cash for additional research and relieved pres-sure on its earnings (which had been exacerbated by Thermedics). This accidental organizational innovation was soon to become the core of Thermo Electron's management philosophy. 'Our purpose,' Hatsopoulos said, 'is to found and grow new companies.'

A crucial component of the spin-out idea was also to provide a reward mech-anism for the leadership of the new company. Hatsopoulos and his brother John were concerned that those developing new ideas for the company's technologies would choose to leave the company and form their own ventures. The brothers found that they were unable to properly reward the leadership of small, high-growth-potential areas of the company with stock options because of the relative size of Thermo Electron. The spin-out mechanism, born of desperation, proved to be a very attractive solution. As George Hatsopoulos reflected 10 years after the idea was born, 'There's no better way to stimulate creativity than to see a guy next to you get $500,000 in options for a great idea.'

Thermo Electron repeated the spin-out twice in 1985. In August it took Thermo Analytical (which provided hazardous waste and nuclear contamination analyses) public, raising $9.6 million for one-third of the company, and in September it organized Tecogen, the company's co-generation division, which generated $1 million for a 5 per cent stake that Thermo Electron sold privately. (It took the company public in 1987.)

By 1986, Thermo Electron was growing rapidly again, profiting from its spin-out strategy and the general improvement in the economy, which left it with $250 million in back orders for its electricity-generating equipment. And from 1977 to 1987 it yielded a 12.2 per cent return on average to shareholders, at a time when the broader market returned 9.3 per cent. Giving permission to the operating companies through the mechanism of the spin-out was working beautifully.

Thermo's share price continued to climb in 1990, helped along by its majority stakes in its spin-outs (among them Thermo Cardiosystems, a 1989 spin-out from Thermedics, Thermo Electron's first 'grandchild'). But the market was beginning to have its doubts about the sustainability of Thermo's strategy. By 1990, Thermo Electron was valued by the market at 23 per cent less than the value of its holdings in its spin-outs (and their spin-outs), in spite of the fact that Thermo Electron had several strong divisions of its own that it had yet to spin out.

While the approach worked well for Thermo Electron and its 'children', the increasing complexity of the system as it grew larger was beginning to have an effect. In 1993, Hatsopoulos made the decision to stop serving on the board of directors of Thermo Electron's 'grandchildren'. 'There's a physical limit to the number of board meetings one man can attend in a single week.' John Hatsopoulos, however, continued to serve as CFO to all of the Thermo companies.

As Thermo grew, the various spin-off offspring began to lose contact with one another. Conversations and chance meetings that occurred easily when the corporation was smaller were less likely to happen as the size and complexity of the corporation increased. Some of the freedom that had been the foundation of Thermo was beginning to be sacrificed in the name of efficiency and managerial control. As the company continued to grow, it was increasingly difficult for even Thermo's talented top management to stay on top of what was going on, which proved to be unnerving.

In 1997, as some of the share prices of Thermo companies began to sag, Thermo Electron stepped in and used its cash to extend its ownership of the companies. Hatsopoulos explained these steps as good investment practice. 'The first reason we buy back all of these shares of spin-offs is very simple – we buy them when we think they are undervalued.' By 1998 shareholders of Thermo Electron were complaining that the company's structure was too complex and was holding it back. Trying to satisfy its corporate shareholders and the minority shareholders of its 22 Thermo companies was proving impossible.

Additionally, financial troubles in Asia were dragging down the company's sales. In July 1998, Thermo Electron's stock fell 17 per cent after it announced it would miss its earnings estimate due to a delay in a new spin-out. The company responded in September 1998 by announcing a reorganization that would cut 700 jobs. It also announced that John Hatsopoulos would be replaced as president of Thermo Electron by Arvin Smith, CEO of Thermo Instruments. At the end of 1998, John Hatsopoulos stepped down from his nearly two dozen CFO roles.

But shareholders were not satisfied that significant changes had been made, and on the back of a boom in US share prices, Thermo Electron's share price continued to fall to $12.50 a share in April 1999, from $40 a share a year earlier. In March 1999, the company announced that founder and CEO George Hatsopoulos would retire, to be replaced by Richard F. Syron, chief executive of the American Stock Exchange.

Within months, Syron announced that he would begin to simplify the company, indicating that 'the risk is [that] the complexity of the structure can deflect management attention'. Syron announced that it would reduce its family of companies down from 23 to 11, by 'spinning in' some units, divesting others, and closing some entirely, including ThermoLase. By February 2000, Thermo Electron extended the plan, announcing that its divestment would exceed $1 billion in assets by year end, and increase the number of 'spin-ins' to 19, effectively eliminating the family structure altogether. In response to its increasing complexity, Thermo Electron has opted for control.

For a long time, Thermo Electron appeared to have a winning formula. It produced very strong results for almost 20 years. But ultimately the increasing complexity of the organization overwhelmed management capacity. While the strategy of permission helped the company weather early crises and grow at a rate that it might not otherwise have been able to achieve, in the end the company simply could not find a way to allow for the entrepreneurial spirit that had been its foundation and control operations as the corporation grew larger.

As earnings began to slip, so too did Wall Street's confidence. Hatsopoulos's strategy clearly had the advantage of retaining creative and entrepreneurial talent – yet perhaps oddly, in this environment of entrepreneurial encouragement, Thermo management were unwilling to give up full control (by spinning companies *out* rather than *off*) and created excessive organizational complexity as the parent grew larger. In this

Thermo management were unwilling to give up full control (by spinning companies *out* rather than *off*) and created excessive organizational complexity as the parent grew larger.

case, the battle between permission and control was won, at least for the time being, by control. The future will tell whether Syron's simplification will allow Thermo to create and grow again.

MAKING CHANGES WORK

How, practically, can these ideas be implemented? Thermo Electron shows us that despite the best intentions, the job of balancing permission and control is quite complex. The key questions concern where to minimize classical controls and where to increase permission, how much permission to give, what mechanisms to use, and how to reserve the right to take it back if things don't work out. The model for making these decisions is always the market, rather than some internal notion of control. If in doubt, one should ask: what processes take place in the market? We think there are six key guidelines to use in answering this question:

1. **Determine what to measure and control.** There are five levels to examine when seeking to minimize controls: corporate, business unit, functional (e.g., marketing or operations), project, and general coordination and control (finance). The task at each level is unique to itself.

   - *At the corporate level*: As discussed in Chapter 8, a substantial portion of the management committee agenda should be devoted to ensuring that the pace and scale of creating and trading matches the pace of change in the market. The amount of time the management committee spends on these issues should be at least equal to the amount of time spent on operating issues. For example, the management committee might regularly review the rate of entry and exit of new companies at the periphery. Among the questions the committee might focus on are: Is the company as a whole moving at the pace and scale of the market in these areas? Should it move more aggressively? What is the key information needed to assess the answer to this question? Which divisions are pursuing business models that may have long-term economic potential? What is the minimum amount of control required to exercise oversight? What processes can be totally eliminated without cutting the effectiveness of oversight?

   - *At the business level*: Most of the managerial effort of existing business units is expended on operations. The business unit leaders are the ones who 'own' these P&Ls. On the other hand, business units cannot abdicate the responsibility for growth. Quite obviously, they need to understand their future sources of growth and understand how they are going to attain them. In some ways, making room for growth is more difficult at the business unit level than it is at the corporate level. In addition to traditional operations-oriented questions, one should ask: Are growth plans realistic? Are companies at the periphery well enough understood (e.g., does senior management personally know the top management people of the most powerful peripheral companies?) What customers are buying the products from peripheral companies, and what value do those customers see in the products? Does senior management personally know the lead customers for the peripheral companies? Do we understand their vision for the evolution of the business? Does it conflict with ours? Under what circumstances could our company become vulnerable to attack from these peripheral players? Typically, these are very difficult questions for existing businesses to answer objectively.

- *At the functional level*: The functions (e.g., marketing, sales, production, procurement, development) have operating responsibility for execution, and thus are in charge of achieving excellence. But that excellence can be elusive. Expertise may become rapidly obsolete. New areas of expertise may be required to develop and launch new business models. Thus, performance at the functional level must be understood both in terms of the daily operating level (upon which traditional benchmarking is based) and in terms of the corporation's ability to adapt to an ever-changing market.

   In addition to traditional questions about cost competitiveness, one might ask: How 'fresh' is our skill base? Do we know what new approaches are being tried? Do we understand new emerging areas with growth potential? Do we have the expertise we need in these areas? What do we plan to get rid of over the next two years? What new expertise do we need? What are we doing to get such expertise? Are we making enough progress in those areas?

- *At the project level*: At the project level, ask managers to design their own control and review processes. What are the key variables to watch? What are the critical milestones? What is the earliest time at which progress should be measured? How will they know if things are on track or not (most normal project-tracking systems are notoriously inadequate)? How frequently should the manager hold reviews? What are the two or three goals that must be accomplished? Are they being realistic about costs, timing, and results? What would it take to cut the complexity of this project in half?

- *At the coordination and control level*: The finance and information management groups are traditionally responsible for oversight of the metrics in the corporation – that is, for gathering data in specific formats at specific times, evaluating budgets, and helping steer capital allocation and set performance standards. Finance also plays a critical role in the control and permission systems of the corporation, and that's why it must be at the centre of the redesign effort.

2. **Measure and control what you must, not what you can.** Clearly, control systems are required. The task is to make the required necessary control systems as simple as possible. Harvard's Robert Simons points out: 'The information processing systems of our contemporary world swim in an exceedingly rich soup of information, of symbols. In a world of this kind, the scarce resource is not information; it is the processing capacity to attend to information. Attention is the chief bottleneck in organizational activity, and the bottleneck becomes narrower and narrower as we move to the top of organizations.' Adopting the slogan 'measure and control what you must, not what you can' directly addresses the dilemma Simons identifies.

   To implement this guideline, the corporation will need to take an inventory of the existing control processes and document how they work (what data they require, when they require it, how the data is analyzed, what decisions are enabled by the data and analysis, what the system costs to gather the data, analyze the data, distribute the data, and make changes based on the data) and the benefits they bring. The analysis of the costs and benefits of current control systems should be conducted by the people who are expected to produce the results and those who carry the 'official' responsibility for the results. This guideline for redesign – 'measure what you must, not what you can' – should be applied to each control process of the corporation. It should be applied to the scope of measurements taken, the frequency of measurement, the breadth of distribution of the data, the frequency of required feedback once the data is reported, and the extent of data review.

   Additionally, key managers with control responsibility should be selected with great care. Their understanding of the need to balance divergent and convergent thinking in their areas of responsibility should be probed before they are selected.

3. **Increase flexibility of information systems.** One of the greatest barriers to change is the cost and time required to update information systems. The systems for gathering, transforming, transmitting, and using information are often quite expensive. Although new technologies are reducing the costs, switching costs are still high.

   This has significant implications for competitive adaptiveness. New companies forming at the periphery don't have the burden of old information systems. These companies have no switching costs.

Management should ask itself about how the corporation is positioned in terms of information management. What information is likely to be permanent and which may change? Which is likely to become obsolete? What new information might be required, and how can the architecture of the system be accommodated to provide that? Does the firm have the skills to make full, intelligent use of the new information?

4. **Increase permission for experimentation.** As discussed above, the corporation needs to provide permission and resources for experimentation at the pace and scale of the market. Specifically, this means permission to explore to the same extent that exploration takes place in the capital markets, permission to pursue a goal without undue interference from control systems, permission to experiment with business concepts at the same rate as the market, and permission to raise funds externally if strong ideas are developed and subsequently turned down by the corporation.

5. **Change the range of reward and risk in the incentive system to reflect and amplify permission.** There are two elements of the incentive system that have to be thought through in addition to the standard monetary elements. They are the nature of non-monetary rewards and the existence of risk with the associated possibility of failure.

   - *Nature of rewards*: Redesigning the evaluation and compensation systems are examples of useful 'enablers'. But many executives feel that compensation is not the most important part of the incentive system – that more important is creating passion around innovation in the company. As one executive observed: 'The type of people who really drive innovation don't do it because of rewards, they do it because they strongly and passionately believe in the idea.'

     Indeed, at the average start-up, particularly a high-tech firm, one will more likely hear people speaking about 'dreams', 'passion', 'trust', 'degree of freedom', and 'autonomy' than money. Monetary compensation, whether delivered in the form of bonuses, options, and other equity-participation plans, is just one among many factors driving decisions.

   - *Risk and failure*: The existence of risk (the unknowability of the future) and the possibility of failure that accompanies it, is the second element that has to be thought through for incentive systems.

Nike uses a team approach to syndicate risk. When an employee has an idea, he or she recruits others to further it. Once others sign on, they share the risk. No one gets credit for a major success or takes the blame for a failure alone.

A few years ago, for example, Nike attempted a foray into the rough-and-tumble arena of street hockey, a far cry from the more traditional sports Nike had become extraordinarily adept at supporting. The company assembled a team to go out and learn about the market, develop some concepts, and test them out. Despite the best of intentions, the team couldn't figure out a way to win. So Nike withdrew the effort. A failure? Nike regarded the effort as part of the learning process. In fact, one of the key players in this 'failure' was promoted.

Thinking through how to deal with failure is an important element in the design of incentive systems. As Roberto Goizueta, former chairman of Coca-Cola, noted: 'We became uncompetitive by not being tolerant of mistakes. The moment you let avoiding failure become your motivation, you are going down the path of inactivity. You can stumble only if you are moving.'

Nike president Tom Clark noted that teams help people 'learn from the past, admit mistakes, and then move ahead. Nothing happens to people who fail,' he added. 'I don't think Phil Knight ever trusted anyone entirely who didn't suffer through a significant failure on his or her watch.'

As Henry Ford noted a half century ago: 'Failure is only an opportunity to begin again more intelligently.'

These approaches can be used to increase the range of risk and reward permitted in the corporation without sacrificing adequate controls.

6. **Establish a process for ongoing senior support, with a focus on its impact on divergence and creation.** To get the foregoing measures accepted by employees at the more junior levels, top management will have to convince them that they are serious, and that the penalties for blocking change are greater than the penalties for trying new ideas and failing.

At Pepsi, for example, Chairman Roger Enrico holds sessions with junior members of the organization, listening to their ideas and assuring them that he stands squarely with them in their aspirations. The goal is to encourage risk taking in the middle-management ranks, and to break down the self-censorship that often blocks good ideas. Of course, holding such sessions in and of itself is not magic. The magic comes in the content of the sessions, and Enrico is widely admired for his ability to make them interactive and intimate.

Opening up conversations between senior management and the rest of the organization is, in fact, one of the most powerful mechanisms for giving permission. This is not 'presentation and response', the closed conversations that are simply another form of control. (There are many linguistic devices for 'controlling' individual conversations, for example, 'Now, really, let's be practical.' Translation: 'I am tired of what you are talking about, let's talk about what I want to talk about.') Instead, Pepsi fosters real conversation.

These six guidelines provide a starting point for rethinking how the corporation could work if assumption of continuity were replaced with the assumption of discontinuity.

The dilemma facing General Motors in the 1940s – how to manage the tension between centralized control (an assertion of the importance of continuity) and local initiative (in the spirit of discontinuity and change) – is strikingly similar to the dilemma facing many large and successful companies today. The question is whether today's corporation, with the evidence of long-term performance before it, will choose continuity or change as its operating paradigm. Is it willing to transform itself from an operating model to a 'create–operate–trade' model? If it is to do so, it will have to adjust its control systems. A corporation cannot declare itself in favour of decentralization and then refuse to give up control. It will not work.

Now that we have a better grasp on the needs of the new corporation, the question remains how we go about delivering them. We address that question in the next chapter.

11

Setting the pace and scale of change

All learning is rooted in conversation.

JOHN SEELY BROWN,

president of Xerox's Palo Alto Research Center (PARC)

A long with General Electric, most analysts would consider Johnson & Johnson, one of the world's largest health-care companies, to be a very well-managed corporation. Lauded in the press as the role model company for entrepreneurial decentralization, J&J is a symphony orchestra of operating companies competing aggressively in the marketplace. Over the past 20 years, J&J has increased sales by more than tenfold, has doubled the number of its employees, has entered many multi-hundred-million-dollar businesses such as blood glucose monitoring and disposable contact lenses, has exited such businesses as disposable diapers, ocular lenses, and CT scanning, has survived and triumphed over the 1982 and 1986 Tylenol scares, has expanded sales internationally, and has, in general, shifted from a mainly consumer-products company to one whose profits are dominated by a rapidly growing pharmaceutical business.

> Lauded in the press as the role model company for entrepreneurial decentralization, J&J is a symphony orchestra of operating companies competing aggressively in the marketplace.

The source of J&J's strong sustained performance is the industries it has chosen to compete in (consumer health care products, medical products, and pharmaceuticals), the countries it has chosen to compete in, and its strong performance in each of those sectors and countries. J&J is well known for its values, as expressed in its Credo, first penned in the mid-1940s by Robert Wood Johnson.

The 1972 Annual Report laid out some of the principles of the Credo, still present more than 25 years later:

- 'It has always been our management philosophy to look beyond the immediate problems of running a business so that our broader vision would include the backdrop of changing social conditions that reflect the interests and concerns of our customers as well as our employees.'

- 'Johnson & Johnson has typically grown over the years by creating new companies built around a particular technology or group of products. These companies, often previously units of a larger organization, are able to concentrate on a special area of business. [This approach allows the new companies to focus on] its own specific and identifiable market, which it can respond to more quickly than a larger organization.'

- 'The Company is organized on the principles of decentralized management and conducts its business through operating divisions and subsidiaries, which are themselves integral, autonomous operations. While direct line management of these units is maintained through the Executive Committee of the Board of Directors of the Company, operational responsibility lies with each operating management.'

J&J's keen sense of the need to balance operational excellence as well as to change at the pace and scale of the market, goes a long way in explaining why it has done as well as it has. J&J is always on the lookout for both opportunities and sources of potential trouble, and then is ready to take action to either capitalize on the opportunities or avert the dangers.

But how does J&J do it? How does it set the pace and scale of change necessary to keep up with the markets? Answers to this question are instructive as other corporations seek to mimic J&J's record of performance.

Perhaps no example of the J&J approach to setting and managing the pace and scale of change is better illustrated than the history of the evolution of the 'FrameworkS' process at J&J. The story begins with a call that

Chairman Ralph Larsen gave one of us early in 1993 when he had become concerned about 'clouds on the horizon'.

ASKING THE QUESTION

The focal point of Larsen's concerns was the collapse in IBM's perform-ance. John Akers, well-known chairman of IBM, had resigned. Lou Gerstner had been brought in to salvage what had once been viewed as the blue chip of blue chips. Like J&J, IBM was for years everybody's favourite company. It represented technological virtue. Innovation. An aggressive American spirit. It was an American juggernaut. Not only had IBM failed, but DEC, Unisys, and Sperry Rand had failed before it; NCR, Siemens, and even Toshiba had lost considerable ground in the 1980s and early 1990s. What had happened at IBM seemed much bigger than the com-pany itself. When James Burke, former chairman of J&J, was appointed head of the search committee for a new CEO at IBM, it would have been hard for the J&J top team not to wonder if what had happened to IBM might not also be possible at J&J. After all, IBM had been caught in the downdraught of the computer hardware industry, and now J&J was facing a new Democratic administration with a clear focus on reforming health care in the United States, not unlike the reform that the market had forced on the computer hardware industry. Moreover, the increase in political risk was matched by an increase in managed care. Managed care companies were the hot companies of the early 1990s. The parallels with the rise of software companies in the computer industry were not hard to make. These factors and others made Larsen question the impact of health care reform on J&J. Could J&J's valued prin-ciples be sustained? Did they need to be reinterpreted or applied in new ways, given the challenges of the 1990s? Did these principles still work for a company that had grown to the size of J&J? These were some of the fun-damental questions on Larsen's mind. Larsen possessed one of the essential skills of a strong divergent thinker – the ability to ask the right questions, no matter how disturbing.

> Larsen possessed one of the essential skills of a strong divergent thinker – the ability to ask the right questions, no matter how disturbing.

Knowing that McKinsey was studying long-term corporate performance during discontinuity, Chairman Larsen asked us to work with him, along with Roger Fine (then VP of administration, and now General Counsel) and members of the Johnson & Johnson Executive Committee. Larsen wanted us to help him assess and reduce the threat facing J&J.

SETTING THE INQUIRY INTO MOTION

In our ongoing discussions with Larsen and Fine, we suggested that the dangers facing large companies as a result of discontinuity are not those that are unknown but those that are undervalued. But few corporations provide a forum to talk in an extended and exploratory manner about the potential impact of future discontinuities. Because there is no forum for dialogue, there is little possibility of changing one's mental model (which we then called one's mental frameworks) about the future evolution of the industry. No matter how many rounds of presentation and response one goes through, it is not the same as a personal exploration of the issues over an extended period of time. We explained that the conventional presentation-and-response approach afforded no time for the search for new ideas, for new ways of looking at the future. Nor does presentation and response allow sufficient time for incubation – for new patterns to fall into place. Without changing its mental models, changing its dialogue, changing the information available to it, there could be no changes in systems or action. Accordingly, the first thing to do was to meet with the Executive Committee, the highest managerial committee at J&J, to lay out this diagnosis of the problem, agree on an approach to fixing it, and lay out a plan for getting started. Larsen agreed that the analysis made sense, and suggested that the ideas should be exposed to, and discussed with, the Executive Committee at a retreat they were planning to have a few months later.

DESIGNING THE DESIGN PHASE

To prepare the Executive Committee for this meeting, individual discussions were held with each member to determine their agreement or disagreement with the basic line of thinking we were pursuing, as well as to hear the issues they thought the corporation faced in the next three to five years.

Armed with these insights, we, along with Fine, developed an agenda – really a sequence of conversations – for the Executive Committee meeting. The meeting would begin with a few case studies of other corporations that had faced this dilemma, discuss how they dealt with it, assess the results of their efforts, and then draw lessons from those cases. Among the specific questions we agreed to discuss were these:

How did these companies come to the danger point? Did they simply become too big? Did they become too bureaucratic? Did their technology lose its edge? Did their sales force lose its edge? Did the company lose touch with its customers? What happened?

Why couldn't the company management see the risks emerging until they were in the vortex of discontinuous change? How could so many intelligent and accomplished individuals, individuals not unlike the J&J team, misread the situation for so long? Why could the leadership not shape an effective programme to deal with the problem when it did see the threat?

Finally, fully anchored in the thinking about the successes and failures of others in dealing with this issue, the Executive Committee would address their perceptions of the most pressing issues facing J&J over the next five years that could have potentially similar effects if not dealt with. The vehicle for doing this was a set of questions for discussion, selected to meet the test of the defining question mentioned below:

Identify in your mind the 100 most talented, thoughtful, and creative people in the organization, regardless of tenure or position. Now imagine that you can bring them together a few at a time for a conversation, an intimate conversation similar to one you might have with friends in your living room after dinner. In this conversation, nothing is sacred. All taboos are off. Everyone is equal, limited only by his or her cognitive and verbal abilities. The agenda is yours. You can raise any issue you want to raise to this august and candid group of experienced advisors. What would you ask them? What are the six most important issues to raise with the most intelligent people you can find in your organization?

At the end of the meeting, an action programme would be sketched out, but the intent was not to design the long-term future. It was only to determine the topic, timing, location, and chairman for the next session.

The purpose of the 'design' meeting was to set the stage for changing the mental models of the corporation. The criteria for the meeting's success were to be the openness and the range of topics discussed. The criteria did not include 'closing' on issues, but rather the opposite. The intent was to 'suspend disbelief' about what the 'right' answers might be. The focus was on finding the right questions.

The purpose of the 'design' meeting was to set the stage for changing the mental models of the corporation. The criteria for the meeting's success were to be the openness and the range of topics discussed.

The discussion was intended to have only the lightest architecture. It was intended to be very open, and only loosely moderated. The agenda contained a great deal of 'white space', unprogrammed time to spot and discuss issues. We anticipated that many of the issues identified could not be resolved during the meeting, because there would be insufficient data or expertise among the members of the Executive Committee to address them. Such questions would simply be tabled. The fact was, we knew that if all the questions raised could already be answered so easily, the right questions were not being asked. The intent of the meeting was simply to pick issues for later resolution.

THE DESIGN MEETING

The design meeting was held a long way from the J&J headquarters to increase the chances of devoting every available moment to the conversations. It is hard to have this kind of conversation when faxes are being delivered, people are stepping out to take phone calls, and side meetings are being held. Meeting at a remote site gave us a chance to control those risks.

The meeting was judged a success, and resulted in unanimous agreement on a specific action programme that addressed the most basic concerns of the Executive Committee. The feeling at the meeting was both positive and collegial. There was little pressure, since current performance was strong and was forecast to remain strong (the forecasts turned out to be accurate) for the coming quarters. It was more like an informal gathering of interesting, intelligent peers cross-stimulating each other with their insights, speculations, and stories. During the meeting, the Executive Committee was able to reach some conclusions about key risks and opportunities for the future. The greatest risk was to stay exclusively focused on operations, fixed on one mental model of how the industry would evolve and how the position of the lead competitor would evolve along with it, rather than to recognize that there were many possible ways the industry could evolve. Rather than look to 'expertise' for the answer, the real answer was to be found in observation, reflection, and conversation. Vice-Chairman Robert Wilson captured the spirit of the meeting when he observed that J&J needed to think about multiple frameworks for the future rather than just one idea. So central was this idea to the spirit of the task that Wilson suggested the process be known as the 'FrameworkS' process (the 'S' was added to emphasize the multiplicity of future possibilities), and everyone quickly agreed.

Given this general conclusion, the Executive Committee identified and selected a series of critical issues that had the potential to alter the competitive environment of their industry. Among the issues were the implications, both long and short term, of managed care on health care suppliers; the impact of the European Union on health care in Europe; growth in emerging markets; the use of advanced information technology, and in particular the Internet, on the delivery of health care; and the changing perception by consumers of their role in the delivery and evaluation of that care. The intent was to construct a 'conversation' around each of these issues after there had been sufficient observation and reflection. Moreover, the participants in the conversation would be picked from all parts of J&J, independent of their position in the corporate hierarchy, dependent only on their ability to contribute to the discussion and the changing FrameworkS of the corporation.

At the end of the meeting, Ralph Larsen summarized by saying: 'We need to think about running the business in a different way. We don't want to be the management group that presides. We want a process that makes sure we don't miss the boat.' General Counsel George Frazza put it this way: 'I think of it in family terms. We are a family of companies. What are our aspirations for our children? We want them to exist, be successful, and be creative. We need to create the environment where our children can be successful. We must not become too specific. The seven of us can't come up with the answer for the other 83,000. We have to make it more likely for the other 83,000 people to contribute. We want to remain a great company. We want to be the challenger, not the challenged. We have to think the opposite of the "great man" theory of history. It is more likely that the key insights for the future lie out in the corporation than it is that they lie here in the EC . . . My biggest concerns are the ABCs of failure: A = Arrogance, B = Bureaucracy, C = Complacency. They can be the dark side of success.'

'My biggest concerns are the ABCs of failure: A = Arrogance, B = Bureaucracy, C = Complacency. They can be the dark side of success.'

In addition to the specific issues and the general sense of commitment to the effort, the Executive Committee committed to some basic principles. First and foremost, it wanted a process that got the Executive Committee started on its basic role of 'looking though the eyes of others' and putting a structure to it. The idea would be to generate multiple frameworks for viewing the market, the competition, and the company.

Moreover, a series of objectives were laid out for the process:

1. Ensure that J&J's direction for its future is based on a realistic, up-to-date view of the world, and especially of its customers and markets.

2. Identify the key business imperatives for coping with the next three to five years (i.e., cost reduction, more innovation, proposed government reform, the emergence of the Internet) rather than a longer-term future, and build the consensus needed for addressing these imperatives in a decentralized environment.

3. Identify the areas where J&J's existing or potential core skills/competencies and major health needs can intersect to provide an element of renewal and synergy for J&J. In particular, identify those areas that might otherwise fall through the cracks because of J&J's decentralized organizational structure and management philosophy.

4. Build a generation of J&J executives who are better equipped to think widely, to recognize discontinuities early in their development, and to seek out, understand, internalize, and act on new ways of viewing J&J's markets and customers.

5. Disseminate a real understanding of J&J's direction and underlying perspective on its markets and customers (and how they will evolve) widely enough to ensure that J&J executives and managers in all sectors and geographies can pursue it independently yet appropriately.

Given the design principles laid out in the initial Executive Committee meeting, a template for future meetings was developed. The template included three phases, each with its own objectives:

Phase 1: Discovery

This phase, devoted to search and incubation, sought to replicate the fairly lengthy search for anomalies in select sets of issues. Its purpose was to expose J&J executives to a wide range of perspectives on health care; open up issues that had been discussed in private; expose J&J executives to a wide range of cultures, political beliefs, and market structures, leading to a more insightful view of J&J's current and future markets and customers; the collection of relevant demographic, social, and market facts whenever feasible, while allowing for intensive periods to collect, disseminate, and discuss information as well as periods of 'gestation'. And, importantly, J&J should focus on searching the periphery for insight. The Executive Committee knew that it would not generate any bold new visions or plans just sitting in 'The Tower' in its world headquarters in New Brunswick. It had to go to the source. If the subject was growth in China, then the session should be held in China. If it was to examine innovation, then the members had to go see how other innovative companies really worked.

Members of the Executive Committee chaired the discussion sessions. The session chairman personally lined up outside speakers who were experts in their fields, and briefed these speakers beforehand on the meeting's objectives. These pre-meeting sessions served the important function of grounding the official sessions in current data, whether it was pleasant or unpleasant.

Phase 2: The 'forcing event'

The conversation itself becomes the equivalent of the 'deadline', where all the divergent thinking is brought together in the context of the group. The goal is to obtain that 'collision of perspectives' that may produce the 'ah-hah!' moment. Meetings should therefore be as open and non-hierarchical as possible, to ensure that the best ideas and conceptual frameworks are brought to light and considered as the process unfolds; involve as many of the key leaders (present and future) of J&J as possible; and seriously and visibly wrestle with the most fundamental, gut-wrenching issues. To achieve this purpose, a somewhat artificial but effective device was used. For the purposes of the FrameworkS meetings, all participants (roughly 20 in number) were designated members of the Executive Committee. As members of the Executive Committee they could not use the FrameworkS process as a bully pulpit for their own points of view. They had to adopt the corporate point of view. And with this, the official meeting concluded.

Phase 3: Synthesis

During this phase, which occurred after the meeting, the thinking and insights developed in the first two phases are reduced to practice. The focus there is on both short-term actions and long-term issues. Task forces would take charge of making things happen.

J&J had known about the dangers of management excessively focused on operations. Now it set out to create a continually self-transforming company, one that thrived on its own creative destruction.

J&J had known about the dangers of management excessively focused on operations. Now it set out to create a continually self-transforming company, one that thrived on its own creative destruction.

THE EARLY YEARS

Once committed to this new process, the J&J Executive Committee began what has turned into a series of focused dialogues examining the changing US health care marketplace. The first meeting was called FrameworkS 1, the second FrameworkS 2, and so on. There have been more than a dozen FrameworkS altogether.

The first FrameworkS

The first FrameworkS, FrameworkS 1, produced a more urgent and more specific understanding of the threats to J&J's businesses. In order to look ahead over the next five years, the Executive Committee and other FrameworkS task-force members sought to put the next few years in a longer-term context. They asked themselves: What will the demographics of 2010 look like? What might the customer look like in 20 years? What will a typical doctor's office look like? What role will governments play? What will be the role and power of the payors in 2010? If regulatory models change to a much more regional approach, it could change all of our prior assumptions. What should we do? What will the technology look like in 2010? Who is on the cutting edge of change now? What unconventional approaches are being tried, for example, wiring the doctor's office? Who are the leaders?

After the session, they concluded that:

> the traditional ways of doing business are eroding. We used to rely on doctors and nurses as our customers. Now those positions are being taken over by managers whose role is to negotiate with us. In our consumer business we are faced with a shift in power between the manufacturer and the retailer. There is a dramatic power shift going on in all of our businesses, which will deeply affect the way we do business in every way.
>
> I'm worried about the issue of complacency. With our profit margins and growth, we have a credibility gap with our own employees who do not understand we are under attack and that the profits we have could get shot very quickly. We have to become more efficient and effective. Being the low-cost producer has historically been tough for us.
>
> A lot of us realize the way the world is going, but are we preparing ourselves for it?

First steps in the transformation: launching businesses and cutting costs

Three themes came out of the FrameworkS 1 effort.

1. **Understanding the 'new American customers'**: who are they? How do they think? What drives them? What drives their economics? What drives their customers? How can J&J sell to them? How can it develop new products for them? How well positioned are we to meet their future needs compared to other suppliers/partners?

2. **Reducing the cost of doing business** throughout the corporation so that the products delivered to the 'new American customers' will be both low-cost for them and profitable for J&J. A great deal of work seemed to be ongoing in this area. Thus it was incumbent only to make sure everything that could be done was being done.

3. **Improving innovativeness** throughout the corporation – both to meet the needs of the 'new American customers' and existing customers, and to increase the speed and competitive impact of innovation in the corporation. In particular, pursuing new business opportunities, especially those relating to the 'new customers' and 'new technologies' emerging in the United States.

The primary focus resulting from this first FrameworkS session was building 'new businesses for the new marketplace'. One of the conclusions teams reached was that J&J's largest customers, such as hospital networks, managed care plans, and government organizations, were increasingly pressing for a single J&J contact to coordinate purchases from its diverse operating companies. As a result, just three months after the task forces met to review their findings, J&J combined several US operating companies to create Health Care Systems, Inc., the coordinating point customers were asking for. 'It's a truly unique and innovative structure, the perfect vehicle to address customer needs while retaining the culture of autonomous operating companies,' wrote David Cassak, editor of *In Vivo: The Business and Medicine Report*, a magazine that tracks the medical industry. Duke University's integrated health care delivery network was one of the J&J customers whose feedback led to the creation of Health Care Systems. 'We are thrilled with the result of that dialogue,' said Duke's Peter Nyberg, assistant operating officer for the corporate programme. 'Health Care Systems help us be more efficient, to make the most of our resources. That ultimately benefits our patients.'

At the same time, a consensus emerged to undertake a massive re-engineering and cost-avoidance effort. This was not the first time that J&J executives had talked about improving cost performance, but it was the first time they were able to make such radical progress on the issue. Over the course of the next 18 months, J&J quite rapidly extracted some $2 billion in cost savings that went straight to the bottom line. Some of the savings involved elimination of jobs, but much of it came from doing more with the same, using assets more efficiently to grow. What made the difference this time? First, the entire Executive Committee aligned itself around the challenge. Through the process of discovery in FrameworkS 1, they were each deeply, personally committed to the fact that something had to be done. Second, Vice-Chairman Bob Wilson took on the mantle of leader of the cost-reduction effort, holding regular meetings with designated managers from each of the major franchises, demanding each business set targets (though not specifying what those targets should be), pushing people to consider non-incremental solutions, and, in general, keeping the sense of urgency and importance high. During those eighteen months, Bob Wilson saw to it that cost avoidance and cost reduction never left the radar screen.

At the outset, we had conceived of the process as largely a creative effort. Destruction would be, we believed, at best an afterthought. One of the most important pieces of information that we took away from implementing the process was that it naturally produces both creation and destruction, because it produces *change*.

Ralph Larsen said at the time: 'Health-care reform will be one of the greatest energizing forces we have ever had.' Fear of the potential negative consequences of health care reform had become an energizing force for the future of J&J.

Next steps

Following this initial success, the Executive Committee launched several more FrameworkS efforts, covering such diverse areas as the 'new American consumer' (a follow-up from the FrameworkS 1 effort), information management, organization, leadership, and several focused efforts on regional growth in Europe, China, Korea, and Japan (each held in the relevant region). The results of these conversations varied by topic. In Europe, the primary outcome was the launching of 17 pilot businesses. In these, J&J would step out of its traditional role as a product supplier and involve itself in health services. In China, investments increased dramatically and an Executive Committee liaison for China was appointed. In regard to finding talented people, J&J set up J&J Standards of Leadership. Henceforth, management teams in each of the approximately 175 operating companies would use these standards to evaluate their own record of leadership development. The discussion on information management led to the creation of the chief information officer position on the Executive Committee.

These accomplishments proved that the FrameworkS process was anything but formulaic. By breaking the mental models and seeing the world as others see it, J&J created a striking diversity of solutions to the most fundamental challenges facing the corporation.

In 1995, stepping back from a few years of considerable change, the Executive Committee felt a sense of accomplishment. FrameworkS by this time had become a new managerial process within J&J. It had, by design, a very light architecture. It was designed to draw the best from the entire organization. It was neither top-down nor bottom-up nor middle-out; rather, it was infused throughout the entire corporation. It required people to think deeply rather than simply to respond in some standard way, and it gave them the time and permission to do this thinking.

As a result of FrameworkS, time was spent differently, old information was used in new ways, new information was used in practical ways, and the evaluation of ideas was conducted based on new criteria. The elaboration and implementation of these ideas at J&J followed a radically different path from that practised in most corporations today.

Changing the old mental models was an emotionally charged experience for the J&J Executive Committee and the other highly successful, effective, intelligent people involved. Denial, defensive routines, rationalization, and avoidance were part of the arsenal brought to bear against the often uncomfortable facts and disconcerting, even disorienting, conclusions that emerged from the process. Yet these reactions did not prove insurmountable. Part of the importance of FrameworkS at J&J was in creating a forum where participants could overcome their prior conceptual frameworks. In the end, FrameworkS gave 'permission' to the organization to break out of old thinking habits and to create new habits. The Executive Committee explicitly relinquished some of its power and authority – even if that power and authority was more in the eyes of the operating company management than in the eyes of the Executive Committee itself – to the operating management of the corporation.

Persuading participants to allow sufficient time for incubation was sometimes an uphill struggle. It was critical that the company induce participants to shrug off years of training, to abstain from seeking closure or a rush to judgment, to seek questions, not answers. Participants had to learn to refrain from planning an outcome, and from defining 'action steps' based on decisions they felt obliged to make, based on information that had been gathered years before.

> Participants had to learn to refrain from planning an outcome, and from defining 'action steps' based on decisions they felt obliged to make, based on information that had been gathered years before.

Most of the credit for overcoming these obstacles was due to the support provided by Ralph Larsen and Bob Wilson, the chairman and vice chairman, who remained enthusiastic proponents of the programme even in the face of resistance. For example, the first geographically oriented FrameworkS dealt with the challenge of growth in Europe. While the first conversation generated a sense that real growth opportunities existed, six months later little had happened. European management had not had the true 'wake-up call'. They felt that they could cover the growth expectations within their existing plans. In this case, the Executive Committee proved willing to go to the mat in their insistence that such a response was not sufficient. They asked the European management to organize a second session. And again they found resistance. But three was the lucky charm: This time the European executives realized the Executive Committee meant business, that they were not going to accept incremental solutions, that henceforth they must think about their businesses differently. And this time they came up with 17 ideas for new growth businesses that would take J&J far beyond the realm in which it had operated until then – away from being a pure product company and into services that would be part of the transformation in health care delivery in Europe. Europe went from being the laggard to being a bed of experimentation for the entire corporation. But it was a nearly-four-year process and took the undying commitment of the Executive Committee to make sure real change happened.

At the same time, Larsen and Wilson stressed that participation was strictly voluntary. They knew that if they had attempted to make it mandatory, they would have encountered a whole new set of difficulties. They went to some lengths to stress that taking part in FrameworkS wouldn't be easy, efficient, or comfortable. It would not be a process for which success or failure would be easily determined.

And yet the participants were deeply engaged in the process. Despite having very full plates, executives made room for FrameworkS. In some cases, this meant getting on a plane and travelling across the Atlantic, and in one case from China, in order to attend.

Fortunately, both the chairman and the vice-chairman were prepared to wait for the results to come in. While they did insist on evaluations of the FrameworkS process at the end of each conversation, they did not force a broader assessment of the impact in the early days. It could have been tempting for them to pull this particular carrot out of the ground every day to ask, 'How's it growing?' Instead, they proved willing to wait 18 or even 24 months for results – at which point a few visible successes could be ascribed to insights achieved through the program.

LATER YEARS

Two years after the first FrameworkS sessions, J&J's Executive Committee realized that some of the original issues raised in the FrameworkS design session – increasing innovation and improving operational effectiveness – remained unsolved. Despite specific progress on growth in various regions, despite some marked success in launching new businesses, and despite some profound cultural changes related to leadership, they felt that the corporation needed to push itself further on both the innovation and operations fronts. The low-hanging fruit had been plucked, and the Executive Committee had the sense that this next round of efforts would be more daunting.

Stimulating innovation

The ninth FrameworkS was thus focused entirely on innovation and aimed at uncovering some of the deeper mysteries about what it takes to up the innovation ante. By surveying executives across the corporation, holding focus groups of employees, conducting intensive diagnostics of three critical businesses, gathering the input of leading academics and experts, and, most important, visiting innovative companies in very different industries (Nike, Pepsi and Enron), the participants in FrameworkS 9 challenged some of the institutionalized patterns of innovation in the corporation: incremental innovation in the operating companies, reliance on licensing and acquisition for more substantial innovation, focus on product innovation at the expense of other dimensions, and heavy reliance on a few 'big bang' innovations for sales growth. There was a general sense that the past pace of innovation, while admired externally and appropriate for the size and scale of the corporation, would no longer be adequate in the changing health care marketplace as J&J continued to grow larger and more complex.

The members of the 'extended Executive Committee' (the participants in this newest FrameworkS project) developed a strong understanding of the challenges Johnson & Johnson faced in achieving higher levels of innovation. And they became highly committed to meeting this challenge. They clarified their understanding of the different levels of innovation and made substantial innovation *the* major upcoming challenge. Next, they mapped out a set of behaviours and actions that are conducive to top innovation performance. And they gained a sense of what it would take to make individual operating companies and franchises more innovative.

There was an electric excitement coming out of that meeting. The participants, having gone on the site visits, having participated in the innovation diagnostics, having held discussions with people across the corporation, had a personal, tangible, first-hand understanding of the issues. Many described the experience in nearly religious terms.

Their next step was to translate this understanding and commitment to the broader management in the corporation. The task Johnson & Johnson executives faced was by no means simple. They were challenging themselves to sustained levels of growth and innovation that have rarely been achieved in the business world. They were seeking to change at the pace and scale of the markets in which they had chosen to compete. And they rightly saw themselves as but 30 (admittedly senior) people in a corporation of more than 87,000. Could they imbue the rest of the businesses and the rest of the workforce with the same feeling of commitment and the same personal understanding of innovation?

It was eminently clear that improving innovativeness was not simply an intellectual issue, a matter of understanding the definitions of innovation and the principles of innovativeness better. The participants in FrameworkS 9 were just that – participants. They had personally engaged in the experience. They had seen how other companies worked from the inside. They had seen for themselves how their employees talked about their fear of risk taking. One might argue, in fact, that none of the concepts or principles was particularly new. While it was certainly useful to have all the facts in one place and the principles articulated clearly, this was not what made the difference. The difference was the experience.

At the end of the FrameworkS 9 meeting, the discussion turned to how to make an impact on the corporation given this new-found commitment. One member of the Executive Committee suggested that they re-create the experience for the entire corporation – for all of the presidents or managing directors and the boards of all of the operating companies around the world. It seemed a fairly audacious suggestion, but the more they discussed it, the more they liked it.

They named the project What's New? as a symbol of the different kind of dialogue they were hoping to engender in the corporation. It was the question that Dr Paul Janssen, a prolific inventor and founder of J&J's Janssen Pharmaceutica, asked of his people as he walked around the lab. It also echoes the sentiments of former CEO and chairman Jim Burke:

When I visit our companies around the world, I try to discourage managers from telling me what the business is like today. I'm not really interested. It's only natural for people to want to tell me how things are going at the moment, but I tell them to talk about the future. This is hard for them, but by my taking this attitude, I am sending a signal that we are primarily interested in long-term growth, and we want to know how it is going to be achieved. This focus on the future forces our managers out of the rut of simply running the business as it is today. We must keep moving on to new things. If we are going to have a future, then we must concentrate on it.

Scaling a 30-person event to an 800-person event was not simple, but a year later, in 1997, more than 800 leaders at J&J met in Los Angeles for three days, the largest event of its kind in the company's history. All of the participants did pre-meeting work – assessments of their own businesses, reading about other innovative companies, and surveying their organization for perceptions about the effectiveness of current innovation processes. At the meeting itself, they held small group FrameworkS-style discussions about what they had learned. Since not everyone could go on a site visit, the organizing team brought the site visits to the executives, using elaborate multimedia presentations so that the presidents and CEOs of these leading companies could talk about their businesses and re-create some of the feel of the company itself.

The Executive Committee members spoke about the importance of innovation for the continued success of the corporation. And, by all accounts, it was a successful meeting. Most came away energized and committed. They understood that the team at the top was universally supportive of innovation efforts and they felt new freedom to press their growth agendas in their own businesses.

The meeting generated a great deal of excitement about the future. Some businesses went aggressively forward in making changes. However, not all businesses were able to translate their enthusiasm into action. For those companies, it was business as usual, perhaps because in the following year, 1998, these businesses faced some short-term performance challenges (e.g., falling sales-growth rates) and much of the advocacy for investment in the long term was crowded out by the desire to get the most out of the short term. Not surprisingly, J&J, as a large and complex corporation, has successes and failures just as the market has.

In an effort to keep the energy alive, the Executive Committee asked Group Operating Committees for each sector to appoint a person to take the lead in assuring implementation; all businesses were supposed to report to their groups about the progress that they had made. In an effort to further institutionalize the importance of innovation, the strategic planning requirements, widely criticized as disconnected from the actual running of the business, were revamped. While the intent was to encourage more FrameworkS-style dialogue and challenge in the planning process, the effort to transmit that intent to all of the businesses around the world led to a degree of formality that detracted from the impact. For example, the planning team put a tremendous amount of energy into creating a tool kit with a wide range of options that individual operating companies could use to stimulate innovation in their organizations. Available in hard copy and online, the tool kit was intended to help the companies through the process of self-discovery and change in order to dramatically up the innovation ante.

There were 'wake-up call' tools, such as detailed instructions on how to conduct a site visit, ways to identify potential site visit companies, how to draft introduction letters, suggested discussion guides. There was a diagnostic tool complete with a self-evaluation survey, central data processing support service, and suggested formats for workshops to discuss the findings. There were guidelines for using science advisory councils, for accessing the J&J quality management knowledge network, for setting up 'innovation cells' to protect and accelerate the development of innovative new business ideas, for conducting post-audits of innovation efforts to understand what worked and what did not. All in all, nearly 40 different suggestions were initially included. The idea was to help jump-start the process in the operating companies, to share the insights that had come from the FrameworkS 9 site visits and internal discovery of innovation's best practices.

In many ways, the tool kit was intended to be the linchpin of the implementation effort after the What's New? launch meeting. Concerned about assuring that something happened after the launch, executives planning the meeting hoped that this tool kit would give J&J executives in the nearly 175 operating companies around the world some handholds, some ideas for actions, that could be developed and tailored to the specific situations in each company. No one thought for a moment that there could be a universal process that would work in all situations. And even if there were, J&J was not the kind of company that would set such guidelines top-down. Instead, the idea was to spark a passion and urgency among the more than 800 attendees at the launch meeting and then give them a menu of ideas for making a difference once they got home from Los Angeles.

But the impact of the tool kit has been limited so far. In the end, tools are not the issue. What is critical is the *passion* to innovate. J&J learned that ad hoc, unstructured, exploratory processes are a more powerful force for change than are formalized programmes.

Where the programme had the most effect, it was because the executives took it upon themselves to encourage their organizations to generate their own process, design their own metrics, and develop their own aspirations for success. In these situations, the tools provided through the What's New? effort, such as the innovation diagnostic, and the videos from the What's New? meeting in Los Angeles, proved helpful starting points. Indeed, the diagnostic survey probably got the most traction of any of the tools. Fuelled by the generally self-critical culture and curiosity of managers around the world, and facilitated by a central support system that processed the surveys confidentially and produced management reports of the findings quickly, the vast majority of operating companies or worldwide franchises used the diagnostic survey in a process of discovery about their organizations. Some used the findings as support for quite radical changes; others found the results helpful in adjusting existing efforts.

The real lesson seems to be that best practices discovered by others are not as meaningful to organizations as the discoveries they make themselves. Attempting to codify the insights that generated so much excitement in FrameworkS took the 'ah-hah!' out of them. The diagnostic survey gave managers a chance to make their own discoveries about their organizations. But we (and they) found that real change happened only when organizations generated their own tools and approaches.

> Best practices discovered by others are not as meaningful to organizations as the discoveries they make themselves.

Improving operations

Having focused on innovation for several years, the Executive Committee decided it was time to turn to the other side of the coin – operations – particularly because the initial reengineering effort sparked from the initial FrameworkS meeting seemed to have produced much of its potential benefit. The goal of the next FrameworkS session was to seek out ways to improve operations in the context of balancing operations with innovation, although a simple focus on operations effectiveness probably won out. Not only did this FrameworkS session have a profound cultural impact – the operations executives felt valued in a way that they had not previously been in a marketing- and sales-dominated culture – but it also got a lot of traction throughout the organization. Restructuring major manufacturing quickly followed, which resulted in closing 36 out of 158 plants and reducing 4,100 jobs and taking a significant write-off.

REFLECTING ON THE PROCESS

No one imagined in March of 1993 what the FrameworkS process would become to J&J. While there were many successes, there were also the inevitable bumps in the road. But each bump was squarely addressed by the senior management group and overcome. Without executive intervention, a willingness to take a stand against sources of resistance, and increased visibility on critical change efforts, FrameworkS would not have had the impact that it has had.

Looking back over those years, the following observations stand out:

1. **The pace.** Since 1994, the J&J Executive Committee has conducted 13 different FrameworkS conversations (including the initial design session). When we first began, we expected that perhaps three of these sessions could be done per year. And J&J sustained that pace for the first two years. But eventually it had to slow things down. Part of the reason is that the preparation for the next session began to overlap with the follow-up task forces from the previous one. People found themselves committed to multiple FrameworkS-related task forces, to the point that it was beginning to crowd out too much of their normal operating responsibilities. In addition, they discovered that the process demanded more, rather than less, preparation time. Every time they talked about making the process somehow

more 'efficient' by shortening preparation time, or by having other people go on the site visits and report back, they concluded that efficiency was counter to the objectives of FrameworkS. So even though J&J would have liked FrameworkS to take less time out of people's schedules, they realized that such a change would kill the process. Finally, each of the FrameworkS led to significant change efforts, whether it was cost reduction, innovation, or growth businesses in Europe. Each of these demanded real leadership attention and energy (and political capital). With each succeeding FrameworkS, the number of change efforts demanded multiplied. In some sense, leadership capacity became the scarce resource.

Time and again, we asked: Should we stop FrameworkS? Is J&J's organization exhausted? Are there too many other things to do? And time and again, after serious debate and consideration, the answer came back: No, we can't afford *not* to do FrameworkS. In the early days, it was necessary to hold several in quick succession to get the critical issues on the table, to deal with the rapidly changing health care environment, to signal to the organization that the Executive Committee was serious about making change. But after the first few catalytic years, a more measured pace seemed to make sense.

In the end, FrameworkS turned out to be a direct expression of the pace and scale of change that can be tolerated within the corporation. FrameworkS increased that pace and scale to the point where management felt J&J was changing at least as rapidly as the markets in which it participated.

2. **The evaluation process.** We collectively went into the FrameworkS process not knowing what would result. The Executive Committee believed that an effort like this was essential if J&J was to avoid the fate of IBM in the early 1990s. But short-term attempts to evaluate the efficiency and effectiveness of FrameworkS, had they been attempted, would have been inconclusive. The earliest we were really able to evaluate the process was two to three years into it; before that the benefits would not have been obvious enough to justify continuing the process. Several years later, people began to see what the payoffs really were.

What saved FrameworkS from being evaluated prematurely – this natural tendency by managers everywhere to measure and monitor processes across relatively short time frames – was the early and sustained commitment of Ralph Larsen, Bob Wilson, and Roger Fine. They maintained the company's commitment through the vulnerable first two to three years. They accepted only shorter-term evaluations that were focused on the process of the conversation itself: Have we raised critical issues? Have we challenged our current assumptions? Have we developed aspirations that are orders of magnitude different from those we started out with? Without their willingness to accept the ambiguities of such a non traditional management process, it would have been prematurely closed down, rather than continue as it has for more than six years.

3. **Sources of resistance.** There were, not surprisingly, people who resisted the FrameworkS process. As we pointed out, resistance came in many forms: regional executives who wanted to run their own shows in the way they had always done it; operating company presidents who were convinced intellectually of the need to change, but who could not reinforce such change through behaviour; corporate staff members who wanted to create institutional processes for change rather than support widely varied ad hoc efforts in various companies; even members of the Executive Committee who, once charged with leading change on a particular issue, found themselves unwilling to break down organizational rigidities. These barriers are not unique to J&J. What characterized the FrameworkS process was the unwavering insistence by Larsen, Wilson, Fine, and later Russ Deyo (when he took over administration of the process) that they find a way over or around the barriers.

4. **Going to the source.** Many of the barriers were overcome by 'going to the source' in each of our FrameworkS sessions. The European FrameworkS sessions occurred in Europe, China's in China, Japan's in Japan. The analysis of innovative companies meant having to go to see innovative companies. In the end, we learned that experience is more convincing than analysis no matter how compellingly presented. This was key, and quite a hard sell in the beginning. But it was, in the end, what made FrameworkS real. 'Being there' increased the sense of urgency that in turn increased the passion to implement. It took the subjects covered by FrameworkS out of the intellectual realm and put them into the visceral, emotional realm. This was the way to 'sense the periphery' first hand.

Going to the source meant that preparation took longer, but that preparation was more effective. It meant that Executive Committee members were less concerned with formal evaluations of the

FrameworkS process because they personally experienced the changes and impact themselves. Going to the source helped break down the sources of resistance and build up commitment. And it allowed the Executive Committee to overcome some of the emotional barriers to changing their mental models.

5. **Bringing the rest of the organization along.** If 'going to the source' was critical for the participants in the FrameworkS process, then the challenge was in bringing FrameworkS to the rest of the 87,000-employee organization (or the more than 800 top managers of J&J's far-flung businesses). The answer came in many forms. Perhaps most dramatically, in what we called FrameworkS 9 and ultimately the What's New? effort, it meant bringing the top 800 to Los Angeles to experience things for themselves. It also meant broadcasting the events of the conference back to the operating companies around the world on a daily basis. In terms of formal method, Chairman Ralph Larsen set up a series of regular communications to employees: quarterly video broadcasts about key issues in the company that never failed to high-light FrameworkS efforts; a regular companywide newsletter devoted to FrameworkS; specific attention to FrameworkS in the annual meeting with shareholders. Even more important, Ralph Larsen, Bob Wilson, Jim Lenehan, Roger Fine, Russ Deyo, Bob Darretta, and Ron Gelbman, as well as many other members of the Executive Committee and many of the Company Group Chairmen, who became critical players in the FrameworkS process, spent time in one-to-one conversations with their colleagues, in speeches to their employees, in discussions of strategic plans, in tours of their plants. They passed on the insights generated in the process throughout the organization. They incorporated the company's new aspirations into the ways they managed the businesses they oversaw. And it is mainly in this way that FrameworkS has changed how J&J works.

ASSESSING THE RESULTS

What has been the impact of FrameworkS? Looking back at the progress since the 1992 'wake-up call,' Ralph Larsen, Bob Wilson, and their other senior J&J executives have made J&J into a very different place. Their willingness to reflect on critical, tough issues has played a crucial role in their success.

General accomplishments

Among J&J's accomplishments are:

- highly tangible results, such as the launch of a corporationwide cost-competitiveness effort that eliminated more than $2 billion from the bottom line and created or helped to acquire several new multi-million-dollar businesses

- less intangible results include increased cross-functional and cross-division teamwork, greater risk taking, broader participation in addressing key strategic challenges, increased cohesiveness among senior managers, and better management development

- initiation of high-profile corporate change initiatives focused on such areas as leadership building and innovativeness

- a changed attitude about the pace of change. The rank and file now believe that change is the essence of competitiveness. J&J is more aggressively seeking change in all areas of its businesses: cost structure, products, organization, and people. The role of creative destruction stands alongside operating excellence as the twin pillars on which J&J's success is built.

There are other ways to look at the impact, however. One is to see it through the eyes of J&J executives and employees; the other is through the eyes of the outsider.

How the J&J executives see it

As the FrameworkS process unfolded, here are a few of the comments and assessments J&J's CEO and other members of the top team have made:

- 'FrameworkS is not a finite project designed to produce a single new strategy or business venture by a certain date. Rather, it is an open-ended, ongoing process that is changing the way we think about our businesses, changing the way we relate to and work with one another, and encouraging the confidence and commitment that will be necessary for us to renew ourselves and remain a great and growing enterprise.'

- 'My reaction is that it has brought hundreds of executives into dealing with the complicated and profound issues we've got to deal with. FrameworkS has built a broad base of support for change. FrameworkS has changed my job as chairman. I've moved from a role of being a pusher and shover to the role of encouraging. I've never seen anything like it. I've never seen an organization as driven and self-motivated as the organization is today, and I attribute a lot of that to FrameworkS.'

I've moved from a role of being a pusher and shover to the role of encouraging. I've never seen anything like it. I've never seen an organization as driven and self-motivated as the organization is today.

- 'We are now looking much more across the corporation as a global entity versus staying within our silos. This is a chance for participants to step back and look at the whole competitive scene, and also to learn from executives within other parts of the organization. We are more likely to identify synergies. It finally puts the spotlight on key areas of opportunity. When you put a spotlight on it, turn it upside down, and look at it more closely, you get more insights.'

- 'FrameworkS has brought a fresh awareness of the implications of fundamental changes in industry structure, for example, increasing consolidation of competitors and increasing power of purchasers to the corporation. People are electrified by these changes, and they are willing to co-operate in ways they were unwilling to just a year ago.'

- 'It was very exciting to see people at all levels of the organization actively involved in shaping, and reshaping, the company.'

Among the comments from participants who were not members of the Executive Committee:

- 'Without FrameworkS, we wouldn't take much of a risk. What this has done is raise the risk profile at the top, and the perception of the [company's] willingness to take risks lower down – as a middle manager, I will be willing to put something forward now.'

- 'FrameworkS increased learning among the business heads and greatly increased communication. I learned things during FrameworkS that I just did not learn over my prior 20 years with the company. It empowered – a word I hate – the general managers a lot. Having the Executive Committee lay out what they expected was very helpful. It raised expectations a lot. It was a very motivational experience.'

- 'FrameworkS is a means of communicating with the Executive Committee and injecting reality into the decision-making process. The Executive Committee went out of touch five years ago, and FrameworkS has brought it into touch. Some terrific people need to be heard out on key issues, and this is a way to do that.'

- 'A collateral benefit is exposure to the Executive Committee, and vice versa. This makes other business interactions easier.'

- 'The cross-functional dialogue that has started and continues is fantastic. The Executive Committee's stock has gone up because of this. This has been very good for them. Their willingness to listen and take action has been seen by everybody.'

Our view

We have been very pleased with the overall impact FrameworkS has had on J&J, although perhaps J&J's executives have expressed the impact more poignantly than we could. This has been a long journey. Certainly the efforts aimed at improving the adaptability of the corporation have had some measure of success. That is not to say, however, that there is not more to do. There is. The effort to dramatically increase the pace and scale of creative destruction, without sacrificing operational effectiveness, will remain a difficult balance to strike. More has to be done, particularly to stimulate substantial and transformational innovation. Perhaps some of the difficulty can be attributed to the difficulty of leading adaptive work. As Ralph Larsen said: 'The last thing they need is someone at headquarters telling them what to do.' It will take more time to perfect the skills of leading adaptive work.

From the experience at J&J, however, we see that change is most effective when the people who drive the change have been personally engaged in generating urgency and in determining the shape and aspirations for change. We feel convinced that the semi-structured, open-ended nature of the FrameworkS process is the kind of jumping-off point that is necessary for companies like J&J that want to revolutionize the corporation and alter the pace and scale of both creation and destruction.

Intellectual stagnation is the great problem of large organizations. It is paramount to increase fertility in the field of ideas. The greatest responsibility of modern management is to develop the human intellect in order that it may express its talent.

ROBERT WOOD JOHNSON, 1959

Ralph Larsen summarized the impact the programme has had in an assessment for *Chief Executive* magazine: 'Is FrameworkS a single, simple approach to equipping an organization to deal with change? Absolutely not. But within the decentralized management structure of Johnson & Johnson, it has become a proven means of releasing energy throughout the corporation and focusing the eyes of the organization and its leadership on the two most important issues central to our future innovation and growth.'

FrameworkS can be an important step in 'increasing fertility in the field of ideas', a critical step in helping the corporation make the transformation from an operating organization to one that creates, operates, and trades at the pace and scale of the market, remaining fresh and vibrant for the future.

12 The ubiquity of creative destruction

J oseph Schumpeter's ideas about the central role of entre-
preneurism came into public debate in the 1930s but were
drowned out by the vision and hope of John Maynard Keynes. The rivalry
between Schumpeter and Keynes was intense and well known. As the
Great Depression sucked half of the GDP out of the United States and left
a quarter of its workforce unemployed, Schumpeter's concepts were not
seen as being as productive for reviving the weakened economy as were
Keynes' proposals to use strong fiscal policy to cure the Depression.
Schumpeter was bitterly disappointed that his voice had not been more
widely heard.

But that was 70 years ago. Keynes' ideas, formed in the crucible of the
depression, found their métier in the middle of the twentieth century. Most
nations have now absorbed Keynes' lessons. Today, general economic conditions are quite different from those that dominated thinking during the
Depression. Then companies remained on the S&P for a half century or
more. Now companies remain on the list for two decades on average, and
the average is rapidly falling. Investment in venture capital funds is at an
unprecedented high level, as are venture capital expenditures. The level is

Fig. 12.1 Merger and acquisition, 1890–1998

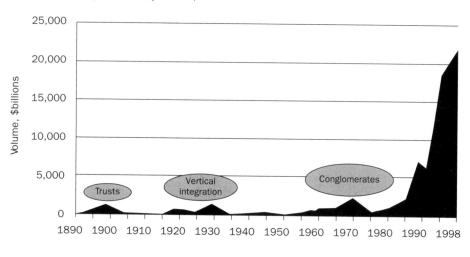

Source: Nelson Series, Thorpe Series, FTC, 'Broad' Series, IRF, Europe Team

so high, in fact, that one wonders whether the nation has sufficient talent to productively use these expenditures. Other signs of change are at all-time-high levels, as well, including the rate of mergers and acquisitions and the rate of corporate spin-offs (see Figiure 12.1).

While this pace of change probably will not be sustained in the long run, neither will it return to the levels of the 1970s. There is simply too much potential for productive change for that to happen. The game of creative destruction will continue – and probably quicken in pace – in the United States.

THE FUTURE OF THE NEW ECONOMY

The New Economy is the dramatic manifestation of Schumpeter's ideas. We doubt that even Schumpeter anticipated a rate of change as extensive as the one we are currently experiencing.

The revolution is far from over. The economic and technological forces are working to accelerate it. In the key technologies driving the economy forward, each advance provides the basis for future advances. The cycle will last for a very long time. We are on the front end of a broad curve, which will continue to accelerate through our lifetimes. The Internet represents the most visible example. It has already begun to change virtually all industries in a permanent way. It has created the potential for both more efficient markets (as the 2,000 or so exchanges that have been established in the past five years indicate) and the more effective marketing of consumer goods and services.

Moreover, the technology underpinning the Internet – communications, computers, and software – is not yet nearing its limits. Broadband and wireless communications will increase the pace and utility of telecommunications for many years to come. It will take decades to build the necessary communication systems in the United States, Europe, and Japan, and perhaps more time to build them in the countries of Latin America, Southeast Asia, the Middle East, and in China. On the back of these new capabilities will come new services and new levels of business efficiency. The cost of interaction, that is, the cost of buying, selling, and delivering products among businesses and between businesses and their consumers, will continue to decrease.

> The technology underpinning the Internet is not yet nearing its limits. Broadband and wireless communications will increase the pace and utility of telecommunications for many years to come.

Based on the advances in genetics (which themselves are enabled by better computer and software technology) we can expect substantial advances in health care, probably starting with diagnostic businesses and later involving whole new families of pharmaceuticals. The flow of new devices, drugs, and businesses coming from these advances can be expected to continue over several decades at the very least.

The path from where we are to where we will go will not be smooth, as we have pointed out many times. New companies will bring new ideas to the marketplace, and with them the inevitable reversal of fortunes that first attracted them. Losses will be an inevitable part of the march to a higher standard of living. The increasing pace of change, coupled with the increasing complexity of our society and our inability to accurately forecast the future, will assure that. Investors and managers can expect more turbulent markets as a permanent feature of the future. We have already seen spectacular price increases and decreases in many Internet stocks, such as Priceline.com and Amazon.com. More will certainly come. As a consequence, it will be more important than ever to find ways to hedge our investments, perhaps through the increasing use of derivative financial instruments such as options. But in the long run, enormous new value will be created in the economy as the new technologies are developed, combined, and exploited.

THE FAILURE OF INCREMENTALISM

The United States is not the first, or only, place where innovation has flourished, but it is the place where the processes of creative destruction have been maintained for the longest period of time and have affected the most people. The two are not the same. Japan is an instructive example. In the late nineteenth century and again in the mid-twentieth century, Japan rose to the ranks of a great power with breathtaking speed by determinedly applying Western technologies and methods. Once Japan became a world-class manufacturer in the late 1970s, however, further economic success demanded that it embrace creative destruction at the pace and scale of international markets. Japan attempted to compete by encouraging incremental innovation in important economic sectors, such as steel, shipbuilding, automobiles, and electronics. While they have been very successful in these areas, no one would claim that the Japanese have embraced the spirit of creative destruction. Quite the opposite. They have gone to great lengths to consolidate the power of the great companies and maintain the status quo. They are still wrestling with the issue today. They have aggressively tried to protect the assumption of continuity rather than embrace discontinuity. The Japanese approach, which couples a yearning for centralized control with incremental change, will be increasingly vulnerable. Now the world has moved ahead, and the Japanese are having trouble keeping up. It may take them decades to sort this out and reach a 'new way'.

South Korea provides a similar story. One of us attended a small breakfast a few years ago with former South Korean prime minister H. K. Lee, who made the point that the number one issue facing South Korea, in his view, was increasing South Korea's innovativeness. He pointed out that the Korean 'miracle' was based on copying the Japanese industrialization strategy. That strategy had now reached its limits. Korean labour rates had reached world levels, but productivity was below world-class levels, and technology access was being denied by non-Korean companies (most technology these days is traded for other technology rather than bought and sold). Moreover, Korean companies were extremely highly leveraged as a result of government-subsidized interest rates that were well below real market rates. The dam was bound to burst at some point, and Prime Minister Lee felt that innovation was the only way out. Since that time, the dam has burst, and many Korean companies had to seek bankruptcy protection. The failure to provide for indigenous capacity for creative destruction undermined the Korean miracle.

Lee recalled being present in the early days after the Korean War, when the economic policy of the country was being shaped. He said: 'We felt that if we only achieved world-scale operations we would have a seat at the table. We would be respected members of the international economic community, and that was our goal. We were successful in reaching our goal.' He went on: 'Our strategy of industrial organization gave us the scale we sought. But when we got to the table, we found we had no seat. We were not welcome because we had copied what others had done. We had not built a capability to contribute to further advances, because we did not know how to innovate. Now we must learn.' Since that time Korea has made progress in learning how to innovate, but to be competitive in the future, Koreans will have to do more than innovate – they, too, will have to learn to become masters of creative destruction.

Until now, developing countries seeking to bolster their economic standing have adopted the strategy of replicating existing innovations rather than attempting to develop the capability to nurture and develop new ones. While this strategy has proven temporarily successful, it has failed in the longer term, as the cases of Japan and Korea illustrate.

> Developing countries seeking to bolster their economic standing have adopted the strategy of replicating existing innovations rather than attempting to develop the capability to nurture and develop new ones.

THE AMERICAN SYSTEM – DESIGNED FOR CREATIVE DESTRUCTION

In the United States we have been more aggressive in adopting the assumption of discontinuity. We have been much more willing to give up the reins of control to the individual. Why?

There are several policies that have been effective in providing a more permissive environment in the United States that encourages economic development, and thus fosters creative destruction. First, our capital markets are the most transparent and developed in the world. Investors have confidence in the information provided by our companies, and that gives them the confidence to invest. Without honest corporate reporting, there can be no honest investing. Second, our trade policies, by and large, encourage foreign competition, perhaps more so than many other countries' policies do. Foreign competition exposes our companies to the realities of global competition and keeps the incentives aligned for continual improvement. Third, we have, for now, a series of government policies – for example, tax policies that encourage capital investment, and provide tax credits for R&D expenditures, as well as patent laws – that encourage risk capital investment and establish the value of intellectual capital more aggressively than other countries' policies do. In addition, we have bankruptcy laws that provide for an orderly process of disposal of assets in the event that a company cannot continue to operate successfully. Moreover, our labour laws provide a safety net for our workforce, but also provide for more labour mobility than is seen in other countries. Finally, as difficult as our legislative processes are, they do allow for more rapid adjustment of our legal framework than is seen in other countries.

While improvements can be made in all these areas, the collective effect of the laws is a more aggressive acceptance, perhaps even encouragement, of creative destruction and the assumption of discontinuity than is seen in any other country in the world. The economic system that has evolved in the United States confers an advantage on US corporations that other countries find difficult to match.

Economic systems that tie up or centralize the access to capital, or that have an insufficient base of scientific knowledge, or that try too hard to maintain continuity of employment or protect themselves from the force of external competition, find that in the long run their national economic productivity falters. This has been the case in many European, Asian, and Latin American countries. Releasing the forces of creative destruction is neither simple nor often sought by those in control.

The changes coming to Europe may rock current social and economic institutions to the core, including labour. Trying to hold off the inevitable pressure will not work; the capital markets are too powerful. Even with vast changes in the tax structure of Germany, it may be years yet until investors are convinced that the change is real and values are raised accordingly. When this does take place, one can look forward to a rapid change in the established competitive order in Germany, and perhaps the rest of Europe.

In the developed world, we are in a time when a country's capacity to innovate has become one of the most important sources of its national power. The ability to accommodate creative destruction as a central element of national economic policy, whether explicitly or implicitly, has become one of the major drivers of economic growth. It will only increase in importance in the future.

COVERING THE COSTS OF CREATIVE DESTRUCTION

The benefits of creative destruction are apparent: the potential for low inflation, low unemployment, and budget surpluses. But the forces of creative destruction, as we know, can also wreak havoc. In the 1930s, the great objection to Joseph Schumpeter's ideas was that they did not deal with the consequences of the social upheaval they implied. And indeed that was the case. If the pace of change is going to increase, and it seems that it inevitably will, the social costs of industrial disruption – the number of people 'left behind' – could also increase. Issues of retirement benefits, educational costs, medical costs, and social 'safety nets' could all increase in intensity. We will need approaches to these problems, and today there is no agreement on these policies.

THE UBIQUITY OF CREATIVE DESTRUCTION

We believe that all institutions benefit from the refreshing processes of creative destruction. We also believe that the forces of creative destruction are impossible to resist in the long term.

Failure to provide avenues for sufficient continual change – to create new options and to rid the system of old processes – eventually results in organizational failure, whether at the national, institutional, or individual level. If the forces of creative destruction are suppressed for long periods, the resulting ruptures can destroy institutions and individuals with astonishing speed and

> Failure to provide avenues for sufficient continual change eventually results in organizational failure, whether at the national, institutional, or individual level.

cruelty, as political and military revolutions have taught us consistently – from the time of the Reformation to the most recent revolutions in the Soviet Union and Serbia.

The benefit of legitimate capital markets is that they co-ordinate the wishes and capabilities of millions of individuals and through their relatively peaceful processes set an appropriate pace and scale of change. Legitimate capital markets allow divergent thinking to flourish if there is the potential for it. Without an active market, entrepreneurship can be suppressed, sometimes for decades.

This requires all organizations and institutions to think through how they will create a 'place' for divergent thinking, how they will allow the competition between new and old ideas to take place. It will also require these institutions to determine when and how to let the forces of destruction act.

We believe that the lessons that hold for our organizations hold for the individual as well. Finding the time for divergent thinking while still holding a job or mastering a discipline at school is at least as difficult on the personal level as it is on the institutional level. Remaining open to new ideas without prematurely rejecting existing ones; maintaining a bias toward change rather than the status quo; changing at the pace and scale of our environment – all are personal challenges that we face as individuals. There are no easy prescriptions to offer, apart from recognizing and accepting such change and finding ways to adapt and respond to it.

In 1939, Schumpeter observed that 'it is not [price and output] competition which counts, but the competition from the new commodity, the new technology, the new source of supply, the new type of organization.' His observation, however, went unheard by policy makers concerned with the Depression and the onset of war. Today the importance of his insight cannot be overstated.

Whether we like it or not, we live in the discontinuous age. Corporate position and prestige are increasingly fleeting; cannibalization is critical; turnover is normal. We are a long way from the 1930s, when the ideas of Schumpeter and Keynes fought for attention. Long ago we learned the lessons of Keynes. Today we have to learn and digest Schumpeter's lessons.

Some object to applying Schumpeter's economic ideas to individual corporations, arguing that one should leave to the markets that which they do best – the reallocation of resources. Corporations, such thinkers argue, not only cannot do this but should not do this, since it will divert their attention from the corporation's central task of managing or administering the operations of highly efficient companies.

We cannot accept this argument. It is an argument first made in Keynesian times, a time of continuity. Under the assumption of continuity, the lifeblood of the corporation was efficient operations. Corporations gave up very little if they abdicated the allocation of resources to the markets. Today the reverse is true. It is no longer good enough simply to operate well. Corporations have to operate and manage creative destruction at the pace and scale of the market, without losing control, or they will falter and fade.

Managing for creative destruction is a substantial challenge that will increase in intensity in the coming years. Those corporations that abdicate the responsibility for resource reallocation to the markets are co-operating in their own demise. Companies unwilling or unable to play the game of creative destruction will inevitably be replaced. Like it or not, the age of continuity is gone for ever. The very forces that make our capital economy so vibrant and resilient are the same forces that spawn discontinuity and creative destruction. Rather than simply acting as custodians of operational excellence, and being buffeted by the winds of change, we urge corporations and their leaders to be the captains of their fate, the masters of the forces of creative destruction that shape and renew the markets into the new millennium.

Appendix A

List of companies

AEROSPACE AND DEFENCE

ATLANTIC RESEARCH CORP.
AVONDALE INDUSTRIES INC.
BANGOR PUNTA CORP.
BOEING CO.
CESSNA AIRCRAFT CO.
CORDANT TECHNOLOGIES INC.
FAIRCHILD INDUSTRIES INC.
GATES LEARJET CORP.
GENCORP. INC.
GENERAL DYNAMICS CORP.
GRUMMAN CORP.
GULFSTREAM AEROSPACE
HALTER MARINE GROUP INC.
HEICO CORP.

HOWMET INTERNATIONAL INC.
LOCKHEED MARTIN
MARTIN MARIETTA CORP.
MCDONNELL DOUGLAS CORP.
NEWPORT NEWS SHIPBUILDING
NORTHROP GRUMMAN.
RAYTHEON CO. − CL B
ROCKWELL INTL CORP.
ROHR INC.
TEXTRON INC.
TRACOR INC.
TRIUMPH GROUP INC.
WOODWARD GOVERNOR CO.

AIRLINES

AIRTRAN HOLDINGS INC.
ALASKA AIRGROUP INC.
AMERICA WEST AIRLINES INC.
AMR CORP. − DEL
ASA HOLDINGS
ATLANTIC COAST AIRLINES HLDG.
COMAIR HOLDINGS INC.
CONTINENTAL AIRLINES INC.
DELTA AIR LINES INC.
EASTERN AIR LINES
MESA AIR GROUP INC.

MIDWEST EXPRESS HOLDINGS
   INC.
NORTHWEST AIRLINES CORP.
PAN AM CORP.
PEOPLE EXPRESS AIRLINES INC.
PIEDMONT AVIATION INC.
SOUTHWEST AIRLINES
TIGER INTERNATIONAL
TRANS WORLD AIRLINES
UAL CORP.
USAIR GROUP

CHEMICALS, COMMODITY

AIR PRODUCTS & CHEMICALS INC.	MONSANTO CO.
AIRCO INC.	NL INDUSTRIES
ALBEMARLE CORP.	OLIN CORP.
ALLIEDSIGNAL INC.	OM GROUP INC.
ARCO CHEMICAL CO.	PENNWALT CORP.
ARISTECH CHEMICAL CORP.	PRAXAIR INC.
BORDEN CHEM & PLAST – LP COM	QUANTUM CHEMICAL CORP.
CALGON CARBON CORP.	REICHHOLD CHEMICALS INC.
CYTEC INDUSTRIES INC.	ROHM & HAAS CO.
DOW CHEMICAL	SCHULMAN (A.) INC.
DU PONT (E.I.) DE NEMOURS	SOLUTIA INC.
ETHYL CORP.	STAUFFER CHEMICAL CO.
GEON COMPANY	STERLING CHEMICALS INC.
GEORGIA GULF CORP.	UNION CARBIDE CORP.
HERCULES INC.	VALHI INC.
LAWTER INTERNATIONAL INC.	VISTA CHEMICAL CO.
MILLENNIUM CHEMICALS INC.	WELLMAN INC.
MINERALS TECHNOLOGIES INC.	WITCO CORP.

CHEMICALS, SPECIALTY

AGRIUM INC.	FOSTER GRANT INC. – CL A
AKZONA	FREEPORT MCMORAN INC.
BAROID CORP.	FULLER (H. B.) CO.
BEKER INDUSTRIES	G-I HOLDINGS INC.
BETZ DEARBORN INC.	GRACE (W.R.) & CO.
BUSH BOAKE ALLEN INC.	GREAT LAKES CHEMICAL CORP.
CABOT CORP.	IMC GLOBAL INC.
CAMBEX CORP.	INMONT CORP.
CELANESE CORP.	INTL FLAVORS & FRAGRANCES
CHEMFIRST INC.	INTL SPECIALTY PRODS INC.
CK WITCO CORP.	LILLY INDS INC. – CL A
DE SOTO INC.	LOCTITE CORP.
EMERY INDUSTRIES INC.	LUBRIZOL CORP.
FERRO CORP.	LYONDELL CHEMICAL CO.

CHEMICALS, SPECIALTY *(CONTINUED)*

MACDERMID INC.

METHANEX CORP.

MISSISSIPPI CHEMICAL CORP.

MOORE (BENJAMIN) & CO.

MORTON INTL INC.

NALCO CHEMICAL CO.

NATIONAL STARCH & CHEMICAL

PETROLITE CORP.

PHOSPATES RES PARTNERS — LP

PPG INDUSTRIES INC.

RPM INC. OHIO

SCOTTS COMPANY

SEQUA CORP. CL A

SHERWIN-WILLIAMS CO.

TERRA CHEMICALS INTL.

THIOKOL CORP.

VALSPAR CORP.

VIGORO CORP.

WD-40 CO.

COMPUTER HARDWARE

AMDAHL CORP.

APEX INC.

APOLLO COMPUTER INC.

APPLE COMPUTER INC.

ASCEND COMMUNICATIONS INC.

AST RESEARCH INC.

BAY NETWORKS INC.

CABLETRON SYSTEMS

CASCADE COMMUNICATIONS CORP.

CHIPCOM CORP.

CIPHER DATA PRODUCTS INC.

CIRRUS LOGIC INC.

CISCO SYSTEMS INC.

COMMODORE INTL LTD.

COMPAQ COMPUTER CORP.

COMPUTER CONSOLES

CONNER PERIPHERALS

CONVEX COMPUTER CORP.

CRAY RESEARCH

CREATIVE TECHNOLOGY LTD.

CYLINK CORP.

DATA GENERAL CORP.

DATAPOINT CORP.

DATAPRODUCTS CORP.

DELL COMPUTER CORP.

DIALOGIC CORP.

DIGI INTERNATIONAL INC.

DIGITAL EQUIPMENT

DYNATECH CORP.

DYSAN CORP.

ELECTRONICS FOR IMAGING
   INC.

EMC CORP./MA

EMULEX CORP.

EXABYTE CORP.

FLOATING POINT SYSTEMS INC.

FORE SYSTEMS INC.

GATEWAY INC.

GOULD INC.

HEWLETT-PACKARD CO.

HMT TECHNOLOGY CORP.

INTELLIGENT SYSTEM CP.

INTERGRAPH CORP.

INTL BUSINESS MACHINES CORP.

IOMEGA CORP.

ISC SYSTEMS CORP.

JTS CORP.

LEXMARK INTL GRP INC. — CL A

COMPUTER HARDWARE *(CONTINUED)*

MAXTOR CORP.

MICRON ELECTRONICS INC.

MINISCRIBE CORP.

MIPS COMPUTER SYSTEMS INC.

MMC NETWORKS INC.

MTI TECHNOLOGY CORP.

NCR CORP.

NETWORK APPLIANCE INC.

NETWORK EQUIPMENT TECH INC.

NETWORK GENERAL CORP.

NETWORK SYSTEMS CORP.

QANTEL CORP.

QUANTUM CORP.

ROLM CORP.

RSA SECURITY INC.

S3 INC.ORP.ORATED

SANDISK CORP.

SCI SYSTEMS INC.

SCM MICROSYSTEMS INC.

SEAGATE TECHNOLOGY

SECURE COMPUTING CORP.

SEQUENT COMPUTER SYSTEMS
    INC.

SILICON GRAPHICS INC.

SPERRY CORP.

STANDARD MICROSYSTEMS
    CORP.

STORAGE TECHNOLOGY CP

STRATUS COMPUTER INC.

SUN MICROSYSTEMS INC.

SYMBOL TECHNOLOGIES

SYNOPTICS COMMUNICATIONS
    INC.

TANDEM COMPUTERS INC.

TANDY CORP.

TELEX CORP.

TERADATA CORP.

TSL HOLDINGS INC.

UNISYS CORP.

VERBATIM CORP.

WANG LABS INC.

WESTERN DIGITAL CORP.

WYSE TECHNOLOGY INC.

XIRCOM INC.

XYLAN CORP.

COMPUTER SOFTWARE

ACCLAIM ENT INC.

ACXIOM CORP.

ADOBE SYSTEMS INC.

ADVANTAGE LEARNING SYSTEMS
    INC.

ADVENT SOFTWARE INC.

ALDUS CORP.

ALLERION INC.

AMERICAN SOFTWARE – CL A

ARDENT SOFTWARE INC.

ASHTON-TATE CO.

ASK GROUP INC.

ASPECT DEVELOPMENT INC.

ASPEN TECHNOLOGY INC.

AUTODESK INC.

AUTOMATIC DATA PROCESSING.

AVANT CORP.

AVT CORP.

COMPUTER SOFTWARE *(CONTINUED)*

AXENT TECHNOLOGIES INC.

BANYAN SYSTEMS INC.

BBN CORP.

BDM FEDERAL — CL A

BEA SYSTEMS INC.

BISYS GROUP INC.

BMC SOFTWARE INC.

BOOLE & BABBAGE INC.

BROADVISION INC.

BRODERBUND SOFTWARE INC.

CADENCE DESIGN SYSTEMS INC.

CCC INFORMATION SVCS GRP
    INC.

CHECK POINT SOFTWARE

CHEYENNE SOFTWARE INC.

CITRIX SYSTEMS INC.

CLARIFY INC.

COGNOS INC.

COMPUTER ASSOCIATES INTL INC.

COMPUTERVISION CORP.

COMPUWARE CORP.

CONCORD COMMUNICATIONS
    INC.

CONTINUUM INC.

COREL CORP.

CSG SYSTEMS INTL INC.

CULLINET SOFTWARE INC.

DAISY SYSTEMS CORP.

DAVIDSON & ASSOCIATES INC.

DENDRITE INTERNATIONAL INC.

DISCREET LOGIC INC.

DOCUMENTUM INC.

DST SYSTEMS INC.

EDWARDS J D & CO.

ELECTRONIC ARTS INC.

ENGINEERING ANIMATION INC.

EPICOR SOFTWARE CORP.

FILENET CORP.

FISERV INC.

FORTE SOFTWARE INC.

FTP SOFTWARE INC.

GENESYS TELECOMM LABS INC.

GT INTERACTIVE SOFTWARE

HARBINGER CORP.

HBO & CO.

HENRY (JACK) & ASSOCIATES

HNC SOFTWARE INC.

HOGAN SYSTEMS INC.

HUMMINGBIRD COMMUNICATNS
    LTD.

HYPERION SOFTWARE CORP.

HYPERION SOLUTIONS CORP.

I2 TECHNOLOGIES INC.

IDX SYSTEMS CORP.

INDUS-MATEMATIK INTL

INFORMIX CORP.

INPRISE CORP.

INSO CORP.

INTEGRATED SYSTEMS INC.

INTUIT INC.

LANDMARK GRAPHICS CORP.

LEARNING COMPANY INC.

LEGATO SYSTEMS INC.

LEGENT CORP.

LHS GROUP INC.

LOTUS DEVELOPMENT CORP.

MACROMEDIA INC.

MANAGEMENT SCIENCE AMERICA

MANUGISTICS GROUP INC.

MAPICS INC.

MEDIC COMPUTER SYSTEMS INC.

MENTOR GRAPHICS CORP.

COMPUTER SOFTWARE *(CONTINUED)*

MERCURY INTERACTIVE CORP.

MICROS SYSTEMS INC.

MICROSOFT CORP.

MIDWAY GAMES INC.

NATIONAL INSTRUMENTS CORP.

NETMANAGE INC.

NETSCAPE COMMUNICATION

NETWORKS ASSOCIATES INC.

NEW ERA OF NETWORKS INC.

NOVELL INC.

ORACLE SYSTEMS CORP.

PANSOPHIC SYSTEMS INC.

PARAMETRIC TECHNOLOGY

PEOPLESOFT INC.

PLATINUM TECHNOLOGY INTL
   INC.

PROGRESS SOFTWARE CORP.

PROJECT SOFTWARE & DEV INC.

QAD INC.

QUADRAMED CORP.

RADIANT SYSTEMS INC.

RATIONAL SOFTWARE CORP.

REALNETWORKS INC.

REMEDY CORP.

SABRE HLDGS CORP. – CL A

SAGA SYSTEMS INC.

SANCHEZ COMPUTER ASSOCS
   INC.

SAPIENT CORP.

SHARED MEDICAL SYSTEMS CORP.

SHL SYSTEMHOUSE INC.

SIEBEL SYSTEMS INC.

SOFTWARE PUBLISHING CORP.

SPYGLASS INC.

STERLING COMMERCE INC.

STERLING SOFTWARE INC.

STRUCTURAL DYNAMICS
   RESEARCH

SUNGARD DATA SYSTEMS INC.

SYBASE INC.

SYMANTEC CORP.

SYNOPSYS INC.

SYSTEM SOFTWARE ASSOCIATION

SYSTEMS & COMPUTER TECH
   CORP.

TECHNOLOGY SOLUTIONS CO.

THQ INC.

TOTAL SYSTEM SERVICES INC.

TRANSITION SYSTEMS INC./MA

TRNSACTN SYS ARCHTCTS – CL A

TSI INTL SOFTWARE LTD.

TYMSHARE INC.

UCCEL CORP.

USWEB CORP.

VANTIVE CORP.

VERITAS SOFTWARE CO.

VIASOFT INC.

VIEWLOGIC SYSTEMS INC.

VISIO CORP.

CRUDE OIL EXTRACTION AND REFINING

ADOBE OIL & GAS CORP.

ADOBE RESOURCES CORP.

ALBERTA ENERGY CO LTD.

AMAREX INC.

AMERAC ENERGY CORP.

AMERADA HESS CORP.

AMOCO CORP.

ANADARKO PETROLEUM CORP.

APACHE CORP.

APACHE PETROLEUM – LP

APCO OIL CORP.

ASAMERA INC.

ASHLAND OIL INC.

ATLANTIC RICHFIELD CO.

ATWOOD OCEANICS

BARRETT RESOURCES CORP.

BELCO PETROLEUM CORP.

BELCO OIL & GAS CORP.

BERRY PETROLEUM – CL A

BJ SERVICES CO.

BOW VALLEY ENERGY INC.

BROWN (TOM) INC.

BURLINGTON RESOURCES INC.

CABOT OIL & GAS CORP. – CL A

CHESAPEAKE ENERGY CORP.

CHEVRON-GULF

CHIEFTAIN INTL INC.

CITIES SERVICE CO.

CLARK OIL & REFINING CORP.

CLIFFS DRILLING CO.

COASTAL CORP.

CONOCO INC. – OLD

CONSOLIDATED OIL & GAS

CREOLE PETROLEUM CORP.

CROSS TIMBERS OIL CO.

CROWN CENTRAL PETROL – CL B

CRUTCHER RESOURCES CORP.

CRYSTAL GAS STORAGE INC.

DEVON ENERGY CORPORATION

DIAMOND OFFSHRE DRILLING
   INC.

DIAMOND SHAMROCK INC.

DOME PETROLEUM LTD.

DYCO PETROLEUM CORP.

EARTH RESOURCES CO.

EEX CORP.

ENERGY RESERVES GROUP

ENRON CORP.

ENSCO INTERNATIONAL INC.

ENSTAR CORP.-DEL

EOG RESOURCES INC.

EQUITY OIL CO.

EXXON CORP.

FALCON DRILLING COMPANY INC.

FELMONT OIL CO.

FINA INC. – CL A

FORCENERGY INC.

FOREST OIL CORP.

FREEPORT MCMORAN OIL &
   GAS CO.

FRONTIER OIL CORP.

GEARHART INDUSTRIES INC.

GENERAL AMERICAN OIL CO-TX

GETTY-SKELLY

GLOBAL INDUSTRIES LTD.

GLOBAL MARINE INC.

GLOBAL NATURAL RESOURCES
   INC.

GREAT BASINS PETROLEUM

GREY WOLF INC.

CRUDE OIL EXTRACTION AND REFINING *(CONTINUED)*

GULF CORP.

HALLIBURTON CO.

HAMILTON OIL CORP.

HELMERICH & PAYNE

HOLLY CORP.

HOME OIL CO LTD.

HOUSTON OIL & MINERALS CORP.

HOWELL CORP.

HUDSON'S BAY OIL & GAS CO.

HUGHES TOOL CO.

HUSKY OIL LTD.

INEXCO OIL

KELLEY OIL & GAS PTRS – LP

KERR-MCGEE CORP.

LEVIATHAN GAS PIPELINE – LP

LOUIS DREYFUS NAT GAS CORP.

LOUISIANA LAND & EXPLORATION

LOUISIANA LAND OFFSHORE EXPL

MAPCO INC.

MARINE DRILLING CO INC.

MAXUS ENERGY CORP.

MCMORAN OIL & GAS CO.

MESA INC.

MGF OIL CORP. – COM

MITCHELL ENERGY & DEV – CL B

MOBIL CORP.

MORAN ENERGY INC.

MURPHY OIL CORP.

NABORS INDUSTRIES

NATOMAS CO.

NEWFIELD EXPLORATION CO.

NICKLOS OIL & GAS CO.

NOBLE DRILLING CORP.

NOBLE AFFILIATES INC.

NUEVO ENERGY CO.

NUMAC ENERGY INC.

OCCIDENTAL PETROLEUM CORP.

OCEAN DRILLING & EXPLORATION

OCEAN ENERGY INC.

OCEANEERING INTERNATIONAL

OKC CORP.

ORYX ENERGY CO.

PACIFIC RESOURCES INC.

PARKER DRILLING CO.

PATTERSON ENERGY INC.

PENNZ ENERGY CO.

PETRO-LEWIS CORP.

PHILLIPS PETROLEUM CO.

PHOENIX RESOURCES CO.

PIONEER NATURAL RESOURCES CO.

PLAINS PETROLEUM COMPANY

POGO PRODUCING CO.

PRIDE INTERNATIONAL INC.

PRODUCTION OPERATORS CORP.

QUAKER CHEMICAL CORP.

QUAKER STATE CORP.

R & B FALCON CORP.

RANGER OIL LTD.

REMINGTON OIL & GAS CP – CL B

RIGEL ENERGY CORP.

ROWAN COS INC.

ROYAL DUTCH PET – NY REG

SABINE CORP.

SAGE ENERGY CO.

SANTA FE INTERNATIONAL CORP.

SANTA FE ENERGY PRTNRS – LP

SANTA FE SNYDER CORP.

SCEPTRE RESOURCES LTD.

SCHLUMBERGER LTD.

SEDCO INC.

CRUDE OIL EXTRACTION AND REFINING (CONTINUED)

SKELLY OIL CO.

SNYDER OIL CORP.

SOLV EX CORP.

SOUTHLAND ROYALTY CO.

STANDARD OIL CO.

STONE ENERGY CORP.

SUN ENERGY PARTNERS – LP

SUNOCO INC.

SUPERIOR OIL CO.

SUPRON ENERGY CORP.

TALISMAN ENERGY INC.

TELECO OILFIELD SERVICES INC.

TESORO PETROLEUM CORP.

TEXACO-GETTY

TOSCO CORP.

TOTAL PETROLEUM OF N AMERICA

TRANSCO EXPLORATION – LP

TRANSOCEAN OFFSHORE INC.

TRANSTEXAS GAS CORP.

TRITON ENERGY LTD.

ULTRAMAR DIAMOND SHAMROCK

UNION PACIFIC RESOURCES GRP.

UNION TEXAS PETRO HLDGS INC.

UNITED CANSO OIL & GAS LTD.

UNITED MERIDIAN CORP.

UNOCAL CORP.

UNOCAL EXPLORATION CORP.

USX-MARATHON GROUP

VALERO ENERGY CORP.

VASTAR RESOURCES INC.

VINTAGE PETROLEUM INC.

WEATHERFORD ENTERRA INC.

WESTERN ATLAS INC.

WESTERN CO OF NO AMER

WISER OIL CO

ELECTRIC UTILITIES

AES CORP.

ALLEGHENY POWER SYSTEM

ALLIANT CORP.

AMEREN CORP.

AMERICAN ELECTRIC POWER

ATLANTIC ENERGY INC.

AVISTA CORP.

BEC ENERGY

BLACK HILLS CORP.

CAROLINA POWER & LIGHT

CENTERIOR ENERGY CORP.

CENTRAL & SOUTH WEST CORP.

CENTRAL HUDSON GAS & ELEC

CENTRAL VERMONT PUB SERV

CILCORP INC.

CINERGY CORP.

CIPSCO INC.

CITIZENS UTILITIES

CLECO CORP.

CMP GROUP

CMS ENERGY CORP.

COMMONWEALTH ENERGY
· SYSTEM

CONECTIV INC.

CONSOLIDATED EDISON INC.

CONSTELLATION ENERGY CORP.

DESTEC ENERGY INC.

DOMINION RESOURCES INC.

DPL INC.

DQE INC.

ELECTRIC UTILITIES *(CONTINUED)*

DTE ENERGY	NISOURCE INC.
DUKE POWER CO.	NORTHEAST UTILITIES
EASTERN UTILITIES ASSOC.	NORTHERN STATES POWER/MN
EDISON INTERNATIONAL	NORTHWESTERN CORP.
EL PASO ELECTRIC CO.	OGDEN PROJECTS INC.
EMPIRE DISTRICT ELECTRIC CO.	OGE ENERGY CORP.
ENERGY EAST CORP.	ORANGE & ROCKLAND UTILITIES
ENOVA CORP.	OTTER TAIL POWER CO.
ENTERGY CORP.	PACIFICORP
FIRST ENERGY CORP.	PECO ENERGY CO.
FLORIDA PROGRESS CORP.	PENNSYLVANIA POWER & LIGHT
FPL GROUP INC.	PG&E CORP.
GPU INC.	PINNACLE WEST CAPITAL
GULF STATES UTILITIES CO.	PORTLAND GENERAL CORP.
HAWAIIAN ELECTRIC INDS	POTOMAC ELECTRIC POWER
HEIZER CORP.	PSI RESOURCES INC.
IDACORP. INC.	PUBLIC SERVICE CO. OF N. MEX
IES INDUSTRIES INC.	PUBLIC SERVICE ENTRP.
ILLINOVA CORP.	PUGET SOUND POWER & LIGHT
INTERSTATE POWER CO.	RELIANT ENERGY INC.
IOWA RESOURCES INC.	ROCHESTER GAS & ELECTRIC
IOWA SOUTHERN INC.	SCANA CORP.
IOWA-ILLINOIS GAS & ELEC	SIERRA PACIFIC RESOURCES
IPALCO ENTERPRISES INC.	SIGCORP. INC.
KANSAS CITY POWER & LIGHT	SOUTHERN CO.
KANSAS GAS & ELECTRIC	SOUTHWESTERN PUBLIC SVC CO.
KU ENERGY CORP.	TECO ENERGY INC.
LG&E ENERGY CORP.	TEXAS UTILITIES CO.
LONG ISLAND LIGHTING	THERMO ECOTEK CORP.
MADISON GAS & ELECTRIC CO.	TNP ENTERPRISES INC.
MAGMA POWER CO.	UNICOM CORP.
MIDAMERICAN ENERGY HOLDINGS	UNISOURCE ENERGY CORP. HLD CO.
MINNESOTA POWER & LIGHT	UNITED ILLUMINATING CO.
MONTANA POWER CO.	UTAH POWER & LIGHT
NEW CENTURY ENERGIES INC.	WESTERN RESOURCES INC.
NEW ENGLAND ELECTRIC SYSTEM	WISCONSIN ENERGY CORP.
NIAGARA MOHAWK POWER	WPS RESOURCES CORP.

PULP AND PAPER PRODUCTS

ACX TECHNOLOGIES INC.

AMERICAN BUSINESS PRODS/GA

BEMIS CO.

BOHEMIA INC.

BOISE CASCADE CORP.

BOWATER INC.

BOWATER PULP & PAPER

BROOKS-SCANLON INC.

BUCKEYE TECHNOLOGIES INC.

CARAUSTAR INDUSTRIES INC.

CHAMPION INTERNATIONAL CORP.

CHESAPEAKE CORP.

CONSOLIDATED PAPERS INC.

CROWN ZELLERBACH

DENNISON MFG CO.

DIAMOND INTERNATIONAL CORP.

FEDERAL PAPER BOARD CO.

FORT HOWARD CORP.

FORT JAMES CORP.

GAYLORD CONTAINER CP

GLATFELTER (P.H.) CO.

GREAT NORTHERN NEKOOSA CORP.

HAMMERMILL PAPER CO.

INTL PAPER CO.

KIMBERLY-CLARK CORP.

LONGVIEW FIBRE CO.

LOUISIANA-PACIFIC CORP.

MEAD CORP.

OLINKRAFT INC.

PENTAIR INC.

POPE & TALBOT INC.

POTLATCH CORP.

RIVERWOOD INTL CORP.

ROCK-TENN COMPANY

SAXON INDUSTRIES

SCHWEITZER-MAUDUIT INTL INC.

SCOTT PAPER CO.

SMURFIT-STONE CONTAINER CORP.

SOUTHWEST FOREST INDUSTRIES

ST REGIS CORP.

STONE CONTAINER CORP.

TAMBRANDS INC.

TEMPLE-INLAND INC.

UNION CAMP CORP.

WAUSAU-MOSINEE PAPER CORP.

WESTVACO CORP.

WEYERHAEUSER CO.

WILLAMETTE INDUSTRIES

PHARMACEUTICALS

ABBOTT LABORATORIES

ADVANCED TISSUE SCI – CL A

AGOURON PHARMACEUTICALS INC.

ALLERGAN INC.

ALLIANCE PHARMACEUTICAL CP

ALPHARMCA INC. – CLA

ALZA CORP.

AMERICAN HOME PRODUCTS CORP.

AMGEN INC.

ANESTA CORP.

AVIRON

BARR LABORATORIES INC.

BIO TECHNOLOGY GENERAL CORP.

BIOCHEM PHARMA INC.

BIOCRAFT LABORATORIES INC.

BIOGEN INC.

PHARMACEUTICALS *(CONTINUED)*

BOSTON LIFE SCIENCES INC.

BRISTOL MYERS-SQUIBB

CATALYTICA INC.

CENTOCOR INC.

CHATTEM INC.

CHIRON CORP.

CIRCA PHARMACEUTICALS INC.

COLUMBIA LABORATORIES INC.

COOPER LABORATORIES

COR THERAPEUTICS INC.

COULTER PHARMACEUTICAL INC.

CYTOGEN CORP.

DIAGNOSTIC PRODUCTS CORP.

DURA PHARMACEUTICALS INC.

FOREST LABORATORIES – CL A

GELTEX PHARMACEUTICALS INC.

GENENTECH INC.

GENETICS INSTITUTE INC.

GENZYME CORP.

GILEAD SCIENCES INC.

HUMAN GENOME SCIENCES INC.

HYBRITECH INC.

ICN PHARMACEUTICALS INC.-DEL

ICOS CORP.ORATION

IDEC PHARMACEUTICALS CORP.

IDEXX LABS INC.

IMMUNEX CORP.

INHALE THERAPEUTIC SYSTEMS

INTERNEURON
    PHARMACEUTICALS

ISIS PHARMACEUTICALS INC.

IVAX CORP.

JONES PHARMA INC.

KEY PHARMACEUTICALS INC.

LIFE TECHNOLOGIES INC.

LIGAND PHARMACEUTICAL – CL B

LILLY (ELI) & CO.

LIPOSOME COMPANY INC.

LYPHOMED INC.

MARION MERRELL DOW INC.

MEDICIS PHARMACEUT CP – CL A

MEDIMMUNE INC.

MERCK & CO.

MILES LABORATORIES INC.

MILLENNIUM PHARMACTCLS INC.

MOLECULAR BIOSYSTEMS INC.

MYLAN LABORATORIES

NBTY INC.

NORTH AMERICAN VACCINE INC.

PARKE DAVIS & CO.

PATHOGENESIS CORP.

PERRIGO COMPANY

PFIZER INC.

PHARMACIA & UPJOHN INC.

PHARMACYCLICS INC.

PROTEIN DESIGN LABS INC.

QLT PHOTOTHERAPEUTICS

REGENERON PHARMACEUT

REXALL SUNDOWN INC.

RHONE-POULENC RORER

RICHARDSON-VICKS INC.

ROBERTS PHARMACEUTICAL CORP.

ROBINS (A.H.) CO.

SANGSTAT MEDICAL CORP.

SCHERBER (R P)/DE

SCHERING-PLOUGH

SEARLE (G.D.) & CO.

SEPRACOR INC.

SEQUUS PHARMACEUTICALS INC.

SEROLOGICALS CORP.

PHARMACEUTICALS *(CONTINUED)*

SICOR INC.

SIGMA-ALDRICH

SQUIBB CORP.

STERLING DRUG INC.

SYNERGEN INC.

SYNTEX CORP.

TECHNE CORP.

THERAGENICS CORP.

TRANSKARYOTIC THERAPIES INC.

TWINLAB CORP.

U S BIOSCIENCE INC.

VERTEX PHARMACEUTICALS INC.

WARNER-LAMBERT CO.

WATSON PHARMACEUTICALS INC.

XOMA LTD.

ZENITH LABORATORIES

SEMICONDUCTORS

ADVANCED MICRO DEVICES

ALPHA INDUSTRIES INC.

ALTERA CORP.

AMERICAN MICROSYSTEMS

AMKOR TECHNOLOGY INC.

ANALOG DEVICES

ATMEL CORP.

BENCHMARK ELECTRONICS INC.

BURR-BROWN CORP.

CHIPS & TECHNOLOGIES INC.

CREE RESEARCH INC.

CTS CORP.

CYPRESS SEMICONDUCTOR CORP.

CYRIX CORP.

DALLAS SEMICONDUCTOR CORP.

DII GROUP INC.

FLEXTRONICS INTERNATIONAL

GALILEO TECHNOLOGY LTD.

GENESIS MICROCHIP INC.

INTEGRATED DEVICE TECH INC.

INTEL CORP.

INTL RECTIFIER CORP.

JABIL CIRCUIT INC.

JDS UNIPHASE CORP.

KEMET CORP.

LATTICE SEMICONDUCTOR CORP.

LEVEL ONE COMMUNICATIONS INC.

LINEAR TECHNOLOGY CORP.

LSI LOGIC CORP.

M/A-COM INC. .

MAXIM INTEGRATED PRODUCTS

MEMC ELECTRONIC MATRIALS INC.

MICREL INC.

MICROCHIP TECHNOLOGY INC.

MICRON TECHNOLOGY INC.

MONOLITHIC MEMORIES INC.

MOSTEK CORP.

NATIONAL SEMICONDUCTOR
    CORP.

NEOMAGIC CORP.

PLEXUS CORP.

PMC-SIERRA INC.

POWER INTEGRATIONS INC.

REMEC INC.

SANMINA CORP.

SDL INC.

SEMTECH CORP.

SIPEX CORP.

SMART MODULAR TECHNOLGS INC.

SOLECTRON CORP.

SEMICONDUCTORS *(CONTINUED)*

TEXAS INSTRUMENTS INC.

TRANSWITCH CORP.

UNITRODE CORP.

VITESSE SEMICONDUCTOR CORP.

VLSI TECHNOLOGY INC.

XILINX INC.

ZILOG INC.

SOAPS AND DETERGENTS

ALBERTO-CULVER CO — CL B

AVON PRODUCTS

BLOCK DRUG — CL A

CHESEBROUGH-POND'S INC.

CHURCH & DWIGHT INC.

CLOROX CO/DE

COLGATE-PALMOLIVE CO.

DIAL CORP.ORATION

ECOLAB INC.

FABERGE INC.

FACTOR (MAX) CO — CL A

HELENA RUBINSTEIN INC.

HELENE CURTIS INDS.

LANVIN-CHARLES OF THE RITZ

LAUDER ESTEE COS INC. — CL A

MARY KAY CORP.

NCH CORP.

NEUTROGENA CORP.

NOXELL — CL B

PROCTER & GAMBLE CO.

PUREX INDUSTRIES INC.

REVLON INC. — CL A

SHULTON INC.

SURGICAL AND MEDICAL PRODUCTS

ACUSON CORP.

ADAC LABORATORIES

AFFYMETRIX INC.

AMERICAN HOSPITAL SUPPLY

AMERICAN STERILIZER CO.

AMSCO INTERNATIONAL

ARROW INTERNATIONAL

ARTERIAL VASCULAR ENGR INC.

ATL ULTRASOUND INC.

BALLARD MEDICAL PRODUCTS

BARD (C.R.) INC.

BAXTER INTERNATIONAL INC.

BECTON DICKINSON & CO.

BIOMET INC.

BOSTON SCIENTIFIC CORP.

CLOSURE MEDICAL CORP.

COLLAGEN AESTHETIC INC.

CONMED CORP.

CORDIS CORP.

CUTTER LABORATORIES INC. — CL A

DATASCOPE CORP.

DENTSPLY INTERNATL INC.

DEPUY INC.

GRAHAM FIELD HEALTH PDS

GUIDANT CORP.

GULF SOUTH MED SUPPLY INC.

SURGICAL AND MEDICAL PRODUCTS *(CONTINUED)*

HAEMONETICS CORPORATION

HEART TECHNOLOGY INC.

INSTRUMENTATION LABS INC.

INVACARE CORP.

KENDALL CO.

MARQUETTE MEDICAL SYS.

MAXXIM MEDICAL INC.

MEDTRONIC INC.

MENTOR CORP.

MINIMED INC.

MIRVANT MEDICAL TECHNOLOGIES

NARCO SCIENTIFIC INC.

NELLCOR PURITAN BENNETT INC.

OEC MED SYS INC.

PATTERSON DENTAL CO.

PERCLOSE INC.

PHYSIO-CONTROL INTL CORP.

PSS WORLD MEDICAL INC.

PURITAN-BENNETT CORP.

RESMED INC.

RESPIRONICS INC.

SCIMED LIFE SYSTEMS INC.

SCOTT TECHNOLOGIES INC.

SHERWOOD MEDICAL INDS INC.

SOFAMOR/DANEK GROUP INC.

SPACELABS MED INC.

ST JUDE MEDICAL INC.

STERIS CORP.

STRYKER CORP.

SUMMIT TECHNOLOGY INC.

SUNRISE MEDICAL INC.

TECNOL MEDICAL PRODUCTS INC.

THERMEDICS INC.

THERMO CARDIOSYSTEMS

THERMOTREX CORP.

U S SURGICAL CORP.

VENTRITEX INC.

VISX INC./DE

VITAL SIGNS INC.

XOMED SURGICAL PRODS.

TELEPHONE AND TELECOMMUNICATIONS

ACC CORP.

ADVANCED TELECOMMUNICATIONS

ALC COMMUNICATIONS INC.

ALIANT COMMUNICATIONS INC.

ALLTEL CORP.

AMERICAN TELE & TELEGRAPH

AMERITECH CORP.

BELL ATLANTIC CORP.

BELLSOUTH CORP.

C TEC CORP.

CALL-NET ENTERPRISES – CL B

CENTEL CORP.

CENTURY TELEPHONE ENTERPRISE

CINC.INNATI BELL INC.

CONTEL CORP.

E SPIRE COMMUNICATIONS INC.

ELECTRIC LIGHTWAVE – CL A

EXCEL COMMUNICATIONS INC.

FRONTIER CORP.

GTE-CONTEL

ICG COMMUNICATIONS

IDT CORP.

INTERMEDIA COMMUNICATNS INC.

ITC DELTACOM INC.

IXC COMMUNICATIONS INC.

LCI INTERNATIONAL INC.

TELEPHONE AND TELECOMMUNICATIONS *(CONTINUED)*

MCI COMMUNICATIONS

MCI WORLDWIDE
   COMMUNICATIONS

MCLEODUSA INC. – CL A

NEXTLINK COMM INC. – CL A

NTL INC.

NYNEX CORP.

PACIFIC GATEWAY EXCHANGE INC.

PACIFIC TELECOM INC.

PACIFIC TELESIS GROUP

PRIMUS TELECOMM GROUP INC.

QWEST COMMUNICATION
   INTL. INC.

ROSEVILLE COMMUNICATIONS

RSL COMMUNICATIONS – CL A

SBC COMMUNICATIONS

SOUTHERN NEW ENG TELECOMM

SOUTHERN NEW ENG TELEPHONE

SPRINT (CENTEL)

STAR TELECOMMUNICATIONS INC.

TALK.COM INC.

TELEGLOBE INC.

TELEPHONE & DATA

TELEPORT COMM GRP – CL A

U S WEST INC.

VIATEL INC.

WINSTAR COMMUNICATIONS

WUI INC.

TRUCKING AND AIR COURIER

AIRBORNE FREIGHT CORP.

AMERICAN FREIGHTWAYS CORP.

ARKANSAS BEST-NAVAJO

ARNOLD INDUSTRIES INC.

CAROLINA FREIGHT CORP.

CON FRGHTWY-EMERY-PURLTR

CONSOLIDATED FREIGHTWAYS CP

EMERY-PUROLATOR

FEDERAL EXPRESS CORP.

HEARTLAND EXPRESS INC.

HUNT (JB) TRANSPRT SVCS INC.

IU INTERNATIONAL CORP.

KNIGHT TRANSPORTATION INC.

LANDSTAR SYSTEM INC.

LEASEWAY TRANSPORTATION CORP.

LEE WAY MOTOR FREIGHT INC.

M S CARRIERS INC.

MCLEAN TRUCKING CO.

OVERNITE TRANSPORTATION

PUROLATOR COURIER CORP.

ROADWAY SERVICES INC.

SWIFT TRANSPORTATION CO. INC.

USFREIGHTWAYS CORP.

WERNER ENTERPRISES INC.

YELLOW CORP.

Appendix B

Managerial approach of principal investors

	Typical corporations	LBO associations
Purpose and structure	Organized in perpetuity (long holding times – several decades; divisional structure).	Organized for limited life of fund (short holding time – several years; corporate structure with boards).
Control	Controls, often from senior levels. Single management approach; focus on information flows. Old rules hold; rules slow to change. No responsibility for finance and tax at manager level. 'Understanding' rather than contracts. Stability in positions.	Monitors, not controls. Multiple approaches; focus on compensation, key crisis points, and key financings. Managers obliged to assimilate new rules of the game. Responsible for finance and tax. Written contracts. Focus on changing people if they don't perform.
Decentralization	Corporate headquarters; extensive staff.	No corporate headquarters. Very small staff. (Paid for by fee of 2% of assets under management.)
Synergies	Essential to concept of leverage. Cross-subsidization possible. Consolidation accounts.	Not considered; ignored. Cross-subsidization impossible. No consolidated accounts.
Compensation	Complex system using surrogates for market value but often based on assets under management. Narrow range of increases. No decreases.	Simple system, tied to market. Wide range of increases possible. Decreases possible.

Appendix C

Dynamic Performance Analysis (DPA)

Dynamic Performance Analysis, or DPA, is a set of analytic techniques designed to reveal the underlying dynamics of companies, industries, and capital markets. DPA is specifically designed to avoid some of the implicit – and, we believe, limiting – assumptions of conventional analysis, which we will call Static Performance Analysis, or SPA.

We believe that DPA gives a more accurate portrayal of the state of the economy, an industry, or a company than do the conventional SPA analyses, on which DPA builds. There are two essential differences between DPA and SPA. First is the focus DPA places on understanding dynamics – that is, time-dependent cause-and-effect relationships. Unlike SPA, DPA does not presume equilibrium, although equilibrium can be revealed if it is present. Second, DPA explicitly does not assume that the distribution of results from competitive market processes are normally distributed around an average, as often SPA implicitly assumes. DPA goes to great lengths to observe the actual distribution of results from large samples over extended periods of time. Given these two differences, we believe that SPA is a special case of DPA.

The need to understand dynamic performance is clear, but until now most of the methods used extensions of static analysis rather than seeking to develop dynamic methods from the beginning. As a consequence of using DPA, we have reached conclusions about the nature of corporate performance and the forces driving that performance that are different from many others.

LIMITATIONS OF SPA

SPA is the common set of analyses used to diagnose historic corporate performance, and it is sometimes used as a basis for forecasting future corporate performance. Many of these techniques use rules of thumb based either on the past or on simple extrapolations of the past. These techniques are not designed to detect discontinuities or substantial changes in longer-term performance. As a consequence, SPA rarely does detect these discontinuities. Failure to detect discontinuity can lead to forecasting failures, because past relationships between cause and effect are erroneously expected to hold into the future.

SPA analyses typically cover periods of two to five years, and may occasionally extend to 10-year periods, neglecting what we call 'The Minimum Unit of Analysis', or the business cycle. Generally, the time periods are selected with a reference to the current year, so they may go back two, five, or ten years from today, independent of the economy's or industry's position in the current economic cycle. Such comparisons are often misleading about the causes of past performance and therefore misleading about future possibilities and probabilities.

SPA implicitly presumes continuity and thus may produce results that confirm the embedded assumption. SPA can falsely reveal outstanding (or exceptionally poor) corporate performance, which is in fact not due to company actions but to industry or national economic effects, or the time period selected. Classic examples of 'excellence' often err in this way, identifying, for example, SmithKline Beecham or Bristol-Myers Squibb as outstanding performers, when in fact their performance is indistinguishable, in a statistical sense, from that of the pharmaceutical industry overall.

The traditional SPA can misanalyze cause and effect either because a particularly good or bad period in the economic cycle is selected, or because the duration of the period examined is too short to be economically significant. Often SPA techniques fall into the trap of assuming the future will be more like than unlike the past. In making this assumption, SPA ignores the dynamic feedback loops in the economy (for example, between buyers and sellers, or between corporations and their investment analysts or regulators).

SPA is also powerless to explain such phenomena as the regular variation in the returns to investors in cyclical businesses, even though the cycle of the business is relatively well known. Nor does SPA provide a compelling rationale for the existence of 'bubbles' in stock prices and their driving forces. DPA can readily offer explanations for both these phenomena and other complex phenomena like them. As a result, DPA dramatically reduces the rate of false-positive conclusions that are an artifact of the analytic method selected.

Finally, when SPA tackles the topic of statistics they often assume a normal bell-shaped distribution of results. We know, however, from a great deal of experience that often results are not distributed in a bell shape but rather some other shape. These different shapes result in different views on the probability of events occurring (how does the 'once-in-a-century' hurricane occur twice in a decade in the United Kingdom, for example), or different views on the risk one faces or even the potential rewards.

DIFFERENCES BETWEEN DPA AND SPA

DPA does not seek to reject conventional economic analysis, but it does not rely totally on them. Specifically, DPA is built to enhance the understanding of rivalry, barriers to entry and exit, the relationship between industry structure, corporate conduct, and corporate performance, and the role of analyst expectations in influencing outcomes. DPA seeks to place all these effects in an explicitly dynamic context, not in a static context.

DPA is not proposed as a substitute for SPA, just as nuclear physics is not a substitute for Newtonian physics. Indeed, the basic framework for DPA analyses is the same as that for SPA, for example, the key balance of power between suppliers and buyers, the price-setting role of the marginal producer, the importance of barriers to exit and entrance. Rather, DPA builds on SPA and puts it into context. There are many situations where the simpler techniques of SPA will suffice. DPA is most useful in uncovering causes of long-term change and alerting the analyst to potential sources of long-term risk. DPA provides context for SPA.

There are six primary differences between DPA and SPA:

1. DPA's primary focus on investors and their expectations as an explicit part of the analysis of the potential for perhaps temporary value creation.

2. DPA explicitly acknowledges the potential importance of feedback and has developed methods to detect its possible presence. DPA techniques seek to avoid making the assumption of continuity; in fact, they are designed to spot discontinuities such as the oil shocks of the 1970s, or the rapid deterioration of the computer hardware industry of the early 1980s, or the emergence of a restructured telecommunications market after the breakup of the Bell System. DPA finds continuity if it is there. If it is not, then discontinuity is revealed.

3. DPA focuses on the cycle of TRS returns as the basic time unit of analysis. DPA acknowledges that the selection of time period can dramatically affect the conclusions drawn from SPA. For example, if two companies in the same industry are competing but one is early in its cycle and is improving in performance, while the other is late in its cycle and watching performance deteriorate, DPA will not judge one as better than the other until the two are compared at similar points in their cycle. SPA may not consider this possibility, and thus may conclude that one company is inherently superior to the other.

4. DPA seeks to put performance analysis in a dynamic statistical context so that one may easily understand whether, if a change is seen, the change is likely to be meaningful. SPA often does this as well, but there are special problems that have to be solved if one is going to attempt this in a dynamic fashion with a small number of companies. For example, non-bell-shaped (Gaussian) distributions and year-to-year changes in the shape of the distribution itself can play havoc with using common measures such as averages and variations from those averages.

5. Unlike static performance analysis, DPA looks at a wide range of performance periods and examines them from many different perspectives.

6. DPA does not presume a normal distribution of results but rather uses empirical methods to gauge the most probable shape of the distribution.

SPA seems as if it were designed to focus on more mature businesses, operating in a slowly changing environment. SPA is well suited for value investors. DPA is more focused on growth investors – their concerns and their risks. By focusing on the interaction of linear and nonlinear systems, DPA provides more insight into longer-term sources of risk than does SPA.

More advances will be made in DPA techniques over time, since DPA is at a relatively early stage of development.

ORIGINS OF DPA

DPA is an outgrowth of the S-curve and discontinuity analyses that were fashioned in the mid-1980s as a result of the work done to support the writing of *Innovation: The Attacker's Advantage*. Our family of analyses developed incrementally/organically as the needs emerged. We did not know at the beginning that we were going to need to invent a new analytic method.

Fig. AC.1 S-Curve

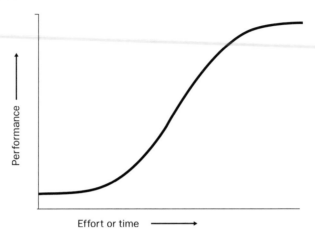

These analyses suggested that there were regular patterns of performance and these patterns were not straight-line projections of the past. Rather, industries start up and follow a very regular pattern of initially slow progress, then a rapid acceleration for a while until the maximum rate of progress is reached, and then a steady decline until equilibrium (either static or dynamic, e.g., cyclical) is established, as their potential or limit is approached. The pattern is shown in Figure AC.1.

One of the implications of the S-curve is that productivity, a key determinant of economic success, varies in a regular but perhaps unexpected way (see Figure AC.2). Productivity is nothing more than output, or performance, divided by input. Put another way, it is the slope of the curve above. It begins at a low level as everyone learns the new approach, then accelerates rapidly as the easier problems are solved, and then begins to collapse, just at the point some expect it to accelerate, because the limits of the S-curve are being reached and only the very tough problems remain to be solved. As the limit is being approached, the problems are getting harder faster than the problem solvers are getting smarter. The result is a dramatic fall-off, which sets up the opportunity for an attacker to enter the field if a better, and often different, approach can be found.

As the evolution begins to approach maturity, a discontinuity can result, changing the basic competitive structure of the industry. This has been the case many times in electronics, pharmaceuticals, consumer products, transportation, and other fields. Discontinuities are the vortex of the 'gales of creative destruction' that Schumpeter described half a century ago. We represent the discontinuity as shown in Figure AC.3.

Fig. AC.2 Productivity

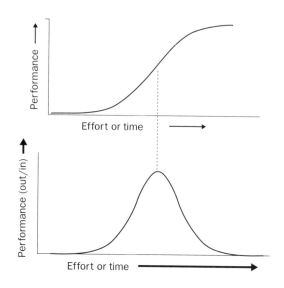

Fig. AC.3 Discontinuity between S-curves

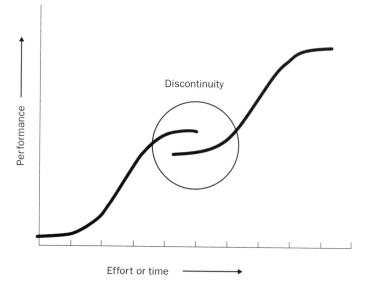

These analyses are not always relevant (for example, in analyzing the performance of the oil industry) because of exogenous events that overwhelm any regular economic process. But if the techniques are not appropriate they automatically demonstrate nonsense results, which indicates to analysts that they have to look elsewhere for answers.

BASIC QUESTIONS DPA SEEKS TO ANSWER

DPA seeks to see the company in an industry context and an industry in a national context.

As with SPA, DPA seeks an answer to the question: How much of the observed company performance is due to managerial action and how much is due to other factors, such as industry or national economic conditions? The question is key, because it underpins the performance evaluation and reward systems (the internal feedback/control systems of the corporation). The answer to this query also shapes the key question management must ask: Should we focus on improving our internal operations or should we be seeking an adjustment in our portfolio (to make an investment or a sale)? If the answer is internal, management can control it. If it is external, management cannot directly control it other than through affecting the industry structure (merger or spin-off) or political action.

The basic question of the sources of performance gives rise to other key questions of concern to management, such as:

- Where is the power – with the attacker or the defender? How has the power changed over time, and why?

- Will the leader lose during a discontinuity, as has often been the case historically? How and when will the transition from defender to attacker occur? What are the economics to the attackers and defenders? What are the economics of attack, and how does profit flow?

- How will the effects of analysts' forecasts affect our strategy?

BASIC DPA ANALYSES

SPA often implicitly imagines relationships in business as 'linear' relationships, that is, the more one puts in, the more one gets out. The proportion does not change over time. These relationships are simple to understand and communicate. They are also simple to analyze, since they involve straightforward, low-level mathematics. Often these simple relationships give rise to rules of thumb, for example, multiply the earnings by a price-to-earnings multiple to get the stock price.

There are some situations in business where these relationships and the shortcuts built on them provide accurate answers, particularly in the very short term. But as the period of analysis extends to multiple years, the probability that relationships will follow these simple linear patterns is greatly reduced. More likely the relationships are more complex, and the complexity confounds accurate, unambiguous interpretation. In the longer term, substantial feedback often exists. For example, analysts begin to expect stocks to outperform and they build these expectations into their models. At some point, the company cannot keep up with the constantly expanding expectations and it underperforms. As it begins to underperform, analysts change their models to reduce their expectations. Feedback between expectations and performance has emerged.

Feedback can, and often does, lead to cycles that are much more complex to analyze than are simple linear relationships. Examples of these more complex patterns include the way in which a new product substitutes for an old one, the way product prices react to the announcement of the construction of a new plant, and the way stock prices react to the emergence of a new category of products (the Internet bubble). Feedback systems can be very complex to analyze, since the strength of the feedback itself can change. Feedback – and the changes in feedback over time – is the explanation behind the admonition to leaders everywhere: 'Beware: the organization you lead contains the seeds of its own destruction.' The job of DPA is to find those seeds early on and to understand how they work in order to enhance their chances of success or to dull them.

Specifically, DPA is a baker's dozen set of basic analyses that are capable of revealing and understanding these underlying patterns and complexities.

1. S-curve Analysis

S-curves represent the relationship between input (e.g., either resources or time) and output (e.g., product performance, or sales, or earnings). These relationships show a classic pattern of slow initiation, followed by rapid progress, which is then followed by deceleration as an asymptote, or limit, is reached. These patterns are called S-curves after their shape, which is an S tacked at the bottom left and drawn out to the top right.

Key questions include: What limits the present approach? How quickly will that limit be approached? What alternatives are available that might exceed the present limit? Who possesses the power to implement those approaches? When are they likely to use that power?

The mathematics of S-curves were best described in 1971 by Fisher and Pry, who asserted that all products grow by substitution for existing products. They imagined that the rate of substitution was proportional to the amount of product that had already been substituted and the proportion of the total product yet to be substituted for. If the amount of product was very small, the rate of substitution would be very small, even though the amount to be substituted for was large because there was so little experience in the art of substitution. As that experience grew, the amount substituted for would be greater and the rate of substitution would rise. Near the end of the cycle the rate would slow.

The approach Fisher and Pry developed has been repeated in many other fields, for example, epidemiology. Diseases spread in exactly the way Fisher and Pry imagined one product substitutes for another. Networks grow this way as well, for example, networks of facsimile machines or Internet sites. In the very early days, there is no one to hook up to so the rate of penetration is slow. After a while, when there are more and more people hooked into the network, the utility of hooking into the network increases, and so does that rate of hookup. Eventually, nearly everyone who is going to hook up has hooked up, and the rate of increase slows again. This is the classic S-curve, which combines both positive and negative feedback systems in its structure.

In verbal mathematical terms the basic (differential) equation is written as:

The rate of change = constant * (the proportion of the total substitution that has occurred) * (the proportion of the substitution that has not occurred)

The constant in this equation relates to the rate of substitution. It is called a rate constant. If it is high, the substitution is fast. If it is low, the substitution is slow.

Since the total amount of substitution is 100 per cent, the proportion not yet substituted for is 100 per cent minus the proportion that has been substituted for.

If the proportion substituted for is x, the constant is k, and time is t, then the mathematical equation is:

$dx/dt = k* (x)* (1 - x)$ Equation 1

This equation can be solved to show the relationship between the proportion substituted and time. That equation is written as:

$x = .5* \{1 - \tanh[(t - t_{mid})/t_{crit}]\}$ Equation 2

t_{mid} and t_{crit} are two time constants that result from solving the equations. t_{mid} is the year the substitution is half completed. t_{crit} is the time it takes for the substitution to go from 10 per cent complete to 90 per cent complete. It is a rate constant. By including t_{mid} and t_{crit}, the rate constant 'k' is eliminated. 'Tanh' is the 'hyperbolic tangent', a basic geometric function that is strange to most people who are not engineers. It is a mathematical *function*. A function is an explicit relationship between two quantities. For example, we can define a function that we will call 2x. What 2x does is convert any value of x into a value of 2˚x. If x = 5, then the function is equal to 10. If x = 200, then the function is equal to 400. Tanh works in exactly the same way, although the results would be different from 2x. In the case of Equation 2, the value for the quantity inside the brackets that come immediately after 'tanh', $[(t − t_{mid})/t_{crit}]$, plays the role of x in 2x. If a value is provided for $[(t − t_{mid})/t_{crit}]$, tanh will give a number that can then be used in Equation 2 to find the answer. All computers have 'tanh' built into their mathematical tables, so the function is easy to use. Equation 2 is the mathematical expression of the S-curve.

Given this equation, the analyst's job is to determine the constants t_{mid} and t_{crit}. Once this is done, the history of the S-curve can be used to forecast the future, if one believes the S-curve forecast will represent the future.

To test the robustness of the S-curve approach, we have determined t_{mid} and t_{crit} for evolution of sales in each industry. The overall fit of the industry experience is quite good, as shown in Figure AC.3.

Fig. AC.3 Sales evolution patterns

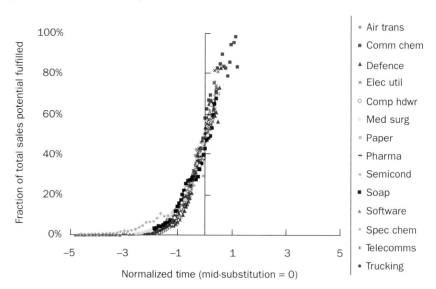

We have not included the oil industry in this analysis, since its prices, and therefore sales, have been so strongly affected by the formation and evolution of OPEC.

The overall pattern is quite clear. It is also clear that the model is not a perfect fit, at least with the constants we used. The semiconductor industry had a bit of a faster start than normal, and the chemical industry in its maturity is acquiring a cyclical pattern, which is not unexpected, rather than the straight-forward 'topping out' that the simple Fisher-Pry model assumes.

The time constants that were used to develop these curves tell us something about the rate at which the industry is changing. It is not surprising that the slowest evolution comes from commodity chemicals and the fastest from software. This is in accord with our intuition.

One final point should be made about this formulation of the S-curve: The slope of the S-curve, as pointed out above, is very similar to the bell-shaped curve commonly associated with random processes. The curve derived from an understanding of randomness is known as a normal distribution, referring to the expected distribution of outcomes if a process is normal. If one assumes that the various companies in the economy are each at some state of their own S-curve, then it is not unreasonable to assume that their growth patterns will be distributed in proportion to the slope of the S-curve. By examining these distributions, one should in principle be able to easily determine whether the underlying processes in the economy derive from random processes or an S-curve. The complication is that the normal distribution and the slope of the S-curve are almost impossible to differentiate, in any practical sense, from one another. Thus it is almost impossible to differentiate between the possible underlying mechanisms producing the results being observed from these distributions alone, since they are indistinguishable. One has to resort to other analyses to argue the differences. We believe that the great weight of the evidence supports the S-curve hypothesis rather than the randomness hypothesis.

2. Discontinuity and long-term-risk analysis

S-curves often end in discontinuity. Discontinuity analysis seeks to understand when a new S-curve is about to begin, and estimates how and when it will interact with the existing S-curve. Discontinuities can occur for a variety of reasons, including the emergence of a new technology (e.g., the

Internet, or computer software); a new approach (e.g., hub-and-spoke reorganization of airline traffic patterns); a change in industry structure (e.g., a merger of two large players; governmental intervention, as in the case of the Department of Justice breaking up the old Bell System; or the formation of a cartel, as in the case of OPEC in the 1970s).

Discontinuities can lead to non-diversifiable risks for the investor and for management. DPA also seeks to identify and classify long-term risks (sudden changes from an apparently regular pattern) rather than shorter-term variations in performance, as is often the case with SPA.

While the discontinuities are wild, they are not without their own predictable characteristics. We believe that discontinuities occur when they do, last as long as they do, and have the effects that they do for fundamental economic reasons – often, at present, discoverable only after the fact, but nevertheless discoverable.

At the simplest level, discontinuities occur when the costs of the attacking business become equal to, and then less than, the costs of the defending business. It is at that moment that cash is being transferred out of the bank accounts of the defenders and into the accounts of the attackers. In reality, one has to consider the specifics of two different costs. The first is the *full cost* necessary to reach the target levels of returns, for example, a 15 per cent return on invested capital. These costs include all the cash costs for supporting the business (including the costs of developing, making, selling, distributing, and servicing the product) as well as depreciation of capital equipment, amortization of goodwill, and profit for the bond and equity holders.

The second cost is the *cash cost*. This is the 'rock-bottom' cost needed to avoid losing cash. Cash costs are always less than the full costs. They do not include depreciation, amortization, and profit for the equity holders (although interest for the debt holders is part of the cash cost in the vast majority of cases). The difference between the cash costs and the full costs is called the *margin*.

In practice, the definition of costs – a seemingly straightforward exercise – can become a bit more complicated. If one is running a nationalized industry, from the point of view of the government, taxes that in a normal business are considered part of cash costs can be, if required, considered part of margin. The government can decide to forgo these payments from the company in order to meet other objectives. This is happening in the

United States, where local authorities give tax abatements to companies to encourage them to locate their facilities in the area. Another example is provided by Internet equity providers, who do not ask that cash costs be returned in the short run, hoping that the company they are investing in will establish such a strong position that it will be able to eventually operate in the black. Normally, an equity provider would insist on profitable operations at the full-cost level, but so eager are investors to capture the value implied by the growth potential of the Internet these days, they are willing to gamble that the payoffs will eventually be there. And for some, but not all, they will be.

In the vast majority of commerce, however, we can understand the essence of what is going on only by considering full and cash costs. These costs are generally declining for both the attacker and the defender, but they are falling faster for attackers, who are earlier in the evolution of their business than are the defenders. On the other hand, the attacker's costs are generally higher in the beginning than the defender's, since the attacker is just getting started. The result is a crossover point, the point where the attacker's cost becomes equal to, and then less than, the defender's cost. Since the attackers and defenders are both concerned with cash and full costs, there are actually four points of intersection, as Figure AC.4 shows.

The simplest point to understand in this exhibit is the 'conservative entry point.' This is the point where the full cost for the defender and attacker are equal. At this point, if the defender wants to defend, it can do so by cut-

Fig. AC.4 Discontinuity timing

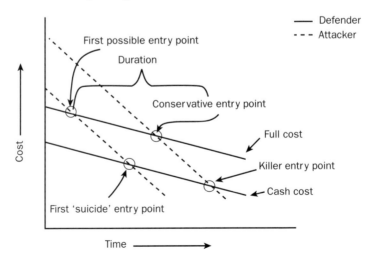

ting prices (or the equivalent move of increasing the value of the product or service to the customer with no increase in price), and thus cut into its margins. To meet this defence, the attacker will have to reciprocate by cutting prices and cutting into its margins. It is a rough game, and the ultimate winner is the competitor with the lowest cash costs.

The earliest point at which it makes conventional economic sense to attack is when the cash costs of the attacker are equal to the full costs of the defender. We call this the 'point of naked attack', because the attacker is economically quite vulnerable at this point. The attacker will sacrifice all profit margin but will not be losing out-of-pocket cash as long as the defender does not react, which is highly unlikely. The defender is much more likely to retaliate by cutting prices without risking negative cash flows, thus bringing real economic harm, and perhaps death, to the attacker. There are few successful attacks at this point, but many are attempted nevertheless.

For the extremely conservative attacker, waiting until full costs are less than the cash costs of the defender is a safe strategy. Few get to pursue it, however, because the game is often over by this point. There is one other significant point at which an attacker can attack, and that is where the cash costs of the attacker are equal to the cash costs of the defender. The full cost of the attacker at this point is usually no less than the full cost of the defender. Often it is more. But the attacker, if it is willing to not recover its full cost, can compete at the defender's price. The defender's main weapon, reducing price to its cash costs in order to bleed the attacker, cannot work at this point, because the attacker has the same cash costs as the defender. The deep-pockets defence is still applicable here, since the defender can subsidize its cash costs from another division or the corporate coffers. But unlike the point of naked attack, the defender will bear real pain here, and thus may be less likely to be as aggressive. There is still plenty of risk and exposure for the attacker here, but less so than at the first, naked, point of attack.

When the discontinuity is over, it will have taken an amount of time roughly equal to that between the points of naked and killer attack. To the customer's benefit, prices will have fallen substantially, by an amount roughly equal to the defender's original margins plus the value of the relative productivity improvements over the duration of the discontinuity. So it can be a meaningful amount – often 25 per cent or more of the price at the beginning of the discontinuity.

Fig. AC.5 Discontinuity timing

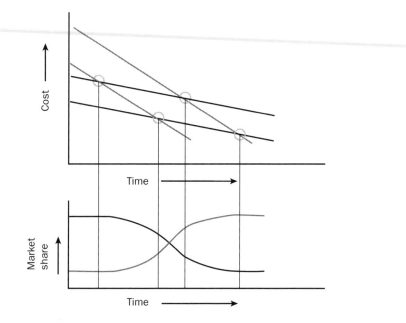

Our empirical market evidence suggests that the transformation of market shares occurs in parallel with the process of price change (see Figure AC.5).

Of course, in real commerce, matters are rarely this simple (if the forego-ing discussion can be called simple). First there is lack of information about the present. The defender and attacker rarely know each other's cost struc-tures. They rarely know each other's productivity rates and how they will play out. They rarely know the proclivity of the other side to take the risk of a price war. Neither knows how the customer will react, and neither can predict the degree of cross-subsidization, willingness to deplete reserves, and cleverness in shifting some of the costs onto others (e.g., suppliers). So the principles outlined above may be hard to apply in practice. Nevertheless, it might be comforting to know that at least there are some principles at work, that they do explain what has happened, and that they can be used to pre-dict what might happen in the future. Having these principles, if not a tool kit for their application, is better, we think, than believing that the disconti-nuity and its effects cannot be understood. They can be.

While there are no systematic statistics that we know of, we believe that one-third of all attackers die in the attack because they attack too early.

They underestimate the resourcefulness and resiliency of the defender. We think another third die because they attack too late. In their efforts to avoid risk, they take the ultimate risk. They wait until positions have been established by others. Of the remaining one-third, the majority fail because while they have a vision of what they would like to accomplish, they cannot put that vision into practice. Most attackers fail. But the attack succeeds. The wave after wave of attackers constitutes Schumpeter's gale.

3. Feedback analysis: the evolution of cycles and self-correcting mechanisms

Each effect has a cause that can ultimately undermine the effect. Prices become too high or low, resources are added too quickly or slowly, and this is what leads to the basic cyclical behavior of all markets. The nature and effects of this feedback cannot be ignored, but are difficult to grasp if one is not trained to look for them. Feedback analyses seek to detect these relationships and understand their consequences, if not their causes. Feedback is ubiquitous because control systems, which are feedback systems, are ubiquitous.

4. Understanding the minimum data unit: cycles of performance

Feedback, and the processes that give rise to it, are responsible for producing cycles in the economy and within industries. These cycles determine the minimum unit of time over which effects have to be measured. Unless one is measuring the cycle itself, it does no good to take one measurement on the upside of a cycle to try to forecast the future. The linear rule of thumb will not work. Thus the minimum unit of analysis in DPA is determined by the length of the business cycle, since this is the only unit that can give insight into the nature of the system. Since, in the United States, the TRS cycle has varied between three and four years, this is the minimum unit of time one must use to draw any conclusions about performance. Analyses that look at shorter periods of time run the risk of mistaking random variation in the system (noise) for meaningful effect. To be safe, one has to look at two cycles, since one cycle can be aberrant. We have used a seven-year period as the basic unit of analysis, since this covers two full cycles of TRS variation.

5. Noise-reduction analysis

Noise (randomness) is always present along with the regularities that the system contains. The noise has to be filtered out before an analysis of the regularities can be made. The trick is to sort out one from the other without confusing them. What is random is dependent on the decision one has to make using the data. What is noise to the CEO is signal to the day trader. A basic filtering method is to use seven-year averages, since this will filter out the noise of the variation in the business cycle. There are other methods available, but they are not explored in this study.

6. Renormalization analysis: the economy, the industry, and the company

To understand the sources of a company's performance, one has to understand the contributions to the company's performance that are made by the overall state of the economy and industry in which the company participates. Industry performance can, and often does, ride on general economy conditions, and one has to account for this. Company performance can, and often does, ride on industry performance, so this gap has to be understood as well. Renormalization analysis allows a visualization of these complex relationships.

7. Investor expectations analysis: the creation of bubbles

DPA takes the investor's perspective, seeking to understand how companies create value over time, not just once. Unlike traditional SPA, DPA focuses as much on the investment community and its expectations (and the changes in its expectations) as it does on the company and industry, since the expectations of future free cash flow influence important strategic variables for the corporation, such as market cap, price-to-earnings ratio, and TRS. There are two specific attributes of DPA that distinguish it:

1. DPA focuses on TRS. As a result, DPA can result in a perspective different from that of methods focused just on EPS, mutiples, growth rates, or market capitalizations.

2. DPA focuses attention on investor forecasting methods, since these methods are intimately related to the values of equities and how those values change over time.

One particular application of our understanding of investor forecasting methods is the way analysts forecast P/E ratios. This is particularly relevant to the understanding of attacker performance that comes directly from an understanding of the inevitable evolution of industries and companies.

Let us apply this approach to the evolution of 'bubbles'. First, assume that the evolution of an industry follows the S-curve that we have described above. Second, assume that analysts, unable to credibly forecast the long-term future of an industry, fall back on 'accepted' approaches, say, multiples analysis, based on current earnings and the short-term forecasts for these earnings. Essentially these analysts forecast the future based on the near-term past. This approach has a long history.

Figure AC.6 shows the S-curve. If one assumes, for the moment, that this curve is both knowable and known, one can use it to calculate the present value of the future cash flow streams of the corporation. This value is conventionally assumed to be equal to the market value of the corporation in any given year. Given the S-curve, the Net Present Value (or NPV) can be calculated for each year, resulting in a new curve, the NPV curve, which is similar to, but not the same as, the S-curve. The difference between the curves stems from the discounting process itself.

The important point is that the discounting process accelerates the evolution of market value. Market value is expected to develop more rapidly than earnings growth due to the discounting process alone.

Fig. AC.6 Evolution of earnings and market value

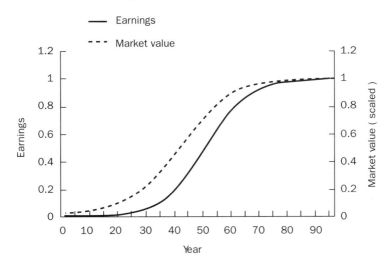

Fig. AC.7 Evolution of earnings, market value, and TRS with perfect forecasting

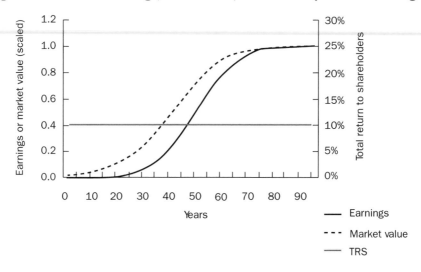

Given the evolution of market value, it is easy to calculate the total return to shareholders in this situation where the analysts have accurately forecasted the future. In this case, as Figure AC.7 shows, the total return to shareholders will always be exactly equal to the cost of equity – which, in this example, is assumed to be 10 per cent.

This result often surprises executives, many of whom may not believe it is realistic. The TRS should reflect the growth, but this is not the case. Rather, if analysts can correctly foresee the future, they can value it – in so doing, they can make sure that at all points in time the annual returns will be equal. The implication is that the P/E ratio will be very high in the early years. After all, no matter how small the sales base is, if the next 50 years of sales could be accurately foreseen – because that is our assumption in this case – then the value would be very high, as Figure AC.8 shows.

But this is clearly not a reasonable case. No analyst ever gets it right for the future of the industry, much less the company. Analysts are human, with all the failings of any other human. Recency and anchoring are two of them. *Recency* is the error that most of us make when we pay more attention to recent data than all the data. *Anchoring* is a state of mind that makes it difficult for us to change our minds once we make a choice about how we think the world works. These two well-known cognitive errors often combine to produce an analysis method that takes the present and applies it to the future. This method is often eminently reasonable at the time but inconsistent with knowledge about the S-curve.

Fig. AC.8 Evolution of earnings, market value, TRS, and P/E with perfect foreknowledge

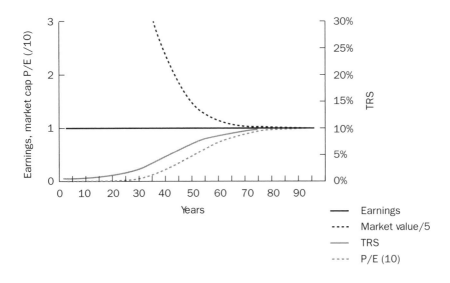

We call this forecasting approach the LINE approach, because it asserts that the investment analyst forecasts in a straight line from the past into the future. LINE stands for Linear INvestor Expectations. How does LINE work? At the beginning of the curve, the analyst forecasts a low rate of growth. The forecast will turn out to be very low – an insight we gain because we understand how the S-curve evolves. As time passes, the analyst forecasts higher growth because the business has evolved more quickly than expected. This happy situation persists until the midpoint of the S-curve, where the extrapolated growth of the business starts to exceed the actual potential of the business. Saturation has been reached. After this point, analyst forecasts are in excess of the actual evolution of the business, causing persistent disappointment (often called the 'hockey stick' curve). This scenario is illustrated in Figure AC.9.

The evolution of systematic, if complex, forecasting errors can easily be seen in this exhibit.

What is the impact of these changes on the evolution of market capitalization (net present value)? Let's refer to Figure AC.10.

The low early earnings forecast turns into lower net present value forecasts until the midpoint of the market capitalization cycle, which evolves earlier than the earnings, at which point the market capitalization forecasts begin to exceed the 'perfect foreknowledge' case. One might think of the

Fig. AC.9 Evolution of bubbles

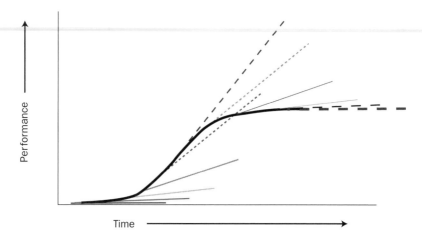

Fig. AC.10 Evolution of earnings and market capitalization with and without accurate foreknowledge

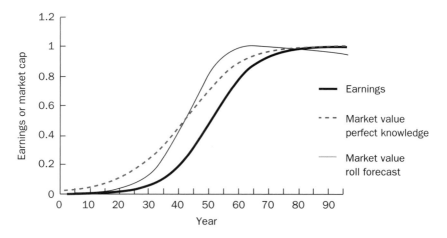

gap between the 'accurate foreknowledge' case and the actual (if 'actual' is adequately represented by the LINE methodology) as a 'bubble'. After the midpoint of the market value curve, the bubble is positive – that is, the estimated value is in excess of the fair value. Before the midpoint the bubble is negative – the estimated value is below the fair value.

Of course, the gaps between estimated and fair value translate into changes in the observed total return to shareholders. The 'perfect foreknowledge' case and the LINE case are compared in Figure AC. 11.

As Figure AC.11 demonstrates, with LINE forecasting, the TRS is above the levels of 'perfect foreknowledge' until the midpoint of the earning evolution (not the market value), and then it dips slightly below the 'perfect foreknowledge' case, at least in this case, where we assume that 15 years has elapsed between 10 per cent saturation and 90 per cent saturation.

What are the implications of the LINE approach for the P/E ratio? The answer can be seen in Figure AC.12.

Fig. AC.11 Evolution of earnings, market value, and TRS with perfct foreknowledge and LINE estimates

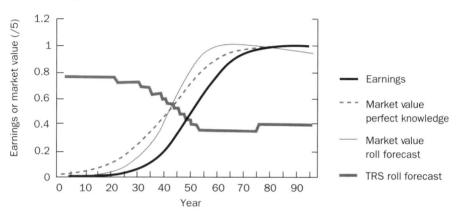

Fig. AC.12 Evolution of earnings, market value, TRS and P/E with perfect foreknowledge and LINE forecasts

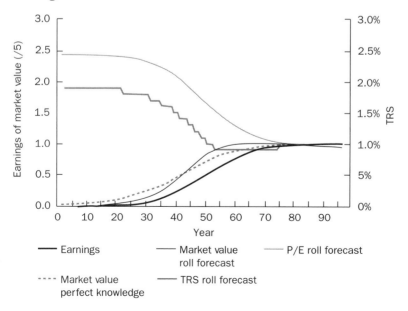

Here we see that P/E is much lower than that in the 'perfect foreknowledge' case. In fact, this case would look much more reasonable to the typical senior executive, except that it forecasts long periods when high TRS is associated with high P/E, a case the typical value investor would not recognize. LINE forecasts do support the intuitions of the growth investor more than those of the value investor.

The case that we have developed above has assumed, as we have said, a 15-year transition time. However, as we have seen, transition times have been shrinking. What happens if the transition time is, say, three years rather than 15? The answers are as follows. First, with perfect foreknowledge the evolution of market value occurs, as before, sooner than the evolution of earnings, but the differences are more pronounced (see Figure AC.13). Second, when fast transitions are combined with LINE forecasts, the evolution of market capitalization shows the formation of a very dangerous situation – the existence of a period of time when the estimated market capitalization is substantially in excess of the long-term-equilibrium market capitalization. This is depicted as the peak in Figure AC.14. In this particular case, with a three-year transition time, the peak is more than double the final market value, indicating that at some point there will be a collapse of stock price of 50 per cent or more. This is a period of great risk for shareholders and for management, which can be caught unawares.

Fig. AC.13 Evolution of earnings and market value with fast transitions time and perfect foreknowledge

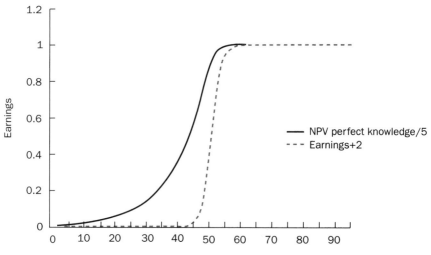

Fig. AC.14 Fast evolution of earnings and TRS with perfect foreknowledge and LINE forecast

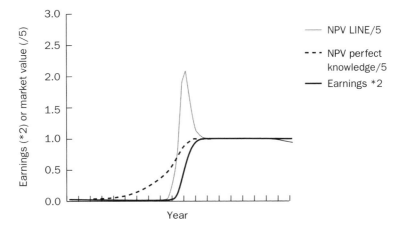

The period has a substantial duration – about 10 years in this case – and occurs before market saturation has occurred. In fact, the initial period of risk occurs at about the midpoint of the earnings evolution. It is important to note that this bubble is entirely due to forecasting errors about the unknowability, at least at this point in time, of what the future will bring. These behaviours have been seen in our case studies, and we have described and analyzed them. Now, however, we are able to say that these behaviours may result directly from forecasting inadequacies rather than from managerial action. This may have implications for management, including management incentives, if executives come to believe that it is, in fact, the cause of the collapse.

Of course, this sinuous development of market capitalization will be reflected in the total return to shareholders (see Figure AC.15).

Initial TRS is very high, as all venture capitalists know, and then crashes well into negative ranges. The risk for new investors here is extreme. Not only is past performance not a guarantee of future performance, but if past performance has been strong, it is a warning signal – although, due to the long duration of high TRS, an ambiguous warning signal – of impending trouble. The period of consistently declining returns can last for several years, as many high-tech investors know. Someone who is very adventurous can 'buy on the dip', but laser-precision forecasting is necessary to avoid getting killed.

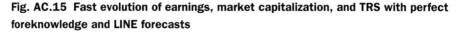

Fig. AC.15 Fast evolution of earnings, market capitalization, and TRS with perfect foreknowledge and LINE forecasts

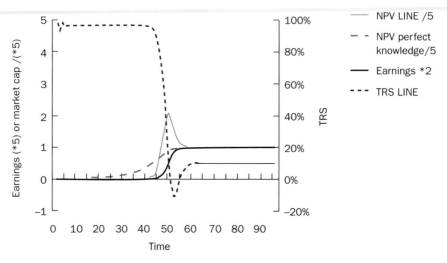

Fig. AC.16 Fast evolution of earnings, market capitalization, TRS, and P/E with perfect foreknowledge and LINE forecasts

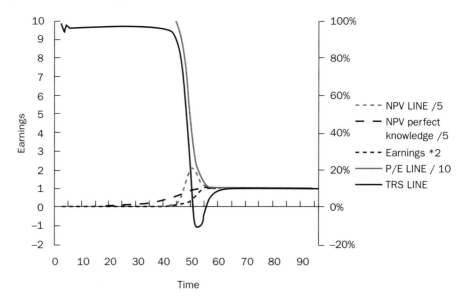

A similar picture emerges for the P/E ratio, as Figure AC.16 shows.

Price-to-earnings ratios in the early days can be exceptionally high, as recent events show, but they too come crashing down as realistic expectations begin to set in. In fact, it is the crashing P/E ratio, combined with the moderately slowing earnings growth rates, that squash the market capitalization and historic TRS results.

The point is that as the pace of change in the economy accelerates, one can anticipate more of these 'risks' – which are really inevitabilities unless the state of forecasting changes – rather than less.

These bubbles, then, are an inevitable consequence of the evolution of industries and the inability of analysts to correctly forecast the future. Understood in this way, a bubble actually has some analytic value. When the bubble is bursting, it may be a strong signal that the S-curve of the present business model is coming to an end.

8. Entry and exit analysis: avoiding survivor bias

Determined to avoid the problems of 'survivor bias' that often plague analysts, DPA explicitly focuses on rates of entry and exit. These dynamics are crucially important in determining or reflecting (it is not yet clear which) industry performance. In doing so, DPA places more emphasis on understanding the entrants and leavers in an industry.

9. Periphery analysis: analyzing the practices of entrants

We characterize entrants as being at the periphery of an industry. Entrants have been found to account for most of the excess performance in an industry or an economy. Hence the periphery is extremely important to an understanding of the economics of industry dynamics. The periphery is a vital part of Schumpeter's 'gales of creative destruction'. Understanding how companies at the periphery create value, how long they are able to create value, and why they cease creating excess value is at the heart of DPA.

10. Barriers to entry analysis

Not all industries welcome new entrants. Understanding which industries welcome new entrants, and which do not, is an important part of DPA.

11. Confidence analysis

This is a set of analyses developed to determine the confidence one has that the results being observed are real and are not due to an artifact. These analyses will be explained in more detail below. There is, we think, an analogy in the science of meteorology. What is 'normal' weather for this time of year, or for the year in general? This question, as we all know in this era of global warming, is not unimportant. Governments are spending millions of dollars trying to tease the answer out of nature. New evidence is being gathered that, in addition to helping resolve this environmental debate, may also illustrate the difficulty in understanding 'normalcy' in the capital markets. As *Science* magazine reported in mid-1999:

George Washington's winter at Valley Forge in 1777–78, when temperatures fell as low as –15 degrees C, was relatively mild for those days; some years, New York Harbor froze solid. Indeed, so bitter were the centuries from about 1400 until 1900 that they have been dubbed the 'little ice age.' But new evidence appears to confirm that the long cold snap was nothing exceptional. Instead, it was only the most recent swing in a climate oscillation that has been alternately warming and cooling the North Atlantic region, if not the globe, for ages upon ages.

Just as meteorologists and earth scientists have to sort out the 'normal' weather cycles to determine what portion of global warming is due to nature and what is due to man, so we have to be able to take into account the 'normal' oscillations of the capital markets to sort out what is extraordinary. What do these 'normal' oscillations or cycles look like? Our technique for addressing this question is the confidence analysis.

12. Non-Gaussian analysis: the real frequency of events

Unlike the distribution of events in the natural world (e.g., distribution of intelligence around the average), events in the capital markets can often be distributed in unusual patterns – with many more events occurring above or below the average than one might suspect. Moreover, these distributions themselves can and do change over time. Understanding these distributions and the way they change is critical to an accurate interpretation of representative statistics such as averages and standard deviations.

13. Dynamic financial analyses

DPA focuses on the standard SPA financial analysis (EPS growth rates, margins, EBITDA, free cash flows, etc.), but also on more dynamic variables such as the reinvestment ratio (and its stability), the growth return on capital investment, and the amount of EBITDA growth that results from each new dollar of capital.

USEFULNESS OF DPA

DPA allows one to clearly see the periods of continuity and to distinguish them from the periods of change. It helps one to separate the 'random from the regular,' to quote Murray Gell-Mann, Nobel Prize-winning physicist and student of complexity.

DPA is helpful in determining and understanding the historic context (envelope) in which change has taken place, and thus setting limits on likely change in the future. It allows one to make judgements about the probable sustainability of long-term performance based on a clear understanding of the precedents of the past. It provides us with an automatic control sample – the market as a whole – which minimizes the chances of false attribution of cause and effect.

We believe that DPA is useful to CEOs and CFOs who want to understand how their investors are looking at their results – both the corporate results and the stock market interpretation of those results. These corporate officers also want to understand the forces at work on their industries.

WHAT DPA HAS TAUGHT US

We focused in Chapter 2 on some of the lessons of DPA. The following is a snapshot of our conclusions:

- Over the period of our analysis the economy has been in two regimes: one before 1974–75, and one since. Since 1976, the TRS cycles of the economy have been quite consistent.
- Most industries do not differ statistically from the overall economy. Only those industries in which there has been substantial change demonstrate any statistically significant superior performance. However, there are industries that have consistently underperformed the economy.
- Exceptional performance, as determined by long-term (two-cycle) total return to shareholders, is driven by earnings growth and ROI to a much greater extent than can be explained by P/Es.
- Exceptional performance is never sustained. Whether it is an industry that is outperforming or a company, high performance always comes to an end. The end of excellence is a good proxy for long-term risk to the investor.

- Company performance deteriorates over the longer run because the market is more dynamic than the corporation.

- Companies don't outperform the market except in rare non-generalizable situations like Berkshire-Hathaway.

- Rates of entry and exit from an industry are very strongly correlated with industry performance. What is cause and what is effect is not always clear. Usually both play a role.

- The best chance to beat the markets is early on, when the potential of a change is far greater than the market estimates.

- The difficulty of understanding the future, along with the difficulties in executing a programme of change within a corporation, makes leadership the key resource.

Notes

INTRODUCTION

THE GAME OF CREATIVE DESTRUCTION

2 'The farther backward': There is some doubt that Churchill actually said this, but it is broadly attributed to him. According to Richard M. Langworth, editor, *Finest Hour*, The Churchill Center, 'I've heard it often but have never been able to attribute it. I suspect it's one of those generic quotes ascribed to many people.'

2 We selected: See Appendix C for a list of the variables covered in our data collection effort.

4 The capital markets provide: The objective of the regulators of the capital markets is to provide for a 'level playing field,' that is, no unfair informational advantage to any one player. A key mechanism for achieving that objective is to establish and enforce standards for information quality and transparency – that is, clear definitions of standards for the information, and clear rules for its access, use, and dissemination. Compliance with these standards is often carefully monitored and enforced. Compliance is enforced by a (hopefully) neutral judicial system reporting to or operated by the state. The rules governing the capital markets can be changed through discussion and dialogue among legislative, judicial, and executive bodies reporting to the state. The discussion about change will often solicit the opinions of players in the capital markets. The change processes can extend for decades or more.

4 'Control, which essentially means': Merchant, Kenneth A. *Control in Business Organizations*. Boston: Pittman, 1985.

4 'Measurement focuses': Simons, Robert. *Levers of Control: How Managers Use Innovative Control Systems to Drive Strategic Renewal*. Boston: Harvard Business School Press, 1995.

CHAPTER 1

SURVIVAL AND PERFORMANCE IN THE ERA OF DISCONTINUITY

7 As a group: Throughout the book we will define the long-term return to investors as the total return to shareholders, or TRS. This measure, which is common in finance, is the sum of the annual increase in stock price for the corporation plus the dividends and special payments distributed to investors. It is the single best measure of the increase in wealth of the investor.

8 One reaches: The original S&P index was formed in 1926 and was made up of 90 companies.

15 'When the millennium arrived': Reston, James. *The Last Apocalypse: Europe at the Year 1000 A.D.* New York: Doubleday, 1998.

18 'Theoretical frameworks': Munger, C., 'A Lesson in Elementary, Worldly Wisdom As It Relates to Investment Management and Business,' *Outstanding Investor Digest*, 1995, as cited by Mauboussin, *On the Shoulders of Giants – Mental Models for a New Millennium*, Vol. 2. Credit Suisse First Boston, 16 Nov. 1998.

19 Unfortunately, conventional: Merchant, 1985.

21 They keep the pipeline: It is true that these partnerships, because of the special laws under which they operate (as we will discuss in Chapter 7), also operate outside of the day-to-day scrutiny of the capital markets, giving them valuable time to focus on the fundamentals of their businesses without having to continuously worry about how the capital markets will interpret their actions. That being said, at some point all these intermediaries sell their properties to others – sometimes through a well-orchestrated auction among publicly traded companies, and sometimes through a public offering of the securities (known as the initial public offering, or IPO). At the time of the sale, they realize their gains and calculate their returns, just as an investor in a public company would.

23 'The test of a first-rate': F. Scott Fitzgerald, 'The Crack Up,' cited in Collins, J., and Porras, J., *Built to Last*, Harper Business: A Division of HarperCollins Publishers, 1994.

24 'The adaptive demands': Heifetz, Ronald A. *Leadership Without Easy Answers.* Cambridge: Belknap Press – Harvard University Press, 1994.

CHAPTER 2

HOW CREATIVE DESTRUCTION WORKS: THE FATE OF THE EAST RIVER SAVINGS BANK

27 The new name reflected: 'East River Savings' New Name,' *The Wall Street Journal*, 18 Oct. 1988.

27 'The Marine Midland Bank': Allon, J., 'Neighborhood Report for the Upper West Side,' *The New York Times*, 9 Nov. 1997.

27 Six months later: When it became clear that the bank was going to become a drugstore, local conservationists swung into action, gaining a landmark designation for the exterior of the building. The fate of the building's interior has not yet been decided. But according to one local resident, the outlook was not favourable: 'What are they going to do, landmark the Tylenol?'

28 Yet in light of the numbers: This is not the only indicator one could use. We have also tracked the number of companies on the major stock exchanges, and similar, if a bit less dramatic, patterns have been observed. Another indicator is the number of companies in our sample of 15 industries. This has increased from about 250 per year, in the beginning of our database, to more than six hundred in 1998.

30 'the . . . process of industrial': Schumpeter, Joseph A. *Business Cycles: A Theoretical, Historical and Statistical Analysis of the Capitalist Process.* 2 vols. New York and London: McGraw-Hill Book Co., Inc., 1939.

31 The exact position: The exact formula is:

Ii = (Pi – Pe)/Ce

where:

Ii = performance index
Pi = industry or company performance
Pe = economy or industry performance
Ce = 90% confidence interval for the economy or industry

38 Interpreting these potentially: *Standard and Poor's Industry Survey of Computer and Office Equipment*, 6/6/85, p. C83.

53 'The real trouble': G.K. Chesterton as sited by Bernstein, Peter L. *Against the Gods: The Remarkable Story of Risk*. New York: John Wiley & Sons, Inc., 1996.

54 Here is a distillation of Sterman's findings: Sterman, John D. *Business Dynamics: Systems Thinking and Modeling for a Complex World*. New York: Irwin/McGraw-Hill, 2000.

CHAPTER 3

CULTURAL LOCK-IN

61 'Things should be': As cited in Medio, Alfredo, and Gallo, Giampaolo. *Chaotic Dynamics: Theory and Applications to Economics*. Cambridge: Cambridge University Press, 1995.

61 'When John Akers took over': 'What Went Wrong at IBM: The Toughest Job in American Business,' *The Economist*, 16 Jan. 1993.

64 'Man seeks for himself': As cited in Medio and Gallo. Ibid.

64 'Small scale models': Kenneth Craik as cited by Johnson-Laird, Philip N. *Mental Models*. Cambridge, MA: Harvard University Press, 1983.

65 'If there is one gift': Virginia Woolf as cited by Ippolito, Maria F., and Tweney, Ryan D. 'The Inception of Insight.' *Nature of Insight* eds. Robert J. Sternberg and Janet E. Davidson. Cambridge, MA: MIT Press, 1995, pp. 433–62.

66 'We have limitations': Johnson-Laird, 1983.

66 'Mental models play': Johnson-Laird, 1983.

66 'A tight analogy or model': Simonton, Dean Keith. *Scientific Genius: A Psychology of Science*. Cambridge: Cambridge University Press, 1988.

67 'Language is used to create': March, James G. *A Primer on Decision Making: How Decisions Happen*. New York: The Free Press – Macmillan, 1994.

70 'Consequently, if the existing': See Johnson-Laird for experiments with Wason cards that demonstrate this point.

70 'The NASA scientists' belief': March, 1994.

71 'To give up one's': Simonton, 1988.

71 'Do we have to change?': Leonhardt, David. 'McDonald's: Can It Regain Its Golden Touch?' *Business Week*, 9 Mar. 1998, p. 70.

72 'A mental model changes': Forrester, Jay W. *World Dynamics*. Cambridge, MA: Wright-Allen Press, Inc., 1971.

72 'Myths, symbols, rituals': March, 1994.

72 'They give context': March, 1994.

73 'Active modeling occurs well before': Sterman, 2000.

73 'The constructive process': Johnson-Laird, 1983.

73 Language, visual imagery: This may be tautological. Beliefs are themselves mental models. But they can be the machine tools of mental models, useful for assembling other mental models, just as machine tools are useful in assembling other machines.

80 'In the start-up phase': Simons, 1995.

82 'In mature firms': Simons, 1995.

83 Often, the only real: See Appendix C for an analytical description of the economics of transition.

84 'Everyone is too damned': Markoff, John. 'I.B.M.'s Chief Criticizes Staff Again', *The New York Times*, 19 June 1991.

84 'We know from common sense': Vail, Priscilla L. *Emotion : The On/OFF Switch for Learning*. Rosemont, NJ: Modern Learning Press, 1994.

87 'When a problem arises': Cited by Sterman, 2000.

88 The capital markets: 'Manage' comes from the Italian *maneggio*, which means 'to train a horse!' Source: WWWebster.

88 'Every individual is continually exerting': Smith, Adam. *The Wealth of Nations: An Inquiry into the Nature and Causes*. (1776) New York: Everyman's Library, 1991.

CHAPTER 4

OPERATING VS. CREATING: THE CASE OF STORAGE TECHNOLOGY CORPORATION

90 'To compete with IBM': 'A Corny (But True) Story,' *Forbes*, 15 Oct 1977.

92 His new goal: 'Buying Magnuson and Its Problems,' *The New York Times*, 21 Dec 1981.

93 'We said to ourselves': Blumenthal, Karen. 'At a Crossroads: Storage Technology, In a Slump, Pins Hope On New Data Device – Firm's Woes Show Hazards Of Battling With IBM; It Pushes Optical System – Technological Glitches Hurt,' *The Wall Street Journal*, 16 Aug. 1984.

94 'Maybe that made us': Blumenthal, Karen. Ibid.

94 'I want to bring': Atchison, Sandra D., Mary J. Pitzer and Marilyn A. Harris. 'Storage Technology Found Its Iacocca?' *Business Week*, 4 Feb 1985.

94 Poppa's approach didn't: Ivey, Mark. 'Storage Technology Is Turning Around – But Where's It Headed?' *Business Week*, 24 Feb 1986.

96 Poppa was so impressed: Lancaster, Hal. 'Storage Technology to Launch Its Vaunted Iceberg – Many Rave About the Data-Storing Device, but Some Doubts Linger,' *The Wall Street Journal*, 24 Jan. 1992.

96 'I told Dick Egan': Lancaster, Hal. Ibid.

100 In a recent series: These discussions were conducted in cooperation with the Center for Corporate Innovation, Inc., 10835 West Olympic Boulevard, Suite 835, Los Angeles, CA 90064, (310) 575-1444.

101 In this sense, innovation: These views are wholly consistent with Schumpeter's original thinking. Although Schumpeter did not use the word 'innovation' directly, he attributed the economic effects he saw to 'the introduction of a new good, the introduction of a new method of production, the opening of a new market, the conquest of

a new source of supply of raw materials or half-manufactured goods, and the carrying out of the new organization of any industry, such as the creation or breakup of a monopoly.' Certainly technical and product advance was part of Schumpeter's concept, but was only a part.

105 'Measurement focuses on': Simons, 1995.

105 Once the variables are selected: Simons, 1995.

107 As the cellular: See box on the definition of innovation at the end of this chapter (p. 125).

114 Transformational innovations: Tushman, Michael L., and Philip Anderson. 'Technological Discontinuities and Organization Environments.' *Administrative Science Quarterly.* Sept. 1986, pp. 439–68.

116 But the word *creativity*: Modern reflection on the nature of creativity begins in the mid- to late-nineteenth century as Europe was going through an explosion of creativity in the arts, and the beginnings of the second real revolution in the sciences in Europe. In art, Impressionism was on the rise. Monet settled in Giverny in 1863. De Maupassant and other writers were actively thinking and writing about the essence of creativity. In music, Bruckner, Bartok, Mahler, Satie, and Sibelius were all in their ascendancy. Verdi and Wagner were battling to see who could sit at the pinnacle of operatic achievement. In science, Darwin was newly popular, and the theory of electromagnetism was capturing the imagination of more than a few entrepreneurs. In mathematics, number theory, which eventually helped pave the way for quantum mechanics, was getting its start in Vienna through the work of Cauchy and others.

116 'Instead of thoughts': Simonton, p. 24.

116 'To say that Thomas Edison': Csikszentmihalyi, Mihaly. *Creativity: Flow and the Psychology of Discovery and Invention.* New York: HarperCollins, 1997.

117 They are trained in diverse: Epstein, Robert. *Cognition, Creativity and Behavior.* Westport, Connecticut: Praeger, 1996.

117 'It is evident that': Simonton, p. 43.

119 'These anomalies provide': Csikszentmihalyi, Mihaly, and Keith Sawyer. 'Creative Insight: The Social Dimension of a Solitary Moment.' *Nature of Insight.* Eds. Robert J. Sternberg and Janet E. Davidson. Cambridge, MA: MIT Press, 1995.

118 'Fleming was not the first': Simonton, 1988.

118 'The accumulation of anomalies': Simonton, 1988.

119 'I keep the subject': Ippolito and Tweney.

120 'where beliefs, lifestyles': Csikszentmihalyi, 1997.

120 'irrational and rational aspects': Csikszentmihalyi, 1997.

120 'What is so difficult': Csikszentmihalyi, 1997.

121 Chess masters call this: Winsemius, Peter. *The Emotional Revolution,* Amsterdam: McKinsey & Company, 1999.

122 'constricted scan that screens': Amabile, Teresa M., et al., eds. *Creativity in Context: Update to the Social Psychology of Creativity.* Boulder, CO: Westview Press – Perseus Books, 1996.

123 'While many would be': This is wholly consistent with the observations of Kahneman and Tversky that the relationship between creativity and risk is U-shaped. When people are operating near their targets they are risk averse. When they are far behind or far ahead of their targets, they employ more creative strategies. This seems to fit the creative personality closely, since they are rarely at a point of satisfaction.

123 'In innovation you have': Csikszentmihalyi, 1997.

125 'Conversion of a creative idea': Isaak, M. I., and Just, M. M. 'Constraints on Thinking in Insight and Invention.' *Nature of Insight*, eds Robert J. Sternberg and Janet E. Davidson. Cambridge, MA: MIT Press, 1995, pp. 281–326.

CHAPTER 5

THE GALES OF DESTRUCTION

128 'This deal will get done': Hardy, Quentin. 'Technology & Science: McAfee Will Lobby Stockholders in Bid to Get Cheyenne,' *The Wall Street Journal*, 17 Apr. 1996.

128 'absolutely inadequate': Ibid.

128 'The long-term prospects': Ibid.

128 'false and misleading public statements': 'Technology & Telecommunications: Cheyenne Sues McAfee, Chief on Fraud Charges,' *The Wall Street Journal*, 19 Apr 1996.

128 'Sanjay called and said': Weber, Thomas E., and Steven Lipin. 'Computer Associates to Buy Cheyenne – Pact for $1.2 Billion Comes Half Year After Target Spurned McAfee's Offer,' *The Wall Street Journal*, 8 Oct. 1996.

130 By 1972, Intel's: 'Strategic Exit and Corporate Transformation: Evolving Links of Technology Strategy and Substantive Generic Corporate Strategies,' Robert A. Burgelman, George W. Cogan, Bruce K. Graham, Research Paper Series, Graduate School of Business, Stanford University, No. 1406, Sept. 1996.

132 'As the debates raged': Ibid.

132 Grove turned to Moore: Ibid.

132 After a few moments: Ibid.

133 'Intel equaled memories': Ibid.

133 It was a classic case: Ibid.

133 The company had: Ibid.

134 'fabrication facilities in': Ibid.

137 'The difficulty lies not': Winsemius, 1999.

137 'Our organizations tend': Winsemius, 1999.

138 'a normal, healthy one': Kübler-Ross, Elisabeth. *On Death and Dying*. New York: Collier Books – Macmillan, 1969.

138 Egyptian and Greek history: The range is from 250 years, as asserted by Tacitus, to 1500 years, according to Lipsius. The historic average range of dynasties in Egypt and Rome was closer to 300 years.

143 Closing down a heritage product line: While from time to time major companies do go bankrupt, in the United States the bankruptcy laws slow this process down. The major source of transformational destruction is acquisition.

CHAPTER 6

BALANCING DESTRUCTION AND CREATION

148 As CEO Ackerman decided: CNNfn, 3/6/00.

149 'The largest position in the world': CNBC, 12/6/99.

149 'Well beyond optical fiber': CNNfn, 7/20/99.

149 'Corning leads primarily': Corning's website.

153 'nothing was sacred': All statements drawn from a 'values document' prepared at the time by Welch's strategic team.

156 'We knew we were going': Anderson, Michael A., and Gordon Bock. 'Information Processing: Sequent Discovers Talents It Didn't Know It Had – Its Fast-Thinking Computer Hasn't Done Well In The Scientific Market – But It's A Surprise Hit In Offices,' *Business Week*, 19 May 1986.

157 'Of the six people': Heins, John. 'Many Hands Make Light Work. (Sequent Computer Systems Inc.),' *Forbes*, 29 May 1989.

159 'It's pretty clear': 'Sequent Computer Posts Quarterly Loss, Cites Major Charge,' *The Wall Street Journal*, 21 Oct. 1991.

159 'When other people': Hof, Robert D. 'Information Processing: Just When Sequent Thought It Was Safe . . . The Computer Maker's Once-Cozy Turf Is Being Invaded,' *Business Week*, 9 Nov. 1992.

161 'I'm big, big, big': 'Sequent Goes It Alone In Bid For Top Spot: Ignores The Industry Trends Of Volume And Commodity,' *Computergram International*, 17 Mar. 1997.

CHAPTER 7

DESIGNED TO CHANGE

168 'What we do is look': Peltz, Michael. 'High Tech's Premier Venture Capitalist,' *Institutional Investor*, June 1996.

168 'The valuation process': Ibid.

168 'There are four hundred': Perkins, Anthony B. 'The Thinker – Interview with John Doerr, General Partner in Charge of Investments in Information Technology at Kleiner Perkins CauWeld & Byers,' *The Red Herring*, 1 Mar. 1995.

168 'We didn't execute': Rutter, Nancy. 'Fastest VC in the West,' *Forbes*, 25 Oct. 1993.

169 'At first I thought': Perkins, Anthony B. 'The Thinker – Interview with John Doerr, General Partner in Charge of Investments in Information Technology at Kleiner Perkins CauWeld & Byers,' *The Red Herring*, 1 Mar. 1995.

169 'In the 1980s, PC hardware': Peltz, Michael. 'High Tech's Premier Venture Capitalist,' *Institutional Investor*, June 1996.

170 'Not once did Henry': Baker, George P., and George David Smith. *The New Financial Capitalists: Kohlberg Kravis Roberts and the Creation of Corporate Value*. Cambridge: Cambridge University Press, 1998.

171 The Securities Act of 1933: Now amended by the National Securities Markets Improvement Act of 1996.

173 The 'leveraged buyout association': Baker and Smith, 1998.

173 Roughly half of that: Pricewaterhouse Coopers MoneyTree® survey.

176 Though the closing: Baker and Smith, 1998.

182 Should they be able to do: The Street.com.

182 At this writing, there are: According to the National Business Incubator Association.

CHAPTER 8

LEADING CREATIVE DESTRUCTION

189 'In a complex social system': Heifetz, 1994.

189 Order – orienting people: Heifetz, 1994.

192 'Authorities, under pressure': Heifetz, 1994.

199 'We noticed that': Hall, Cheryl. 'When the parts are greater than the sum; Some of Safeguard Scientifics' spinoffs reap big rewards for investors,' *The Dallas Morning News*, 12 Mar. 1995.

202 'We are active': CNBC/Dow Jones Business Video, 03/16/1999.

203 'We asked Jim': Bulkeley, William M. 'Tech IPOs Put Unsung Backer In the Limelight,' *The Wall Street Journal*, 14 Oct. 1999.

204 'In the early 1990s, we helped': Press Release from website, 5/26/99.

204 'Shareholders should be evaluating': CNBC/Dow Jones Business Video, 03/16/99.

207 'To me, being truly': Born, Pete. 'Lindsay Owen-Jones: a world vision for L'Oreal,' *Women's Wear Daily*, 12 Oct. 1990.

208 'Our labs have a basic rule': Barrett, Amy. 'L'Oreal's Pretty Face Veils Growth Drive – Research Arm Helps Maintain Its Global Position,' *The Wall Street Journal*, 16 Jan. 1998.

CHAPTER 9

INCREASING CREATION TENFOLD

222 More latitude to invest risk capital: Lerner, Josh, *Venture Capital & Private Equity*, New York: John Wiley, 2000.

231 At McKinsey, our partners: First developed by Kevin Coyne and others in the McKinsey Atlanta office in 1996.

232 'In cultures that are uniform': Csikszentmihalyi, 1997.

232 A fourth trick is: Smith, Steven. 'Getting into and out of mental ruts: A theory of Fixation, incubation, and insight.' *Nature of Insight*, eds Robert J. Sternberg and Janet E. Davidson. Cambridge, MA: MIT Press, 1995.

233 'When Einstein burst in': Everdell, William R. *The First Moderns: Profiles in the Origins of Twentieth-Century Thought*. Chicago: University of Chicago Press, 1997.

233 'It takes two': Simonton, Dean Keith. 'Foresight in insight? A Darwinian answer.' *Nature of Insight*, eds Robert J. Sternberg and Janet E. Davidson. Cambridge, MA: MIT Press, 1995, pp. 465–94.

233 'Poetry is about': Csikszentmihalyi, 1997.

237 Together these functions may work: The work was originally led by Lothar Stein in the McKinsey Munich Office.

CHAPTER 10

CONTROL, PERMISSION, AND RISK

241 General Motors could not: Originally published in 1946 by John Day Company; 1993 edition Transaction Publishers, New Brunswick, NJ.

243 'Control, which essentially means': Merchant, 1985.

243 The purpose of divergent: Simons, 1995.

244 Can be abused by 'gaming the system': In one study of the budgeting practices of more than four hundred US firms, almost all respondents stated that they engaged in one or more budget games. Managers either did not accept the budgetary targets and opted to beat the system, or they felt pressures to achieve the budgetary targets at any cost.

245 'If people have a standard': *Business Month*, Dec. 1989, p. 33, and *Management Review*, 1986, p. 49.

245 Capital markets are the opposite: We are not making a case here for not planning and controlling, we are simply trying to clarify the differences between markets and corporations, and the absence of planning and control in markets is one of its distinctive features.

245 'We need to give up': Tom Peters, Conference Board Review, 1991.

248 At the time of publication: Pinchot, Gifford. *Intrapreneuring : Why You Don't Have to Leave the Corporation to Become an Entrepreneur*. New York: Harper & Row, 1985.

250 When decision makers are: Bernstein, 1996.

252 Because of this: CCi Interviews.

253 The world little knows: Simonton, 1998.

255 Thermo Electron was founded: Baldwin, William. 'Serendipity,' *Forbes*, 16 Nov 1987.

256 'Then all hell broke loose': *New England Business*, Dec. 1989.

257 'There's no better way': Wilke, John R. 'Innovative Ways: Thermo Electron Uses An Unusual Strategy To Create Products – It "Spins Out" New Companies To the Public but Retains A Majority of the Stocks – For Sale: Core Technologies,' *The Wall Street Journal*, 5 Aug. 1993.

257 'There's a physical limit': *The Wall Street Journal*, 8/5/93, p. A1.

258 'The risk is': Bulkeley, William M. 'Thermo Electron to Take Pretax Charge, Reacquire Stakes in Four Subsidiaries,' *The Wall Street Journal*, 25 May 1999.

264 'We became uncompetitive': Sellers, Patricia. 'So You Fail. Now Bounce Back!' *Fortune*, 1 May 1995.

264 'Failure is only an opportunity': Ford, Cameron, M., and Dennis A. Giola. *Creative Actions in Organizations: Ivory Tower Visions & Real World Voices*. Thousand Oaks: Sage Publications, 1995.

CHAPTER 11

SETTING THE PACE AND SCALE OF CHANGE

267 Johnson & Johnson has typically grown: Source: 1972 Johnson & Johnson Annual Report, Chairman's Letter to Shareholders.

272 'We need to think about': All quotes from private meetings and correspondence unless otherwise noted.

277 'We are thrilled': Jones, Gladys Montgomery, 'Framing the future: How Johnson & Johnson executives keep in touch with the changing marketplace – and one another,' *Continental Airlines*, March 1999.

277 Some of the savings: 18 August 1993, *Chemical Week* reports that J&J announced the elimination of 3,000 jobs and a related $200 million write-off.

286 Restructuring major manufacturing: Barrett, Amy. 'J&J Stops Babying Itself,' *Business Week*, 13 Sept. 1999.

287 What saved FrameworkS: Subsequently Russell Deyo took over responsibility for the programme in 1998 from Roger Fine.

289 Even more important: Daretta and Gelbman played key leadership roles in later FrameworkS sessions.

293 'Is FrameworkS a single, simple approach': Ralph S. Larsen, 'FrameworkS: Turning the Challenges of Change into Opportunities for Growth,' *Chief Executive* (US), 05/01/1999.

APPENDIX C

DYNAMIC PERFORMANCE ANALYSIS (DPA)

327 The mathematics of S-curves: Fisher, J.C., and R.H. Pry. 'A Simple Substitution Model for Technological Change.' *Technological Forecasting and Social Change* 3: 1971, pp. 75–88.

337 This approach has: Kahnemann, Daniel, Paul Slovic and Amos Tversky, eds. *Judgment Under Uncertainty: Heuristics and Biases.* Cambridge: Cambridge University Press, 1982.

338 *Recency* is the error: Kerr, Richard A. 'The Little Ice Age – Only the Latest Big Chill,' *Science*, 25 June 1999.

346 'George Washington's winter': *Science*, June 1999.

Selected Sources

Overall we have drawn on more than 500 references to inform our work. We have chosen not to publish that full list here, but rather to focus on the works that have been the most influential in our thinking

Amabile, Teresa M., et al., eds. *Creativity in Context: Update to the Social Psychology of Creativity*. Boulder, CO: Westview Press/Perseus Books, 1996.

Argyris, Chris. *Reasoning, Learning and Action: Individual and Organizational*. Jossey-Bass Series in Social and Behavioral Science and Jossey-Bass Series in Management. San Francisco: Jossey-Bass, Inc., 1982.

— *Overcoming Organizational Defenses: Facilitating Organizational Learning*. Boston: Allyn & Bacon, 1990.

Arthur, W. Brian. *Increasing Returns and Path Dependence in the Economy*. Ann Arbor: University of Michigan Press, 1994.

Baker, George P., and George David Smith. *The New Financial Capitalists: Kohlberg Kravis Roberts and the Creation of Corporate Value*. Cambridge: Cambridge University Press, 1998.

Bernstein, Peter L. *Against the Gods: The Remarkable Story of Risk*. New York: John Wiley & Sons, Inc., 1996.

Christensen, Clayton M. *The Innovator's Dilemma: When New Technologies Cause Great Firms to Fail*. Boston: Harvard Business School Press, 1997.

Csikszentmihalyi, Mihaly. *Creativity: Flow and the Psychology of Discovery and Invention*. New York: HarperCollins, 1997.

— *Flow: The Psychology of Optimal Experience*. New York: HarperCollins, 1991.

— and Keith Sawyer. 'Creative Insight: The Social Dimension of a Solitary Moment.' *Nature of Insight*. eds Robert J. Sternberg and Janet E. Davidson. Cambridge, MA: MIT Press, 1995.

Drucker, Peter F. *The Age of Discontinuity: Guidelines to Our Changing Society*. (1969) New Brunswick: Transaction Publishers, 1992.

— *Concept of the Corporation*. (1946) New Brunswick: Transaction Publishers, 1993.

Dunbar, Kevin. 'How Scientists Really Reason: Scientific Reasoning in Real-World Laboratories.' *Nature of Insight*. eds Robert J. Sternberg and Janet E. Davidson. Cambridge, MA: MIT Press, 1995.

Epstein, Robert. *Cognition, Creativity and Behavior*. Westport, CT: Praeger, 1996.

Everdell, William R. *The End of Kings: A History of Republics and Republicans*. New York: The Free Press, 1983.

— *The First Moderns: Profiles in the Origins of Twentieth-Century Thought*. Chicago: University of Chicago Press, 1997.

Ford, Cameron M., and Dennis A. Giola. *Creative Actions in Organizations: Ivory Tower Visions and Real World Voices*. Thousand Oaks: Sage Publications, 1995.

Forrester, Jay W. *World Dynamics*. Cambridge, MA: Wright-Allen Press, Inc., 1971.

Foster, Richard N. *Innovation: The Attacker's Advantage*. New York: Summit Books/Simon & Schuster, 1986.

Heifetz, Ronald A. *Leadership Without Easy Answers*. Cambridge: Belknap Press/Harvard University Press, 1994.

Ippolito, Maria F., and Ryan D. Tweney. 'The Inception of Insight.' *Nature of Insight*. eds Robert J. Sternberg and Janet E. Davidson. Cambridge, MA: MIT Press, 1995.

Isaak, M. I., and M. M. Just. 'Constraints on Thinking in Insight and Invention.' *Nature of Insight*. eds Robert J. Sternberg and Janet E. Davidson. Cambridge, MA: MIT Press, 1995.

Johnson-Laird, Philip N. *Mental Models*. Cambridge, MA: Harvard University Press, 1983.

Kahnemann, Daniel, Paul Slovic, and Amos Tversky, eds. *Judgment Under Uncertainty: Heuristics and Biases*. Cambridge: Cambridge University Press, 1982.

Kübler-Ross, Elizabeth. *On Death and Dying*. New York: Collier Books/Macmillan, 1969.

Lerner, Josh. *Venture Capital and Private Equity: A Casebook*. New York: John Wiley, 2000.

March, James G. *A Primer on Decision Making: How Decisions Happen*. New York: The Free Press – Macmillan, 1994.

Merchant, Kenneth A. *Control in Business Organizations*. Boston: Pittman, 1985.

Pinchot, Gifford. *Intrapreneuring: Why You Don't Have to Leave the Corporation to Become an Entrepreneur*. New York: Harper & Row, 1985.

Reston, James. *The Last Apocalypse: Europe at the Year 1000 A.D.* New York: Doubleday, 1998.

Schumpeter, Joseph A. *Business Cycles: A Theoretical, Historical and Statistical Analysis of the Capitalist Process*. 2 vols. New York and London: McGraw-Hill Book Co., Inc., 1939. Revised edition published in 1964.

— *Capitalism, Socialism and Democracy*. (1942) New York: Harper & Row, 1976.

Senge, Peter M. *The Fifth Discipline: The Art and Practice of the Learning Organization*. New York: Currency/Doubleday, 1990.

— et al., eds *The Fifth Discipline Fieldbook: Strategies and Tools for Building a Learning Organization*. New York: Currency/Doubleday, 1994.

Simons, Robert. *Levers of Control: How Managers Use Innovative Control Systems to Drive Strategic Renewal*. Boston: Harvard Business School Press, 1995.

Simonton, Dean Keith. *Genius, Creativity, and Leadership*. Cambridge, MA: Harvard University Press, 1984.

— *Scientific Genius: A Psychology of Science*. Cambridge: Cambridge University Press, 1988.

— 'Foresight in Insight? A Darwinian Answer.' *Nature of Insight*, eds Robert J. Sternberg and Janet E. Davidson. Cambridge, MA: MIT Press, 1995.

Smith, Steven. 'Getting Into and Out of Mental Ruts: A Theory of Fixation, Incubation, and Insight.' *Nature of Insight*, eds Robert J. Sternberg and Janet E. Davidson. Cambridge, MA: MIT Press, 1995.

Sterman, John D. *Business Dynamics: Systems Thinking and Modeling for a Complex World*. New York: Irwin/McGraw-Hill, 2000.

Sternberg, Robert J., and Janet E. Davidson, eds, *Nature of Insight*. Cambridge, MA: MIT Press, 1995.

Tushman, Michael L., and Philip Anderson. 'Technological Discontinuities and Organization Environments.' *Administrative Science Quarterly*, September 1986, pp. 439–68.

Vail, Priscilla L. *Emotion: The On/Off Switch for Learning*. Rosemont, NJ: Modern Learning Press, 1994.

Winsemius, Peter. *The Emotional Revolution*. Amsterdam: McKinsey & Company, 1999.

Index